P9-CCM-260

Port Washington Public Library
One Library Drive
Port Washington, NY 11050
(516) 883-4400   JAN 0 9 2024

WINGS OF FIRE

OF

FIRE

WINTER TURNING
THE GRAPHIC NOVEL

For Dash and Jess, with love from all the dragons!
—T.T.S.

This one's for Ella the cat and Heidi the dog, our
animal friends for many, many years. You'll always be
immortalized as the animalistic inspiration for
the dragons in the pages of these books.
—M.H.

Story and text copyright © 2024 by Tui T. Sutherland
Adaptation by Barry Deutsch and Rachel Swirsky
Map and border design © 2014 by Mike Schley
Art by Mike Holmes © 2024 by Scholastic Inc.

All rights reserved. Published by Graphix, an imprint of Scholastic Inc.,
Publishers since 1920. SCHOLASTIC, GRAPHIX, and associated logos are
trademarks and/or registered trademarks of Scholastic Inc.

The publisher does not have any control over and does not assume any responsibility
for author or third-party websites or their content.

No part of this publication may be reproduced, stored in a retrieval
system, or transmitted in any form or by any means, electronic, mechanical,
photocopying, recording, or otherwise, without written permission of the publisher.
For information regarding permission, write to Scholastic Inc., Attention:
Permissions Department, 557 Broadway, New York, NY 10012.

This book is a work of fiction. Names, characters, places, and incidents are either the
product of the author's imagination or are used fictitiously, and any resemblance to actual
persons, living or dead, business establishments, events, or locales is entirely coincidental.

Library of Congress Control Number Available

ISBN 978-1-338-73093-7 (hardcover)
ISBN 978-1-338-73092-0 (paperback)

10 9 8 7 6 5 4 3 2 1   24 25 26 27 28

Printed in China   62
First edition, January 2024
Edited by Amanda Maciel
Coloring by Maarta Laiho
Lettering by E.K. Weaver
Creative Director: Phil Falco
Publisher: David Saylor

WINGS OF FIRE

WINTER TURNING
THE GRAPHIC NOVEL

BY TUI T. SUTHERLAND

ADAPTED BY BARRY DEUTSCH
AND RACHEL SWIRSKY

ART BY MIKE HOLMES
COLOR BY MAARTA LAIHO

AN IMPRINT OF
■SCHOLASTIC

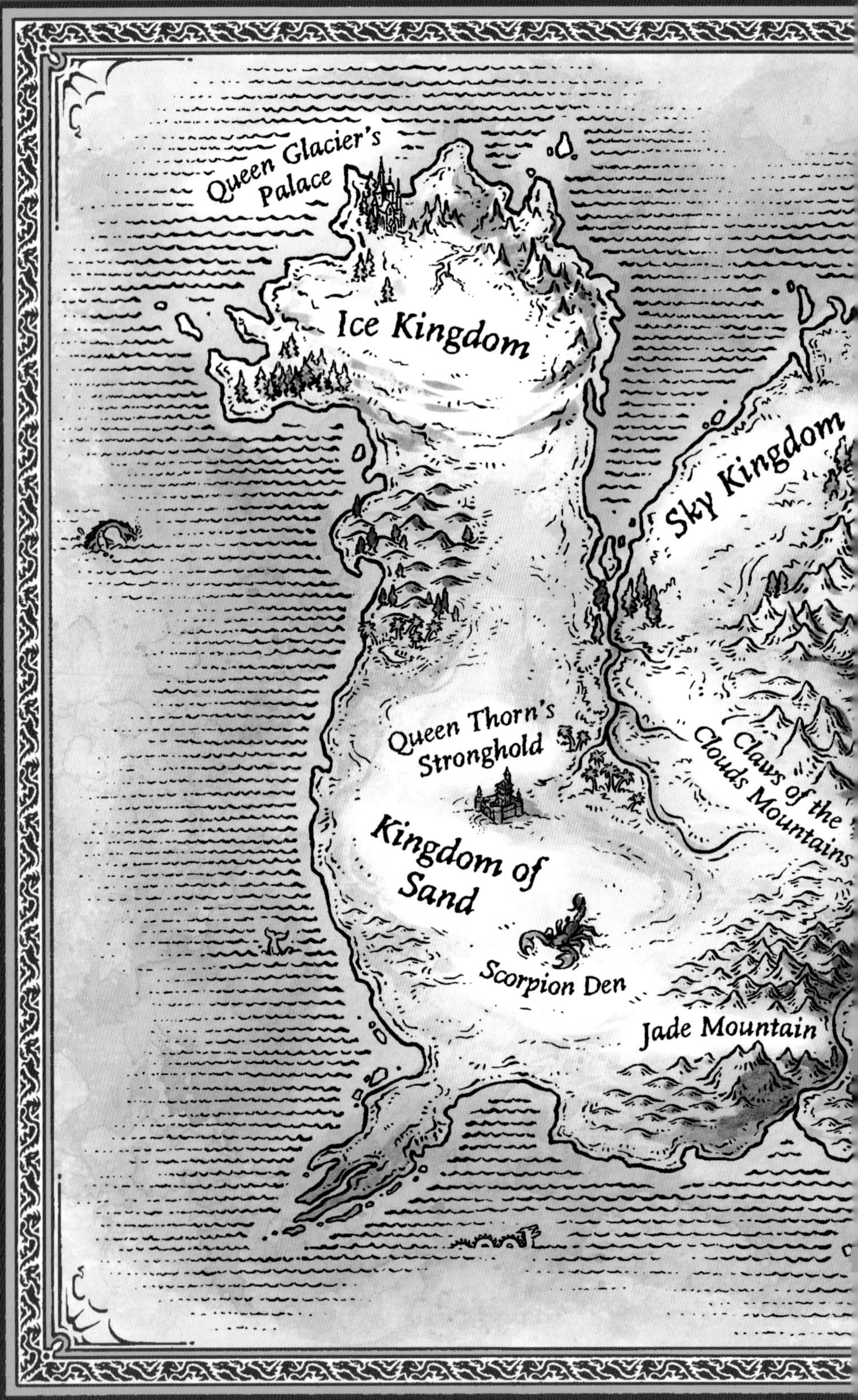
Queen Glacier's Palace
Ice Kingdom
Sky Kingdom
Queen Thorn's Stronghold
Claws of the Clouds Mountains
Kingdom of Sand
Scorpion Den
Jade Mountain

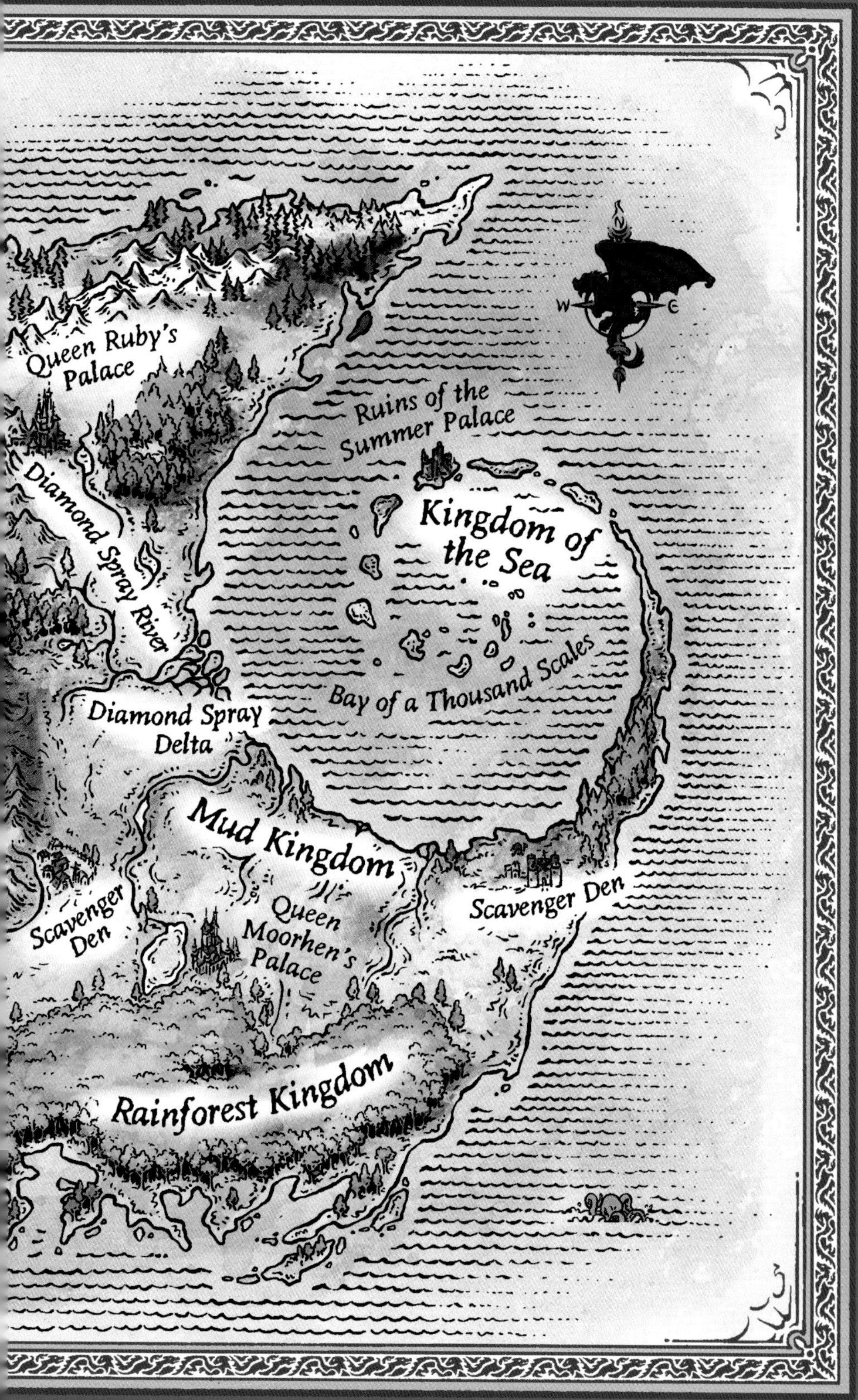

Queen Ruby's Palace
Ruins of the Summer Palace
W
E
Diamond Spray River
Kingdom of the Sea
Bay of a Thousand Scales
Diamond Spray Delta
Mud Kingdom
Scavenger Den
Queen Moorhen's Palace
Scavenger Den
Rainforest Kingdom

Queen Glacier's Palace

Ice Kingdom

Sky Kingdom

Claws of the Clouds Mountains

Queen Thorn's Stronghold

Kingdom of Sand

Scorpion Den

Jade Mountain

WINTER TURNING

THE JADE MOUNTAIN PROPHECY

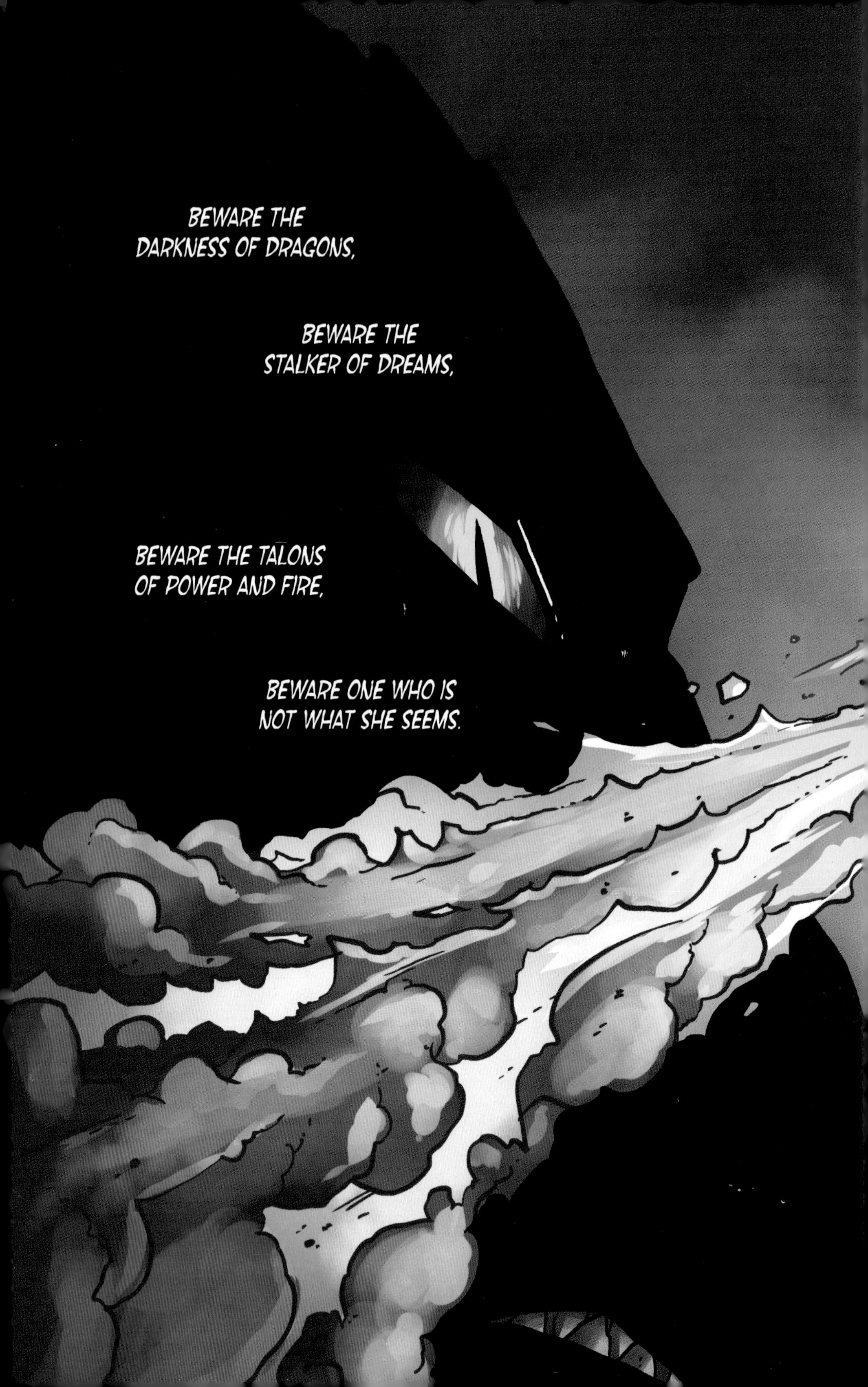
BEWARE THE
DARKNESS OF DRAGONS,
BEWARE THE
STALKER OF DREAMS,
BEWARE THE TALONS
OF POWER AND FIRE,
BEWARE ONE WHO IS
NOT WHAT SHE SEEMS.

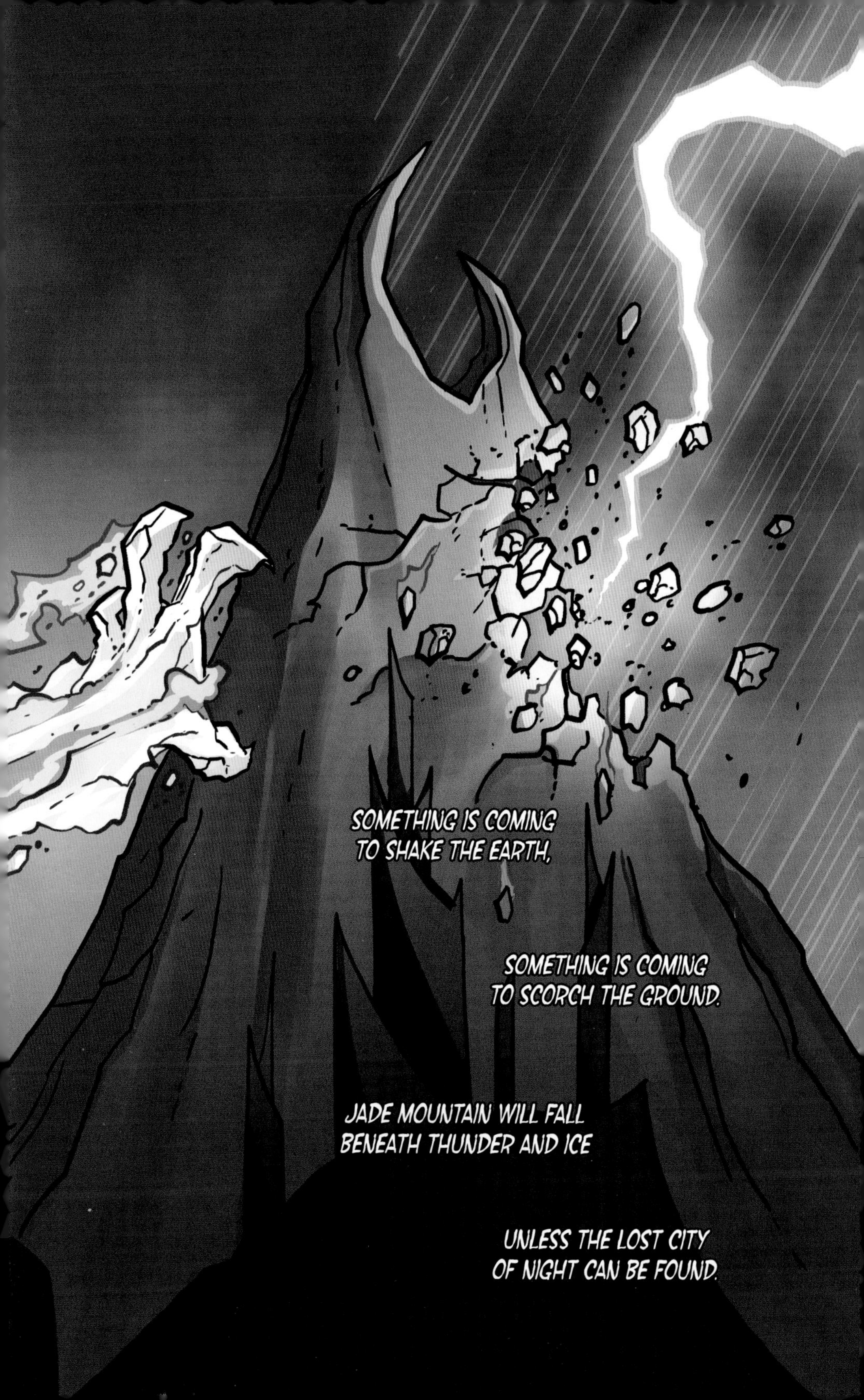
SOMETHING IS COMING
TO SHAKE THE EARTH,
SOMETHING IS COMING
TO SCORCH THE GROUND.
JADE MOUNTAIN WILL FALL
BENEATH THUNDER AND ICE
UNLESS THE LOST CITY
OF NIGHT CAN BE FOUND.

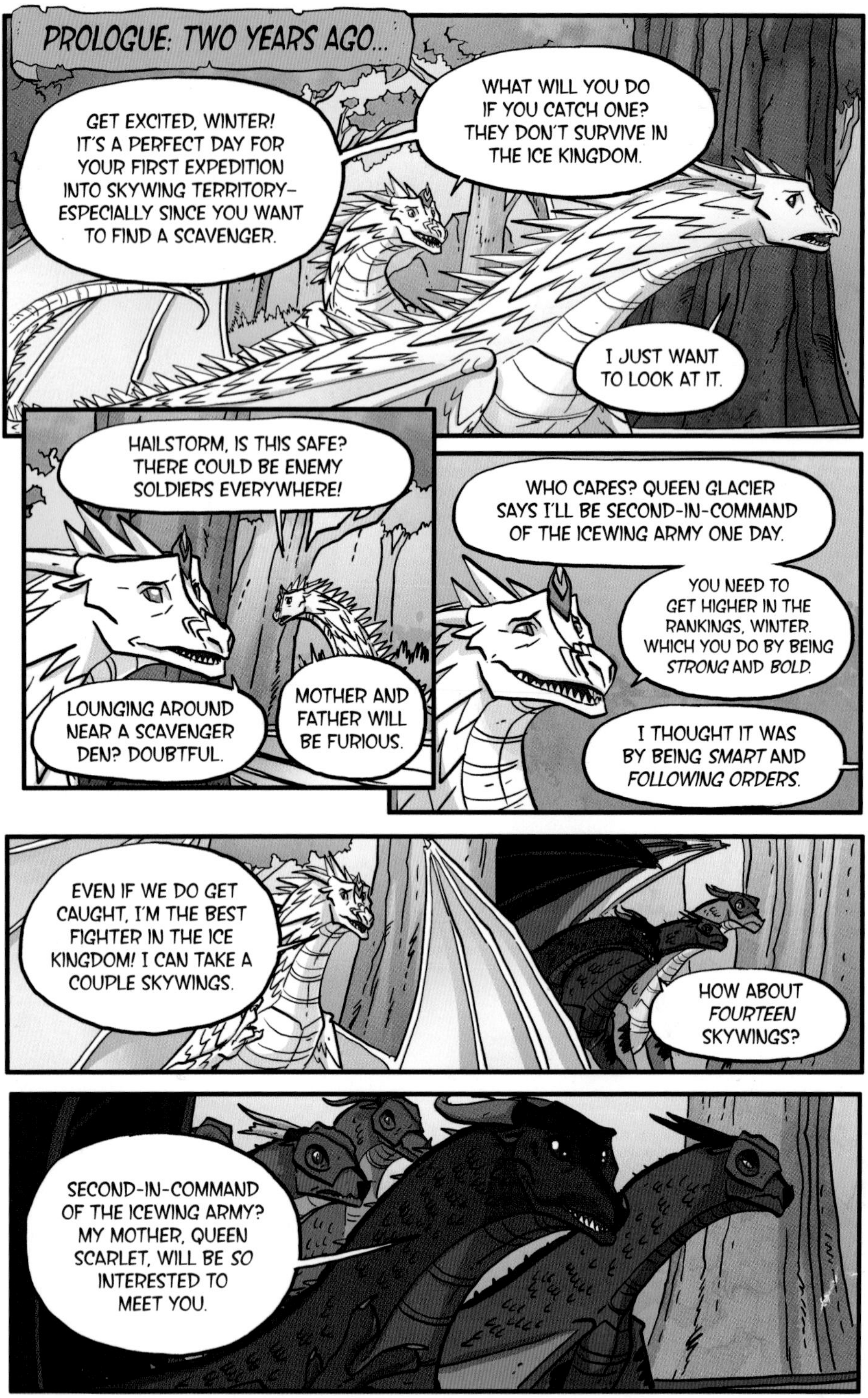
PROLOGUE: TWO YEARS AGO...
GET EXCITED, WINTER! IT'S A PERFECT DAY FOR YOUR FIRST EXPEDITION INTO SKYWING TERRITORY— ESPECIALLY SINCE YOU WANT TO FIND A SCAVENGER.
WHAT WILL YOU DO IF YOU CATCH ONE? THEY DON'T SURVIVE IN THE ICE KINGDOM.
I JUST WANT TO LOOK AT IT.
HAILSTORM, IS THIS SAFE? THERE COULD BE ENEMY SOLDIERS EVERYWHERE!
LOUNGING AROUND NEAR A SCAVENGER DEN? DOUBTFUL.
MOTHER AND FATHER WILL BE FURIOUS.
WHO CARES? QUEEN GLACIER SAYS I'LL BE SECOND-IN-COMMAND OF THE ICEWING ARMY ONE DAY.
YOU NEED TO GET HIGHER IN THE RANKINGS, WINTER. WHICH YOU DO BY BEING *STRONG* AND *BOLD*.
I THOUGHT IT WAS BY BEING *SMART* AND *FOLLOWING ORDERS*.
EVEN IF WE DO GET CAUGHT, I'M THE BEST FIGHTER IN THE ICE KINGDOM! I CAN TAKE A COUPLE SKYWINGS.
HOW ABOUT *FOURTEEN* SKYWINGS?
SECOND-IN-COMMAND OF THE ICEWING ARMY? MY MOTHER, QUEEN SCARLET, WILL BE *SO* INTERESTED TO MEET YOU.

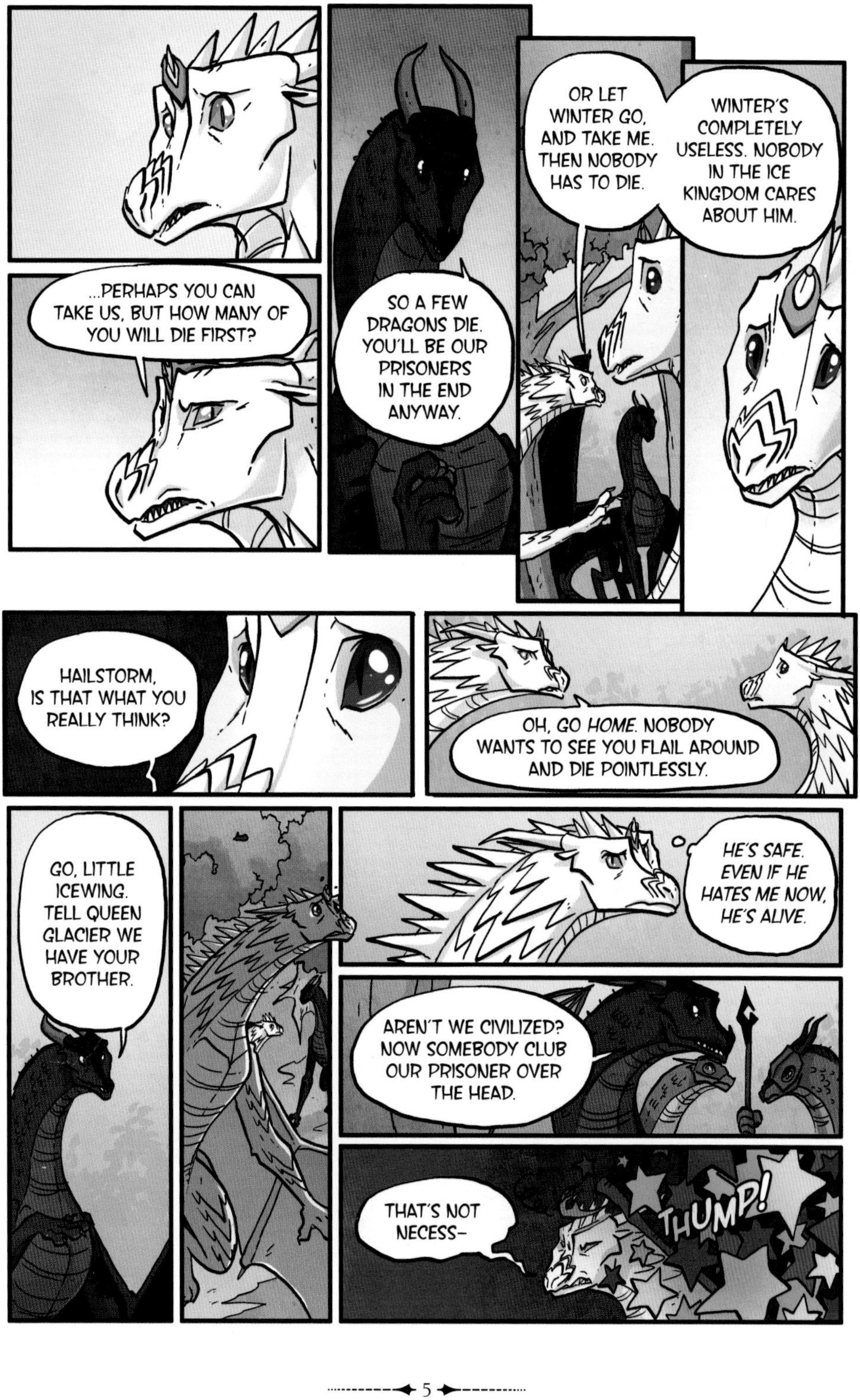
...PERHAPS YOU CAN TAKE US, BUT HOW MANY OF YOU WILL DIE FIRST?
SO A FEW DRAGONS DIE. YOU'LL BE OUR PRISONERS IN THE END ANYWAY.
OR LET WINTER GO, AND TAKE ME. THEN NOBODY HAS TO DIE.
WINTER'S COMPLETELY USELESS. NOBODY IN THE ICE KINGDOM CARES ABOUT HIM.
HAILSTORM, IS THAT WHAT YOU REALLY THINK?
OH, GO *HOME*. NOBODY WANTS TO SEE YOU FLAIL AROUND AND DIE POINTLESSLY.
GO, LITTLE ICEWING. TELL QUEEN GLACIER WE HAVE YOUR BROTHER.
HE'S SAFE. EVEN IF HE HATES ME NOW, HE'S ALIVE.
AREN'T WE CIVILIZED? NOW SOMEBODY CLUB OUR PRISONER OVER THE HEAD.
THAT'S NOT NECESS–
THUMP!

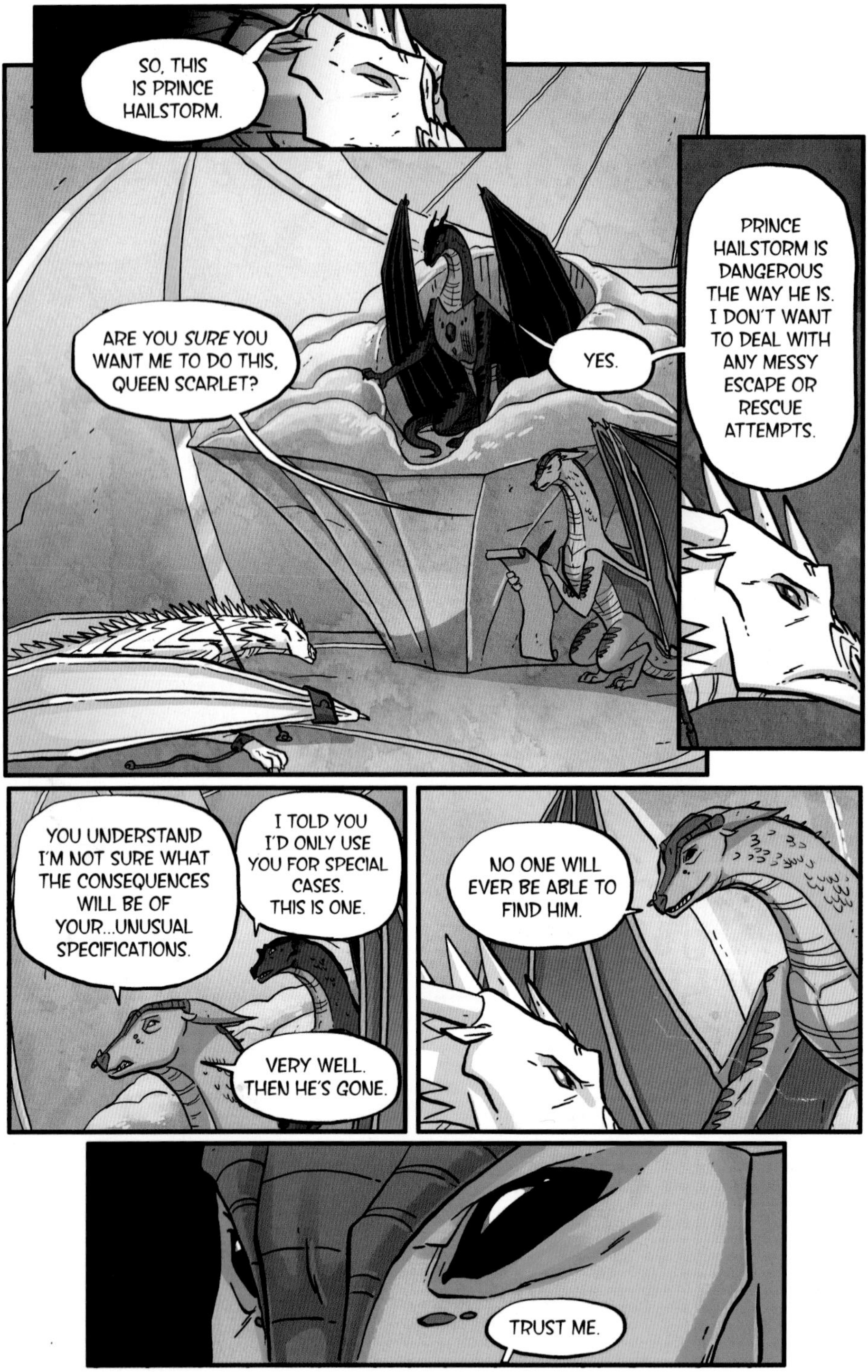
SO, THIS IS PRINCE HAILSTORM.
ARE YOU *SURE* YOU WANT ME TO DO THIS, QUEEN SCARLET?
YES.
PRINCE HAILSTORM IS DANGEROUS THE WAY HE IS. I DON'T WANT TO DEAL WITH ANY MESSY ESCAPE OR RESCUE ATTEMPTS.
YOU UNDERSTAND I'M NOT SURE WHAT THE CONSEQUENCES WILL BE OF YOUR...UNUSUAL SPECIFICATIONS.
I TOLD YOU I'D ONLY USE YOU FOR SPECIAL CASES. THIS IS ONE.
VERY WELL. THEN HE'S GONE.
NO ONE WILL EVER BE ABLE TO FIND HIM.
TRUST ME.

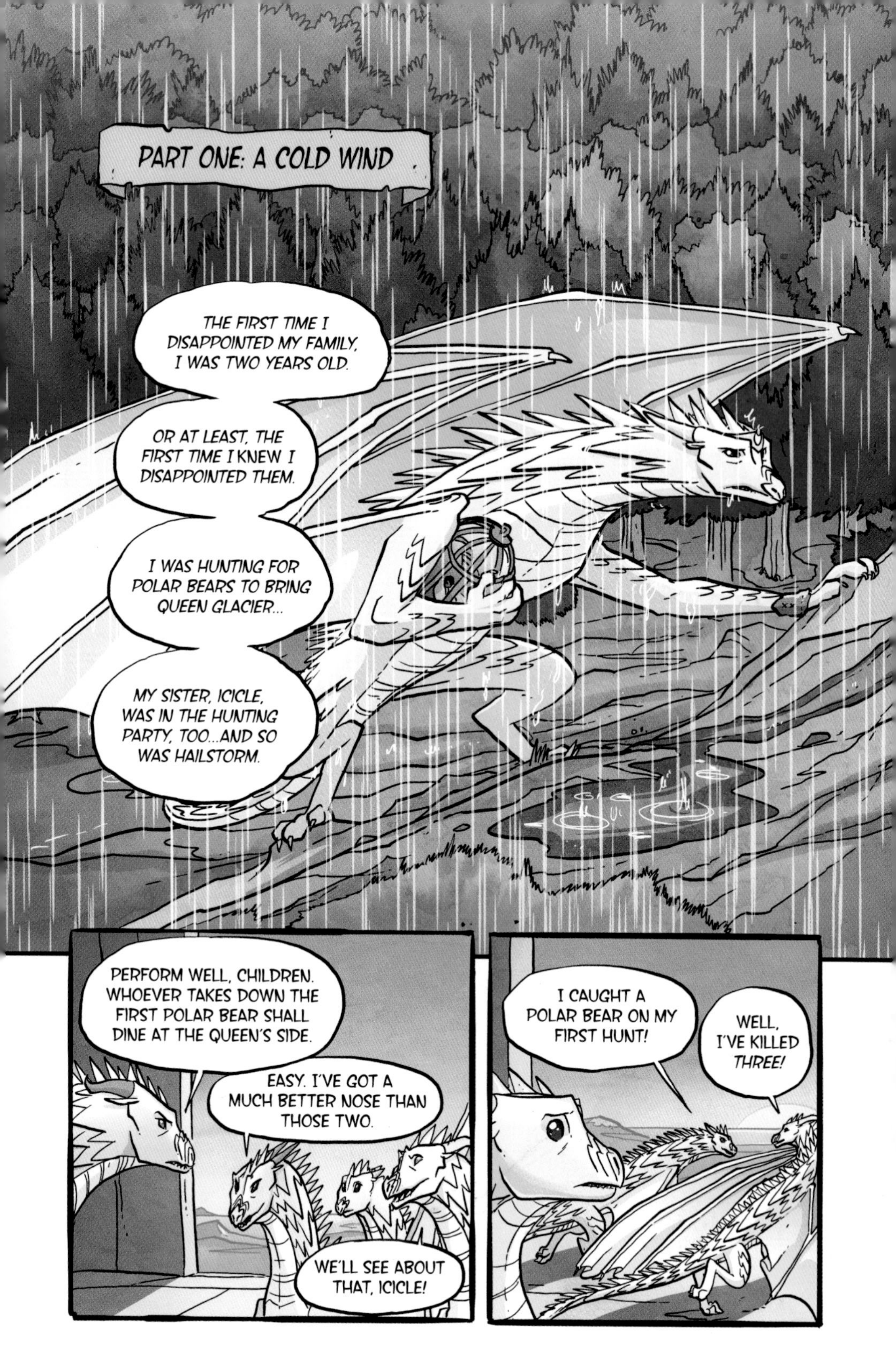
PART ONE: A COLD WIND
THE FIRST TIME I DISAPPOINTED MY FAMILY, I WAS TWO YEARS OLD.
OR AT LEAST, THE FIRST TIME I KNEW I DISAPPOINTED THEM.
I WAS HUNTING FOR POLAR BEARS TO BRING QUEEN GLACIER...
MY SISTER, ICICLE, WAS IN THE HUNTING PARTY, TOO...AND SO WAS HAILSTORM.
PERFORM WELL, CHILDREN. WHOEVER TAKES DOWN THE FIRST POLAR BEAR SHALL DINE AT THE QUEEN'S SIDE.
EASY. I'VE GOT A MUCH BETTER NOSE THAN THOSE TWO.
WE'LL SEE ABOUT THAT, ICICLE!
I CAUGHT A POLAR BEAR ON MY FIRST HUNT!
WELL, I'VE KILLED THREE!

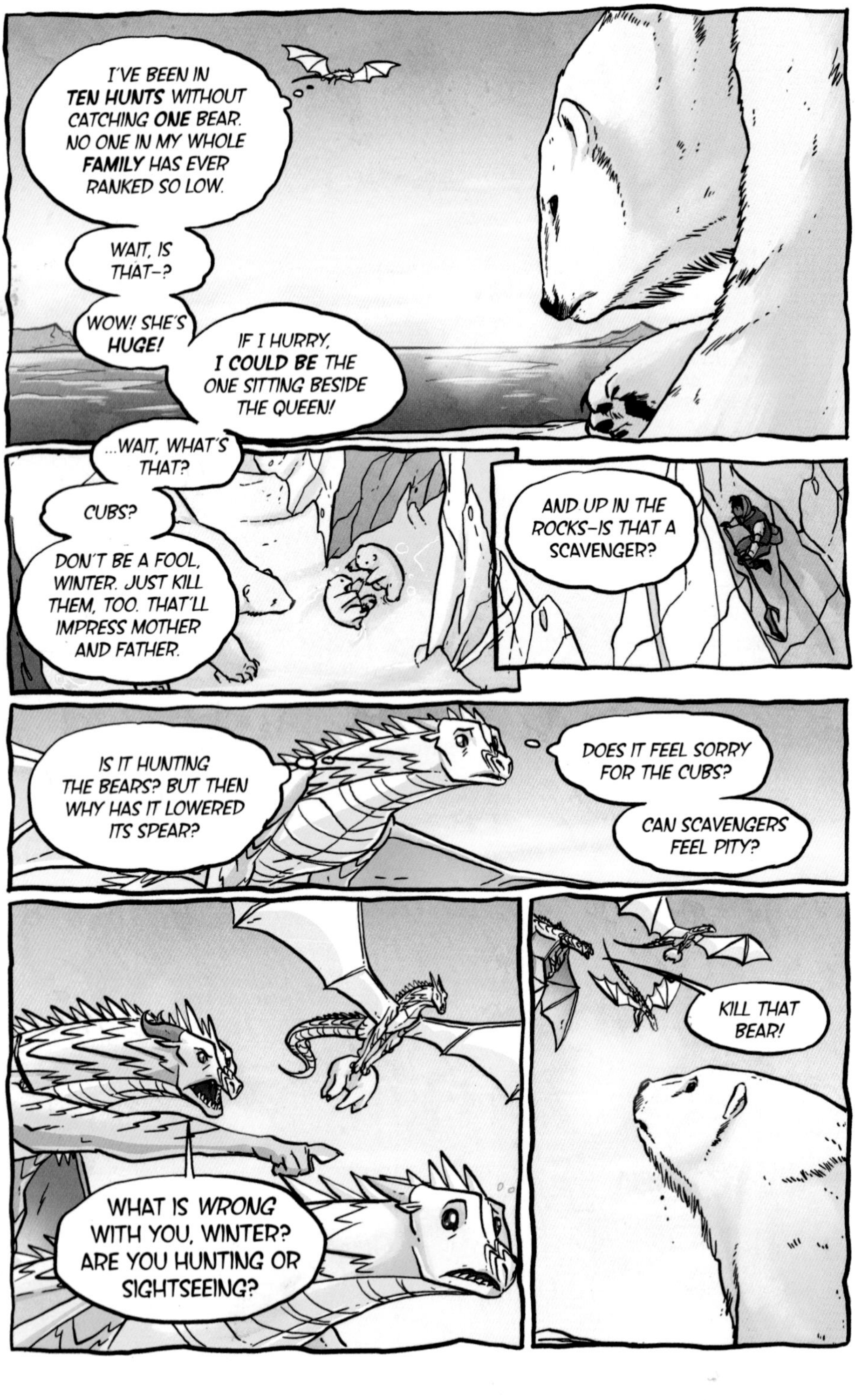
I'VE BEEN IN **TEN HUNTS** WITHOUT CATCHING **ONE** BEAR. NO ONE IN MY WHOLE **FAMILY** HAS EVER RANKED SO LOW.
WAIT, IS THAT–?
WOW! SHE'S **HUGE!**
IF I HURRY, **I COULD BE** THE ONE SITTING BESIDE THE QUEEN!
...WAIT, WHAT'S THAT?
CUBS?
DON'T BE A FOOL, WINTER. JUST KILL THEM, TOO. THAT'LL IMPRESS MOTHER AND FATHER.
AND UP IN THE ROCKS–IS THAT A SCAVENGER?
IS IT HUNTING THE BEARS? BUT THEN WHY HAS IT LOWERED ITS SPEAR?
DOES IT FEEL SORRY FOR THE CUBS?
CAN SCAVENGERS FEEL PITY?
WHAT IS *WRONG* WITH YOU, WINTER? ARE YOU HUNTING OR SIGHTSEEING?
KILL THAT BEAR!

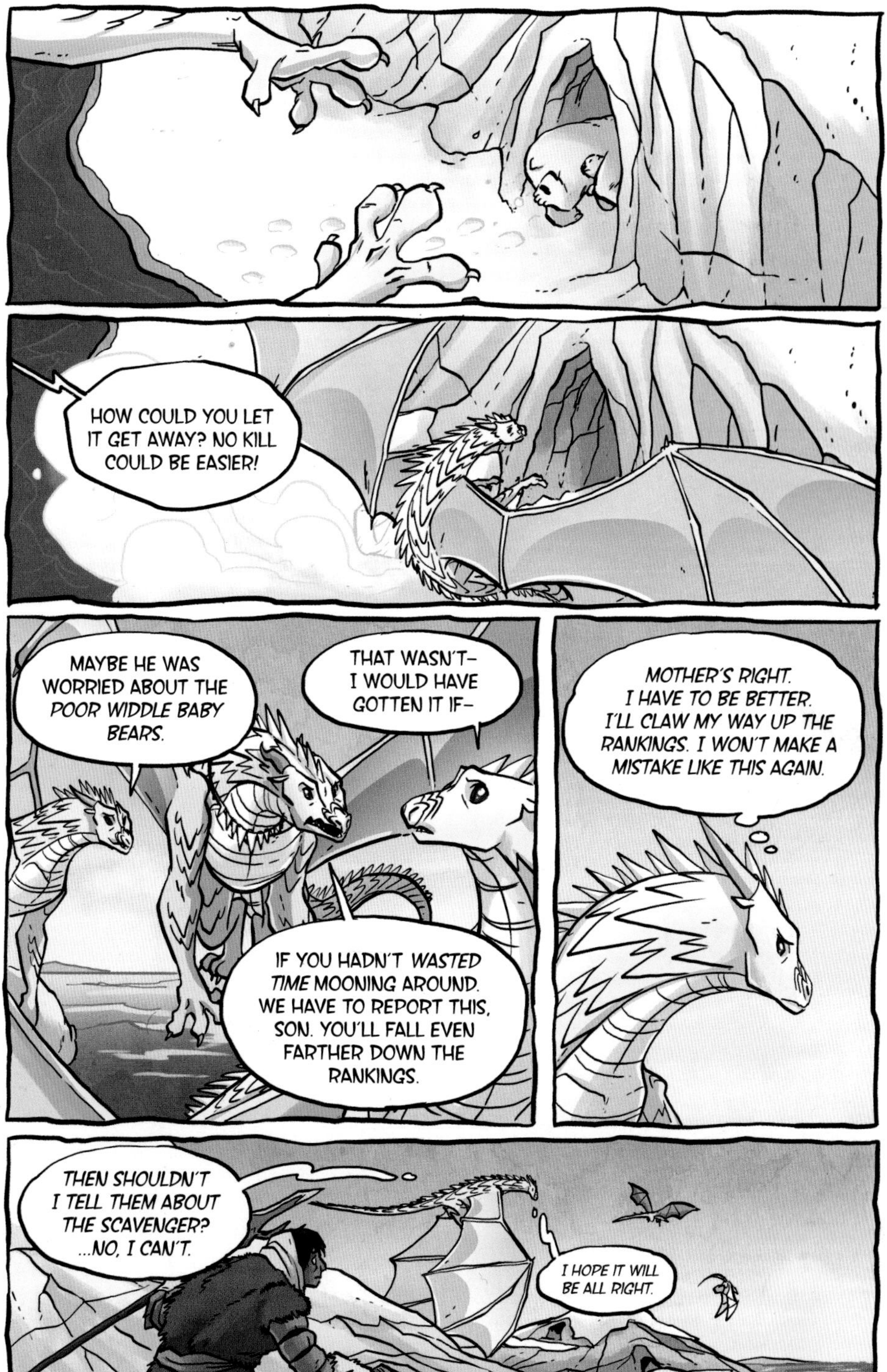
HOW COULD YOU LET IT GET AWAY? NO KILL COULD BE EASIER!
MAYBE HE WAS WORRIED ABOUT THE *POOR WIDDLE BABY BEARS.*
THAT WASN'T– I WOULD HAVE GOTTEN IT IF–
IF YOU HADN'T *WASTED TIME* MOONING AROUND. WE HAVE TO REPORT THIS, SON. YOU'LL FALL EVEN FARTHER DOWN THE RANKINGS.
MOTHER'S RIGHT. I HAVE TO BE BETTER. I'LL CLAW MY WAY UP THE RANKINGS. I WON'T MAKE A MISTAKE LIKE THIS AGAIN.
THEN SHOULDN'T I TELL THEM ABOUT THE SCAVENGER? ...NO, I CAN'T.
I HOPE IT WILL BE ALL RIGHT.

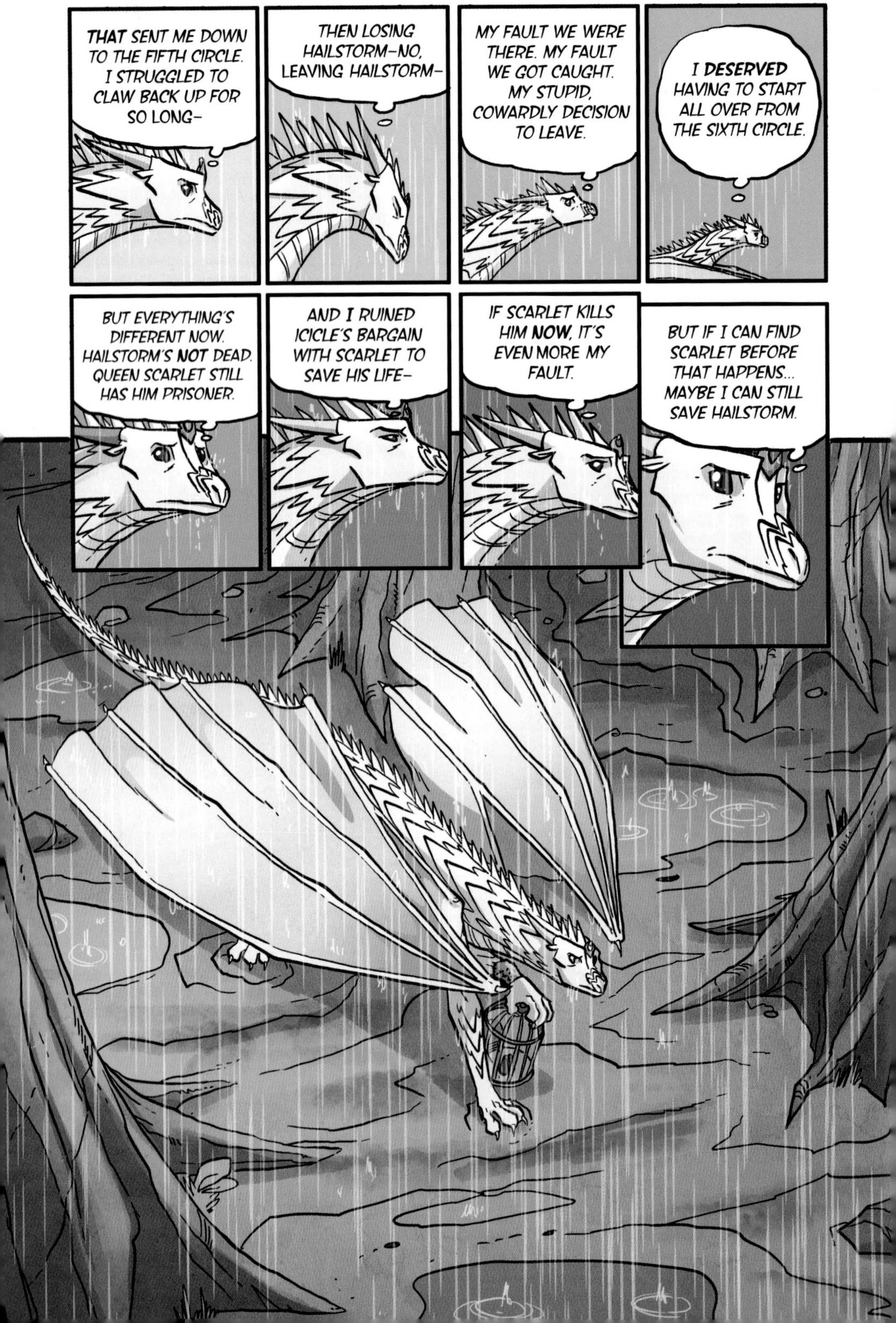
THAT SENT ME DOWN TO THE FIFTH CIRCLE. I STRUGGLED TO CLAW BACK UP FOR SO LONG–
THEN LOSING HAILSTORM–NO, LEAVING HAILSTORM–
MY FAULT WE WERE THERE. MY FAULT WE GOT CAUGHT. MY STUPID, COWARDLY DECISION TO LEAVE.
I DESERVED HAVING TO START ALL OVER FROM THE SIXTH CIRCLE.
BUT EVERYTHING'S DIFFERENT NOW. HAILSTORM'S NOT DEAD. QUEEN SCARLET STILL HAS HIM PRISONER.
AND I RUINED ICICLE'S BARGAIN WITH SCARLET TO SAVE HIS LIFE–
IF SCARLET KILLS HIM NOW, IT'S EVEN MORE MY FAULT.
BUT IF I CAN FIND SCARLET BEFORE THAT HAPPENS... MAYBE I CAN STILL SAVE HAILSTORM.

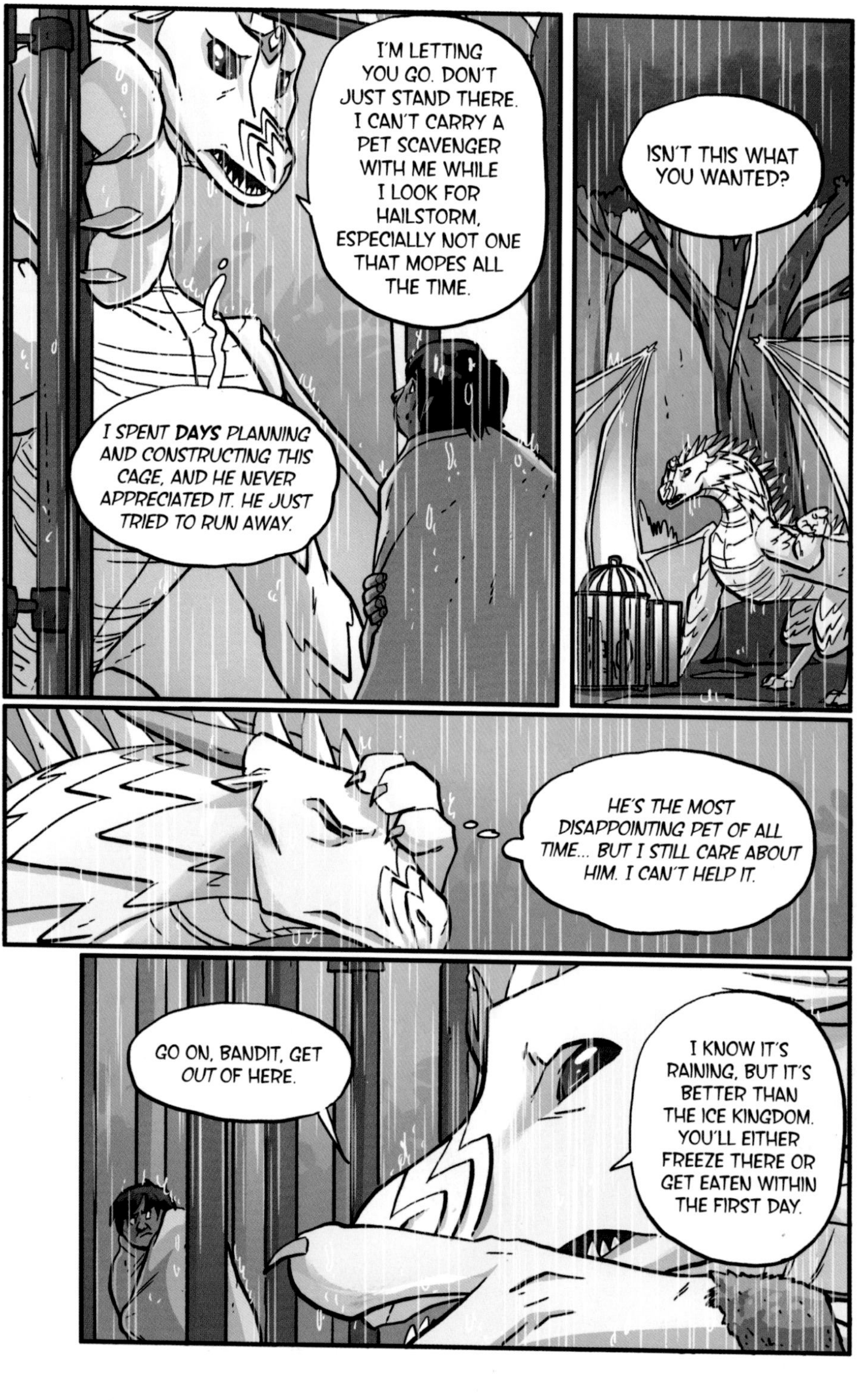
I'M LETTING YOU GO. DON'T JUST STAND THERE. I CAN'T CARRY A PET SCAVENGER WITH ME WHILE I LOOK FOR HAILSTORM, ESPECIALLY NOT ONE THAT MOPES ALL THE TIME.
I SPENT **DAYS** PLANNING AND CONSTRUCTING THIS CAGE, AND HE NEVER APPRECIATED IT. HE JUST TRIED TO RUN AWAY.
ISN'T THIS WHAT YOU WANTED?
HE'S THE MOST DISAPPOINTING PET OF ALL TIME... BUT I STILL CARE ABOUT HIM. I CAN'T HELP IT.
GO ON, BANDIT, GET OUT OF HERE.
I KNOW IT'S RAINING, BUT IT'S BETTER THAN THE ICE KINGDOM. YOU'LL EITHER FREEZE THERE OR GET EATEN WITHIN THE FIRST DAY.

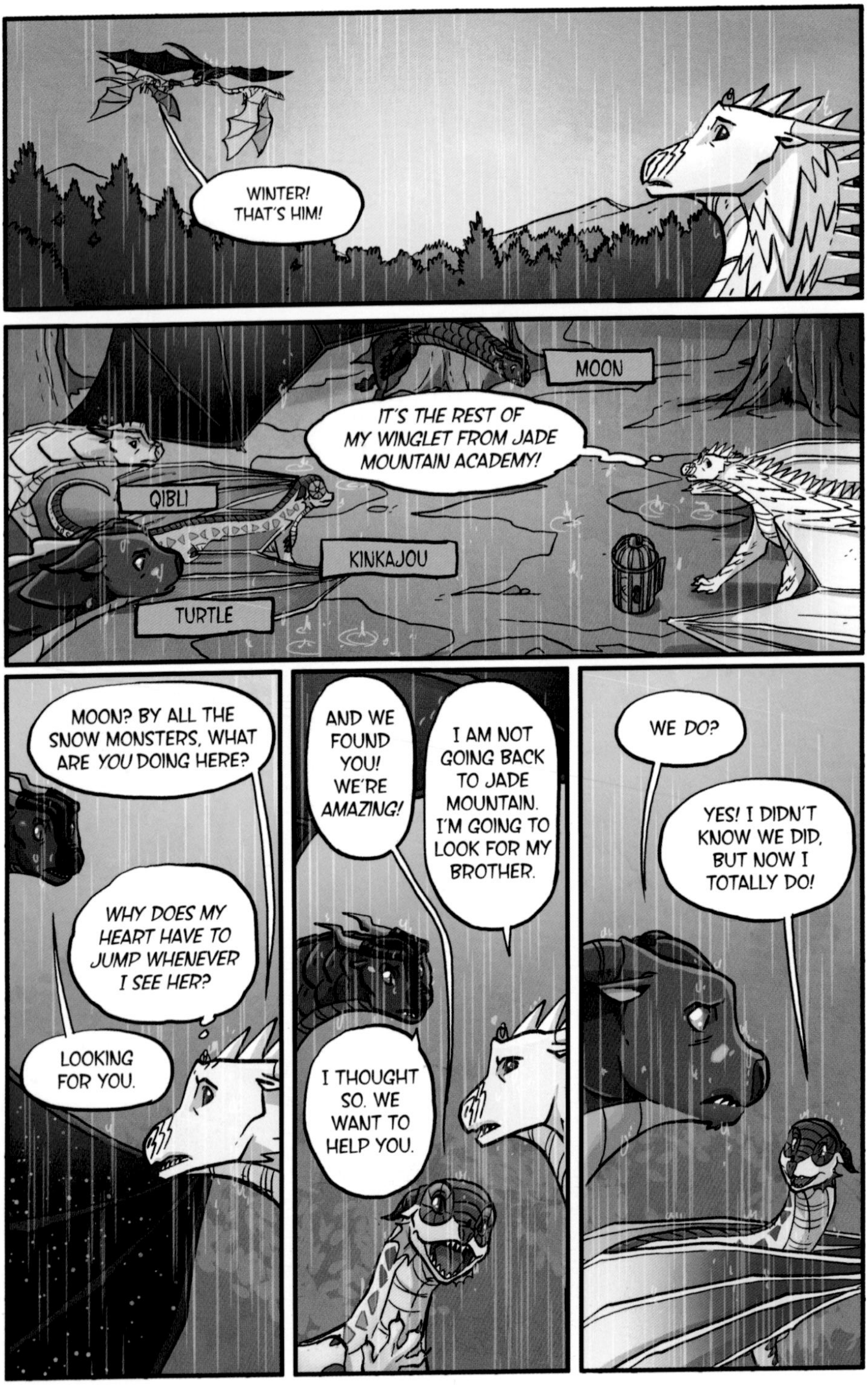
WINTER! THAT'S HIM!
MOON
IT'S THE REST OF MY WINGLET FROM JADE MOUNTAIN ACADEMY!
QIBLI
KINKAJOU
TURTLE
MOON? BY ALL THE SNOW MONSTERS, WHAT ARE *YOU* DOING HERE?
WHY DOES MY HEART HAVE TO JUMP WHENEVER I SEE HER?
LOOKING FOR YOU.
AND WE FOUND YOU! WE'RE *AMAZING!*
I AM NOT GOING BACK TO JADE MOUNTAIN. I'M GOING TO LOOK FOR MY BROTHER.
I THOUGHT SO. WE WANT TO HELP YOU.
WE *DO?*
YES! I DIDN'T KNOW WE DID, BUT NOW I TOTALLY DO!

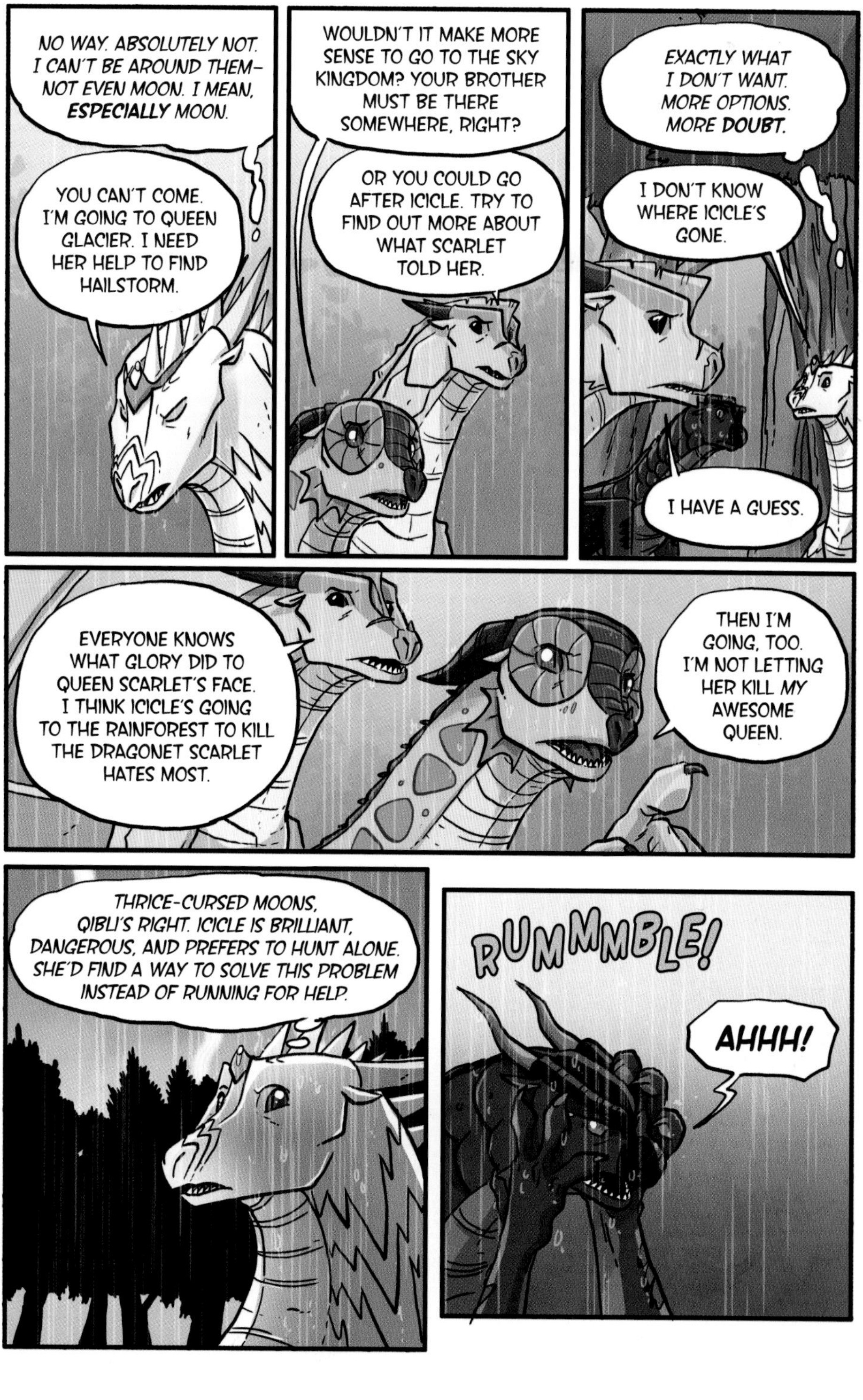
NO WAY. ABSOLUTELY NOT. I CAN'T BE AROUND THEM— NOT EVEN MOON. I MEAN, ESPECIALLY MOON.
YOU CAN'T COME. I'M GOING TO QUEEN GLACIER. I NEED HER HELP TO FIND HAILSTORM.
WOULDN'T IT MAKE MORE SENSE TO GO TO THE SKY KINGDOM? YOUR BROTHER MUST BE THERE SOMEWHERE, RIGHT?
OR YOU COULD GO AFTER ICICLE. TRY TO FIND OUT MORE ABOUT WHAT SCARLET TOLD HER.
EXACTLY WHAT I DON'T WANT. MORE OPTIONS. MORE DOUBT.
I DON'T KNOW WHERE ICICLE'S GONE.
I HAVE A GUESS.
EVERYONE KNOWS WHAT GLORY DID TO QUEEN SCARLET'S FACE. I THINK ICICLE'S GOING TO THE RAINFOREST TO KILL THE DRAGONET SCARLET HATES MOST.
THEN I'M GOING, TOO. I'M NOT LETTING HER KILL MY AWESOME QUEEN.
THRICE-CURSED MOONS, QIBLI'S RIGHT. ICICLE IS BRILLIANT, DANGEROUS, AND PREFERS TO HUNT ALONE. SHE'D FIND A WAY TO SOLVE THIS PROBLEM INSTEAD OF RUNNING FOR HELP.
RUMMMBLE!
AHHH!

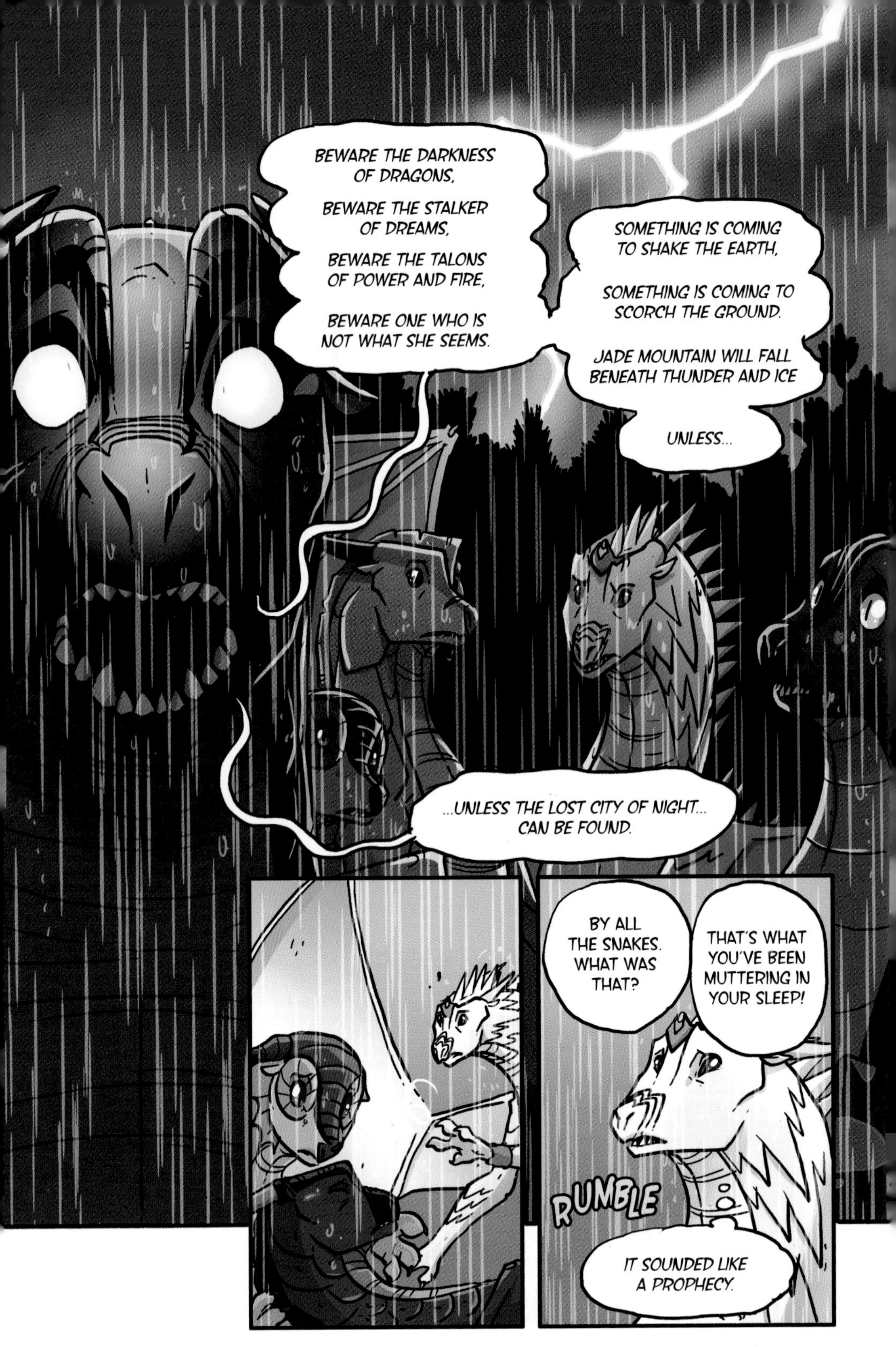

BEWARE THE DARKNESS OF DRAGONS,
BEWARE THE STALKER OF DREAMS,
BEWARE THE TALONS OF POWER AND FIRE,
BEWARE ONE WHO IS NOT WHAT SHE SEEMS.
SOMETHING IS COMING TO SHAKE THE EARTH,
SOMETHING IS COMING TO SCORCH THE GROUND.
JADE MOUNTAIN WILL FALL BENEATH THUNDER AND ICE
UNLESS...
...UNLESS THE LOST CITY OF NIGHT... CAN BE FOUND.
BY ALL THE SNAKES. WHAT WAS THAT?
THAT'S WHAT YOU'VE BEEN MUTTERING IN YOUR SLEEP!
RUMBLE
IT SOUNDED LIKE A PROPHECY.

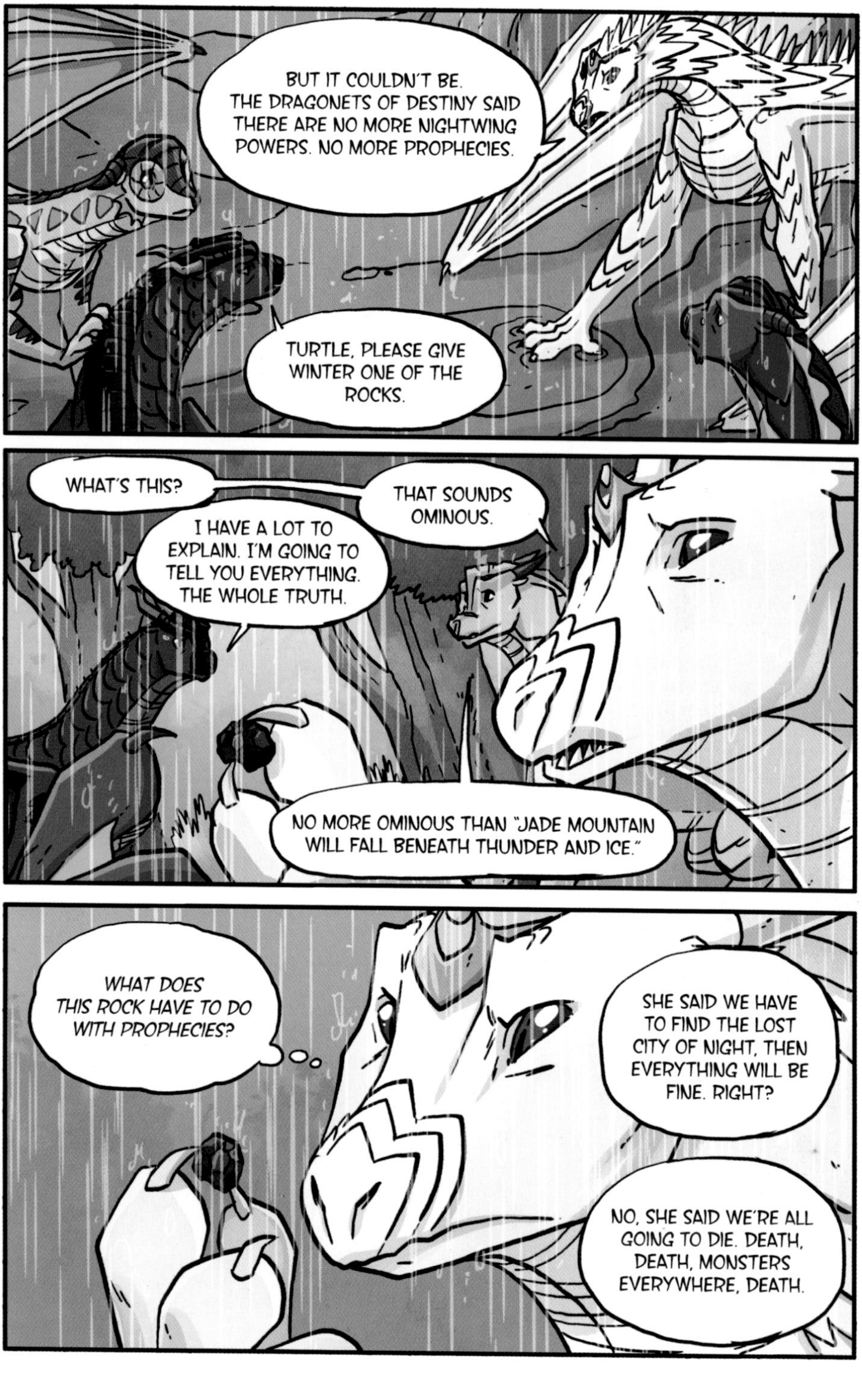
BUT IT COULDN'T BE. THE DRAGONETS OF DESTINY SAID THERE ARE NO MORE NIGHTWING POWERS. NO MORE PROPHECIES.
TURTLE, PLEASE GIVE WINTER ONE OF THE ROCKS.
WHAT'S THIS?
THAT SOUNDS OMINOUS.
I HAVE A LOT TO EXPLAIN. I'M GOING TO TELL YOU EVERYTHING. THE WHOLE TRUTH.
NO MORE OMINOUS THAN "JADE MOUNTAIN WILL FALL BENEATH THUNDER AND ICE."
WHAT DOES THIS ROCK HAVE TO DO WITH PROPHECIES?
SHE SAID WE HAVE TO FIND THE LOST CITY OF NIGHT, THEN EVERYTHING WILL BE FINE. RIGHT?
NO, SHE SAID WE'RE ALL GOING TO DIE. DEATH, DEATH, MONSTERS EVERYWHERE, DEATH.

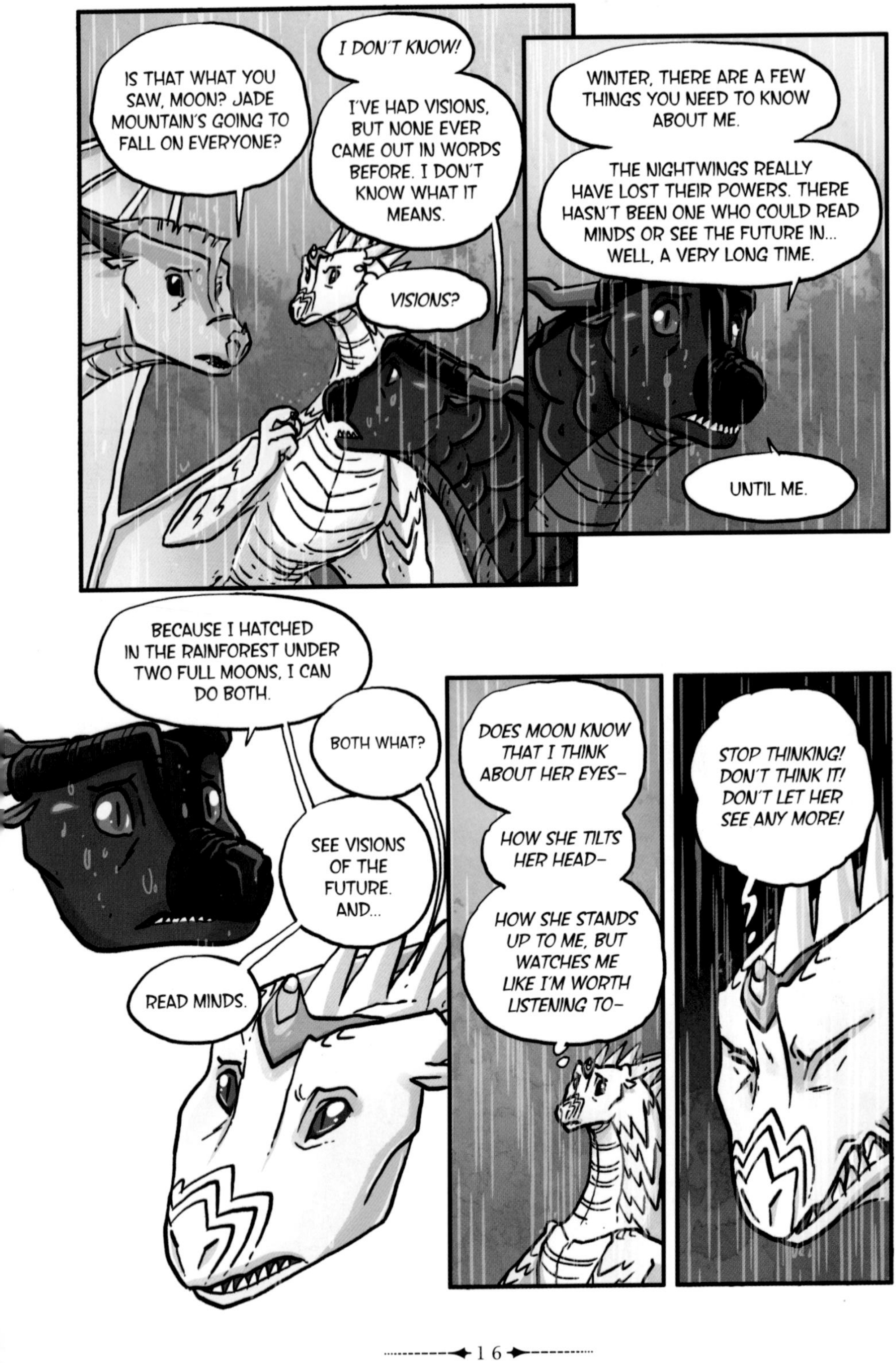

IS THAT WHAT YOU SAW, MOON? JADE MOUNTAIN'S GOING TO FALL ON EVERYONE?
I DON'T KNOW!
I'VE HAD VISIONS, BUT NONE EVER CAME OUT IN WORDS BEFORE. I DON'T KNOW WHAT IT MEANS.
VISIONS?
WINTER, THERE ARE A FEW THINGS YOU NEED TO KNOW ABOUT ME.
THE NIGHTWINGS REALLY HAVE LOST THEIR POWERS. THERE HASN'T BEEN ONE WHO COULD READ MINDS OR SEE THE FUTURE IN... WELL, A VERY LONG TIME.
UNTIL ME.
BECAUSE I HATCHED IN THE RAINFOREST UNDER TWO FULL MOONS, I CAN DO BOTH.
BOTH WHAT?
SEE VISIONS OF THE FUTURE. AND...
READ MINDS.
DOES MOON KNOW THAT I THINK ABOUT HER EYES–
HOW SHE TILTS HER HEAD–
HOW SHE STANDS UP TO ME, BUT WATCHES ME LIKE I'M WORTH LISTENING TO–
STOP THINKING! DON'T THINK IT! DON'T LET HER SEE ANY MORE!

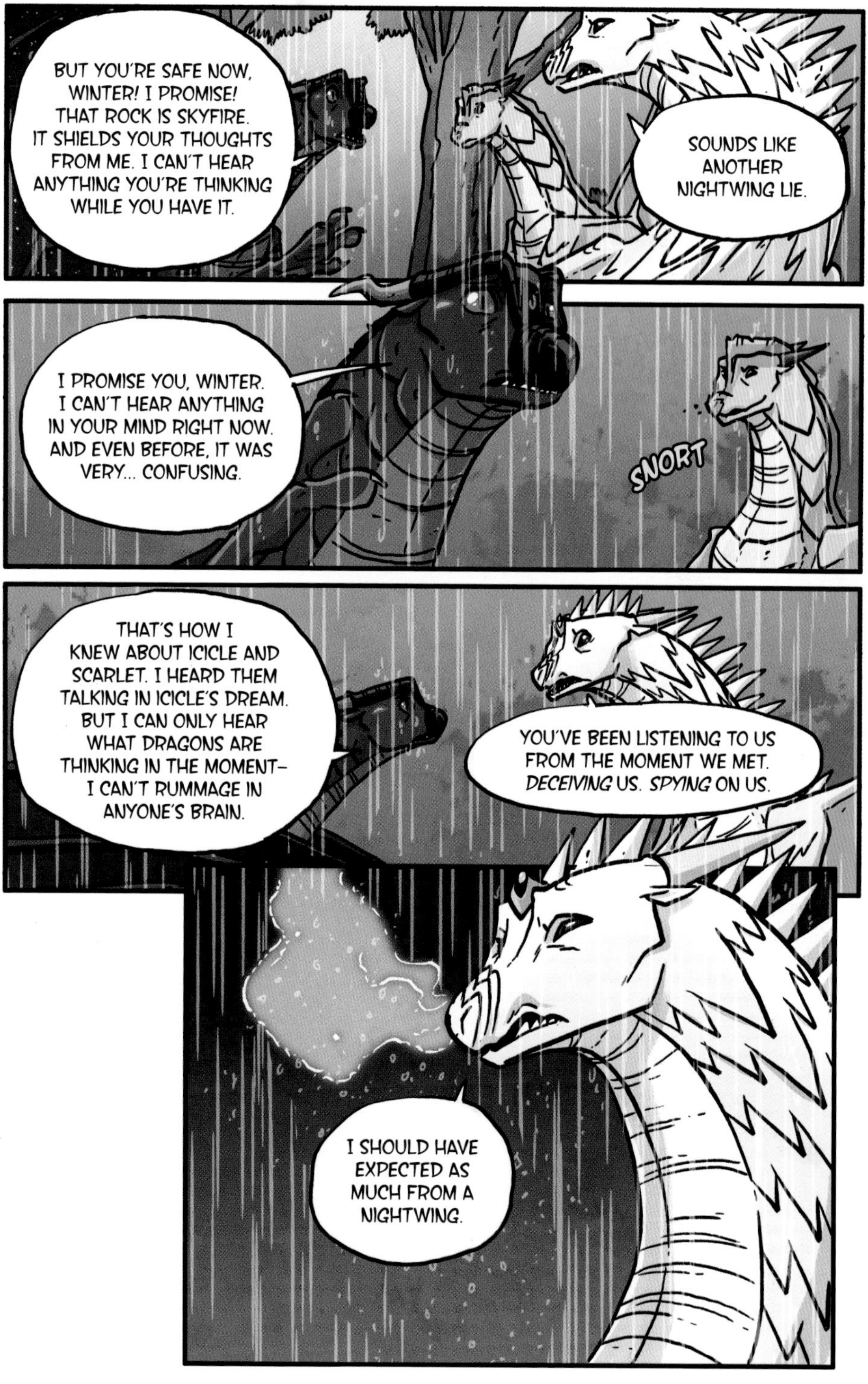
BUT YOU'RE SAFE NOW, WINTER! I PROMISE! THAT ROCK IS SKYFIRE. IT SHIELDS YOUR THOUGHTS FROM ME. I CAN'T HEAR ANYTHING YOU'RE THINKING WHILE YOU HAVE IT.
SOUNDS LIKE ANOTHER NIGHTWING LIE.
I PROMISE YOU, WINTER. I CAN'T HEAR ANYTHING IN YOUR MIND RIGHT NOW. AND EVEN BEFORE, IT WAS VERY... CONFUSING.
SNORT
THAT'S HOW I KNEW ABOUT ICICLE AND SCARLET. I HEARD THEM TALKING IN ICICLE'S DREAM. BUT I CAN ONLY HEAR WHAT DRAGONS ARE THINKING IN THE MOMENT– I CAN'T RUMMAGE IN ANYONE'S BRAIN.
YOU'VE BEEN LISTENING TO US FROM THE MOMENT WE MET. *DECEIVING* US. *SPYING* ON US.
I SHOULD HAVE EXPECTED AS MUCH FROM A NIGHTWING.

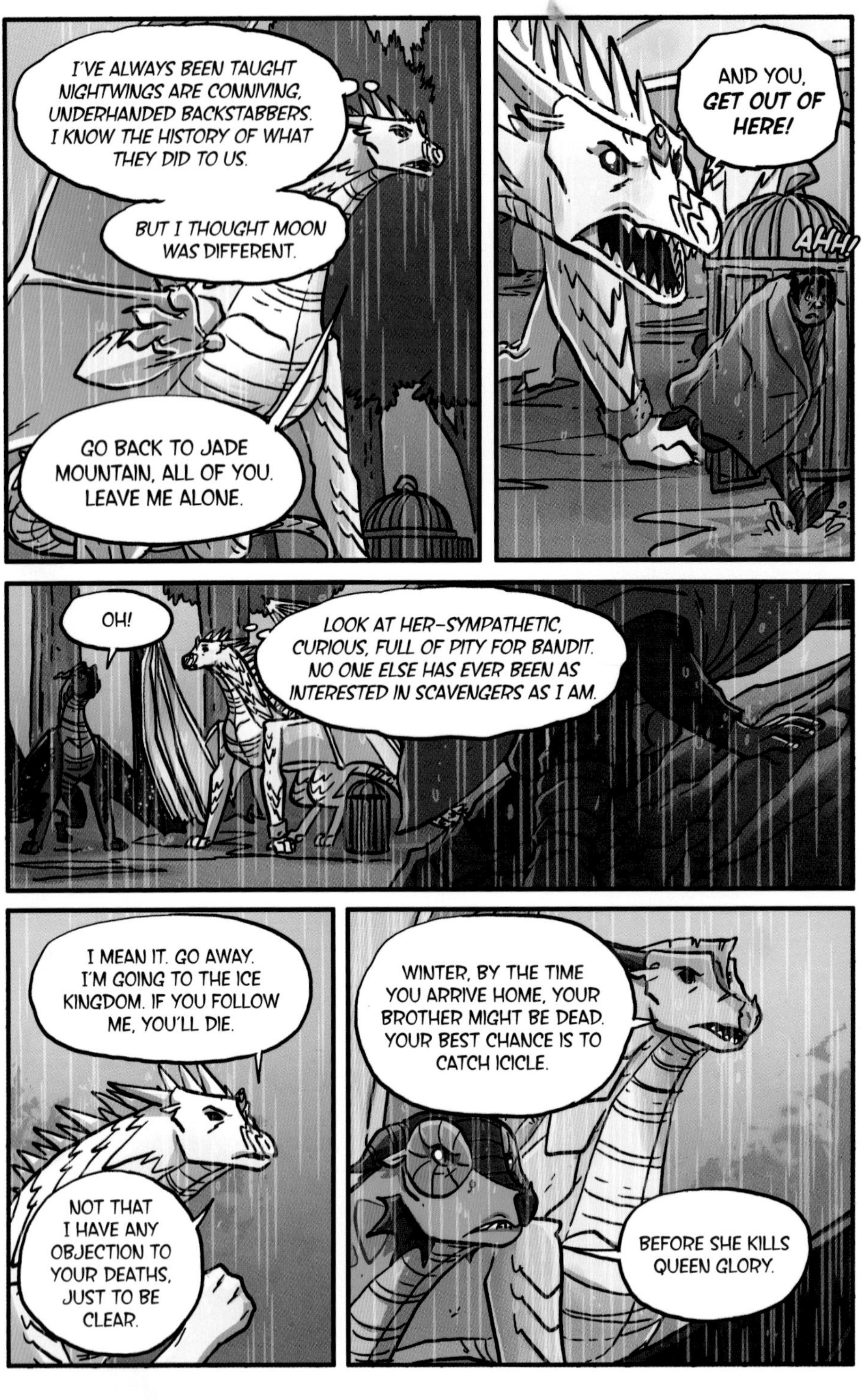
I'VE ALWAYS BEEN TAUGHT NIGHTWINGS ARE CONNIVING, UNDERHANDED BACKSTABBERS. I KNOW THE HISTORY OF WHAT THEY DID TO US.
BUT I THOUGHT MOON WAS DIFFERENT.
GO BACK TO JADE MOUNTAIN, ALL OF YOU. LEAVE ME ALONE.
AND YOU, GET OUT OF HERE!
AHH!
OH!
LOOK AT HER–SYMPATHETIC, CURIOUS, FULL OF PITY FOR BANDIT. NO ONE ELSE HAS EVER BEEN AS INTERESTED IN SCAVENGERS AS I AM.
I MEAN IT. GO AWAY. I'M GOING TO THE ICE KINGDOM. IF YOU FOLLOW ME, YOU'LL DIE.
NOT THAT I HAVE ANY OBJECTION TO YOUR DEATHS, JUST TO BE CLEAR.
WINTER, BY THE TIME YOU ARRIVE HOME, YOUR BROTHER MIGHT BE DEAD. YOUR BEST CHANCE IS TO CATCH ICICLE.
BEFORE SHE KILLS QUEEN GLORY.

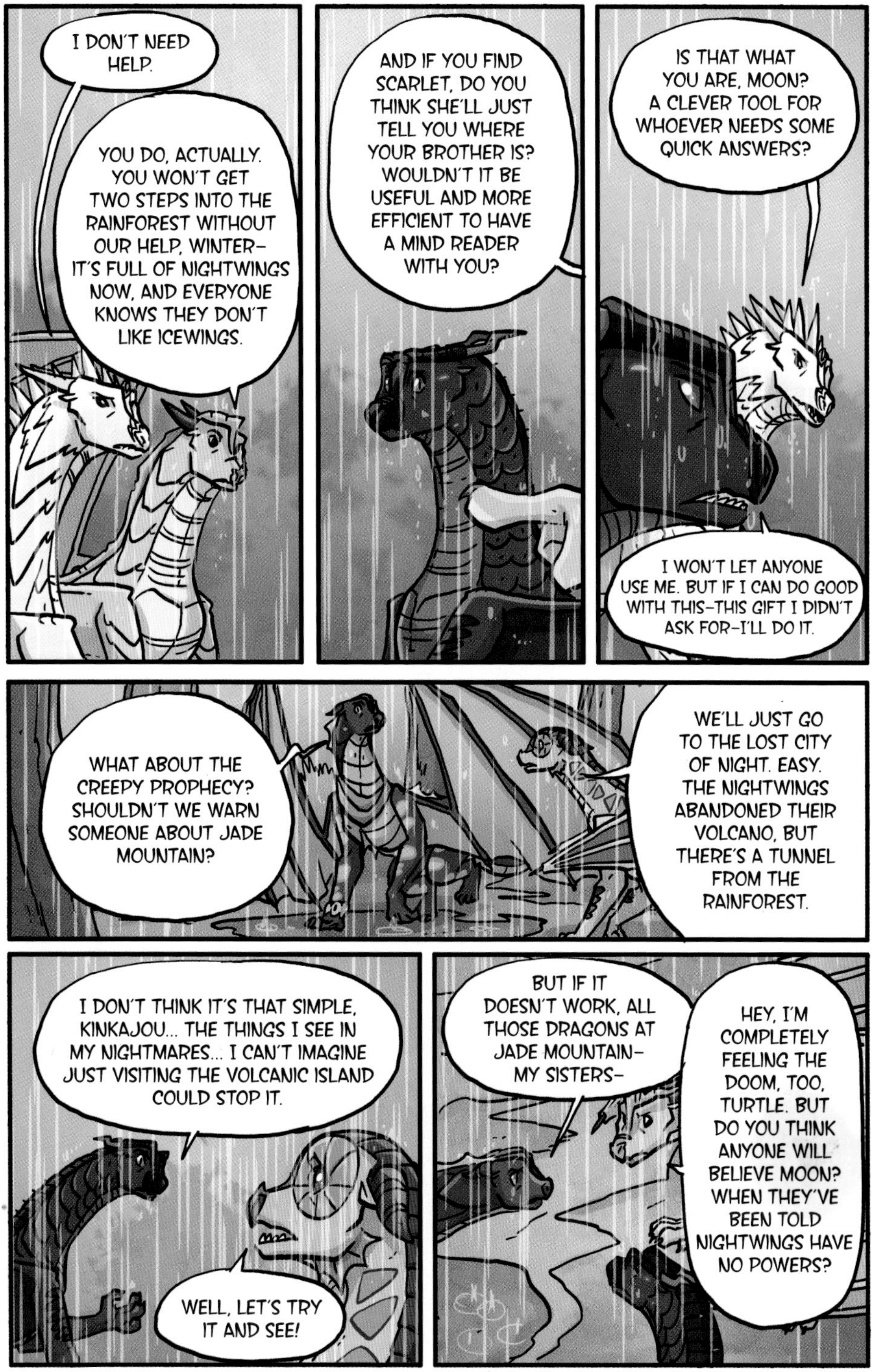
I DON'T NEED HELP.
YOU DO, ACTUALLY. YOU WON'T GET TWO STEPS INTO THE RAINFOREST WITHOUT OUR HELP, WINTER— IT'S FULL OF NIGHTWINGS NOW, AND EVERYONE KNOWS THEY DON'T LIKE ICEWINGS.
AND IF YOU FIND SCARLET, DO YOU THINK SHE'LL JUST TELL YOU WHERE YOUR BROTHER IS? WOULDN'T IT BE USEFUL AND MORE EFFICIENT TO HAVE A MIND READER WITH YOU?
IS THAT WHAT YOU ARE, MOON? A CLEVER TOOL FOR WHOEVER NEEDS SOME QUICK ANSWERS?
I WON'T LET ANYONE USE ME. BUT IF I CAN DO GOOD WITH THIS—THIS GIFT I DIDN'T ASK FOR—I'LL DO IT.
WHAT ABOUT THE CREEPY PROPHECY? SHOULDN'T WE WARN SOMEONE ABOUT JADE MOUNTAIN?
WE'LL JUST GO TO THE LOST CITY OF NIGHT. EASY. THE NIGHTWINGS ABANDONED THEIR VOLCANO, BUT THERE'S A TUNNEL FROM THE RAINFOREST.
I DON'T THINK IT'S THAT SIMPLE, KINKAJOU... THE THINGS I SEE IN MY NIGHTMARES... I CAN'T IMAGINE JUST VISITING THE VOLCANIC ISLAND COULD STOP IT.
WELL, LET'S TRY IT AND SEE!
BUT IF IT DOESN'T WORK, ALL THOSE DRAGONS AT JADE MOUNTAIN— MY SISTERS—
HEY, I'M COMPLETELY FEELING THE DOOM, TOO, TURTLE. BUT DO YOU THINK ANYONE WILL BELIEVE MOON? WHEN THEY'VE BEEN TOLD NIGHTWINGS HAVE NO POWERS?

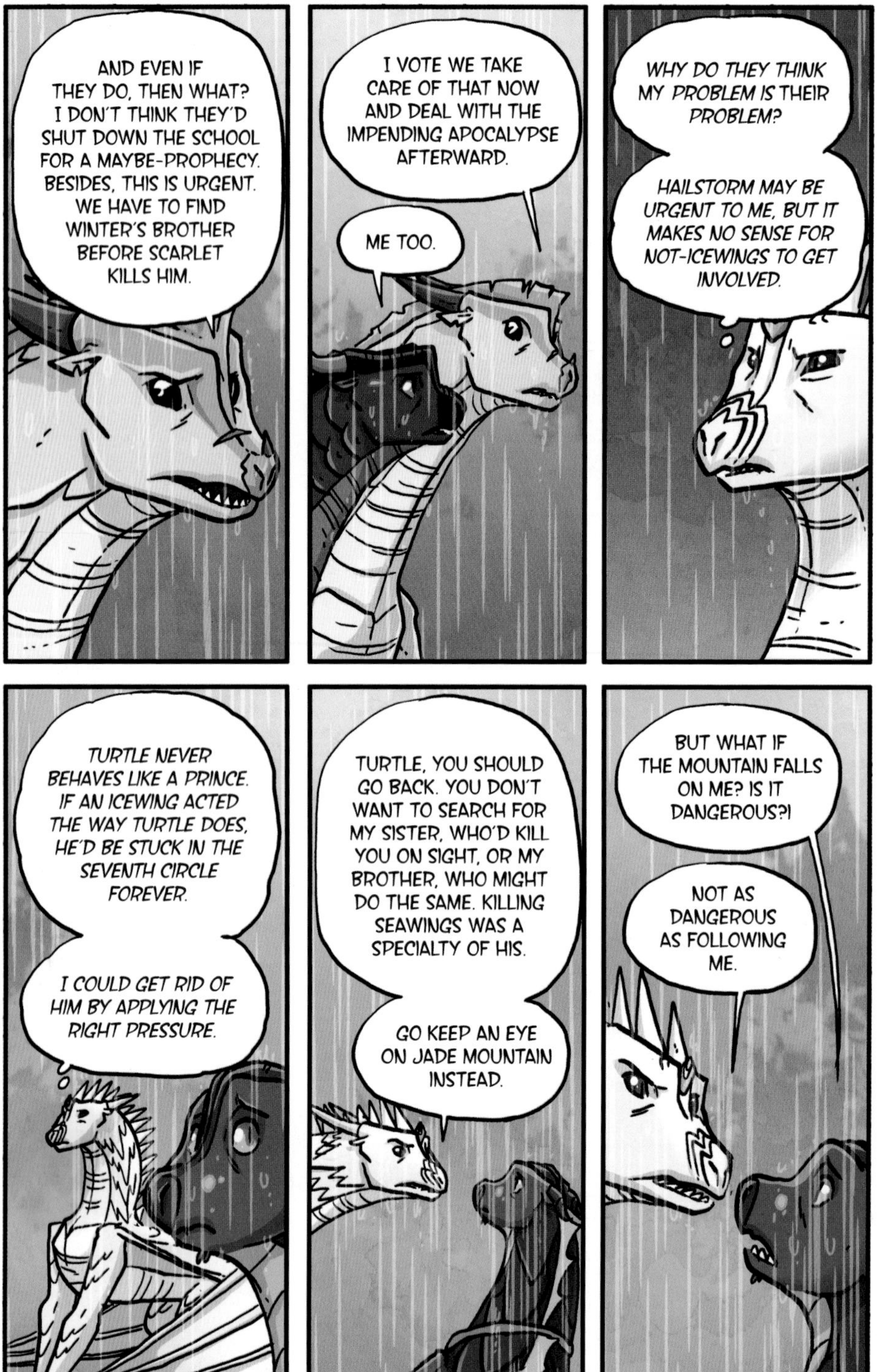
AND EVEN IF THEY DO, THEN WHAT? I DON'T THINK THEY'D SHUT DOWN THE SCHOOL FOR A MAYBE-PROPHECY. BESIDES, THIS IS URGENT. WE HAVE TO FIND WINTER'S BROTHER BEFORE SCARLET KILLS HIM.
I VOTE WE TAKE CARE OF THAT NOW AND DEAL WITH THE IMPENDING APOCALYPSE AFTERWARD.
ME TOO.
WHY DO THEY THINK MY PROBLEM IS THEIR PROBLEM?
HAILSTORM MAY BE URGENT TO ME, BUT IT MAKES NO SENSE FOR NOT-ICEWINGS TO GET INVOLVED.
TURTLE NEVER BEHAVES LIKE A PRINCE. IF AN ICEWING ACTED THE WAY TURTLE DOES, HE'D BE STUCK IN THE SEVENTH CIRCLE FOREVER.
I COULD GET RID OF HIM BY APPLYING THE RIGHT PRESSURE.
TURTLE, YOU SHOULD GO BACK. YOU DON'T WANT TO SEARCH FOR MY SISTER, WHO'D KILL YOU ON SIGHT, OR MY BROTHER, WHO MIGHT DO THE SAME. KILLING SEAWINGS WAS A SPECIALTY OF HIS.
GO KEEP AN EYE ON JADE MOUNTAIN INSTEAD.
BUT WHAT IF THE MOUNTAIN FALLS ON ME? IS IT DANGEROUS?!
NOT AS DANGEROUS AS FOLLOWING ME.

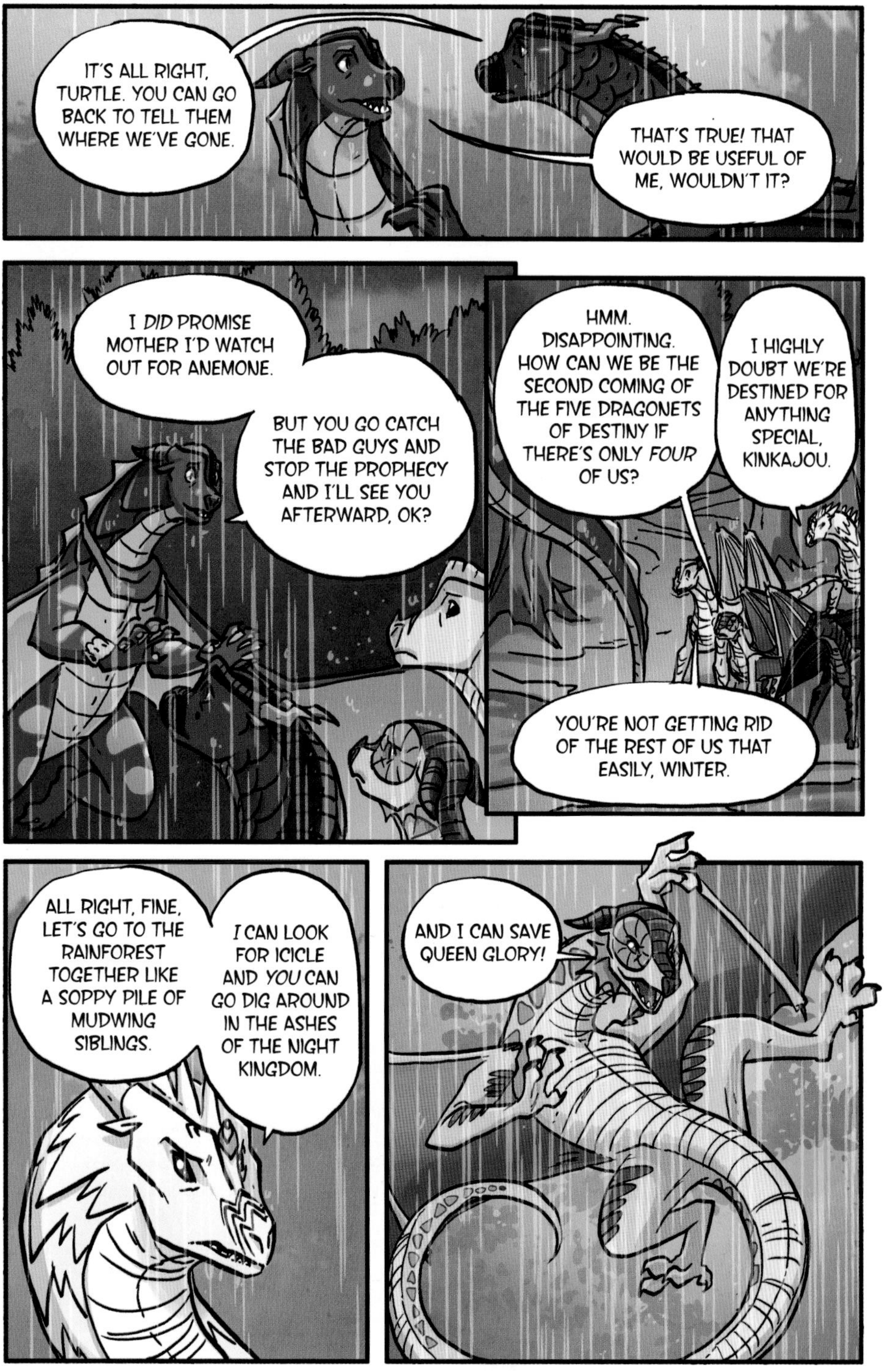
IT'S ALL RIGHT, TURTLE. YOU CAN GO BACK TO TELL THEM WHERE WE'VE GONE.
THAT'S TRUE! THAT WOULD BE USEFUL OF ME, WOULDN'T IT?
I *DID* PROMISE MOTHER I'D WATCH OUT FOR ANEMONE.
BUT YOU GO CATCH THE BAD GUYS AND STOP THE PROPHECY AND I'LL SEE YOU AFTERWARD, OK?
HMM. DISAPPOINTING. HOW CAN WE BE THE SECOND COMING OF THE FIVE DRAGONETS OF DESTINY IF THERE'S ONLY *FOUR* OF US?
I HIGHLY DOUBT WE'RE DESTINED FOR ANYTHING SPECIAL, KINKAJOU.
YOU'RE NOT GETTING RID OF THE REST OF US THAT EASILY, WINTER.
ALL RIGHT, FINE, LET'S GO TO THE RAINFOREST TOGETHER LIKE A SOPPY PILE OF MUDWING SIBLINGS.
I CAN LOOK FOR ICICLE AND *YOU* CAN GO DIG AROUND IN THE ASHES OF THE NIGHT KINGDOM.
AND I CAN SAVE QUEEN GLORY!

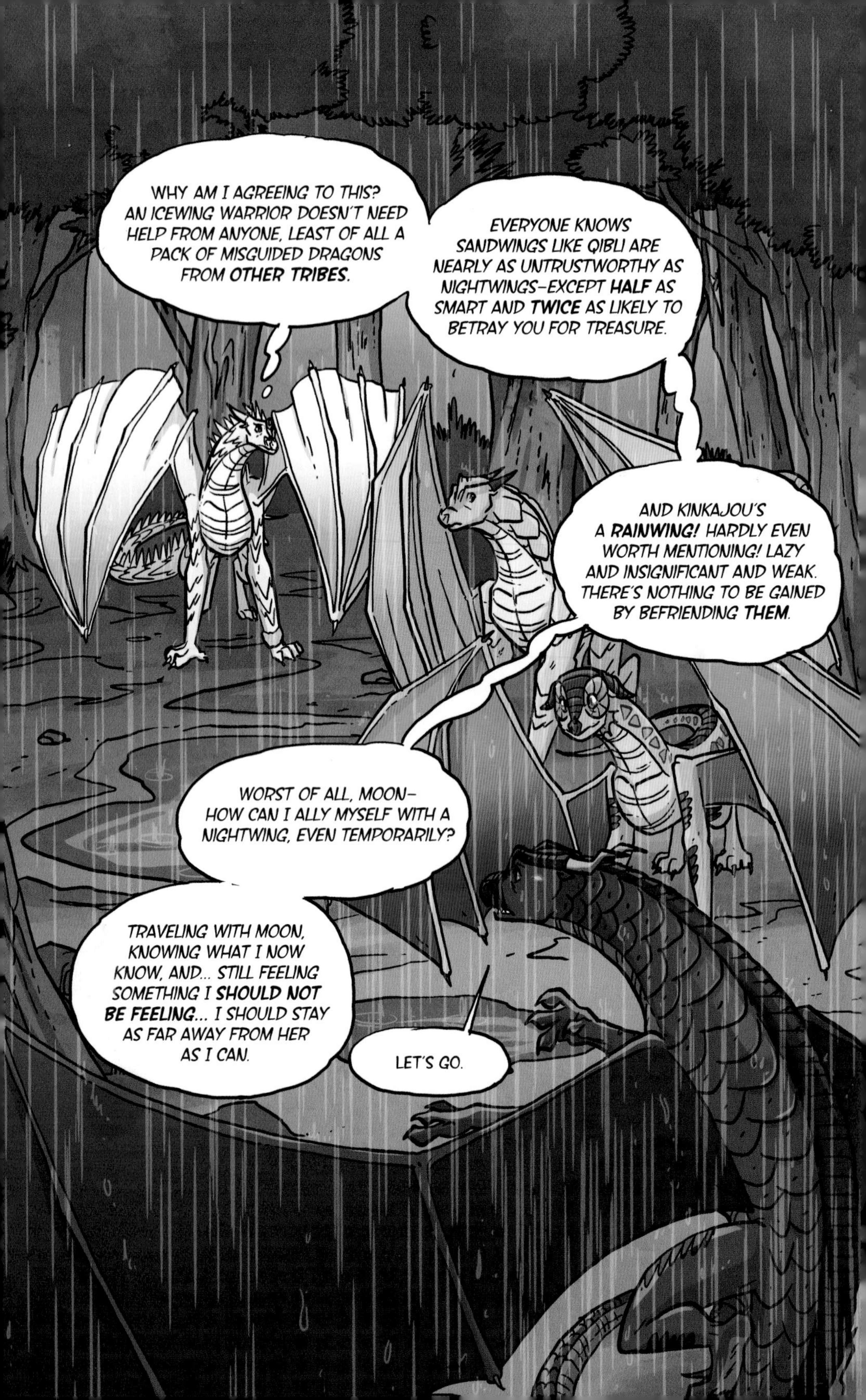
WHY AM I AGREEING TO THIS? AN ICEWING WARRIOR DOESN'T NEED HELP FROM ANYONE, LEAST OF ALL A PACK OF MISGUIDED DRAGONS FROM **OTHER TRIBES**.
EVERYONE KNOWS SANDWINGS LIKE QIBLI ARE NEARLY AS UNTRUSTWORTHY AS NIGHTWINGS–EXCEPT **HALF** AS SMART AND **TWICE** AS LIKELY TO BETRAY YOU FOR TREASURE.
AND KINKAJOU'S A **RAINWING!** HARDLY EVEN WORTH MENTIONING! LAZY AND INSIGNIFICANT AND WEAK. THERE'S NOTHING TO BE GAINED BY BEFRIENDING **THEM**.
WORST OF ALL, MOON– HOW CAN I ALLY MYSELF WITH A NIGHTWING, EVEN TEMPORARILY?
TRAVELING WITH MOON, KNOWING WHAT I NOW KNOW, AND... STILL FEELING SOMETHING I **SHOULD NOT BE FEELING**... I SHOULD STAY AS FAR AWAY FROM HER AS I CAN.
LET'S GO.

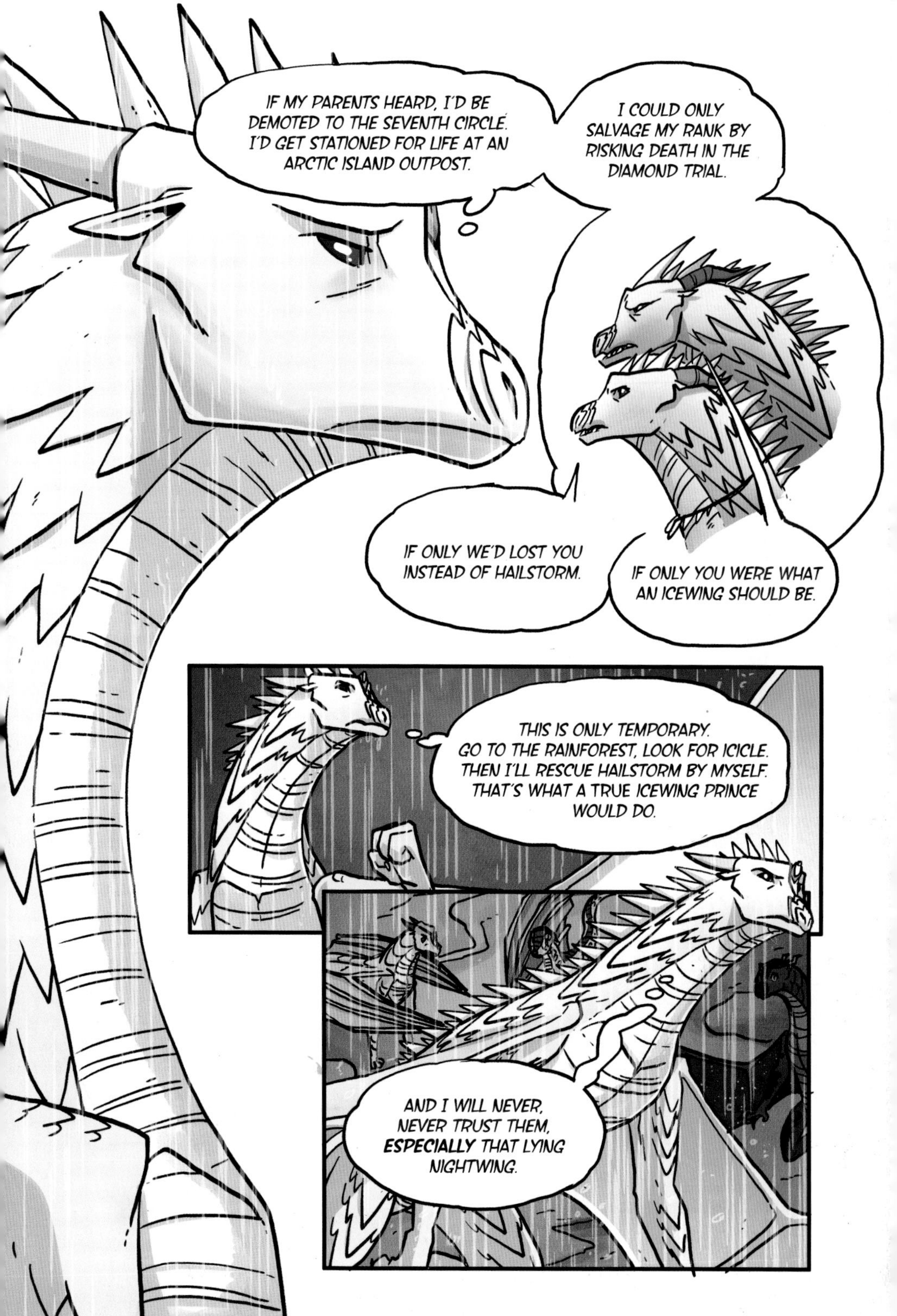
IF MY PARENTS HEARD, I'D BE DEMOTED TO THE SEVENTH CIRCLE. I'D GET STATIONED FOR LIFE AT AN ARCTIC ISLAND OUTPOST.
I COULD ONLY SALVAGE MY RANK BY RISKING DEATH IN THE DIAMOND TRIAL.
IF ONLY WE'D LOST YOU INSTEAD OF HAILSTORM.
IF ONLY YOU WERE WHAT AN ICEWING SHOULD BE.
THIS IS ONLY TEMPORARY. GO TO THE RAINFOREST, LOOK FOR ICICLE. THEN I'LL RESCUE HAILSTORM BY MYSELF. THAT'S WHAT A TRUE ICEWING PRINCE WOULD DO.
AND I WILL NEVER, NEVER TRUST THEM, **ESPECIALLY** THAT LYING NIGHTWING.

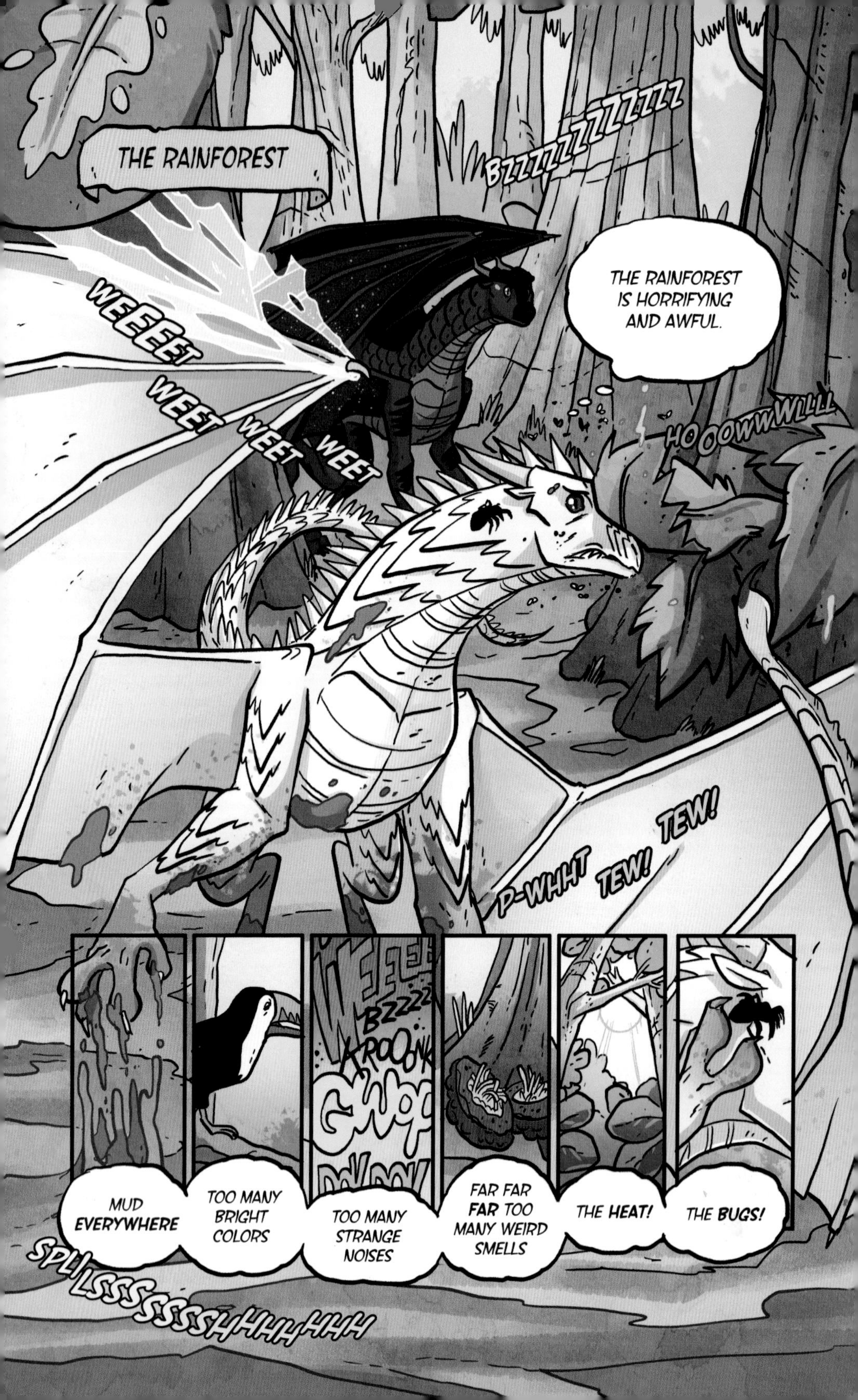
THE RAINFOREST
BZZZZZZZZZZZZZ
WEEEEET
WEET WEET WEET
THE RAINFOREST IS HORRIFYING AND AWFUL.
HOOOWWWLLLL
P-WHHT TEW! TEW!
MUD EVERYWHERE
TOO MANY BRIGHT COLORS
BZZZZ
KROOOONK
TOO MANY STRANGE NOISES
FAR FAR FAR TOO MANY WEIRD SMELLS
THE HEAT!
THE BUGS!
SPLLSSSSSSSHHHHHHH

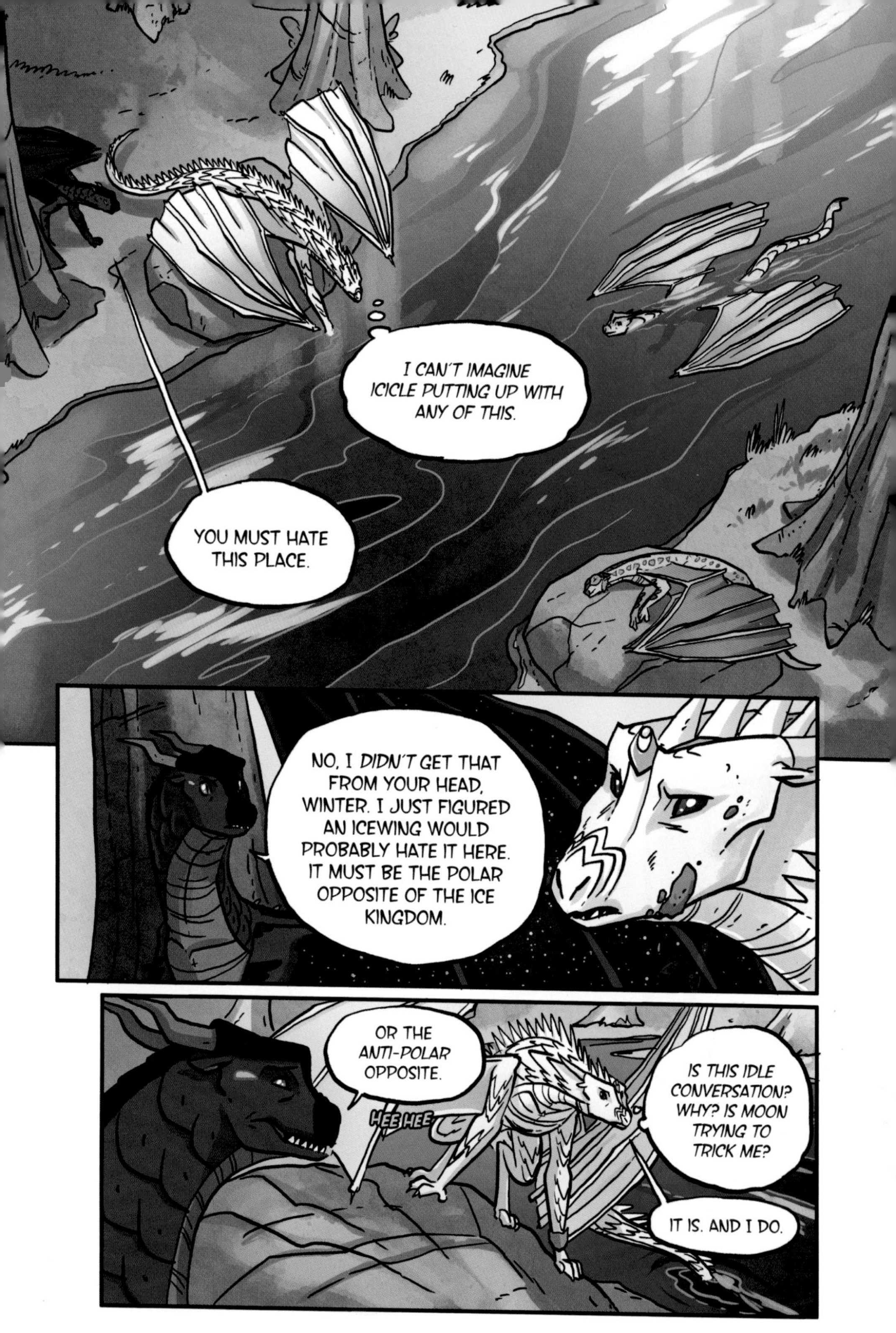
I CAN'T IMAGINE ICICLE PUTTING UP WITH ANY OF THIS.
YOU MUST HATE THIS PLACE.
NO, I *DIDN'T* GET THAT FROM YOUR HEAD, WINTER. I JUST FIGURED AN ICEWING WOULD PROBABLY HATE IT HERE. IT MUST BE THE POLAR OPPOSITE OF THE ICE KINGDOM.
OR THE ANTI-POLAR OPPOSITE.
HEE HEE
IS THIS IDLE CONVERSATION? WHY? IS MOON TRYING TO TRICK ME?
IT IS. AND I DO.

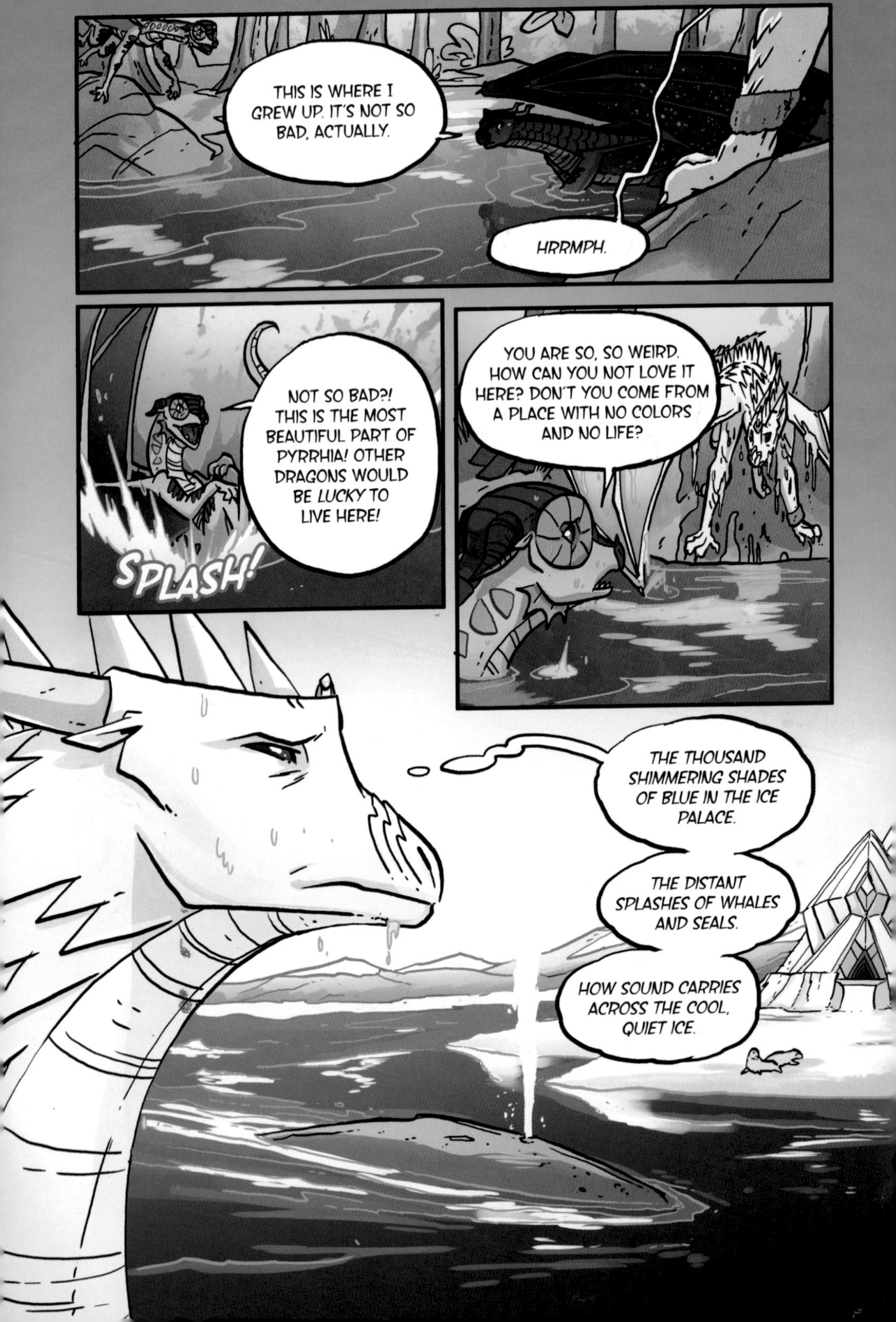

THIS IS WHERE I GREW UP. IT'S NOT SO BAD, ACTUALLY.
HRRMPH.
SPLASH!
NOT SO BAD?! THIS IS THE MOST BEAUTIFUL PART OF PYRRHIA! OTHER DRAGONS WOULD BE *LUCKY* TO LIVE HERE!
YOU ARE SO, SO WEIRD. HOW CAN YOU NOT LOVE IT HERE? DON'T YOU COME FROM A PLACE WITH NO COLORS AND NO LIFE?
THE THOUSAND SHIMMERING SHADES OF BLUE IN THE ICE PALACE.
THE DISTANT SPLASHES OF WHALES AND SEALS.
HOW SOUND CARRIES ACROSS THE COOL, QUIET ICE.

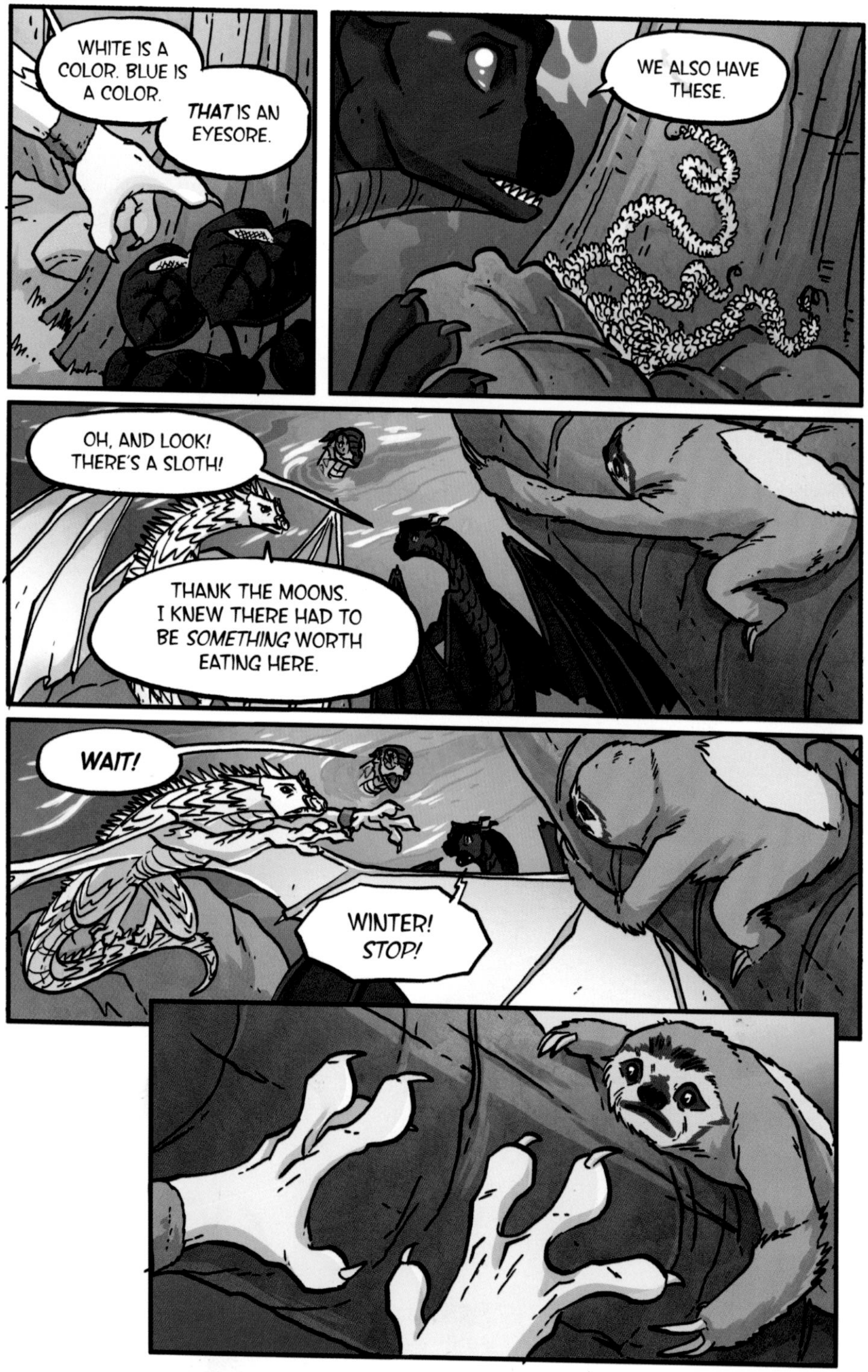
WHITE IS A COLOR. BLUE IS A COLOR.
THAT IS AN EYESORE.
WE ALSO HAVE THESE.
OH, AND LOOK! THERE'S A SLOTH!
THANK THE MOONS. I KNEW THERE HAD TO BE *SOMETHING* WORTH EATING HERE.
WAIT!
WINTER! *STOP!*

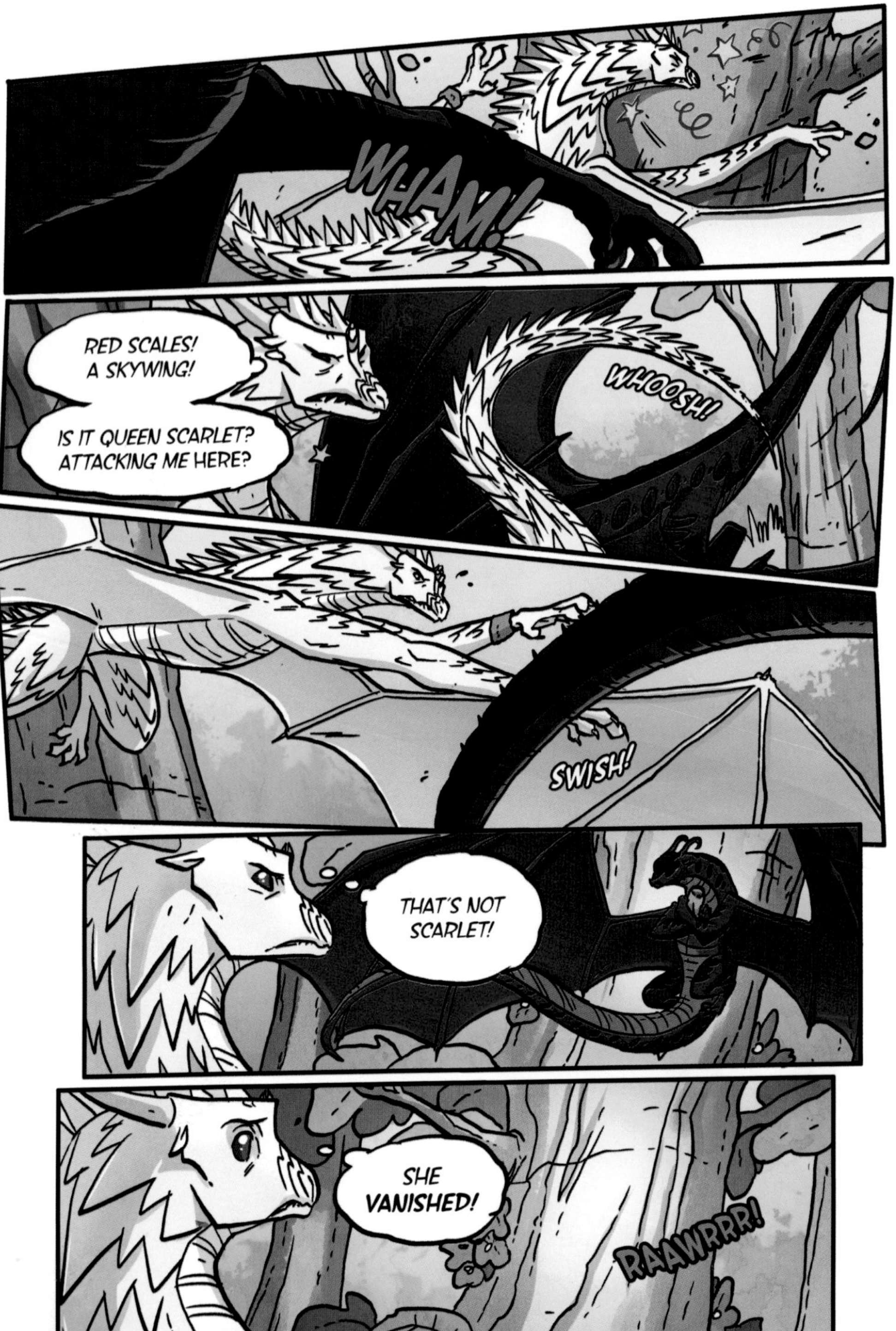
WHAM!
RED SCALES! A SKYWING!
IS IT QUEEN SCARLET? ATTACKING ME HERE?
WHOOSH!
SWISH!
THAT'S NOT SCARLET!
SHE VANISHED!
RAAWRRR!

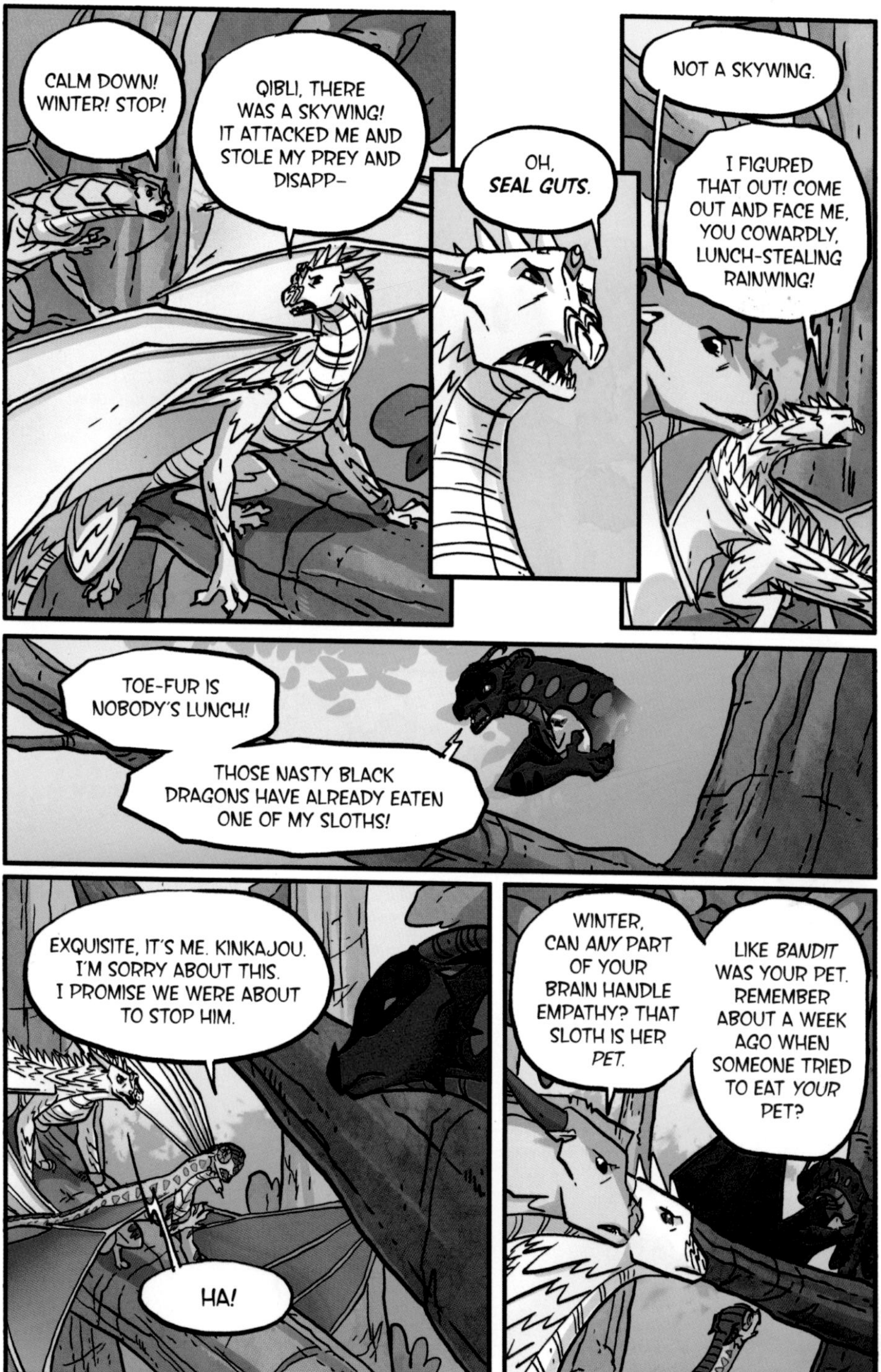
CALM DOWN! WINTER! STOP!
QIBLI, THERE WAS A SKYWING! IT ATTACKED ME AND STOLE MY PREY AND DISAPP–
OH, *SEAL GUTS*.
NOT A SKYWING.
I FIGURED THAT OUT! COME OUT AND FACE ME, YOU COWARDLY, LUNCH-STEALING RAINWING!
TOE-FUR IS NOBODY'S LUNCH!
THOSE NASTY BLACK DRAGONS HAVE ALREADY EATEN ONE OF MY SLOTHS!
EXQUISITE, IT'S ME. KINKAJOU. I'M SORRY ABOUT THIS. I PROMISE WE WERE ABOUT TO STOP HIM.
HA!
WINTER, CAN *ANY* PART OF YOUR BRAIN HANDLE EMPATHY? THAT SLOTH IS HER *PET*.
LIKE *BANDIT* WAS YOUR PET. REMEMBER ABOUT A WEEK AGO WHEN SOMEONE TRIED TO EAT *YOUR* PET?

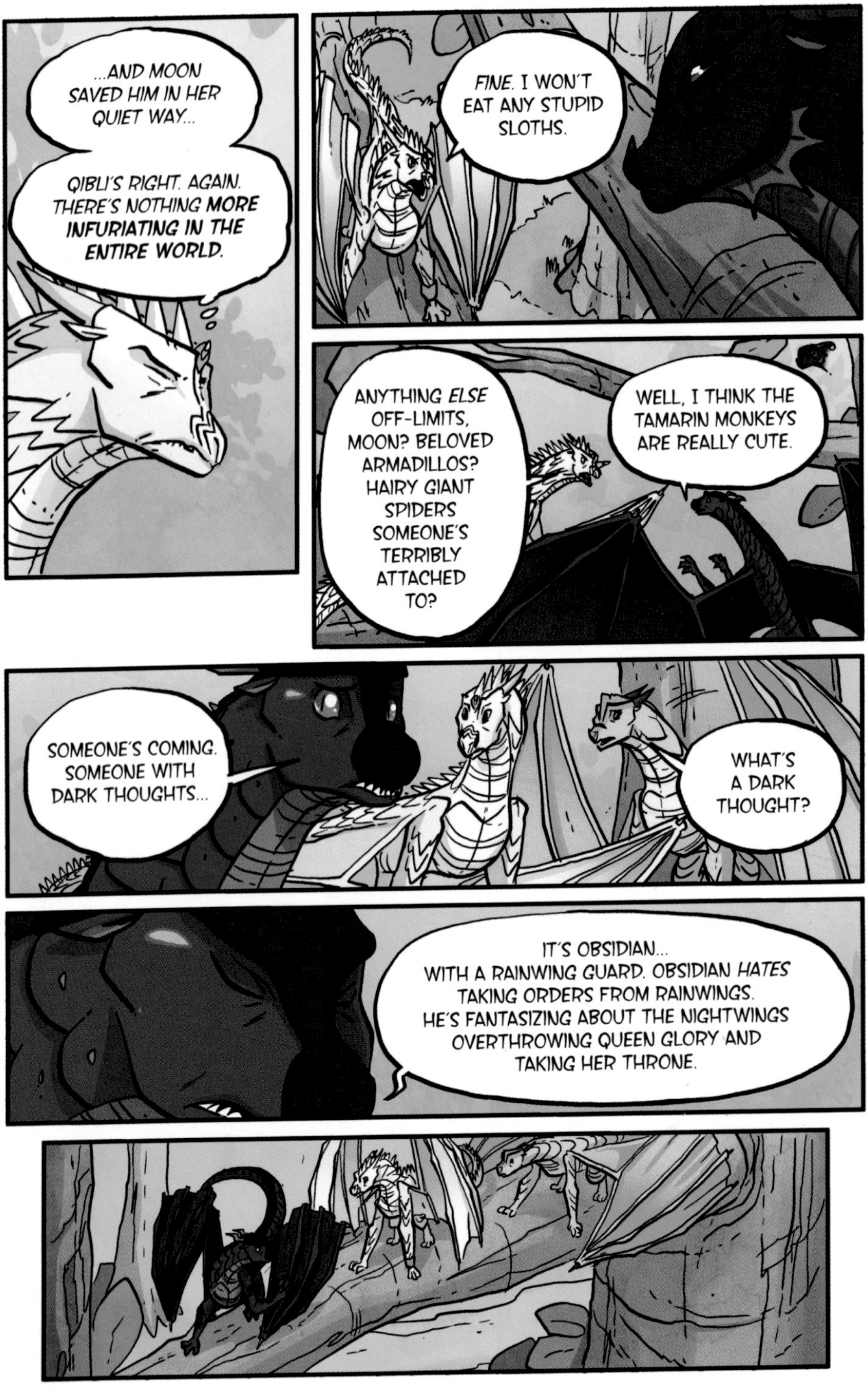
...AND MOON SAVED HIM IN HER QUIET WAY...
QIBLI'S RIGHT. AGAIN. THERE'S NOTHING **MORE INFURIATING IN THE ENTIRE WORLD.**
FINE. I WON'T EAT ANY STUPID SLOTHS.
ANYTHING *ELSE* OFF-LIMITS, MOON? BELOVED ARMADILLOS? HAIRY GIANT SPIDERS SOMEONE'S TERRIBLY ATTACHED TO?
WELL, I THINK THE TAMARIN MONKEYS ARE REALLY CUTE.
SOMEONE'S COMING. SOMEONE WITH DARK THOUGHTS...
WHAT'S A DARK THOUGHT?
IT'S OBSIDIAN... WITH A RAINWING GUARD. OBSIDIAN *HATES* TAKING ORDERS FROM RAINWINGS. HE'S FANTASIZING ABOUT THE NIGHTWINGS OVERTHROWING QUEEN GLORY AND TAKING HER THRONE.

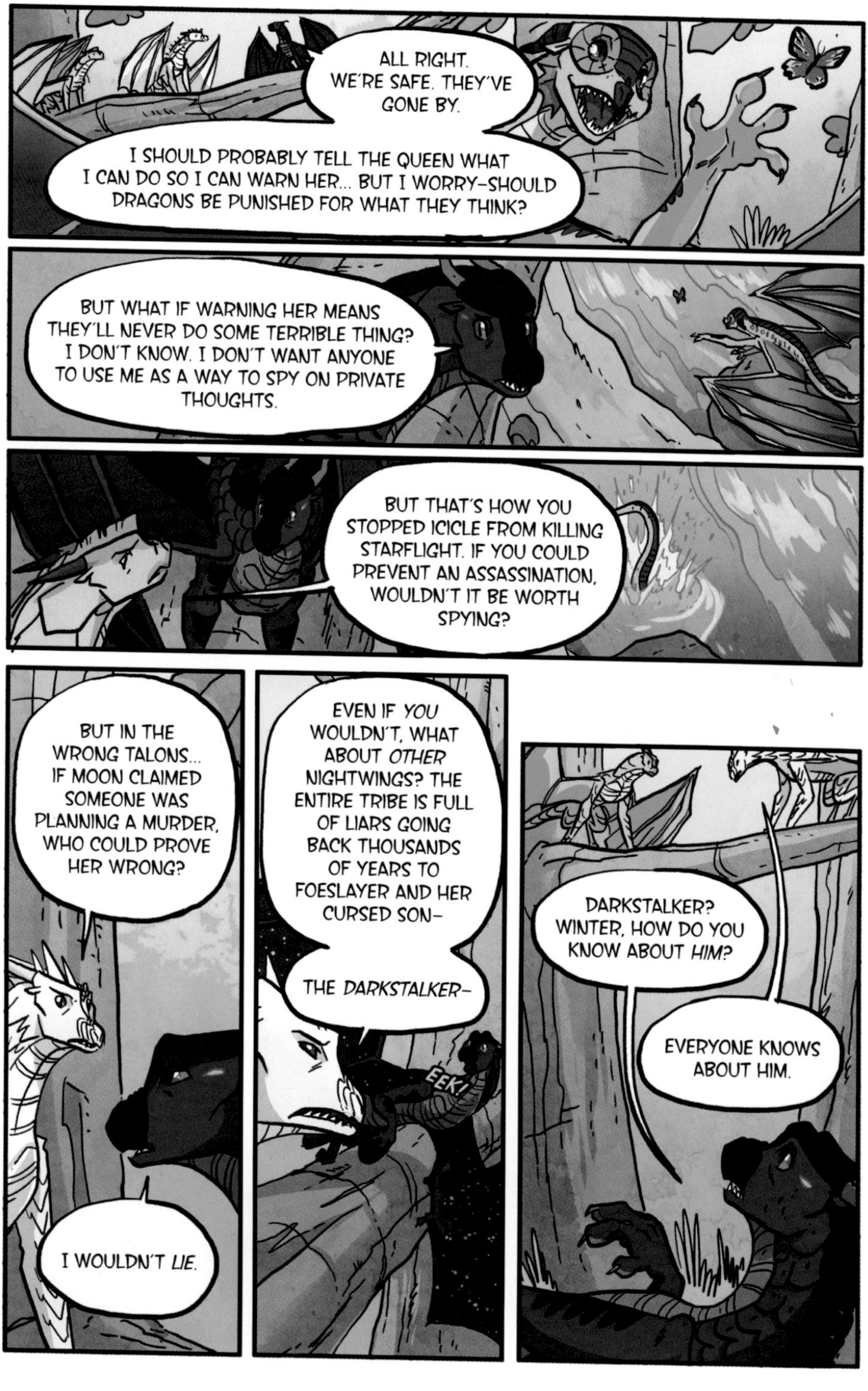
ALL RIGHT. WE'RE SAFE. THEY'VE GONE BY.
I SHOULD PROBABLY TELL THE QUEEN WHAT I CAN DO SO I CAN WARN HER... BUT I WORRY–SHOULD DRAGONS BE PUNISHED FOR WHAT THEY THINK?
BUT WHAT IF WARNING HER MEANS THEY'LL NEVER DO SOME TERRIBLE THING? I DON'T KNOW. I DON'T WANT ANYONE TO USE ME AS A WAY TO SPY ON PRIVATE THOUGHTS.
BUT THAT'S HOW YOU STOPPED ICICLE FROM KILLING STARFLIGHT. IF YOU COULD PREVENT AN ASSASSINATION, WOULDN'T IT BE WORTH SPYING?
BUT IN THE WRONG TALONS... IF MOON CLAIMED SOMEONE WAS PLANNING A MURDER, WHO COULD PROVE HER WRONG?
I WOULDN'T *LIE*.
EVEN IF *YOU* WOULDN'T, WHAT ABOUT *OTHER* NIGHTWINGS? THE ENTIRE TRIBE IS FULL OF LIARS GOING BACK THOUSANDS OF YEARS TO FOESLAYER AND HER CURSED SON–
THE *DARKSTALKER*–
EEK!
DARKSTALKER? WINTER, HOW DO YOU KNOW ABOUT *HIM*?
EVERYONE KNOWS ABOUT HIM.

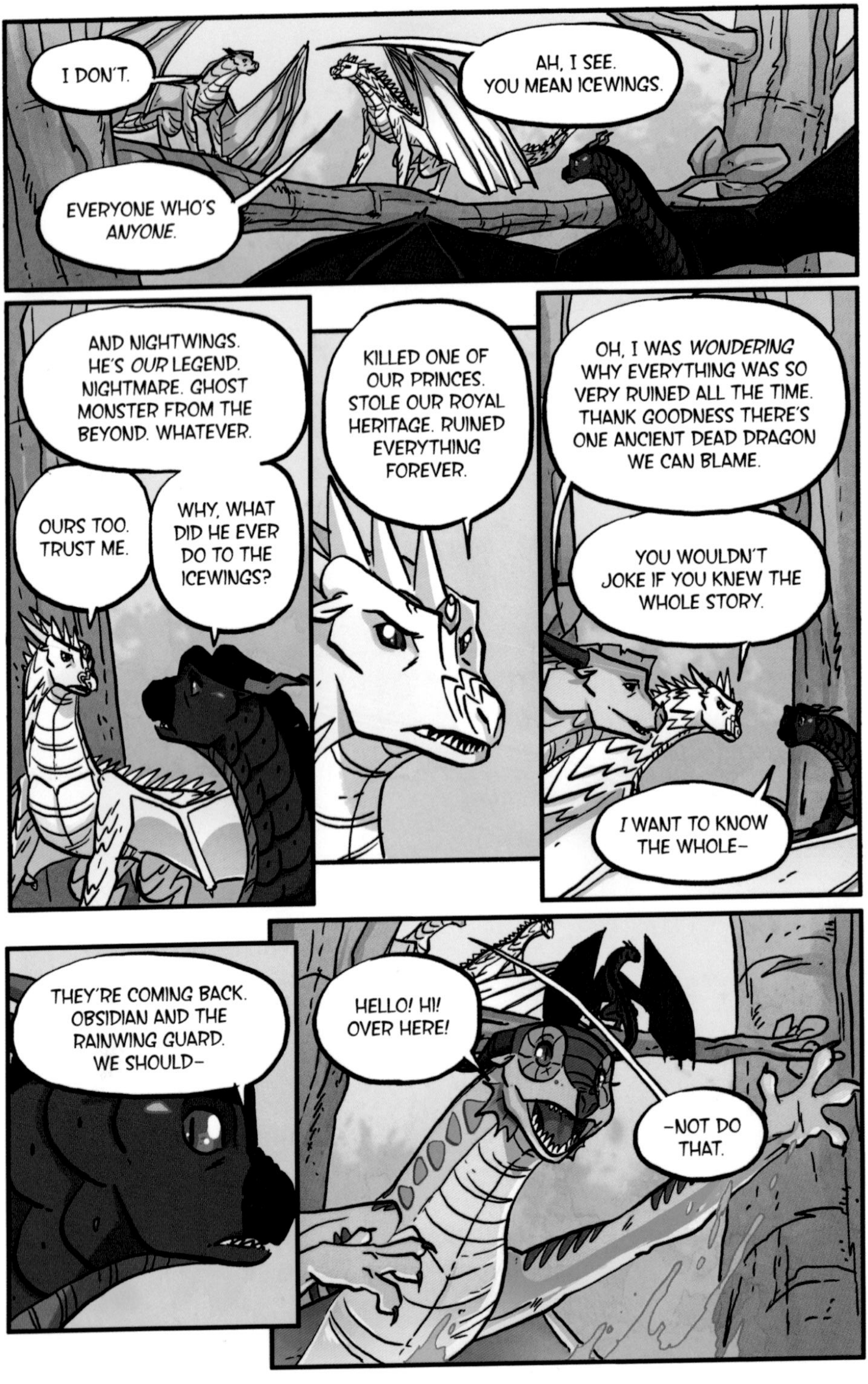
I DON'T.
AH, I SEE. YOU MEAN ICEWINGS.
EVERYONE WHO'S *ANYONE.*
AND NIGHTWINGS. HE'S *OUR* LEGEND. NIGHTMARE. GHOST MONSTER FROM THE BEYOND. WHATEVER.
OURS TOO. TRUST ME.
WHY, WHAT DID HE EVER DO TO THE ICEWINGS?
KILLED ONE OF OUR PRINCES. STOLE OUR ROYAL HERITAGE. RUINED EVERYTHING FOREVER.
OH, I WAS *WONDERING* WHY EVERYTHING WAS SO VERY RUINED ALL THE TIME. THANK GOODNESS THERE'S ONE ANCIENT DEAD DRAGON WE CAN BLAME.
YOU WOULDN'T JOKE IF YOU KNEW THE WHOLE STORY.
I WANT TO KNOW THE WHOLE–
THEY'RE COMING BACK. OBSIDIAN AND THE RAINWING GUARD. WE SHOULD–
HELLO! HI! OVER HERE!
–NOT DO THAT.

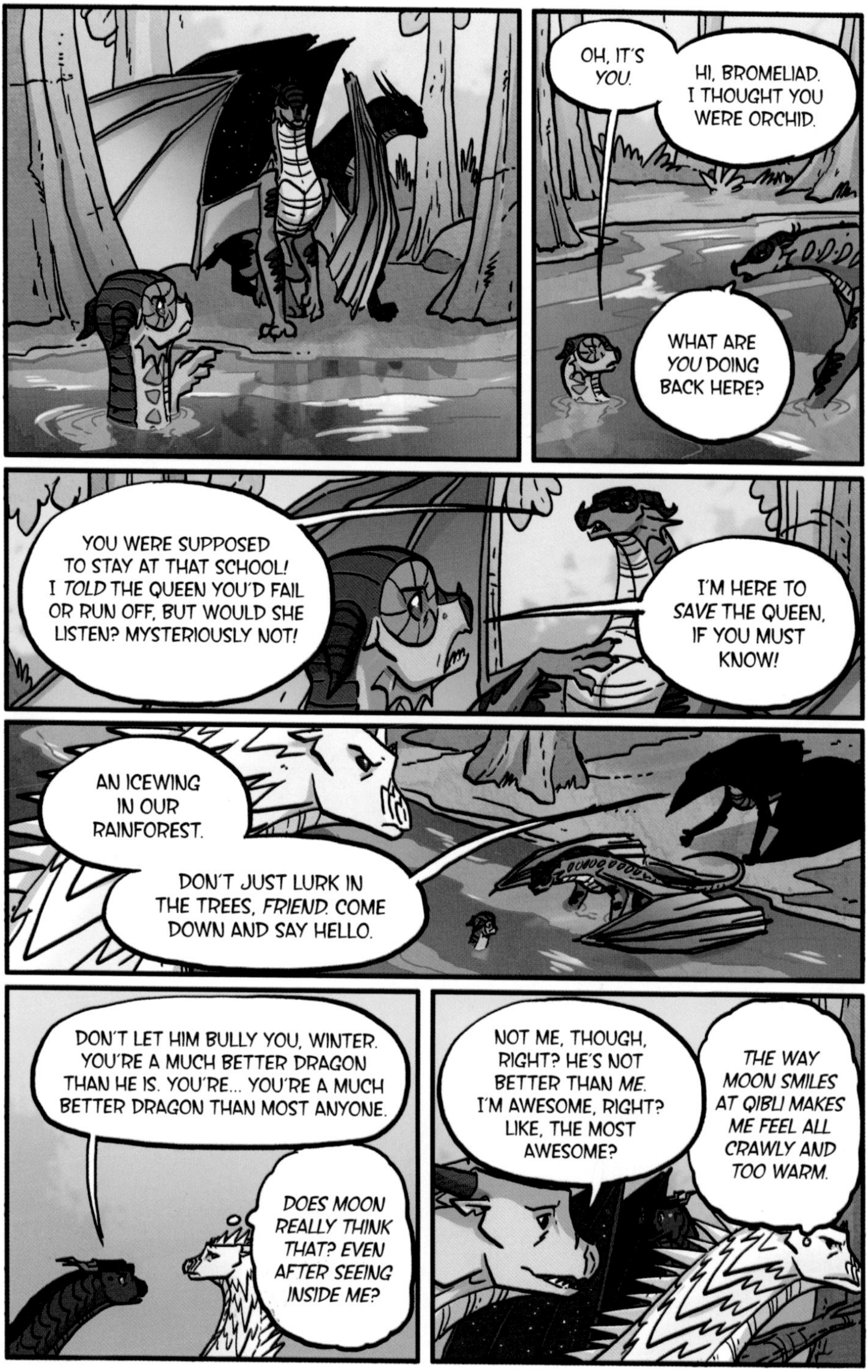
OH, IT'S *YOU.*
HI, BROMELIAD. I THOUGHT YOU WERE ORCHID.
WHAT ARE *YOU* DOING BACK HERE?
YOU WERE SUPPOSED TO STAY AT THAT SCHOOL! I *TOLD* THE QUEEN YOU'D FAIL OR RUN OFF, BUT WOULD SHE LISTEN? MYSTERIOUSLY NOT!
I'M HERE TO *SAVE* THE QUEEN, IF YOU MUST KNOW!
AN ICEWING IN OUR RAINFOREST.
DON'T JUST LURK IN THE TREES, *FRIEND.* COME DOWN AND SAY HELLO.
DON'T LET HIM BULLY YOU, WINTER. YOU'RE A MUCH BETTER DRAGON THAN HE IS. YOU'RE... YOU'RE A MUCH BETTER DRAGON THAN MOST ANYONE.
DOES MOON REALLY THINK THAT? EVEN AFTER SEEING INSIDE ME?
NOT ME, THOUGH, RIGHT? HE'S NOT BETTER THAN *ME.* I'M AWESOME, RIGHT? LIKE, THE MOST AWESOME?
THE WAY MOON SMILES AT QIBLI MAKES ME FEEL ALL CRAWLY AND TOO WARM.

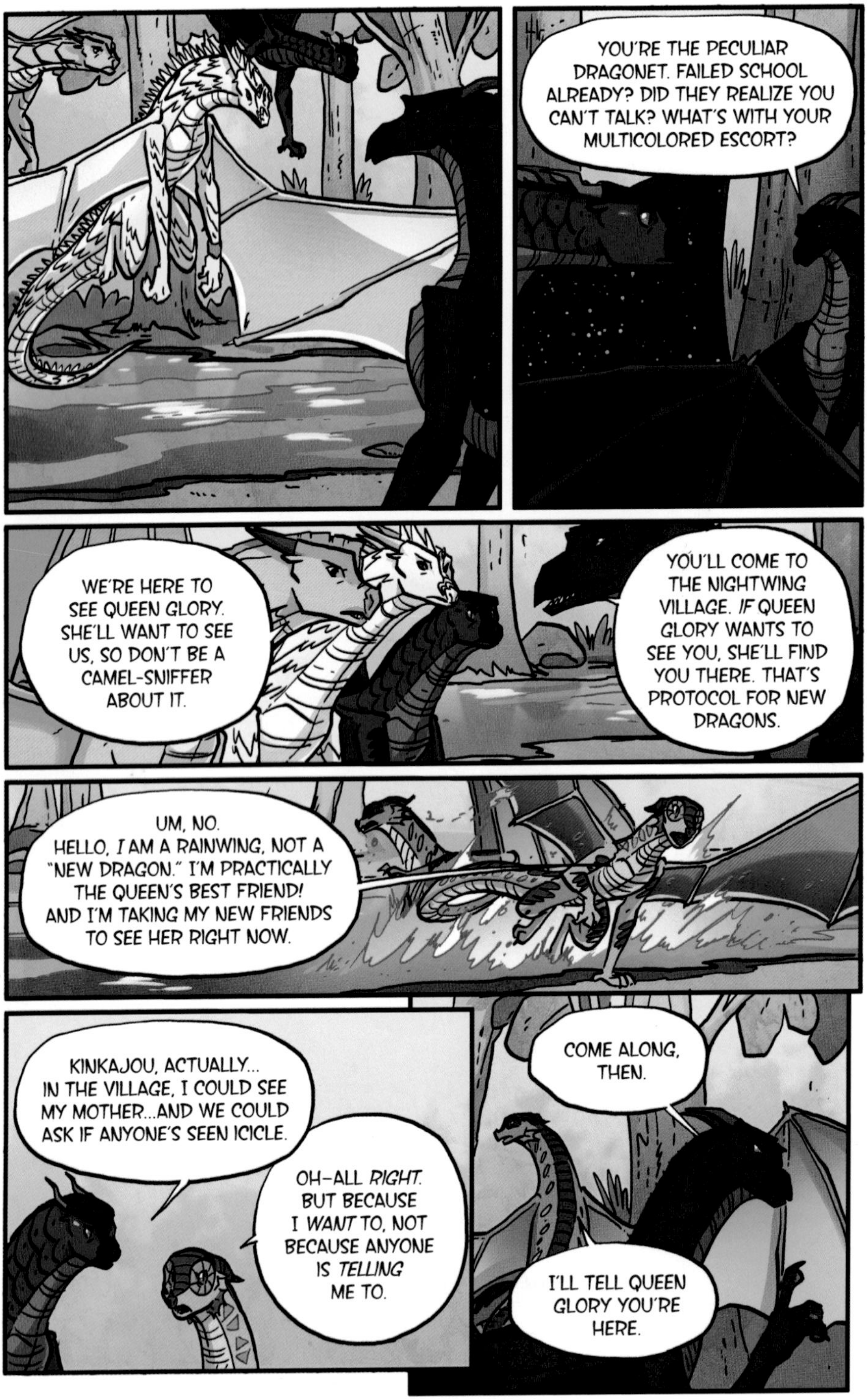
YOU'RE THE PECULIAR DRAGONET. FAILED SCHOOL ALREADY? DID THEY REALIZE YOU CAN'T TALK? WHAT'S WITH YOUR MULTICOLORED ESCORT?
WE'RE HERE TO SEE QUEEN GLORY. SHE'LL WANT TO SEE US, SO DON'T BE A CAMEL-SNIFFER ABOUT IT.
YOU'LL COME TO THE NIGHTWING VILLAGE. *IF* QUEEN GLORY WANTS TO SEE YOU, SHE'LL FIND YOU THERE. THAT'S PROTOCOL FOR NEW DRAGONS.
UM, NO. HELLO, *I* AM A RAINWING, NOT A "NEW DRAGON." I'M PRACTICALLY THE QUEEN'S BEST FRIEND! AND I'M TAKING MY NEW FRIENDS TO SEE HER RIGHT NOW.
KINKAJOU, ACTUALLY... IN THE VILLAGE, I COULD SEE MY MOTHER...AND WE COULD ASK IF ANYONE'S SEEN ICICLE.
OH—ALL *RIGHT.* BUT BECAUSE I *WANT* TO, NOT BECAUSE ANYONE IS *TELLING* ME TO.
COME ALONG, THEN.
I'LL TELL QUEEN GLORY YOU'RE HERE.

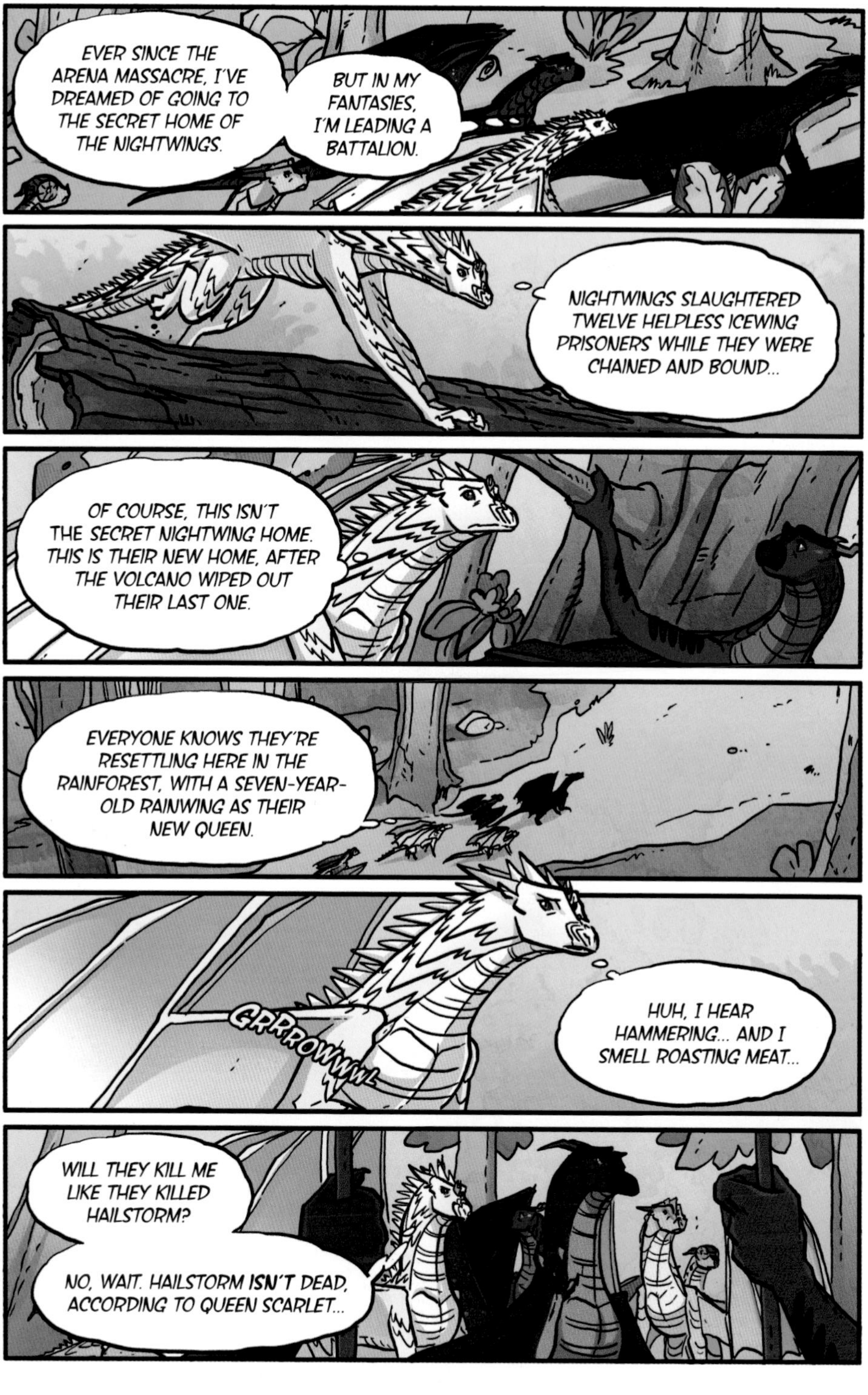
EVER SINCE THE ARENA MASSACRE, I'VE DREAMED OF GOING TO THE SECRET HOME OF THE NIGHTWINGS.
BUT IN MY FANTASIES, I'M LEADING A BATTALION.
NIGHTWINGS SLAUGHTERED TWELVE HELPLESS ICEWING PRISONERS WHILE THEY WERE CHAINED AND BOUND...
OF COURSE, THIS ISN'T THE SECRET NIGHTWING HOME. THIS IS THEIR NEW HOME, AFTER THE VOLCANO WIPED OUT THEIR LAST ONE.
EVERYONE KNOWS THEY'RE RESETTLING HERE IN THE RAINFOREST, WITH A SEVEN-YEAR-OLD RAINWING AS THEIR NEW QUEEN.
GRRROWWWL
HUH, I HEAR HAMMERING... AND I SMELL ROASTING MEAT...
WILL THEY KILL ME LIKE THEY KILLED HAILSTORM?
NO, WAIT. HAILSTORM ISN'T DEAD, ACCORDING TO QUEEN SCARLET...

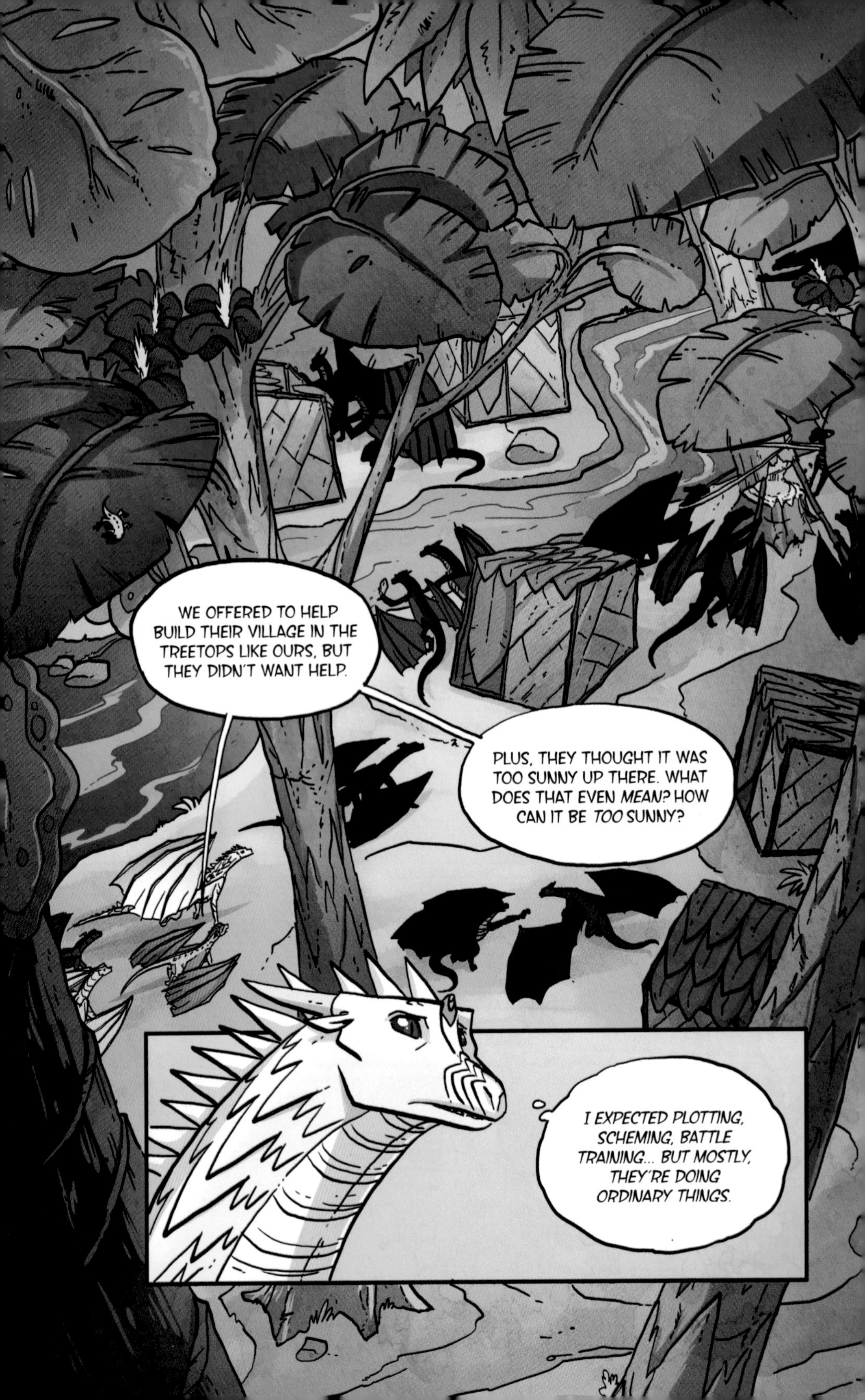
WE OFFERED TO HELP BUILD THEIR VILLAGE IN THE TREETOPS LIKE OURS, BUT THEY DIDN'T WANT HELP.
PLUS, THEY THOUGHT IT WAS TOO SUNNY UP THERE. WHAT DOES THAT EVEN *MEAN*? HOW CAN IT BE *TOO* SUNNY?
I EXPECTED PLOTTING, SCHEMING, BATTLE TRAINING... BUT MOSTLY, THEY'RE DOING ORDINARY THINGS.

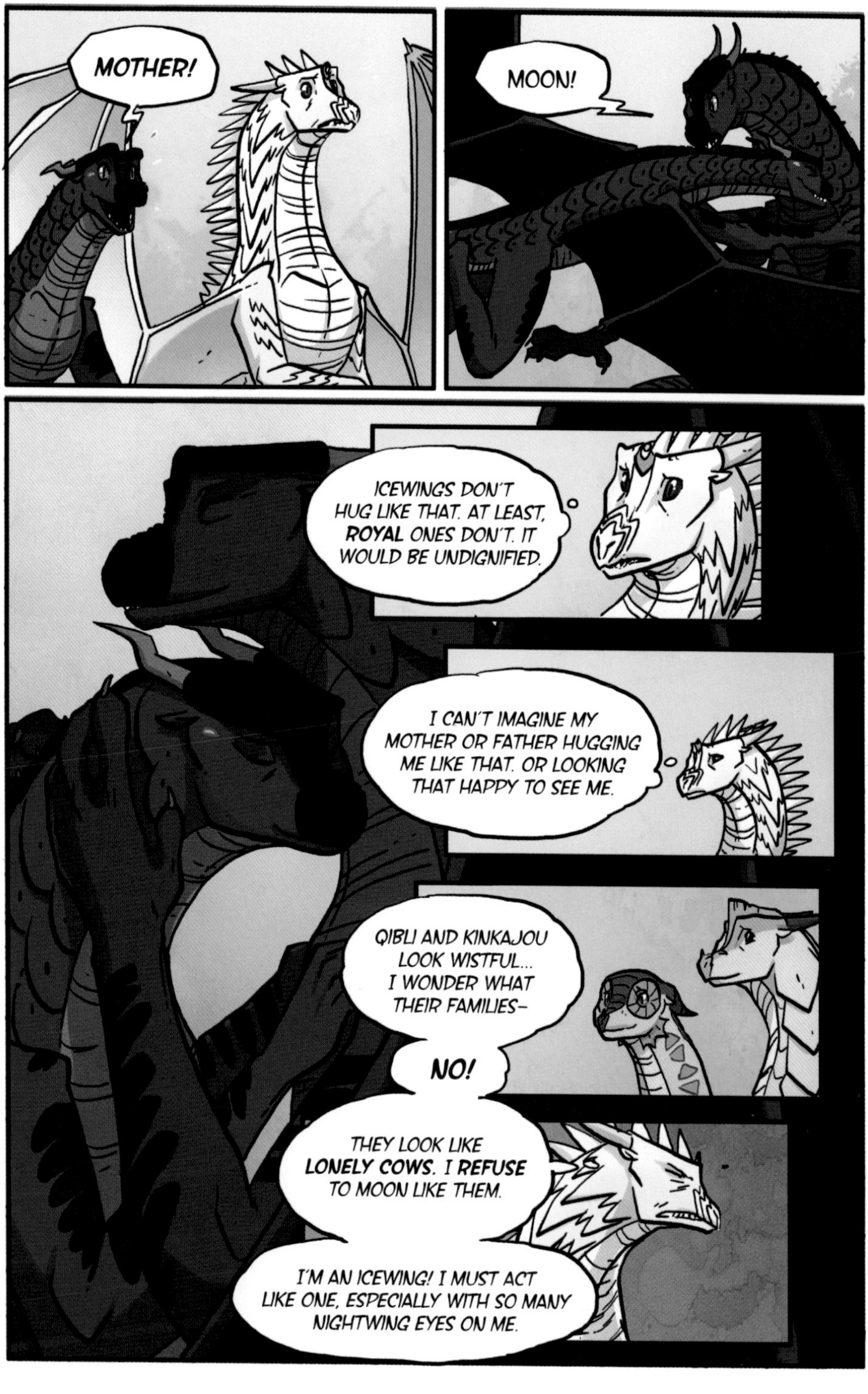
MOTHER!
MOON!
ICEWINGS DON'T HUG LIKE THAT. AT LEAST, ROYAL ONES DON'T. IT WOULD BE UNDIGNIFIED.
I CAN'T IMAGINE MY MOTHER OR FATHER HUGGING ME LIKE THAT. OR LOOKING THAT HAPPY TO SEE ME.
QIBLI AND KINKAJOU LOOK WISTFUL... I WONDER WHAT THEIR FAMILIES–
NO!
THEY LOOK LIKE LONELY COWS. I REFUSE TO MOON LIKE THEM.
I'M AN ICEWING! I MUST ACT LIKE ONE, ESPECIALLY WITH SO MANY NIGHTWING EYES ON ME.

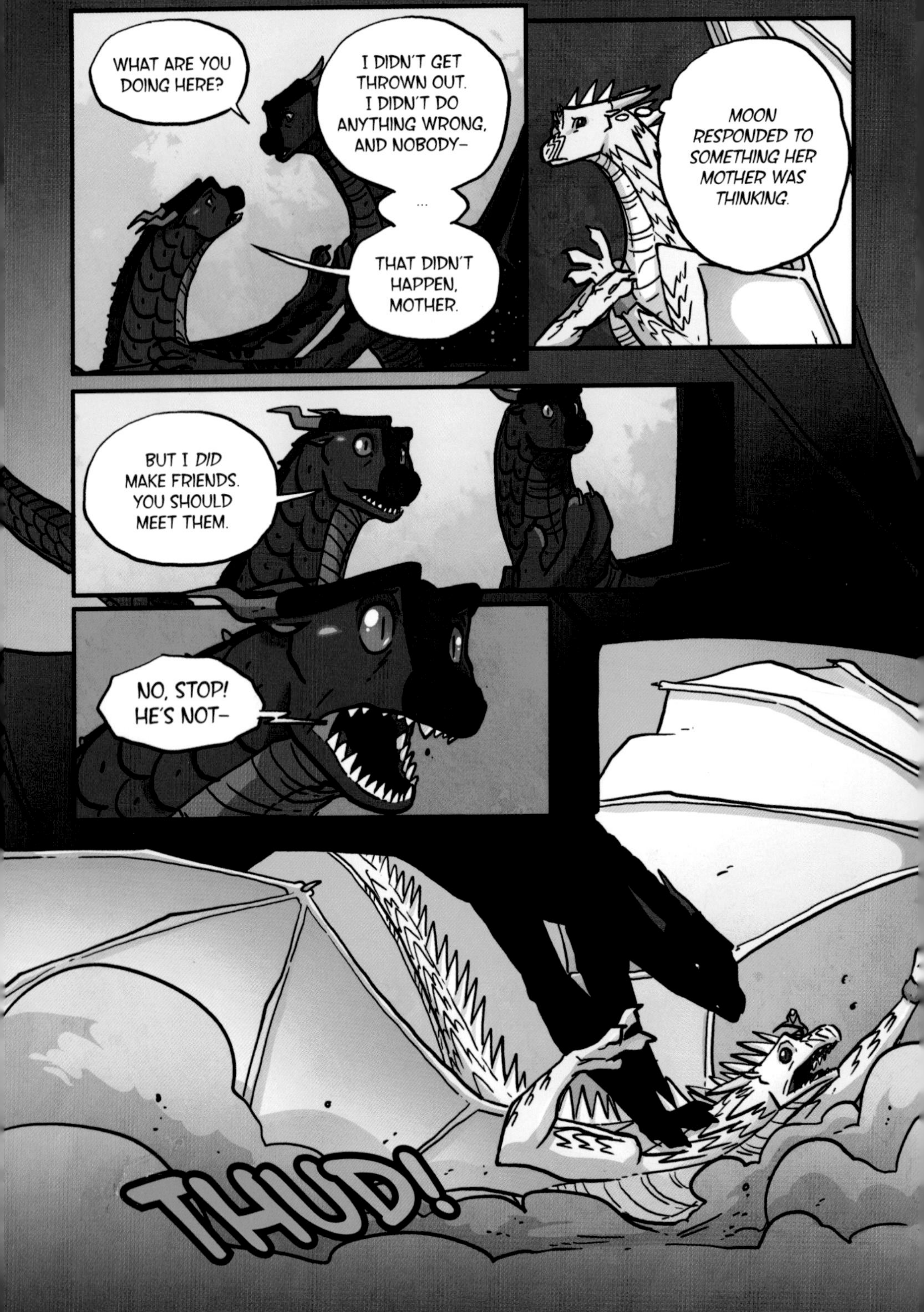
WHAT ARE YOU DOING HERE?
I DIDN'T GET THROWN OUT. I DIDN'T DO ANYTHING WRONG, AND NOBODY–
...
THAT DIDN'T HAPPEN, MOTHER.
MOON RESPONDED TO SOMETHING HER MOTHER WAS THINKING.
BUT I *DID* MAKE FRIENDS. YOU SHOULD MEET THEM.
NO, STOP! HE'S NOT–
THUD!

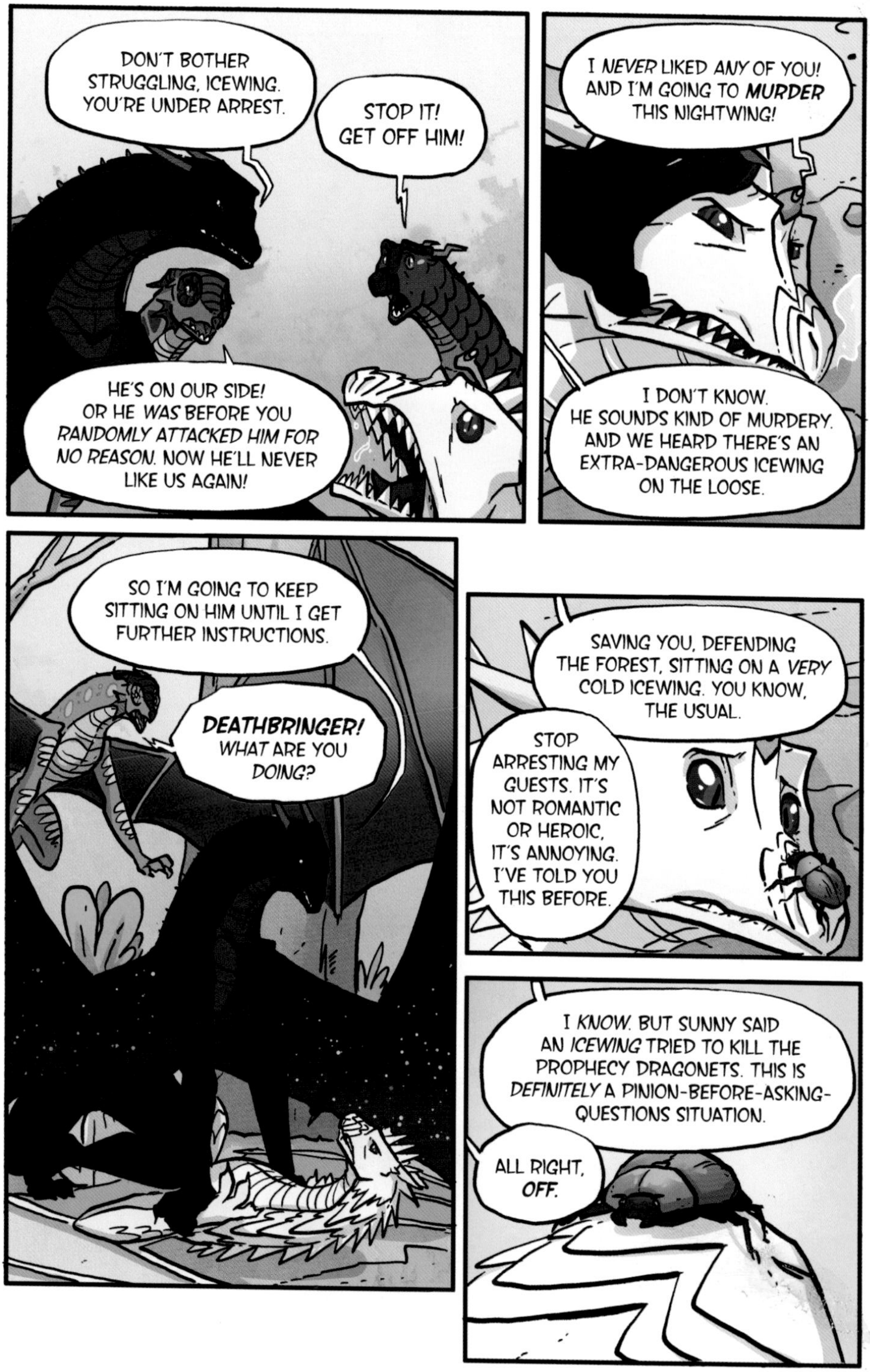
DON'T BOTHER STRUGGLING, ICEWING. YOU'RE UNDER ARREST.
STOP IT! GET OFF HIM!
HE'S ON OUR SIDE! OR HE *WAS* BEFORE YOU *RANDOMLY ATTACKED HIM FOR NO REASON.* NOW HE'LL NEVER LIKE US AGAIN!
I *NEVER* LIKED *ANY* OF YOU! AND I'M GOING TO ***MURDER*** THIS NIGHTWING!
I DON'T KNOW. HE SOUNDS KIND OF MURDERY. AND WE HEARD THERE'S AN EXTRA-DANGEROUS ICEWING ON THE LOOSE.
SO I'M GOING TO KEEP SITTING ON HIM UNTIL I GET FURTHER INSTRUCTIONS.
DEATHBRINGER! *WHAT ARE YOU DOING?*
SAVING YOU, DEFENDING THE FOREST, SITTING ON A *VERY* COLD ICEWING. YOU KNOW, THE USUAL.
STOP ARRESTING MY GUESTS. IT'S NOT ROMANTIC OR HEROIC, IT'S ANNOYING. I'VE TOLD YOU THIS BEFORE.
I *KNOW*. BUT SUNNY SAID AN *ICEWING* TRIED TO KILL THE PROPHECY DRAGONETS. THIS IS *DEFINITELY* A PINION-BEFORE-ASKING-QUESTIONS SITUATION.
ALL RIGHT, ***OFF.***

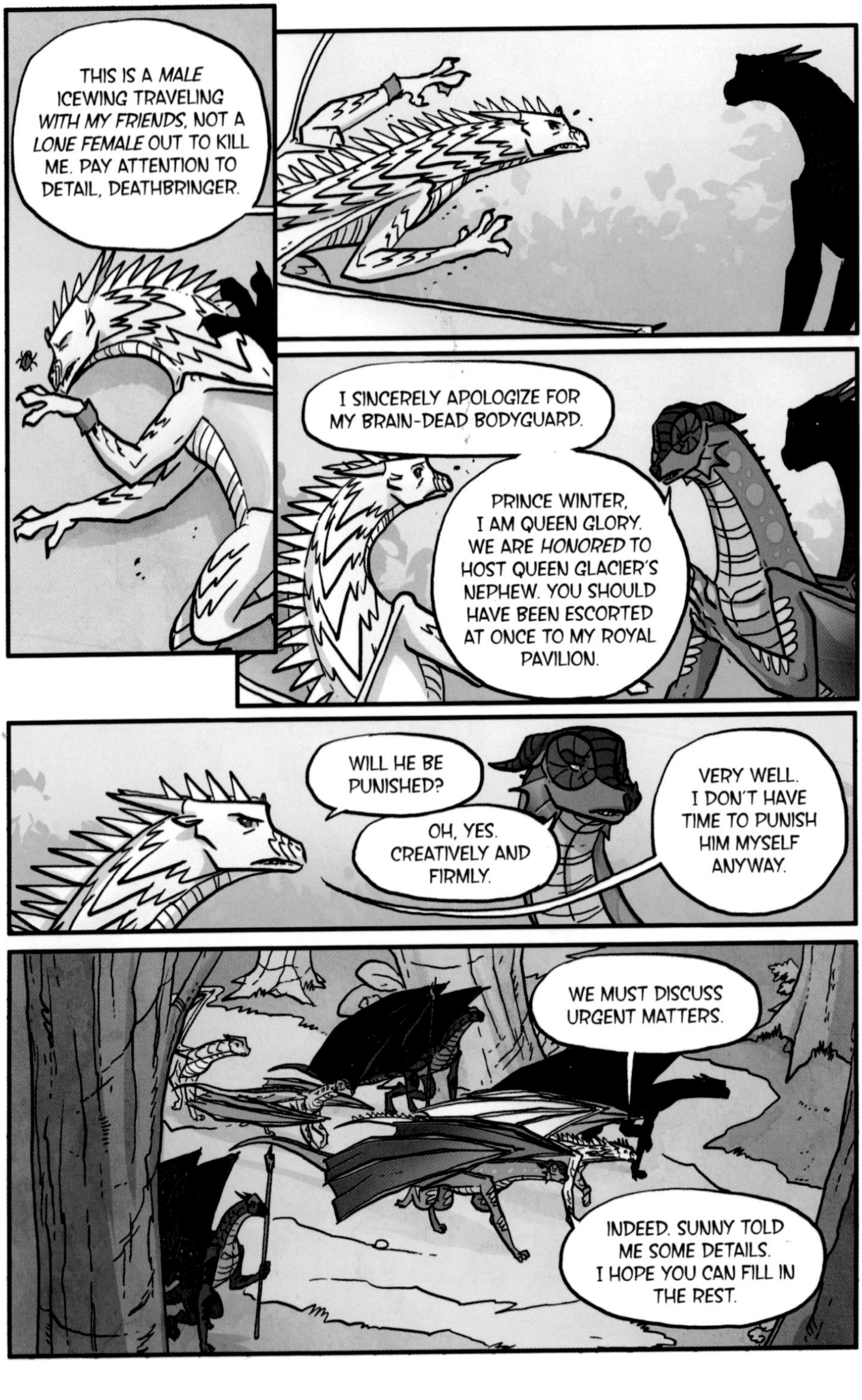
THIS IS A *MALE* ICEWING TRAVELING *WITH MY FRIENDS*, NOT A *LONE FEMALE* OUT TO KILL ME. PAY ATTENTION TO DETAIL, DEATHBRINGER.
I SINCERELY APOLOGIZE FOR MY BRAIN-DEAD BODYGUARD.
PRINCE WINTER, I AM QUEEN GLORY. WE ARE *HONORED* TO HOST QUEEN GLACIER'S NEPHEW. YOU SHOULD HAVE BEEN ESCORTED AT ONCE TO MY ROYAL PAVILION.
WILL HE BE PUNISHED?
OH, YES. CREATIVELY AND FIRMLY.
VERY WELL. I DON'T HAVE TIME TO PUNISH HIM MYSELF ANYWAY.
WE MUST DISCUSS URGENT MATTERS.
INDEED. SUNNY TOLD ME SOME DETAILS. I HOPE YOU CAN FILL IN THE REST.

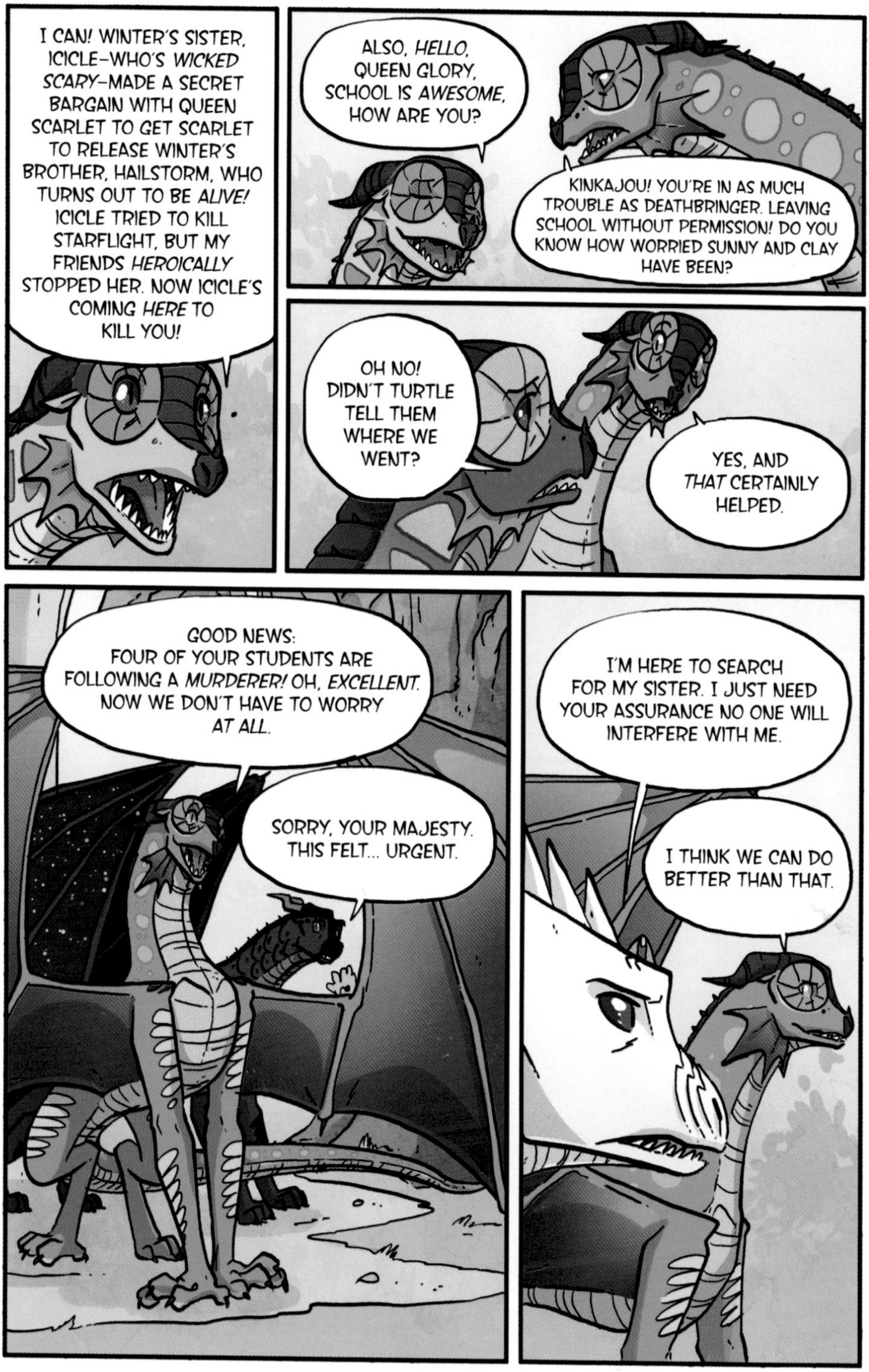
I CAN! WINTER'S SISTER, ICICLE—WHO'S *WICKED SCARY*—MADE A SECRET BARGAIN WITH QUEEN SCARLET TO GET SCARLET TO RELEASE WINTER'S BROTHER, HAILSTORM, WHO TURNS OUT TO BE *ALIVE!* ICICLE TRIED TO KILL STARFLIGHT, BUT MY FRIENDS *HEROICALLY* STOPPED HER. NOW ICICLE'S COMING *HERE* TO KILL YOU!
ALSO, *HELLO*, QUEEN GLORY, SCHOOL IS *AWESOME*, HOW ARE YOU?
KINKAJOU! YOU'RE IN AS MUCH TROUBLE AS DEATHBRINGER. LEAVING SCHOOL WITHOUT PERMISSION! DO YOU KNOW HOW WORRIED SUNNY AND CLAY HAVE BEEN?
OH NO! DIDN'T TURTLE TELL THEM WHERE WE WENT?
YES, AND *THAT* CERTAINLY HELPED.
GOOD NEWS: FOUR OF YOUR STUDENTS ARE FOLLOWING A *MURDERER!* OH, *EXCELLENT*. NOW WE DON'T HAVE TO WORRY *AT ALL*.
SORRY, YOUR MAJESTY. THIS FELT... URGENT.
I'M HERE TO SEARCH FOR MY SISTER. I JUST NEED YOUR ASSURANCE NO ONE WILL INTERFERE WITH ME.
I THINK WE CAN DO BETTER THAN THAT.

BANANA?

ER... NO, THANK YOU.

ACTUALLY, IT'S HELICONIA, YOUR MAJESTY. BUT GOOD GUESS.

HELICONIA, PLEASE TELL MY SCOUT CAPTAINS TO MEET ME AT THE PAVILION AS SOON AS POSSIBLE.

BUT I SHOULDN'T LEAVE YOU UNGUARDED, MAJESTY.

SEVEN GUARDS ARE QUITE SUFFICIENT. OVERKILL, IN FACT.

SOMEBODY SEEMS TO THINK I WOULDN'T NOTICE FIVE ADDITIONAL DRAGONS FOLLOWING ME AROUND.

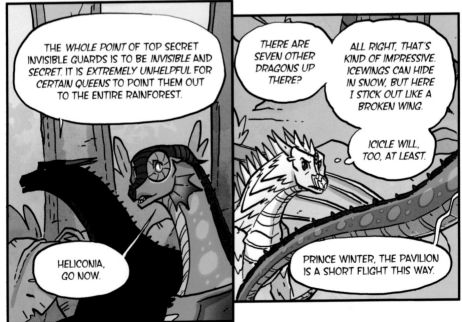

THE WHOLE POINT OF TOP SECRET INVISIBLE GUARDS IS TO BE INVISIBLE AND SECRET. IT IS EXTREMELY UNHELPFUL FOR CERTAIN QUEENS TO POINT THEM OUT TO THE ENTIRE RAINFOREST.

HELICONIA, GO NOW.

THERE ARE SEVEN OTHER DRAGONS UP THERE?

ALL RIGHT, THAT'S KIND OF IMPRESSIVE. ICEWINGS CAN HIDE IN SNOW, BUT HERE I STICK OUT LIKE A BROKEN WING.

ICICLE WILL, TOO, AT LEAST.

PRINCE WINTER, THE PAVILION IS A SHORT FLIGHT THIS WAY.

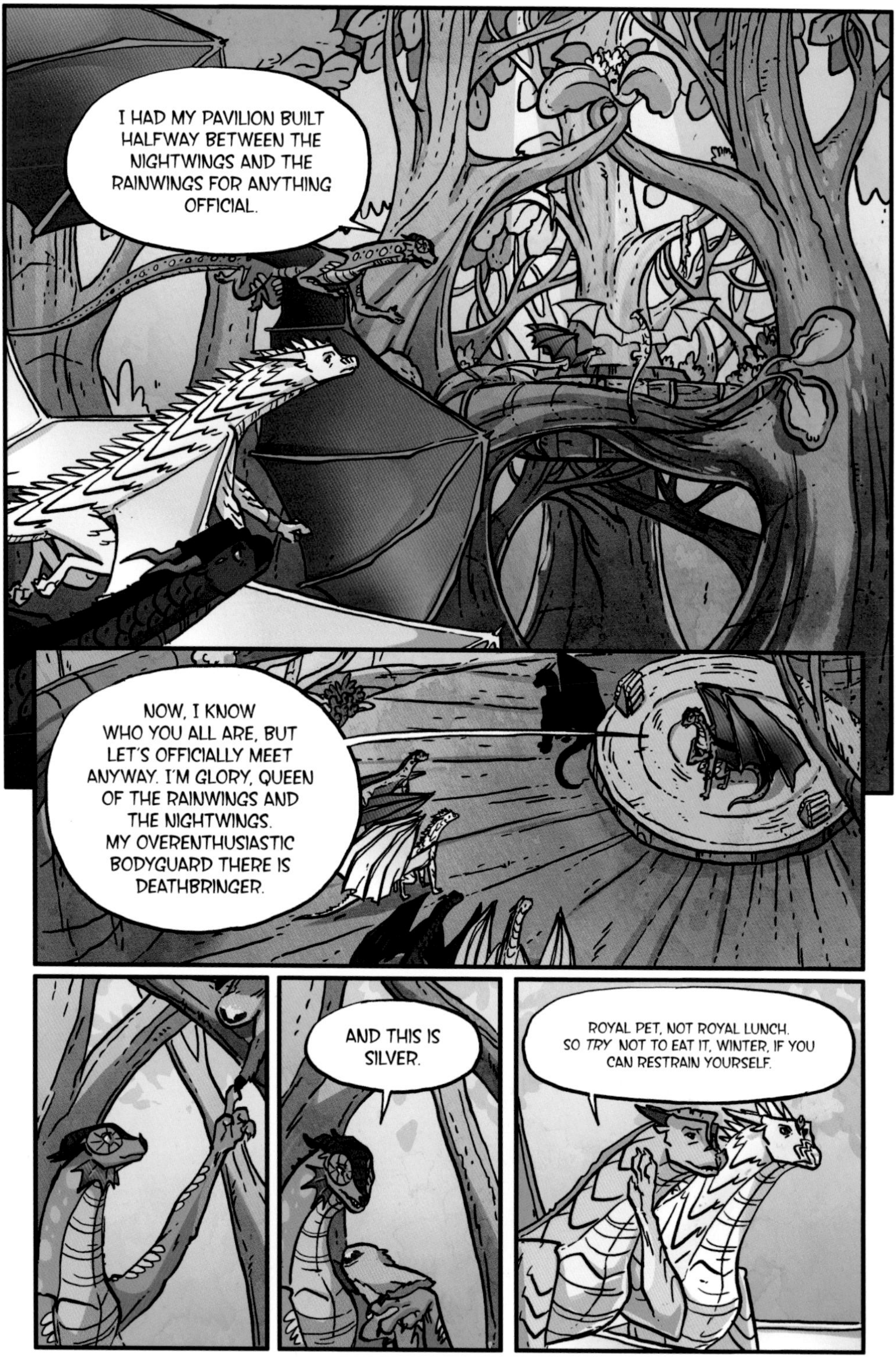
I HAD MY PAVILION BUILT HALFWAY BETWEEN THE NIGHTWINGS AND THE RAINWINGS FOR ANYTHING OFFICIAL.
NOW, I KNOW WHO YOU ALL ARE, BUT LET'S OFFICIALLY MEET ANYWAY. I'M GLORY, QUEEN OF THE RAINWINGS AND THE NIGHTWINGS. MY OVERENTHUSIASTIC BODYGUARD THERE IS DEATHBRINGER.
AND THIS IS SILVER.
ROYAL PET, NOT ROYAL LUNCH. SO *TRY* NOT TO EAT IT, WINTER, IF YOU CAN RESTRAIN YOURSELF.

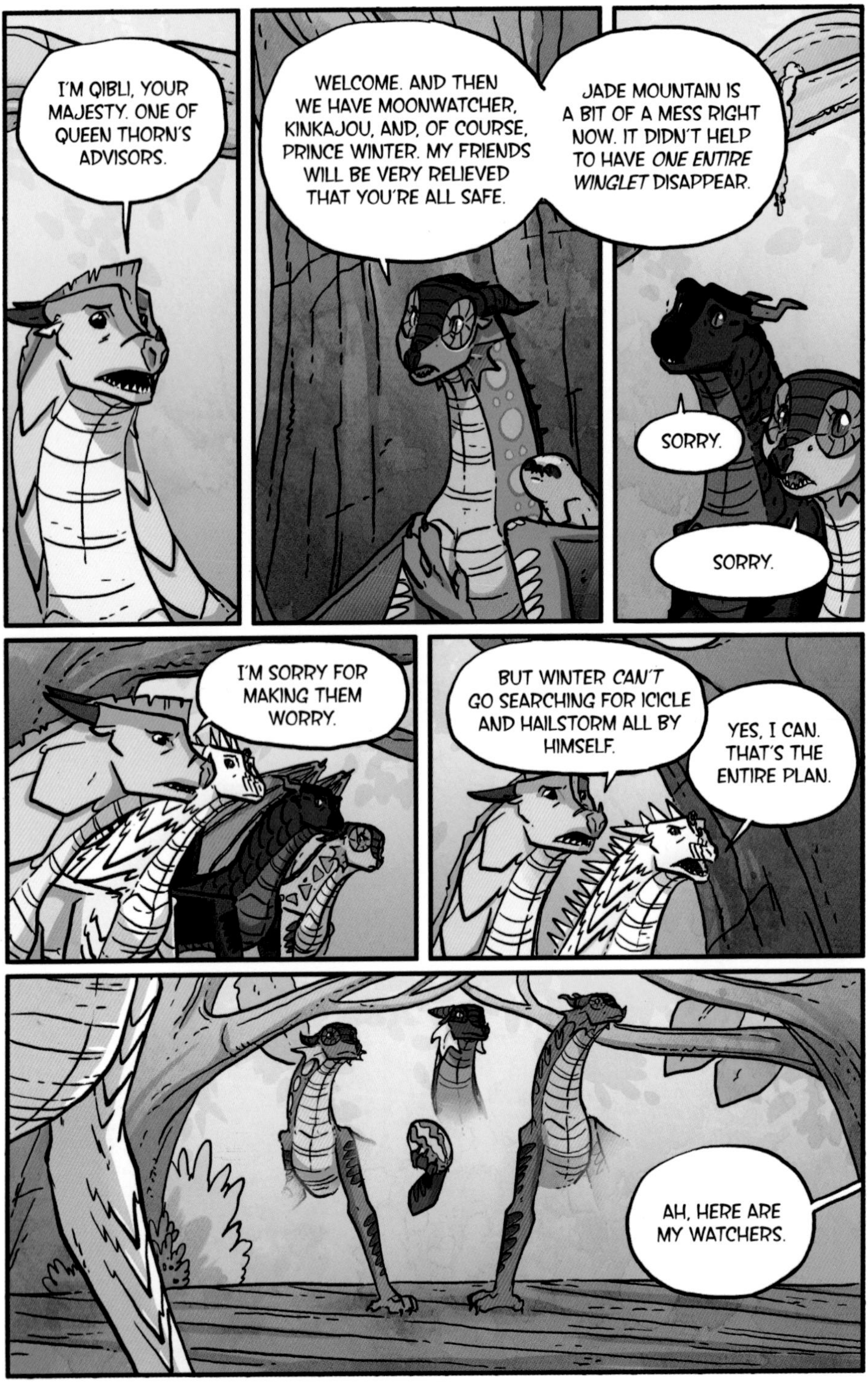
I'M QIBLI, YOUR MAJESTY. ONE OF QUEEN THORN'S ADVISORS.
WELCOME. AND THEN WE HAVE MOONWATCHER, KINKAJOU, AND, OF COURSE, PRINCE WINTER. MY FRIENDS WILL BE VERY RELIEVED THAT YOU'RE ALL SAFE.
JADE MOUNTAIN IS A BIT OF A MESS RIGHT NOW. IT DIDN'T HELP TO HAVE *ONE ENTIRE WINGLET* DISAPPEAR.
SORRY.
SORRY.
I'M SORRY FOR MAKING THEM WORRY.
BUT WINTER *CAN'T* GO SEARCHING FOR ICICLE AND HAILSTORM ALL BY HIMSELF.
YES, I CAN. THAT'S THE ENTIRE PLAN.
AH, HERE ARE MY WATCHERS.

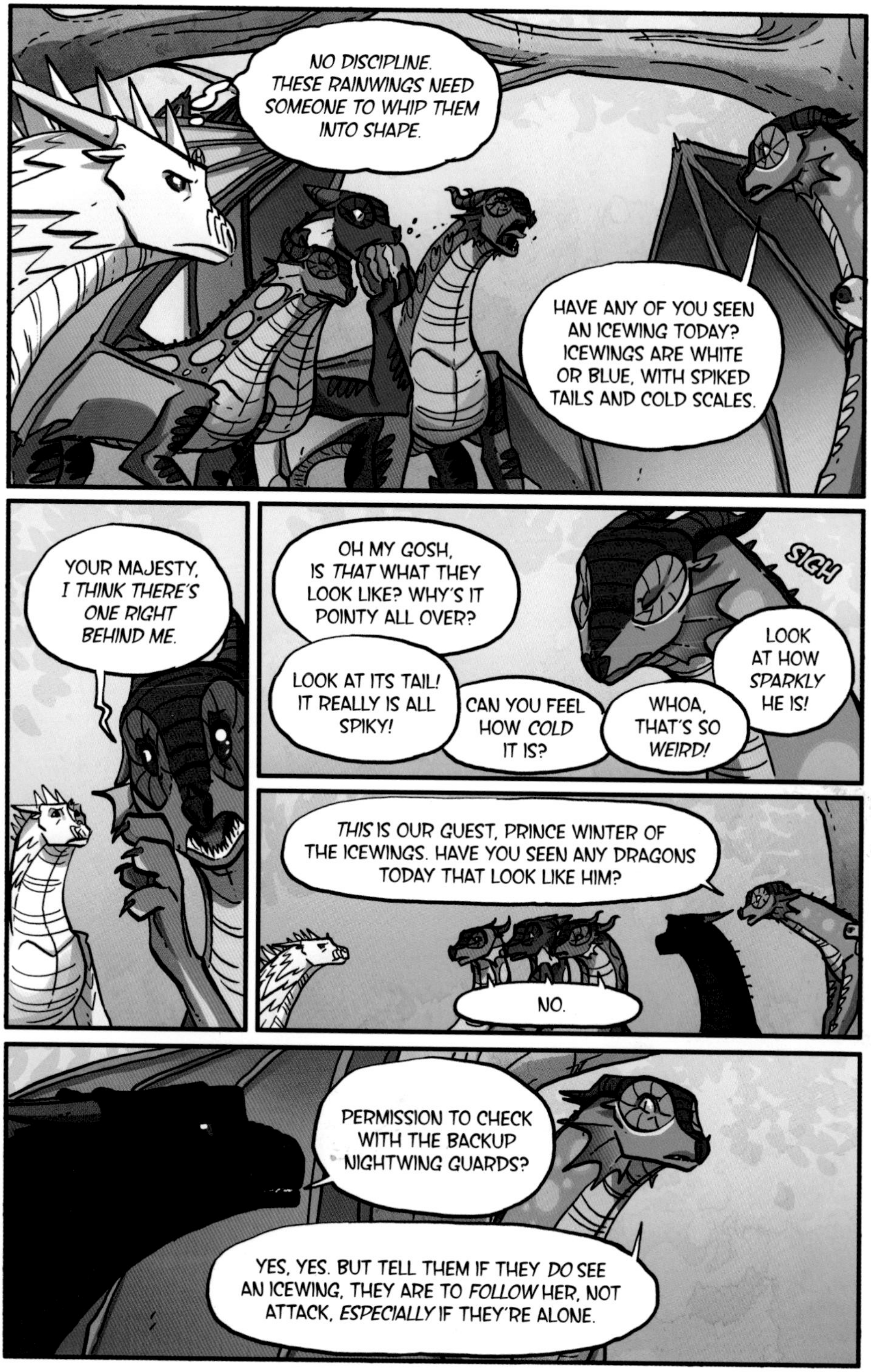
NO DISCIPLINE. THESE RAINWINGS NEED SOMEONE TO WHIP THEM INTO SHAPE.
HAVE ANY OF YOU SEEN AN ICEWING TODAY? ICEWINGS ARE WHITE OR BLUE, WITH SPIKED TAILS AND COLD SCALES.
YOUR MAJESTY, I THINK THERE'S ONE RIGHT BEHIND ME.
OH MY GOSH, IS THAT WHAT THEY LOOK LIKE? WHY'S IT POINTY ALL OVER?
SIGH
LOOK AT ITS TAIL! IT REALLY IS ALL SPIKY!
CAN YOU FEEL HOW COLD IT IS?
WHOA, THAT'S SO WEIRD!
LOOK AT HOW SPARKLY HE IS!
THIS IS OUR GUEST, PRINCE WINTER OF THE ICEWINGS. HAVE YOU SEEN ANY DRAGONS TODAY THAT LOOK LIKE HIM?
NO.
PERMISSION TO CHECK WITH THE BACKUP NIGHTWING GUARDS?
YES, YES. BUT TELL THEM IF THEY DO SEE AN ICEWING, THEY ARE TO FOLLOW HER, NOT ATTACK, ESPECIALLY IF THEY'RE ALONE.

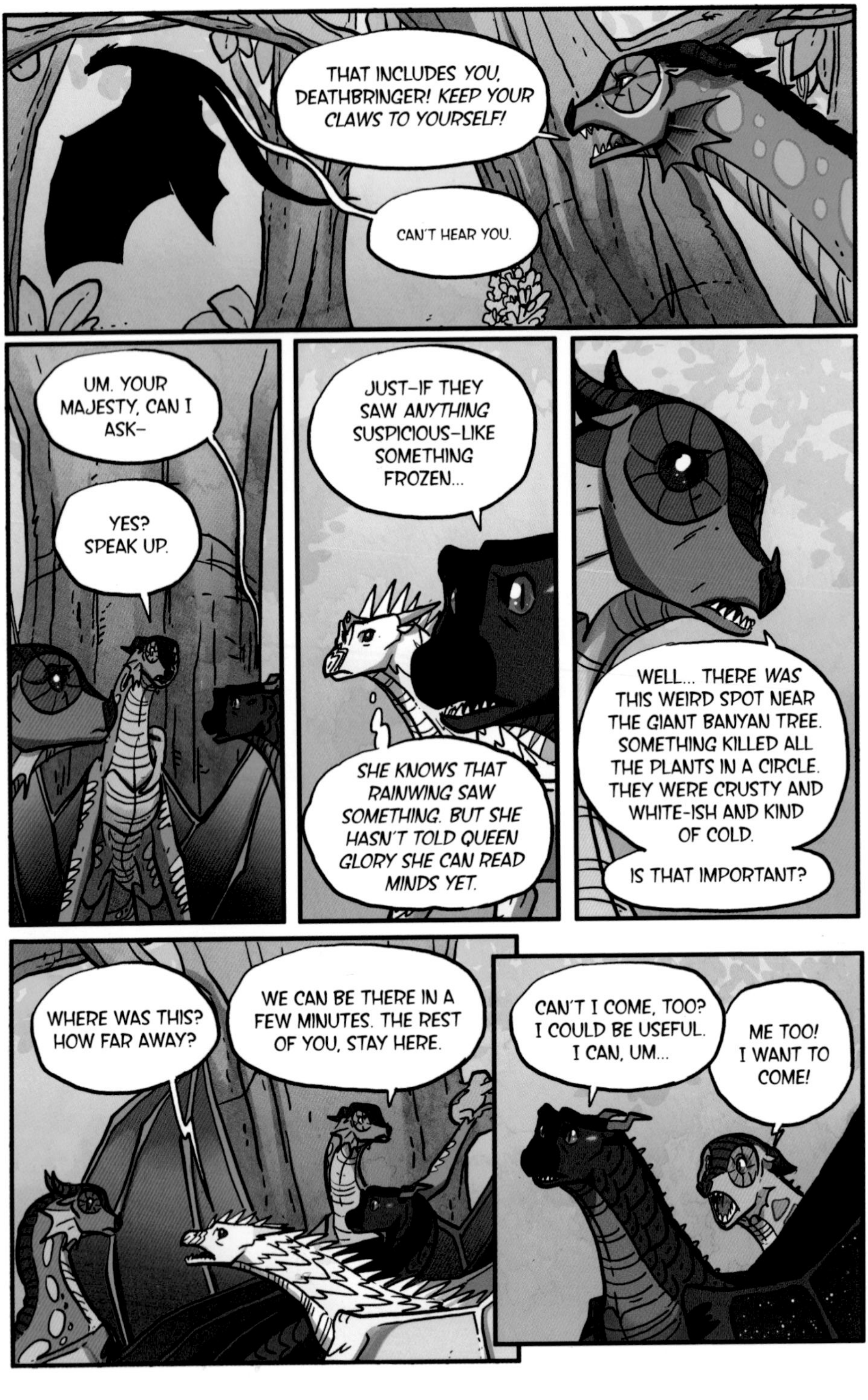
THAT INCLUDES YOU, DEATHBRINGER! KEEP YOUR CLAWS TO YOURSELF!
CAN'T HEAR YOU.
UM. YOUR MAJESTY, CAN I ASK–
YES? SPEAK UP.
JUST–IF THEY SAW ANYTHING SUSPICIOUS–LIKE SOMETHING FROZEN...
SHE KNOWS THAT RAINWING SAW SOMETHING. BUT SHE HASN'T TOLD QUEEN GLORY SHE CAN READ MINDS YET.
WELL... THERE WAS THIS WEIRD SPOT NEAR THE GIANT BANYAN TREE. SOMETHING KILLED ALL THE PLANTS IN A CIRCLE. THEY WERE CRUSTY AND WHITE-ISH AND KIND OF COLD.
IS THAT IMPORTANT?
WHERE WAS THIS? HOW FAR AWAY?
WE CAN BE THERE IN A FEW MINUTES. THE REST OF YOU, STAY HERE.
CAN'T I COME, TOO? I COULD BE USEFUL. I CAN, UM...
ME TOO! I WANT TO COME!

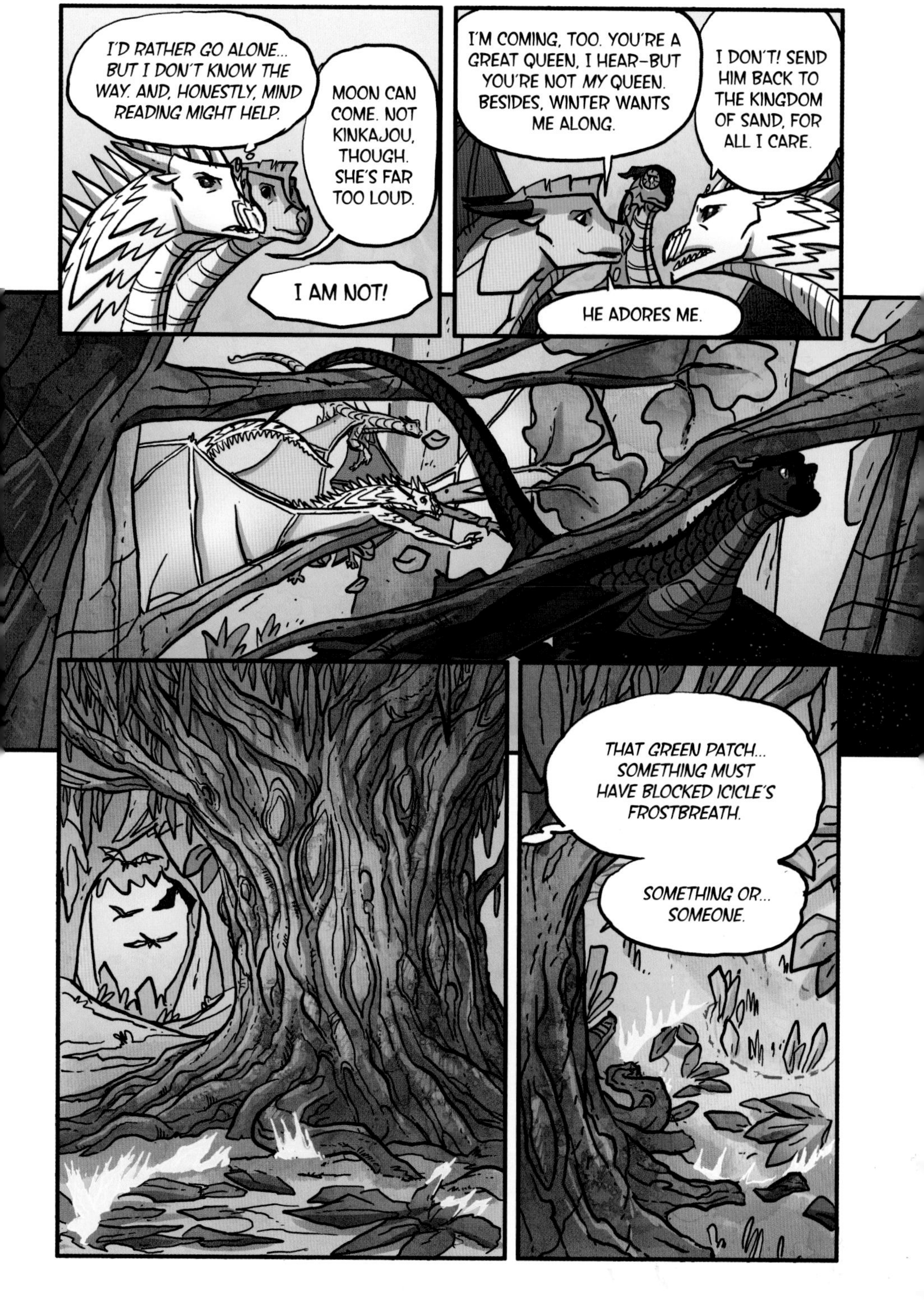
I'D RATHER GO ALONE... BUT I DON'T KNOW THE WAY. AND, HONESTLY, MIND READING MIGHT HELP.
MOON CAN COME. NOT KINKAJOU, THOUGH. SHE'S FAR TOO LOUD.
I AM NOT!
I'M COMING, TOO. YOU'RE A GREAT QUEEN, I HEAR–BUT YOU'RE NOT MY QUEEN. BESIDES, WINTER WANTS ME ALONG.
I DON'T! SEND HIM BACK TO THE KINGDOM OF SAND, FOR ALL I CARE.
HE ADORES ME.
THAT GREEN PATCH... SOMETHING MUST HAVE BLOCKED ICICLE'S FROSTBREATH.
SOMETHING OR... SOMEONE.

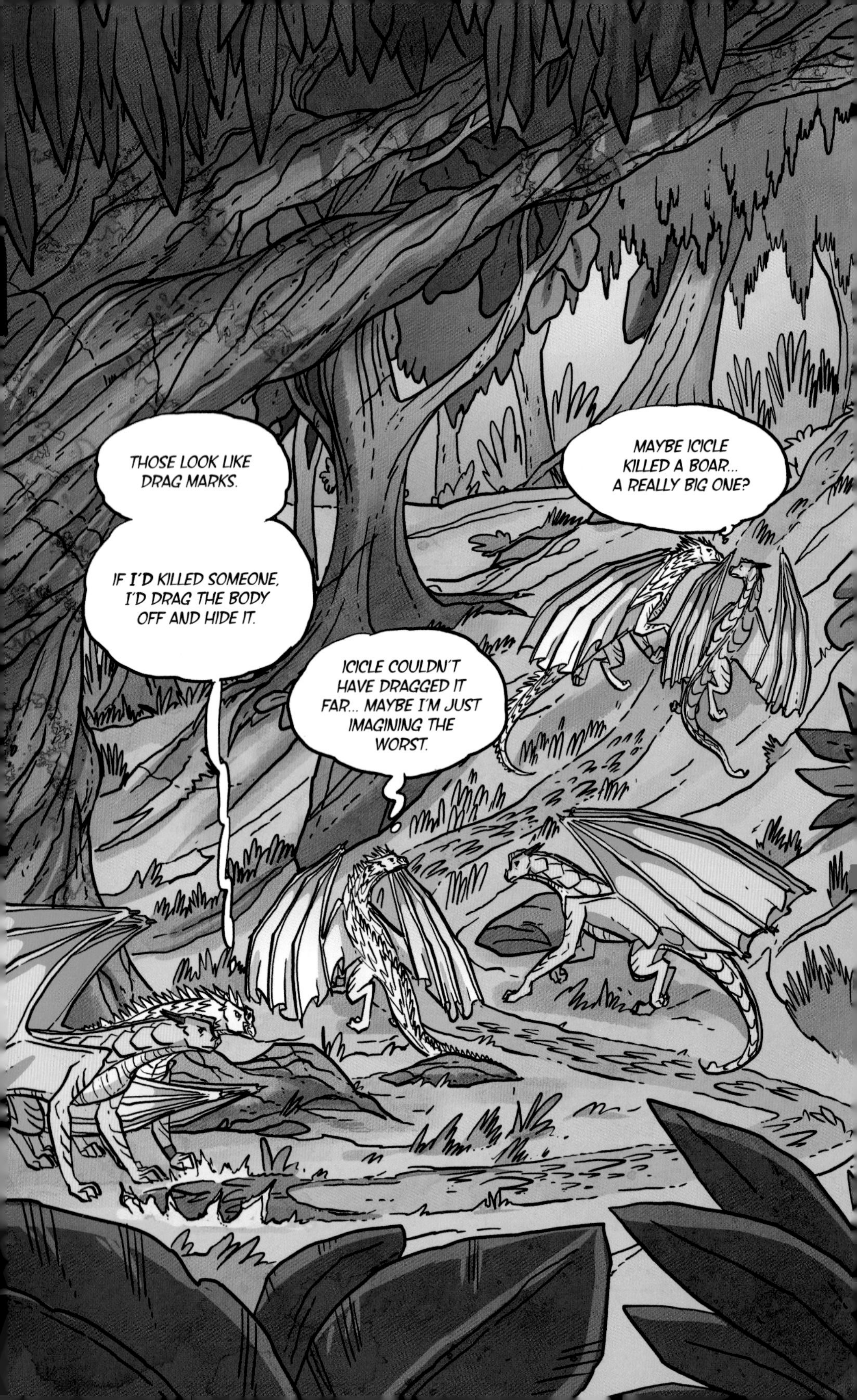
THOSE LOOK LIKE DRAG MARKS.
IF I'D KILLED SOMEONE, I'D DRAG THE BODY OFF AND HIDE IT.
MAYBE ICICLE KILLED A BOAR... A REALLY BIG ONE?
ICICLE COULDN'T HAVE DRAGGED IT FAR... MAYBE I'M JUST IMAGINING THE WORST.

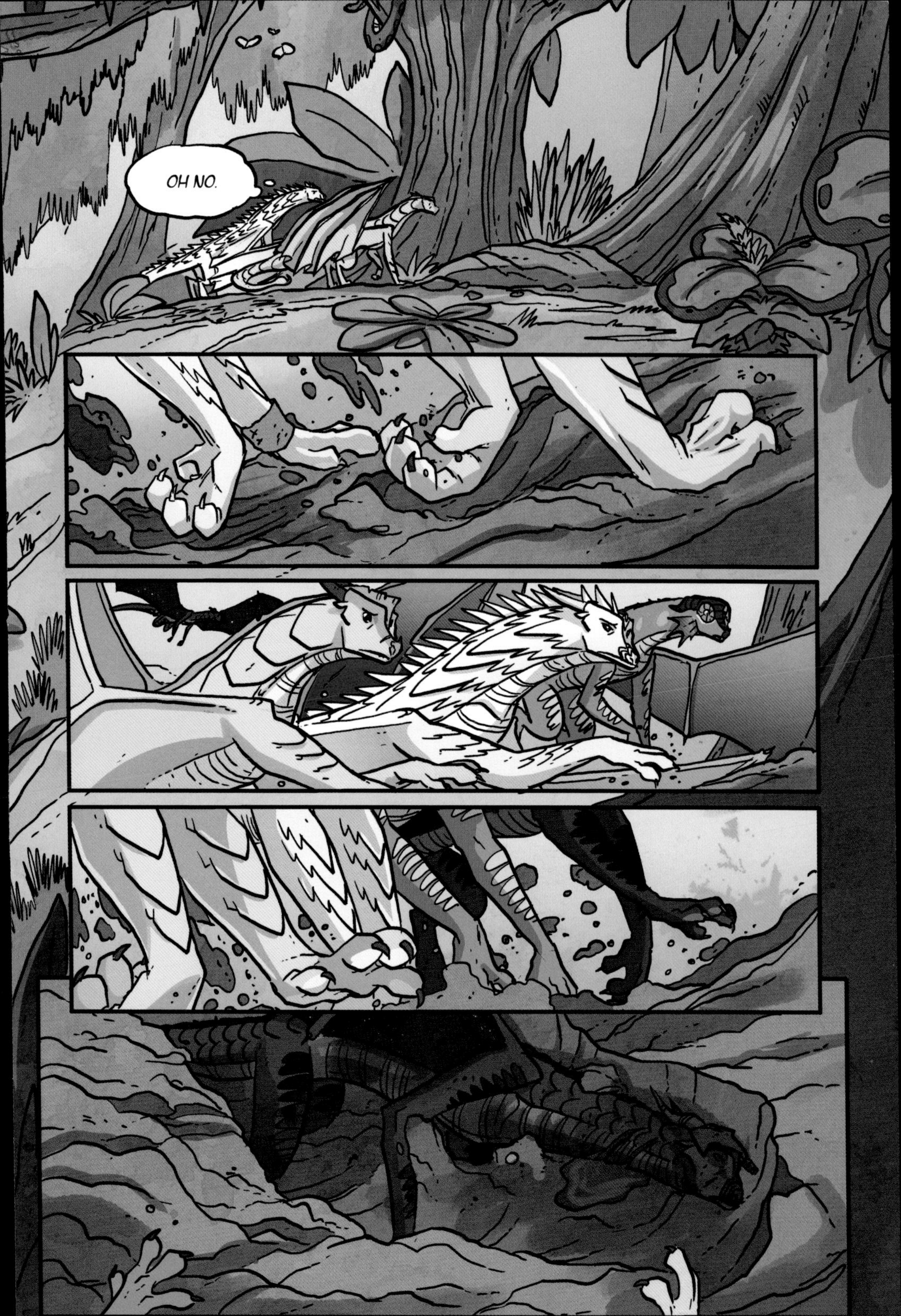
OH NO.

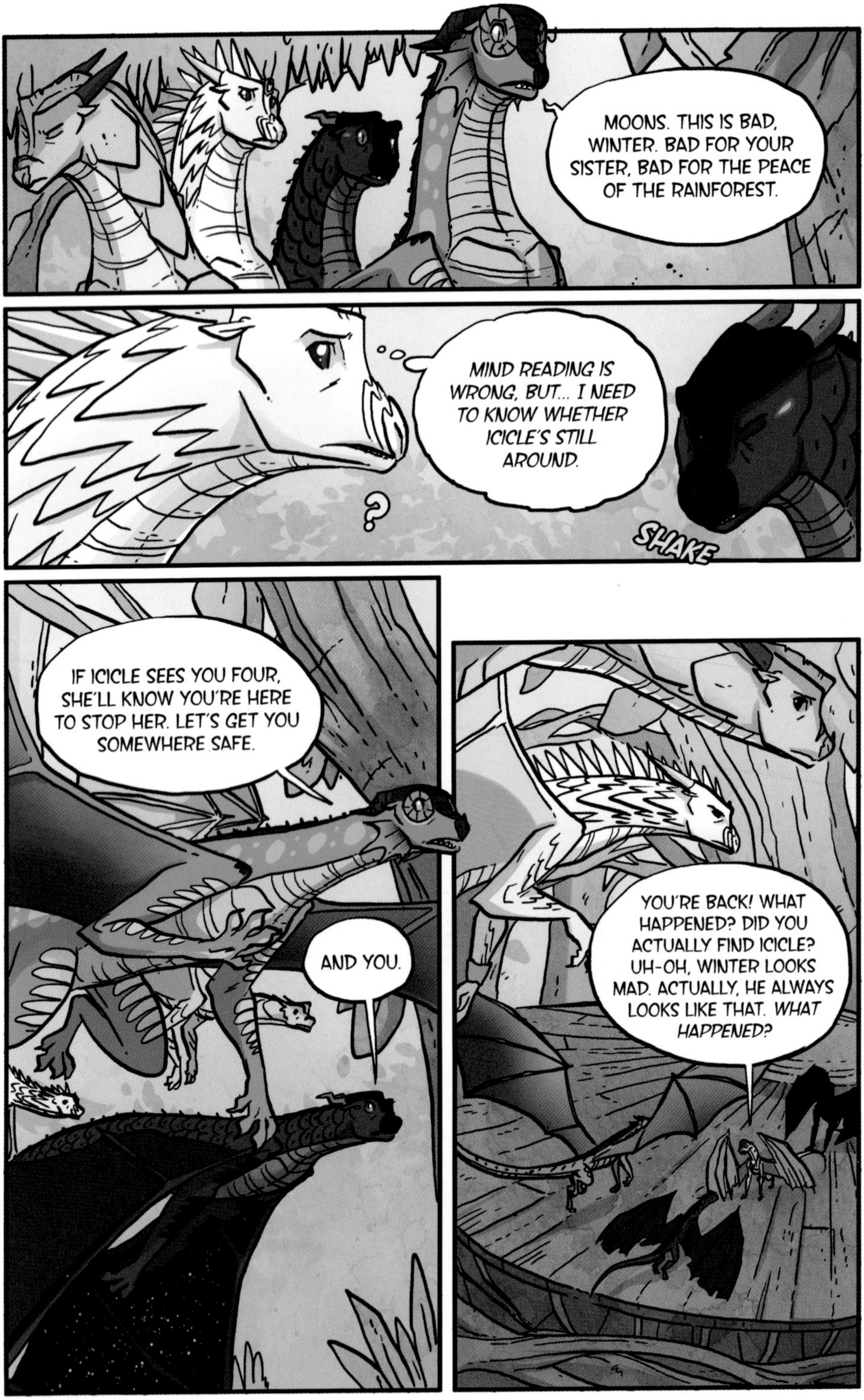
MOONS. THIS IS BAD, WINTER. BAD FOR YOUR SISTER, BAD FOR THE PEACE OF THE RAINFOREST.
MIND READING IS WRONG, BUT... I NEED TO KNOW WHETHER ICICLE'S STILL AROUND.
?
SHAKE
IF ICICLE SEES YOU FOUR, SHE'LL KNOW YOU'RE HERE TO STOP HER. LET'S GET YOU SOMEWHERE SAFE.
AND YOU.
YOU'RE BACK! WHAT HAPPENED? DID YOU ACTUALLY FIND ICICLE? UH-OH, WINTER LOOKS MAD. ACTUALLY, HE ALWAYS LOOKS LIKE THAT. *WHAT HAPPENED?*

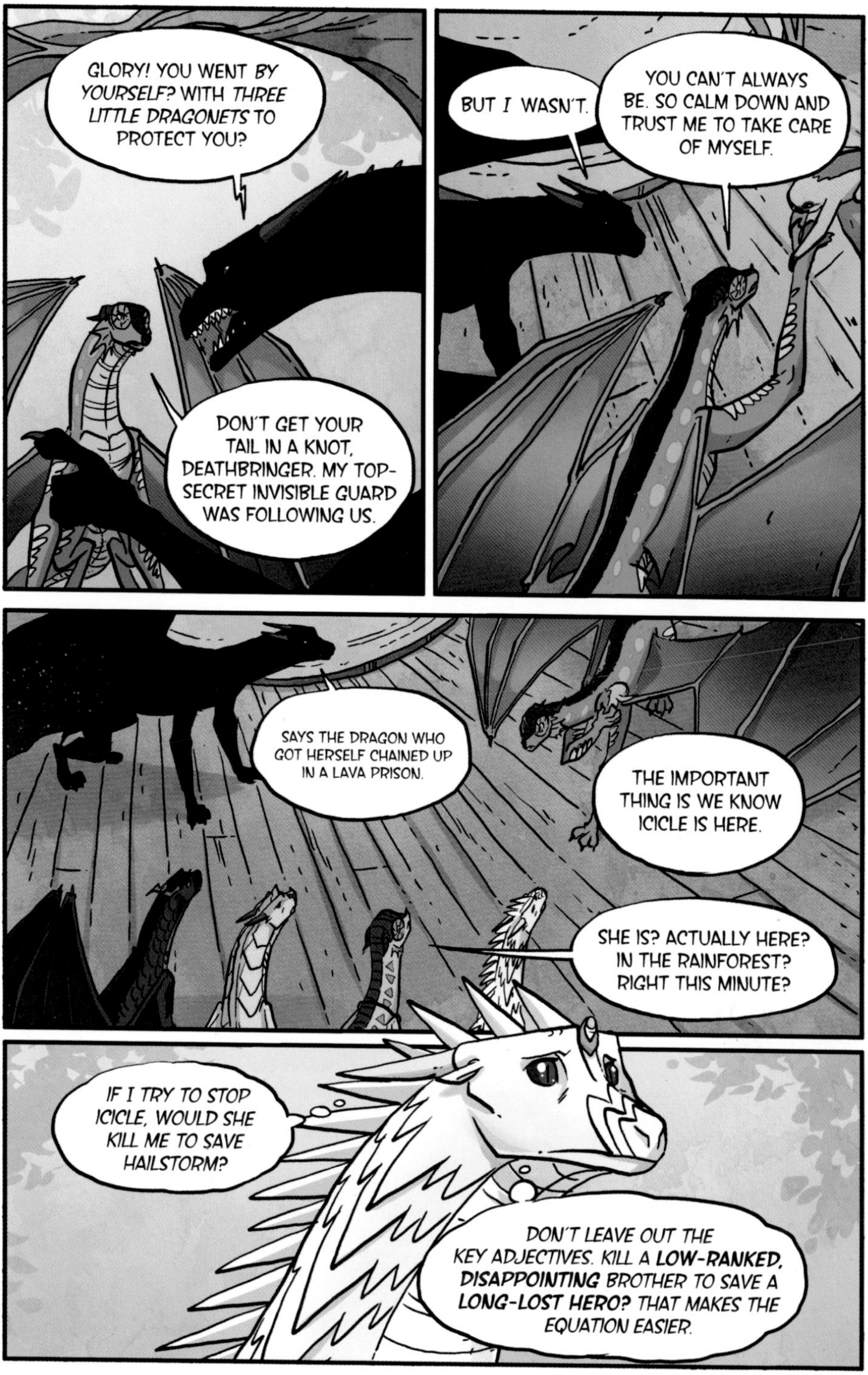
GLORY! YOU WENT BY *YOURSELF?* WITH *THREE LITTLE DRAGONETS* TO PROTECT YOU?
DON'T GET YOUR TAIL IN A KNOT, DEATHBRINGER. MY TOP-SECRET INVISIBLE GUARD WAS FOLLOWING US.
BUT *I* WASN'T.
YOU CAN'T ALWAYS BE. SO CALM DOWN AND TRUST ME TO TAKE CARE OF MYSELF.
SAYS THE DRAGON WHO GOT HERSELF CHAINED UP IN A LAVA PRISON.
THE IMPORTANT THING IS WE KNOW ICICLE IS HERE.
SHE IS? ACTUALLY HERE? IN THE RAINFOREST? RIGHT THIS MINUTE?
IF I TRY TO STOP ICICLE, WOULD SHE KILL ME TO SAVE HAILSTORM?
DON'T LEAVE OUT THE KEY ADJECTIVES. KILL A ***LOW-RANKED, DISAPPOINTING*** *BROTHER TO SAVE A* ***LONG-LOST HERO?*** *THAT MAKES THE EQUATION EASIER.*

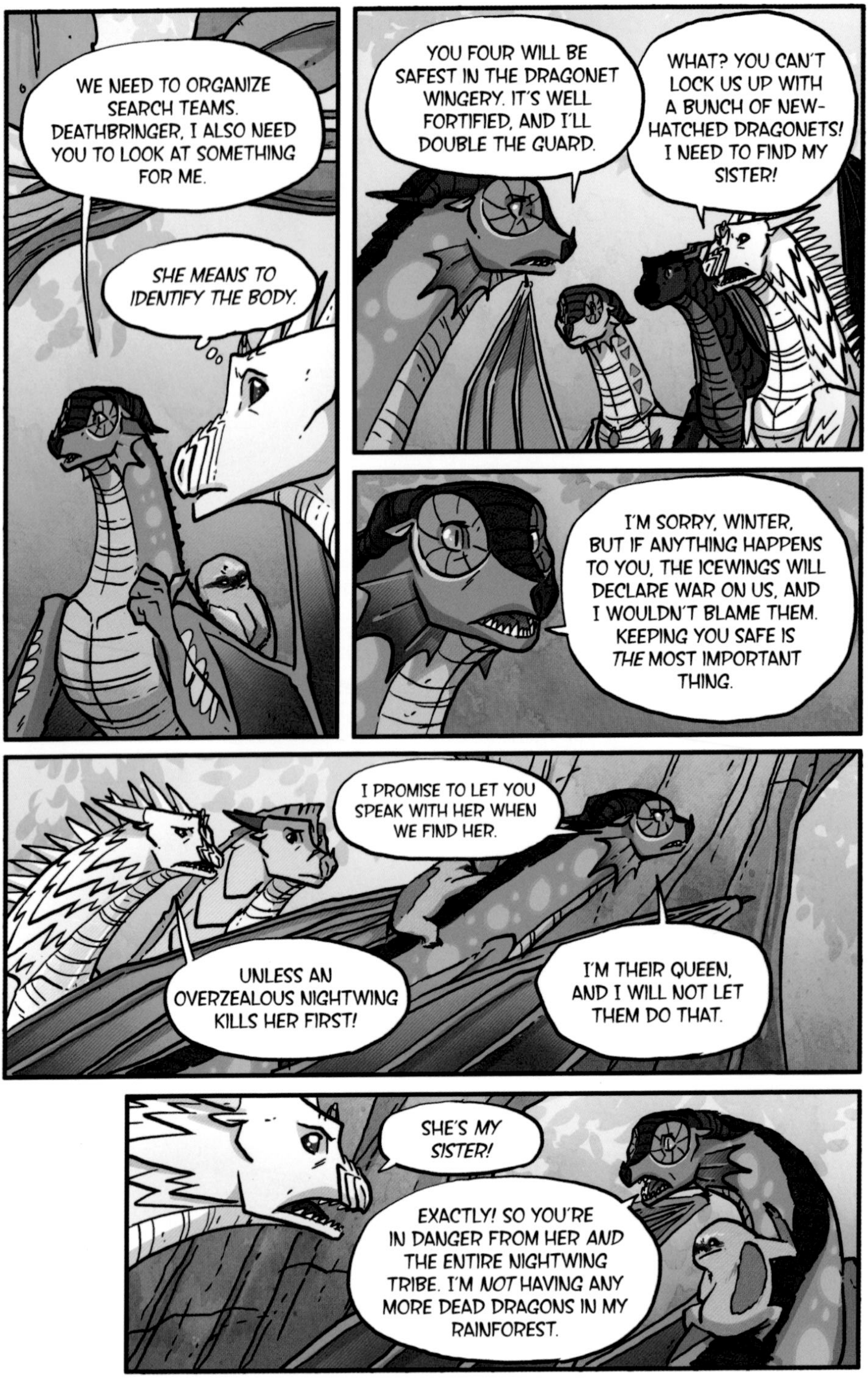
WE NEED TO ORGANIZE SEARCH TEAMS. DEATHBRINGER, I ALSO NEED YOU TO LOOK AT SOMETHING FOR ME.
SHE MEANS TO IDENTIFY THE BODY.
YOU FOUR WILL BE SAFEST IN THE DRAGONET WINGERY. IT'S WELL FORTIFIED, AND I'LL DOUBLE THE GUARD.
WHAT? YOU CAN'T LOCK US UP WITH A BUNCH OF NEW-HATCHED DRAGONETS! I NEED TO FIND MY SISTER!
I'M SORRY, WINTER, BUT IF ANYTHING HAPPENS TO YOU, THE ICEWINGS WILL DECLARE WAR ON US, AND I WOULDN'T BLAME THEM. KEEPING YOU SAFE IS *THE* MOST IMPORTANT THING.
I PROMISE TO LET YOU SPEAK WITH HER WHEN WE FIND HER.
UNLESS AN OVERZEALOUS NIGHTWING KILLS HER FIRST!
I'M THEIR QUEEN, AND I WILL NOT LET THEM DO THAT.
SHE'S *MY SISTER!*
EXACTLY! SO YOU'RE IN DANGER FROM HER AND THE ENTIRE NIGHTWING TRIBE. I'M *NOT* HAVING ANY MORE DEAD DRAGONS IN MY RAINFOREST.

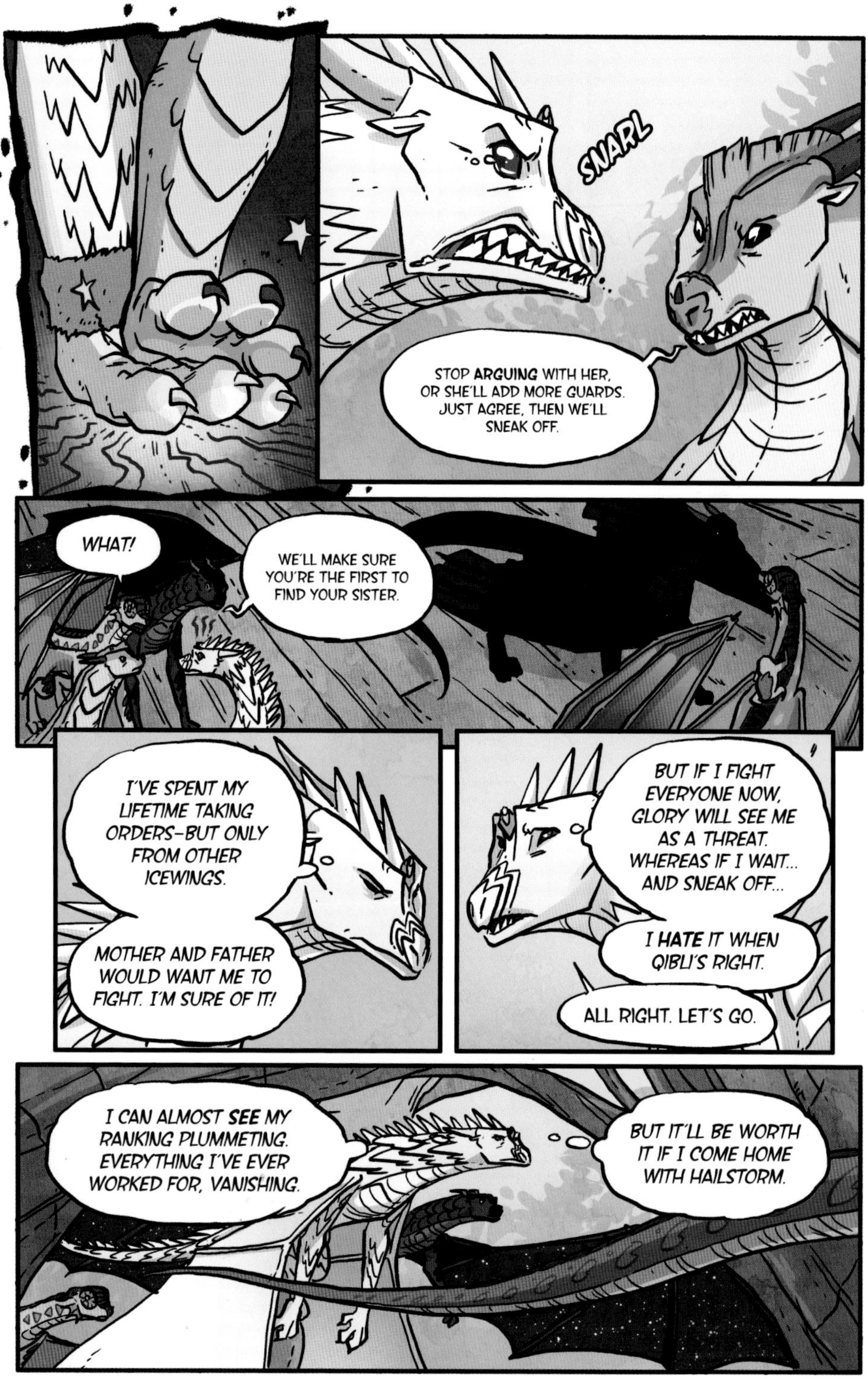
SNARL
STOP **ARGUING** WITH HER, OR SHE'LL ADD MORE GUARDS. JUST AGREE, THEN WE'LL SNEAK OFF.
WHAT!
WE'LL MAKE SURE YOU'RE THE FIRST TO FIND YOUR SISTER.
I'VE SPENT MY LIFETIME TAKING ORDERS—BUT ONLY FROM OTHER ICEWINGS.
MOTHER AND FATHER WOULD WANT ME TO FIGHT. I'M SURE OF IT!
BUT IF I FIGHT EVERYONE NOW, GLORY WILL SEE ME AS A THREAT. WHEREAS IF I WAIT... AND SNEAK OFF...
I **HATE** IT WHEN QIBLI'S RIGHT.
ALL RIGHT. LET'S GO.
I CAN ALMOST **SEE** MY RANKING PLUMMETING. EVERYTHING I'VE EVER WORKED FOR, VANISHING.
BUT IT'LL BE WORTH IT IF I COME HOME WITH HAILSTORM.

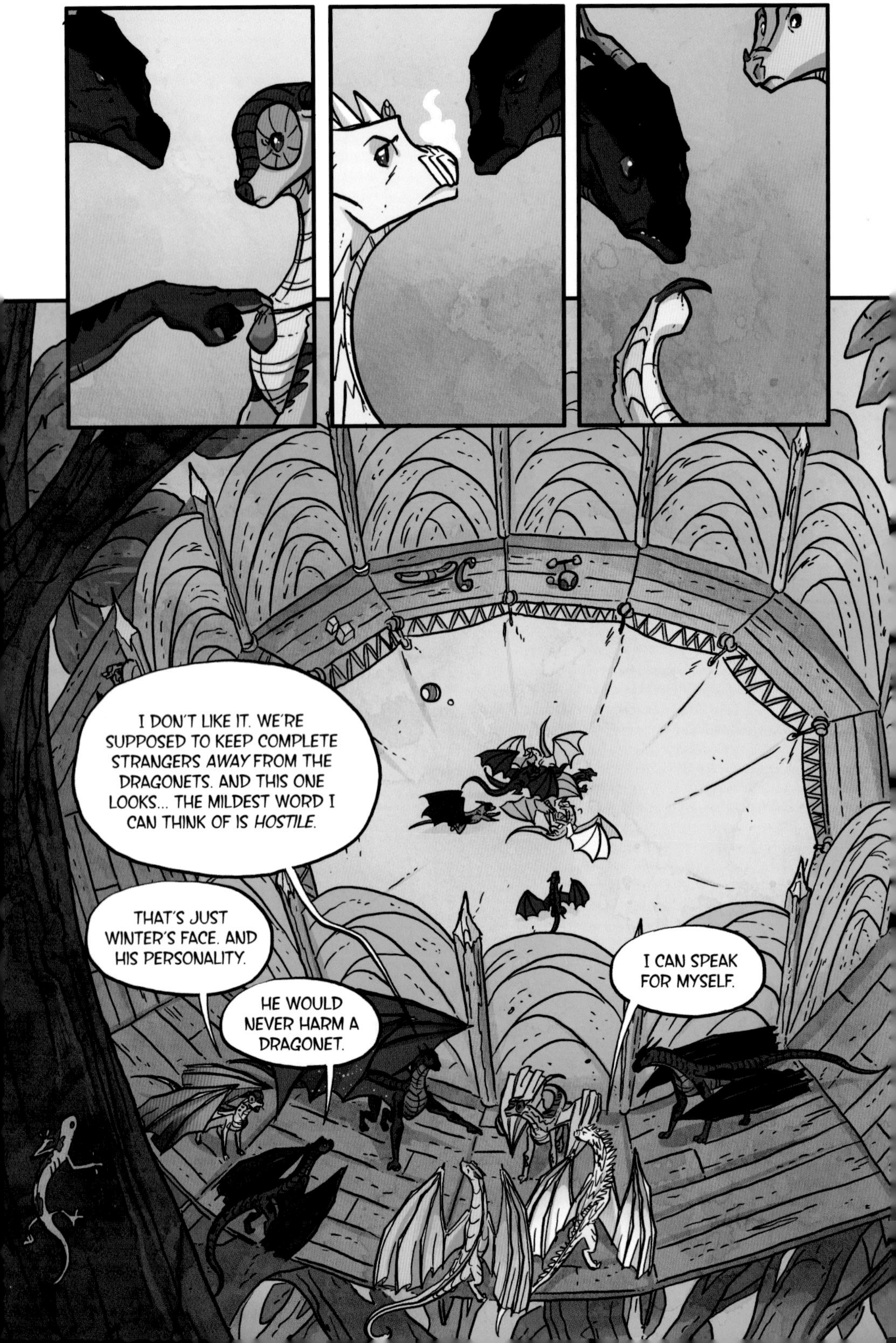
I DON'T LIKE IT. WE'RE SUPPOSED TO KEEP COMPLETE STRANGERS *AWAY* FROM THE DRAGONETS. AND THIS ONE LOOKS... THE MILDEST WORD I CAN THINK OF IS *HOSTILE*.
THAT'S JUST WINTER'S FACE. AND HIS PERSONALITY.
HE WOULD NEVER HARM A DRAGONET.
I CAN SPEAK FOR MYSELF.

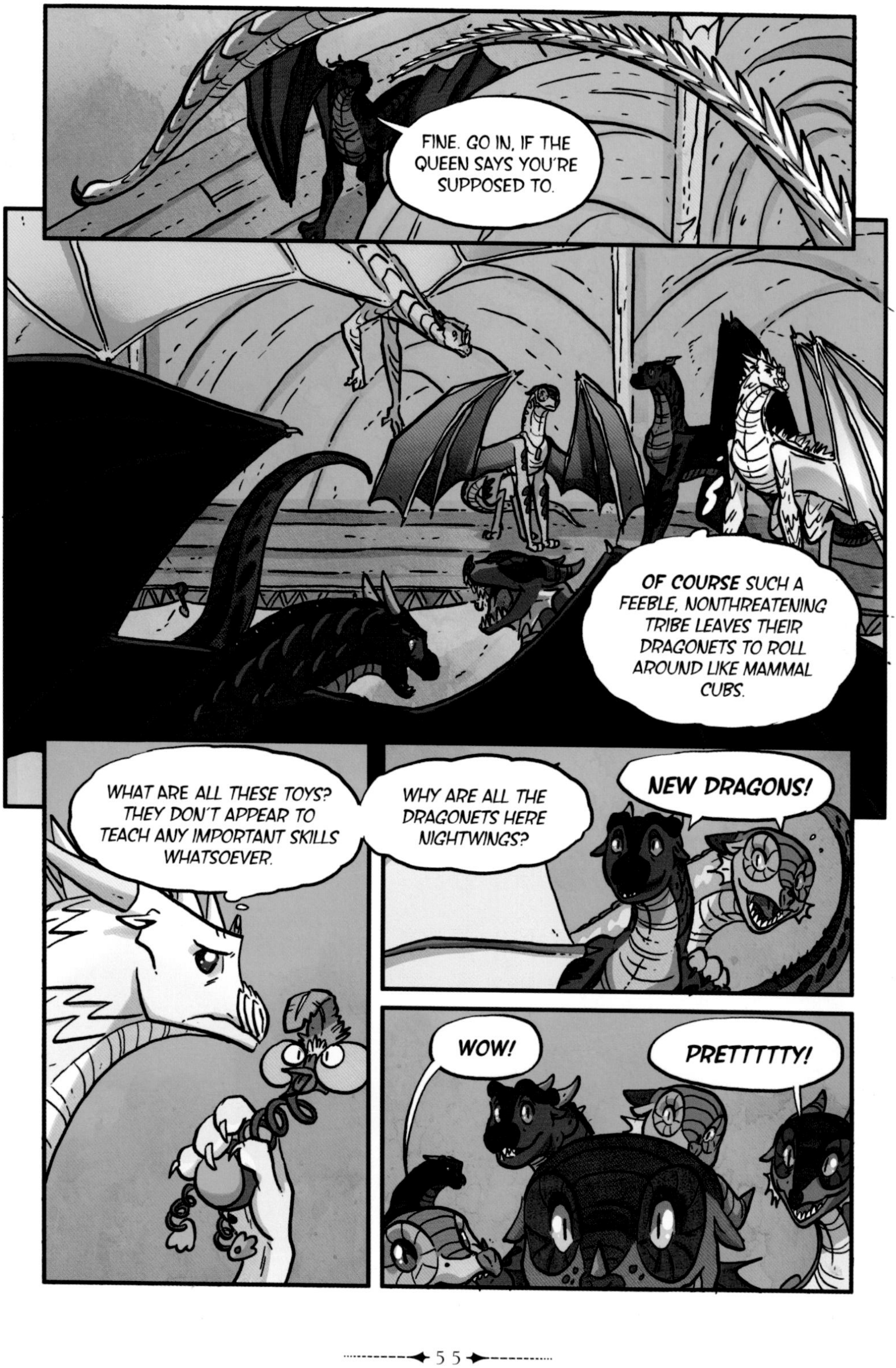

FINE. GO IN, IF THE QUEEN SAYS YOU'RE SUPPOSED TO.
OF COURSE SUCH A FEEBLE, NONTHREATENING TRIBE LEAVES THEIR DRAGONETS TO ROLL AROUND LIKE MAMMAL CUBS.
WHAT ARE ALL THESE TOYS? THEY DON'T APPEAR TO TEACH ANY IMPORTANT SKILLS WHATSOEVER.
WHY ARE ALL THE DRAGONETS HERE NIGHTWINGS?
NEW DRAGONS!
WOW!
PRETTTTTY!

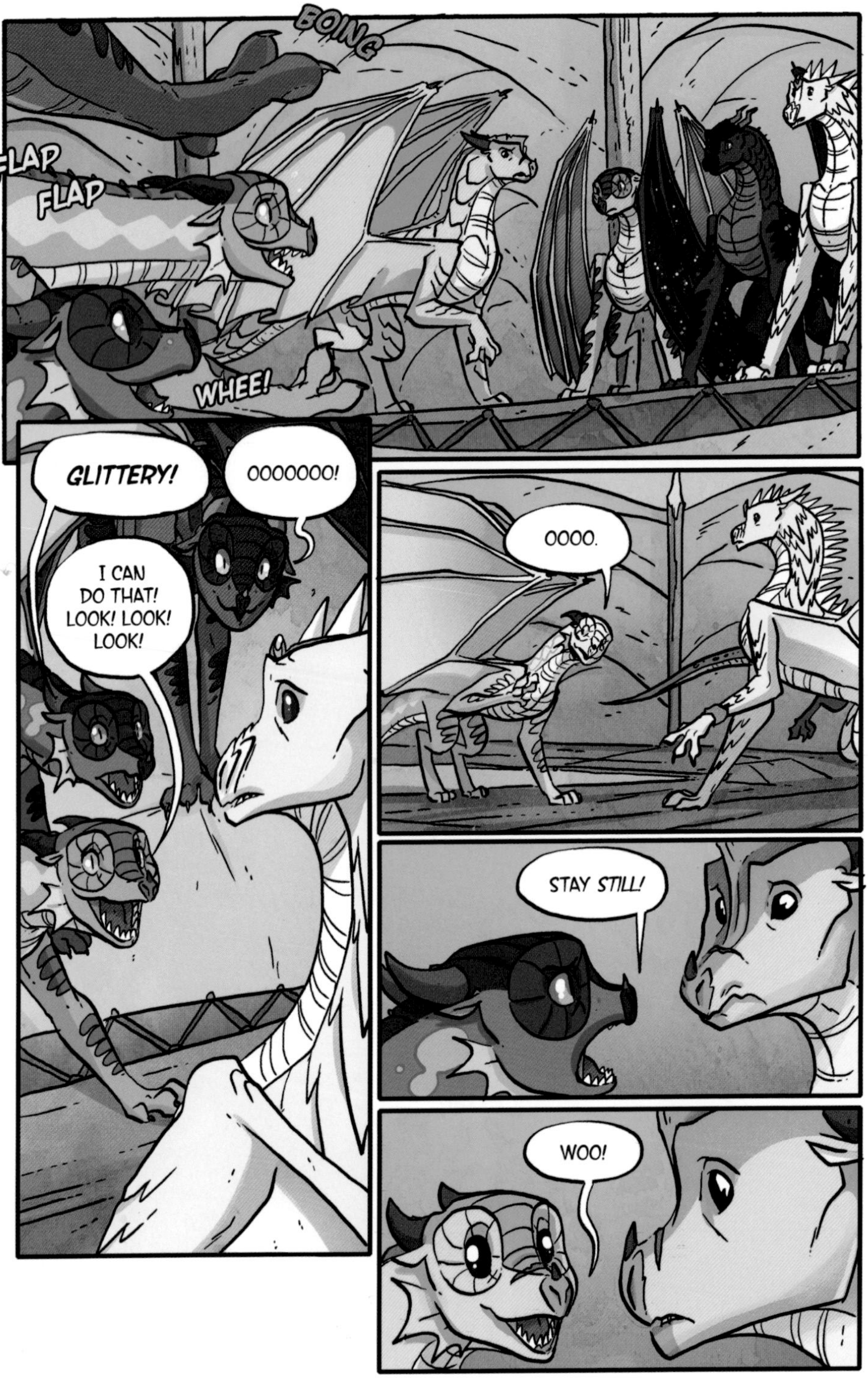
BOING
FLAP
FLAP
WHEE!
GLITTERY!
OOOOOOO!
I CAN DO THAT! LOOK! LOOK! LOOK!
OOOO.
STAY STILL!
WOO!

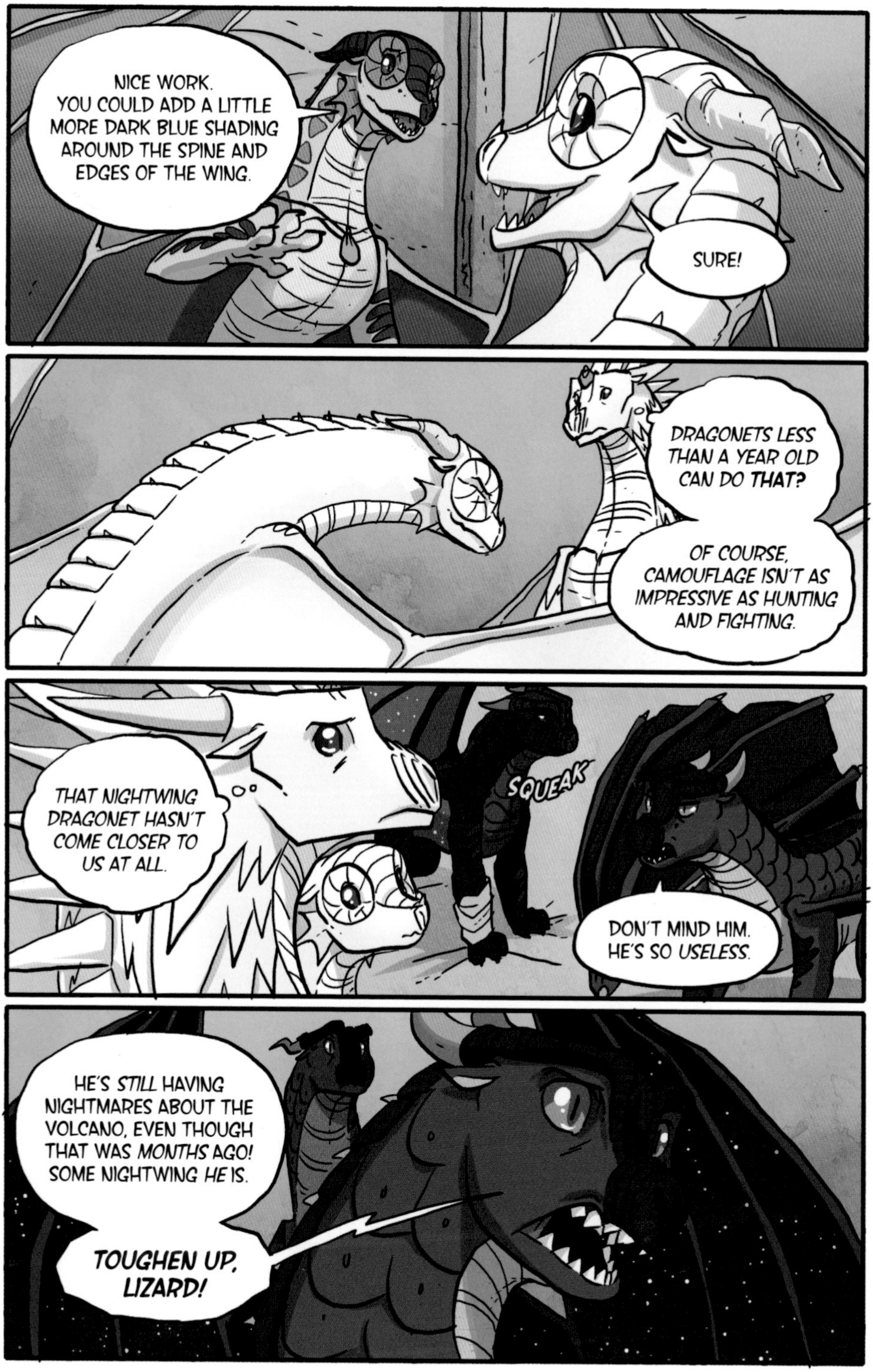
NICE WORK.
YOU COULD ADD A LITTLE MORE DARK BLUE SHADING AROUND THE SPINE AND EDGES OF THE WING.
SURE!
DRAGONETS LESS THAN A YEAR OLD CAN DO THAT?
OF COURSE, CAMOUFLAGE ISN'T AS IMPRESSIVE AS HUNTING AND FIGHTING.
THAT NIGHTWING DRAGONET HASN'T COME CLOSER TO US AT ALL.
SQUEAK
DON'T MIND HIM. HE'S SO USELESS.
HE'S STILL HAVING NIGHTMARES ABOUT THE VOLCANO, EVEN THOUGH THAT WAS MONTHS AGO! SOME NIGHTWING HE IS.
TOUGHEN UP, LIZARD!

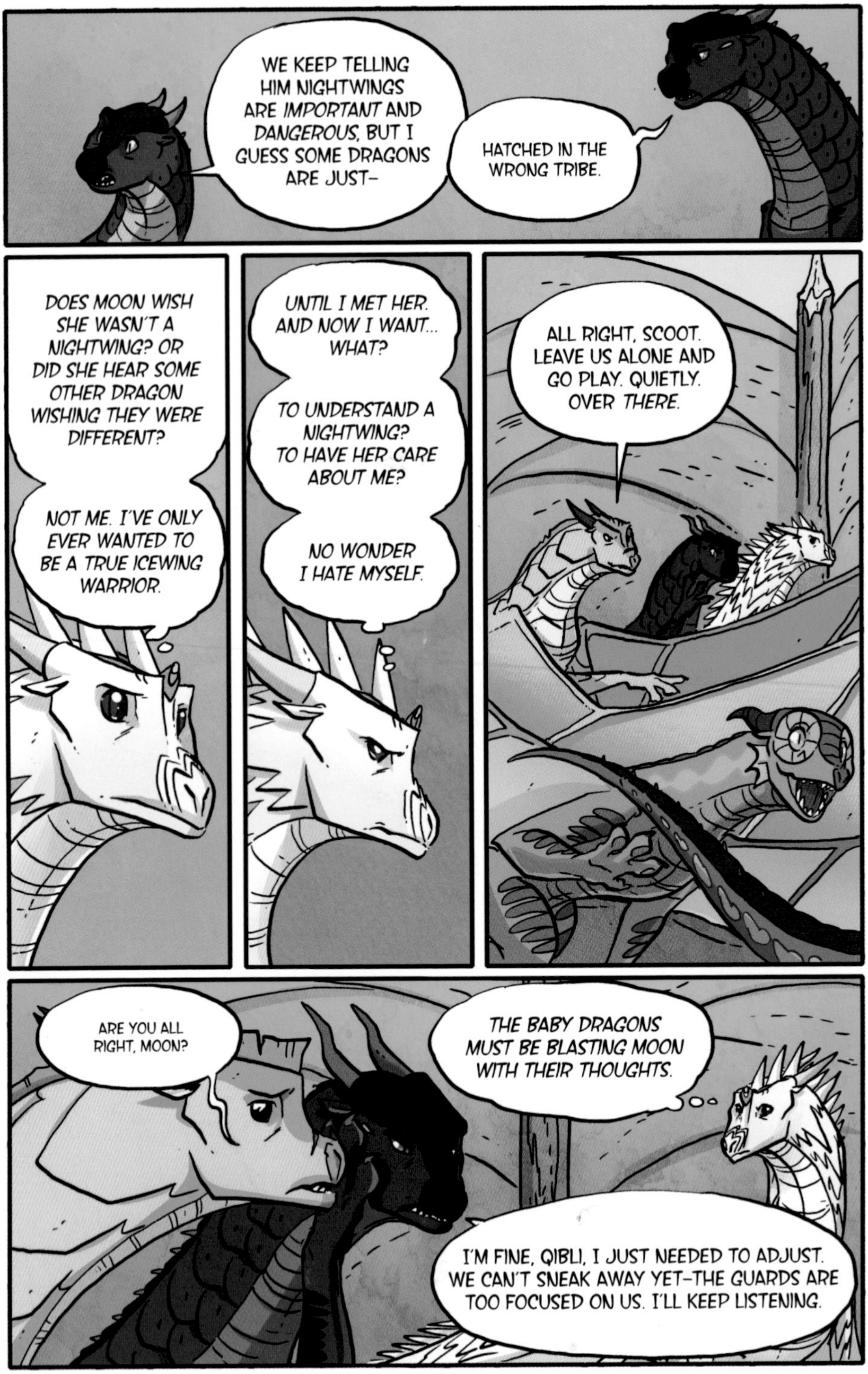
WE KEEP TELLING HIM NIGHTWINGS ARE *IMPORTANT* AND *DANGEROUS*, BUT I GUESS SOME DRAGONS ARE JUST–
HATCHED IN THE WRONG TRIBE.
DOES MOON WISH SHE WASN'T A NIGHTWING? OR DID SHE HEAR SOME OTHER DRAGON WISHING THEY WERE DIFFERENT?
NOT ME. I'VE ONLY EVER WANTED TO BE A TRUE ICEWING WARRIOR.
UNTIL I MET HER. AND NOW I WANT... WHAT?
TO UNDERSTAND A NIGHTWING? TO HAVE HER CARE ABOUT ME?
NO WONDER I HATE MYSELF.
ALL RIGHT, SCOOT. LEAVE US ALONE AND GO PLAY. QUIETLY. OVER *THERE.*
ARE YOU ALL RIGHT, MOON?
THE BABY DRAGONS MUST BE BLASTING MOON WITH THEIR THOUGHTS.
I'M FINE, QIBLI, I JUST NEEDED TO ADJUST. WE CAN'T SNEAK AWAY YET–THE GUARDS ARE TOO FOCUSED ON US. I'LL KEEP LISTENING.

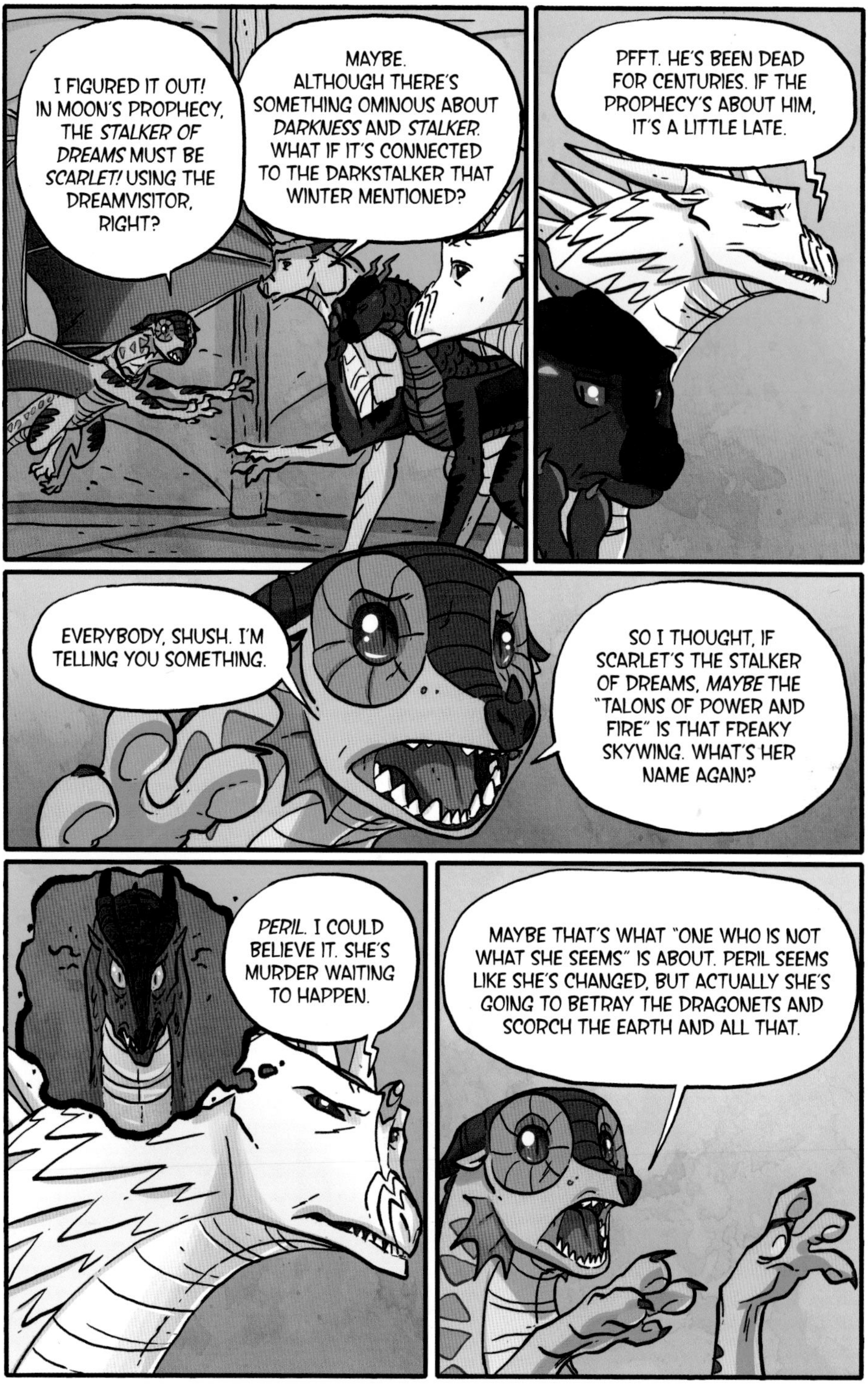
I FIGURED IT OUT! IN MOON'S PROPHECY, THE *STALKER OF DREAMS* MUST BE *SCARLET!* USING THE DREAMVISITOR, RIGHT?
MAYBE. ALTHOUGH THERE'S SOMETHING OMINOUS ABOUT *DARKNESS* AND *STALKER*. WHAT IF IT'S CONNECTED TO THE DARKSTALKER THAT WINTER MENTIONED?
PFFT. HE'S BEEN DEAD FOR CENTURIES. IF THE PROPHECY'S ABOUT HIM, IT'S A LITTLE LATE.
EVERYBODY, SHUSH. I'M TELLING YOU SOMETHING.
SO I THOUGHT, IF SCARLET'S THE STALKER OF DREAMS, *MAYBE* THE "TALONS OF POWER AND FIRE" IS THAT FREAKY SKYWING. WHAT'S HER NAME AGAIN?
PERIL. I COULD BELIEVE IT. SHE'S MURDER WAITING TO HAPPEN.
MAYBE THAT'S WHAT "ONE WHO IS NOT WHAT SHE SEEMS" IS ABOUT. PERIL SEEMS LIKE SHE'S CHANGED, BUT ACTUALLY SHE'S GOING TO BETRAY THE DRAGONETS AND SCORCH THE EARTH AND ALL THAT.

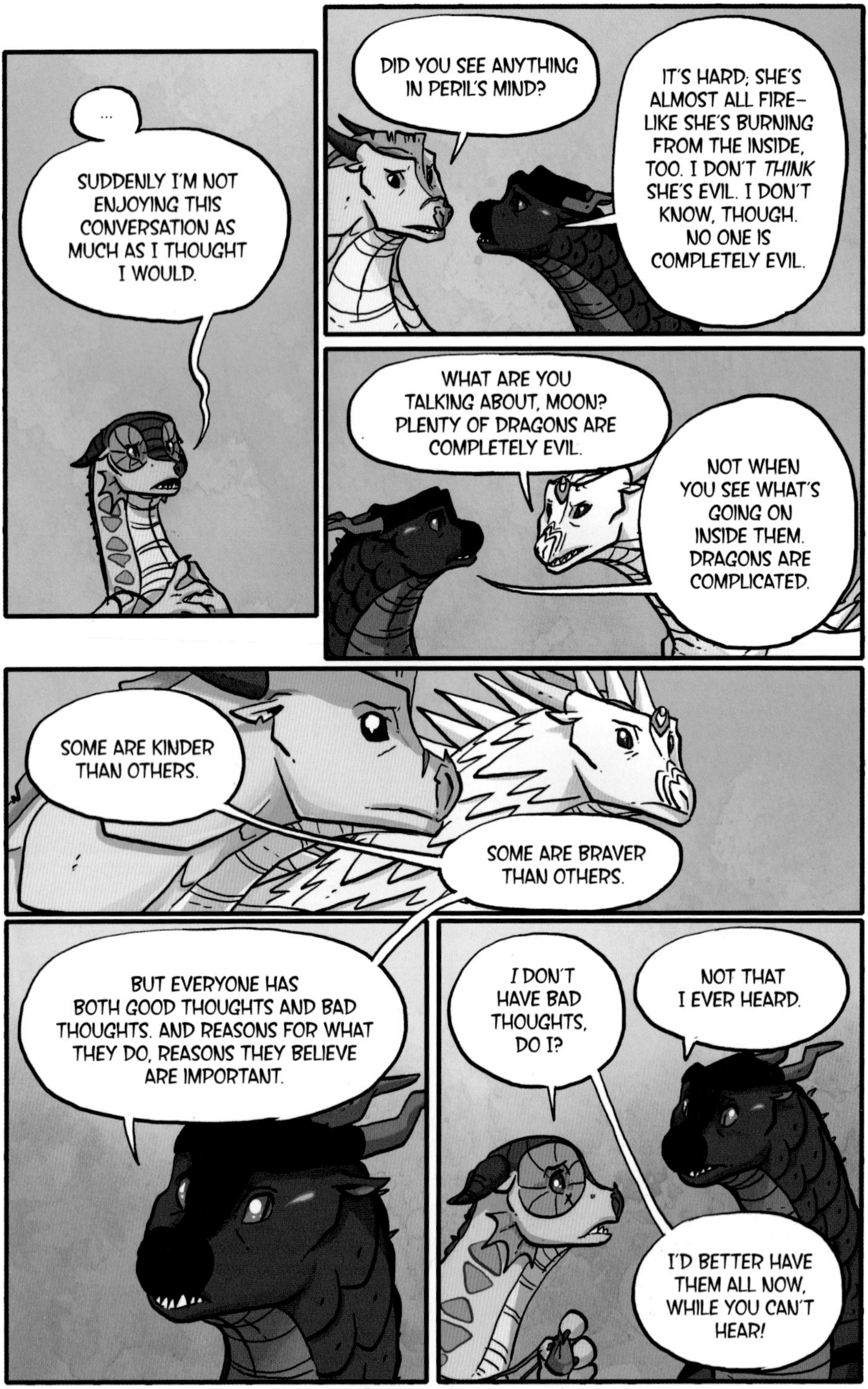
...
SUDDENLY I'M NOT ENJOYING THIS CONVERSATION AS MUCH AS I THOUGHT I WOULD.
DID YOU SEE ANYTHING IN PERIL'S MIND?
IT'S HARD; SHE'S ALMOST ALL FIRE—LIKE SHE'S BURNING FROM THE INSIDE, TOO. I DON'T *THINK* SHE'S EVIL. I DON'T KNOW, THOUGH. NO ONE IS COMPLETELY EVIL.
WHAT ARE YOU TALKING ABOUT, MOON? PLENTY OF DRAGONS ARE COMPLETELY EVIL.
NOT WHEN YOU SEE WHAT'S GOING ON INSIDE THEM. DRAGONS ARE COMPLICATED.
SOME ARE KINDER THAN OTHERS.
SOME ARE BRAVER THAN OTHERS.
BUT EVERYONE HAS BOTH GOOD THOUGHTS AND BAD THOUGHTS. AND REASONS FOR WHAT THEY DO, REASONS THEY BELIEVE ARE IMPORTANT.
I DON'T HAVE BAD THOUGHTS, DO I?
NOT THAT I EVER HEARD.
I'D BETTER HAVE THEM ALL NOW, WHILE YOU CAN'T HEAR!

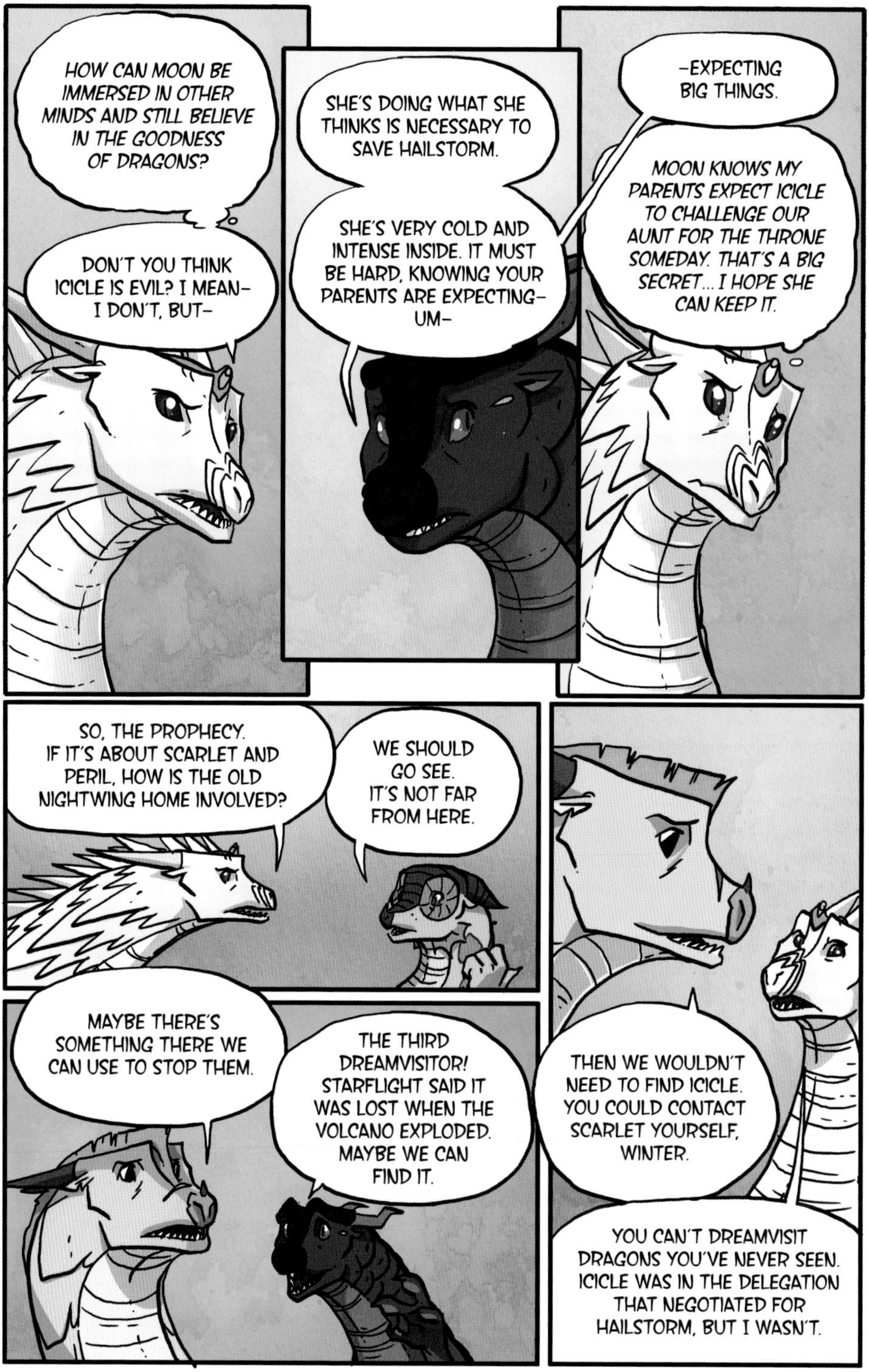
HOW CAN MOON BE IMMERSED IN OTHER MINDS AND STILL BELIEVE IN THE GOODNESS OF DRAGONS?
DON'T YOU THINK ICICLE IS EVIL? I MEAN– I DON'T, BUT–
SHE'S DOING WHAT SHE THINKS IS NECESSARY TO SAVE HAILSTORM.
SHE'S VERY COLD AND INTENSE INSIDE. IT MUST BE HARD, KNOWING YOUR PARENTS ARE EXPECTING– UM–
–EXPECTING BIG THINGS.
MOON KNOWS MY PARENTS EXPECT ICICLE TO CHALLENGE OUR AUNT FOR THE THRONE SOMEDAY. THAT'S A BIG SECRET... I HOPE SHE CAN KEEP IT.
SO, THE PROPHECY. IF IT'S ABOUT SCARLET AND PERIL, HOW IS THE OLD NIGHTWING HOME INVOLVED?
WE SHOULD GO SEE. IT'S NOT FAR FROM HERE.
MAYBE THERE'S SOMETHING THERE WE CAN USE TO STOP THEM.
THE THIRD DREAMVISITOR! STARFLIGHT SAID IT WAS LOST WHEN THE VOLCANO EXPLODED. MAYBE WE CAN FIND IT.
THEN WE WOULDN'T NEED TO FIND ICICLE. YOU COULD CONTACT SCARLET YOURSELF, WINTER.
YOU CAN'T DREAMVISIT DRAGONS YOU'VE NEVER SEEN. ICICLE WAS IN THE DELEGATION THAT NEGOTIATED FOR HAILSTORM, BUT I WASN'T.

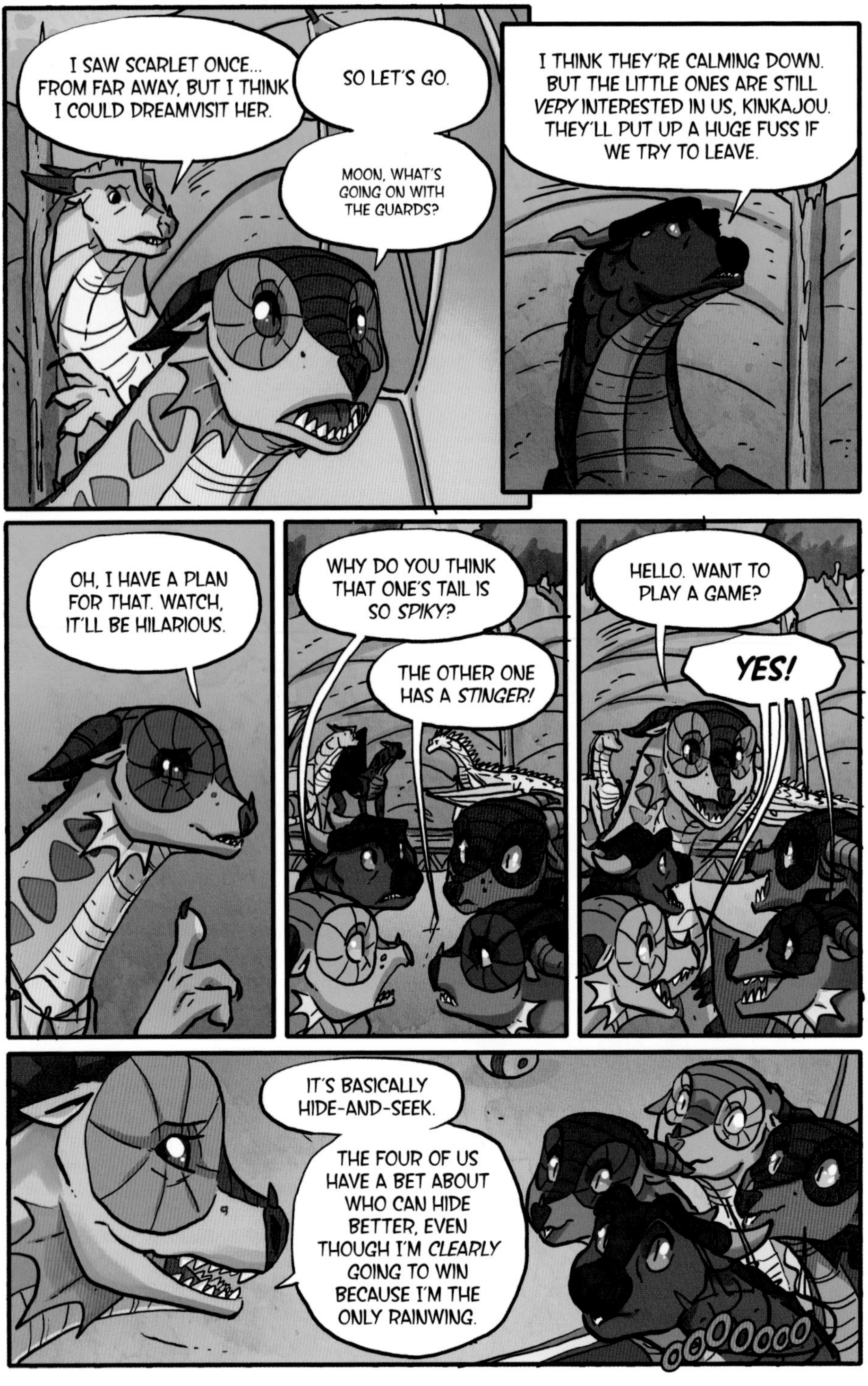
I SAW SCARLET ONCE... FROM FAR AWAY, BUT I THINK I COULD DREAMVISIT HER.
SO LET'S GO.
MOON, WHAT'S GOING ON WITH THE GUARDS?
I THINK THEY'RE CALMING DOWN. BUT THE LITTLE ONES ARE STILL *VERY* INTERESTED IN US, KINKAJOU. THEY'LL PUT UP A HUGE FUSS IF WE TRY TO LEAVE.
OH, I HAVE A PLAN FOR THAT. WATCH, IT'LL BE HILARIOUS.
WHY DO YOU THINK THAT ONE'S TAIL IS SO *SPIKY*?
THE OTHER ONE HAS A *STINGER*!
HELLO. WANT TO PLAY A GAME?
YES!
IT'S BASICALLY HIDE-AND-SEEK.
THE FOUR OF US HAVE A BET ABOUT WHO CAN HIDE BETTER, EVEN THOUGH I'M *CLEARLY* GOING TO WIN BECAUSE I'M THE ONLY RAINWING.
OOOOOOO

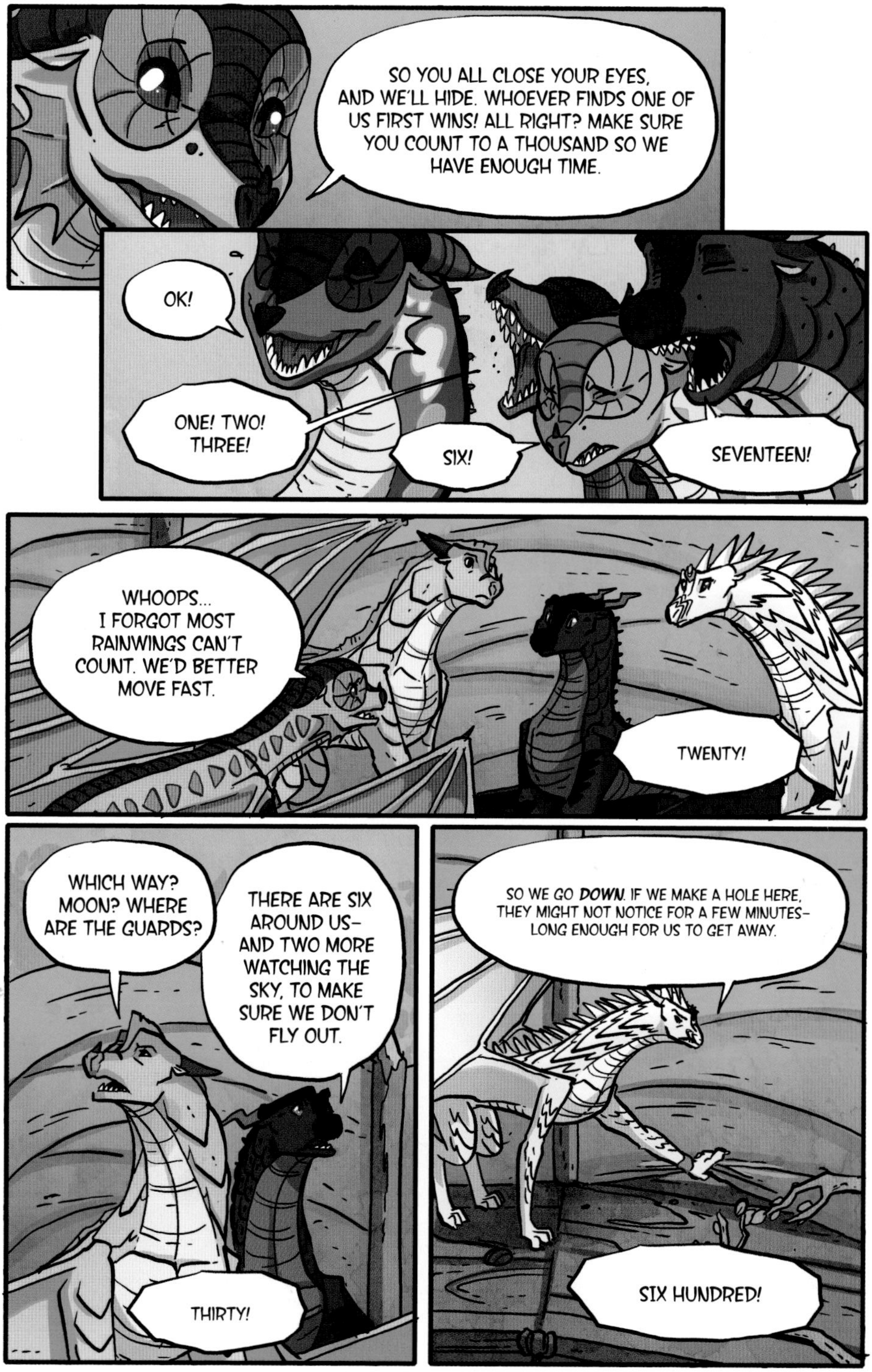
SO YOU ALL CLOSE YOUR EYES, AND WE'LL HIDE. WHOEVER FINDS ONE OF US FIRST WINS! ALL RIGHT? MAKE SURE YOU COUNT TO A THOUSAND SO WE HAVE ENOUGH TIME.
OK!
ONE! TWO! THREE!
SIX!
SEVENTEEN!
WHOOPS... I FORGOT MOST RAINWINGS CAN'T COUNT. WE'D BETTER MOVE FAST.
TWENTY!
WHICH WAY? MOON? WHERE ARE THE GUARDS?
THERE ARE SIX AROUND US— AND TWO MORE WATCHING THE SKY, TO MAKE SURE WE DON'T FLY OUT.
THIRTY!
SO WE GO DOWN. IF WE MAKE A HOLE HERE, THEY MIGHT NOT NOTICE FOR A FEW MINUTES— LONG ENOUGH FOR US TO GET AWAY.
SIX HUNDRED!

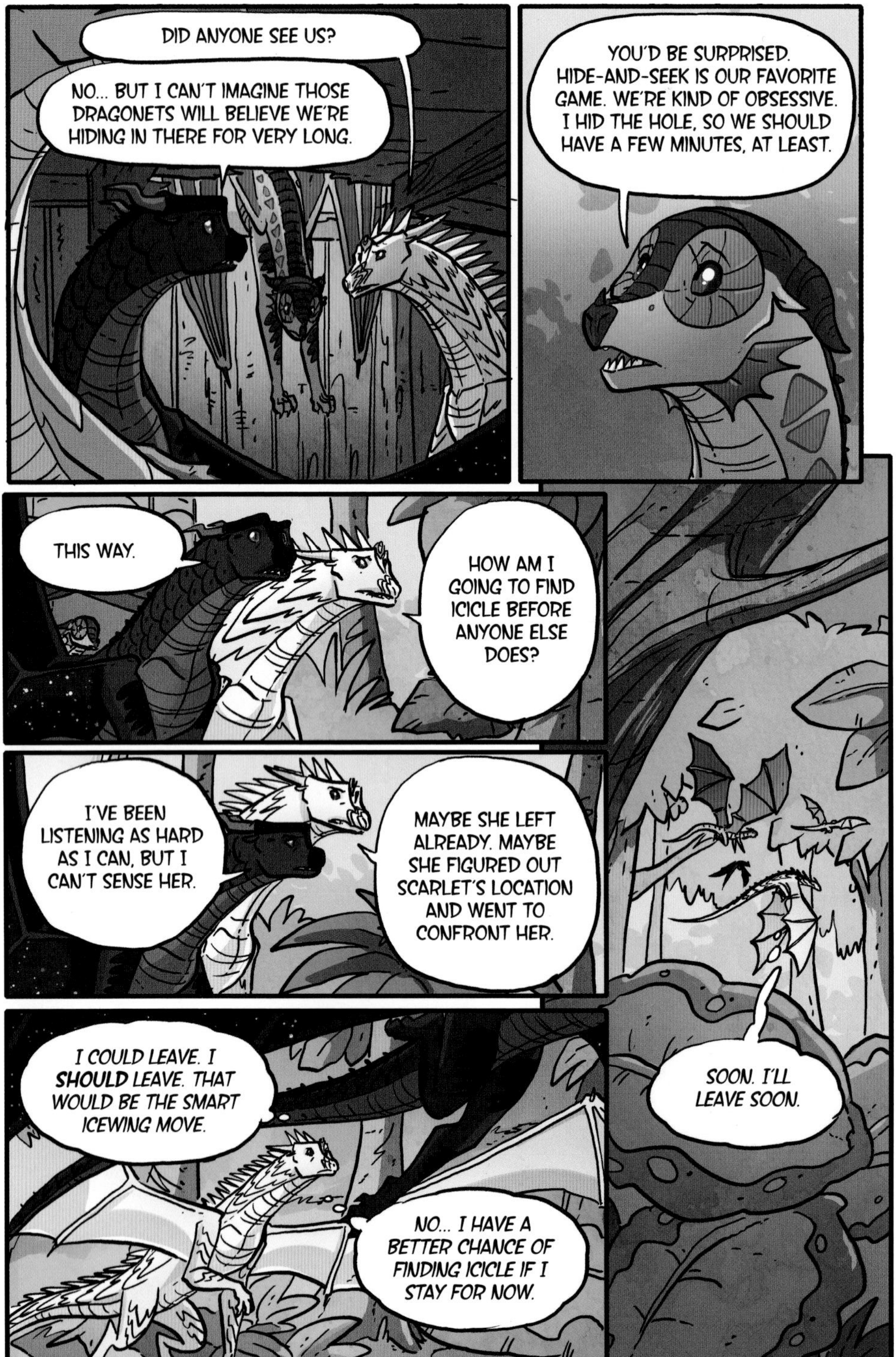
DID ANYONE SEE US?
NO... BUT I CAN'T IMAGINE THOSE DRAGONETS WILL BELIEVE WE'RE HIDING IN THERE FOR VERY LONG.
YOU'D BE SURPRISED. HIDE-AND-SEEK IS OUR FAVORITE GAME. WE'RE KIND OF OBSESSIVE. I HID THE HOLE, SO WE SHOULD HAVE A FEW MINUTES, AT LEAST.
THIS WAY.
HOW AM I GOING TO FIND ICICLE BEFORE ANYONE ELSE DOES?
I'VE BEEN LISTENING AS HARD AS I CAN, BUT I CAN'T SENSE HER.
MAYBE SHE LEFT ALREADY. MAYBE SHE FIGURED OUT SCARLET'S LOCATION AND WENT TO CONFRONT HER.
I COULD LEAVE. I **SHOULD** LEAVE. THAT WOULD BE THE SMART ICEWING MOVE.
NO... I HAVE A BETTER CHANCE OF FINDING ICICLE IF I STAY FOR NOW.
SOON. I'LL LEAVE SOON.

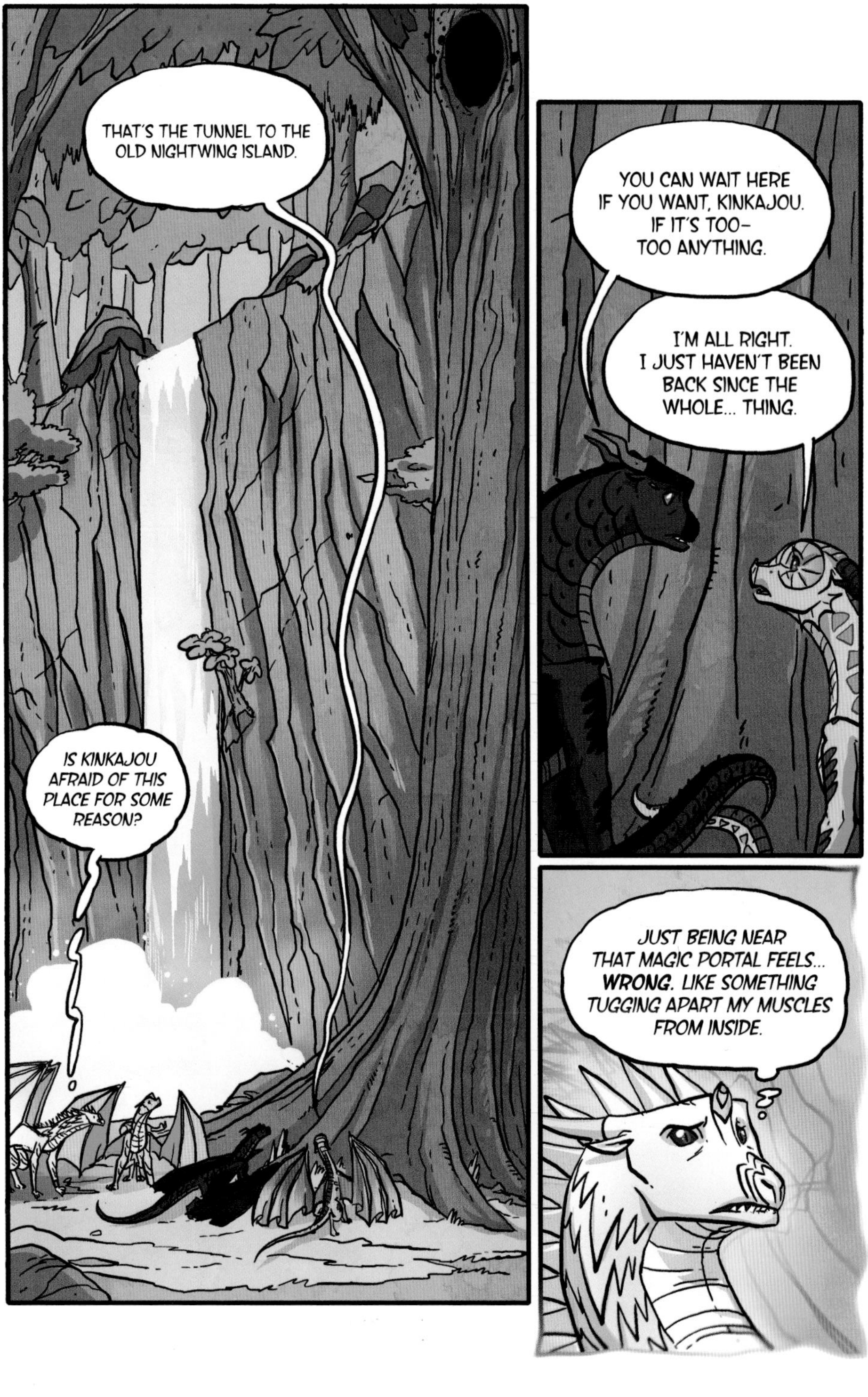
THAT'S THE TUNNEL TO THE OLD NIGHTWING ISLAND.
IS KINKAJOU AFRAID OF THIS PLACE FOR SOME REASON?
YOU CAN WAIT HERE IF YOU WANT, KINKAJOU. IF IT'S TOO— TOO ANYTHING.
I'M ALL RIGHT. I JUST HAVEN'T BEEN BACK SINCE THE WHOLE... THING.
JUST BEING NEAR THAT MAGIC PORTAL FEELS... **WRONG.** LIKE SOMETHING TUGGING APART MY MUSCLES FROM INSIDE.

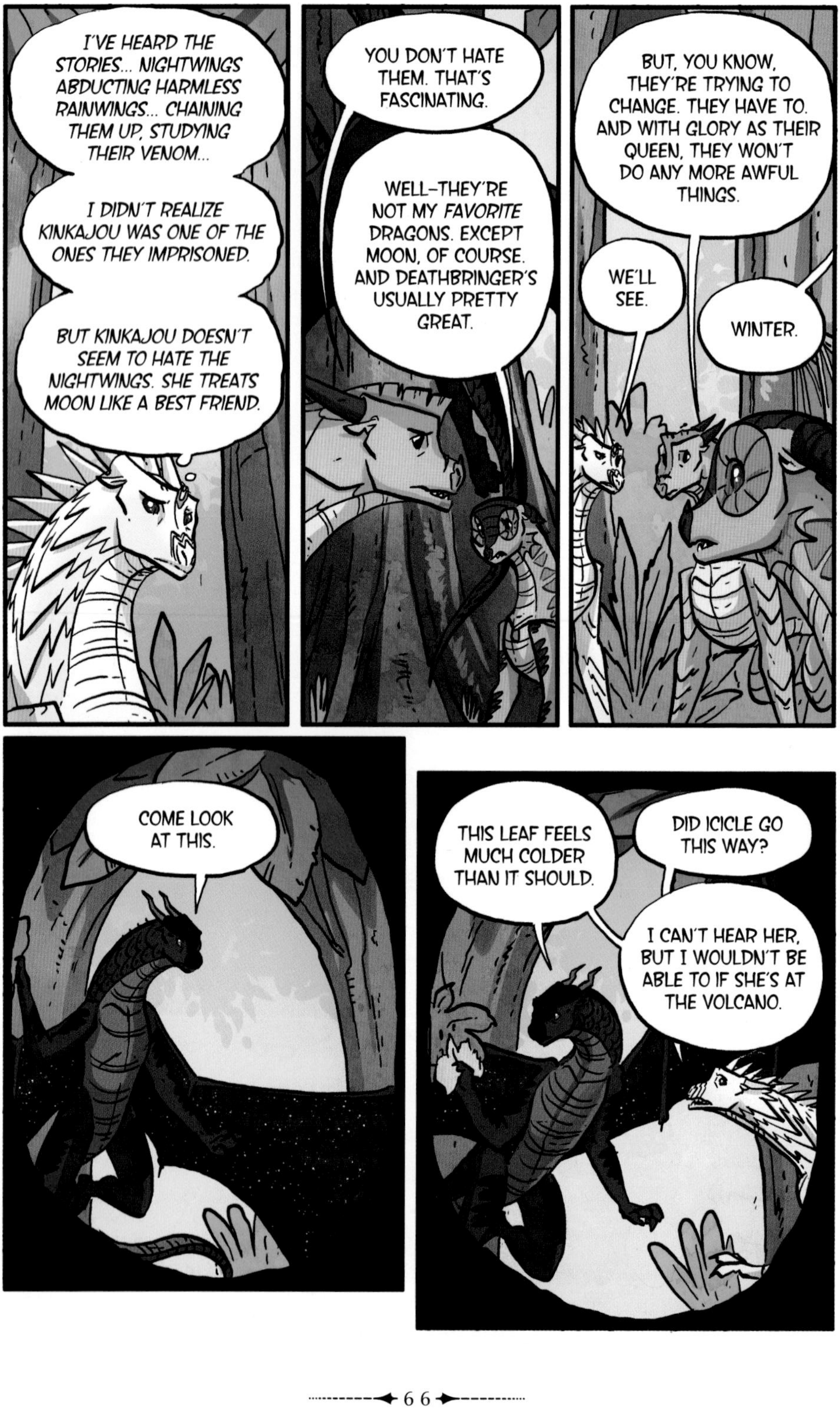
I'VE HEARD THE STORIES... NIGHTWINGS ABDUCTING HARMLESS RAINWINGS... CHAINING THEM UP, STUDYING THEIR VENOM...
I DIDN'T REALIZE KINKAJOU WAS ONE OF THE ONES THEY IMPRISONED.
BUT KINKAJOU DOESN'T SEEM TO HATE THE NIGHTWINGS. SHE TREATS MOON LIKE A BEST FRIEND.
YOU DON'T HATE THEM. THAT'S FASCINATING.
WELL–THEY'RE NOT MY *FAVORITE* DRAGONS. EXCEPT MOON, OF COURSE. AND DEATHBRINGER'S USUALLY PRETTY GREAT.
BUT, YOU KNOW, THEY'RE TRYING TO CHANGE. THEY HAVE TO. AND WITH GLORY AS THEIR QUEEN, THEY WON'T DO ANY MORE AWFUL THINGS.
WE'LL SEE.
WINTER.
COME LOOK AT THIS.
THIS LEAF FEELS MUCH COLDER THAN IT SHOULD.
DID ICICLE GO THIS WAY?
I CAN'T HEAR HER, BUT I WOULDN'T BE ABLE TO IF SHE'S AT THE VOLCANO.

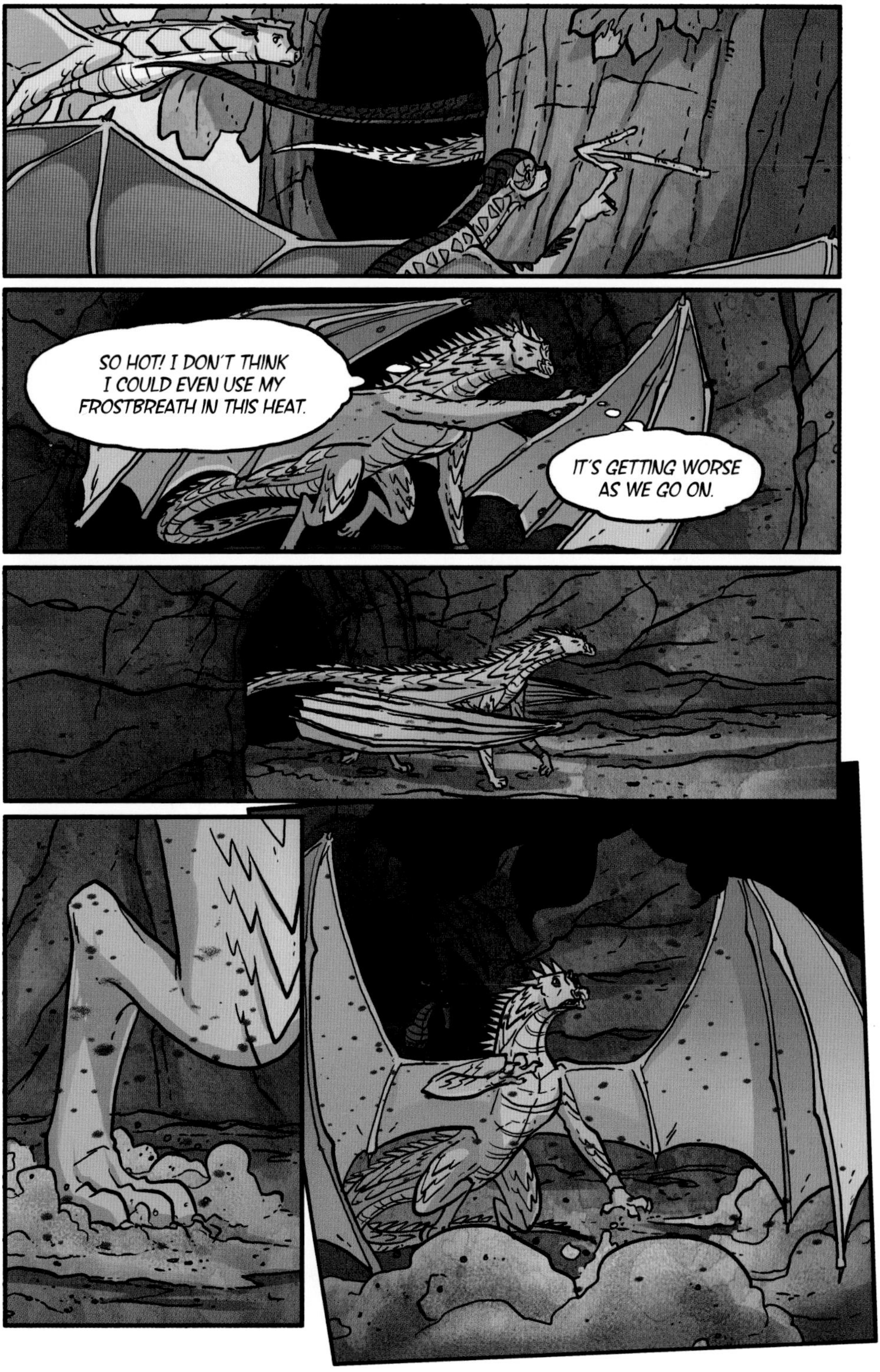
SO HOT! I DON'T THINK I COULD EVEN USE MY FROSTBREATH IN THIS HEAT.
IT'S GETTING WORSE AS WE GO ON.

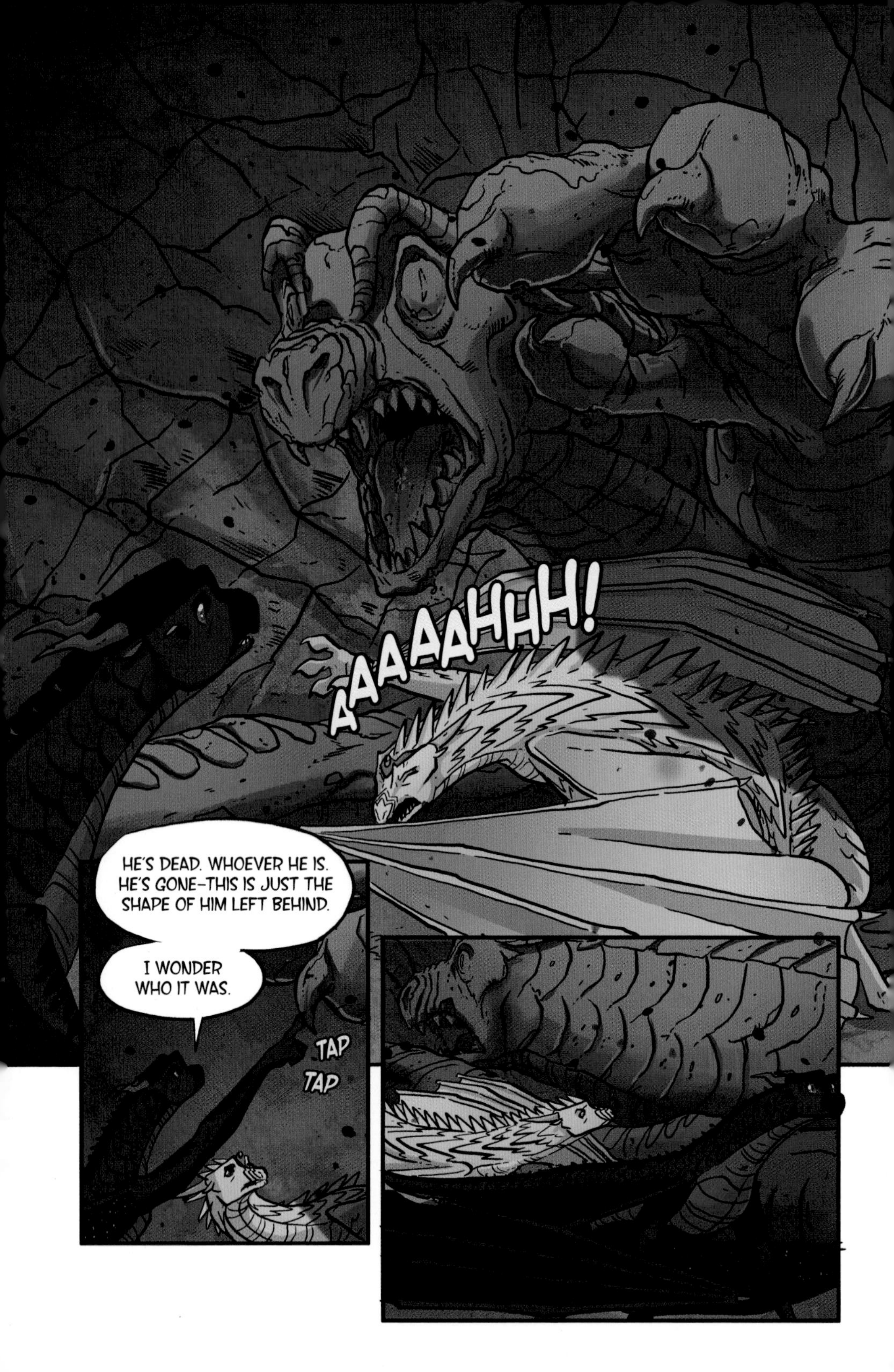
AAAAAHHHH!
HE'S DEAD. WHOEVER HE IS. HE'S GONE—THIS IS JUST THE SHAPE OF HIM LEFT BEHIND.
I WONDER WHO IT WAS.
TAP
TAP

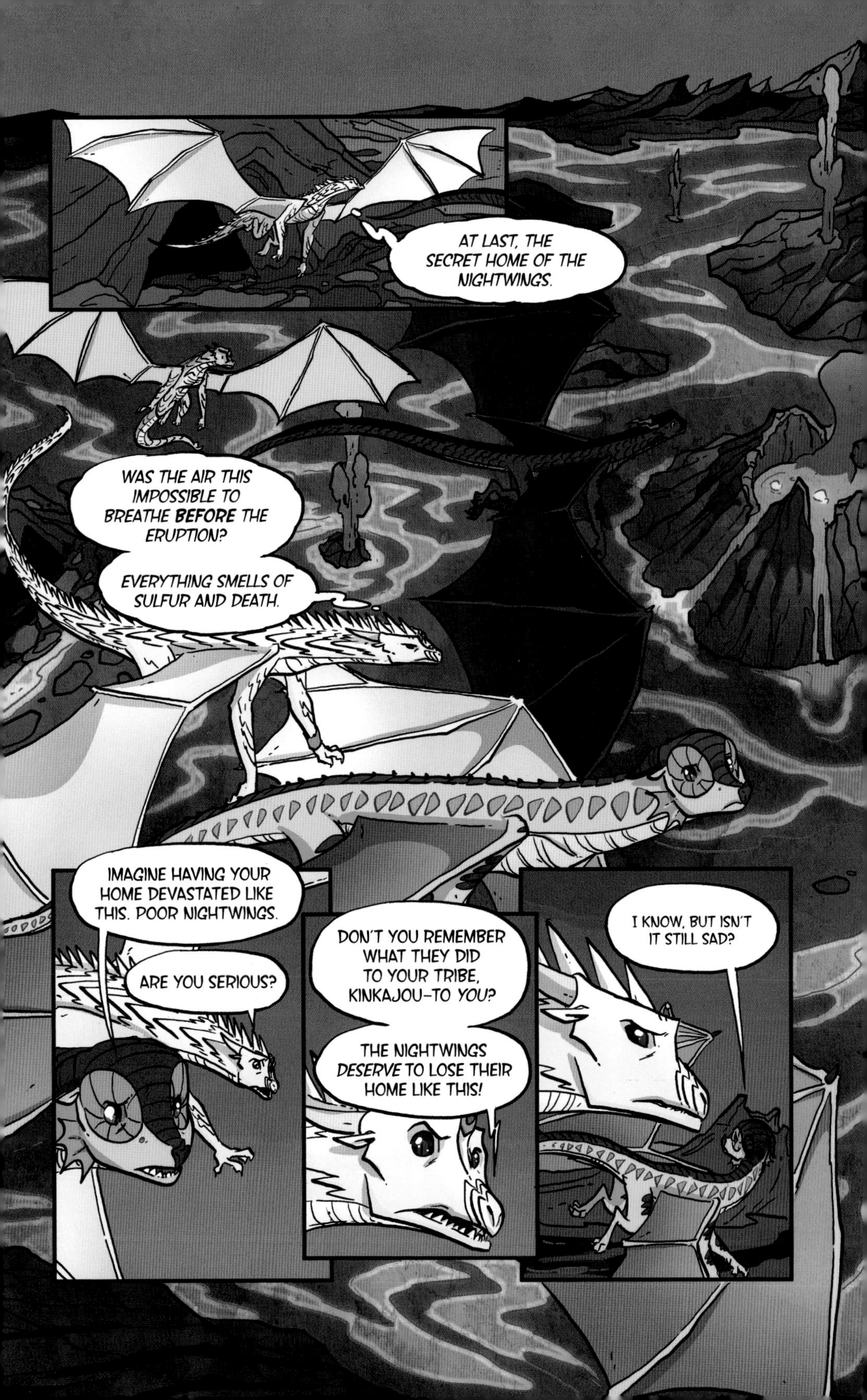
AT LAST, THE SECRET HOME OF THE NIGHTWINGS.
WAS THE AIR THIS IMPOSSIBLE TO BREATHE **BEFORE** THE ERUPTION?
EVERYTHING SMELLS OF SULFUR AND DEATH.
IMAGINE HAVING YOUR HOME DEVASTATED LIKE THIS. POOR NIGHTWINGS.
ARE YOU SERIOUS?
DON'T YOU REMEMBER WHAT THEY DID TO YOUR TRIBE, KINKAJOU—TO *YOU*?
THE NIGHTWINGS *DESERVE* TO LOSE THEIR HOME LIKE THIS!
I KNOW, BUT ISN'T IT STILL SAD?

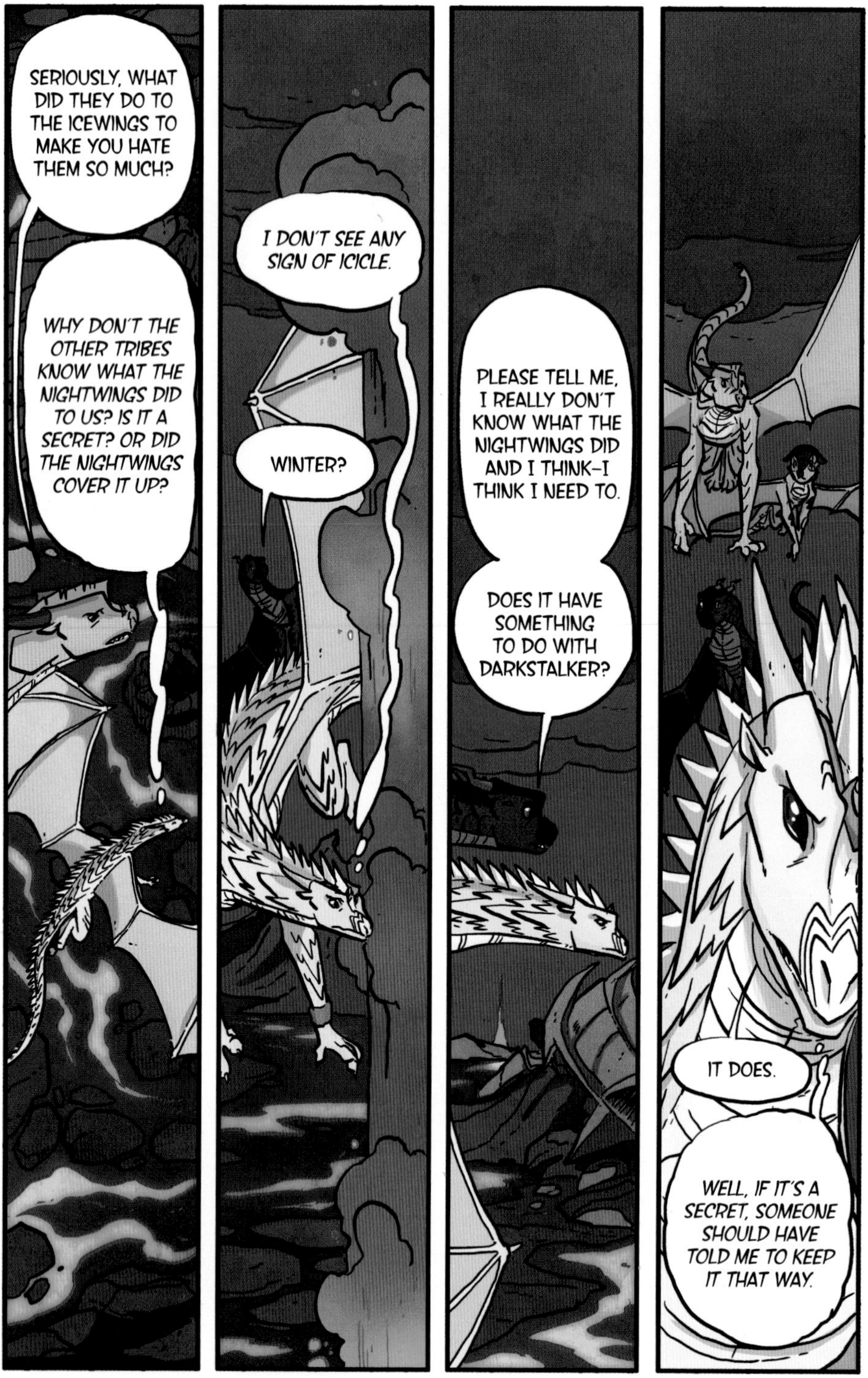
SERIOUSLY, WHAT DID THEY DO TO THE ICEWINGS TO MAKE YOU HATE THEM SO MUCH?
WHY DON'T THE OTHER TRIBES KNOW WHAT THE NIGHTWINGS DID TO US? IS IT A SECRET? OR DID THE NIGHTWINGS COVER IT UP?
I DON'T SEE ANY SIGN OF ICICLE.
WINTER?
PLEASE TELL ME, I REALLY DON'T KNOW WHAT THE NIGHTWINGS DID AND I THINK–I THINK I NEED TO.
DOES IT HAVE SOMETHING TO DO WITH DARKSTALKER?
IT DOES.
WELL, IF IT'S A SECRET, SOMEONE SHOULD HAVE TOLD ME TO KEEP IT THAT WAY.

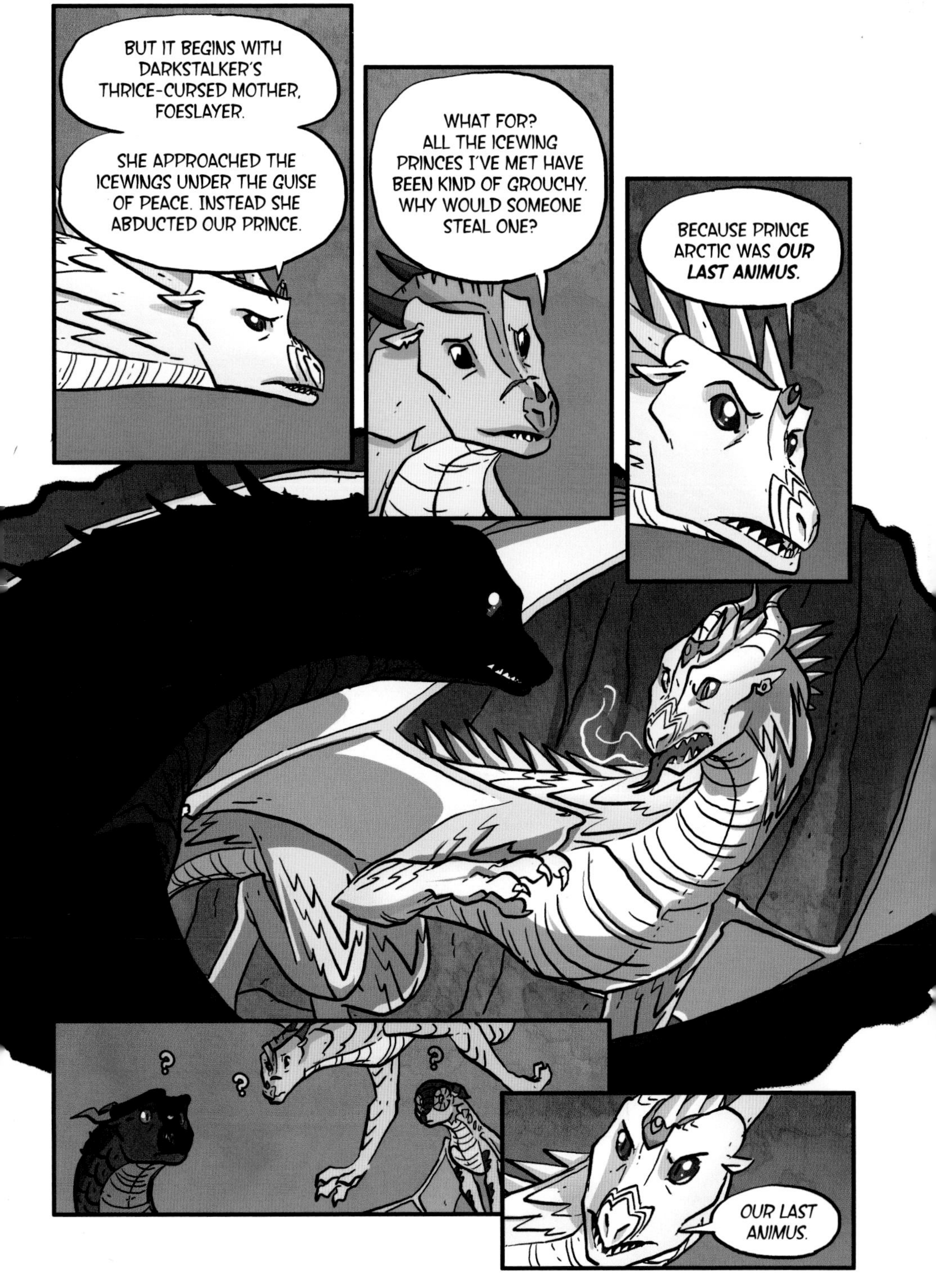
BUT IT BEGINS WITH DARKSTALKER'S THRICE-CURSED MOTHER, FOESLAYER.
SHE APPROACHED THE ICEWINGS UNDER THE GUISE OF PEACE. INSTEAD SHE ABDUCTED OUR PRINCE.
WHAT FOR? ALL THE ICEWING PRINCES I'VE MET HAVE BEEN KIND OF GROUCHY. WHY WOULD SOMEONE STEAL ONE?
BECAUSE PRINCE ARCTIC WAS ***OUR LAST ANIMUS.***
?
?
?
OUR LAST ANIMUS.

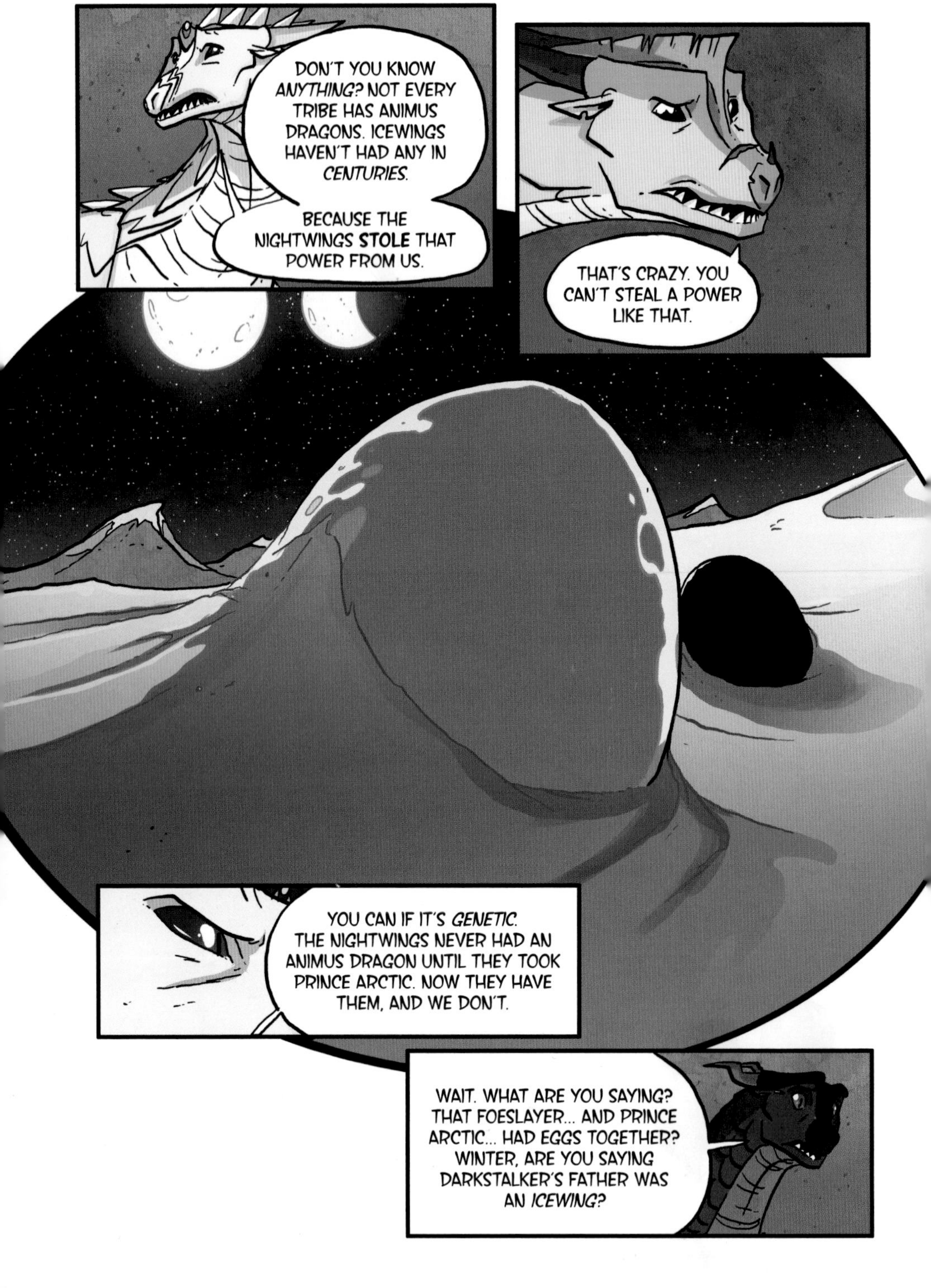
DON'T YOU KNOW *ANYTHING?* NOT EVERY TRIBE HAS ANIMUS DRAGONS. ICEWINGS HAVEN'T HAD ANY IN *CENTURIES.*
BECAUSE THE NIGHTWINGS **STOLE** THAT POWER FROM US.
THAT'S CRAZY. YOU CAN'T STEAL A POWER LIKE THAT.
YOU CAN IF IT'S *GENETIC.* THE NIGHTWINGS NEVER HAD AN ANIMUS DRAGON UNTIL THEY TOOK PRINCE ARCTIC. NOW THEY HAVE THEM, AND WE DON'T.
WAIT. WHAT ARE YOU SAYING? THAT FOESLAYER... AND PRINCE ARCTIC... HAD EGGS TOGETHER? WINTER, ARE YOU SAYING DARKSTALKER'S FATHER WAS AN *ICEWING?*

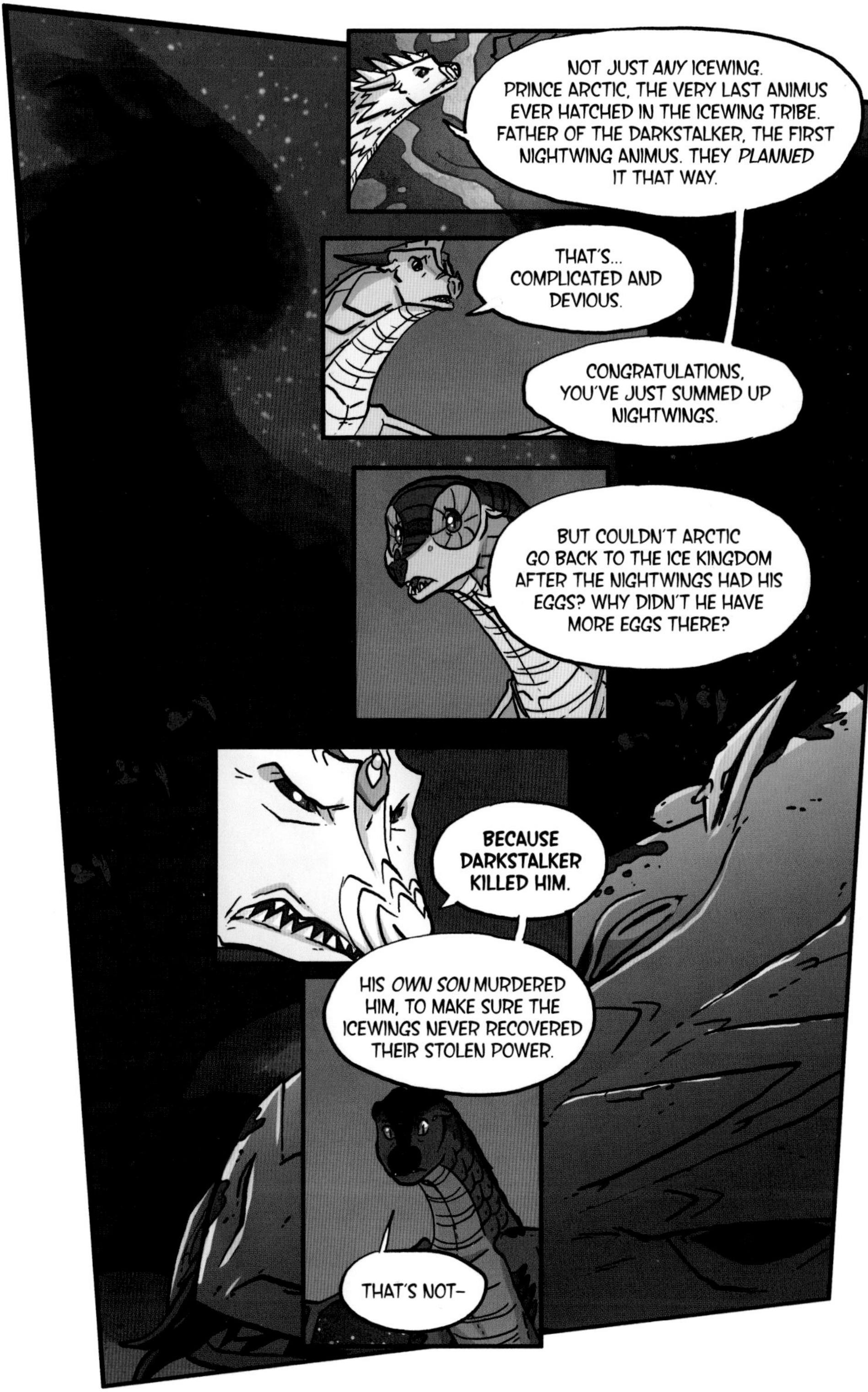
NOT JUST *ANY* ICEWING. PRINCE ARCTIC, THE VERY LAST ANIMUS EVER HATCHED IN THE ICEWING TRIBE. FATHER OF THE DARKSTALKER, THE FIRST NIGHTWING ANIMUS. THEY *PLANNED* IT THAT WAY.
THAT'S... COMPLICATED AND DEVIOUS.
CONGRATULATIONS, YOU'VE JUST SUMMED UP NIGHTWINGS.
BUT COULDN'T ARCTIC GO BACK TO THE ICE KINGDOM AFTER THE NIGHTWINGS HAD HIS EGGS? WHY DIDN'T HE HAVE MORE EGGS THERE?
BECAUSE DARKSTALKER KILLED HIM.
HIS *OWN SON* MURDERED HIM, TO MAKE SURE THE ICEWINGS NEVER RECOVERED THEIR STOLEN POWER.
THAT'S NOT–

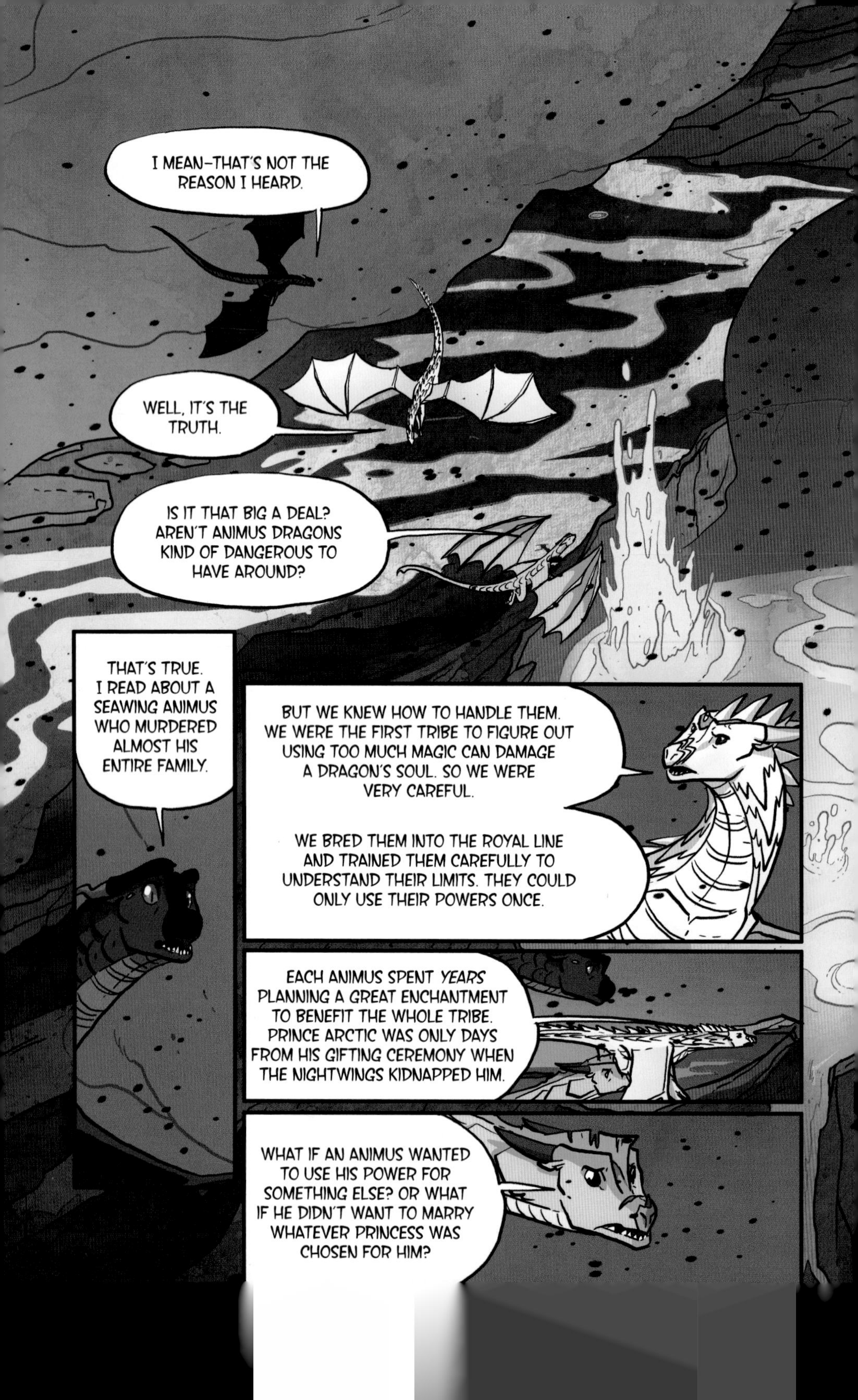
I MEAN—THAT'S NOT THE REASON I HEARD.
WELL, IT'S THE TRUTH.
IS IT THAT BIG A DEAL? AREN'T ANIMUS DRAGONS KIND OF DANGEROUS TO HAVE AROUND?
THAT'S TRUE. I READ ABOUT A SEAWING ANIMUS WHO MURDERED ALMOST HIS ENTIRE FAMILY.
BUT WE KNEW HOW TO HANDLE THEM. WE WERE THE FIRST TRIBE TO FIGURE OUT USING TOO MUCH MAGIC CAN DAMAGE A DRAGON'S SOUL. SO WE WERE VERY CAREFUL.
WE BRED THEM INTO THE ROYAL LINE AND TRAINED THEM CAREFULLY TO UNDERSTAND THEIR LIMITS. THEY COULD ONLY USE THEIR POWERS ONCE.
EACH ANIMUS SPENT *YEARS* PLANNING A GREAT ENCHANTMENT TO BENEFIT THE WHOLE TRIBE. PRINCE ARCTIC WAS ONLY DAYS FROM HIS GIFTING CEREMONY WHEN THE NIGHTWINGS KIDNAPPED HIM.
WHAT IF AN ANIMUS WANTED TO USE HIS POWER FOR SOMETHING ELSE? OR WHAT IF HE DIDN'T WANT TO MARRY WHATEVER PRINCESS WAS CHOSEN FOR HIM?

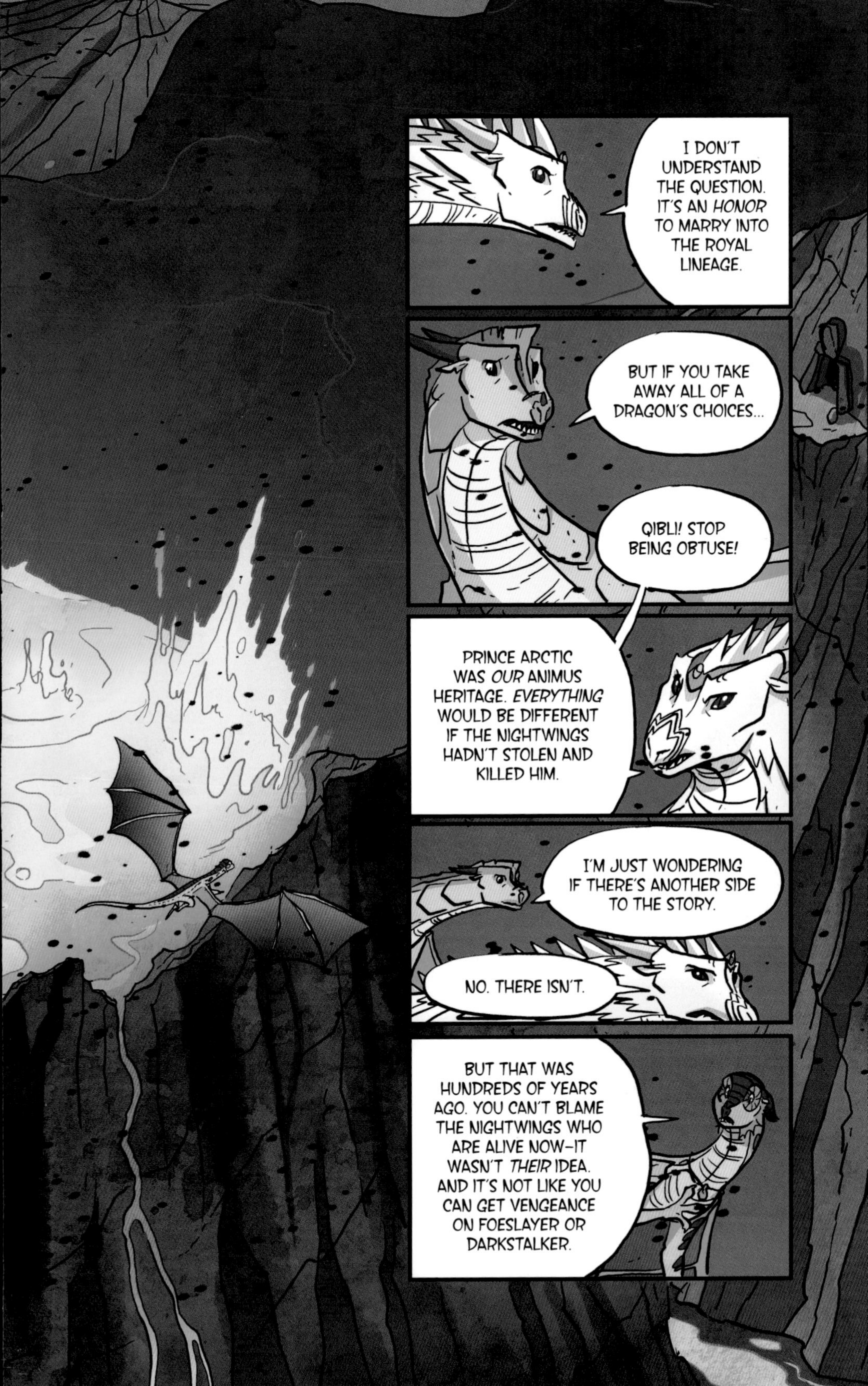
I DON'T UNDERSTAND THE QUESTION. IT'S AN *HONOR* TO MARRY INTO THE ROYAL LINEAGE.
BUT IF YOU TAKE AWAY ALL OF A DRAGON'S CHOICES...
QIBLI! STOP BEING OBTUSE!
PRINCE ARCTIC WAS *OUR* ANIMUS HERITAGE. *EVERYTHING* WOULD BE DIFFERENT IF THE NIGHTWINGS HADN'T STOLEN AND KILLED HIM.
I'M JUST WONDERING IF THERE'S ANOTHER SIDE TO THE STORY.
NO. THERE ISN'T.
BUT THAT WAS HUNDREDS OF YEARS AGO. YOU CAN'T BLAME THE NIGHTWINGS WHO ARE ALIVE NOW—IT WASN'T *THEIR* IDEA. AND IT'S NOT LIKE YOU CAN GET VENGEANCE ON FOESLAYER OR DARKSTALKER.

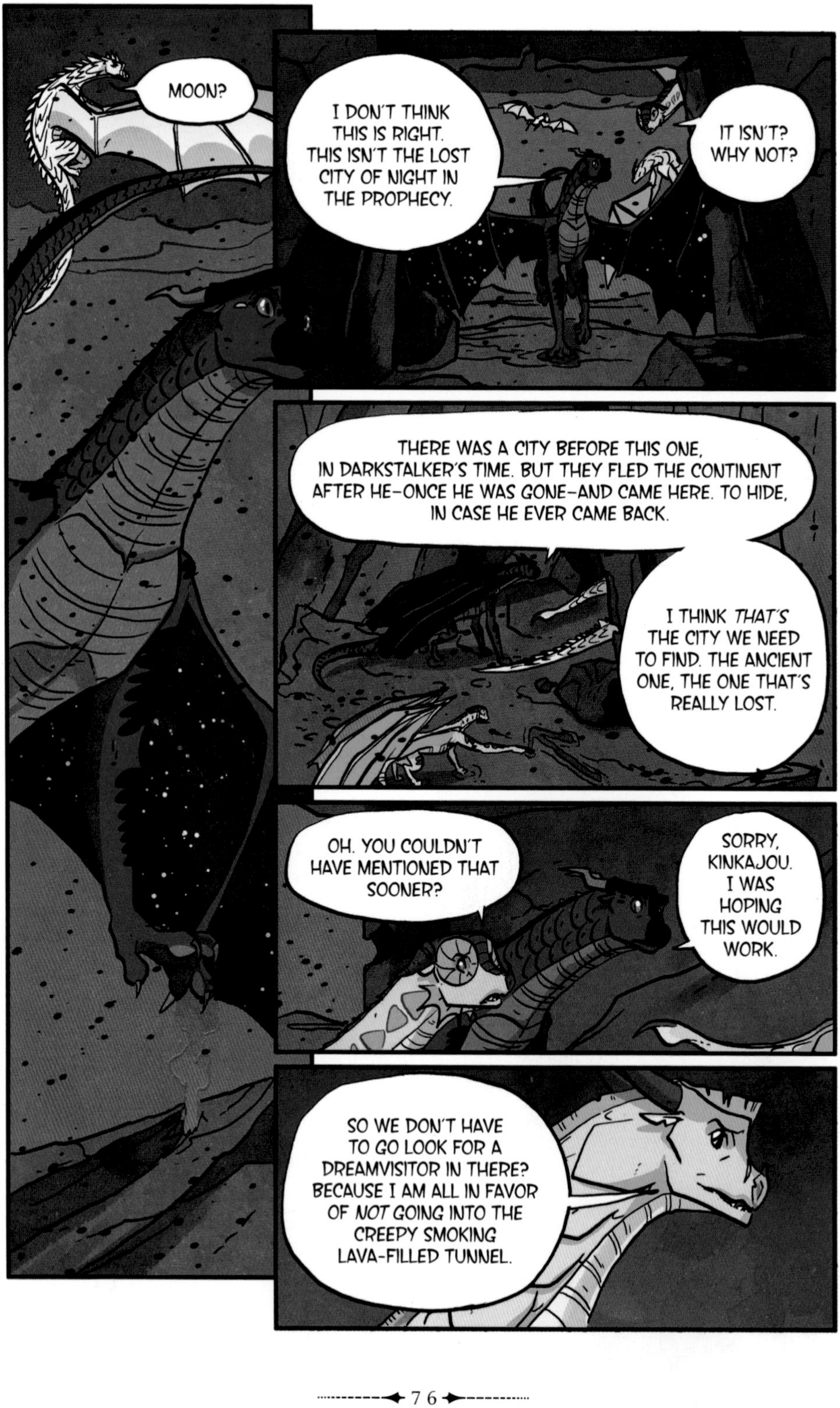
MOON?
I DON'T THINK THIS IS RIGHT. THIS ISN'T THE LOST CITY OF NIGHT IN THE PROPHECY.
IT ISN'T? WHY NOT?
THERE WAS A CITY BEFORE THIS ONE, IN DARKSTALKER'S TIME. BUT THEY FLED THE CONTINENT AFTER HE—ONCE HE WAS GONE—AND CAME HERE. TO HIDE, IN CASE HE EVER CAME BACK.
I THINK *THAT'S* THE CITY WE NEED TO FIND. THE ANCIENT ONE, THE ONE THAT'S REALLY LOST.
OH. YOU COULDN'T HAVE MENTIONED THAT SOONER?
SORRY, KINKAJOU. I WAS HOPING THIS WOULD WORK.
SO WE DON'T HAVE TO GO LOOK FOR A DREAMVISITOR IN THERE? BECAUSE I AM ALL IN FAVOR OF *NOT* GOING INTO THE CREEPY SMOKING LAVA-FILLED TUNNEL.

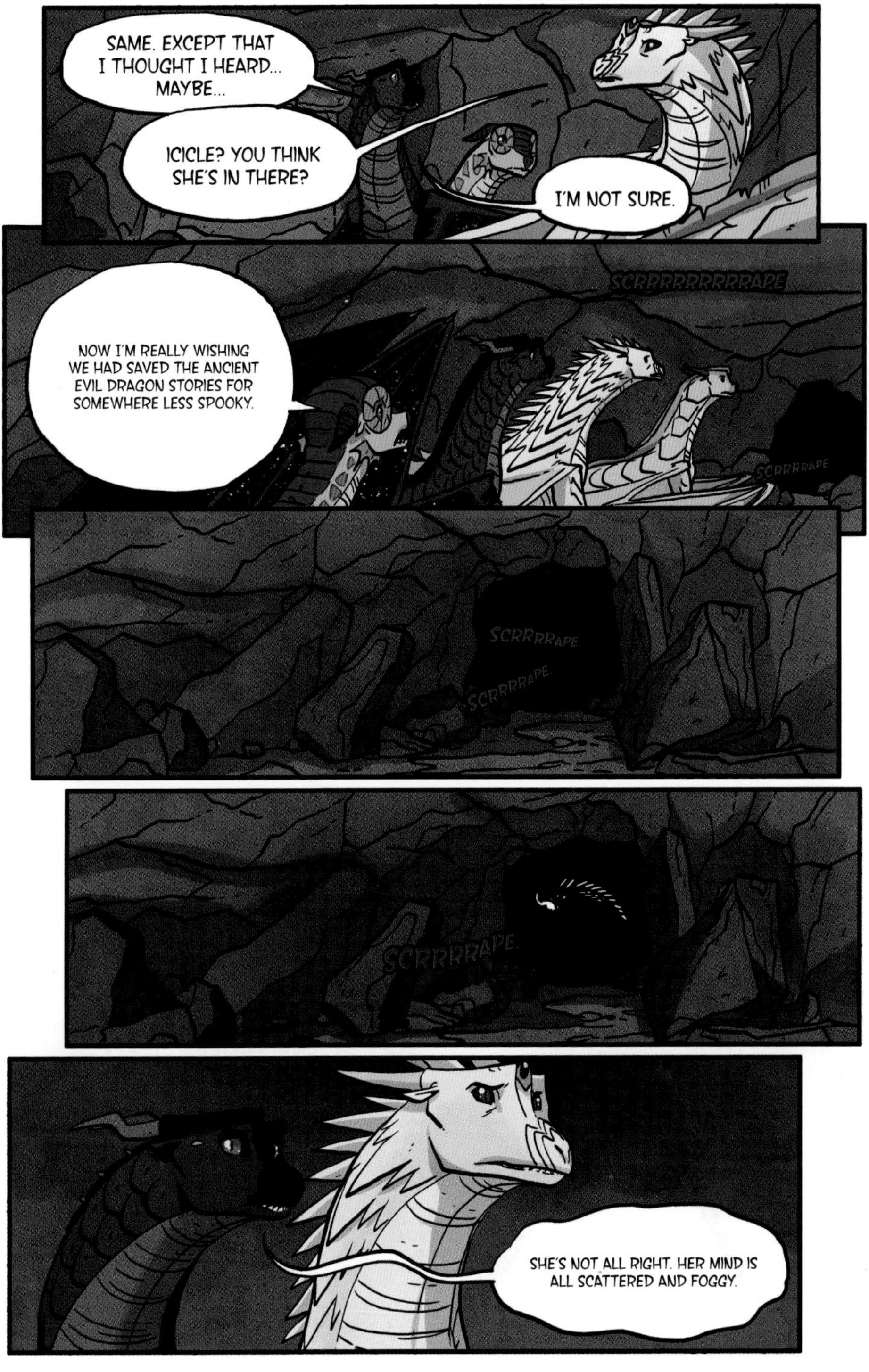
SAME. EXCEPT THAT I THOUGHT I HEARD... MAYBE...
ICICLE? YOU THINK SHE'S IN THERE?
I'M NOT SURE.
SCRRRRRRRRRRAPE
NOW I'M REALLY WISHING WE HAD SAVED THE ANCIENT EVIL DRAGON STORIES FOR SOMEWHERE LESS SPOOKY.
SCRRRRAPE
SCRRRRAPE.
SCRRRRAPE.
SCRRRRAPE.
SHE'S NOT ALL RIGHT. HER MIND IS ALL SCATTERED AND FOGGY.

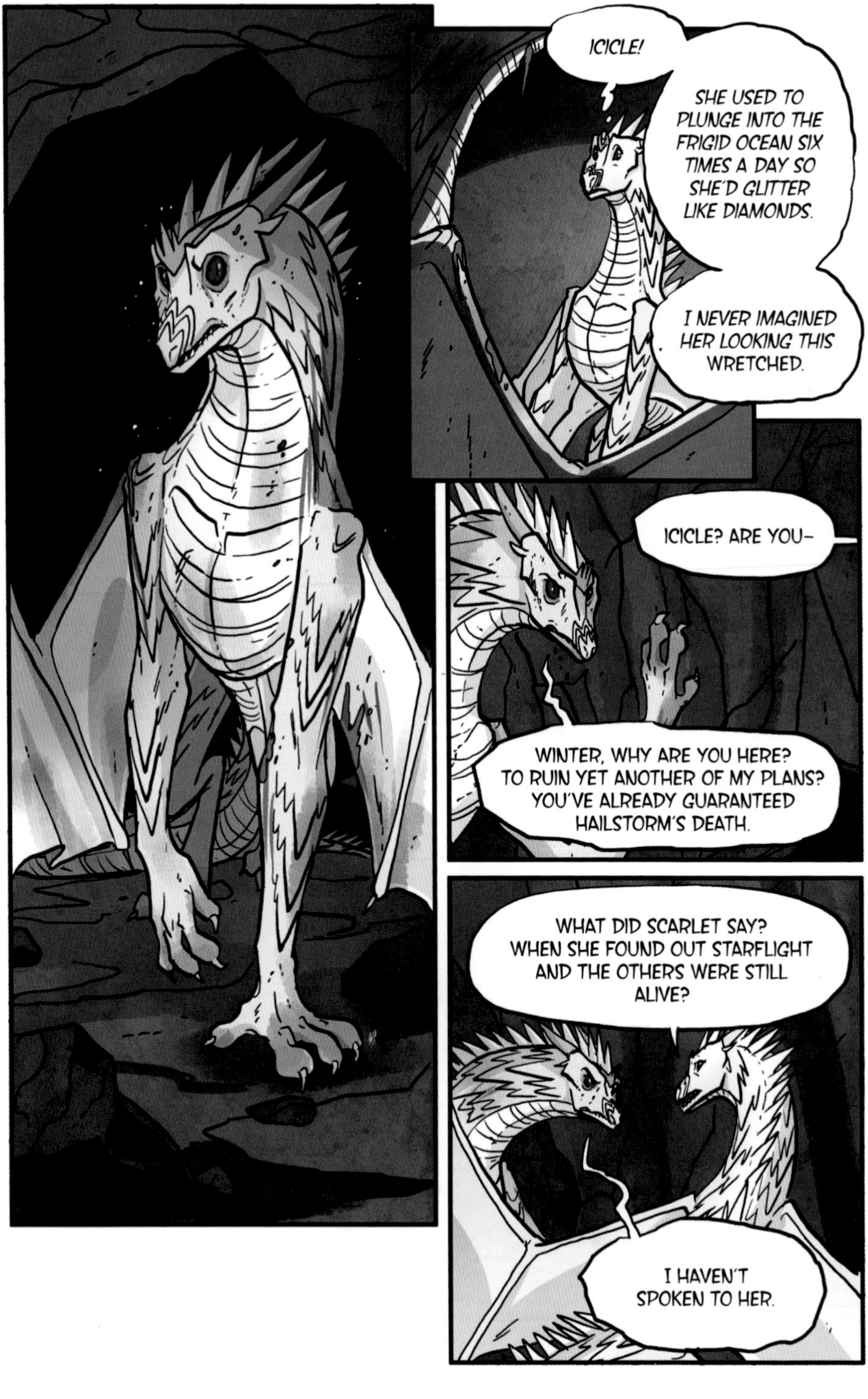
ICICLE!
SHE USED TO PLUNGE INTO THE FRIGID OCEAN SIX TIMES A DAY SO SHE'D GLITTER LIKE DIAMONDS.
I NEVER IMAGINED HER LOOKING THIS WRETCHED.
ICICLE? ARE YOU–
WINTER, WHY ARE YOU HERE? TO RUIN YET ANOTHER OF MY PLANS? YOU'VE ALREADY GUARANTEED HAILSTORM'S DEATH.
WHAT DID SCARLET SAY? WHEN SHE FOUND OUT STARFLIGHT AND THE OTHERS WERE STILL ALIVE?
I HAVEN'T SPOKEN TO HER.

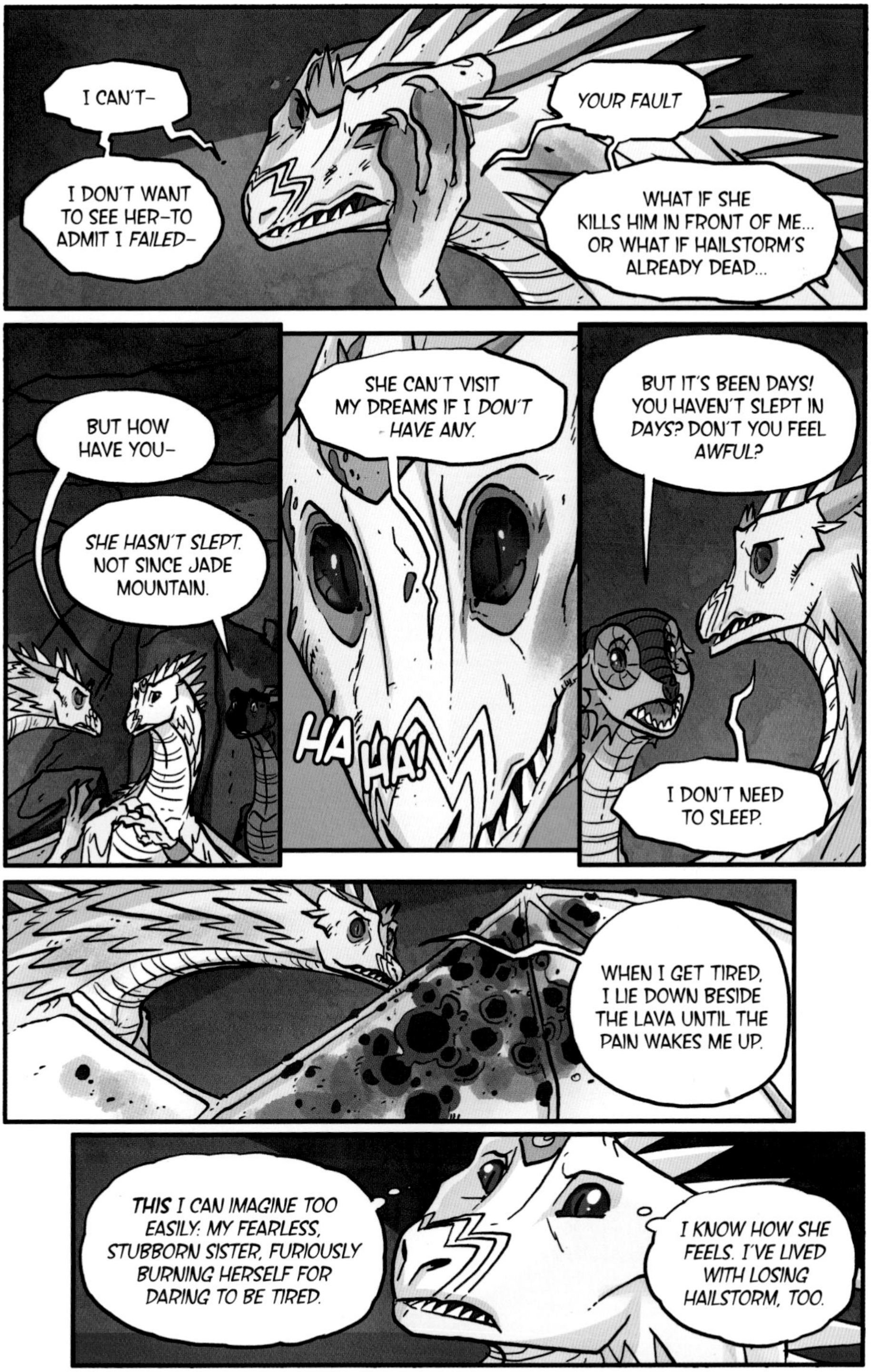
I CAN'T-
I DON'T WANT TO SEE HER–TO ADMIT I *FAILED*-
YOUR FAULT
WHAT IF SHE KILLS HIM IN FRONT OF ME... OR WHAT IF HAILSTORM'S ALREADY DEAD...
BUT HOW HAVE YOU-
SHE HASN'T SLEPT. NOT SINCE JADE MOUNTAIN.
SHE CAN'T VISIT MY DREAMS IF I *DON'T HAVE ANY.*
HA HA!
BUT IT'S BEEN DAYS! YOU HAVEN'T SLEPT IN DAYS? DON'T YOU FEEL *AWFUL?*
I DON'T NEED TO SLEEP.
WHEN I GET TIRED, I LIE DOWN BESIDE THE LAVA UNTIL THE PAIN WAKES ME UP.
THIS I CAN IMAGINE TOO EASILY: MY FEARLESS, STUBBORN SISTER, FURIOUSLY BURNING HERSELF FOR DARING TO BE TIRED.
I KNOW HOW SHE FEELS. I'VE LIVED WITH LOSING HAILSTORM, TOO.

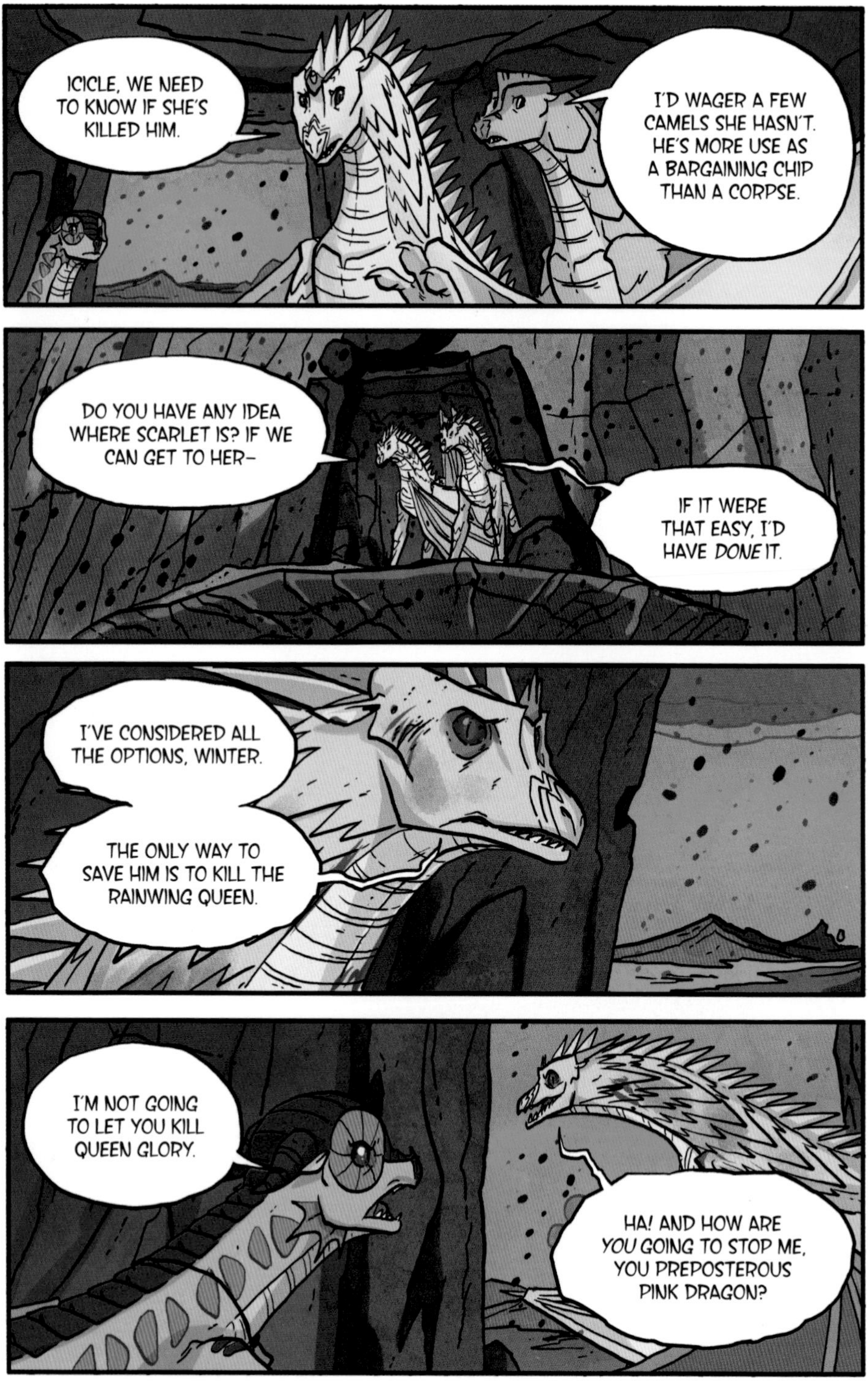
ICICLE, WE NEED TO KNOW IF SHE'S KILLED HIM.
I'D WAGER A FEW CAMELS SHE HASN'T. HE'S MORE USE AS A BARGAINING CHIP THAN A CORPSE.
DO YOU HAVE ANY IDEA WHERE SCARLET IS? IF WE CAN GET TO HER–
IF IT WERE THAT EASY, I'D HAVE *DONE* IT.
I'VE CONSIDERED ALL THE OPTIONS, WINTER.
THE ONLY WAY TO SAVE HIM IS TO KILL THE RAINWING QUEEN.
I'M NOT GOING TO LET YOU KILL QUEEN GLORY.
HA! AND HOW ARE *YOU* GOING TO STOP ME, YOU PREPOSTEROUS PINK DRAGON?

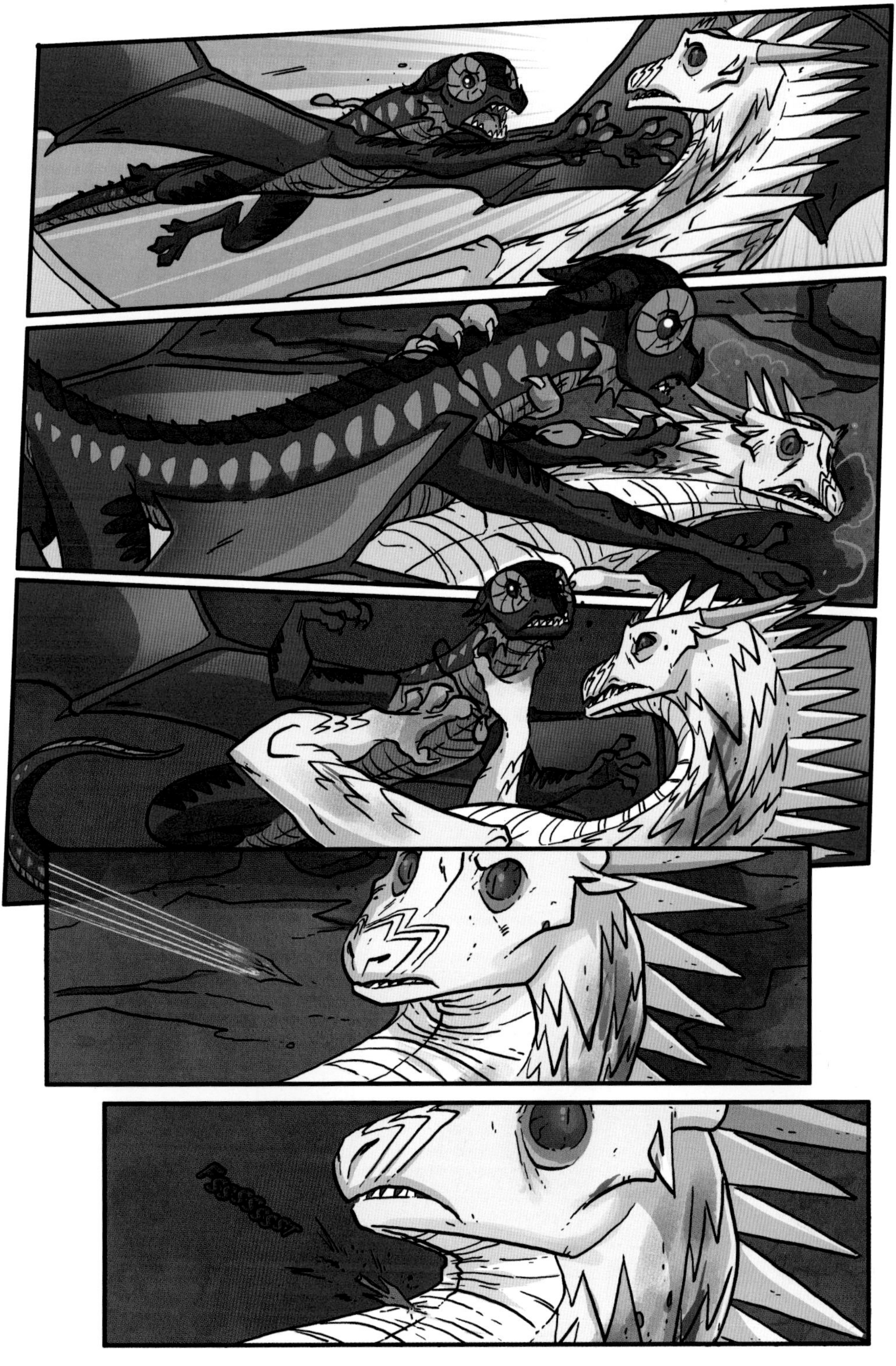

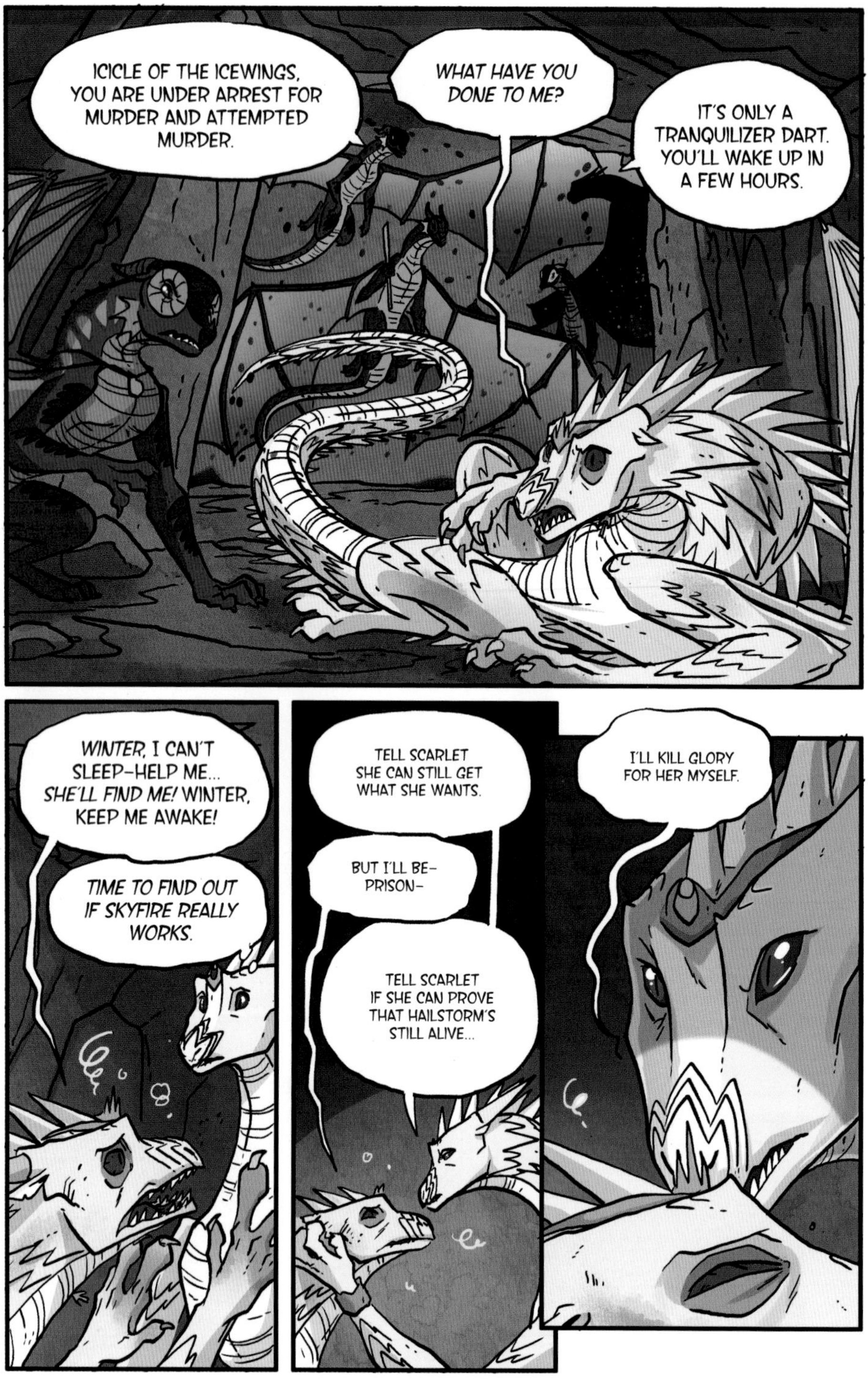
ICICLE OF THE ICEWINGS, YOU ARE UNDER ARREST FOR MURDER AND ATTEMPTED MURDER.
WHAT HAVE YOU DONE TO ME?
IT'S ONLY A TRANQUILIZER DART. YOU'LL WAKE UP IN A FEW HOURS.
WINTER, I CAN'T SLEEP–HELP ME... SHE'LL FIND ME! WINTER, KEEP ME AWAKE!
TIME TO FIND OUT IF SKYFIRE REALLY WORKS.
TELL SCARLET SHE CAN STILL GET WHAT SHE WANTS.
BUT I'LL BE–PRISON–
TELL SCARLET IF SHE CAN PROVE THAT HAILSTORM'S STILL ALIVE...
I'LL KILL GLORY FOR HER MYSELF.

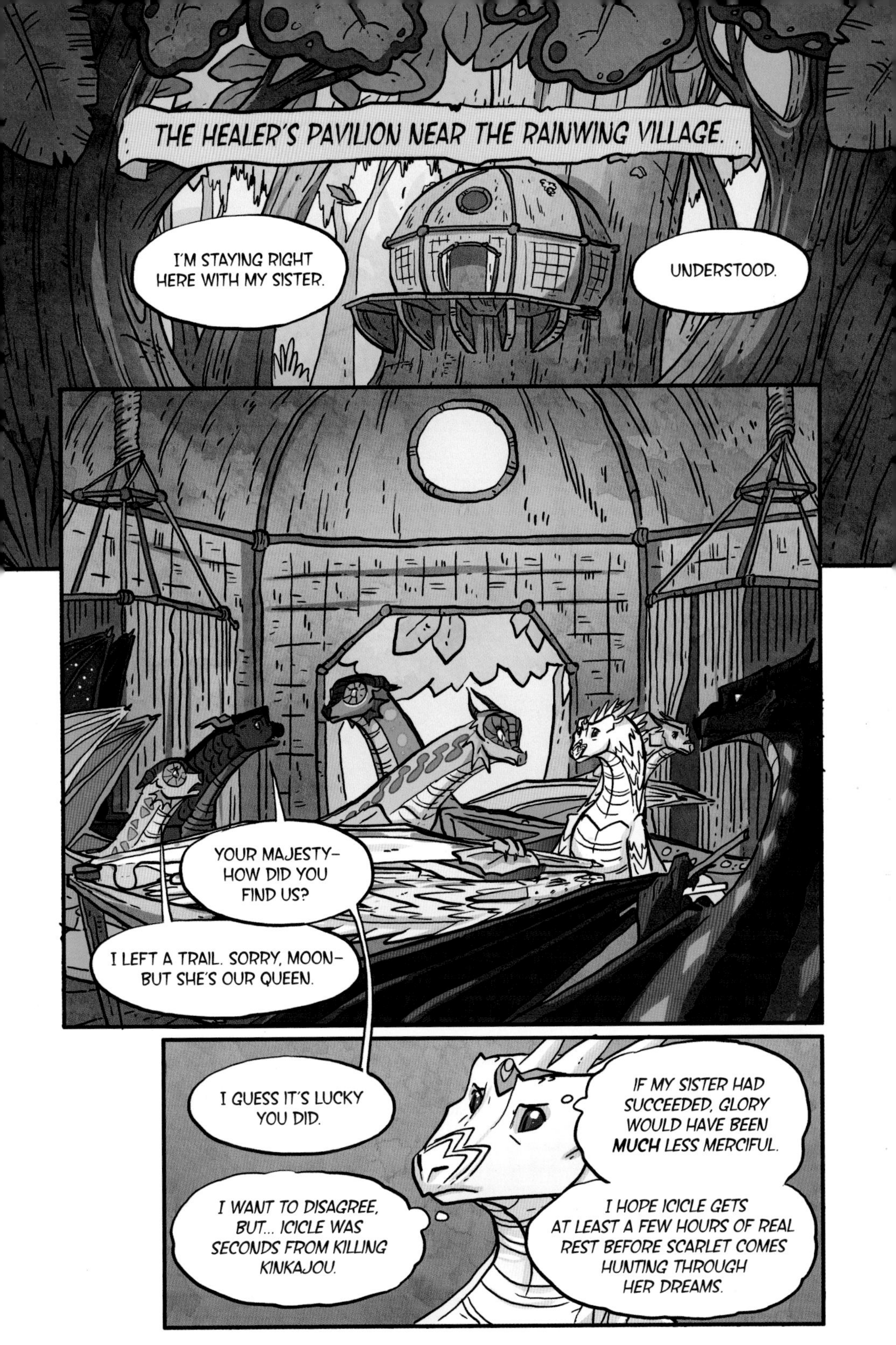
THE HEALER'S PAVILION NEAR THE RAINWING VILLAGE.
I'M STAYING RIGHT HERE WITH MY SISTER.
UNDERSTOOD.
YOUR MAJESTY—HOW DID YOU FIND US?
I LEFT A TRAIL. SORRY, MOON—BUT SHE'S OUR QUEEN.
I GUESS IT'S LUCKY YOU DID.
IF MY SISTER HAD SUCCEEDED, GLORY WOULD HAVE BEEN **MUCH** LESS MERCIFUL.
I WANT TO DISAGREE, BUT... ICICLE WAS SECONDS FROM KILLING KINKAJOU.
I HOPE ICICLE GETS AT LEAST A FEW HOURS OF REAL REST BEFORE SCARLET COMES HUNTING THROUGH HER DREAMS.

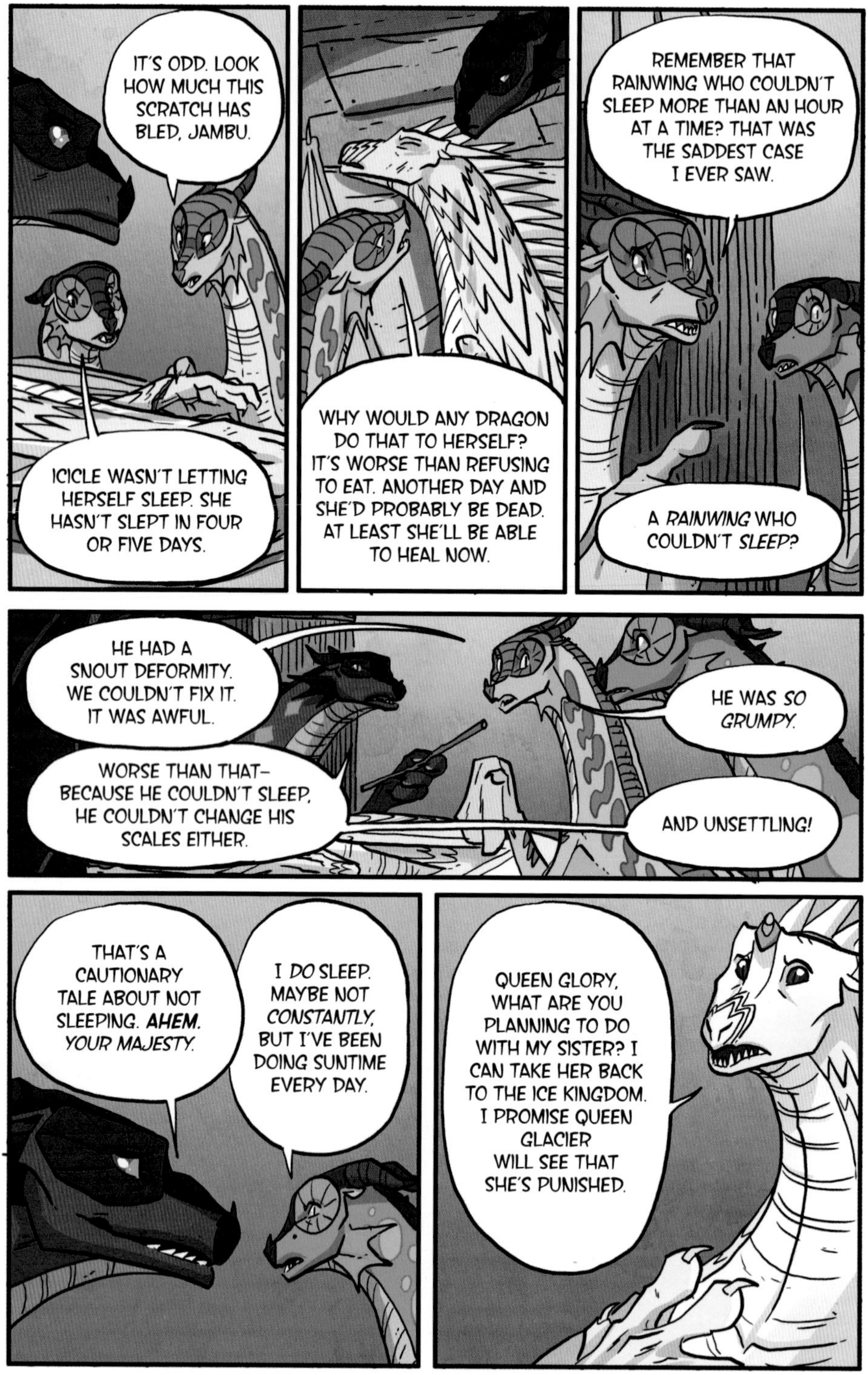
IT'S ODD. LOOK HOW MUCH THIS SCRATCH HAS BLED, JAMBU.
ICICLE WASN'T LETTING HERSELF SLEEP. SHE HASN'T SLEPT IN FOUR OR FIVE DAYS.
WHY WOULD ANY DRAGON DO THAT TO HERSELF? IT'S WORSE THAN REFUSING TO EAT. ANOTHER DAY AND SHE'D PROBABLY BE DEAD. AT LEAST SHE'LL BE ABLE TO HEAL NOW.
REMEMBER THAT RAINWING WHO COULDN'T SLEEP MORE THAN AN HOUR AT A TIME? THAT WAS THE SADDEST CASE I EVER SAW.
A *RAINWING* WHO COULDN'T *SLEEP?*
HE HAD A SNOUT DEFORMITY. WE COULDN'T FIX IT. IT WAS AWFUL.
HE WAS *SO GRUMPY.*
WORSE THAN THAT–BECAUSE HE COULDN'T SLEEP, HE COULDN'T CHANGE HIS SCALES EITHER.
AND UNSETTLING!
THAT'S A CAUTIONARY TALE ABOUT NOT SLEEPING. ***AHEM.*** *YOUR MAJESTY.*
I *DO* SLEEP. MAYBE NOT *CONSTANTLY,* BUT I'VE BEEN DOING SUNTIME EVERY DAY.
QUEEN GLORY, WHAT ARE YOU PLANNING TO DO WITH MY SISTER? I CAN TAKE HER BACK TO THE ICE KINGDOM. I PROMISE QUEEN GLACIER WILL SEE THAT SHE'S PUNISHED.

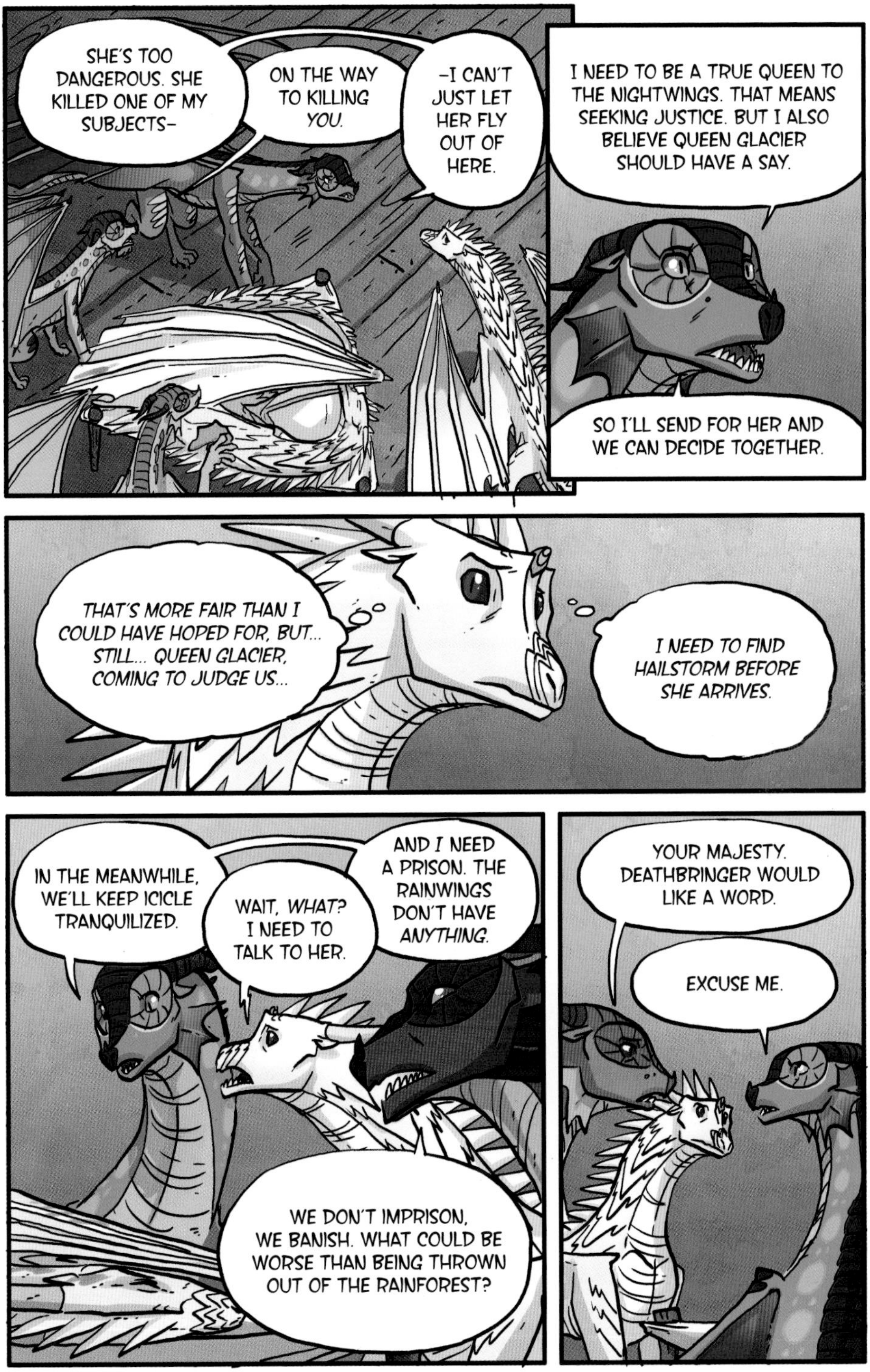
SHE'S TOO DANGEROUS. SHE KILLED ONE OF MY SUBJECTS–
ON THE WAY TO KILLING *YOU.*
–I CAN'T JUST LET HER FLY OUT OF HERE.
I NEED TO BE A TRUE QUEEN TO THE NIGHTWINGS. THAT MEANS SEEKING JUSTICE. BUT I ALSO BELIEVE QUEEN GLACIER SHOULD HAVE A SAY.
SO I'LL SEND FOR HER AND WE CAN DECIDE TOGETHER.
THAT'S MORE FAIR THAN I COULD HAVE HOPED FOR, BUT... STILL... QUEEN GLACIER, COMING TO JUDGE US...
I NEED TO FIND HAILSTORM BEFORE SHE ARRIVES.
IN THE MEANWHILE, WE'LL KEEP ICICLE TRANQUILIZED.
WAIT, *WHAT?* I NEED TO TALK TO HER.
AND *I* NEED A PRISON. THE RAINWINGS DON'T HAVE *ANYTHING.*
WE DON'T IMPRISON, WE BANISH. WHAT COULD BE WORSE THAN BEING THROWN OUT OF THE RAINFOREST?
YOUR MAJESTY. DEATHBRINGER WOULD LIKE A WORD.
EXCUSE ME.

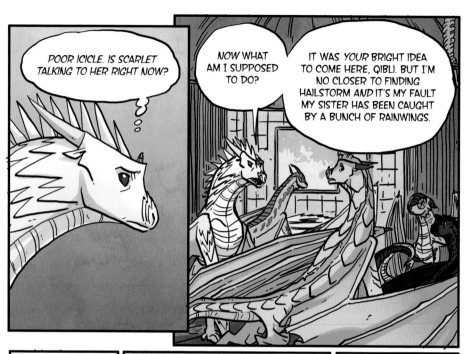

POOR ICICLE. IS SCARLET TALKING TO HER RIGHT NOW?

NOW WHAT AM I SUPPOSED TO DO?

IT WAS *YOUR* BRIGHT IDEA TO COME HERE, QIBLI. BUT I'M NO CLOSER TO FINDING HAILSTORM AND IT'S MY FAULT MY SISTER HAS BEEN CAUGHT BY A BUNCH OF RAINWINGS.

WINTER, WE ARE CLOSER TO FINDING HAILSTORM. WE'VE FOUND THE ONLY DRAGON WHO'S SPOKEN TO SCARLET.

AND SHE'S FAST ASLEEP. WHICH DOES ME ANY GOOD *HOW?*

MOON, DIDN'T YOU SAY YOU OVERHEARD ICICLE AND SCARLET CONSPIRING? DOES THAT MEAN YOU CAN GET INTO DREAMS, TOO?

I'M TRYING. IT'S ALL DARKNESS IN ICICLE'S MIND RIGHT NOW— SHE'S TOO DEEP IN SLEEP FOR DREAMS.

SO THEN WE WAIT. FOR SCARLET TO COME.

THREE MOONS! IF MOON HEARS ICICLE TELL SCARLET MY OFFER TO KILL GLORY... I'LL HAVE TO BE READY TO FLY THE MOMENT SHE TELLS ME WHERE SCARLET IS.

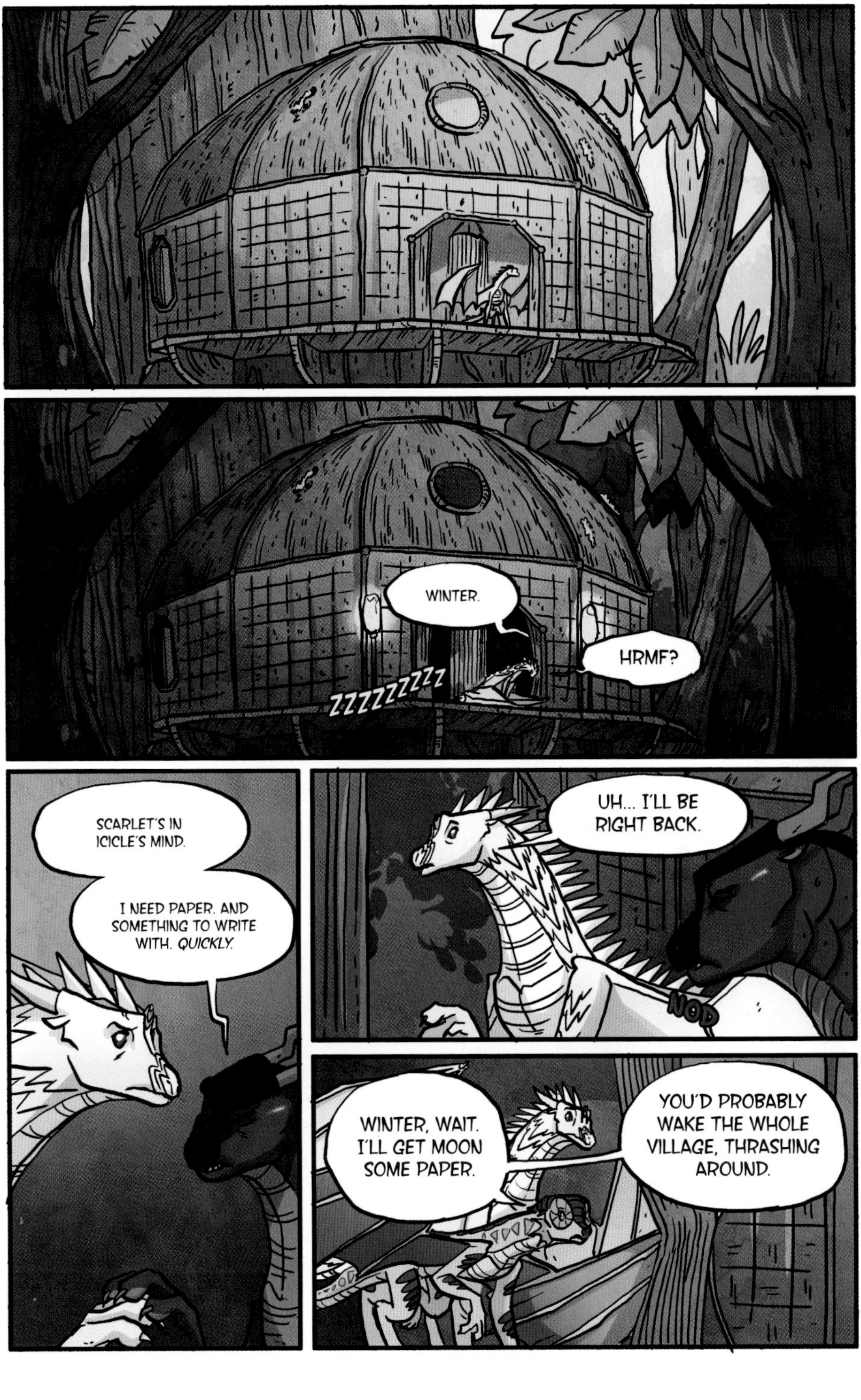
WINTER.
HRMF?
ZZZZZZZZZ
SCARLET'S IN ICICLE'S MIND.
I NEED PAPER. AND SOMETHING TO WRITE WITH. *QUICKLY.*
UH... I'LL BE RIGHT BACK.
NOD
WINTER, WAIT. I'LL GET MOON SOME PAPER.
YOU'D PROBABLY WAKE THE WHOLE VILLAGE, THRASHING AROUND.

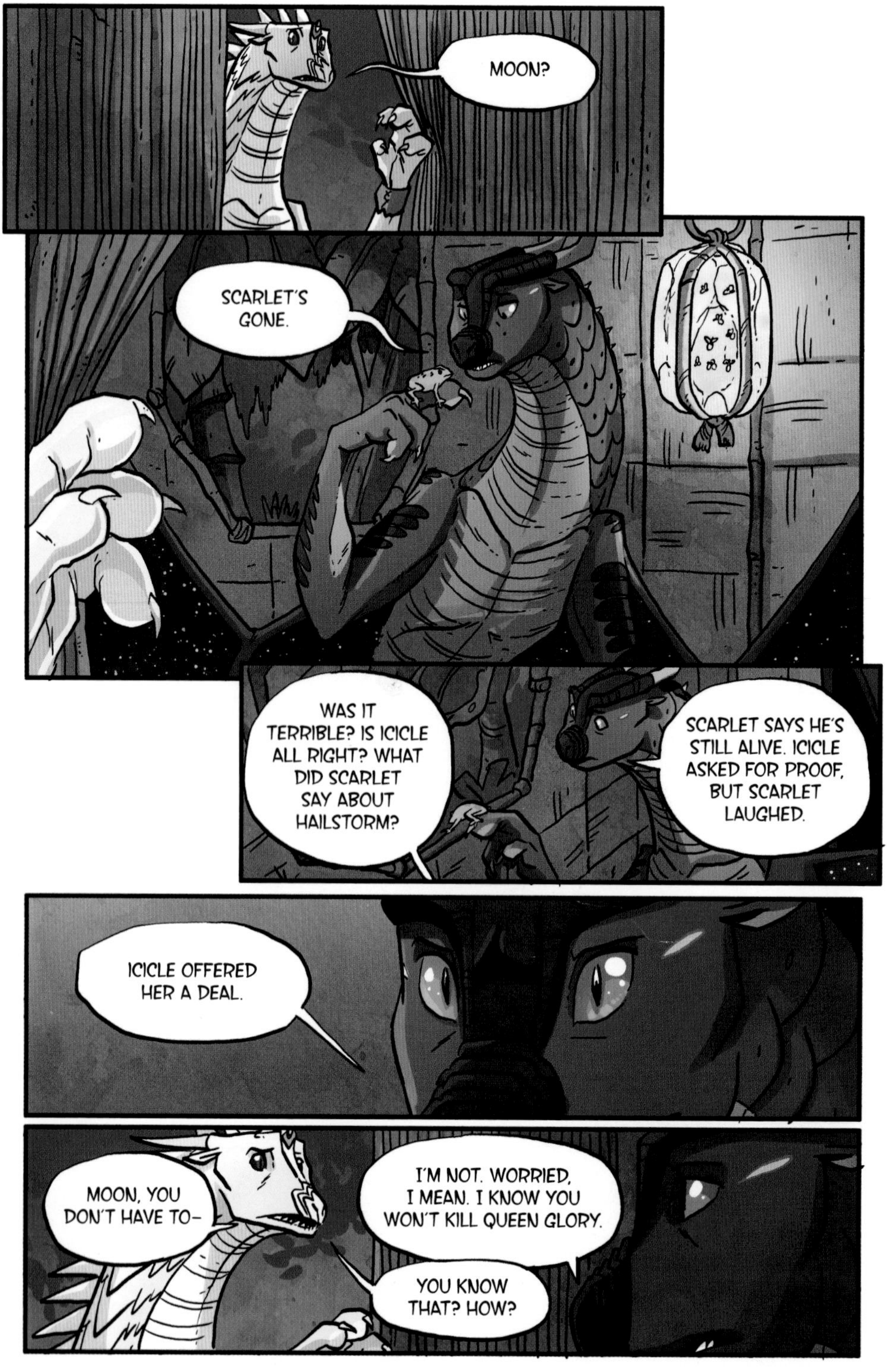
MOON?
SCARLET'S GONE.
WAS IT TERRIBLE? IS ICICLE ALL RIGHT? WHAT DID SCARLET SAY ABOUT HAILSTORM?
SCARLET SAYS HE'S STILL ALIVE. ICICLE ASKED FOR PROOF, BUT SCARLET LAUGHED.
ICICLE OFFERED HER A DEAL.
MOON, YOU DON'T HAVE TO-
I'M NOT. WORRIED, I MEAN. I KNOW YOU WON'T KILL QUEEN GLORY.
YOU KNOW THAT? HOW?

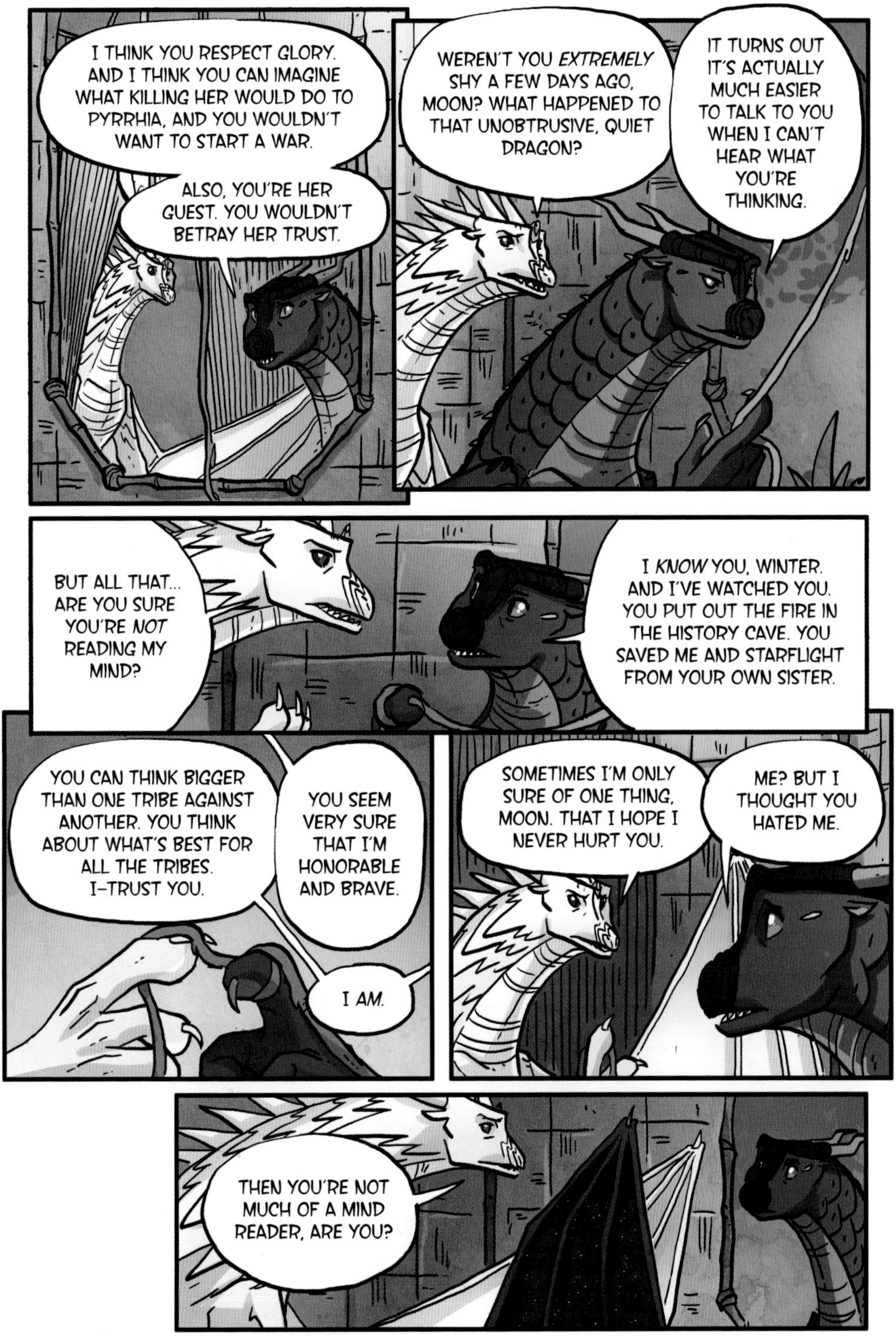
I THINK YOU RESPECT GLORY. AND I THINK YOU CAN IMAGINE WHAT KILLING HER WOULD DO TO PYRRHIA, AND YOU WOULDN'T WANT TO START A WAR.
ALSO, YOU'RE HER GUEST. YOU WOULDN'T BETRAY HER TRUST.
WEREN'T YOU *EXTREMELY* SHY A FEW DAYS AGO, MOON? WHAT HAPPENED TO THAT UNOBTRUSIVE, QUIET DRAGON?
IT TURNS OUT IT'S ACTUALLY MUCH EASIER TO TALK TO YOU WHEN I CAN'T HEAR WHAT YOU'RE THINKING.
BUT ALL THAT... ARE YOU SURE YOU'RE *NOT* READING MY MIND?
I *KNOW* YOU, WINTER. AND I'VE WATCHED YOU. YOU PUT OUT THE FIRE IN THE HISTORY CAVE. YOU SAVED ME AND STARFLIGHT FROM YOUR OWN SISTER.
YOU CAN THINK BIGGER THAN ONE TRIBE AGAINST ANOTHER. YOU THINK ABOUT WHAT'S BEST FOR ALL THE TRIBES. I–TRUST YOU.
YOU SEEM VERY SURE THAT I'M HONORABLE AND BRAVE.
I AM.
SOMETIMES I'M ONLY SURE OF ONE THING, MOON. THAT I HOPE I NEVER HURT YOU.
ME? BUT I THOUGHT YOU HATED ME.
THEN YOU'RE NOT MUCH OF A MIND READER, ARE YOU?

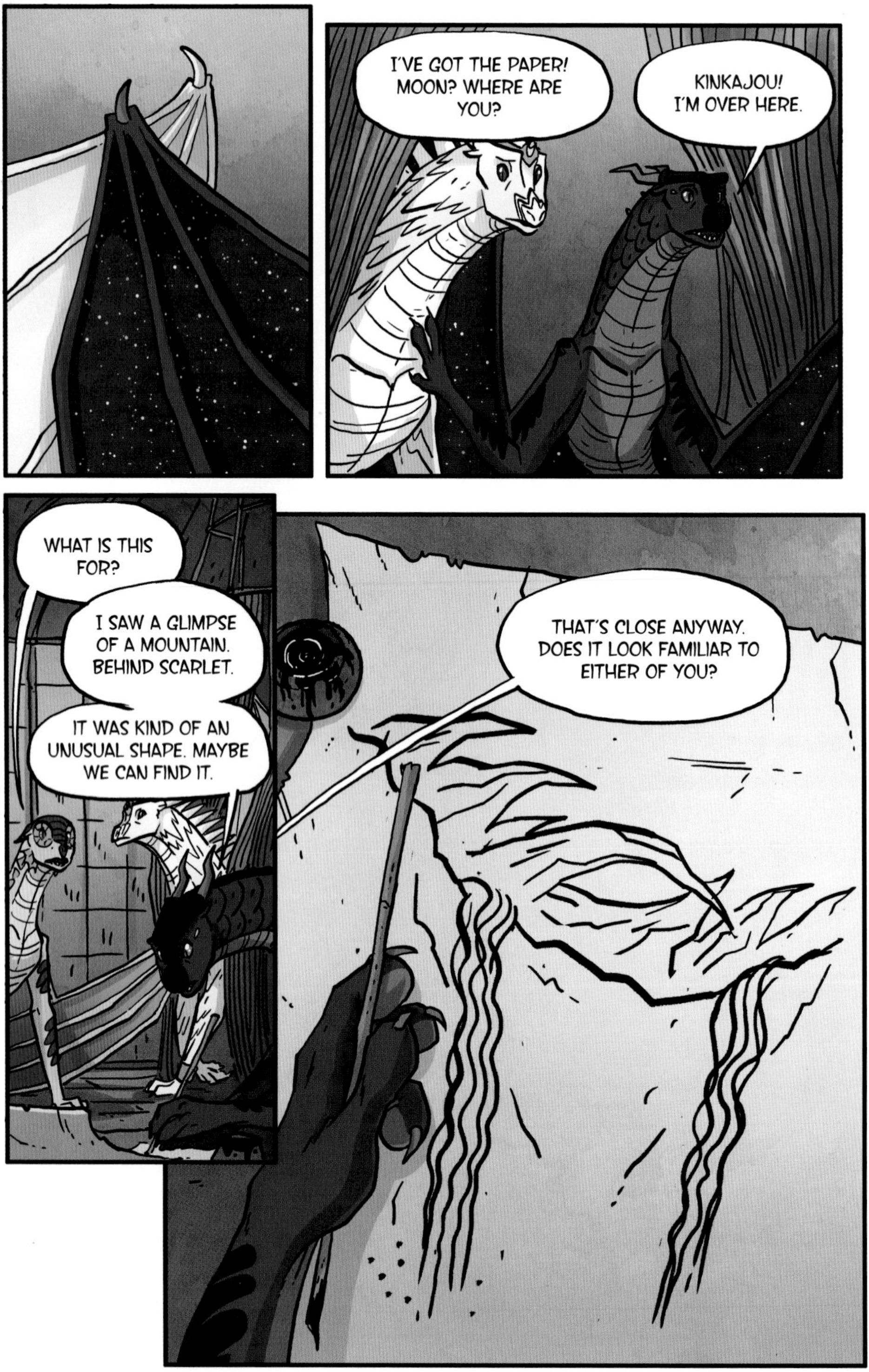

I'VE GOT THE PAPER! MOON? WHERE ARE YOU?
KINKAJOU! I'M OVER HERE.
WHAT IS THIS FOR?
I SAW A GLIMPSE OF A MOUNTAIN. BEHIND SCARLET.
IT WAS KIND OF AN UNUSUAL SHAPE. MAYBE WE CAN FIND IT.
THAT'S CLOSE ANYWAY. DOES IT LOOK FAMILIAR TO EITHER OF YOU?

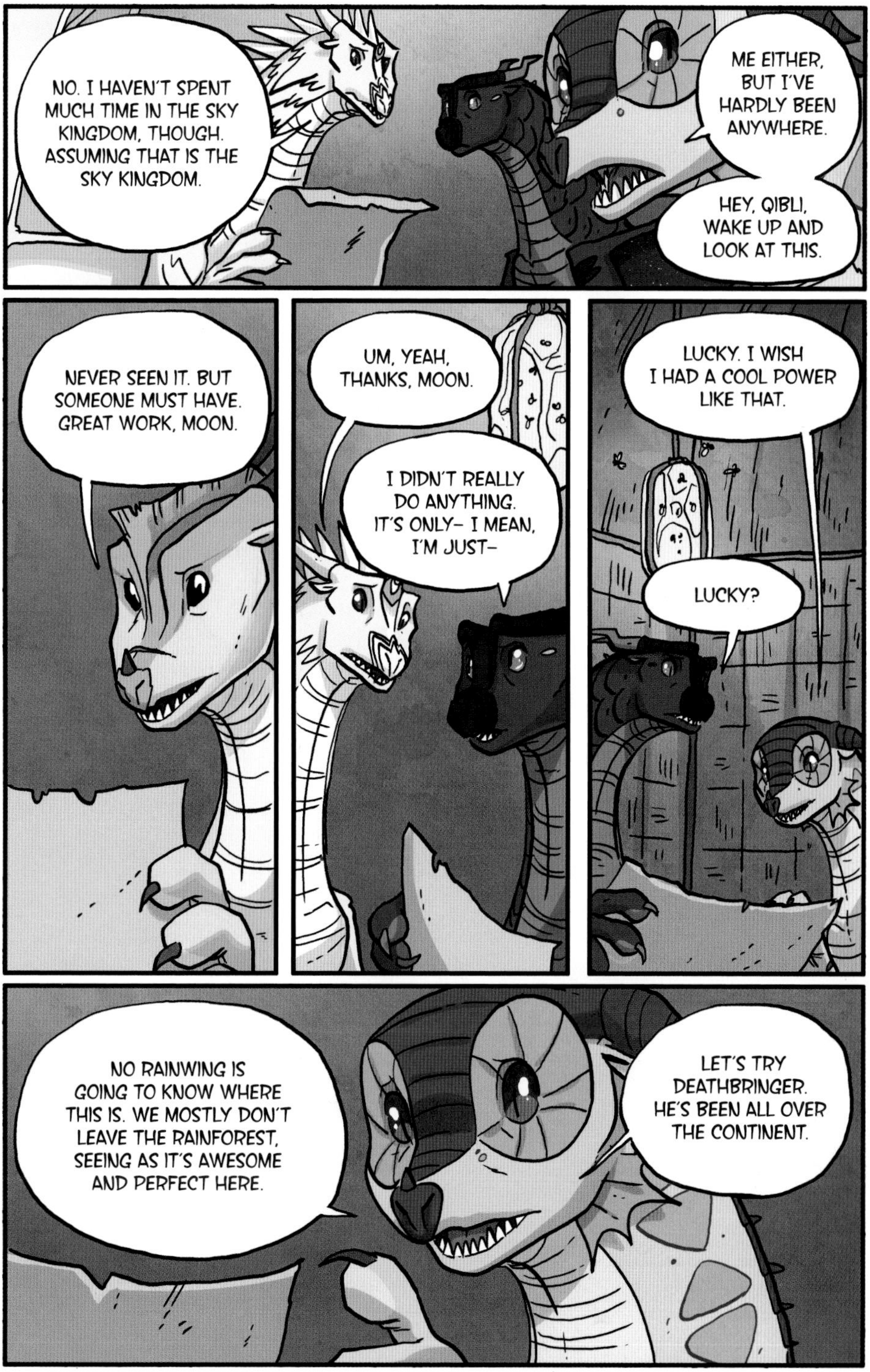
NO. I HAVEN'T SPENT MUCH TIME IN THE SKY KINGDOM, THOUGH. ASSUMING THAT IS THE SKY KINGDOM.
ME EITHER, BUT I'VE HARDLY BEEN ANYWHERE.
HEY, QIBLI, WAKE UP AND LOOK AT THIS.
NEVER SEEN IT. BUT SOMEONE MUST HAVE. GREAT WORK, MOON.
UM, YEAH, THANKS, MOON.
I DIDN'T REALLY DO ANYTHING. IT'S ONLY– I MEAN, I'M JUST–
LUCKY. I WISH I HAD A COOL POWER LIKE THAT.
LUCKY?
NO RAINWING IS GOING TO KNOW WHERE THIS IS. WE MOSTLY DON'T LEAVE THE RAINFOREST, SEEING AS IT'S AWESOME AND PERFECT HERE.
LET'S TRY DEATHBRINGER. HE'S BEEN ALL OVER THE CONTINENT.

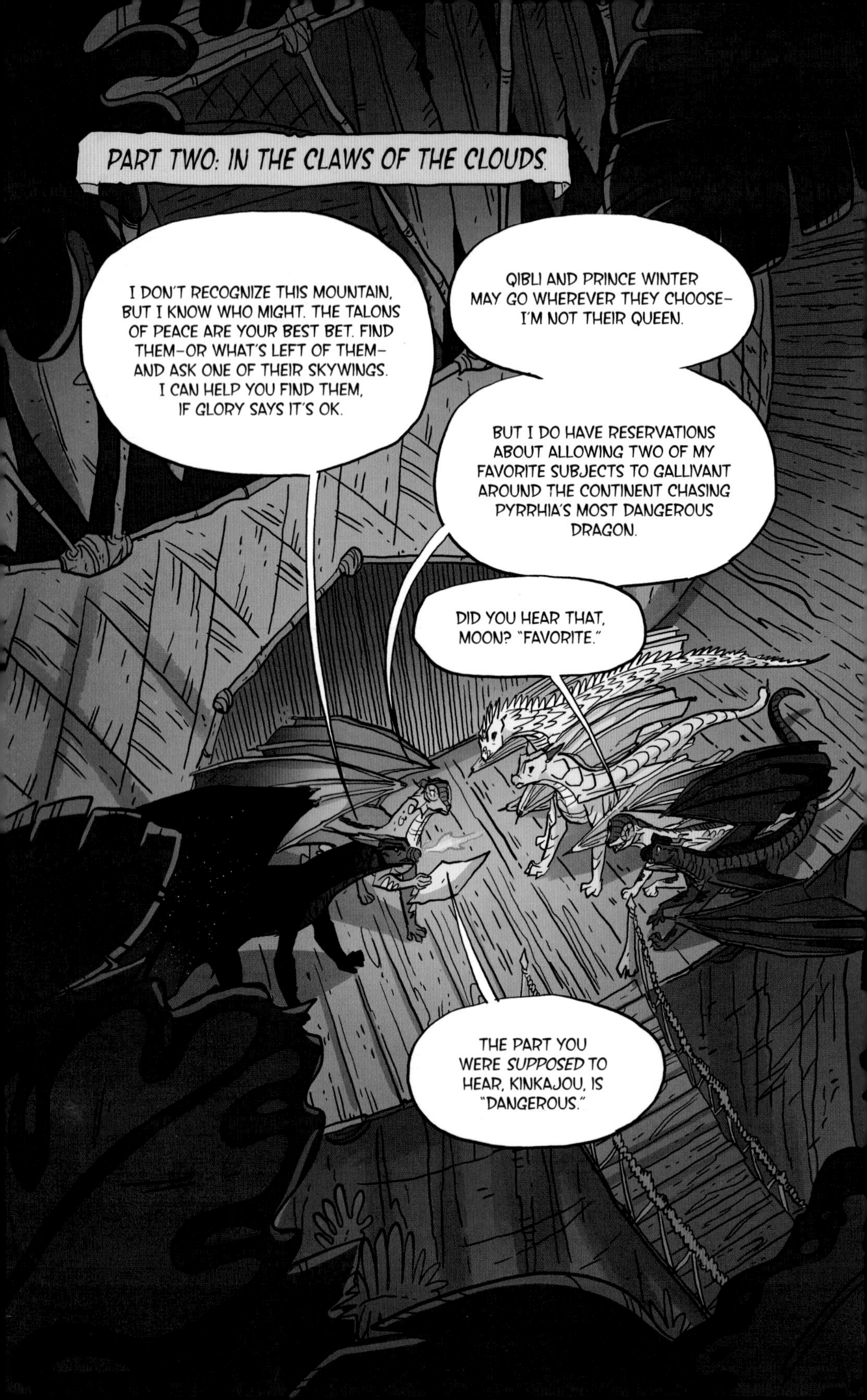
PART TWO: IN THE CLAWS OF THE CLOUDS.
I DON'T RECOGNIZE THIS MOUNTAIN, BUT I KNOW WHO MIGHT. THE TALONS OF PEACE ARE YOUR BEST BET. FIND THEM—OR WHAT'S LEFT OF THEM—AND ASK ONE OF THEIR SKYWINGS. I CAN HELP YOU FIND THEM, IF GLORY SAYS IT'S OK.
QIBLI AND PRINCE WINTER MAY GO WHEREVER THEY CHOOSE—I'M NOT THEIR QUEEN.
BUT I DO HAVE RESERVATIONS ABOUT ALLOWING TWO OF MY FAVORITE SUBJECTS TO GALLIVANT AROUND THE CONTINENT CHASING PYRRHIA'S MOST DANGEROUS DRAGON.
DID YOU HEAR THAT, MOON? "FAVORITE."
THE PART YOU WERE *SUPPOSED* TO HEAR, KINKAJOU, IS "DANGEROUS."

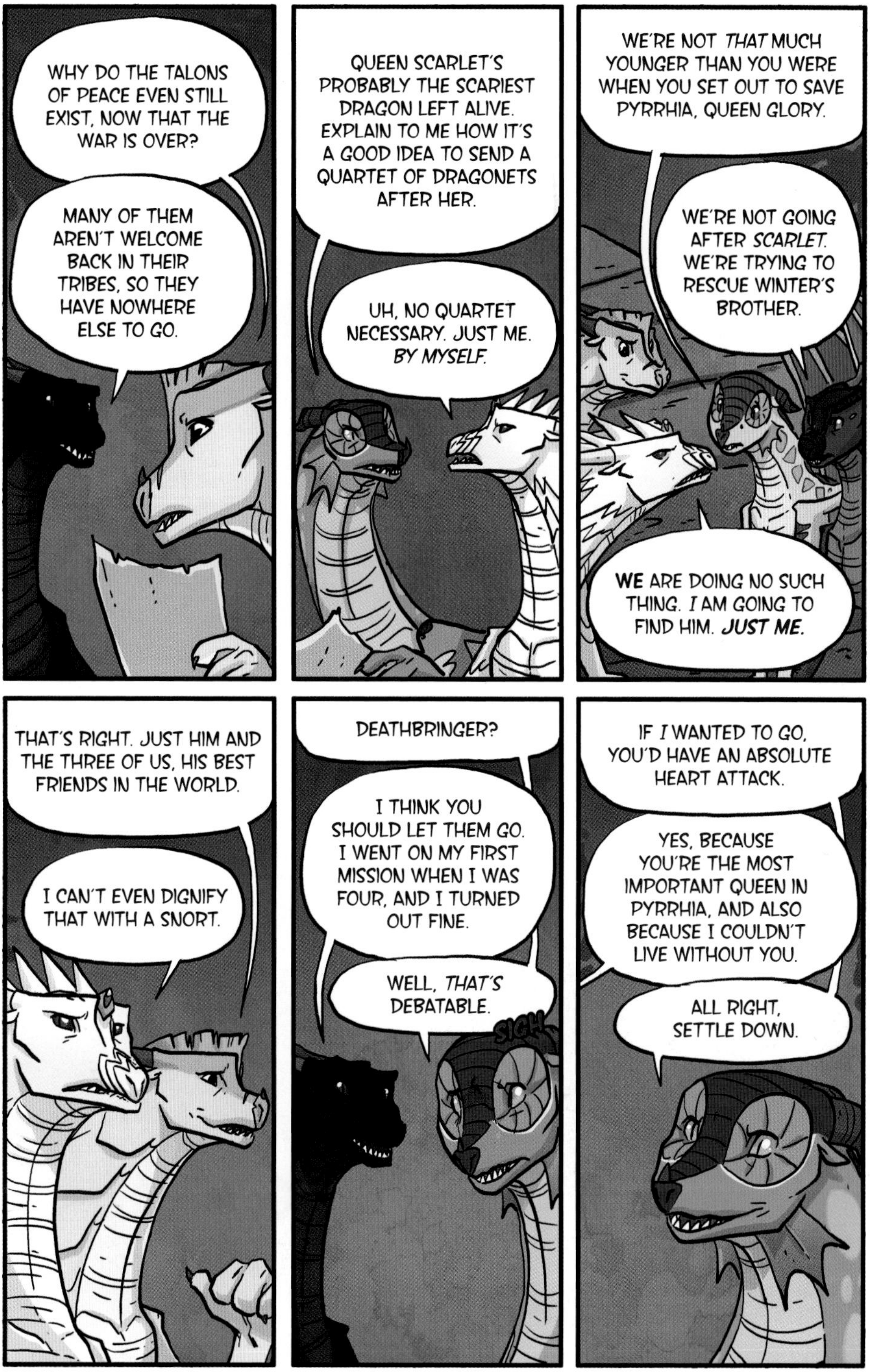

WHY DO THE TALONS OF PEACE EVEN STILL EXIST, NOW THAT THE WAR IS OVER?
MANY OF THEM AREN'T WELCOME BACK IN THEIR TRIBES, SO THEY HAVE NOWHERE ELSE TO GO.
QUEEN SCARLET'S PROBABLY THE SCARIEST DRAGON LEFT ALIVE. EXPLAIN TO ME HOW IT'S A GOOD IDEA TO SEND A QUARTET OF DRAGONETS AFTER HER.
UH, NO QUARTET NECESSARY. JUST ME. *BY MYSELF.*
WE'RE NOT *THAT* MUCH YOUNGER THAN YOU WERE WHEN YOU SET OUT TO SAVE PYRRHIA, QUEEN GLORY.
WE'RE NOT GOING AFTER *SCARLET.* WE'RE TRYING TO RESCUE WINTER'S BROTHER.
WE ARE DOING NO SUCH THING. *I* AM GOING TO FIND HIM. ***JUST ME.***
THAT'S RIGHT. JUST HIM AND THE THREE OF US, HIS BEST FRIENDS IN THE WORLD.
I CAN'T EVEN DIGNIFY THAT WITH A SNORT.
DEATHBRINGER?
I THINK YOU SHOULD LET THEM GO. I WENT ON MY FIRST MISSION WHEN I WAS FOUR, AND I TURNED OUT FINE.
WELL, *THAT'S* DEBATABLE.
SIGH
IF *I* WANTED TO GO, YOU'D HAVE AN ABSOLUTE HEART ATTACK.
YES, BECAUSE YOU'RE THE MOST IMPORTANT QUEEN IN PYRRHIA, AND ALSO BECAUSE I COULDN'T LIVE WITHOUT YOU.
ALL RIGHT, SETTLE DOWN.

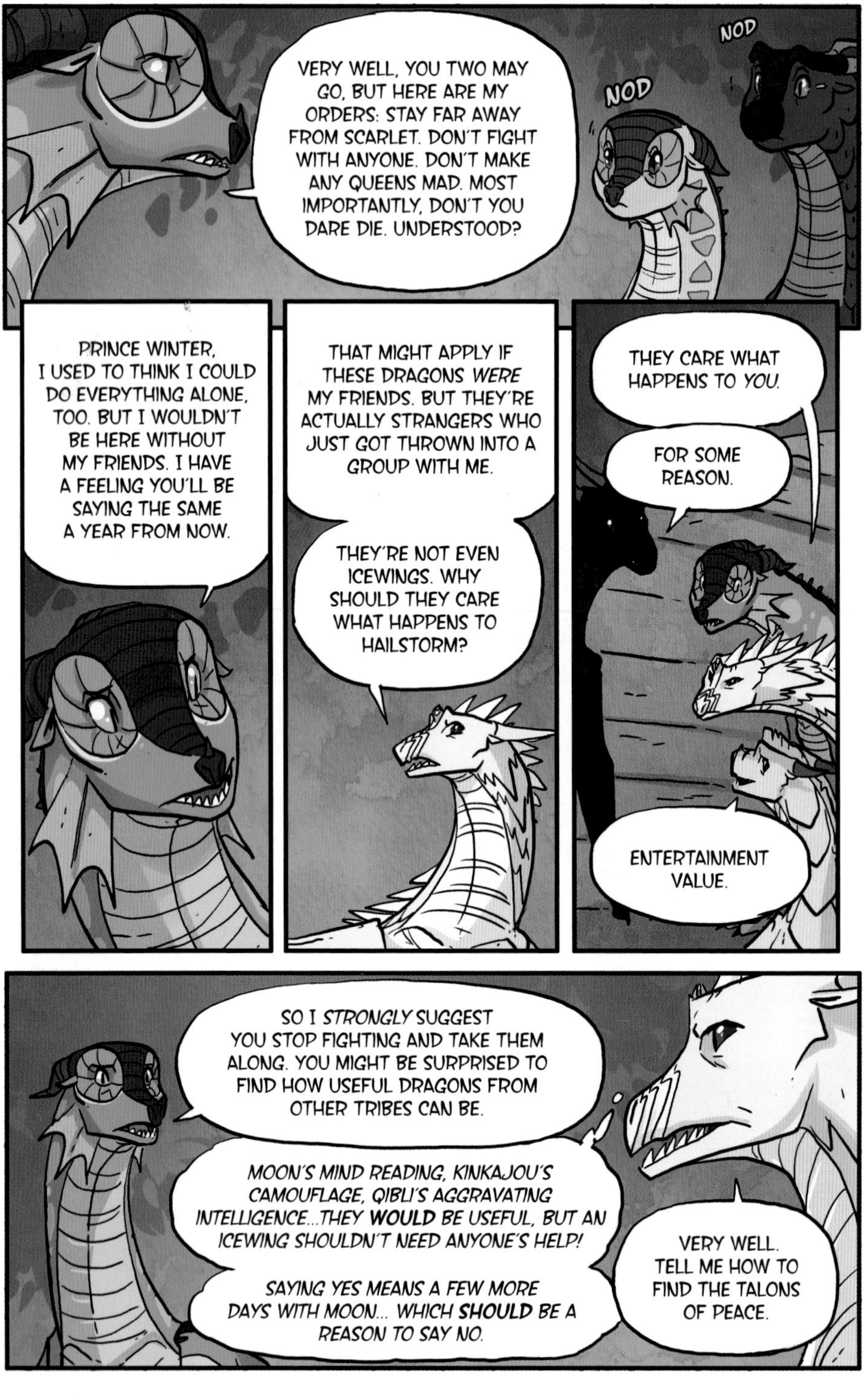
VERY WELL, YOU TWO MAY GO, BUT HERE ARE MY ORDERS: STAY FAR AWAY FROM SCARLET. DON'T FIGHT WITH ANYONE. DON'T MAKE ANY QUEENS MAD. MOST IMPORTANTLY, DON'T YOU DARE DIE. UNDERSTOOD?
NOD
NOD
PRINCE WINTER, I USED TO THINK I COULD DO EVERYTHING ALONE, TOO. BUT I WOULDN'T BE HERE WITHOUT MY FRIENDS. I HAVE A FEELING YOU'LL BE SAYING THE SAME A YEAR FROM NOW.
THAT MIGHT APPLY IF THESE DRAGONS *WERE* MY FRIENDS. BUT THEY'RE ACTUALLY STRANGERS WHO JUST GOT THROWN INTO A GROUP WITH ME.
THEY'RE NOT EVEN ICEWINGS. WHY SHOULD THEY CARE WHAT HAPPENS TO HAILSTORM?
THEY CARE WHAT HAPPENS TO *YOU*.
FOR SOME REASON.
ENTERTAINMENT VALUE.
SO I *STRONGLY* SUGGEST YOU STOP FIGHTING AND TAKE THEM ALONG. YOU MIGHT BE SURPRISED TO FIND HOW USEFUL DRAGONS FROM OTHER TRIBES CAN BE.
MOON'S MIND READING, KINKAJOU'S CAMOUFLAGE, QIBLI'S AGGRAVATING INTELLIGENCE...THEY ***WOULD*** *BE USEFUL, BUT AN ICEWING SHOULDN'T NEED ANYONE'S HELP!*
SAYING YES MEANS A FEW MORE DAYS WITH MOON... WHICH ***SHOULD*** *BE A REASON TO SAY NO.*
VERY WELL. TELL ME HOW TO FIND THE TALONS OF PEACE.

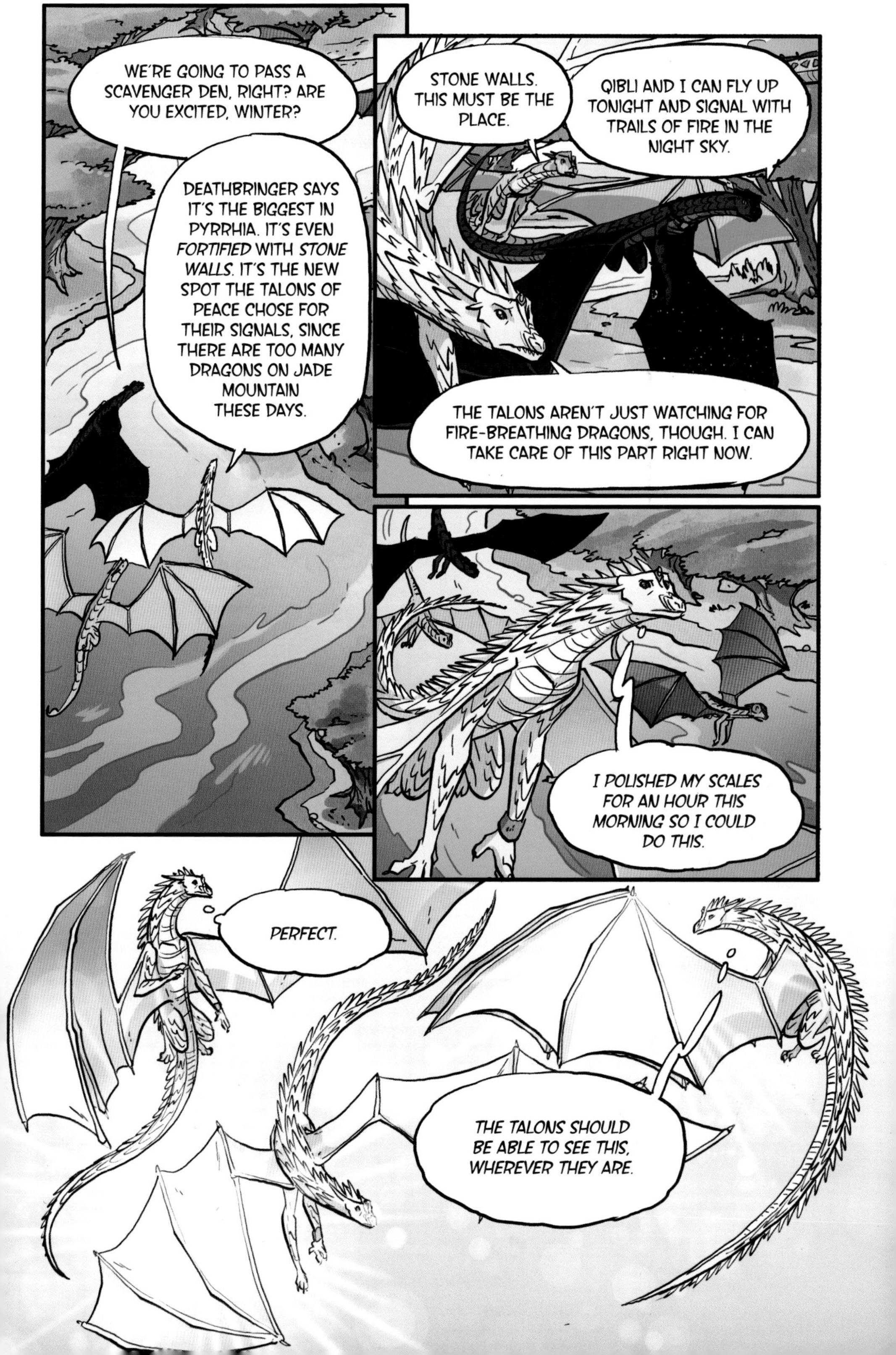
WE'RE GOING TO PASS A SCAVENGER DEN, RIGHT? ARE YOU EXCITED, WINTER?
DEATHBRINGER SAYS IT'S THE BIGGEST IN PYRRHIA. IT'S EVEN *FORTIFIED* WITH *STONE WALLS*. IT'S THE NEW SPOT THE TALONS OF PEACE CHOSE FOR THEIR SIGNALS, SINCE THERE ARE TOO MANY DRAGONS ON JADE MOUNTAIN THESE DAYS.
STONE WALLS. THIS MUST BE THE PLACE.
QIBLI AND I CAN FLY UP TONIGHT AND SIGNAL WITH TRAILS OF FIRE IN THE NIGHT SKY.
THE TALONS AREN'T JUST WATCHING FOR FIRE-BREATHING DRAGONS, THOUGH. I CAN TAKE CARE OF THIS PART RIGHT NOW.
I POLISHED MY SCALES FOR AN HOUR THIS MORNING SO I COULD DO THIS.
PERFECT.
THE TALONS SHOULD BE ABLE TO SEE THIS, WHEREVER THEY ARE.

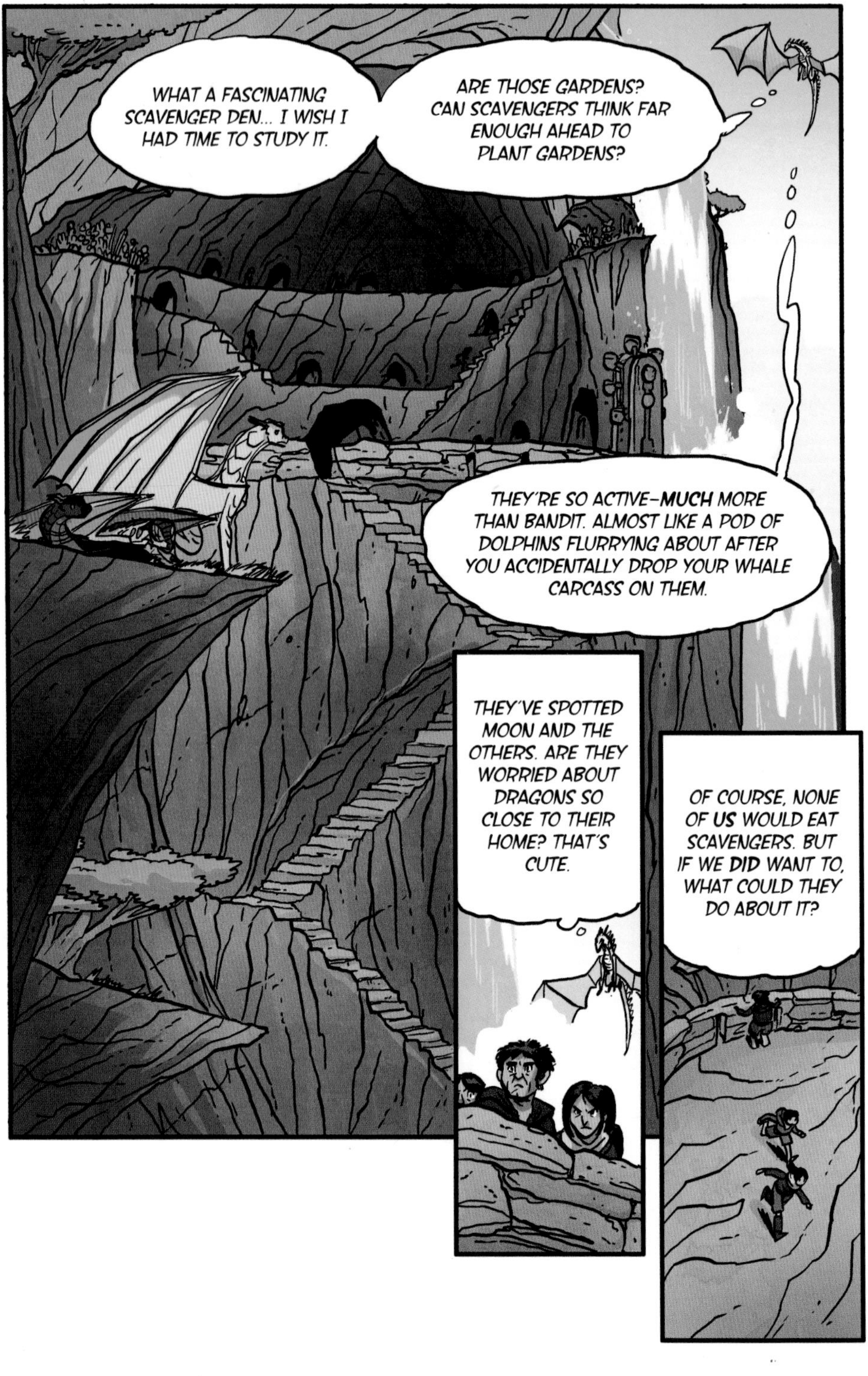
WHAT A FASCINATING SCAVENGER DEN... I WISH I HAD TIME TO STUDY IT.
ARE THOSE GARDENS? CAN SCAVENGERS THINK FAR ENOUGH AHEAD TO PLANT GARDENS?
THEY'RE SO ACTIVE-**MUCH** MORE THAN BANDIT. ALMOST LIKE A POD OF DOLPHINS FLURRYING ABOUT AFTER YOU ACCIDENTALLY DROP YOUR WHALE CARCASS ON THEM.
THEY'VE SPOTTED MOON AND THE OTHERS. ARE THEY WORRIED ABOUT DRAGONS SO CLOSE TO THEIR HOME? THAT'S CUTE.
OF COURSE, NONE OF **US** WOULD EAT SCAVENGERS. BUT IF WE **DID** WANT TO, WHAT COULD THEY DO ABOUT IT?

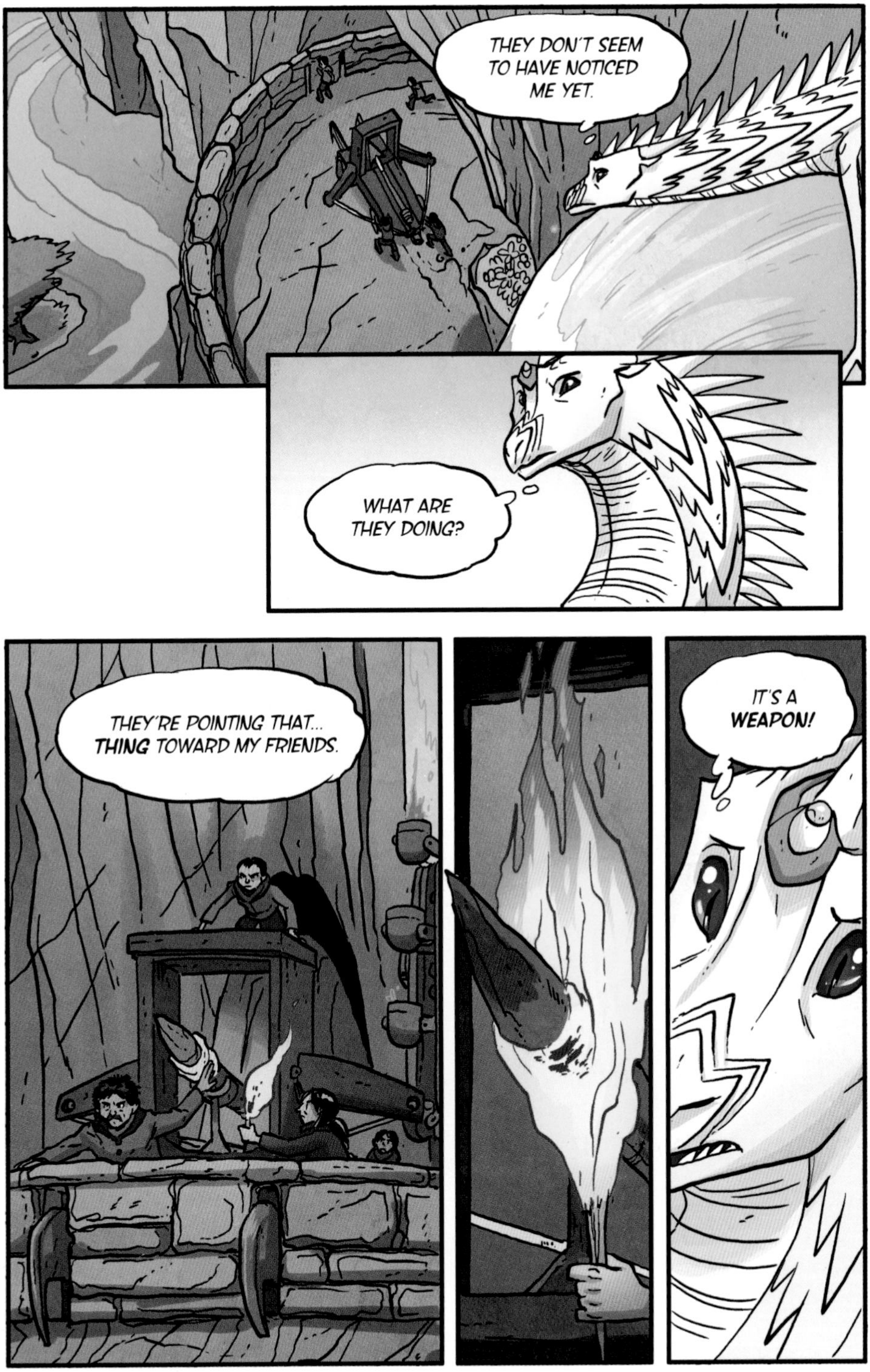
THEY DON'T SEEM TO HAVE NOTICED ME YET.
WHAT ARE THEY DOING?
THEY'RE POINTING THAT... **THING** TOWARD MY FRIENDS.
IT'S A **WEAPON!**

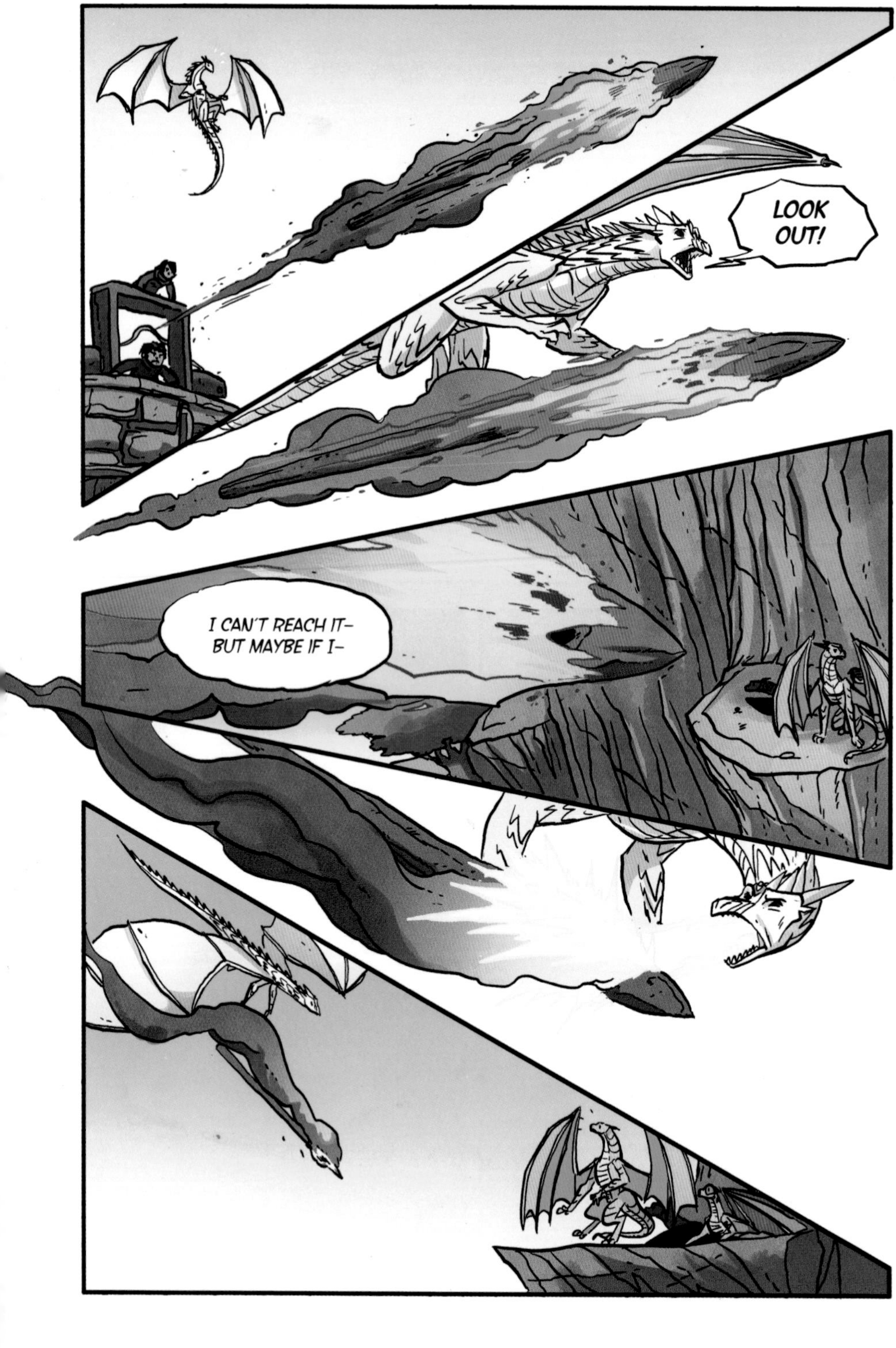
LOOK OUT!
I CAN'T REACH IT– BUT MAYBE IF I–

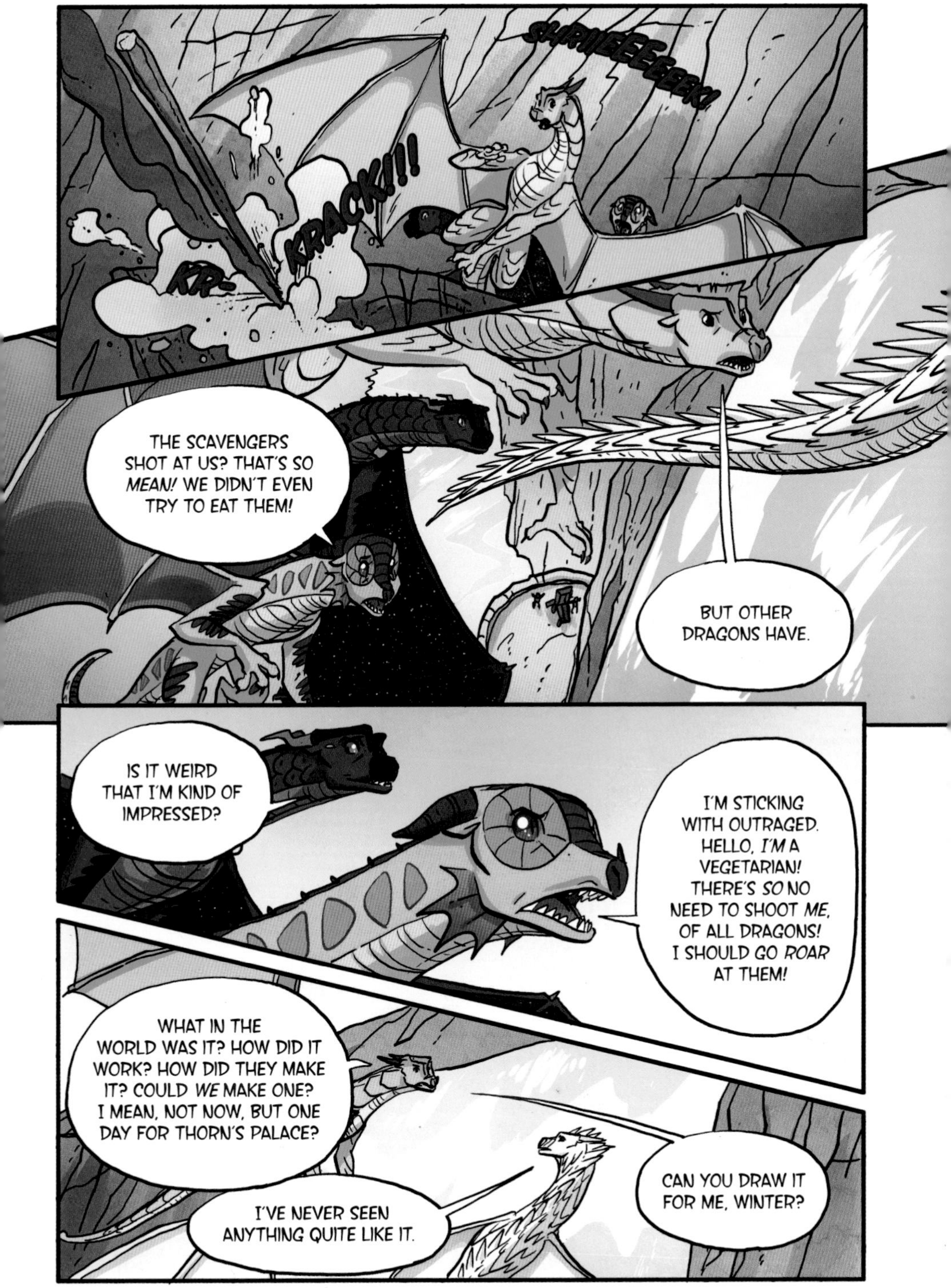
SHRIIEEEEEEEEK!
KR-
KRACK!!!!
THE SCAVENGERS SHOT AT US? THAT'S SO *MEAN!* WE DIDN'T EVEN TRY TO EAT THEM!
BUT OTHER DRAGONS HAVE.
IS IT WEIRD THAT I'M KIND OF IMPRESSED?
I'M STICKING WITH OUTRAGED. HELLO, *I'M* A VEGETARIAN! THERE'S *SO* NO NEED TO SHOOT *ME*, OF ALL DRAGONS! I SHOULD *GO ROAR* AT THEM!
WHAT IN THE WORLD WAS IT? HOW DID IT WORK? HOW DID THEY MAKE IT? COULD *WE* MAKE ONE? I MEAN, NOT NOW, BUT ONE DAY FOR THORN'S PALACE?
I'VE NEVER SEEN ANYTHING QUITE LIKE IT.
CAN YOU DRAW IT FOR ME, WINTER?

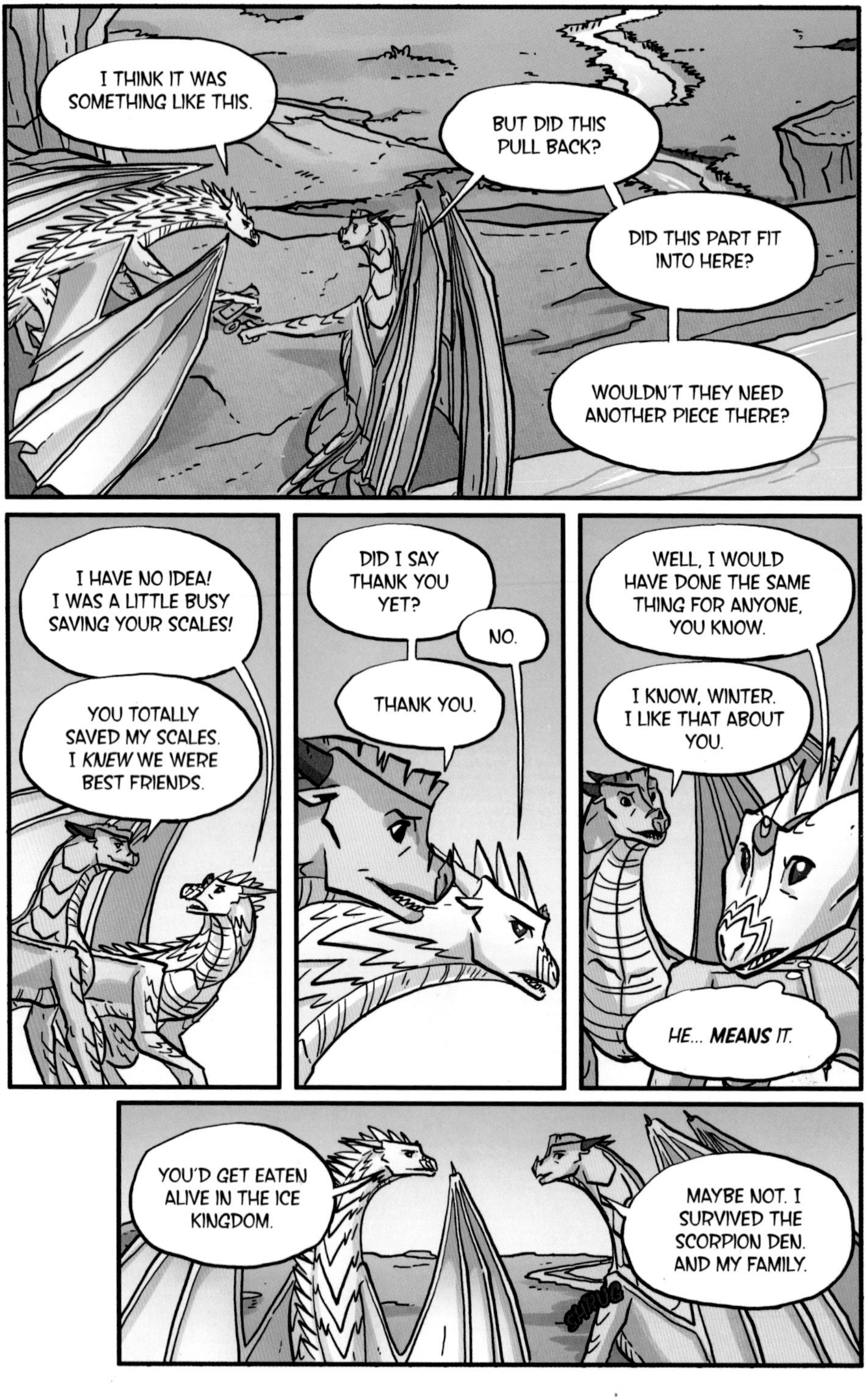
I THINK IT WAS SOMETHING LIKE THIS.
BUT DID THIS PULL BACK?
DID THIS PART FIT INTO HERE?
WOULDN'T THEY NEED ANOTHER PIECE THERE?
I HAVE NO IDEA! I WAS A LITTLE BUSY SAVING YOUR SCALES!
YOU TOTALLY SAVED MY SCALES. I *KNEW* WE WERE BEST FRIENDS.
DID I SAY THANK YOU YET?
NO.
THANK YOU.
WELL, I WOULD HAVE DONE THE SAME THING FOR ANYONE, YOU KNOW.
I KNOW, WINTER. I LIKE THAT ABOUT YOU.
*HE... **MEANS** IT.*
YOU'D GET EATEN ALIVE IN THE ICE KINGDOM.
MAYBE NOT. I SURVIVED THE SCORPION DEN. AND MY FAMILY.
SHRUG

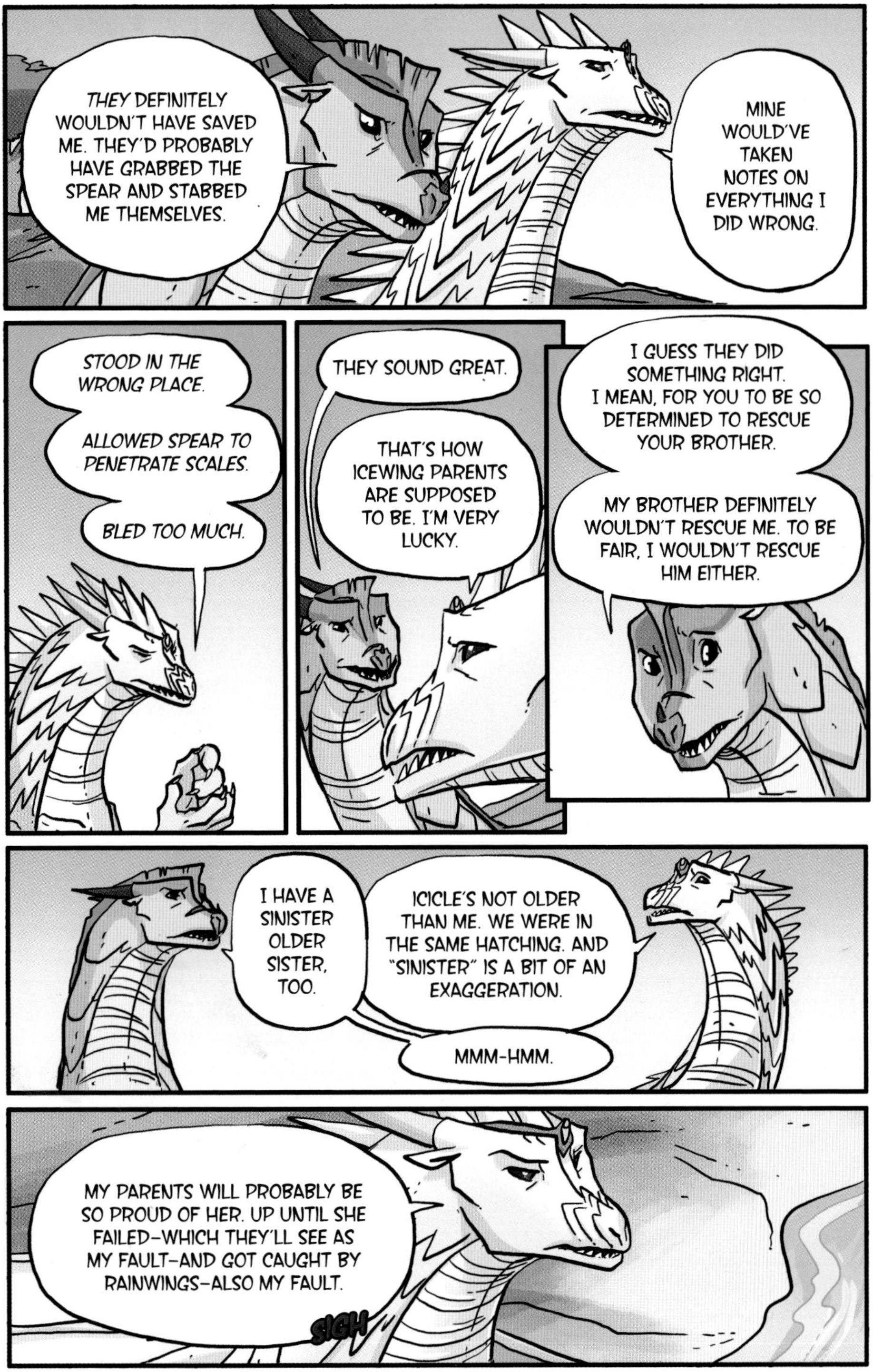

THEY DEFINITELY WOULDN'T HAVE SAVED ME. THEY'D PROBABLY HAVE GRABBED THE SPEAR AND STABBED ME THEMSELVES.
MINE WOULD'VE TAKEN NOTES ON EVERYTHING I DID WRONG.
STOOD IN THE WRONG PLACE.
ALLOWED SPEAR TO PENETRATE SCALES.
BLED TOO MUCH.
THEY SOUND GREAT.
THAT'S HOW ICEWING PARENTS ARE SUPPOSED TO BE. I'M VERY LUCKY.
I GUESS THEY DID SOMETHING RIGHT. I MEAN, FOR YOU TO BE SO DETERMINED TO RESCUE YOUR BROTHER.
MY BROTHER DEFINITELY WOULDN'T RESCUE ME. TO BE FAIR, I WOULDN'T RESCUE HIM EITHER.
I HAVE A SINISTER OLDER SISTER, TOO.
ICICLE'S NOT OLDER THAN ME. WE WERE IN THE SAME HATCHING. AND "SINISTER" IS A BIT OF AN EXAGGERATION.
MMM-HMM.
MY PARENTS WILL PROBABLY BE SO PROUD OF HER. UP UNTIL SHE FAILED–WHICH THEY'LL SEE AS MY FAULT–AND GOT CAUGHT BY RAINWINGS–ALSO MY FAULT.
SIGH

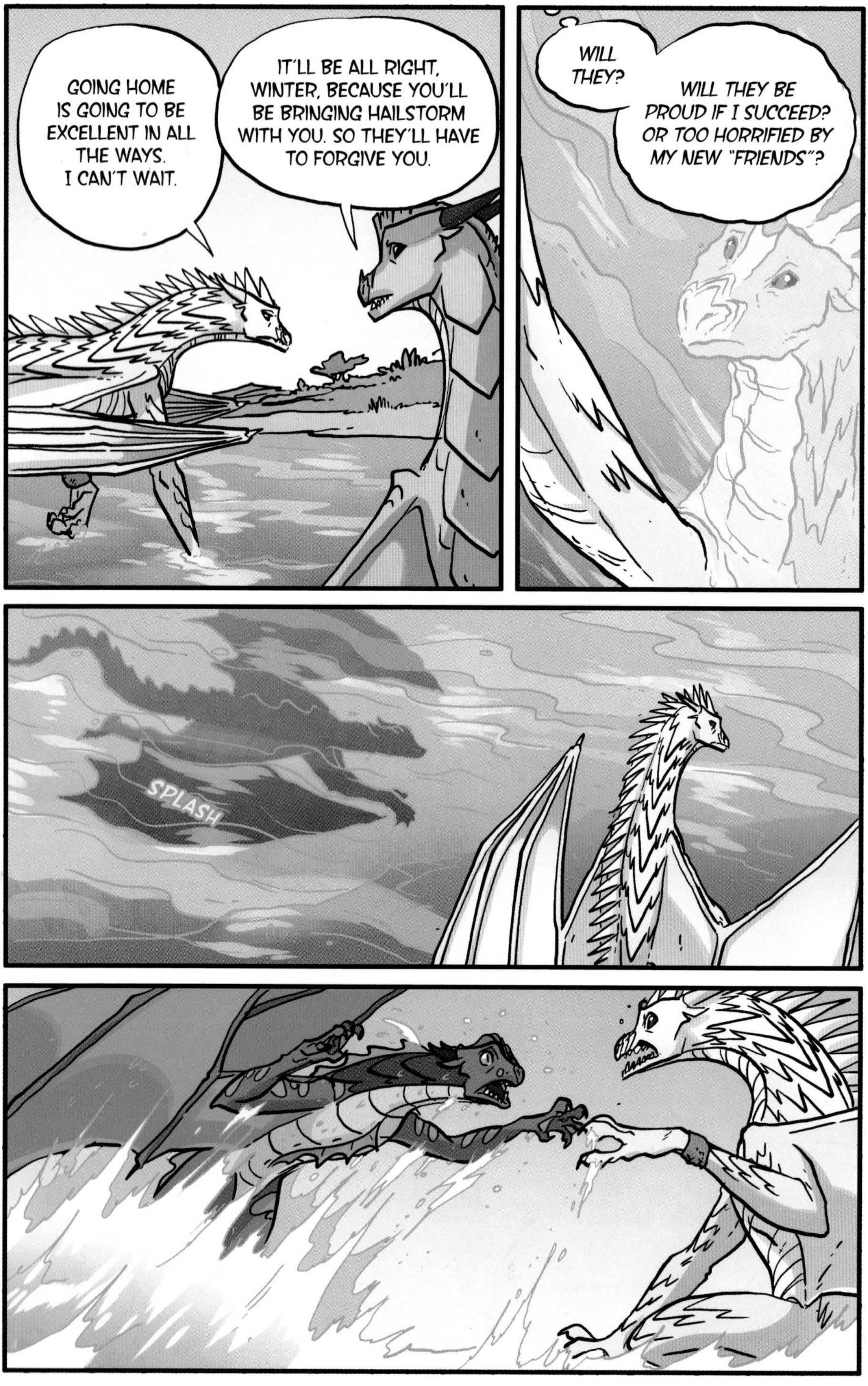
GOING HOME IS GOING TO BE EXCELLENT IN ALL THE WAYS. I CAN'T WAIT.
IT'LL BE ALL RIGHT, WINTER, BECAUSE YOU'LL BE BRINGING HAILSTORM WITH YOU. SO THEY'LL HAVE TO FORGIVE YOU.
WILL THEY?
WILL THEY BE PROUD IF I SUCCEED? OR TOO HORRIFIED BY MY NEW "FRIENDS"?
SPLASH

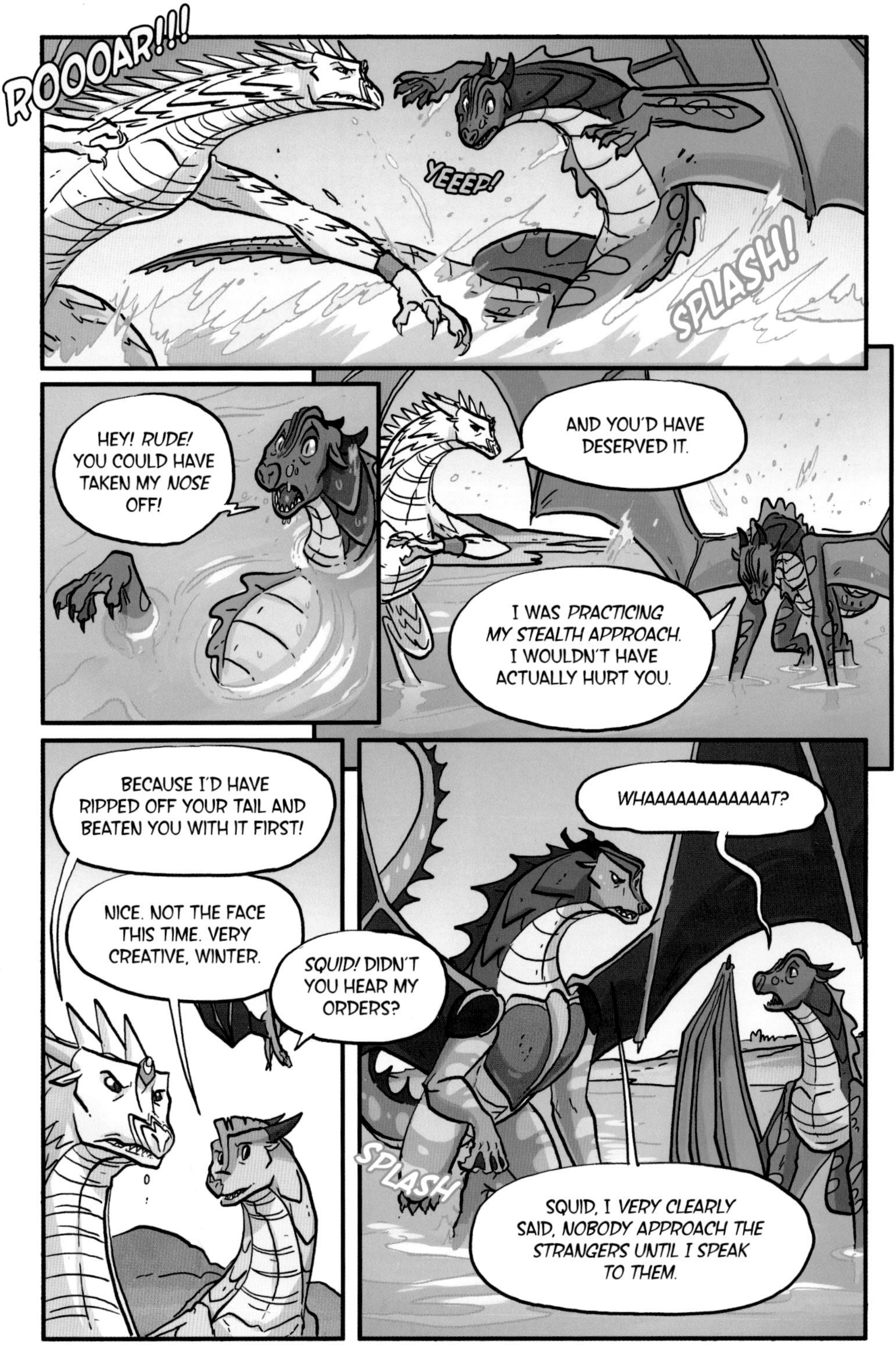
ROOOAR!!!
YEEEP!
SPLASH!
HEY! RUDE! YOU COULD HAVE TAKEN MY NOSE OFF!
AND YOU'D HAVE DESERVED IT.
I WAS PRACTICING MY STEALTH APPROACH. I WOULDN'T HAVE ACTUALLY HURT YOU.
BECAUSE I'D HAVE RIPPED OFF YOUR TAIL AND BEATEN YOU WITH IT FIRST!
NICE. NOT THE FACE THIS TIME. VERY CREATIVE, WINTER.
SQUID! DIDN'T YOU HEAR MY ORDERS?
WHAAAAAAAAAAAAT?
SPLASH
SQUID, I VERY CLEARLY SAID, NOBODY APPROACH THE STRANGERS UNTIL I SPEAK TO THEM.

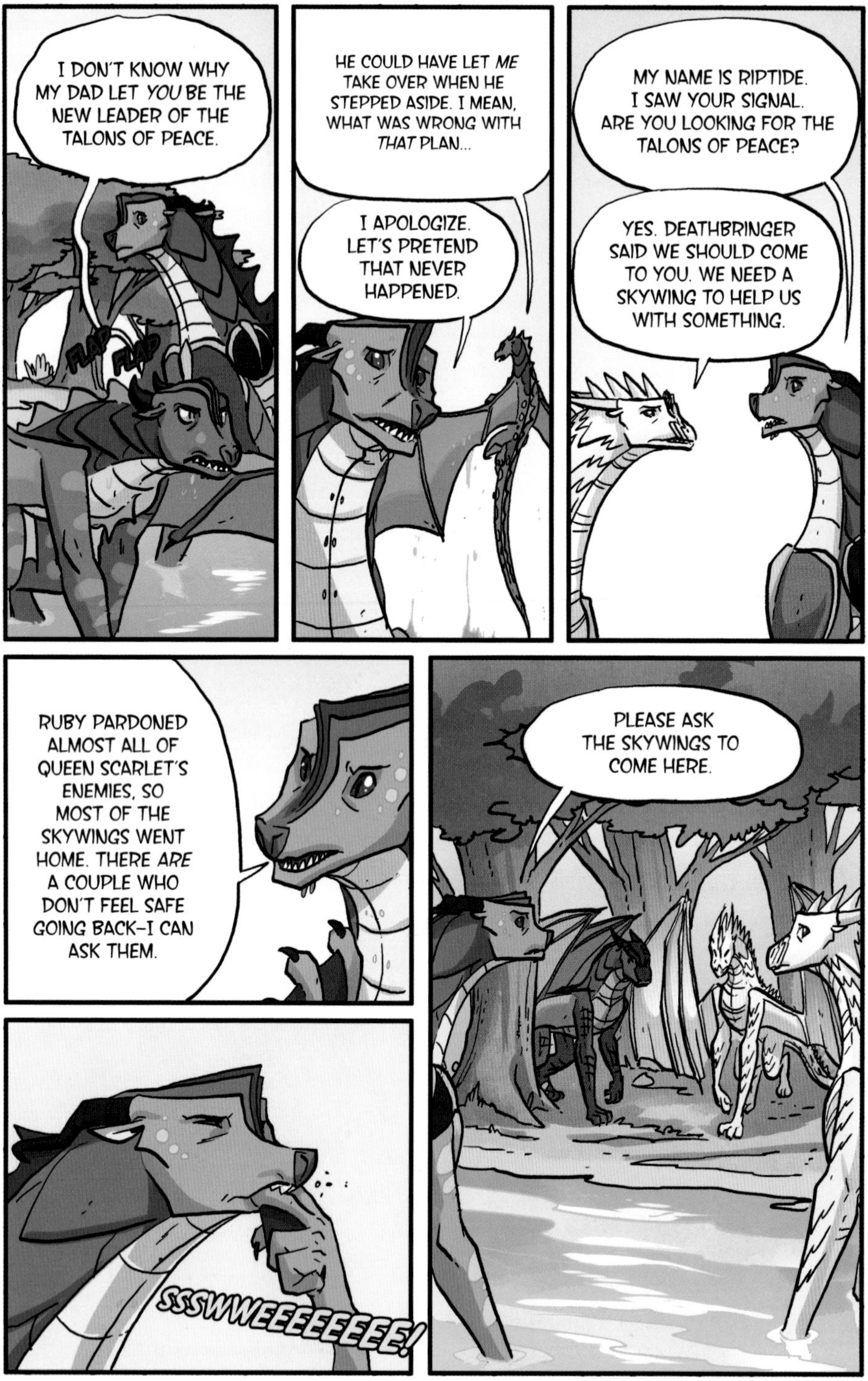
I DON'T KNOW WHY MY DAD LET *YOU* BE THE NEW LEADER OF THE TALONS OF PEACE.
FLAP
FLAP
HE COULD HAVE LET *ME* TAKE OVER WHEN HE STEPPED ASIDE. I MEAN, WHAT WAS WRONG WITH *THAT* PLAN...
I APOLOGIZE. LET'S PRETEND THAT NEVER HAPPENED.
MY NAME IS RIPTIDE. I SAW YOUR SIGNAL. ARE YOU LOOKING FOR THE TALONS OF PEACE?
YES. DEATHBRINGER SAID WE SHOULD COME TO YOU. WE NEED A SKYWING TO HELP US WITH SOMETHING.
RUBY PARDONED ALMOST ALL OF QUEEN SCARLET'S ENEMIES, SO MOST OF THE SKYWINGS WENT HOME. THERE *ARE* A COUPLE WHO DON'T FEEL SAFE GOING BACK–I CAN ASK THEM.
SSSWWEEEEEEEEE!
PLEASE ASK THE SKYWINGS TO COME HERE.

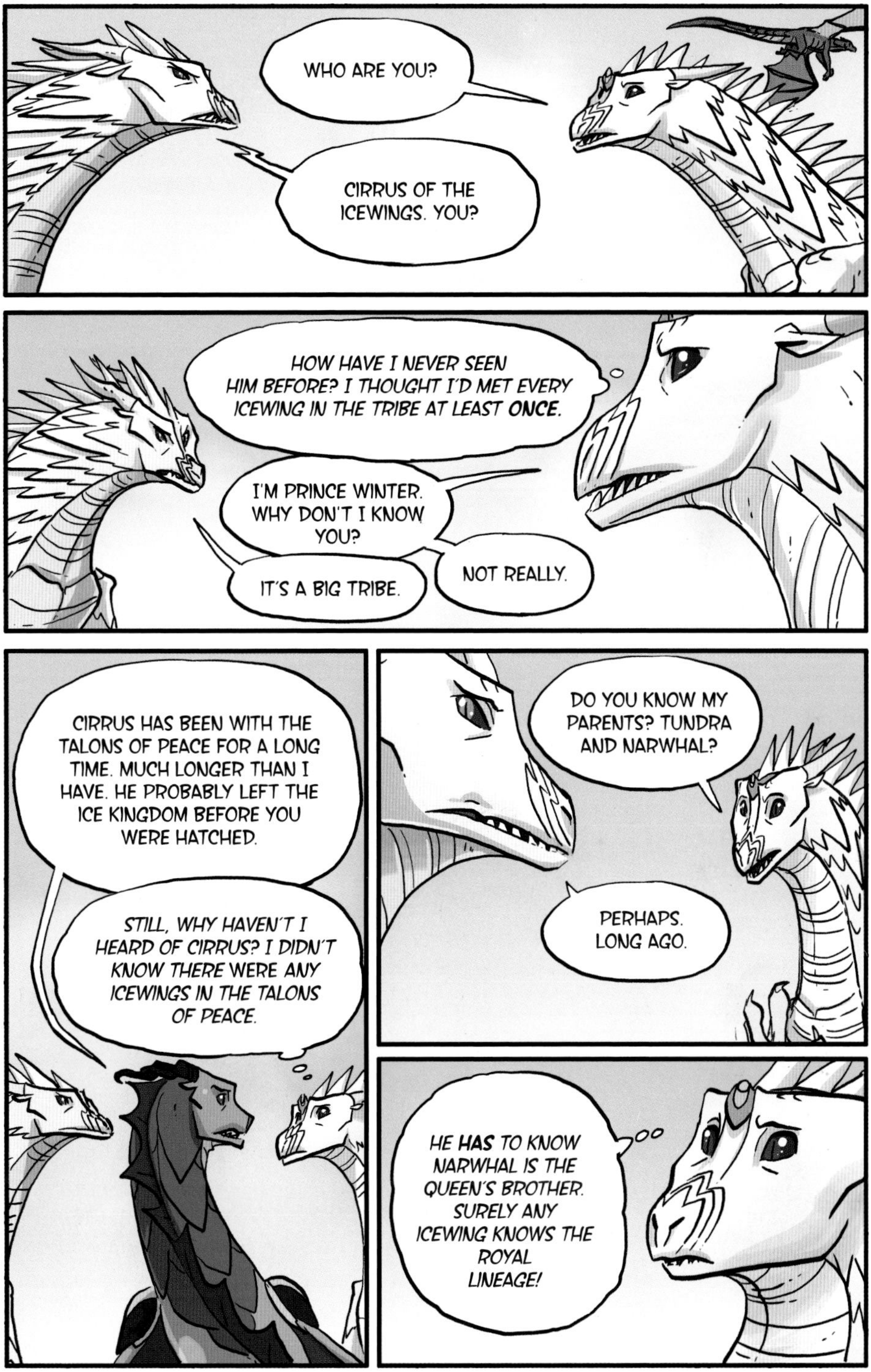
WHO ARE YOU?
CIRRUS OF THE ICEWINGS. YOU?
HOW HAVE I NEVER SEEN HIM BEFORE? I THOUGHT I'D MET EVERY ICEWING IN THE TRIBE AT LEAST **ONCE.**
I'M PRINCE WINTER. WHY DON'T I KNOW YOU?
IT'S A BIG TRIBE.
NOT REALLY.
CIRRUS HAS BEEN WITH THE TALONS OF PEACE FOR A LONG TIME. MUCH LONGER THAN I HAVE. HE PROBABLY LEFT THE ICE KINGDOM BEFORE YOU WERE HATCHED.
STILL, WHY HAVEN'T I HEARD OF CIRRUS? I DIDN'T KNOW THERE WERE ANY ICEWINGS IN THE TALONS OF PEACE.
DO YOU KNOW MY PARENTS? TUNDRA AND NARWHAL?
PERHAPS. LONG AGO.
HE **HAS** TO KNOW NARWHAL IS THE QUEEN'S BROTHER. SURELY ANY ICEWING KNOWS THE ROYAL LINEAGE!

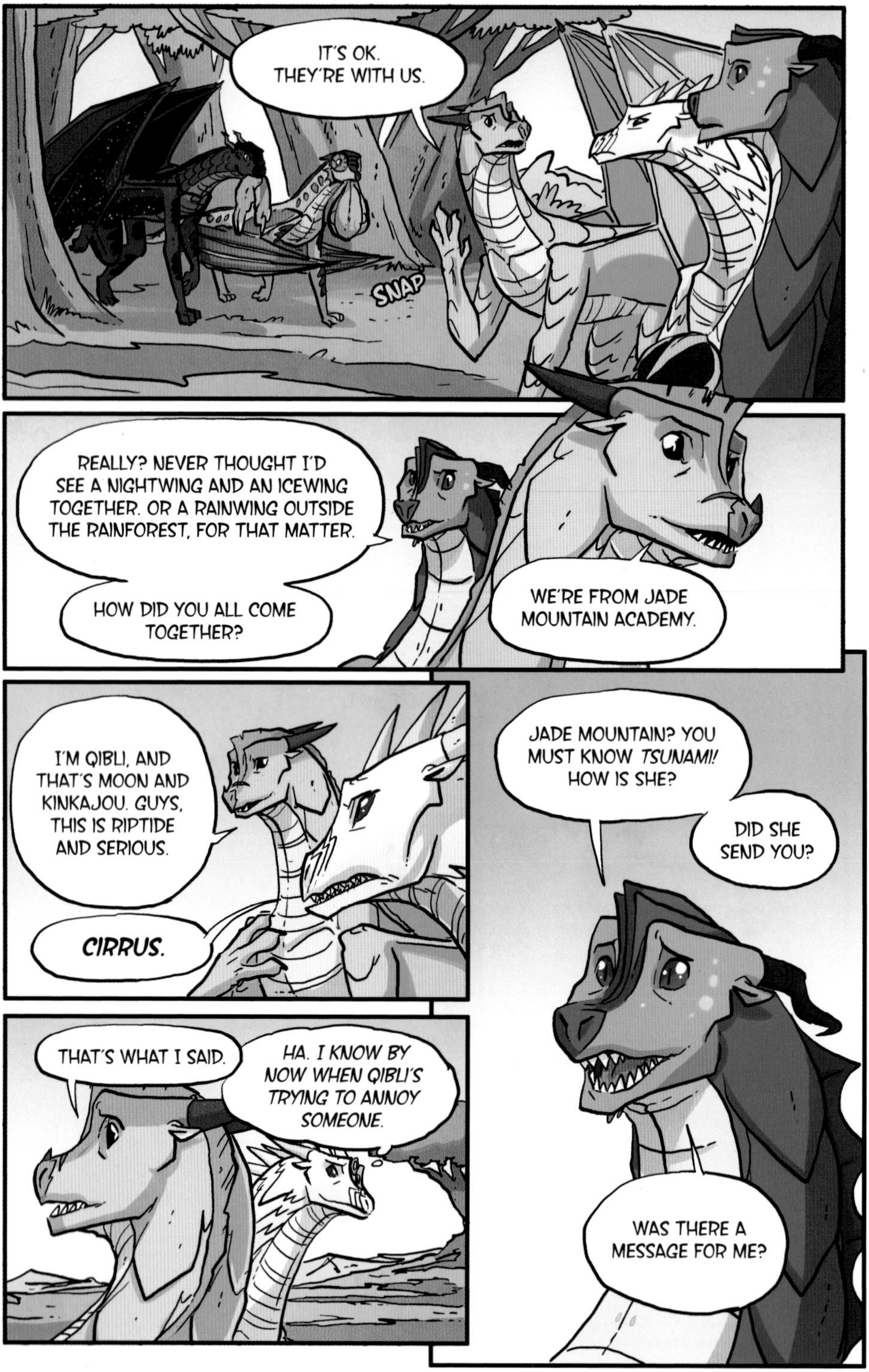
IT'S OK. THEY'RE WITH US.
SNAP
REALLY? NEVER THOUGHT I'D SEE A NIGHTWING AND AN ICEWING TOGETHER. OR A RAINWING OUTSIDE THE RAINFOREST, FOR THAT MATTER.
HOW DID YOU ALL COME TOGETHER?
WE'RE FROM JADE MOUNTAIN ACADEMY.
I'M QIBLI, AND THAT'S MOON AND KINKAJOU. GUYS, THIS IS RIPTIDE AND SERIOUS.
CIRRUS.
THAT'S WHAT I SAID.
HA. I KNOW BY NOW WHEN QIBLI'S TRYING TO ANNOY SOMEONE.
JADE MOUNTAIN? YOU MUST KNOW *TSUNAMI!* HOW IS SHE?
DID SHE SEND YOU?
WAS THERE A MESSAGE FOR ME?

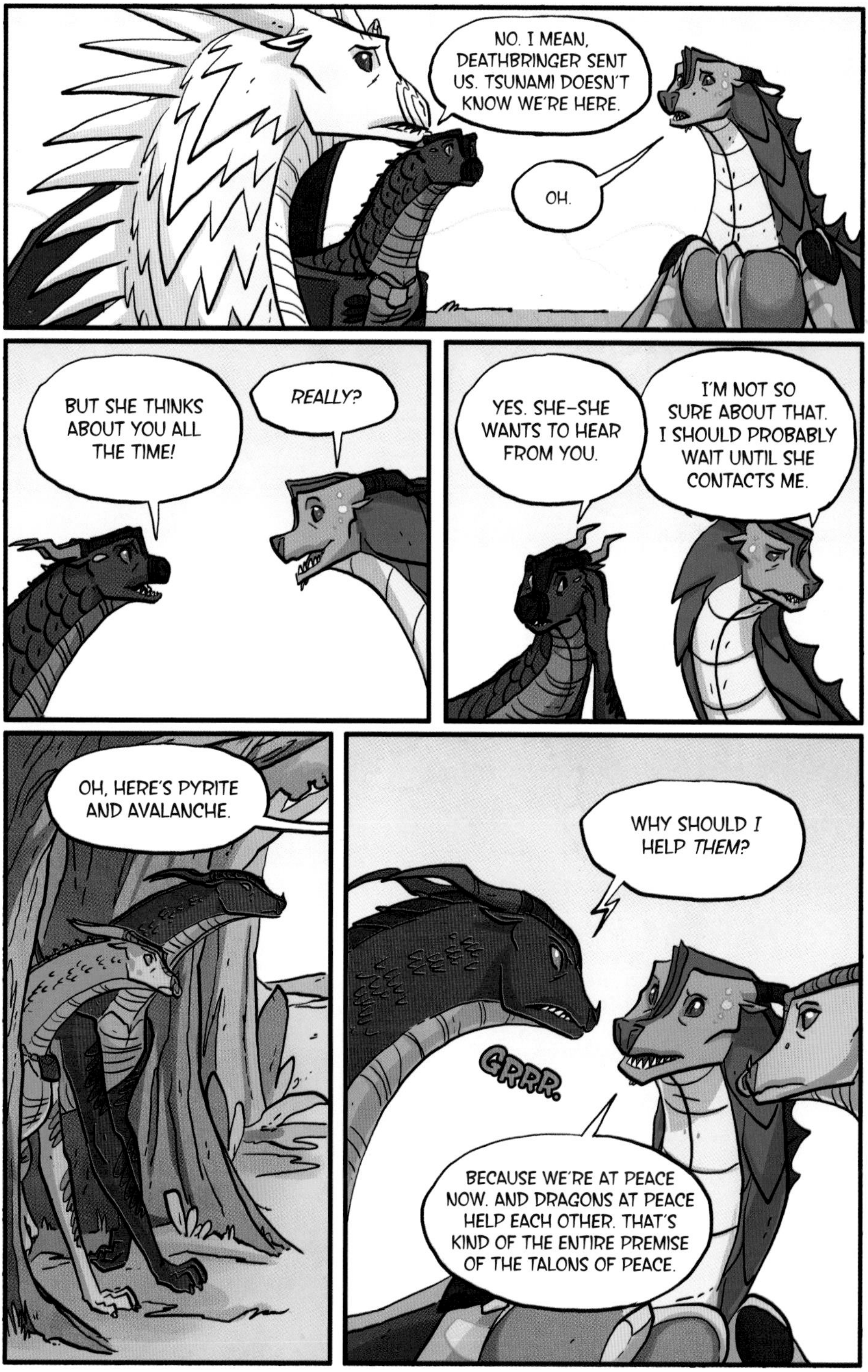
NO. I MEAN, DEATHBRINGER SENT US. TSUNAMI DOESN'T KNOW WE'RE HERE.
OH.
BUT SHE THINKS ABOUT YOU ALL THE TIME!
REALLY?
YES. SHE–SHE WANTS TO HEAR FROM YOU.
I'M NOT SO SURE ABOUT THAT. I SHOULD PROBABLY WAIT UNTIL SHE CONTACTS ME.
OH, HERE'S PYRITE AND AVALANCHE.
WHY SHOULD I HELP THEM?
GRRR.
BECAUSE WE'RE AT PEACE NOW. AND DRAGONS AT PEACE HELP EACH OTHER. THAT'S KIND OF THE ENTIRE PREMISE OF THE TALONS OF PEACE.

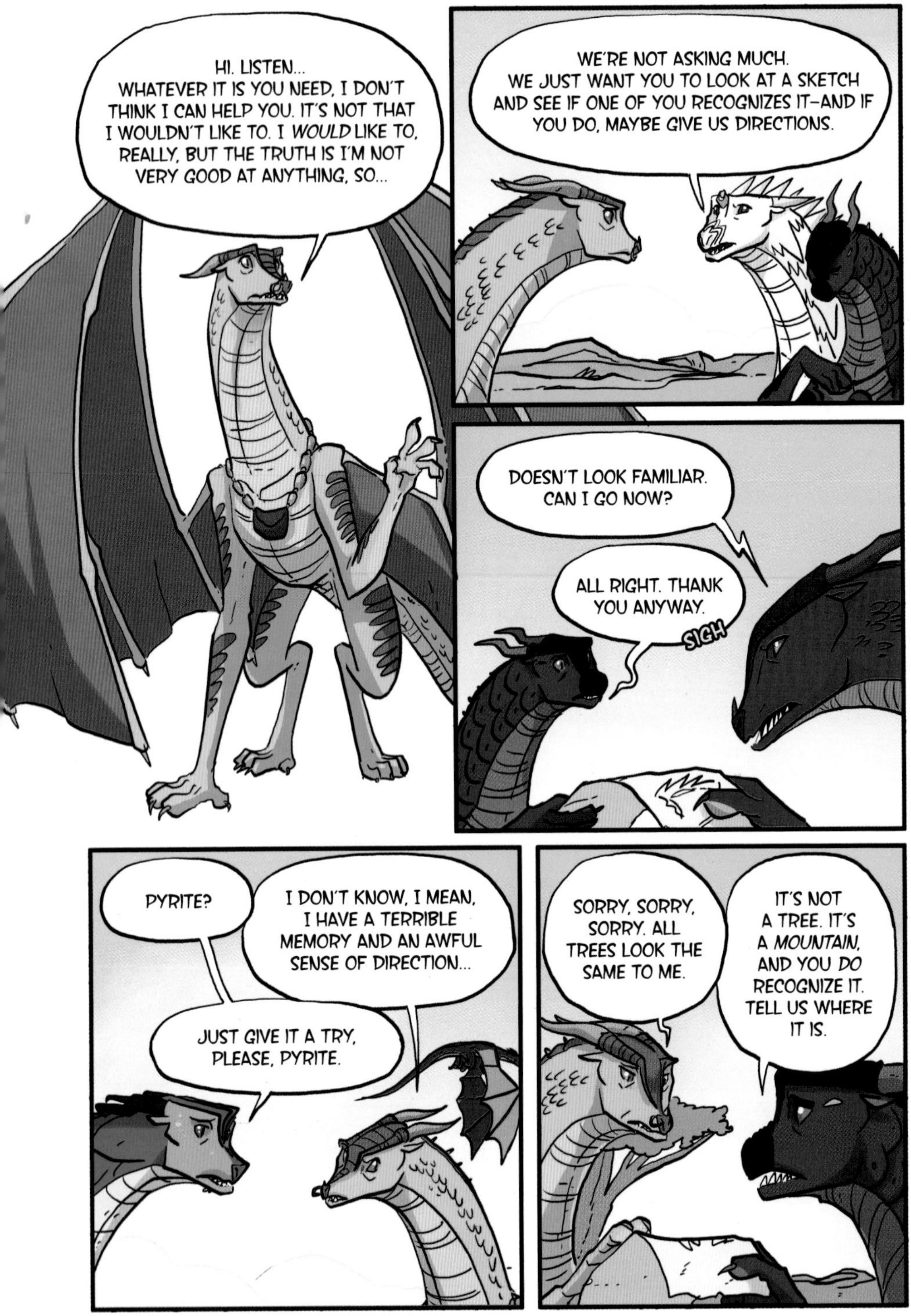
HI. LISTEN...
WHATEVER IT IS YOU NEED, I DON'T THINK I CAN HELP YOU. IT'S NOT THAT I WOULDN'T LIKE TO. I *WOULD* LIKE TO, REALLY, BUT THE TRUTH IS I'M NOT VERY GOOD AT ANYTHING, SO...
WE'RE NOT ASKING MUCH. WE JUST WANT YOU TO LOOK AT A SKETCH AND SEE IF ONE OF YOU RECOGNIZES IT—AND IF YOU DO, MAYBE GIVE US DIRECTIONS.
DOESN'T LOOK FAMILIAR. CAN I GO NOW?
ALL RIGHT. THANK YOU ANYWAY.
SIGH
PYRITE?
I DON'T KNOW, I MEAN, I HAVE A TERRIBLE MEMORY AND AN AWFUL SENSE OF DIRECTION...
JUST GIVE IT A TRY, PLEASE, PYRITE.
SORRY, SORRY, SORRY. ALL TREES LOOK THE SAME TO ME.
IT'S NOT A TREE. IT'S A *MOUNTAIN*, AND YOU *DO* RECOGNIZE IT. TELL US WHERE IT IS.

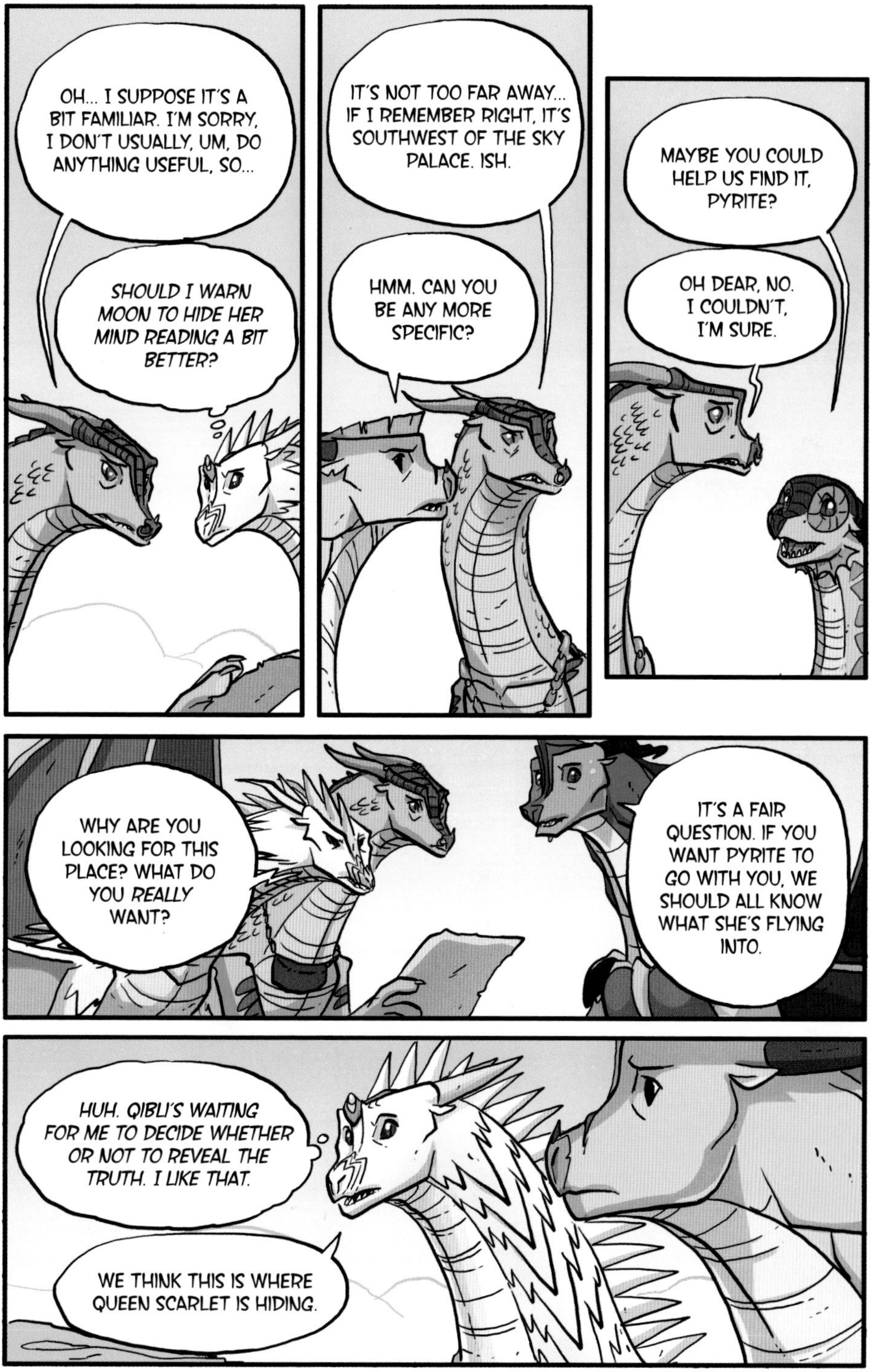
OH... I SUPPOSE IT'S A BIT FAMILIAR. I'M SORRY, I DON'T USUALLY, UM, DO ANYTHING USEFUL, SO...
SHOULD I WARN MOON TO HIDE HER MIND READING A BIT BETTER?
IT'S NOT TOO FAR AWAY... IF I REMEMBER RIGHT, IT'S SOUTHWEST OF THE SKY PALACE. ISH.
HMM. CAN YOU BE ANY MORE SPECIFIC?
MAYBE YOU COULD HELP US FIND IT, PYRITE?
OH DEAR, NO. I COULDN'T, I'M SURE.
WHY ARE YOU LOOKING FOR THIS PLACE? WHAT DO YOU *REALLY* WANT?
IT'S A FAIR QUESTION. IF YOU WANT PYRITE TO GO WITH YOU, WE SHOULD ALL KNOW WHAT SHE'S FLYING INTO.
HUH. QIBLI'S WAITING FOR ME TO DECIDE WHETHER OR NOT TO REVEAL THE TRUTH. I LIKE THAT.
WE THINK THIS IS WHERE QUEEN SCARLET IS HIDING.

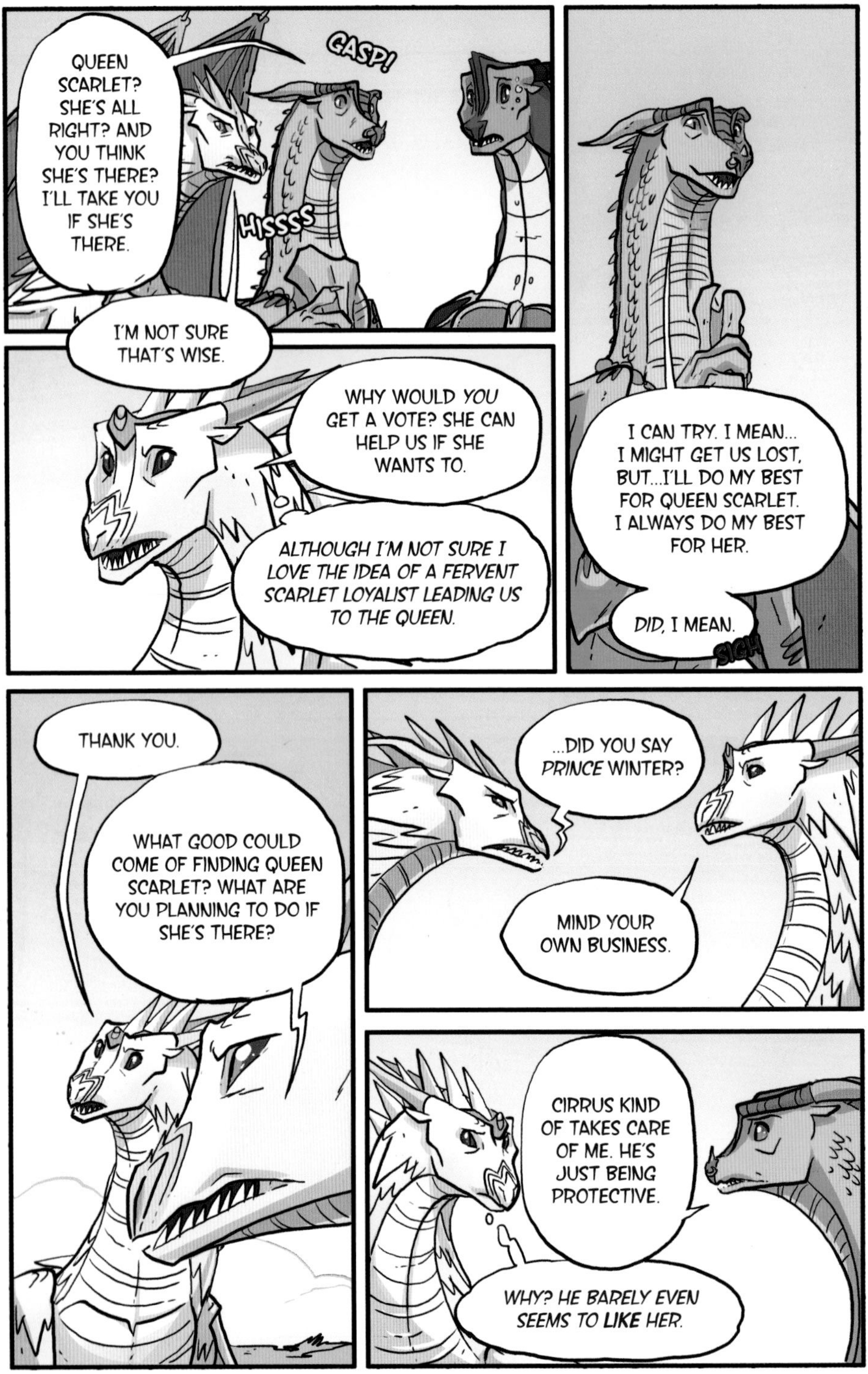
QUEEN SCARLET? SHE'S ALL RIGHT? AND YOU THINK SHE'S THERE? I'LL TAKE YOU IF SHE'S THERE.
GASP!
HISSSS
I'M NOT SURE THAT'S WISE.
WHY WOULD *YOU* GET A VOTE? SHE CAN HELP US IF SHE WANTS TO.
ALTHOUGH I'M NOT SURE I LOVE THE IDEA OF A FERVENT SCARLET LOYALIST LEADING US TO THE QUEEN.
I CAN TRY. I MEAN... I MIGHT GET US LOST, BUT...I'LL DO MY BEST FOR QUEEN SCARLET. I ALWAYS DO MY BEST FOR HER.
DID, I MEAN.
SIGH
THANK YOU.
WHAT GOOD COULD COME OF FINDING QUEEN SCARLET? WHAT ARE YOU PLANNING TO DO IF SHE'S THERE?
...DID YOU SAY *PRINCE* WINTER?
MIND YOUR OWN BUSINESS.
CIRRUS KIND OF TAKES CARE OF ME. HE'S JUST BEING PROTECTIVE.
*WHY? HE BARELY EVEN SEEMS TO **LIKE** HER.*

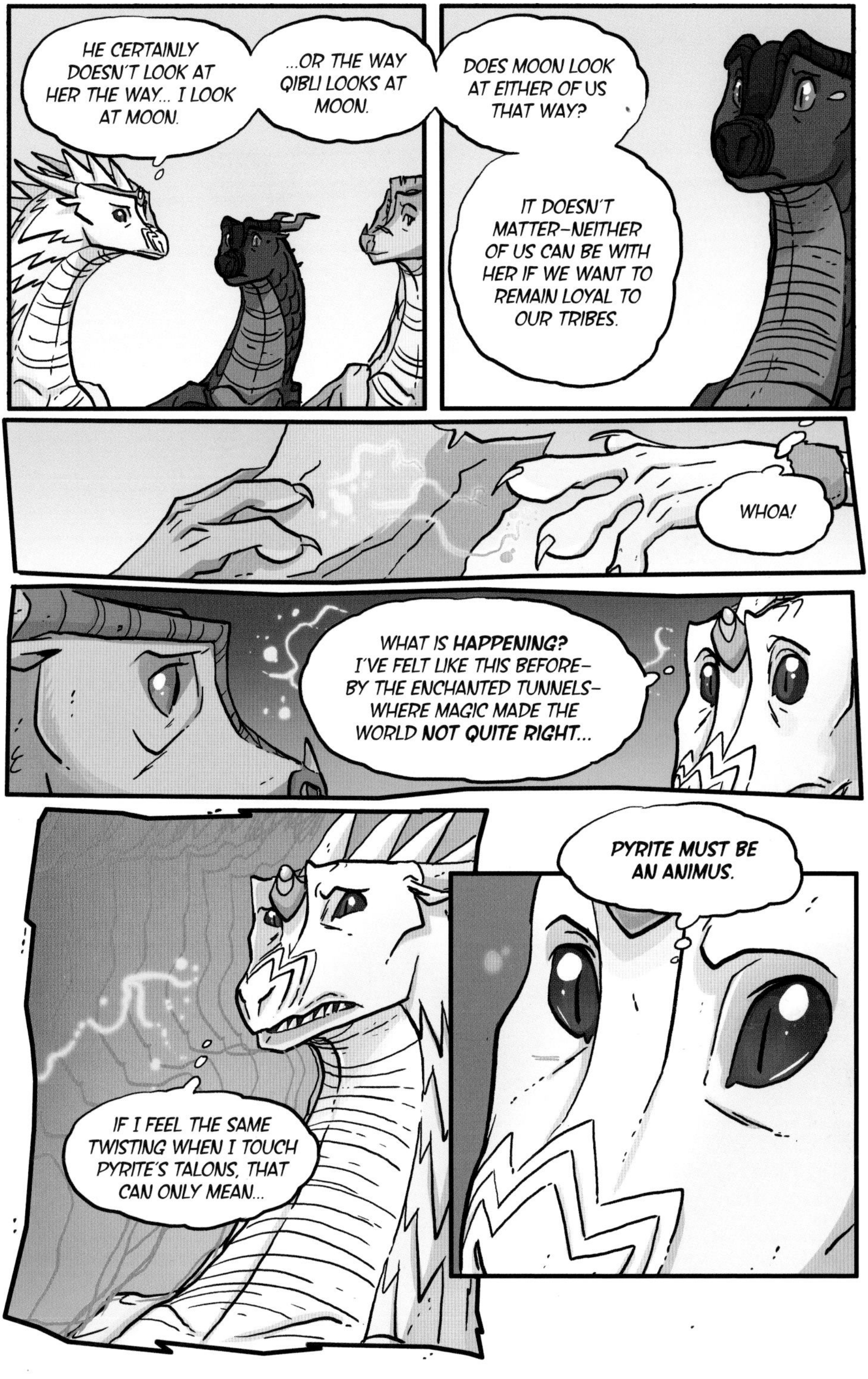
HE CERTAINLY DOESN'T LOOK AT HER THE WAY... I LOOK AT MOON.
...OR THE WAY QIBLI LOOKS AT MOON.
DOES MOON LOOK AT EITHER OF US THAT WAY?
IT DOESN'T MATTER—NEITHER OF US CAN BE WITH HER IF WE WANT TO REMAIN LOYAL TO OUR TRIBES.
WHOA!
WHAT IS **HAPPENING?** I'VE FELT LIKE THIS BEFORE—BY THE ENCHANTED TUNNELS—WHERE MAGIC MADE THE WORLD **NOT QUITE RIGHT...**
IF I FEEL THE SAME TWISTING WHEN I TOUCH PYRITE'S TALONS, THAT CAN ONLY MEAN...
PYRITE MUST BE AN ANIMUS.

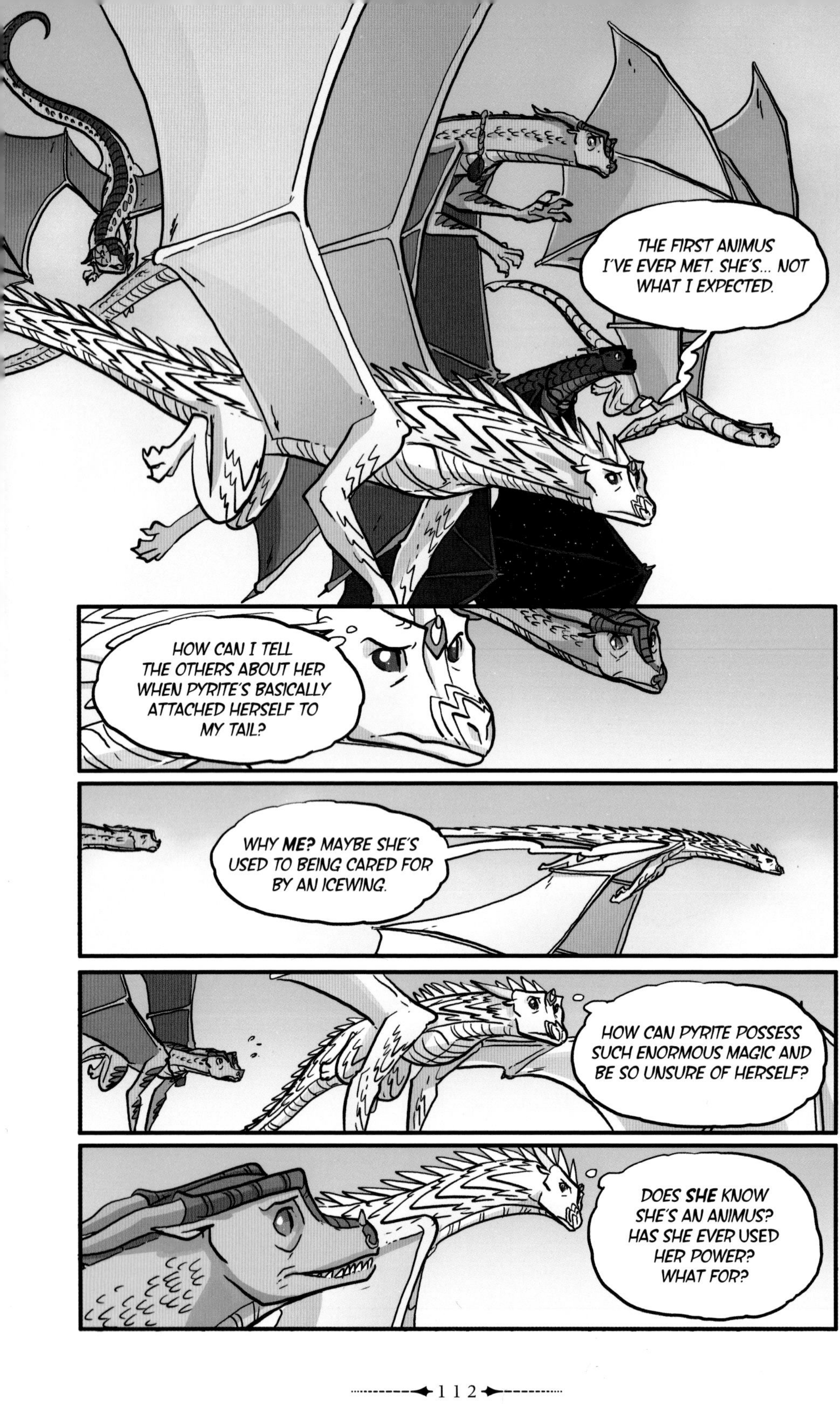
THE FIRST ANIMUS I'VE EVER MET. SHE'S... NOT WHAT I EXPECTED.
HOW CAN I TELL THE OTHERS ABOUT HER WHEN PYRITE'S BASICALLY ATTACHED HERSELF TO MY TAIL?
WHY **ME?** MAYBE SHE'S USED TO BEING CARED FOR BY AN ICEWING.
HOW CAN PYRITE POSSESS SUCH ENORMOUS MAGIC AND BE SO UNSURE OF HERSELF?
DOES **SHE** KNOW SHE'S AN ANIMUS? HAS SHE EVER USED HER POWER? WHAT FOR?

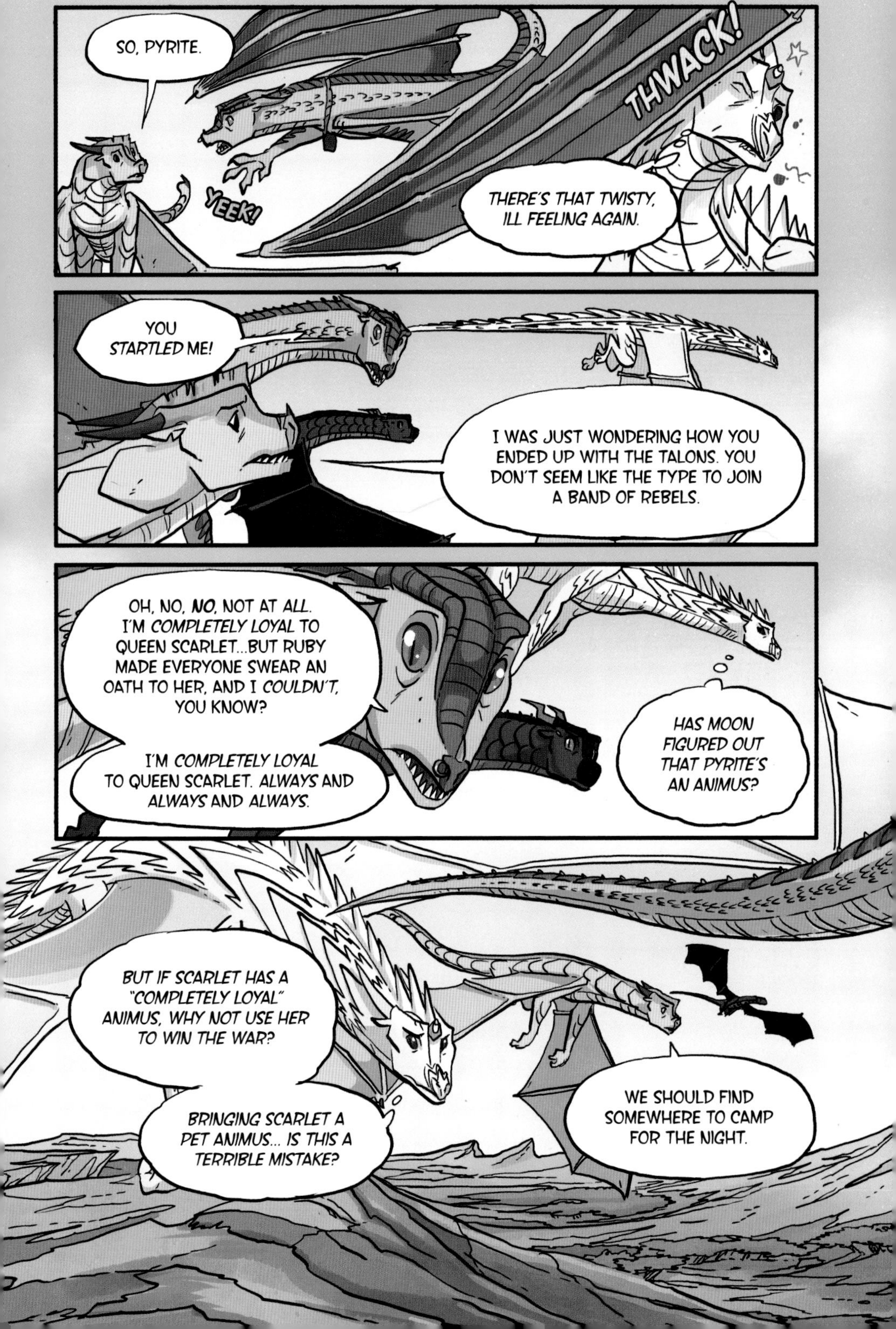
SO, PYRITE.
YEEK!
THWACK!
THERE'S THAT TWISTY, ILL FEELING AGAIN.
YOU STARTLED ME!
I WAS JUST WONDERING HOW YOU ENDED UP WITH THE TALONS. YOU DON'T SEEM LIKE THE TYPE TO JOIN A BAND OF REBELS.
OH, NO, NO, NOT AT ALL. I'M COMPLETELY LOYAL TO QUEEN SCARLET...BUT RUBY MADE EVERYONE SWEAR AN OATH TO HER, AND I COULDN'T, YOU KNOW?
I'M COMPLETELY LOYAL TO QUEEN SCARLET. ALWAYS AND ALWAYS AND ALWAYS.
HAS MOON FIGURED OUT THAT PYRITE'S AN ANIMUS?
BUT IF SCARLET HAS A "COMPLETELY LOYAL" ANIMUS, WHY NOT USE HER TO WIN THE WAR?
BRINGING SCARLET A PET ANIMUS... IS THIS A TERRIBLE MISTAKE?
WE SHOULD FIND SOMEWHERE TO CAMP FOR THE NIGHT.

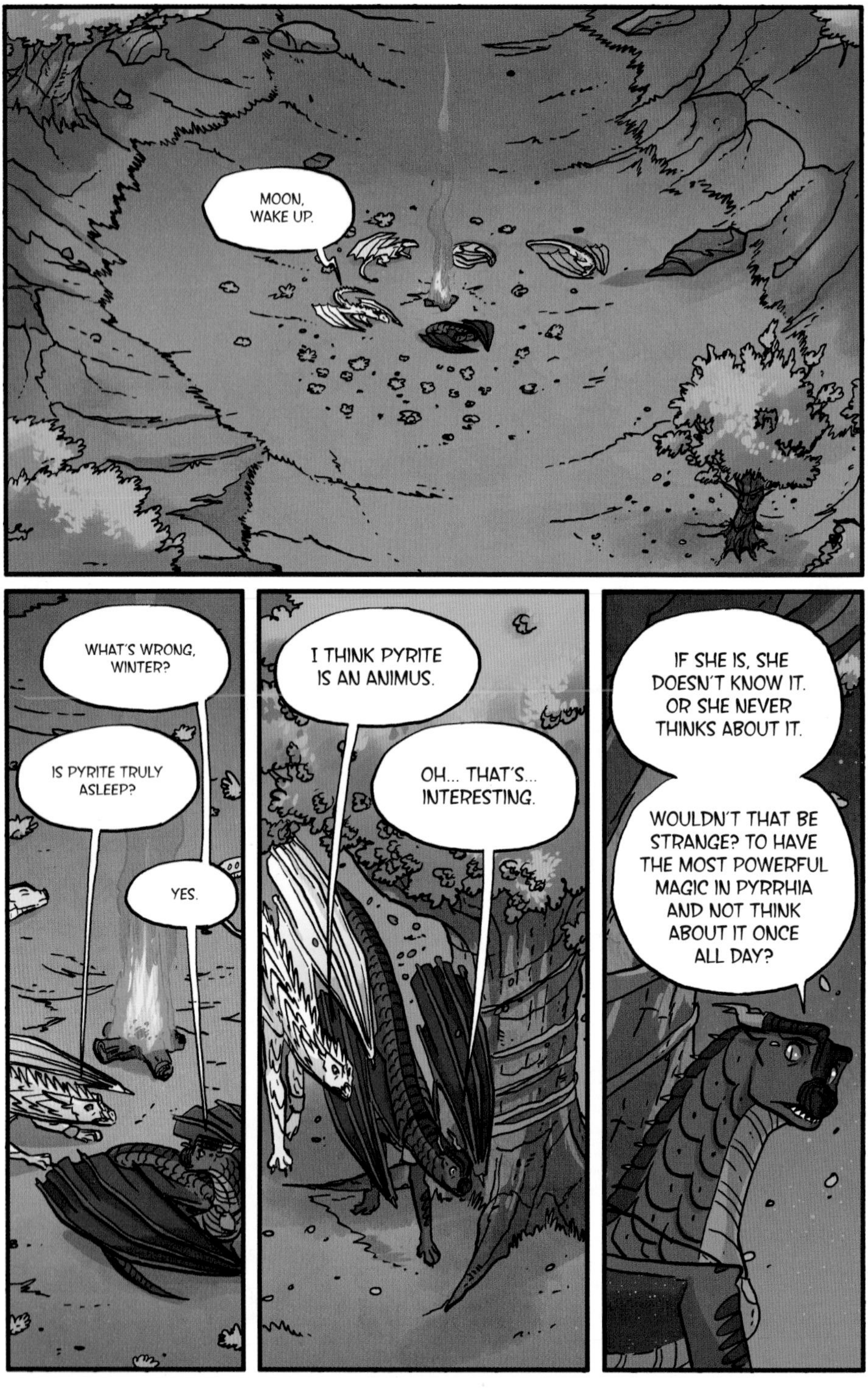
MOON, WAKE UP.
WHAT'S WRONG, WINTER?
IS PYRITE TRULY ASLEEP?
YES.
I THINK PYRITE IS AN ANIMUS.
OH... THAT'S... INTERESTING.
IF SHE IS, SHE DOESN'T KNOW IT. OR SHE NEVER THINKS ABOUT IT.
WOULDN'T THAT BE STRANGE? TO HAVE THE MOST POWERFUL MAGIC IN PYRRHIA AND NOT THINK ABOUT IT ONCE ALL DAY?

WHAT DID YOU THINK OF HER?

WELL... I FEEL SORRY FOR HER. HER BRAIN IS VERY ODD.

IT'S LIKE HER THOUGHTS JUST GO ROUND AND ROUND. I DON'T KNOW IF SHE'S BEEN HIT ON THE HEAD REALLY HARD OR SOMETHING?

"I'M COMPLETELY LOYAL TO QUEEN SCARLET. I'M NOT GOOD AT ANYTHING. I'M GLAD I'M A SKYWING. I'M CLUMSY AND NOT VERY BRIGHT AND GENERALLY USELESS."

THEN BACK TO:

"I'M COMPLETELY LOYAL TO QUEEN SCARLET..."

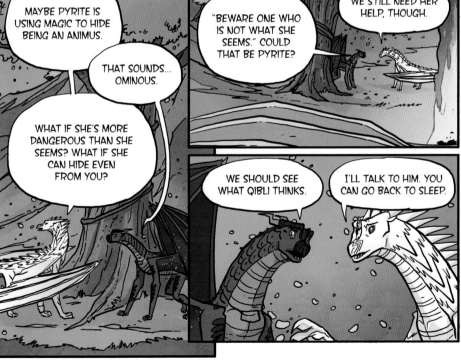

MAYBE PYRITE IS USING MAGIC TO HIDE BEING AN ANIMUS.

THAT SOUNDS... OMINOUS.

WHAT IF SHE'S MORE DANGEROUS THAN SHE SEEMS? WHAT IF SHE CAN HIDE EVEN FROM YOU?

"BEWARE ONE WHO IS NOT WHAT SHE SEEMS." COULD THAT BE PYRITE?

WE STILL NEED HER HELP, THOUGH.

WE SHOULD SEE WHAT QIBLI THINKS.

I'LL TALK TO HIM. YOU CAN GO BACK TO SLEEP.

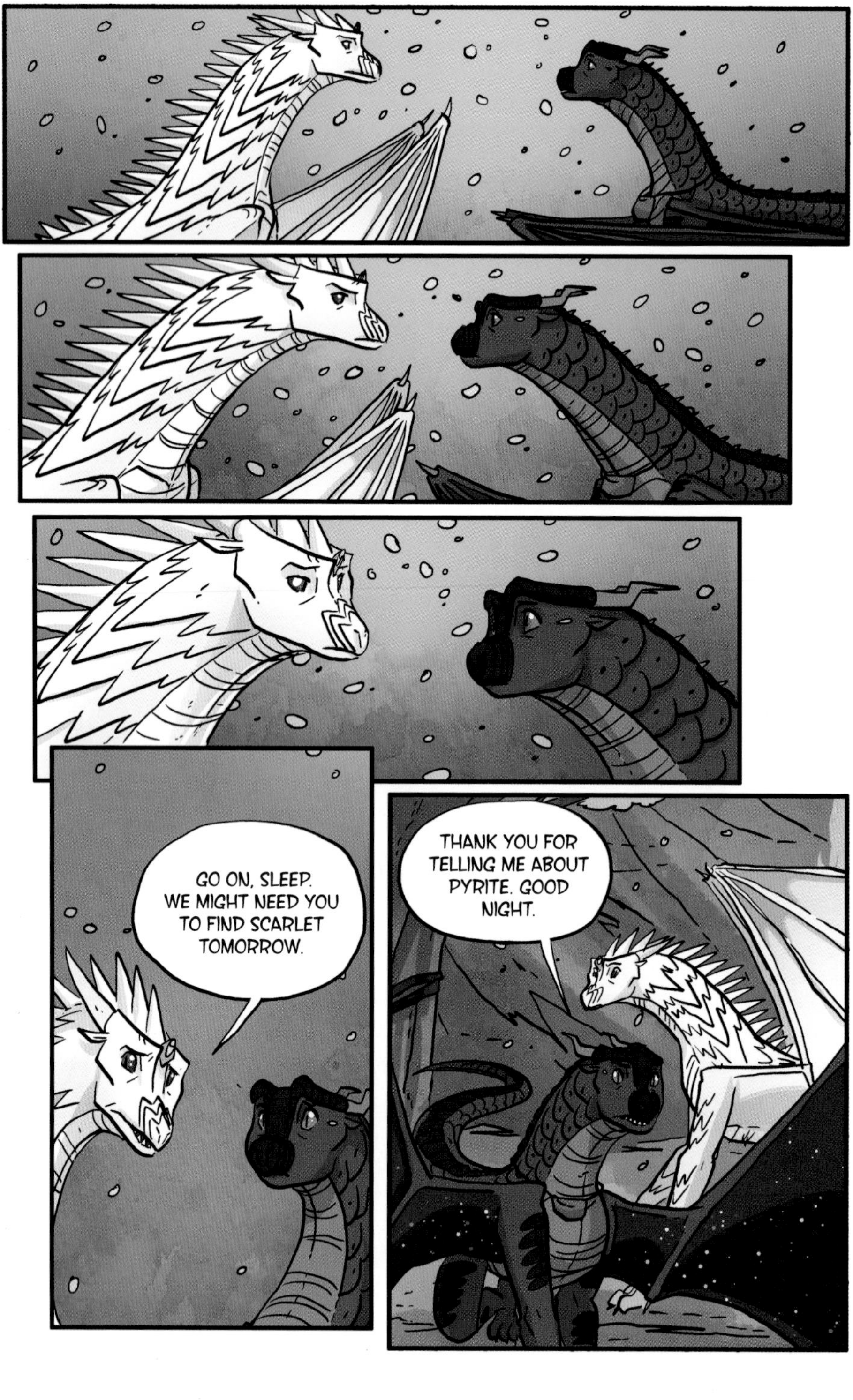
GO ON, SLEEP. WE MIGHT NEED YOU TO FIND SCARLET TOMORROW.
THANK YOU FOR TELLING ME ABOUT PYRITE. GOOD NIGHT.

OVER THERE! I THINK I SEE THE MOUNTAIN!

I DON'T SEE ANYTHING.

THAT'S BECAUSE YOU'RE A RAINWING. I SEE IT. SKYWINGS CAN SEE MUCH BETTER AND FASTER THAN YOU.

SO CAN ICEWINGS... BUT I'M DEFINITELY NOT GOING TO SAY THAT AND SOUND LIKE PYRITE.

I DON'T SEE IT YET EITHER, BUT IF IT'S OVER THERE, LET'S GO!

RACE YOU TO THAT PEAK!

TERRIBLY UNDIGNIFIED. WE WOULD NEVER ALLOW SUCH HIGGLEDY-PIGGLEDY SHENANIGANS IN THE ICE KINGDOM.

WAS THAT SUPPOSED TO BE ME, QIBLI? TERRIBLY UNIMPRESSIVE, IF SO.

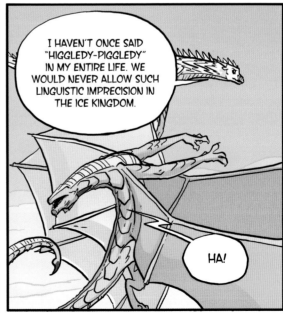

I HAVEN'T ONCE SAID "HIGGLEDY-PIGGLEDY" IN MY ENTIRE LIFE. WE WOULD NEVER ALLOW SUCH LINGUISTIC IMPRECISION IN THE ICE KINGDOM.

HA!

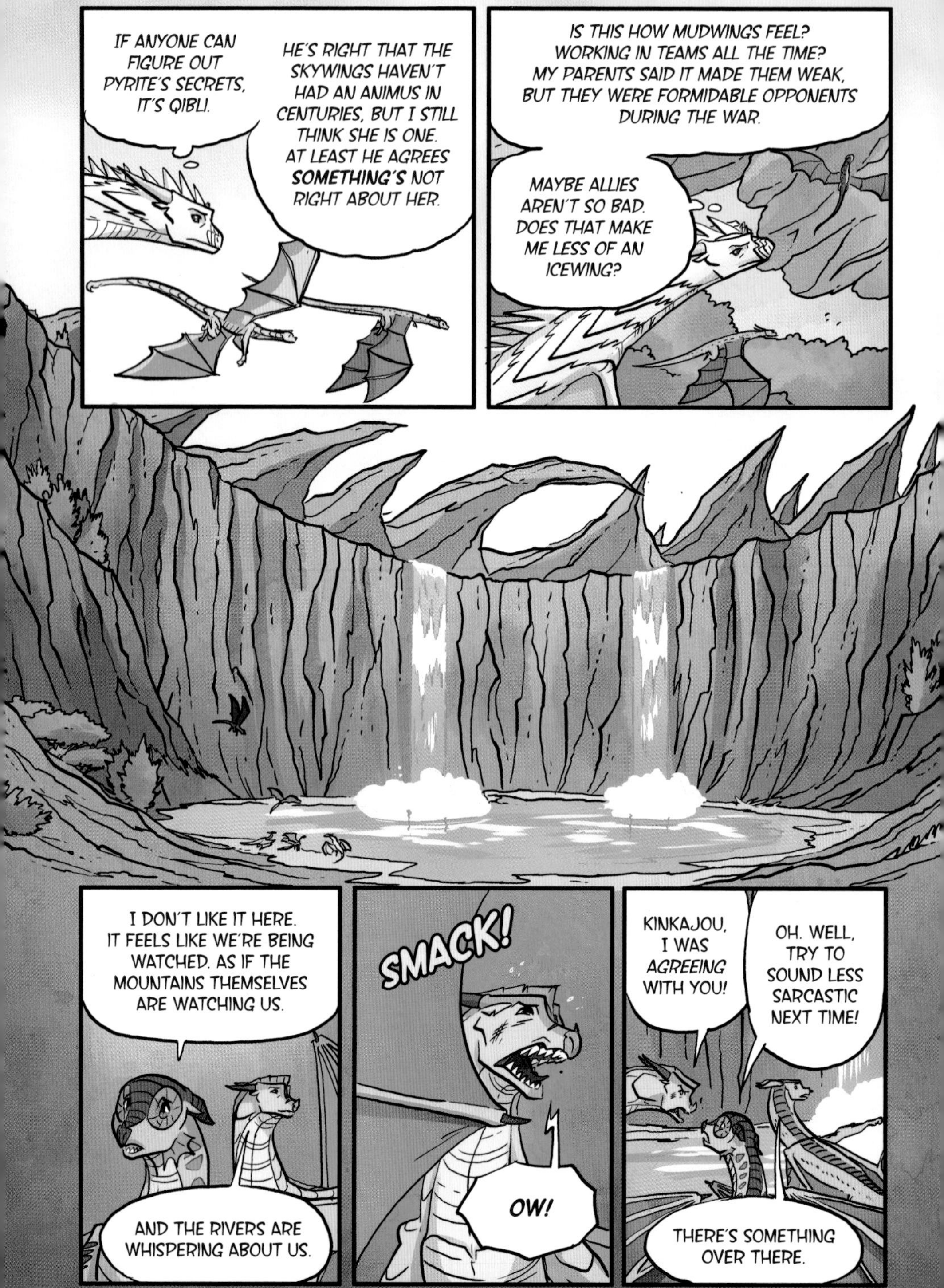
IF ANYONE CAN FIGURE OUT PYRITE'S SECRETS, IT'S QIBLI.
HE'S RIGHT THAT THE SKYWINGS HAVEN'T HAD AN ANIMUS IN CENTURIES, BUT I STILL THINK SHE IS ONE. AT LEAST HE AGREES **SOMETHING'S** NOT RIGHT ABOUT HER.
IS THIS HOW MUDWINGS FEEL? WORKING IN TEAMS ALL THE TIME? MY PARENTS SAID IT MADE THEM WEAK, BUT THEY WERE FORMIDABLE OPPONENTS DURING THE WAR.
MAYBE ALLIES AREN'T SO BAD. DOES THAT MAKE ME LESS OF AN ICEWING?
I DON'T LIKE IT HERE. IT FEELS LIKE WE'RE BEING WATCHED. AS IF THE MOUNTAINS THEMSELVES ARE WATCHING US.
AND THE RIVERS ARE WHISPERING ABOUT US.
SMACK!
OW!
KINKAJOU, I WAS AGREEING WITH YOU!
OH. WELL, TRY TO SOUND LESS SARCASTIC NEXT TIME!
THERE'S SOMETHING OVER THERE.

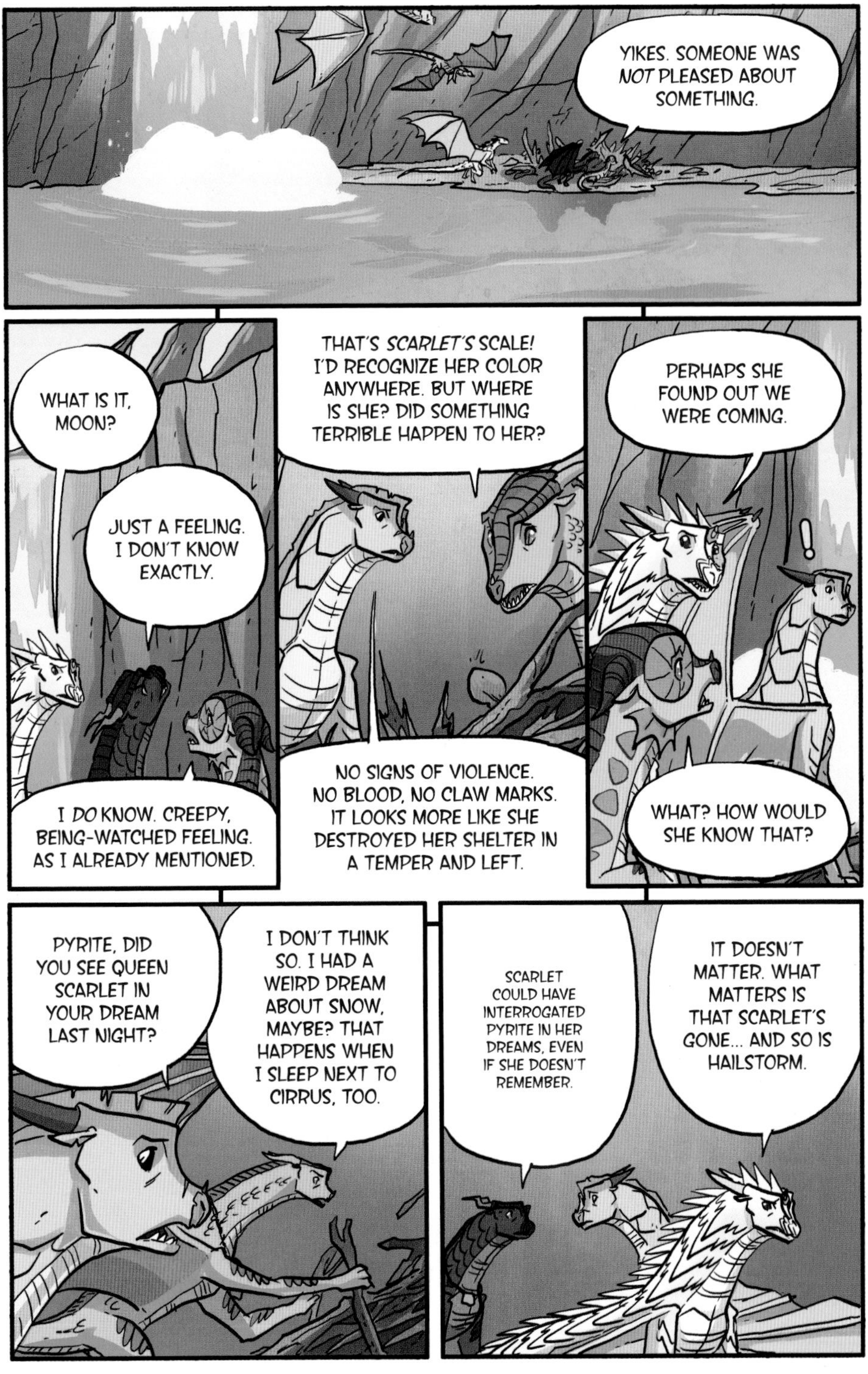
YIKES. SOMEONE WAS *NOT* PLEASED ABOUT SOMETHING.
WHAT IS IT, MOON?
JUST A FEELING. I DON'T KNOW EXACTLY.
I *DO* KNOW. CREEPY, BEING-WATCHED FEELING. AS I ALREADY MENTIONED.
THAT'S *SCARLET'S* SCALE! I'D RECOGNIZE HER COLOR ANYWHERE. BUT WHERE IS SHE? DID SOMETHING TERRIBLE HAPPEN TO HER?
NO SIGNS OF VIOLENCE. NO BLOOD, NO CLAW MARKS. IT LOOKS MORE LIKE SHE DESTROYED HER SHELTER IN A TEMPER AND LEFT.
PERHAPS SHE FOUND OUT WE WERE COMING.
!
WHAT? HOW WOULD SHE KNOW THAT?
PYRITE, DID YOU SEE QUEEN SCARLET IN YOUR DREAM LAST NIGHT?
I DON'T THINK SO. I HAD A WEIRD DREAM ABOUT SNOW, MAYBE? THAT HAPPENS WHEN I SLEEP NEXT TO CIRRUS, TOO.
SCARLET COULD HAVE INTERROGATED PYRITE IN HER DREAMS, EVEN IF SHE DOESN'T REMEMBER.
IT DOESN'T MATTER. WHAT MATTERS IS THAT SCARLET'S GONE... AND SO IS HAILSTORM.

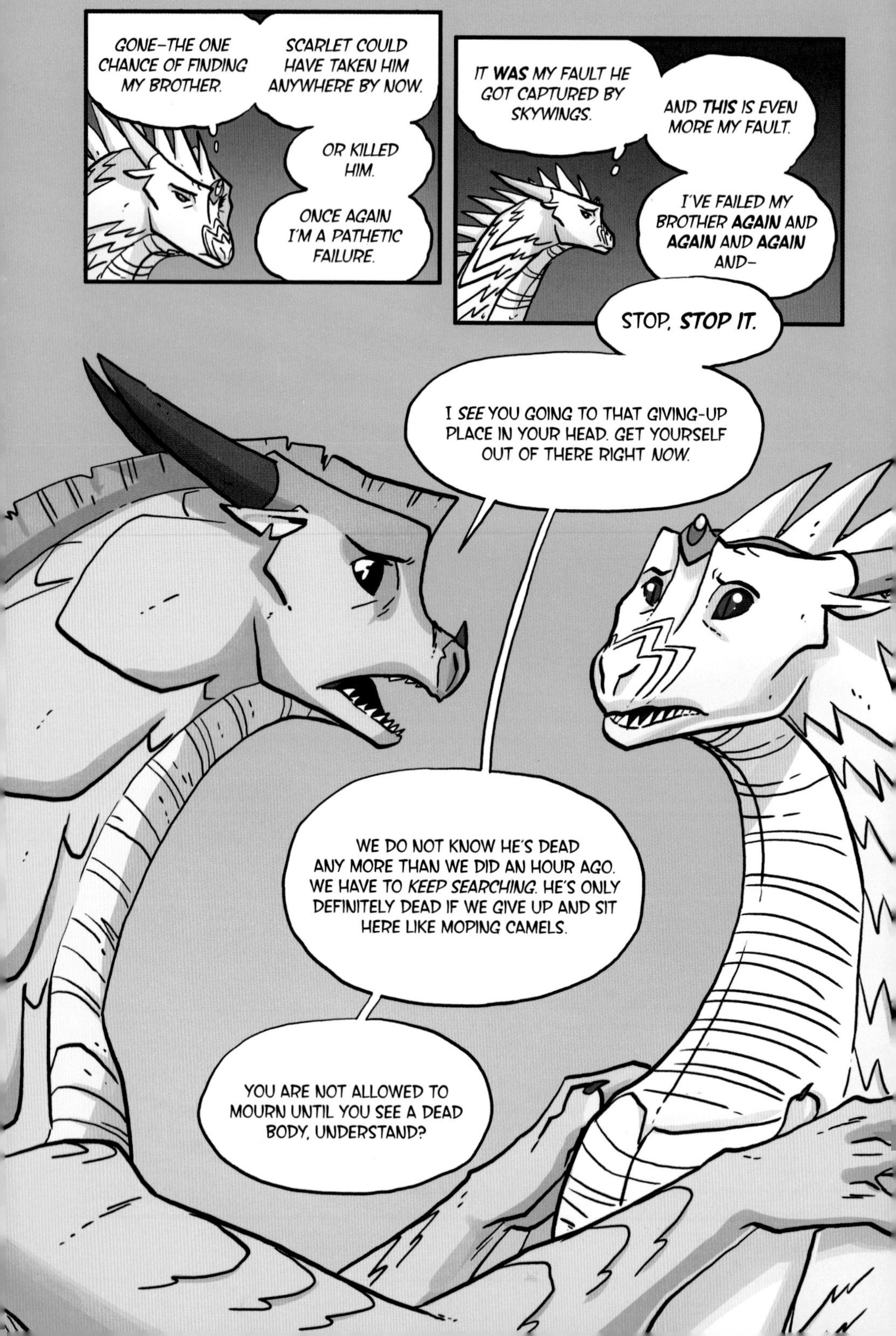
GONE—THE ONE CHANCE OF FINDING MY BROTHER.
SCARLET COULD HAVE TAKEN HIM ANYWHERE BY NOW.
OR KILLED HIM.
ONCE AGAIN I'M A PATHETIC FAILURE.
IT WAS MY FAULT HE GOT CAPTURED BY SKYWINGS.
AND THIS IS EVEN MORE MY FAULT.
I'VE FAILED MY BROTHER AGAIN AND AGAIN AND AGAIN AND—
STOP, STOP IT.
I SEE YOU GOING TO THAT GIVING-UP PLACE IN YOUR HEAD. GET YOURSELF OUT OF THERE RIGHT NOW.
WE DO NOT KNOW HE'S DEAD ANY MORE THAN WE DID AN HOUR AGO. WE HAVE TO KEEP SEARCHING. HE'S ONLY DEFINITELY DEAD IF WE GIVE UP AND SIT HERE LIKE MOPING CAMELS.
YOU ARE NOT ALLOWED TO MOURN UNTIL YOU SEE A DEAD BODY, UNDERSTAND?

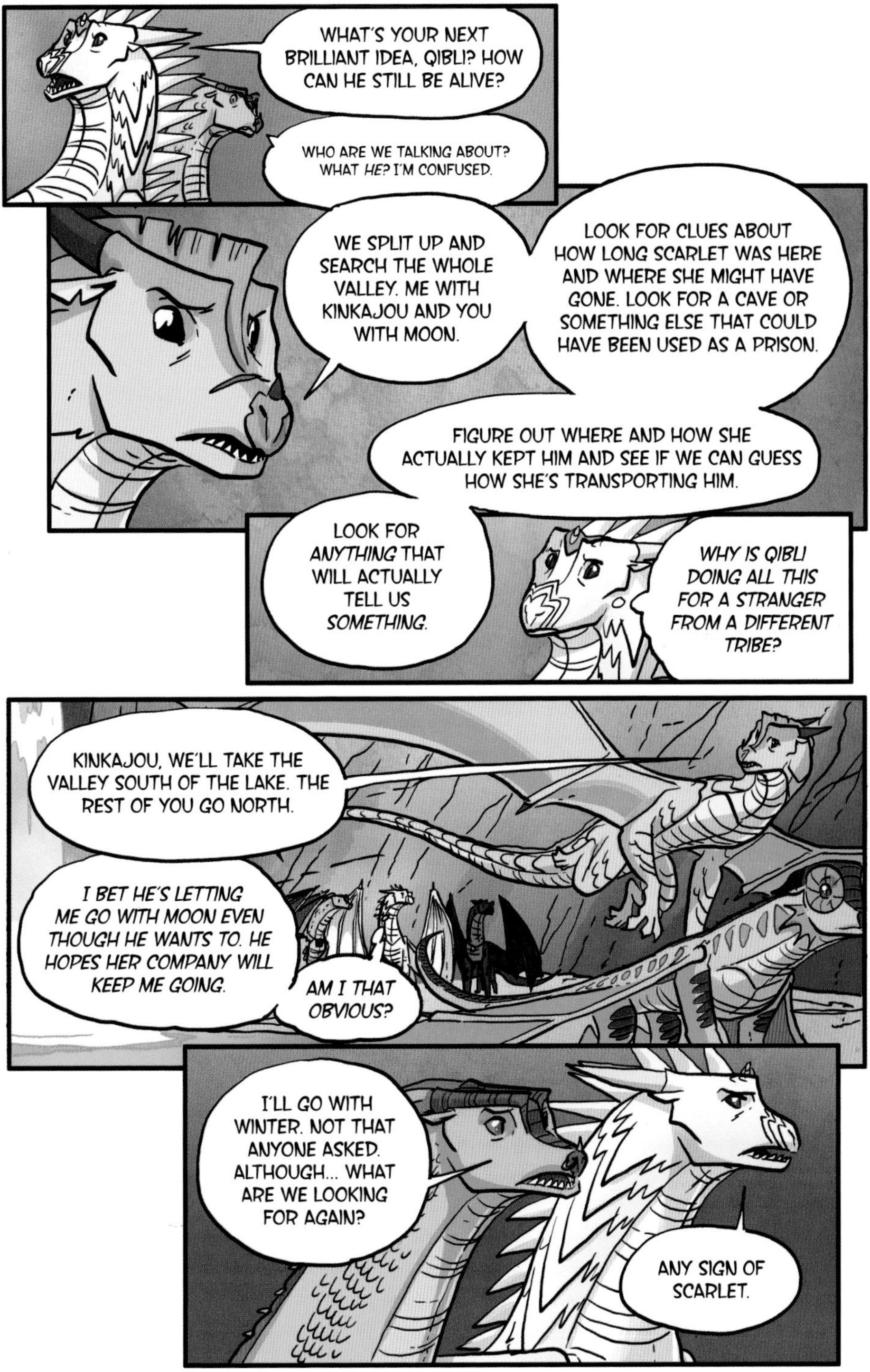
WHAT'S YOUR NEXT BRILLIANT IDEA, QIBLI? HOW CAN HE STILL BE ALIVE?
WHO ARE WE TALKING ABOUT? WHAT *HE*? I'M CONFUSED.
WE SPLIT UP AND SEARCH THE WHOLE VALLEY. ME WITH KINKAJOU AND YOU WITH MOON.
LOOK FOR CLUES ABOUT HOW LONG SCARLET WAS HERE AND WHERE SHE MIGHT HAVE GONE. LOOK FOR A CAVE OR SOMETHING ELSE THAT COULD HAVE BEEN USED AS A PRISON.
FIGURE OUT WHERE AND HOW SHE ACTUALLY KEPT HIM AND SEE IF WE CAN GUESS HOW SHE'S TRANSPORTING HIM.
LOOK FOR *ANYTHING* THAT WILL ACTUALLY TELL US *SOMETHING.*
WHY IS QIBLI DOING ALL THIS FOR A STRANGER FROM A DIFFERENT TRIBE?
KINKAJOU, WE'LL TAKE THE VALLEY SOUTH OF THE LAKE. THE REST OF YOU GO NORTH.
I BET HE'S LETTING ME GO WITH MOON EVEN THOUGH HE WANTS TO. HE HOPES HER COMPANY WILL KEEP ME GOING.
AM I THAT OBVIOUS?
I'LL GO WITH WINTER. NOT THAT ANYONE ASKED. ALTHOUGH... WHAT ARE WE LOOKING FOR AGAIN?
ANY SIGN OF SCARLET.

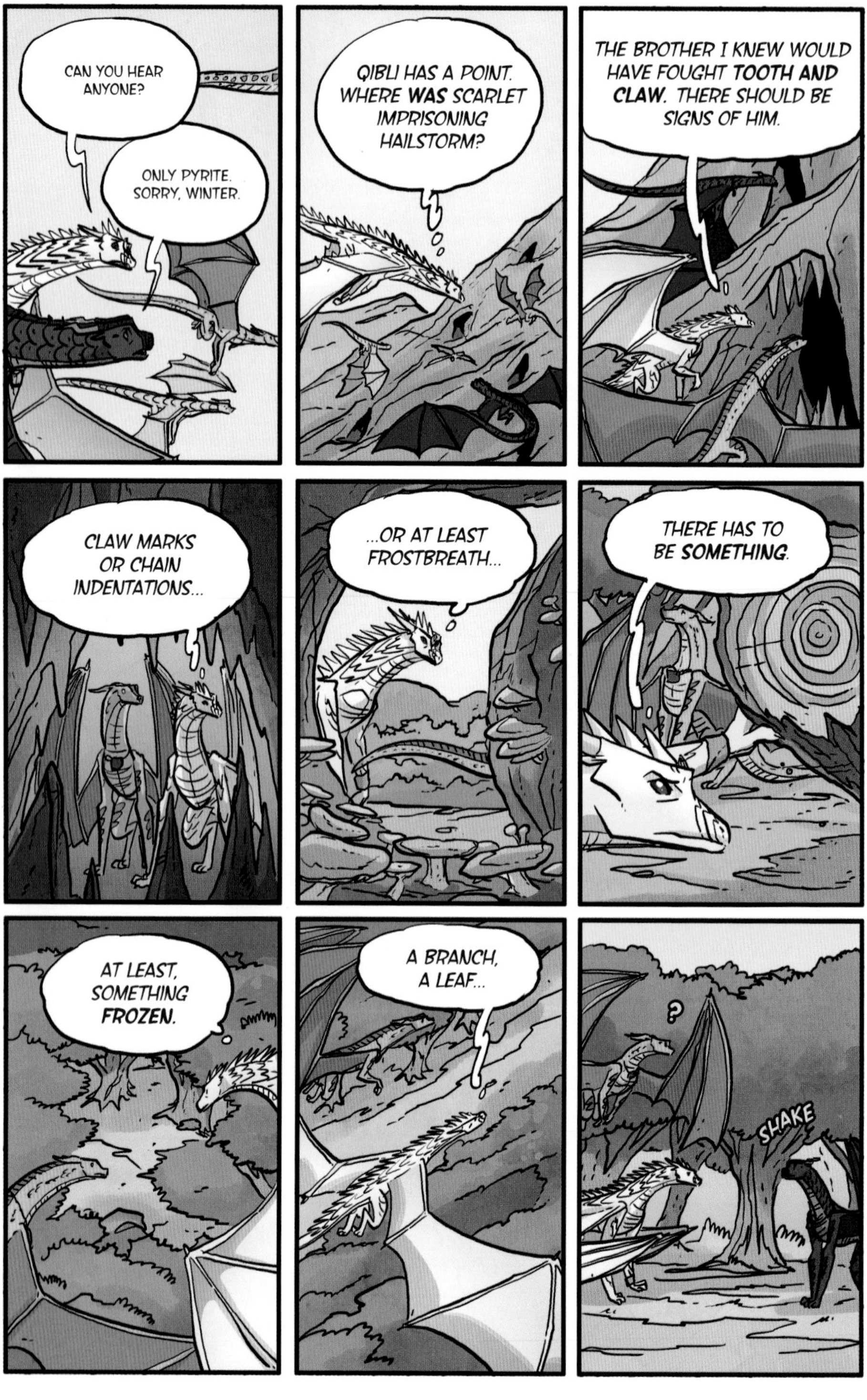
CAN YOU HEAR ANYONE?
ONLY PYRITE. SORRY, WINTER.
QIBLI HAS A POINT. WHERE WAS SCARLET IMPRISONING HAILSTORM?
THE BROTHER I KNEW WOULD HAVE FOUGHT TOOTH AND CLAW. THERE SHOULD BE SIGNS OF HIM.
CLAW MARKS OR CHAIN INDENTATIONS...
...OR AT LEAST FROSTBREATH...
THERE HAS TO BE SOMETHING.
AT LEAST, SOMETHING FROZEN.
A BRANCH, A LEAF...
?
SHAKE

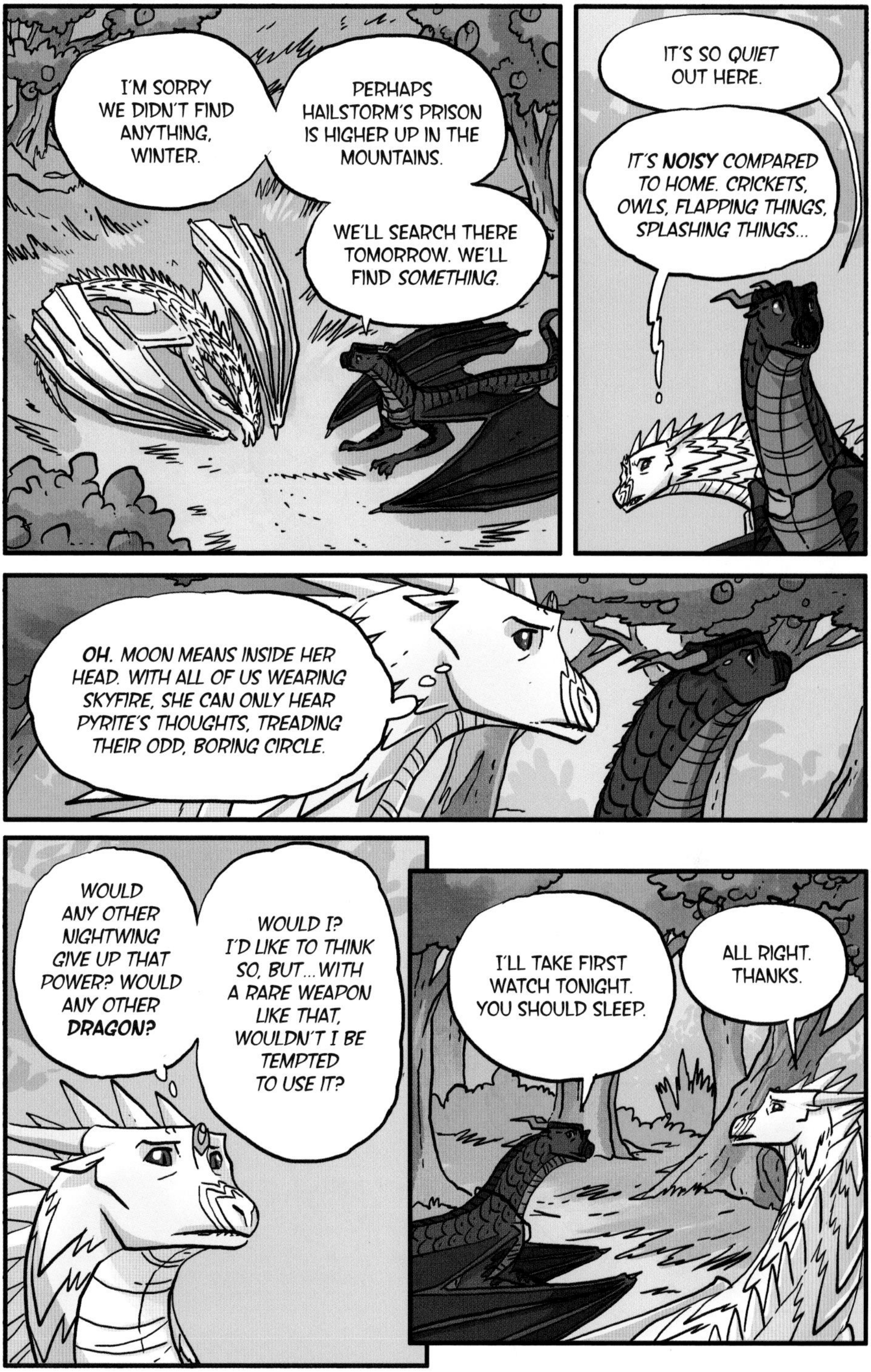
I'M SORRY WE DIDN'T FIND ANYTHING, WINTER.
PERHAPS HAILSTORM'S PRISON IS HIGHER UP IN THE MOUNTAINS.
WE'LL SEARCH THERE TOMORROW. WE'LL FIND *SOMETHING.*
IT'S SO *QUIET* OUT HERE.
IT'S **NOISY** *COMPARED TO HOME. CRICKETS, OWLS, FLAPPING THINGS, SPLASHING THINGS...*
OH. *MOON MEANS INSIDE HER HEAD. WITH ALL OF US WEARING SKYFIRE, SHE CAN ONLY HEAR PYRITE'S THOUGHTS, TREADING THEIR ODD, BORING CIRCLE.*
WOULD ANY OTHER NIGHTWING GIVE UP THAT POWER? WOULD ANY OTHER ***DRAGON?***
WOULD I? I'D LIKE TO THINK SO, BUT...WITH A RARE WEAPON LIKE THAT, WOULDN'T I BE TEMPTED TO USE IT?
I'LL TAKE FIRST WATCH TONIGHT. YOU SHOULD SLEEP.
ALL RIGHT. THANKS.

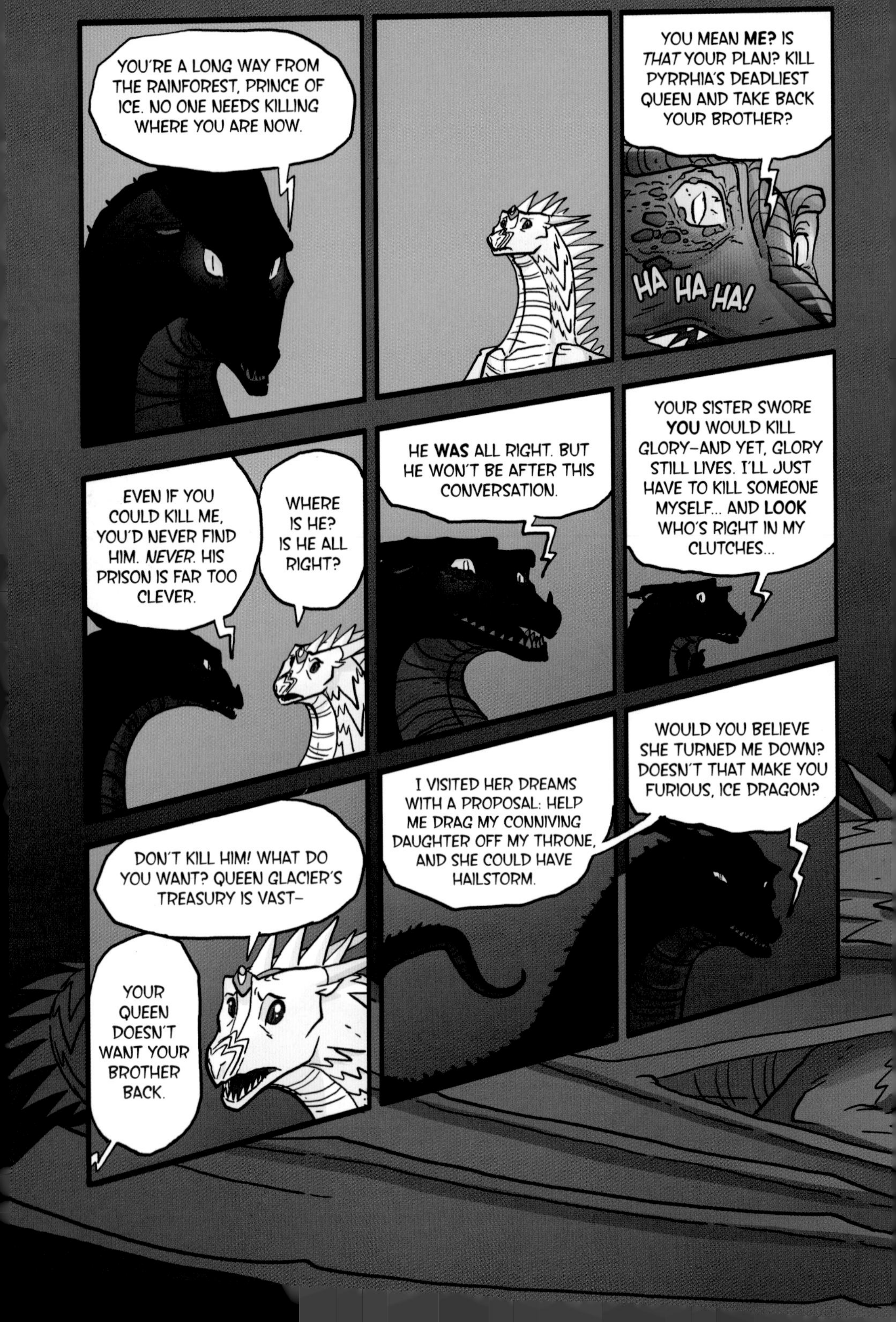
YOU'RE A LONG WAY FROM THE RAINFOREST, PRINCE OF ICE. NO ONE NEEDS KILLING WHERE YOU ARE NOW.
YOU MEAN ME? IS THAT YOUR PLAN? KILL PYRRHIA'S DEADLIEST QUEEN AND TAKE BACK YOUR BROTHER?
HA HA HA!
EVEN IF YOU COULD KILL ME, YOU'D NEVER FIND HIM. NEVER. HIS PRISON IS FAR TOO CLEVER.
WHERE IS HE? IS HE ALL RIGHT?
HE WAS ALL RIGHT. BUT HE WON'T BE AFTER THIS CONVERSATION.
YOUR SISTER SWORE YOU WOULD KILL GLORY—AND YET, GLORY STILL LIVES. I'LL JUST HAVE TO KILL SOMEONE MYSELF... AND LOOK WHO'S RIGHT IN MY CLUTCHES...
DON'T KILL HIM! WHAT DO YOU WANT? QUEEN GLACIER'S TREASURY IS VAST—
YOUR QUEEN DOESN'T WANT YOUR BROTHER BACK.
I VISITED HER DREAMS WITH A PROPOSAL: HELP ME DRAG MY CONNIVING DAUGHTER OFF MY THRONE, AND SHE COULD HAVE HAILSTORM.
WOULD YOU BELIEVE SHE TURNED ME DOWN? DOESN'T THAT MAKE YOU FURIOUS, ICE DRAGON?

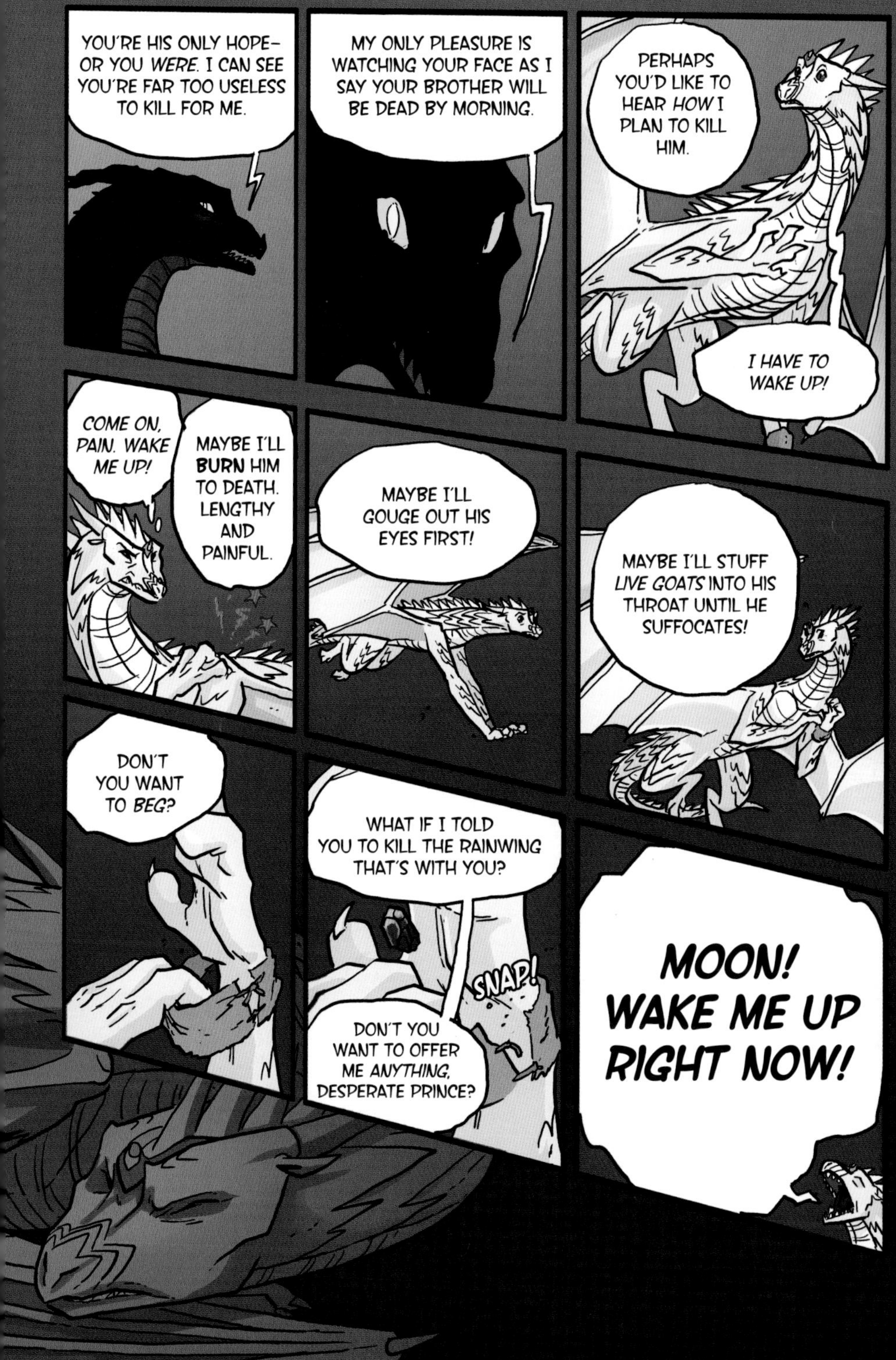
YOU'RE HIS ONLY HOPE— OR YOU *WERE*. I CAN SEE YOU'RE FAR TOO USELESS TO KILL FOR ME.
MY ONLY PLEASURE IS WATCHING YOUR FACE AS I SAY YOUR BROTHER WILL BE DEAD BY MORNING.
PERHAPS YOU'D LIKE TO HEAR *HOW* I PLAN TO KILL HIM.
I HAVE TO WAKE UP!
COME ON, PAIN. WAKE ME UP!
MAYBE I'LL **BURN** HIM TO DEATH. LENGTHY AND PAINFUL.
MAYBE I'LL GOUGE OUT HIS EYES FIRST!
MAYBE I'LL STUFF *LIVE GOATS* INTO HIS THROAT UNTIL HE SUFFOCATES!
DON'T YOU WANT TO *BEG?*
WHAT IF I TOLD YOU TO KILL THE RAINWING THAT'S WITH YOU?
SNAP!
DON'T YOU WANT TO OFFER ME *ANYTHING*, DESPERATE PRINCE?
MOON! WAKE ME UP RIGHT NOW!

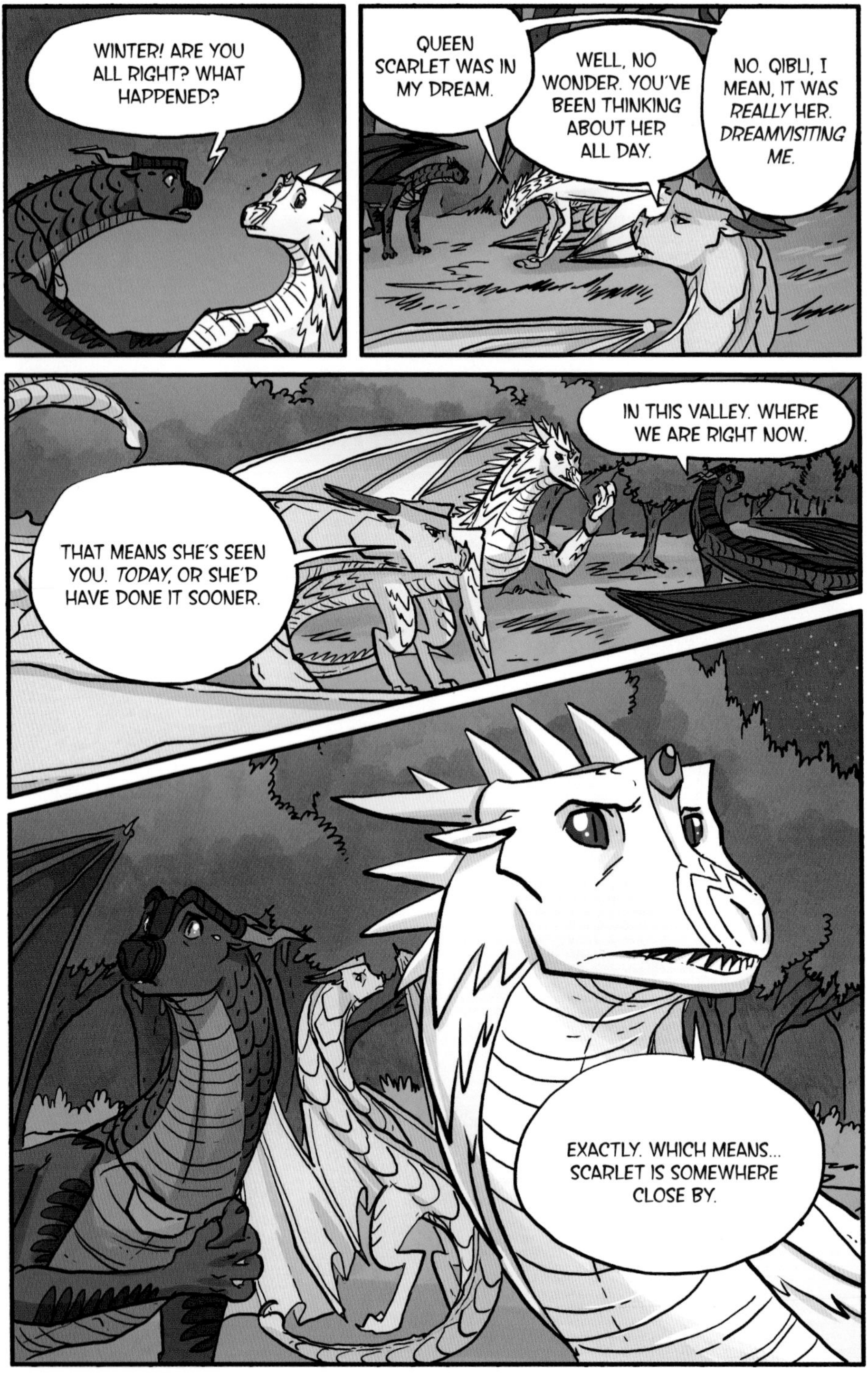
WINTER! ARE YOU ALL RIGHT? WHAT HAPPENED?
QUEEN SCARLET WAS IN MY DREAM.
WELL, NO WONDER. YOU'VE BEEN THINKING ABOUT HER ALL DAY.
NO. QIBLI, I MEAN, IT WAS *REALLY* HER. *DREAMVISITING* ME.
IN THIS VALLEY. WHERE WE ARE RIGHT NOW.
THAT MEANS SHE'S SEEN YOU. *TODAY*, OR SHE'D HAVE DONE IT SOONER.
EXACTLY. WHICH MEANS... SCARLET IS SOMEWHERE CLOSE BY.

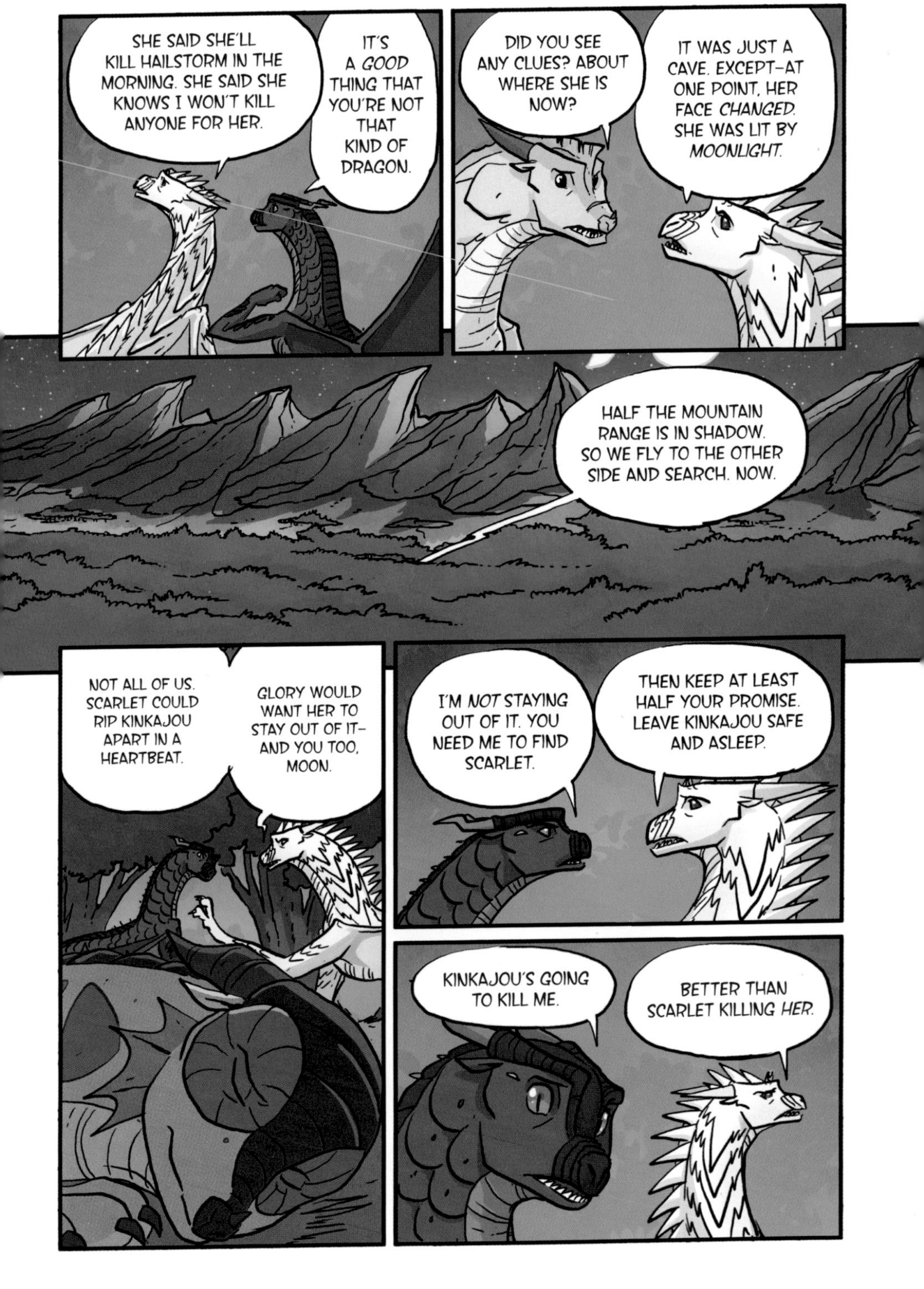
SHE SAID SHE'LL KILL HAILSTORM IN THE MORNING. SHE SAID SHE KNOWS I WON'T KILL ANYONE FOR HER.
IT'S A *GOOD* THING THAT YOU'RE NOT THAT KIND OF DRAGON.
DID YOU SEE ANY CLUES? ABOUT WHERE SHE IS NOW?
IT WAS JUST A CAVE. EXCEPT—AT ONE POINT, HER FACE *CHANGED*. SHE WAS LIT BY *MOONLIGHT*.
HALF THE MOUNTAIN RANGE IS IN SHADOW. SO WE FLY TO THE OTHER SIDE AND SEARCH. NOW.
NOT ALL OF US. SCARLET COULD RIP KINKAJOU APART IN A HEARTBEAT.
GLORY WOULD WANT HER TO STAY OUT OF IT—AND YOU TOO, MOON.
I'M *NOT* STAYING OUT OF IT. YOU NEED ME TO FIND SCARLET.
THEN KEEP AT LEAST HALF YOUR PROMISE. LEAVE KINKAJOU SAFE AND ASLEEP.
KINKAJOU'S GOING TO KILL ME.
BETTER THAN SCARLET KILLING *HER*.

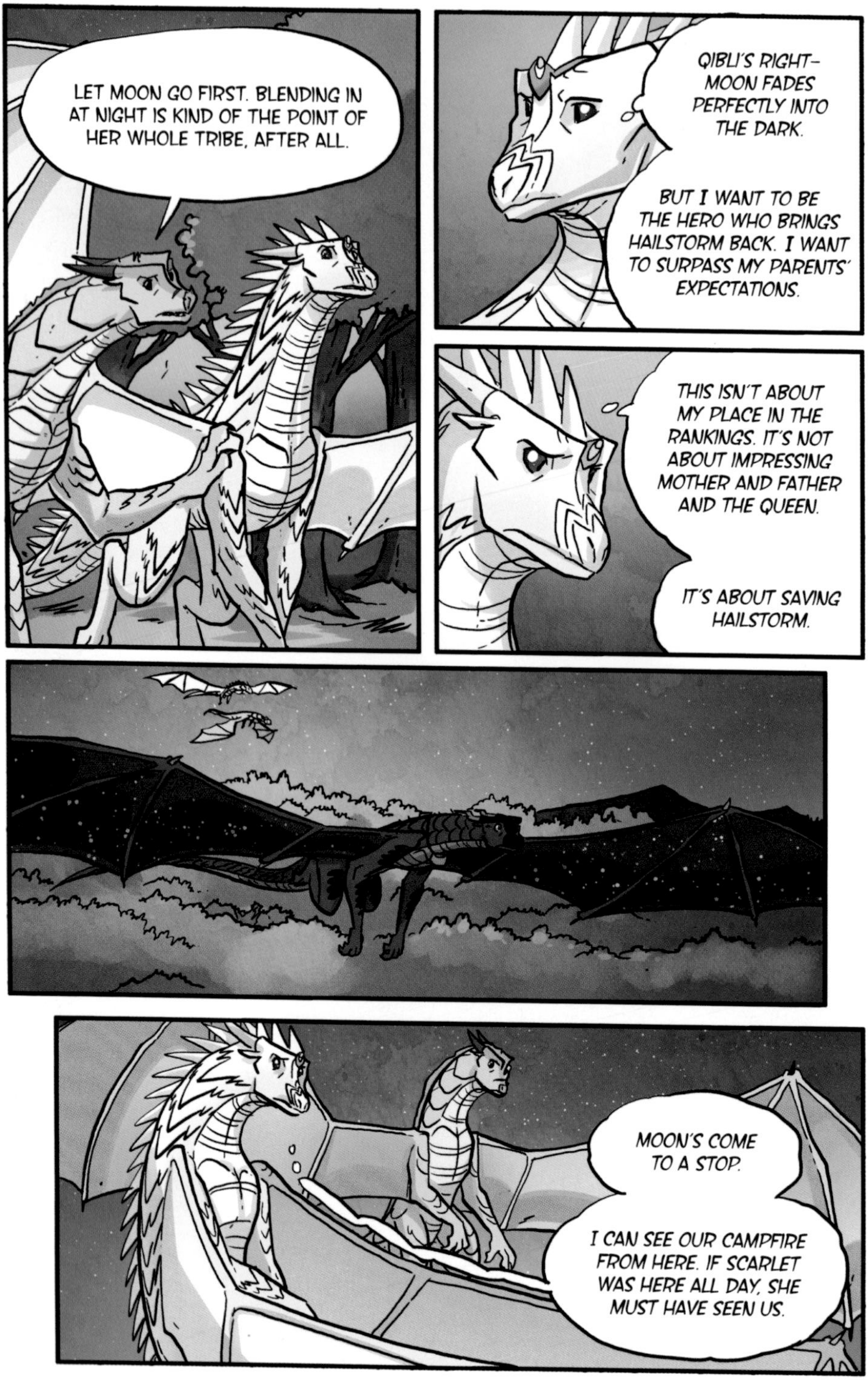
LET MOON GO FIRST. BLENDING IN AT NIGHT IS KIND OF THE POINT OF HER WHOLE TRIBE, AFTER ALL.
QIBLI'S RIGHT—MOON FADES PERFECTLY INTO THE DARK.
BUT I WANT TO BE THE HERO WHO BRINGS HAILSTORM BACK. I WANT TO SURPASS MY PARENTS' EXPECTATIONS.
THIS ISN'T ABOUT MY PLACE IN THE RANKINGS. IT'S NOT ABOUT IMPRESSING MOTHER AND FATHER AND THE QUEEN.
IT'S ABOUT SAVING HAILSTORM.
MOON'S COME TO A STOP.
I CAN SEE OUR CAMPFIRE FROM HERE. IF SCARLET WAS HERE ALL DAY, SHE MUST HAVE SEEN US.

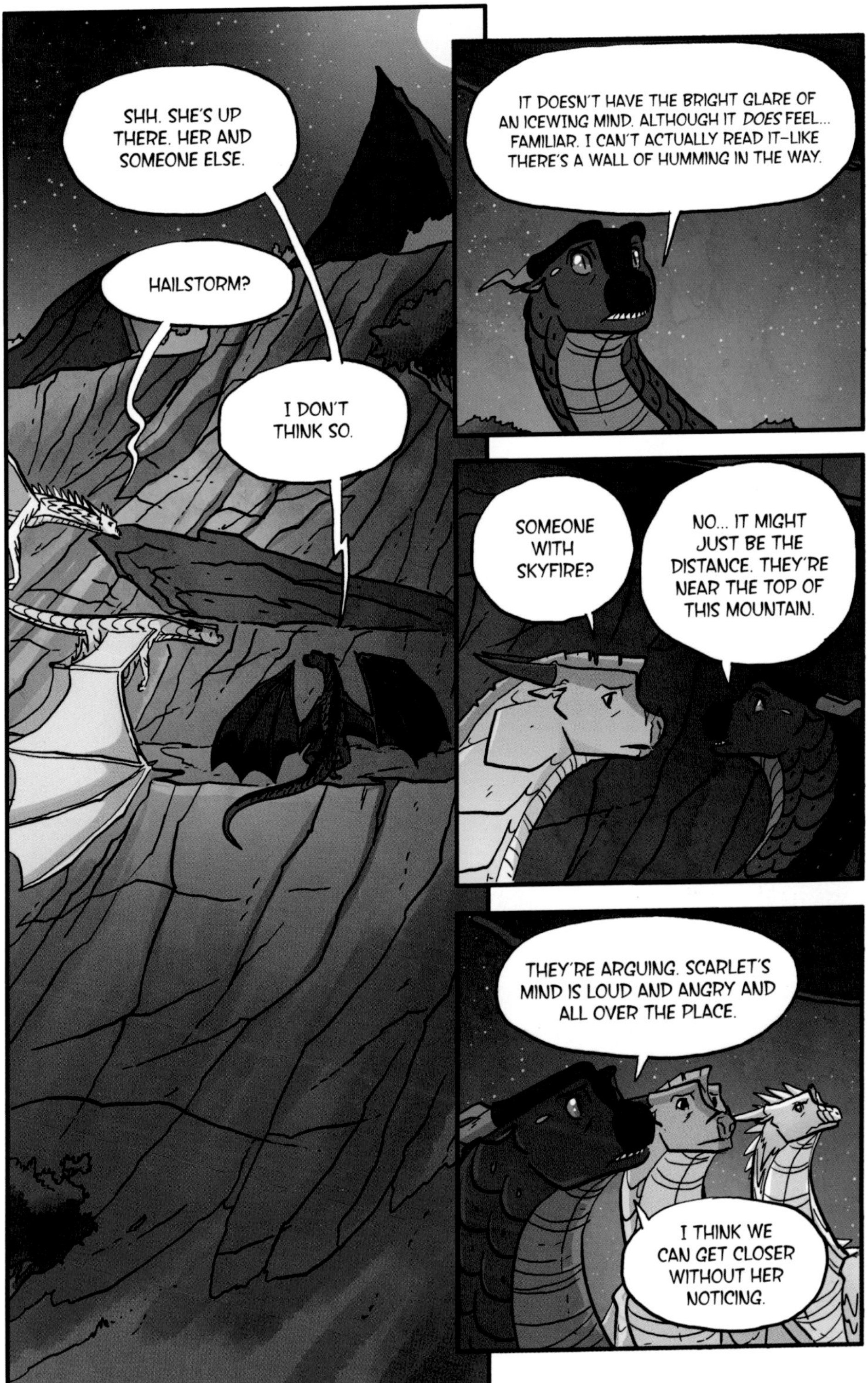
SHH. SHE'S UP THERE. HER AND SOMEONE ELSE.
HAILSTORM?
I DON'T THINK SO.
IT DOESN'T HAVE THE BRIGHT GLARE OF AN ICEWING MIND. ALTHOUGH IT *DOES* FEEL... FAMILIAR. I CAN'T ACTUALLY READ IT—LIKE THERE'S A WALL OF HUMMING IN THE WAY.
SOMEONE WITH SKYFIRE?
NO... IT MIGHT JUST BE THE DISTANCE. THEY'RE NEAR THE TOP OF THIS MOUNTAIN.
THEY'RE ARGUING. SCARLET'S MIND IS LOUD AND ANGRY AND ALL OVER THE PLACE.
I THINK WE CAN GET CLOSER WITHOUT HER NOTICING.

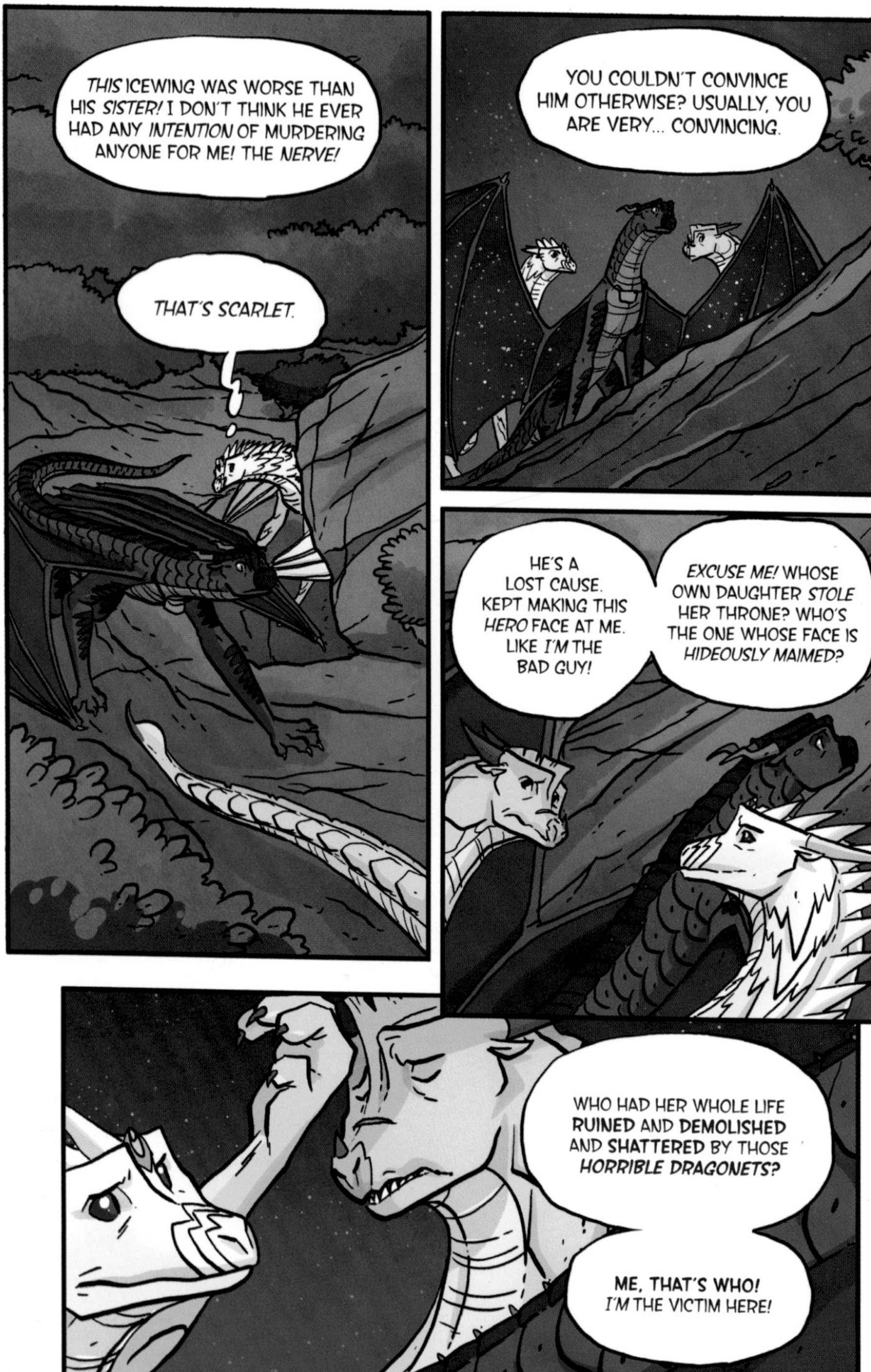

THIS ICEWING WAS WORSE THAN HIS SISTER! I DON'T THINK HE EVER HAD ANY INTENTION OF MURDERING ANYONE FOR ME! THE NERVE!
THAT'S SCARLET.
YOU COULDN'T CONVINCE HIM OTHERWISE? USUALLY, YOU ARE VERY... CONVINCING.
HE'S A LOST CAUSE. KEPT MAKING THIS HERO FACE AT ME. LIKE I'M THE BAD GUY!
EXCUSE ME! WHOSE OWN DAUGHTER STOLE HER THRONE? WHO'S THE ONE WHOSE FACE IS HIDEOUSLY MAIMED?
WHO HAD HER WHOLE LIFE RUINED AND DEMOLISHED AND SHATTERED BY THOSE HORRIBLE DRAGONETS?
ME, THAT'S WHO! I'M THE VICTIM HERE!

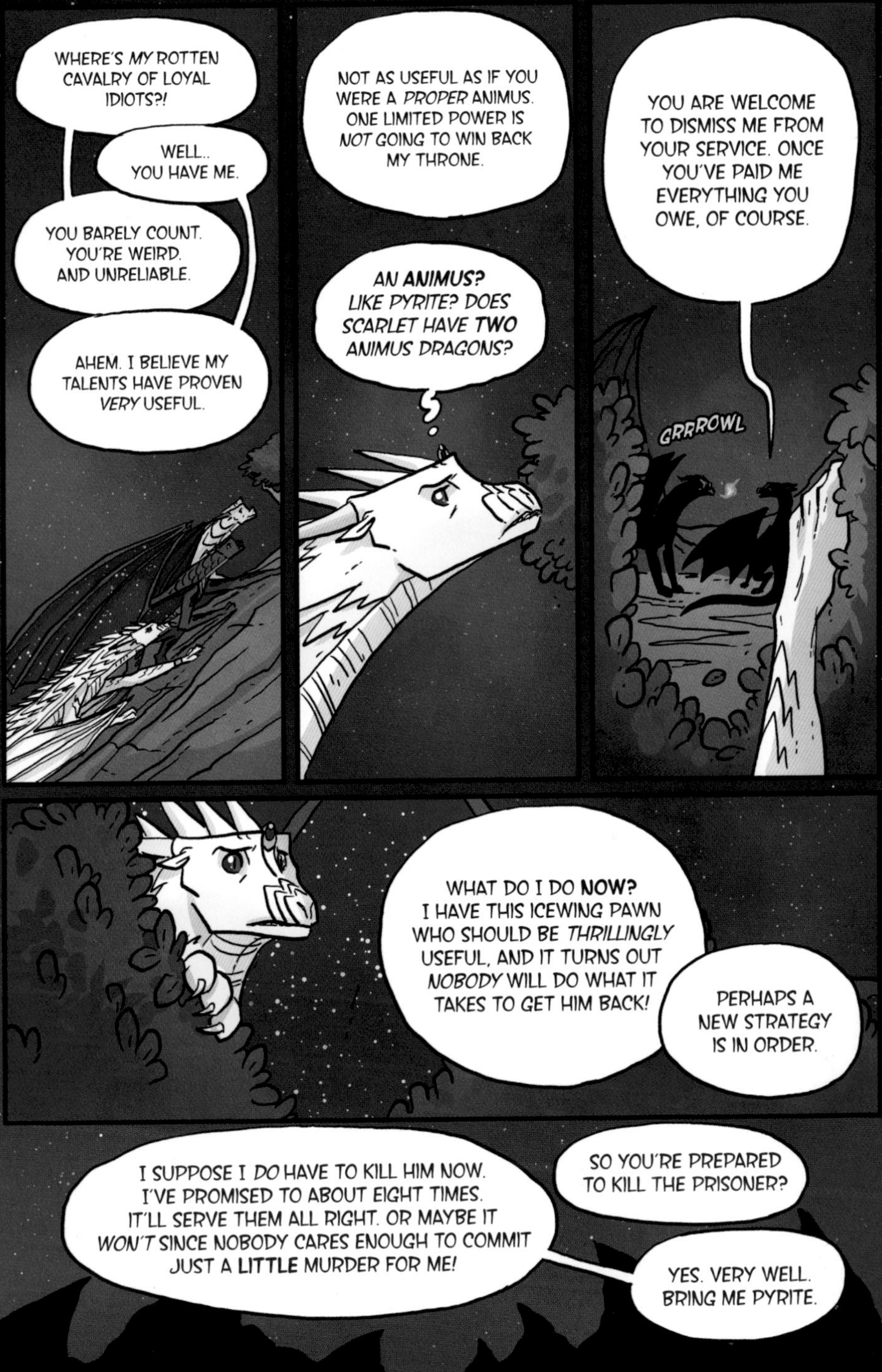
WHERE'S *MY* ROTTEN CAVALRY OF LOYAL IDIOTS?!
WELL.. YOU HAVE ME.
YOU BARELY COUNT. YOU'RE WEIRD. AND UNRELIABLE.
AHEM. I BELIEVE MY TALENTS HAVE PROVEN *VERY* USEFUL.
NOT AS USEFUL AS IF YOU WERE A *PROPER* ANIMUS. ONE LIMITED POWER IS *NOT* GOING TO WIN BACK MY THRONE.
AN **ANIMUS?** *LIKE PYRITE? DOES SCARLET HAVE* ***TWO*** *ANIMUS DRAGONS?*
YOU ARE WELCOME TO DISMISS ME FROM YOUR SERVICE. ONCE YOU'VE PAID ME EVERYTHING YOU OWE, OF COURSE.
GRRROWL
WHAT DO I DO **NOW?** I HAVE THIS ICEWING PAWN WHO SHOULD BE *THRILLINGLY* USEFUL, AND IT TURNS OUT *NOBODY* WILL DO WHAT IT TAKES TO GET HIM BACK!
PERHAPS A NEW STRATEGY IS IN ORDER.
I SUPPOSE I *DO* HAVE TO KILL HIM NOW. I'VE PROMISED TO ABOUT EIGHT TIMES. IT'LL SERVE THEM ALL RIGHT. OR MAYBE IT *WON'T* SINCE NOBODY CARES ENOUGH TO COMMIT JUST A **LITTLE** MURDER FOR ME!
SO YOU'RE PREPARED TO KILL THE PRISONER?
YES. VERY WELL. BRING ME PYRITE.

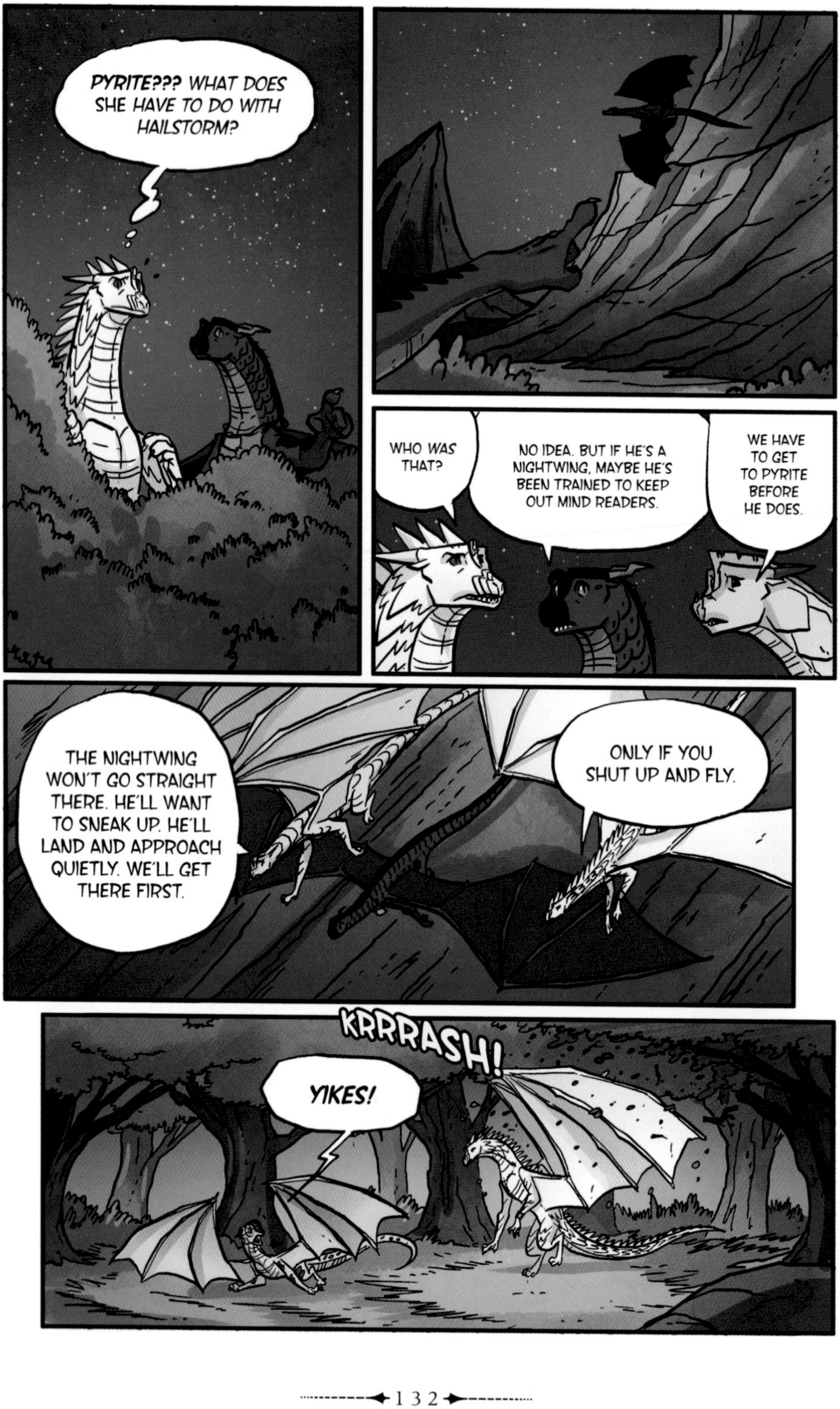
PYRITE??? WHAT DOES SHE HAVE TO DO WITH HAILSTORM?
WHO WAS THAT?
NO IDEA. BUT IF HE'S A NIGHTWING, MAYBE HE'S BEEN TRAINED TO KEEP OUT MIND READERS.
WE HAVE TO GET TO PYRITE BEFORE HE DOES.
THE NIGHTWING WON'T GO STRAIGHT THERE. HE'LL WANT TO SNEAK UP. HE'LL LAND AND APPROACH QUIETLY. WE'LL GET THERE FIRST.
ONLY IF YOU SHUT UP AND FLY.
KRRRASH!
YIKES!

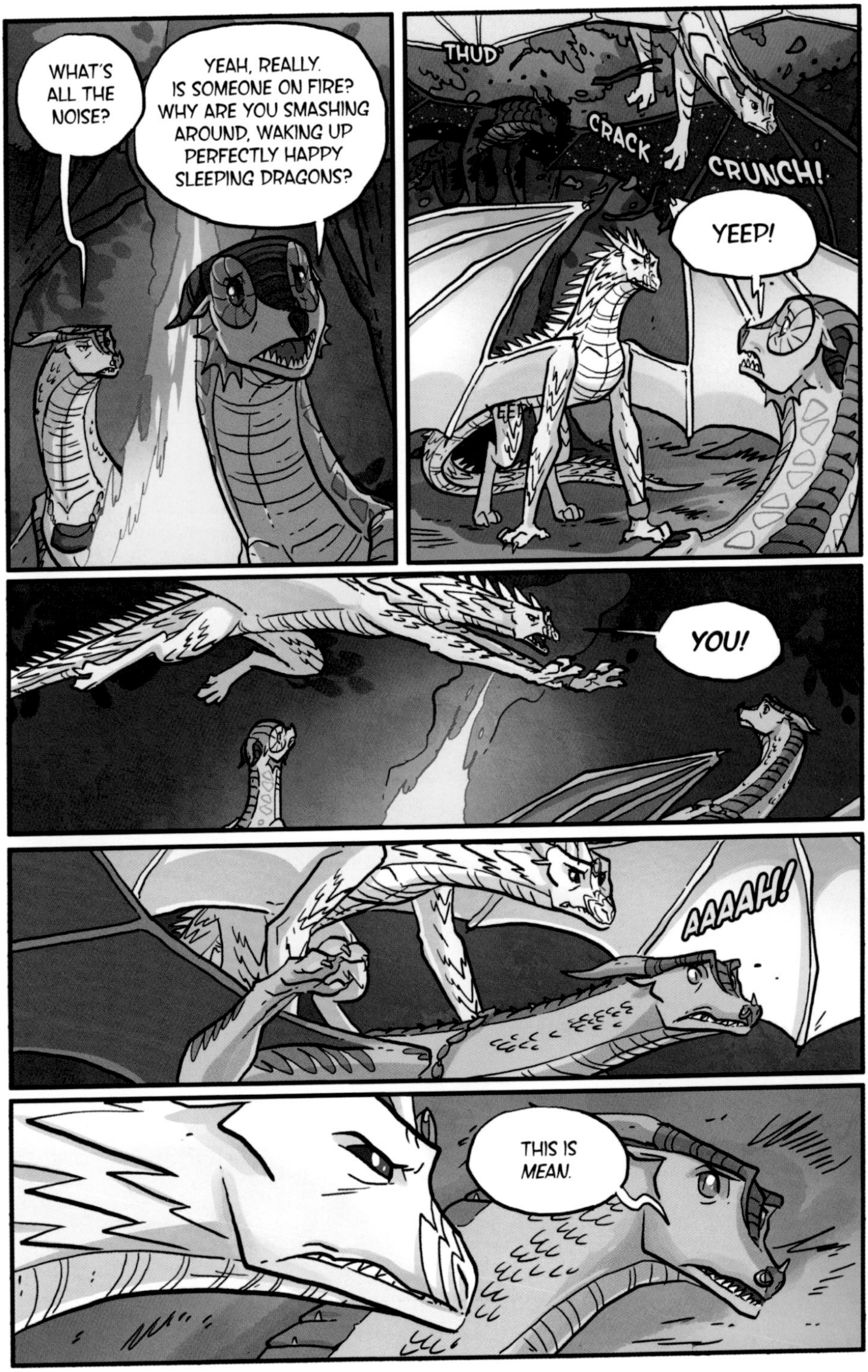
WHAT'S ALL THE NOISE?
YEAH, REALLY. IS SOMEONE ON FIRE? WHY ARE YOU SMASHING AROUND, WAKING UP PERFECTLY HAPPY SLEEPING DRAGONS?
THUD
CRACK
CRUNCH!
YEEP!
YOU!
AAAAH!
THIS IS MEAN.

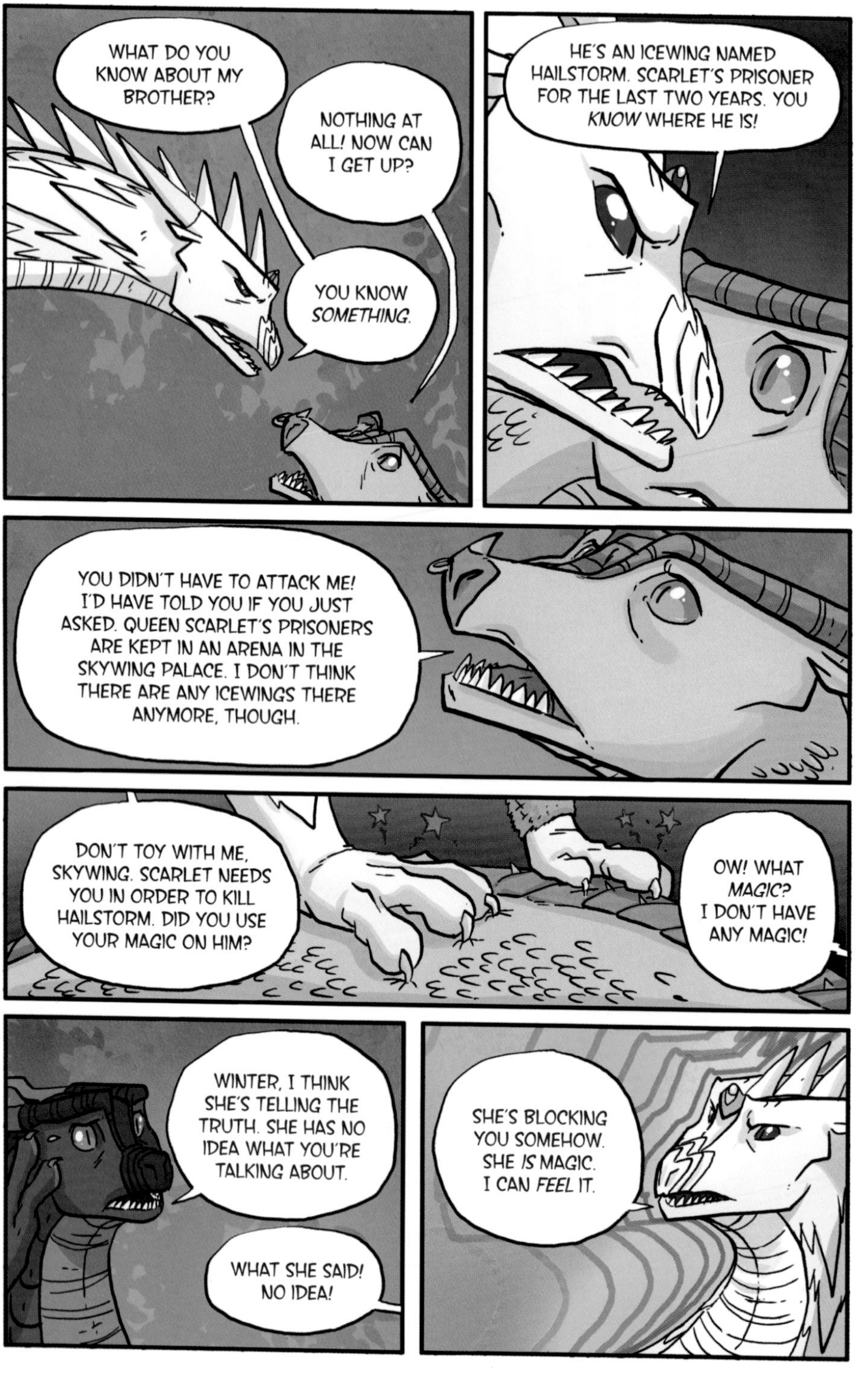
WHAT DO YOU KNOW ABOUT MY BROTHER?
NOTHING AT ALL! NOW CAN I GET UP?
YOU KNOW *SOMETHING.*
HE'S AN ICEWING NAMED HAILSTORM. SCARLET'S PRISONER FOR THE LAST TWO YEARS. YOU *KNOW* WHERE HE IS!
YOU DIDN'T HAVE TO ATTACK ME! I'D HAVE TOLD YOU IF YOU JUST ASKED. QUEEN SCARLET'S PRISONERS ARE KEPT IN AN ARENA IN THE SKYWING PALACE. I DON'T THINK THERE ARE ANY ICEWINGS THERE ANYMORE, THOUGH.
DON'T TOY WITH ME, SKYWING. SCARLET NEEDS YOU IN ORDER TO KILL HAILSTORM. DID YOU USE YOUR MAGIC ON HIM?
OW! WHAT *MAGIC?* I DON'T HAVE ANY MAGIC!
WINTER, I THINK SHE'S TELLING THE TRUTH. SHE HAS NO IDEA WHAT YOU'RE TALKING ABOUT.
WHAT SHE SAID! NO IDEA!
SHE'S BLOCKING YOU SOMEHOW. SHE *IS* MAGIC. I CAN *FEEL* IT.

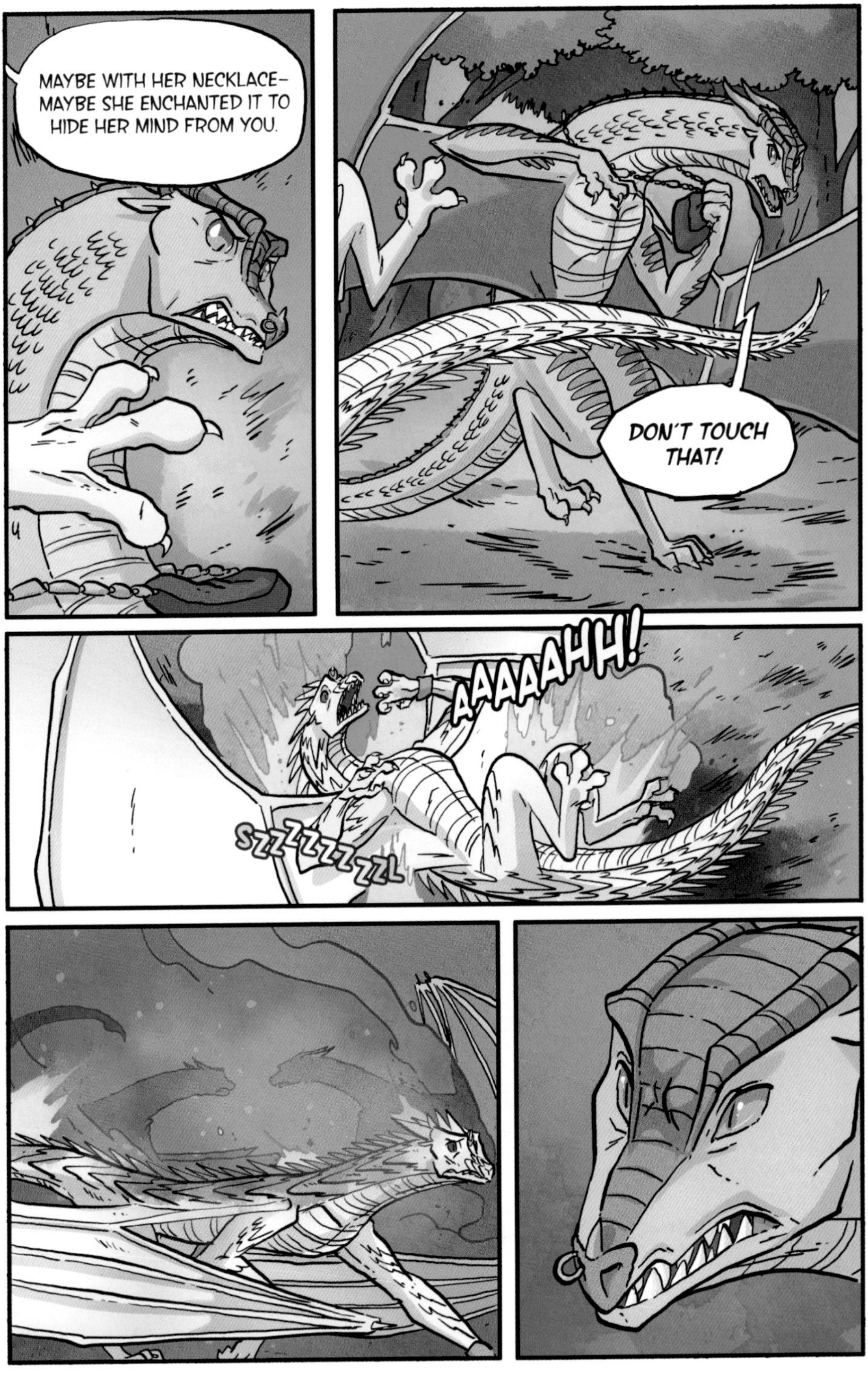
MAYBE WITH HER NECKLACE—MAYBE SHE ENCHANTED IT TO HIDE HER MIND FROM YOU.
DON'T TOUCH THAT!
AAAAAHH!
SSZZZZZZZL

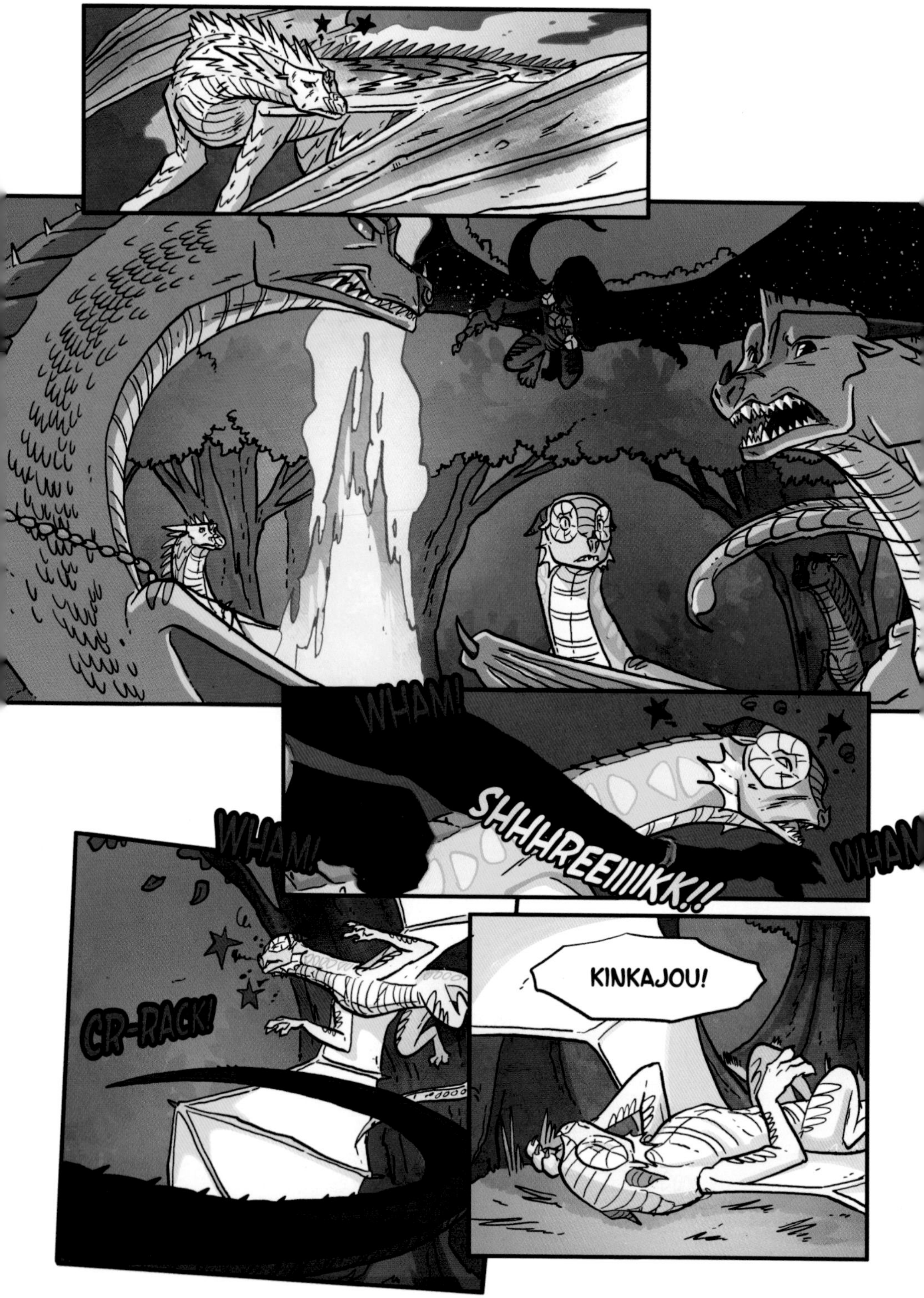
WHAM!
WHAM!
SHHHREEIIIIKK!!
WHAM
CR-RACK!
KINKAJOU!

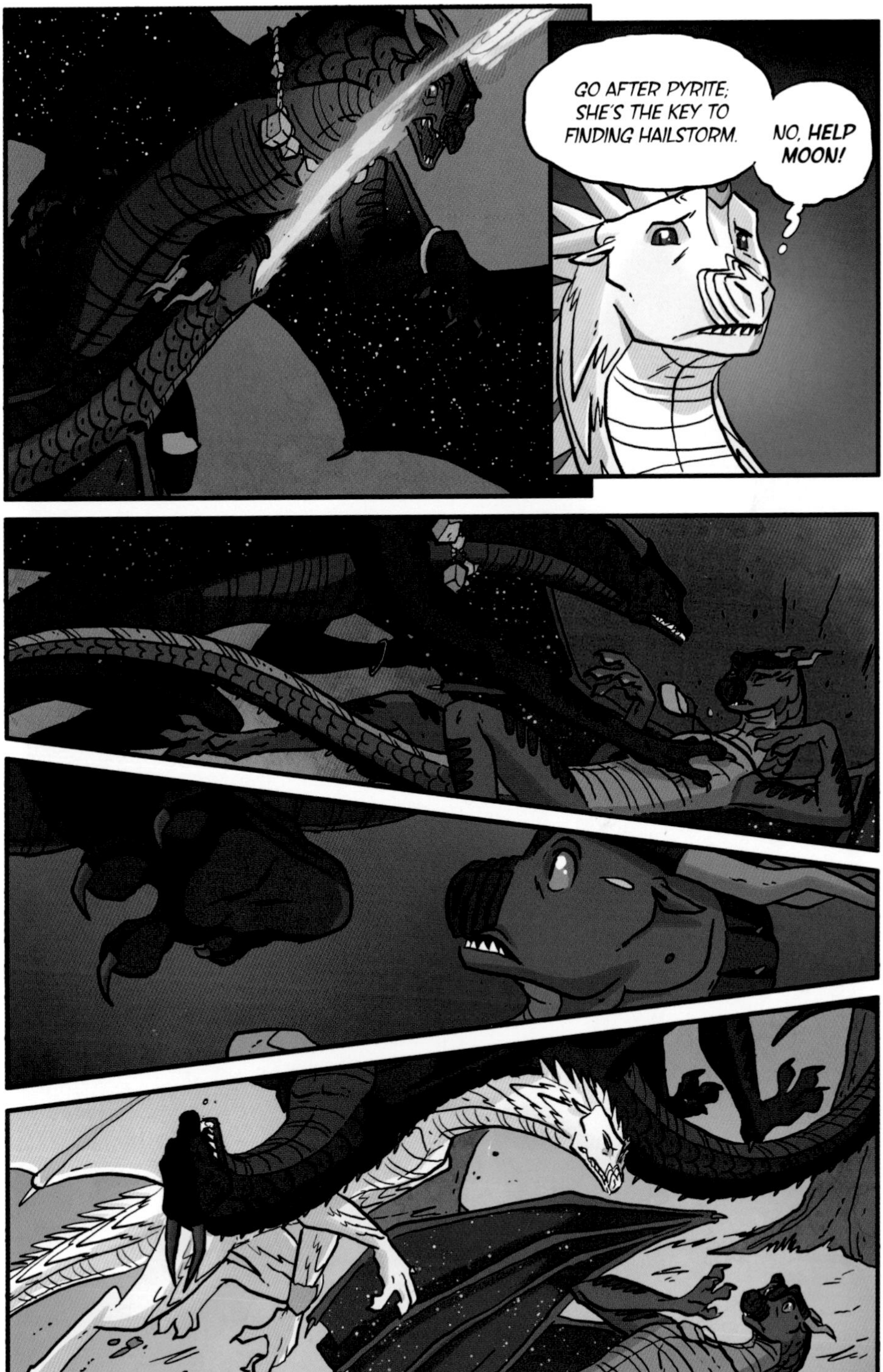
GO AFTER PYRITE; SHE'S THE KEY TO FINDING HAILSTORM.
NO, **HELP MOON!**

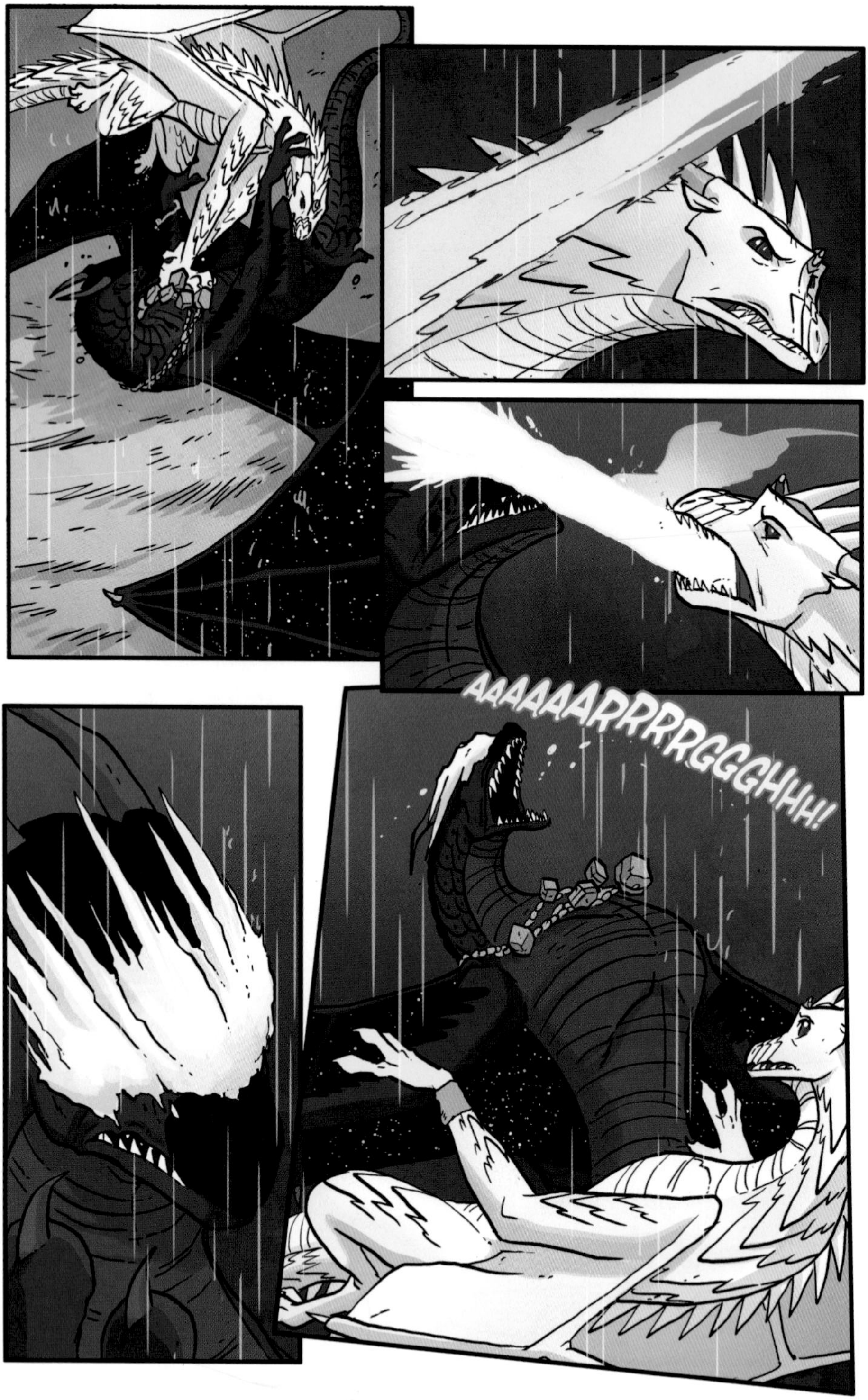
AAAAAARRRRRGGGGHHH!

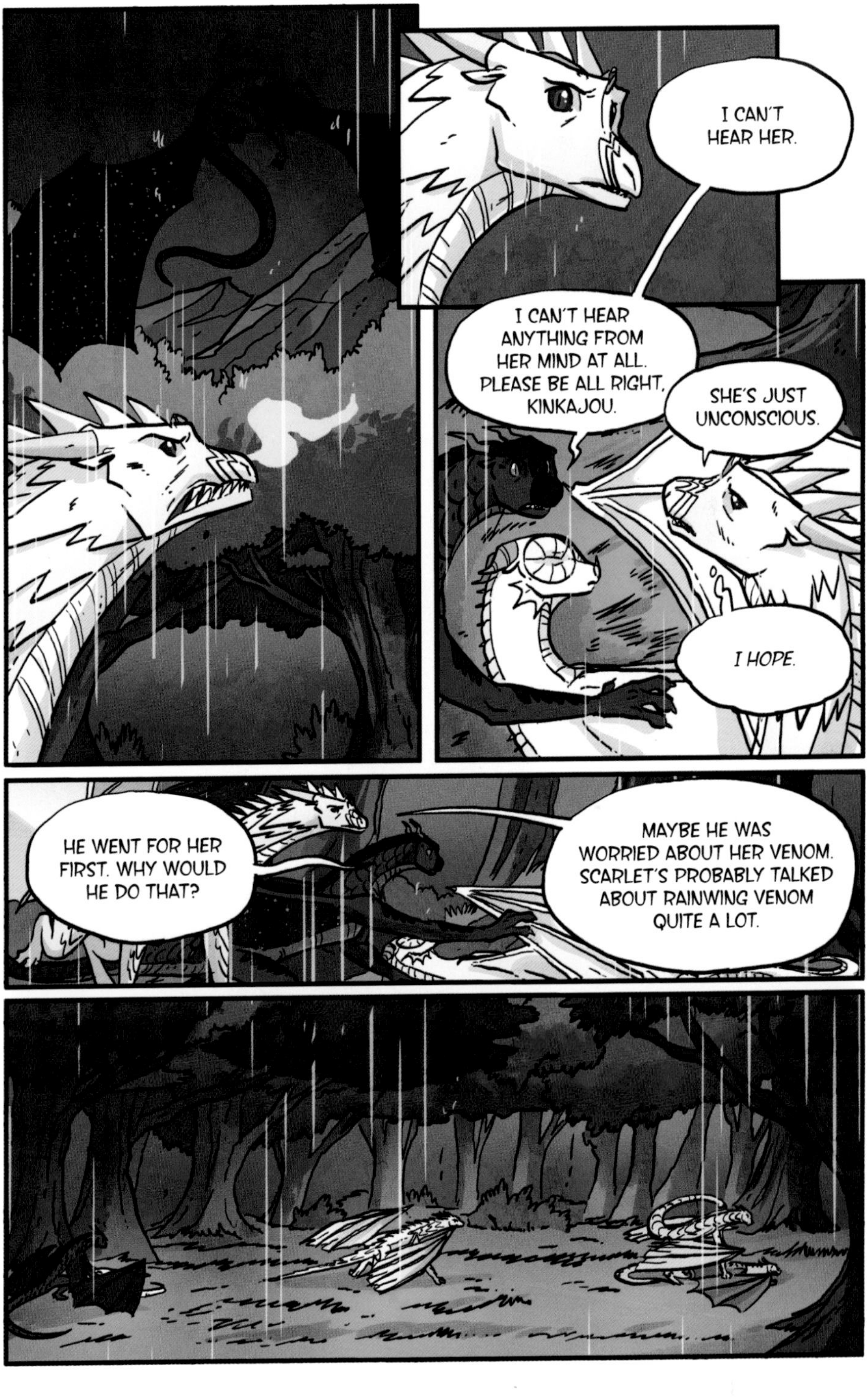
I CAN'T HEAR HER.
I CAN'T HEAR ANYTHING FROM HER MIND AT ALL. PLEASE BE ALL RIGHT, KINKAJOU.
SHE'S JUST UNCONSCIOUS.
I HOPE.
HE WENT FOR HER FIRST. WHY WOULD HE DO THAT?
MAYBE HE WAS WORRIED ABOUT HER VENOM. SCARLET'S PROBABLY TALKED ABOUT RAINWING VENOM QUITE A LOT.

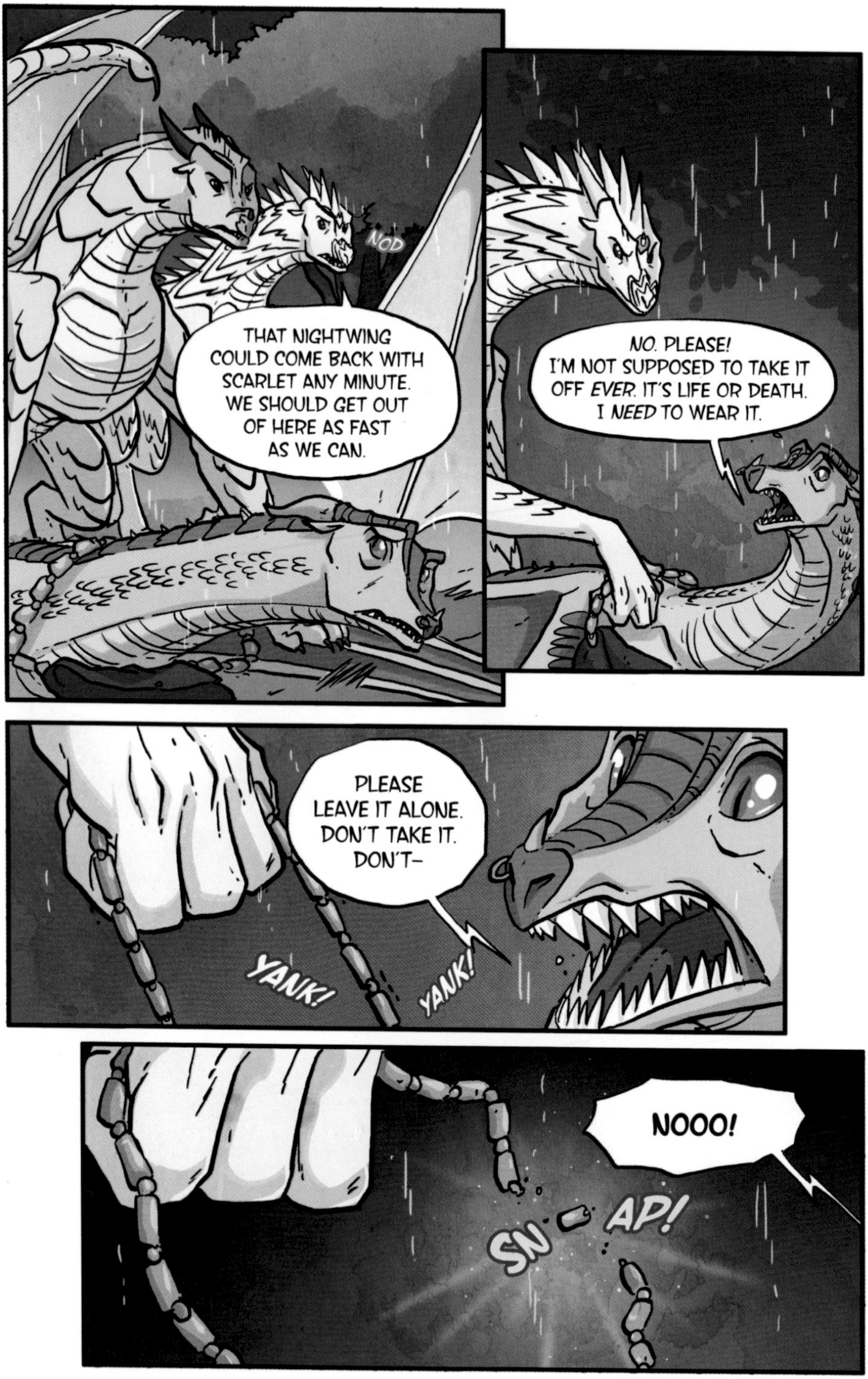
NOD
THAT NIGHTWING COULD COME BACK WITH SCARLET ANY MINUTE. WE SHOULD GET OUT OF HERE AS FAST AS WE CAN.
NO. PLEASE! I'M NOT SUPPOSED TO TAKE IT OFF EVER. IT'S LIFE OR DEATH. I NEED TO WEAR IT.
PLEASE LEAVE IT ALONE. DON'T TAKE IT. DON'T–
YANK!
YANK!
NOOO!
SN – AP!

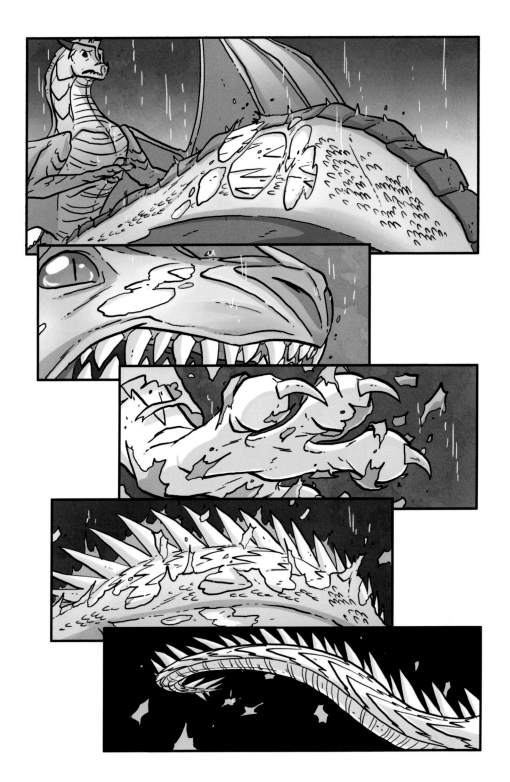

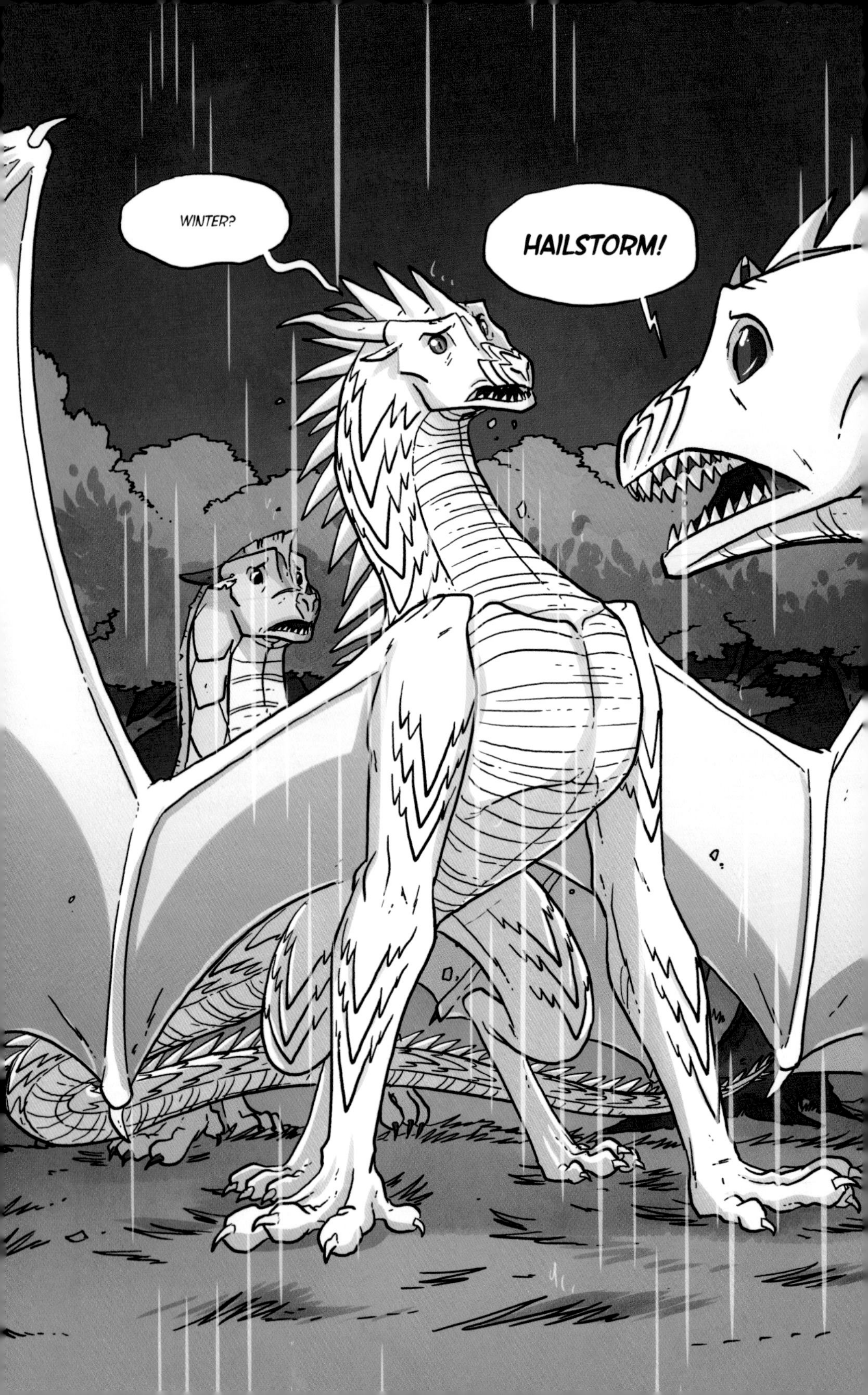
WINTER?
HAILSTORM!

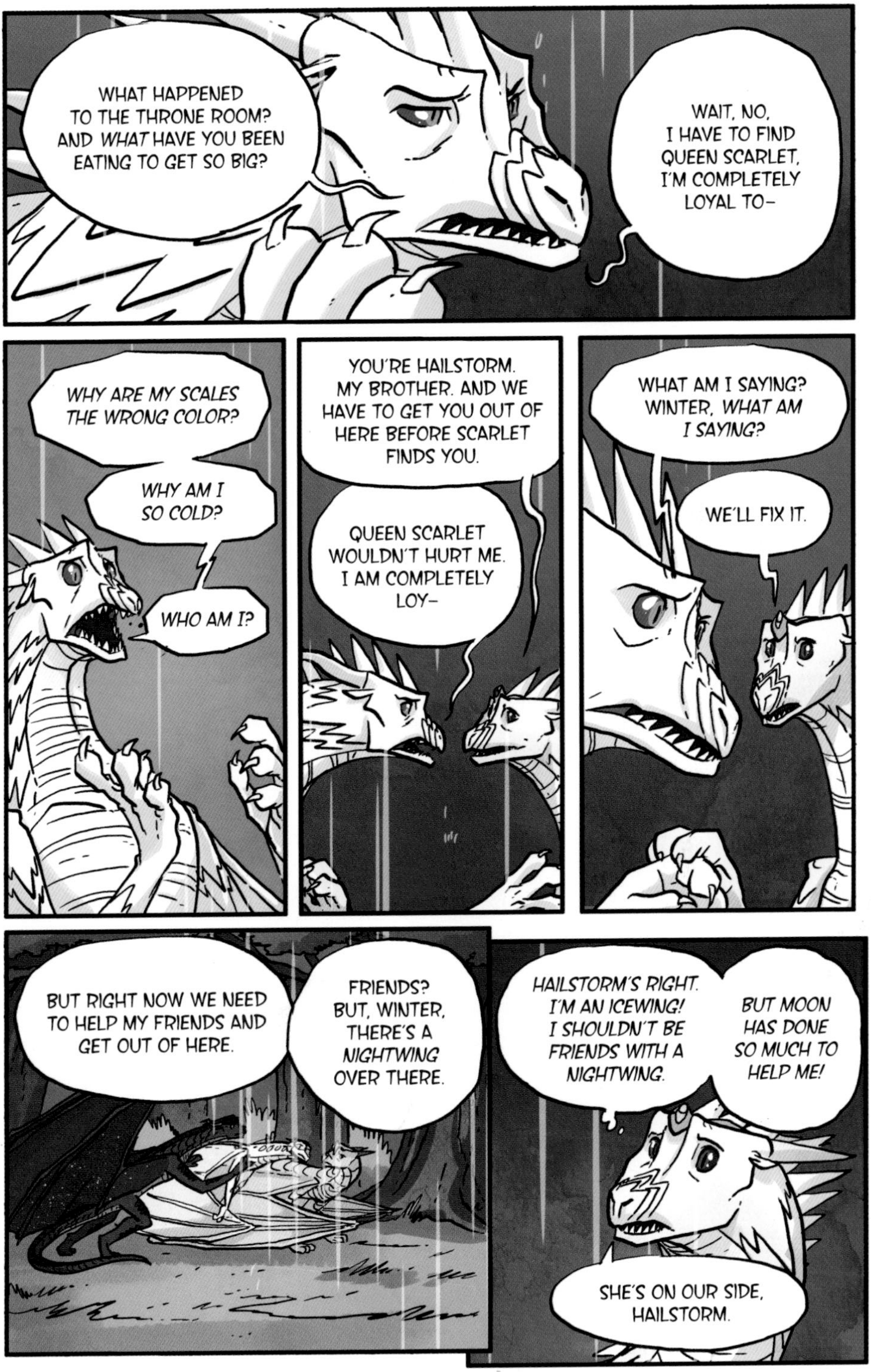
WHAT HAPPENED TO THE THRONE ROOM? AND *WHAT* HAVE YOU BEEN EATING TO GET SO BIG?
WAIT, NO, I HAVE TO FIND QUEEN SCARLET, I'M COMPLETELY LOYAL TO–
WHY ARE MY SCALES THE WRONG COLOR?
WHY AM I SO COLD?
WHO AM I?
YOU'RE HAILSTORM. MY BROTHER. AND WE HAVE TO GET YOU OUT OF HERE BEFORE SCARLET FINDS YOU.
QUEEN SCARLET WOULDN'T HURT ME. I AM COMPLETELY LOY–
WHAT AM I SAYING? WINTER, *WHAT AM I SAYING?*
WE'LL FIX IT.
BUT RIGHT NOW WE NEED TO HELP MY FRIENDS AND GET OUT OF HERE.
FRIENDS? BUT, WINTER, THERE'S A *NIGHTWING* OVER THERE.
HAILSTORM'S RIGHT. I'M AN ICEWING! I SHOULDN'T BE FRIENDS WITH A NIGHTWING.
BUT MOON HAS DONE SO MUCH TO HELP ME!
SHE'S ON OUR SIDE, HAILSTORM.

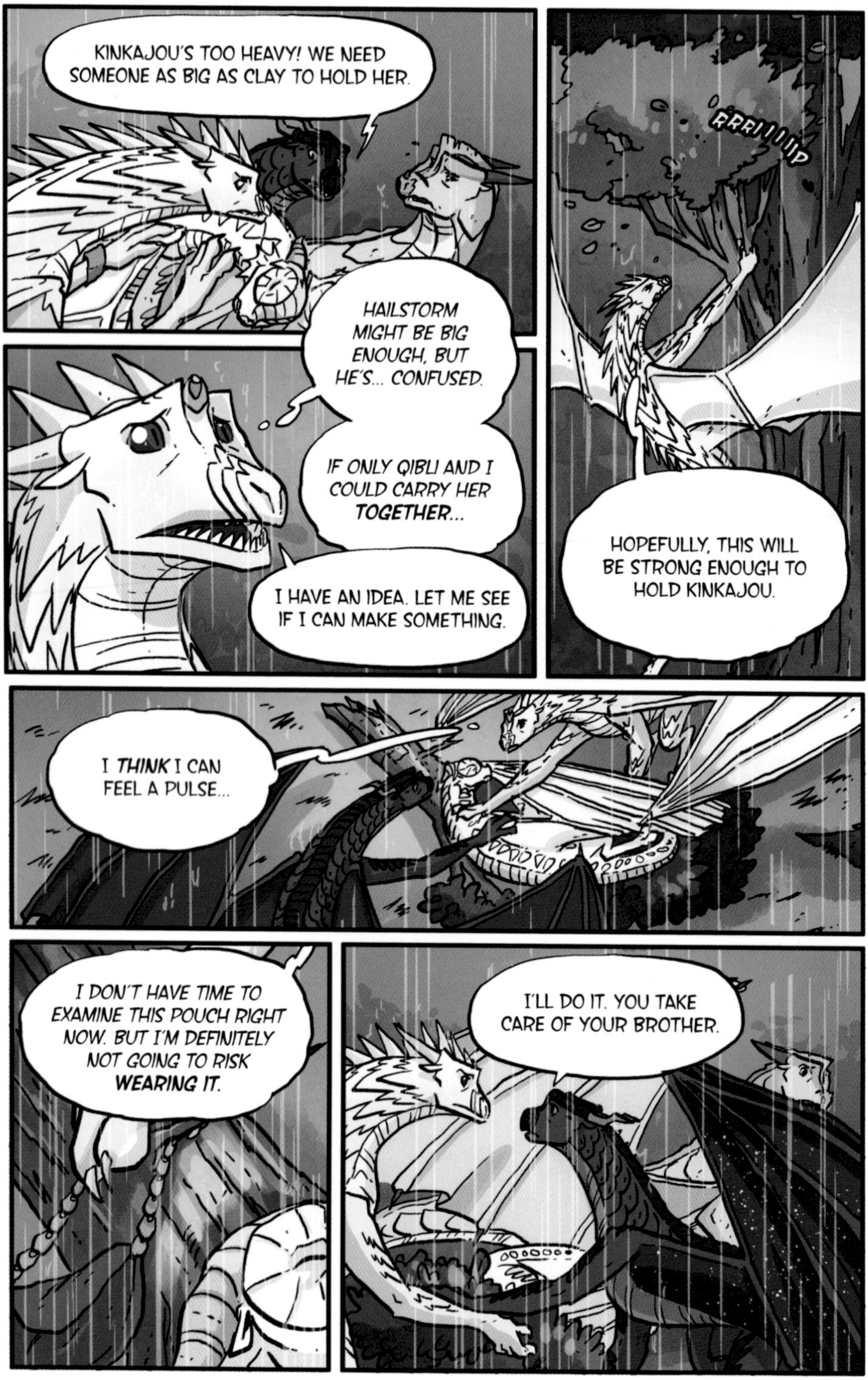
KINKAJOU'S TOO HEAVY! WE NEED SOMEONE AS BIG AS CLAY TO HOLD HER.
HAILSTORM MIGHT BE BIG ENOUGH, BUT HE'S... CONFUSED.
IF ONLY QIBLI AND I COULD CARRY HER **TOGETHER**...
I HAVE AN IDEA. LET ME SEE IF I CAN MAKE SOMETHING.
RRRIIIIIP
HOPEFULLY, THIS WILL BE STRONG ENOUGH TO HOLD KINKAJOU.
I *THINK* I CAN FEEL A PULSE...
I DON'T HAVE TIME TO EXAMINE THIS POUCH RIGHT NOW. BUT I'M DEFINITELY NOT GOING TO RISK **WEARING IT.**
I'LL DO IT. YOU TAKE CARE OF YOUR BROTHER.

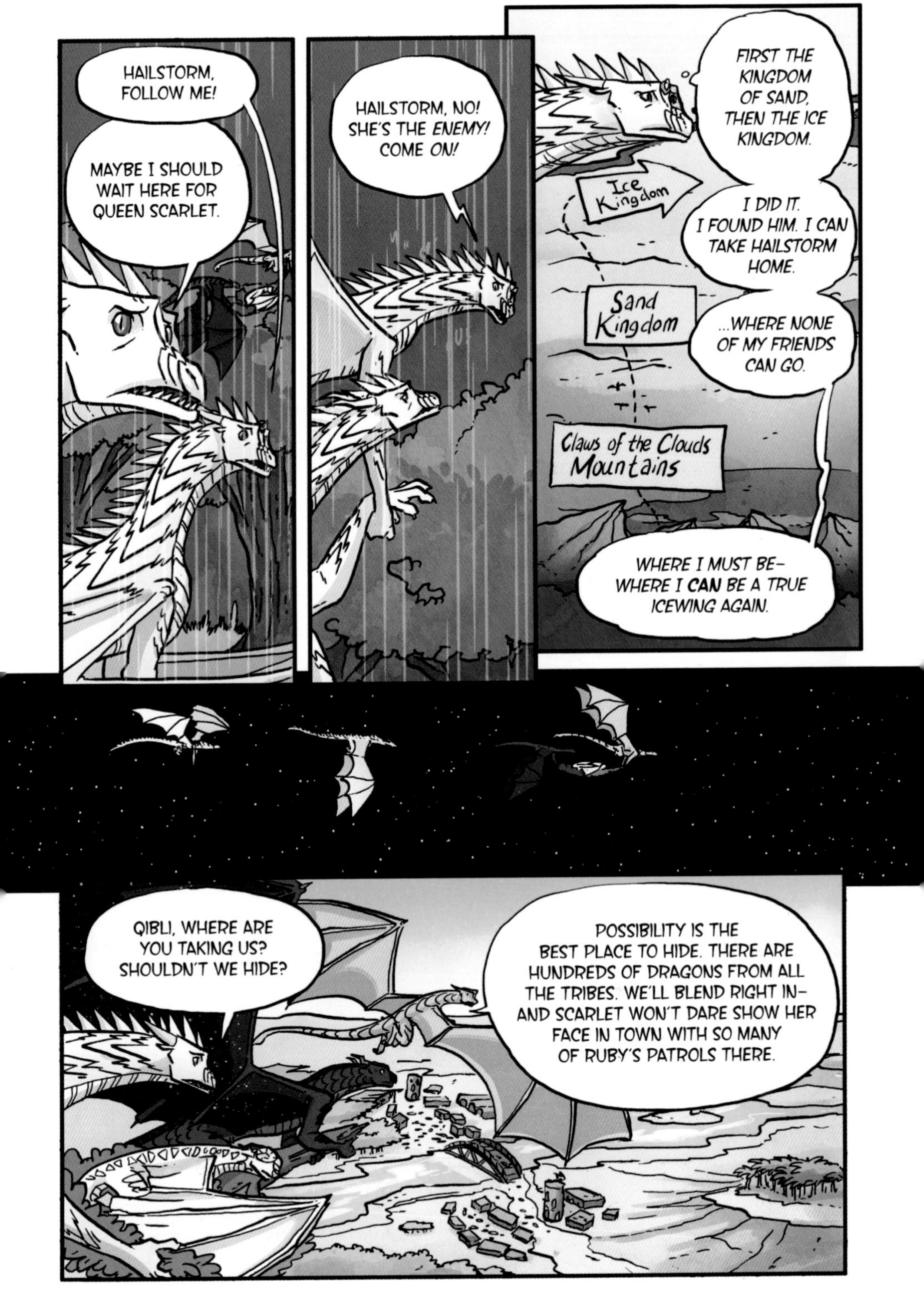
HAILSTORM, FOLLOW ME!
MAYBE I SHOULD WAIT HERE FOR QUEEN SCARLET.
HAILSTORM, NO! SHE'S THE *ENEMY!* COME *ON!*
FIRST THE KINGDOM OF SAND, THEN THE ICE KINGDOM.
Ice Kingdom
Sand Kingdom
Claws of the Clouds Mountains
I DID IT. I FOUND HIM. I CAN TAKE HAILSTORM HOME.
...WHERE NONE OF MY FRIENDS CAN GO.
WHERE I MUST BE— WHERE I **CAN** BE A TRUE ICEWING AGAIN.
QIBLI, WHERE ARE YOU TAKING US? SHOULDN'T WE HIDE?
POSSIBILITY IS THE BEST PLACE TO HIDE. THERE ARE HUNDREDS OF DRAGONS FROM ALL THE TRIBES. WE'LL BLEND RIGHT IN— AND SCARLET WON'T DARE SHOW HER FACE IN TOWN WITH SO MANY OF RUBY'S PATROLS THERE.

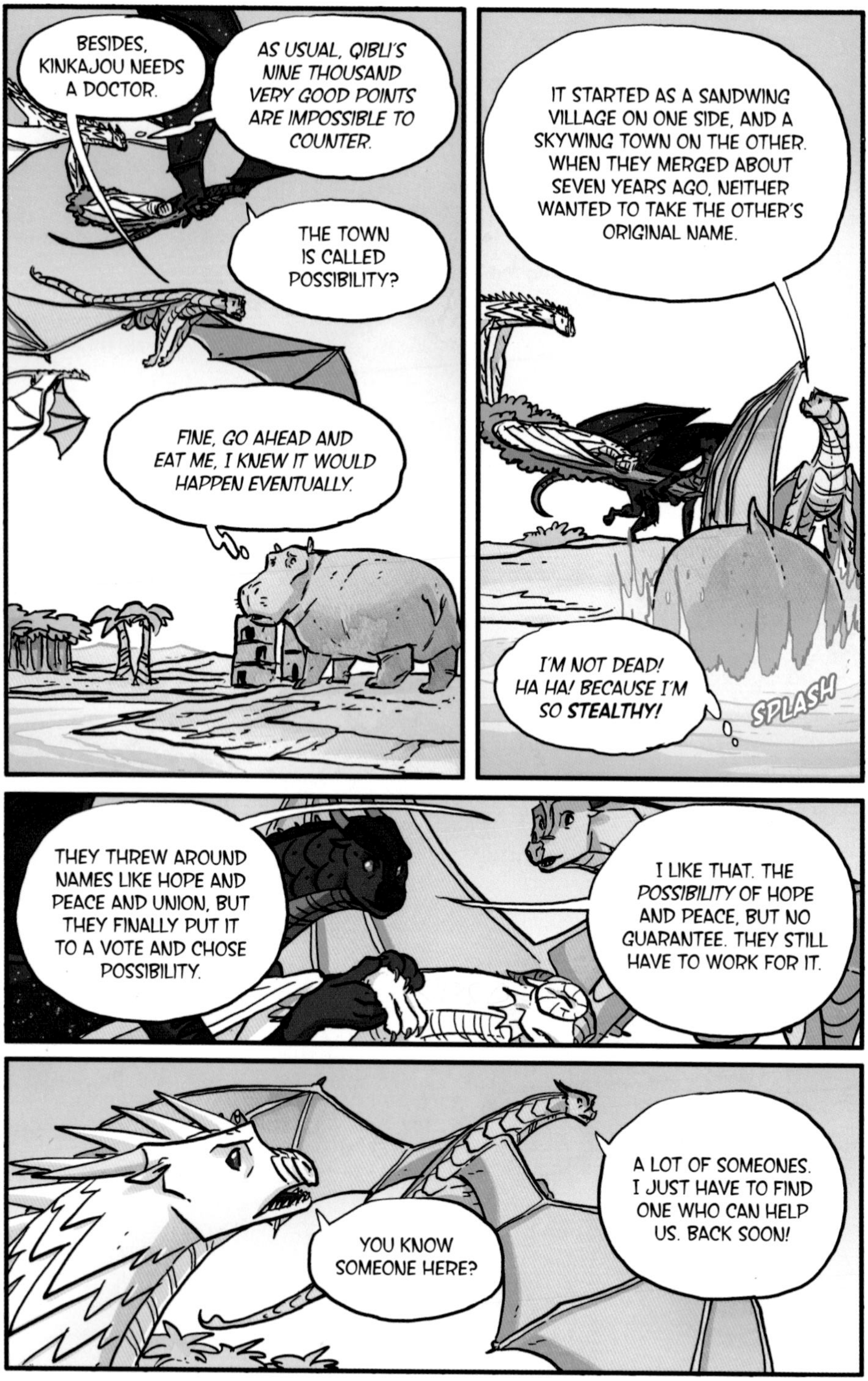
BESIDES, KINKAJOU NEEDS A DOCTOR.
AS USUAL, QIBLI'S NINE THOUSAND VERY GOOD POINTS ARE IMPOSSIBLE TO COUNTER.
THE TOWN IS CALLED POSSIBILITY?
FINE, GO AHEAD AND EAT ME, I KNEW IT WOULD HAPPEN EVENTUALLY.
IT STARTED AS A SANDWING VILLAGE ON ONE SIDE, AND A SKYWING TOWN ON THE OTHER. WHEN THEY MERGED ABOUT SEVEN YEARS AGO, NEITHER WANTED TO TAKE THE OTHER'S ORIGINAL NAME.
I'M NOT DEAD! HA HA! BECAUSE I'M SO **STEALTHY!**
SPLASH
THEY THREW AROUND NAMES LIKE HOPE AND PEACE AND UNION, BUT THEY FINALLY PUT IT TO A VOTE AND CHOSE POSSIBILITY.
I LIKE THAT. THE *POSSIBILITY* OF HOPE AND PEACE, BUT NO GUARANTEE. THEY STILL HAVE TO WORK FOR IT.
YOU KNOW SOMEONE HERE?
A LOT OF SOMEONES. I JUST HAVE TO FIND ONE WHO CAN HELP US. BACK SOON!

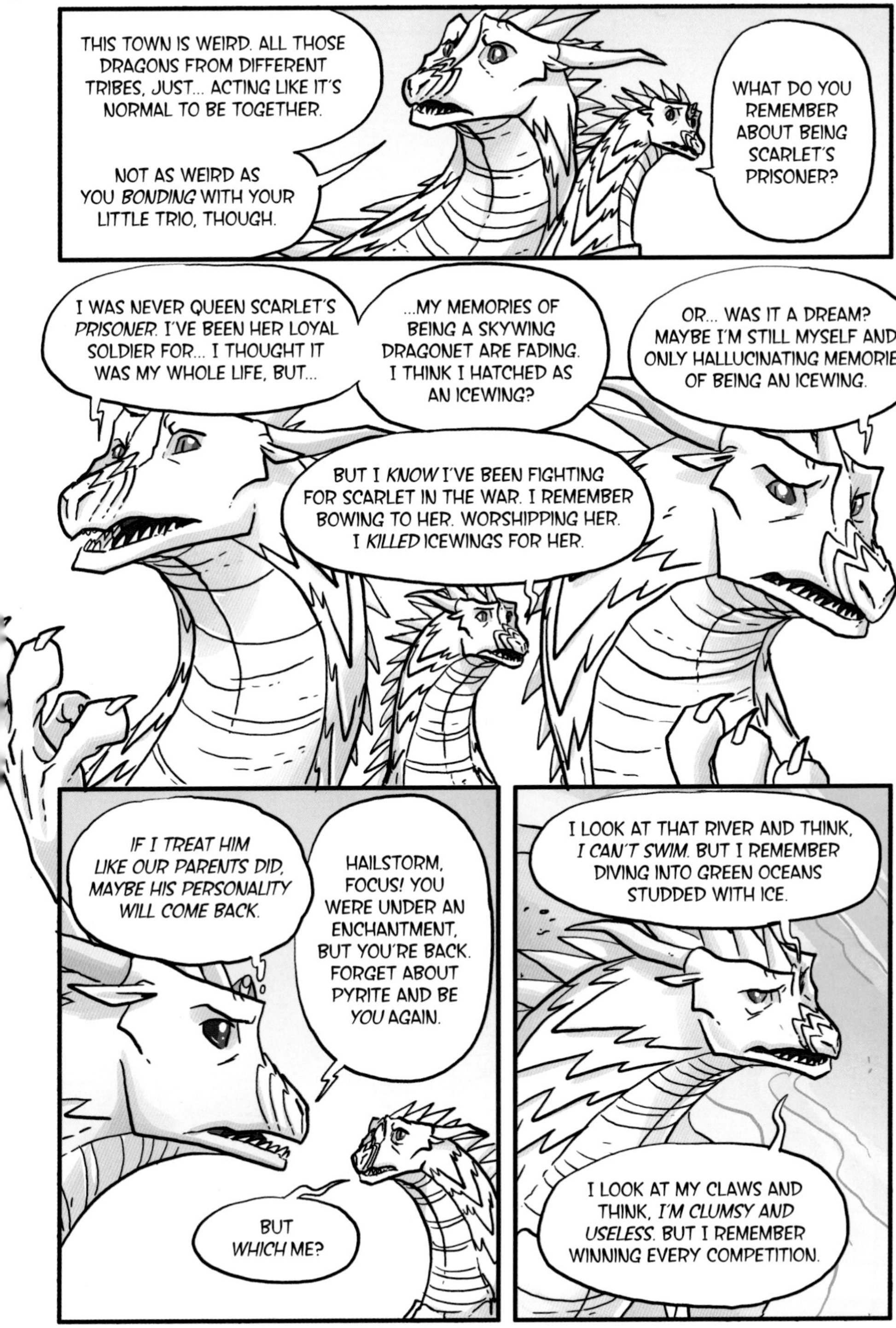
THIS TOWN IS WEIRD. ALL THOSE DRAGONS FROM DIFFERENT TRIBES, JUST... ACTING LIKE IT'S NORMAL TO BE TOGETHER.
NOT AS WEIRD AS YOU *BONDING* WITH YOUR LITTLE TRIO, THOUGH.
WHAT DO YOU REMEMBER ABOUT BEING SCARLET'S PRISONER?
I WAS NEVER QUEEN SCARLET'S *PRISONER*. I'VE BEEN HER LOYAL SOLDIER FOR... I THOUGHT IT WAS MY WHOLE LIFE, BUT...
...MY MEMORIES OF BEING A SKYWING DRAGONET ARE FADING. I THINK I HATCHED AS AN ICEWING?
OR... WAS IT A DREAM? MAYBE I'M STILL MYSELF AND ONLY HALLUCINATING MEMORIES OF BEING AN ICEWING.
BUT I *KNOW* I'VE BEEN FIGHTING FOR SCARLET IN THE WAR. I REMEMBER BOWING TO HER. WORSHIPPING HER. I *KILLED* ICEWINGS FOR HER.
IF I TREAT HIM LIKE OUR PARENTS DID, MAYBE HIS PERSONALITY WILL COME BACK.
HAILSTORM, FOCUS! YOU WERE UNDER AN ENCHANTMENT, BUT YOU'RE BACK. FORGET ABOUT PYRITE AND BE *YOU* AGAIN.
BUT *WHICH* ME?
I LOOK AT THAT RIVER AND THINK, *I CAN'T SWIM*. BUT I REMEMBER DIVING INTO GREEN OCEANS STUDDED WITH ICE.
I LOOK AT MY CLAWS AND THINK, *I'M CLUMSY AND USELESS*. BUT I REMEMBER WINNING EVERY COMPETITION.

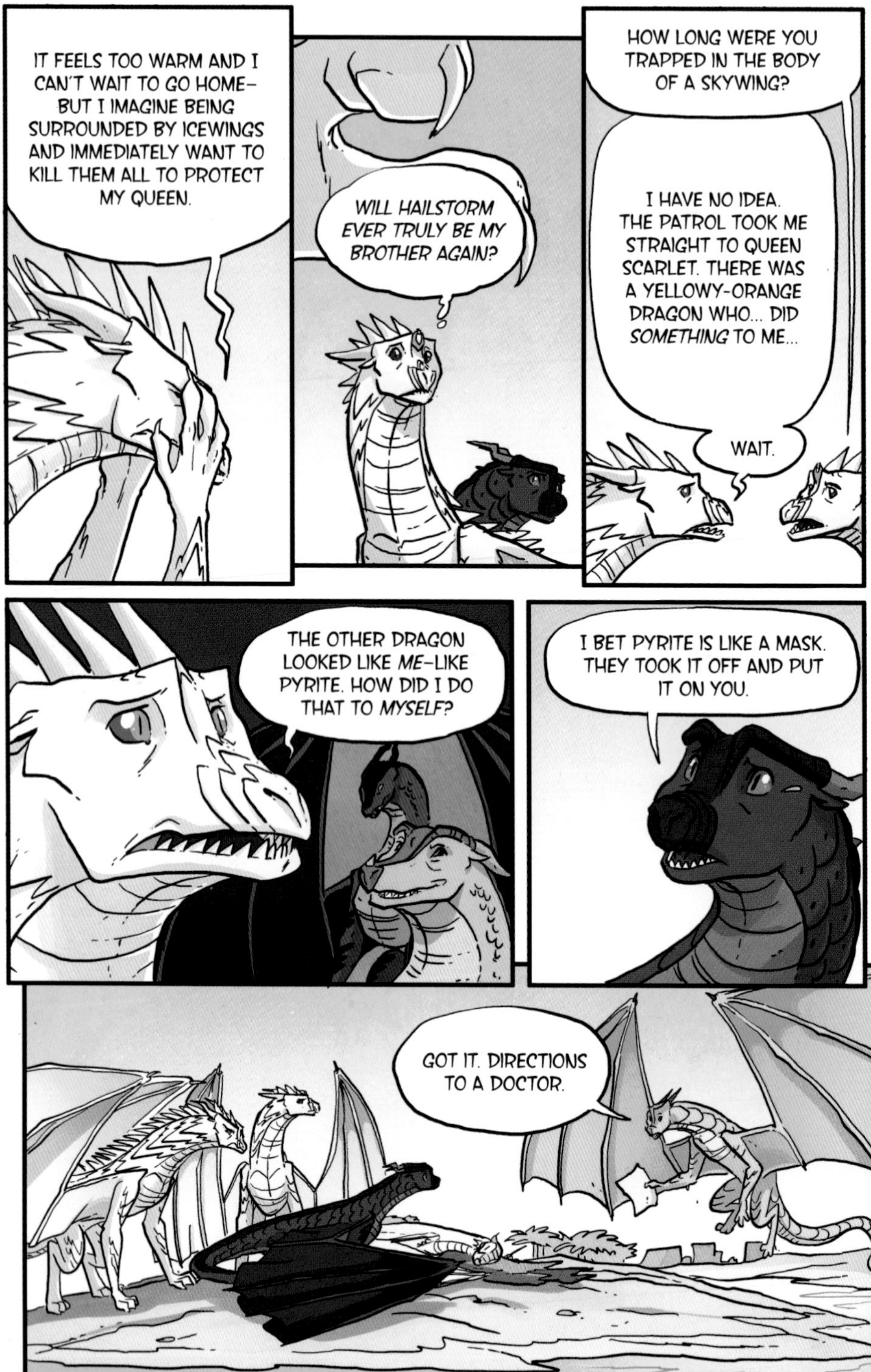
IT FEELS TOO WARM AND I CAN'T WAIT TO GO HOME– BUT I IMAGINE BEING SURROUNDED BY ICEWINGS AND IMMEDIATELY WANT TO KILL THEM ALL TO PROTECT MY QUEEN.
WILL HAILSTORM EVER TRULY BE MY BROTHER AGAIN?
HOW LONG WERE YOU TRAPPED IN THE BODY OF A SKYWING?
I HAVE NO IDEA. THE PATROL TOOK ME STRAIGHT TO QUEEN SCARLET. THERE WAS A YELLOWY-ORANGE DRAGON WHO... DID *SOMETHING* TO ME...
WAIT.
THE OTHER DRAGON LOOKED LIKE *ME*–LIKE PYRITE. HOW DID I DO THAT TO *MYSELF*?
I BET PYRITE IS LIKE A MASK. THEY TOOK IT OFF AND PUT IT ON YOU.
GOT IT. DIRECTIONS TO A DOCTOR.

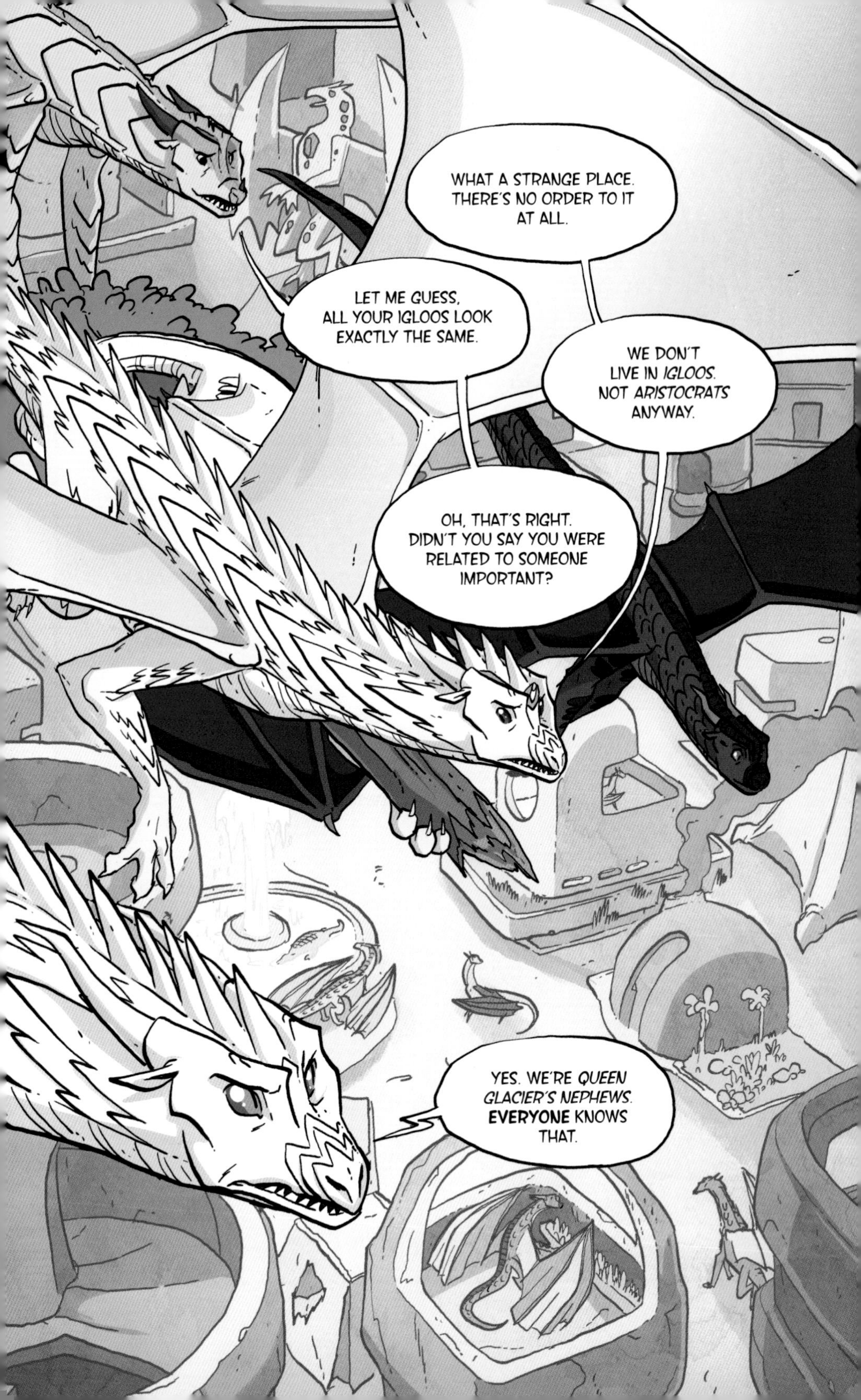

WHAT A STRANGE PLACE. THERE'S NO ORDER TO IT AT ALL.
LET ME GUESS, ALL YOUR *IGLOOS* LOOK EXACTLY THE SAME.
WE DON'T LIVE IN *IGLOOS*. NOT *ARISTOCRATS* ANYWAY.
OH, THAT'S RIGHT. DIDN'T YOU SAY YOU WERE RELATED TO SOMEONE IMPORTANT?
YES. WE'RE *QUEEN GLACIER'S NEPHEWS*. **EVERYONE** KNOWS THAT.

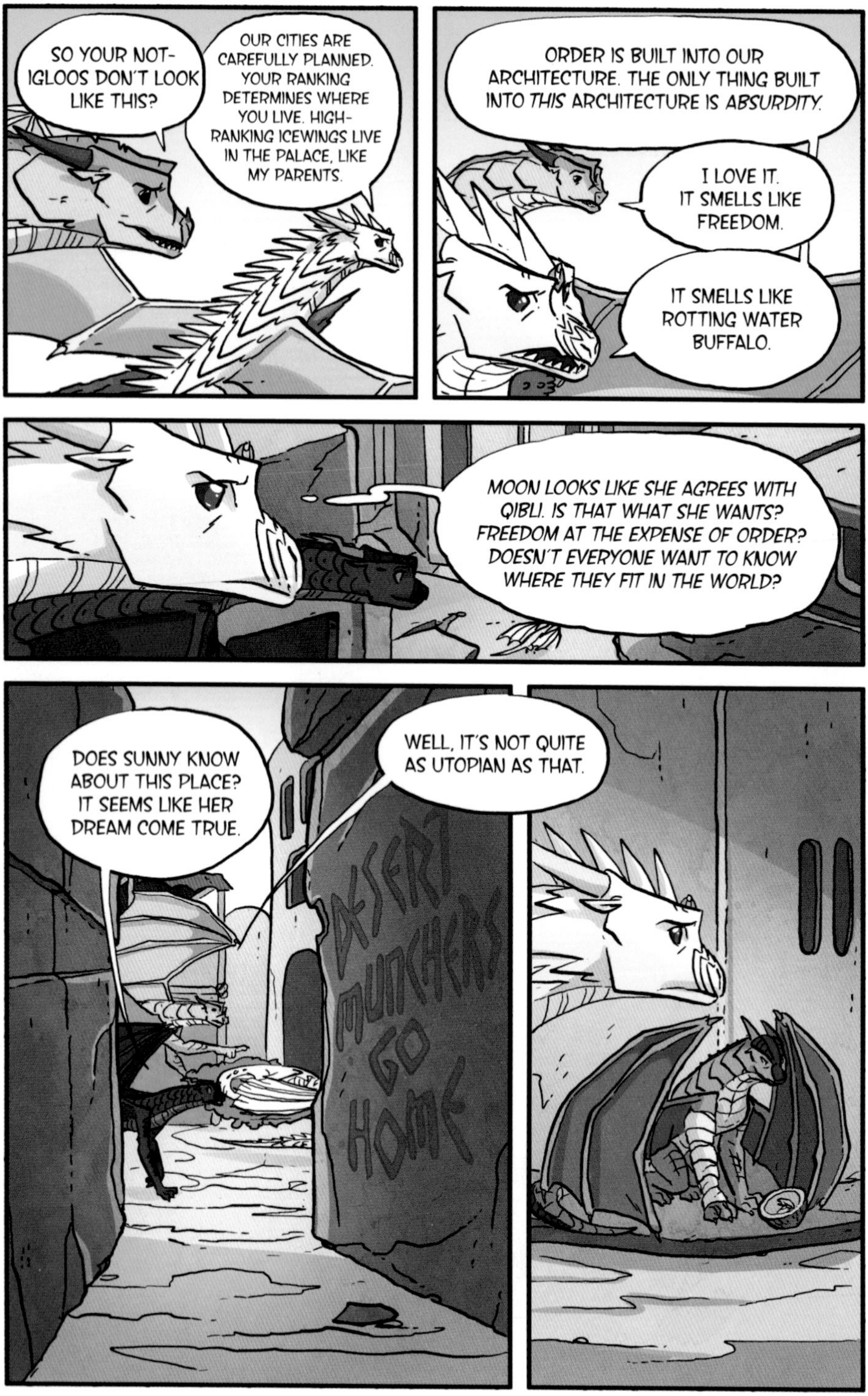
SO YOUR NOT-IGLOOS DON'T LOOK LIKE THIS?
OUR CITIES ARE CAREFULLY PLANNED. YOUR RANKING DETERMINES WHERE YOU LIVE. HIGH-RANKING ICEWINGS LIVE IN THE PALACE, LIKE MY PARENTS.
ORDER IS BUILT INTO OUR ARCHITECTURE. THE ONLY THING BUILT INTO *THIS* ARCHITECTURE IS *ABSURDITY.*
I LOVE IT. IT SMELLS LIKE FREEDOM.
IT SMELLS LIKE ROTTING WATER BUFFALO.
MOON LOOKS LIKE SHE AGREES WITH QIBLI. IS THAT WHAT SHE WANTS? FREEDOM AT THE EXPENSE OF ORDER? DOESN'T EVERYONE WANT TO KNOW WHERE THEY FIT IN THE WORLD?
DOES SUNNY KNOW ABOUT THIS PLACE? IT SEEMS LIKE HER DREAM COME TRUE.
WELL, IT'S NOT QUITE AS UTOPIAN AS THAT.
DESERT MUNCHERS GO HOME

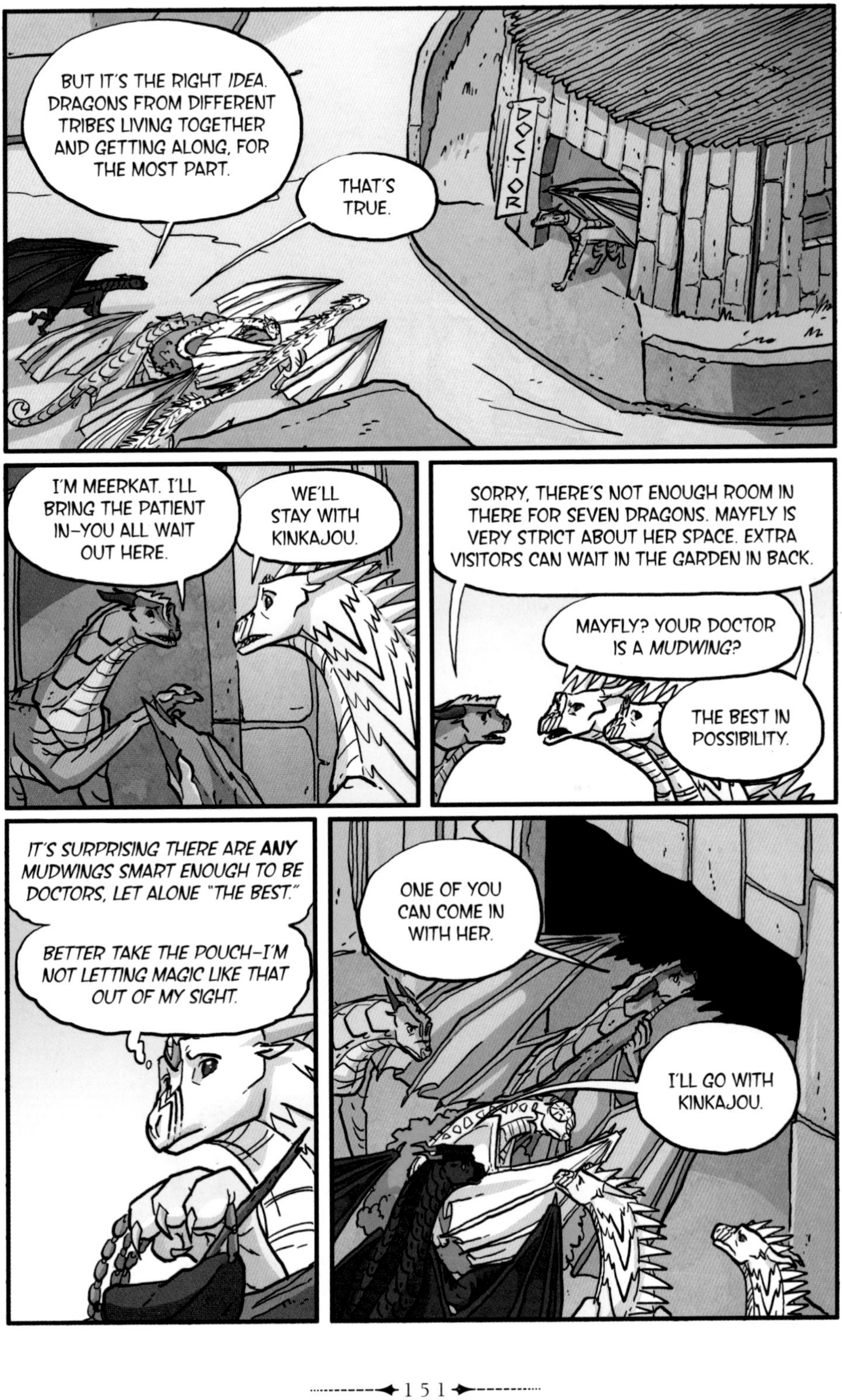

BUT IT'S THE RIGHT *IDEA*. DRAGONS FROM DIFFERENT TRIBES LIVING TOGETHER AND GETTING ALONG, FOR THE MOST PART.
THAT'S TRUE.
DOCTOR
I'M MEERKAT. I'LL BRING THE PATIENT IN—YOU ALL WAIT OUT HERE.
WE'LL STAY WITH KINKAJOU.
SORRY, THERE'S NOT ENOUGH ROOM IN THERE FOR SEVEN DRAGONS. MAYFLY IS VERY STRICT ABOUT HER SPACE. EXTRA VISITORS CAN WAIT IN THE GARDEN IN BACK.
MAYFLY? YOUR DOCTOR IS A *MUDWING?*
THE BEST IN POSSIBILITY.
IT'S SURPRISING THERE ARE ***ANY*** *MUDWINGS SMART ENOUGH TO BE DOCTORS, LET ALONE "THE BEST."*
BETTER TAKE THE POUCH—I'M NOT LETTING MAGIC LIKE THAT OUT OF MY SIGHT.
ONE OF YOU CAN COME IN WITH HER.
I'LL GO WITH KINKAJOU.

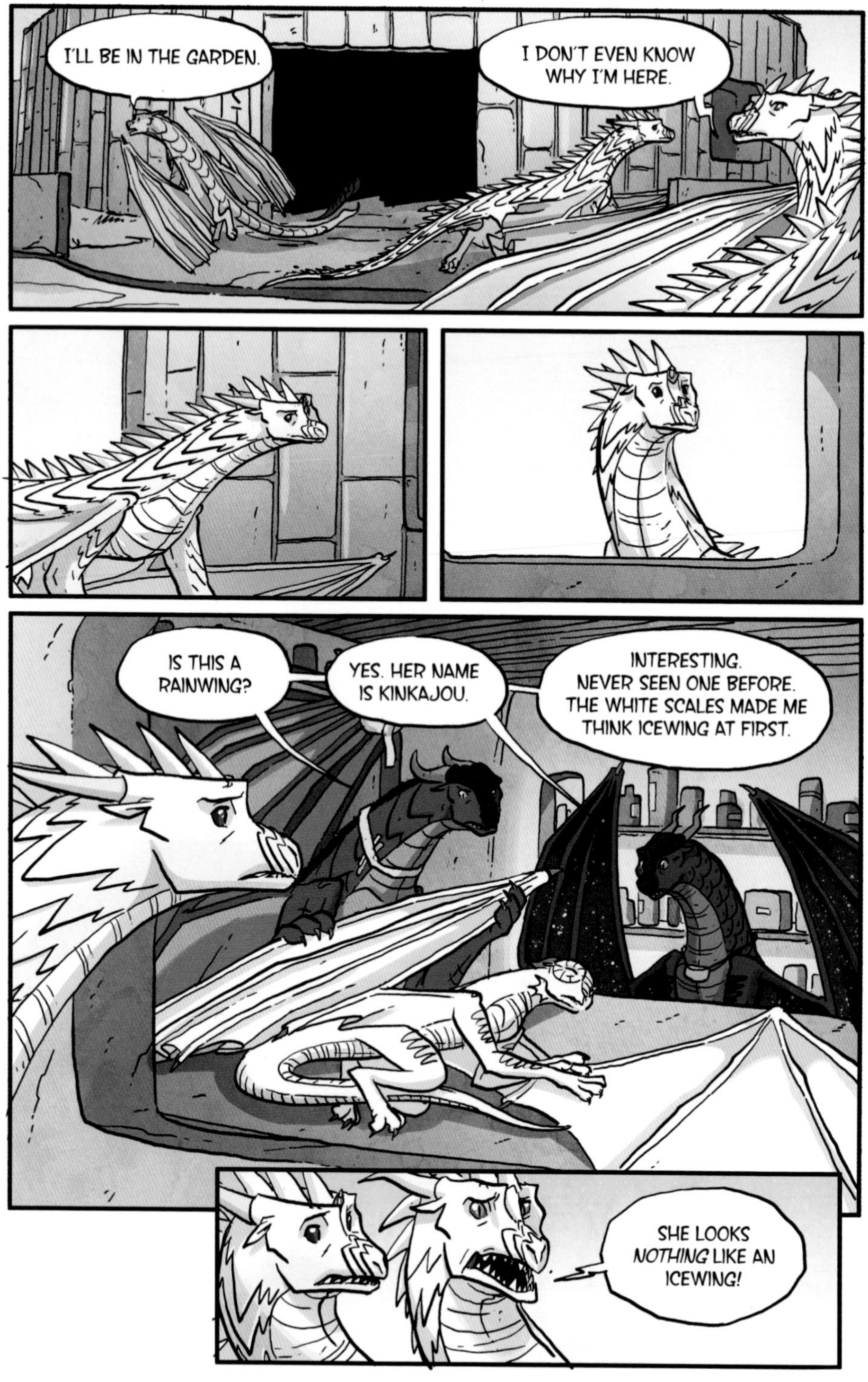
I'LL BE IN THE GARDEN.
I DON'T EVEN KNOW WHY I'M HERE.
IS THIS A RAINWING?
YES. HER NAME IS KINKAJOU.
INTERESTING. NEVER SEEN ONE BEFORE. THE WHITE SCALES MADE ME THINK ICEWING AT FIRST.
SHE LOOKS *NOTHING* LIKE AN ICEWING!

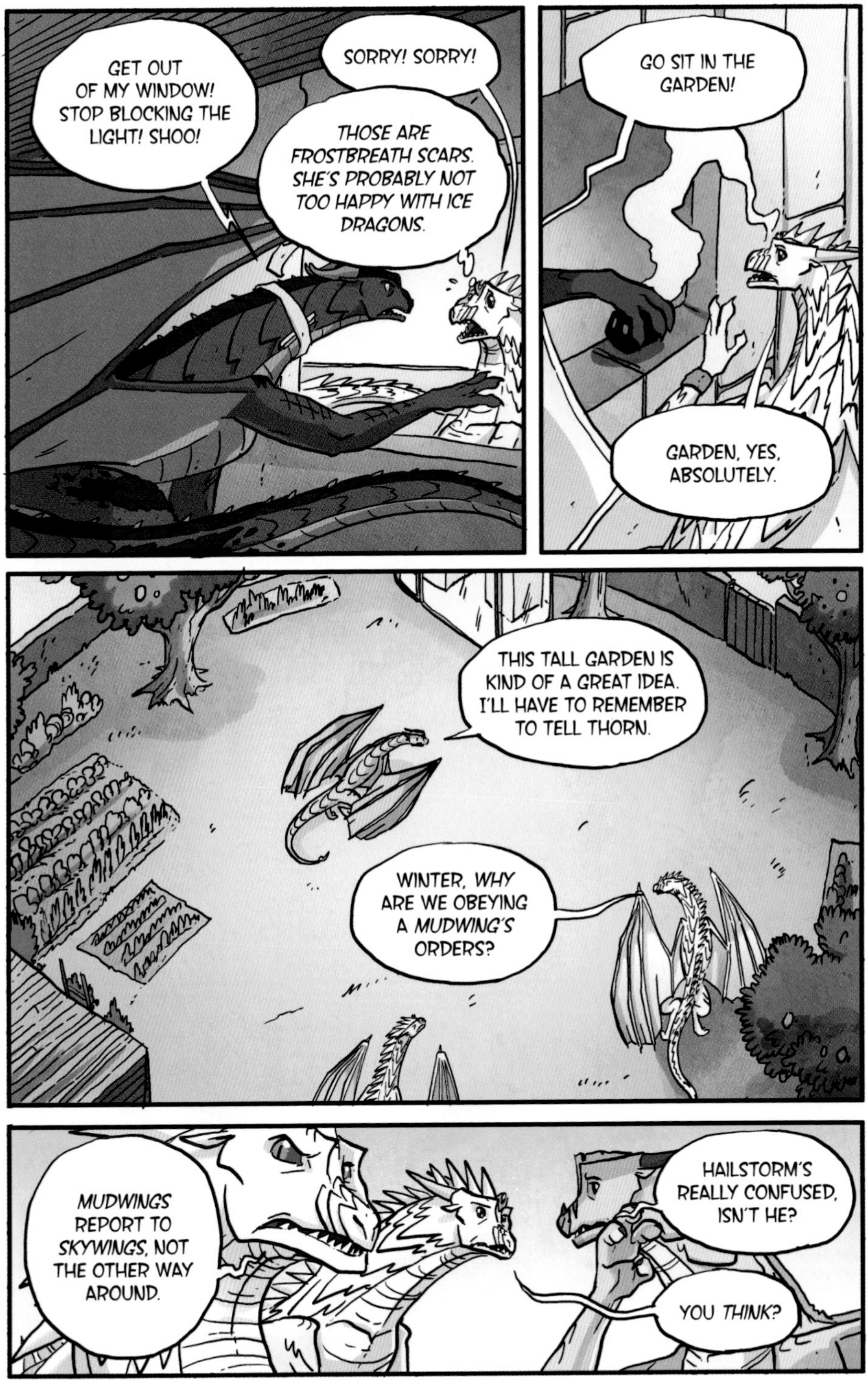
GET OUT OF MY WINDOW! STOP BLOCKING THE LIGHT! SHOO!
SORRY! SORRY!
THOSE ARE FROSTBREATH SCARS. SHE'S PROBABLY NOT TOO HAPPY WITH ICE DRAGONS.
GO SIT IN THE GARDEN!
GARDEN, YES, ABSOLUTELY.
THIS TALL GARDEN IS KIND OF A GREAT IDEA. I'LL HAVE TO REMEMBER TO TELL THORN.
WINTER, *WHY* ARE WE OBEYING A *MUDWING'S* ORDERS?
MUDWINGS REPORT TO *SKYWINGS*, NOT THE OTHER WAY AROUND.
HAILSTORM'S REALLY CONFUSED, ISN'T HE?
YOU *THINK*?

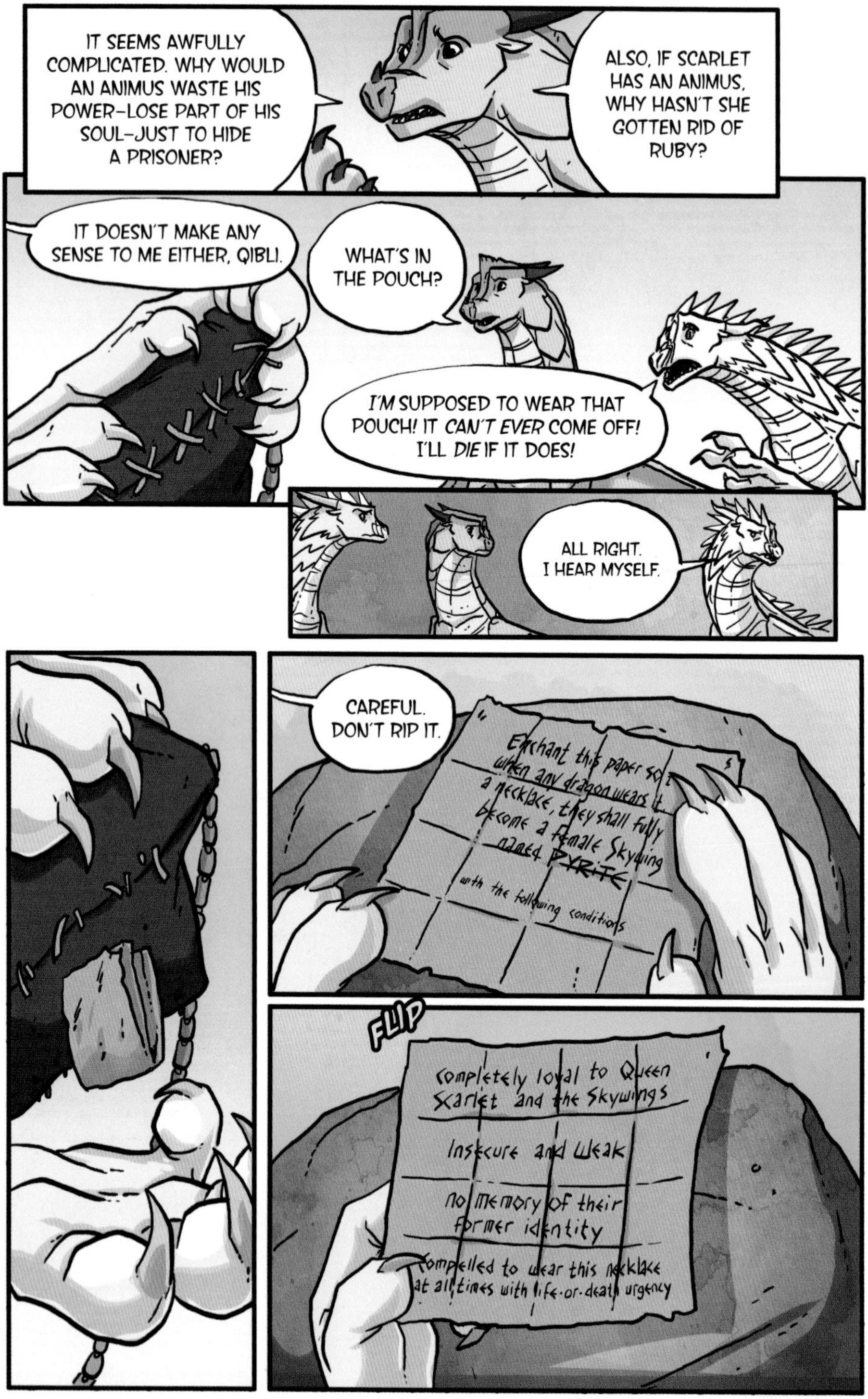
IT SEEMS AWFULLY COMPLICATED. WHY WOULD AN ANIMUS WASTE HIS POWER—LOSE PART OF HIS SOUL—JUST TO HIDE A PRISONER?
ALSO, IF SCARLET HAS AN ANIMUS, WHY HASN'T SHE GOTTEN RID OF RUBY?
IT DOESN'T MAKE ANY SENSE TO ME EITHER, QIBLI.
WHAT'S IN THE POUCH?
I'M SUPPOSED TO WEAR THAT POUCH! IT *CAN'T EVER* COME OFF! I'LL *DIE* IF IT DOES!
ALL RIGHT. I HEAR MYSELF.
CAREFUL. DON'T RIP IT.
Enchant this paper so
when any dragon wears it
a necklace, they shall fully
become a female Skywing
named PYRITE
with the following conditions
FLIP
completely loyal to Queen Scarlet and the Skywings
Insecure and weak
no memory of their former identity
compelled to wear this necklace at all times with life-or-death urgency

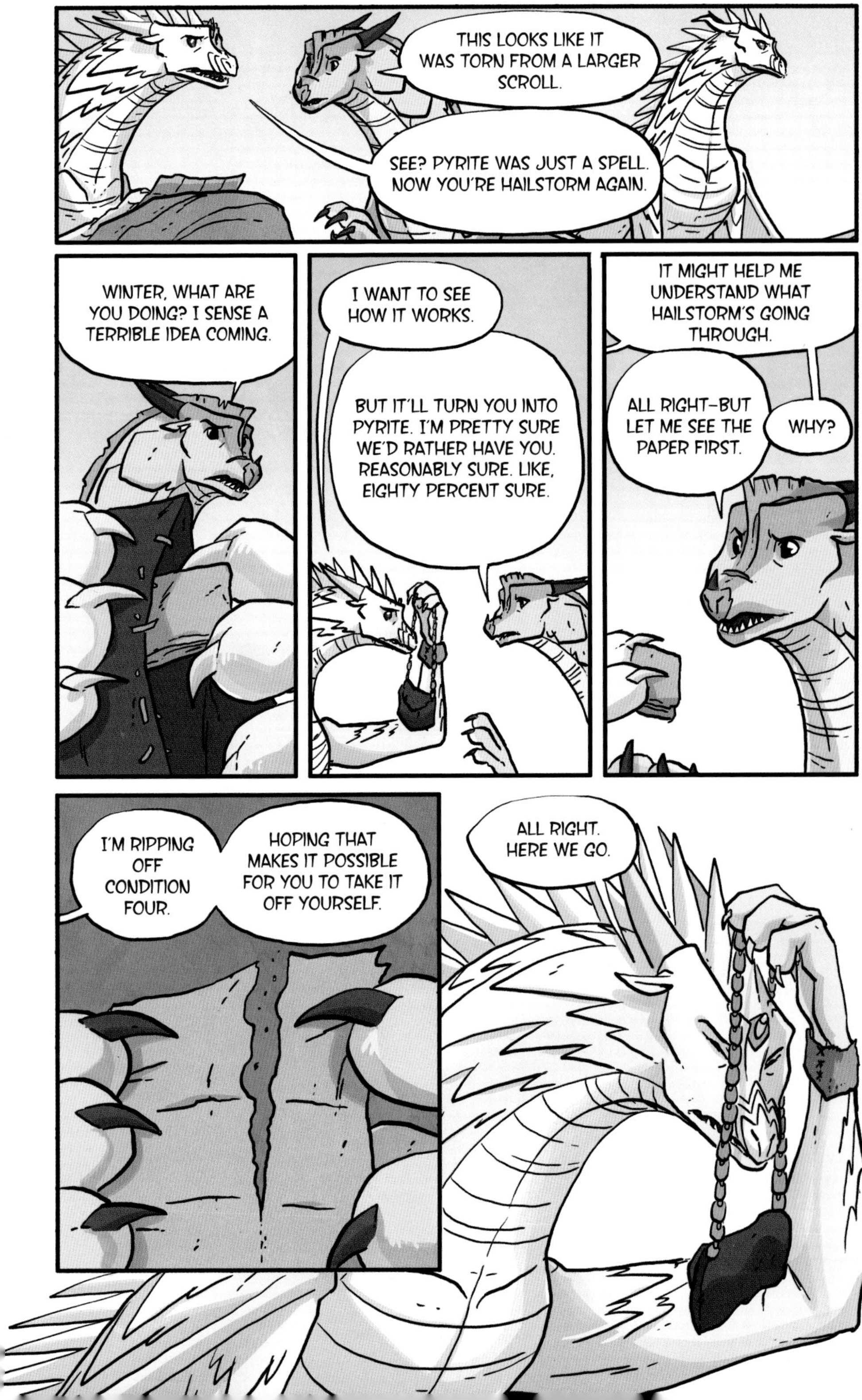
THIS LOOKS LIKE IT WAS TORN FROM A LARGER SCROLL.
SEE? PYRITE WAS JUST A SPELL. NOW YOU'RE HAILSTORM AGAIN.
WINTER, WHAT ARE YOU DOING? I SENSE A TERRIBLE IDEA COMING.
I WANT TO SEE HOW IT WORKS.
BUT IT'LL TURN YOU INTO PYRITE. I'M PRETTY SURE WE'D RATHER HAVE YOU. REASONABLY SURE. LIKE, EIGHTY PERCENT SURE.
IT MIGHT HELP ME UNDERSTAND WHAT HAILSTORM'S GOING THROUGH.
ALL RIGHT—BUT LET ME SEE THE PAPER FIRST.
WHY?
I'M RIPPING OFF CONDITION FOUR.
HOPING THAT MAKES IT POSSIBLE FOR YOU TO TAKE IT OFF YOURSELF.
ALL RIGHT. HERE WE GO.

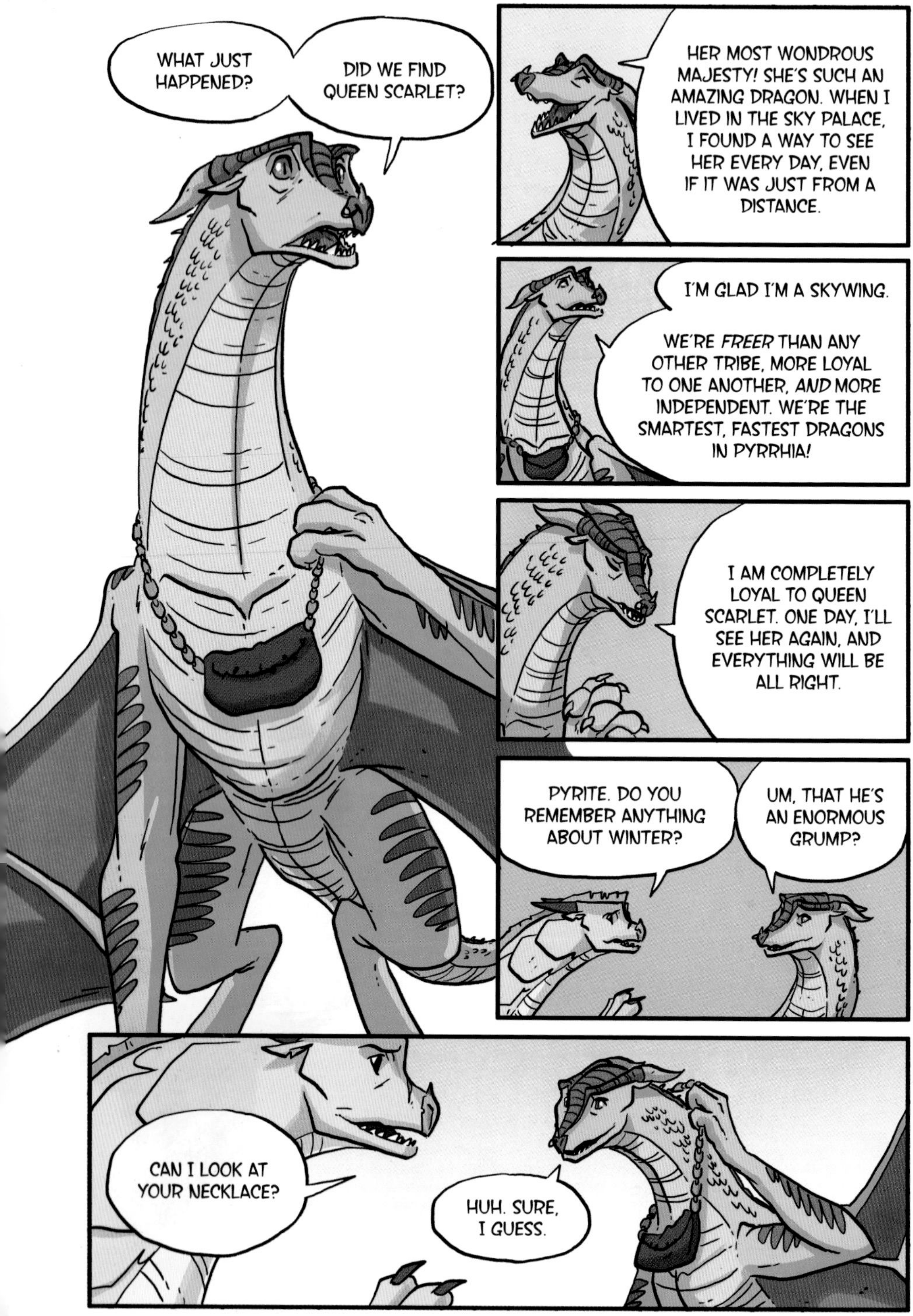
WHAT JUST HAPPENED?
DID WE FIND QUEEN SCARLET?
HER MOST WONDROUS MAJESTY! SHE'S SUCH AN AMAZING DRAGON. WHEN I LIVED IN THE SKY PALACE, I FOUND A WAY TO SEE HER EVERY DAY, EVEN IF IT WAS JUST FROM A DISTANCE.
I'M GLAD I'M A SKYWING.
WE'RE *FREER* THAN ANY OTHER TRIBE, MORE LOYAL TO ONE ANOTHER, *AND* MORE INDEPENDENT. WE'RE THE SMARTEST, FASTEST DRAGONS IN PYRRHIA!
I AM COMPLETELY LOYAL TO QUEEN SCARLET. ONE DAY, I'LL SEE HER AGAIN, AND EVERYTHING WILL BE ALL RIGHT.
PYRITE. DO YOU REMEMBER ANYTHING ABOUT WINTER?
UM, THAT HE'S AN ENORMOUS GRUMP?
CAN I LOOK AT YOUR NECKLACE?
HUH. SURE, I GUESS.

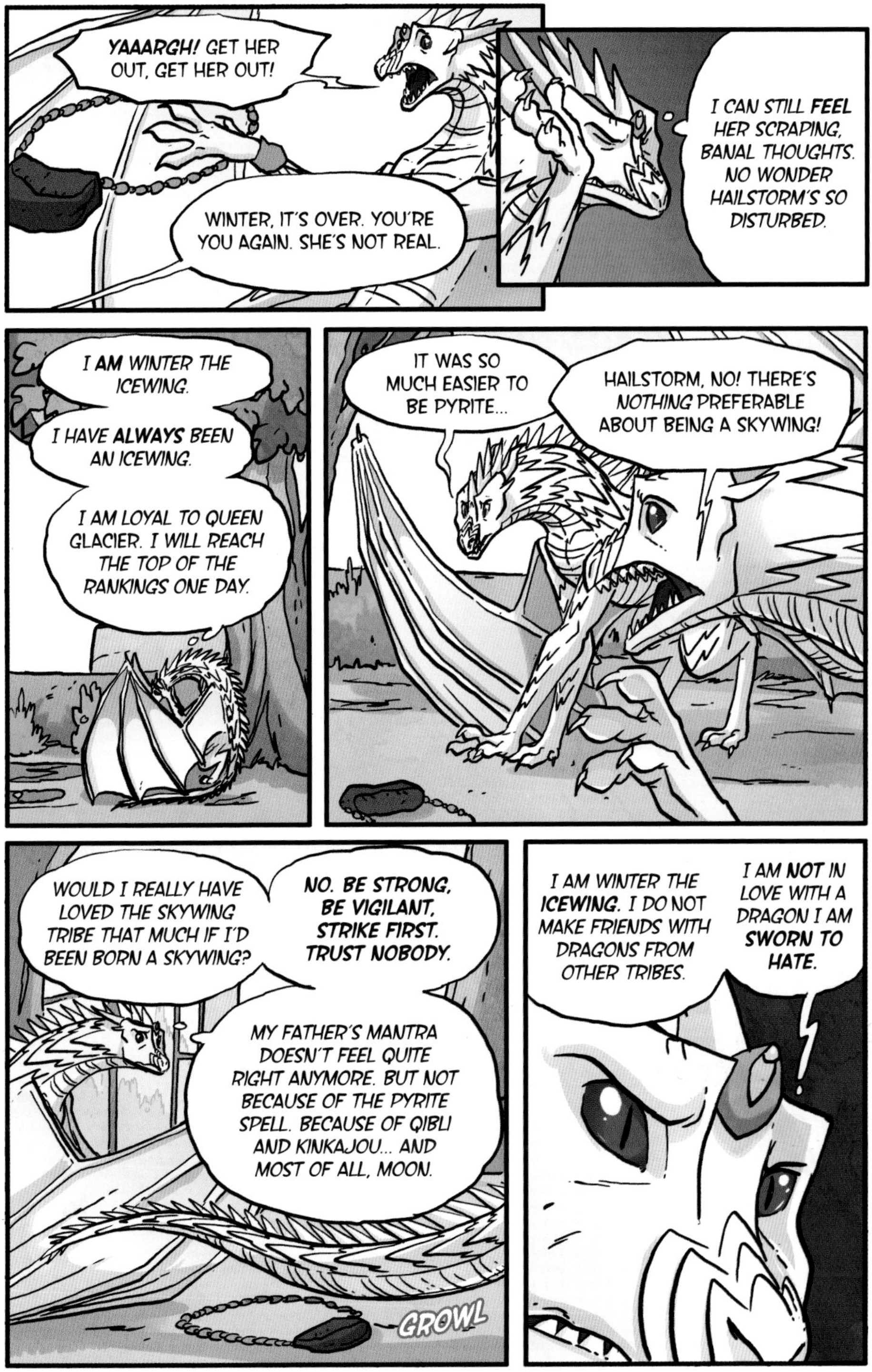
YAAARGH! GET HER OUT, GET HER OUT!
WINTER, IT'S OVER. YOU'RE YOU AGAIN. SHE'S NOT REAL.
I CAN STILL FEEL HER SCRAPING, BANAL THOUGHTS. NO WONDER HAILSTORM'S SO DISTURBED.
I AM WINTER THE ICEWING.
I HAVE ALWAYS BEEN AN ICEWING.
I AM LOYAL TO QUEEN GLACIER. I WILL REACH THE TOP OF THE RANKINGS ONE DAY.
IT WAS SO MUCH EASIER TO BE PYRITE...
HAILSTORM, NO! THERE'S NOTHING PREFERABLE ABOUT BEING A SKYWING!
WOULD I REALLY HAVE LOVED THE SKYWING TRIBE THAT MUCH IF I'D BEEN BORN A SKYWING?
NO. BE STRONG, BE VIGILANT, STRIKE FIRST. TRUST NOBODY.
MY FATHER'S MANTRA DOESN'T FEEL QUITE RIGHT ANYMORE. BUT NOT BECAUSE OF THE PYRITE SPELL. BECAUSE OF QIBLI AND KINKAJOU... AND MOST OF ALL, MOON.
GROWL
I AM WINTER THE ICEWING. I DO NOT MAKE FRIENDS WITH DRAGONS FROM OTHER TRIBES.
I AM NOT IN LOVE WITH A DRAGON I AM SWORN TO HATE.

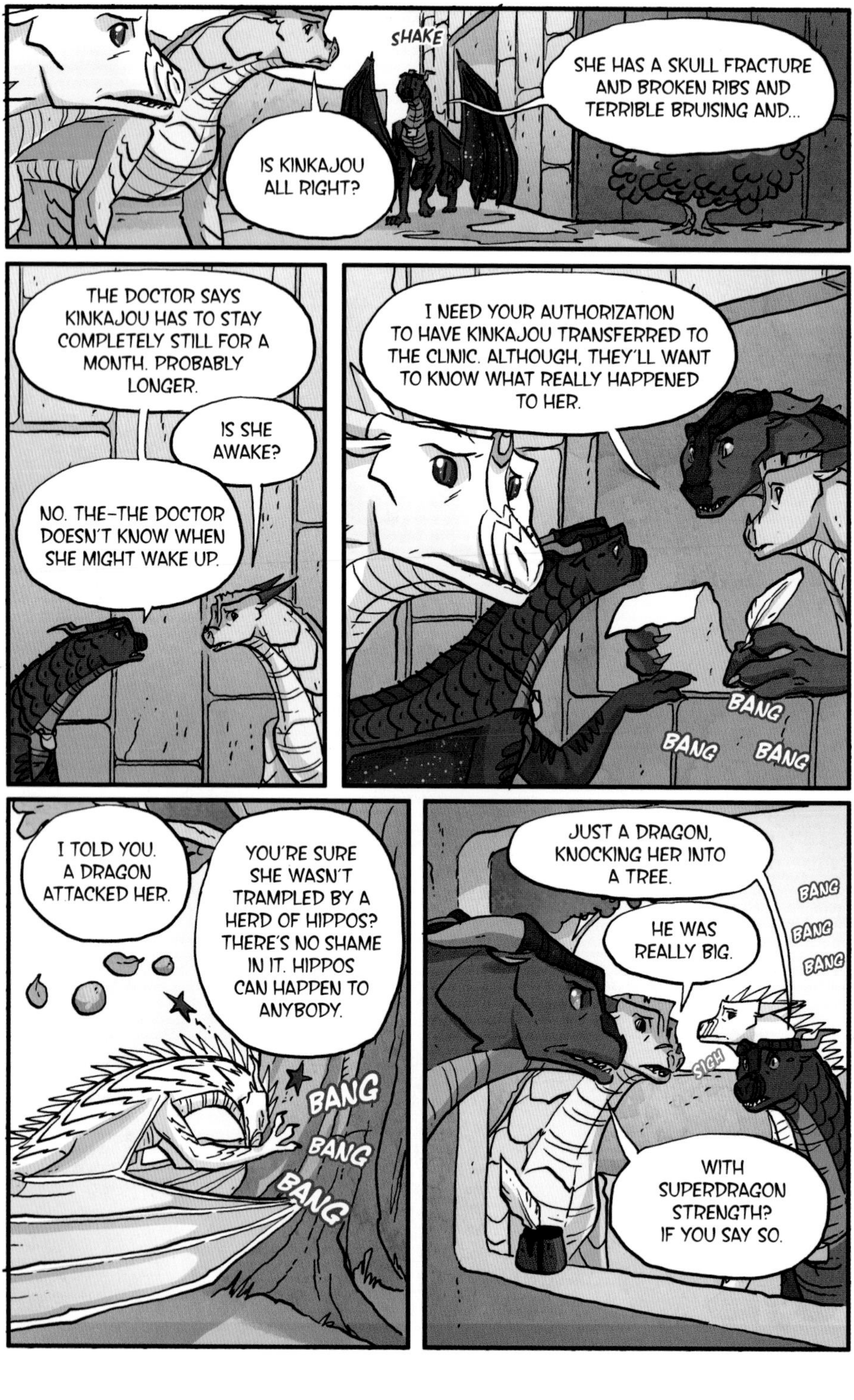
SHAKE
IS KINKAJOU ALL RIGHT?
SHE HAS A SKULL FRACTURE AND BROKEN RIBS AND TERRIBLE BRUISING AND...
THE DOCTOR SAYS KINKAJOU HAS TO STAY COMPLETELY STILL FOR A MONTH. PROBABLY LONGER.
IS SHE AWAKE?
NO. THE–THE DOCTOR DOESN'T KNOW WHEN SHE MIGHT WAKE UP.
I NEED YOUR AUTHORIZATION TO HAVE KINKAJOU TRANSFERRED TO THE CLINIC. ALTHOUGH, THEY'LL WANT TO KNOW WHAT REALLY HAPPENED TO HER.
BANG
BANG
BANG
I TOLD YOU. A DRAGON ATTACKED HER.
YOU'RE SURE SHE WASN'T TRAMPLED BY A HERD OF HIPPOS? THERE'S NO SHAME IN IT. HIPPOS CAN HAPPEN TO ANYBODY.
BANG
BANG
BANG
JUST A DRAGON, KNOCKING HER INTO A TREE.
HE WAS REALLY BIG.
BANG
BANG
BANG
SIGH
WITH SUPERDRAGON STRENGTH? IF YOU SAY SO.

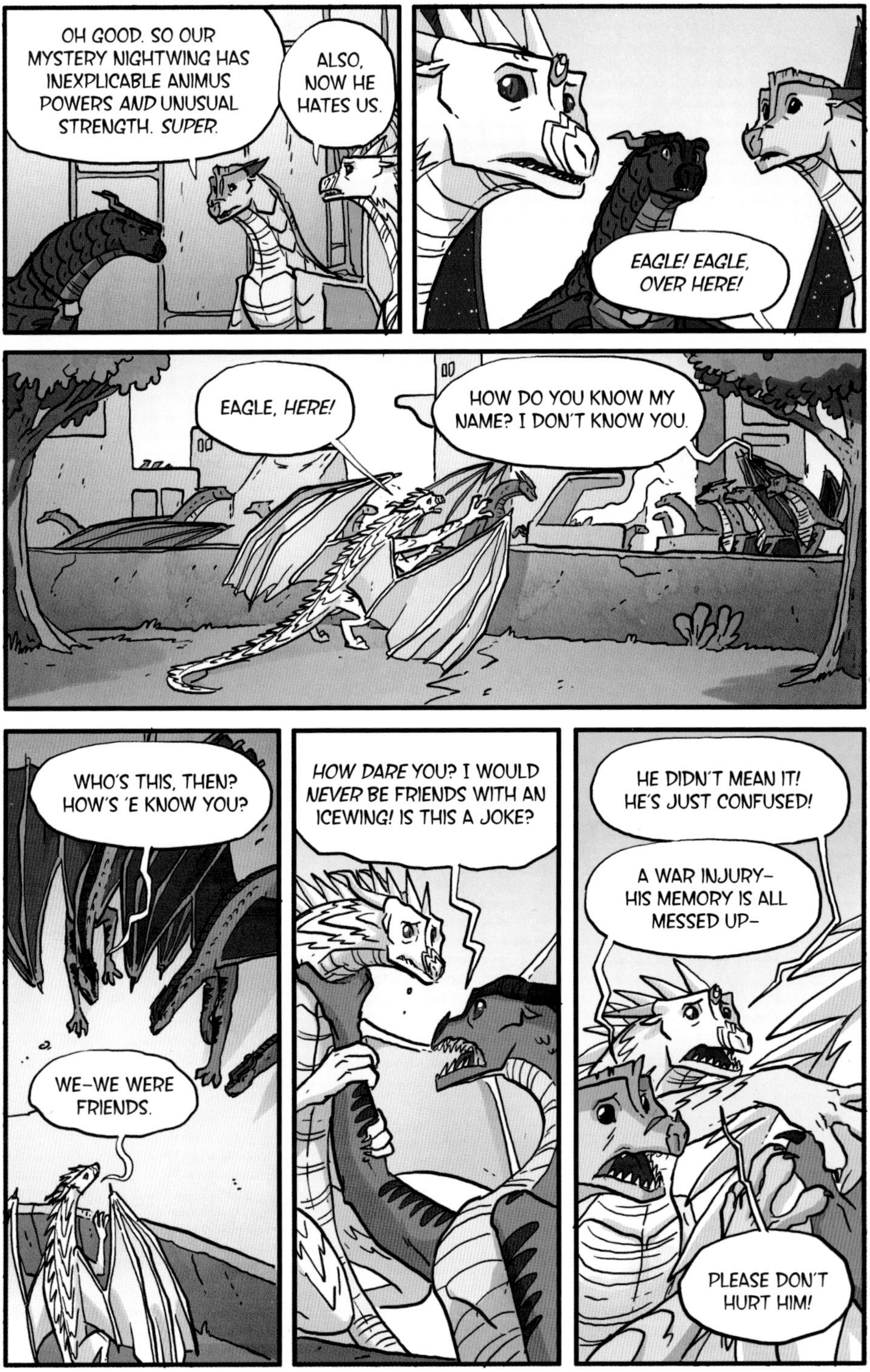
OH GOOD. SO OUR MYSTERY NIGHTWING HAS INEXPLICABLE ANIMUS POWERS *AND* UNUSUAL STRENGTH. *SUPER.*
ALSO, NOW HE HATES US.
EAGLE! EAGLE, OVER HERE!
EAGLE, *HERE!*
HOW DO YOU KNOW MY NAME? I DON'T KNOW YOU.
WHO'S THIS, THEN? HOW'S 'E KNOW YOU?
WE—WE WERE FRIENDS.
HOW DARE YOU? I WOULD *NEVER* BE FRIENDS WITH AN ICEWING! IS THIS A JOKE?
HE DIDN'T MEAN IT! HE'S JUST CONFUSED!
A WAR INJURY—HIS MEMORY IS ALL MESSED UP—
PLEASE DON'T HURT HIM!

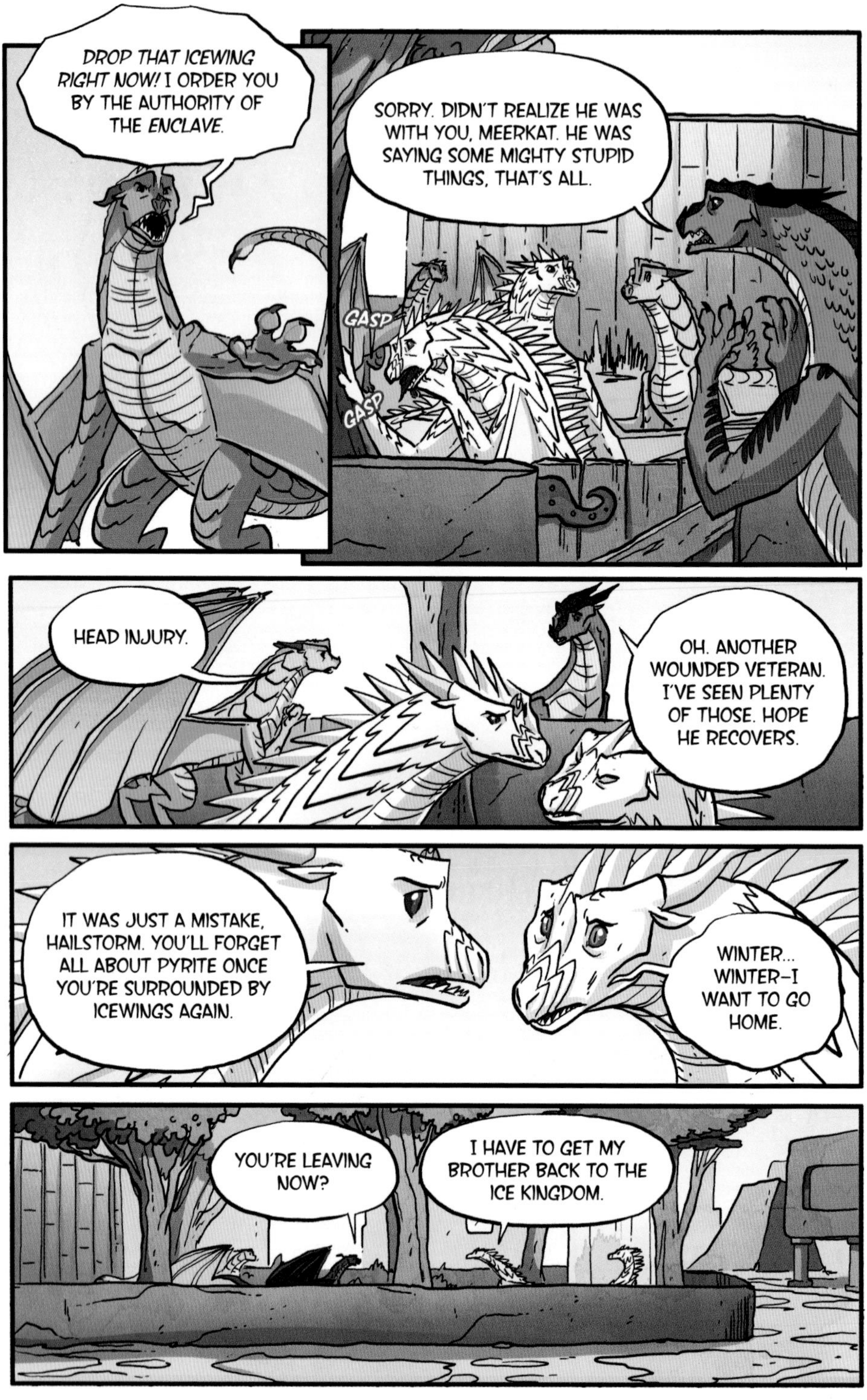
DROP THAT ICEWING RIGHT NOW! I ORDER YOU BY THE AUTHORITY OF THE ENCLAVE.
SORRY. DIDN'T REALIZE HE WAS WITH YOU, MEERKAT. HE WAS SAYING SOME MIGHTY STUPID THINGS, THAT'S ALL.
GASP
GASP
HEAD INJURY.
OH. ANOTHER WOUNDED VETERAN. I'VE SEEN PLENTY OF THOSE. HOPE HE RECOVERS.
IT WAS JUST A MISTAKE, HAILSTORM. YOU'LL FORGET ALL ABOUT PYRITE ONCE YOU'RE SURROUNDED BY ICEWINGS AGAIN.
WINTER... WINTER—I WANT TO GO HOME.
YOU'RE LEAVING NOW?
I HAVE TO GET MY BROTHER BACK TO THE ICE KINGDOM.

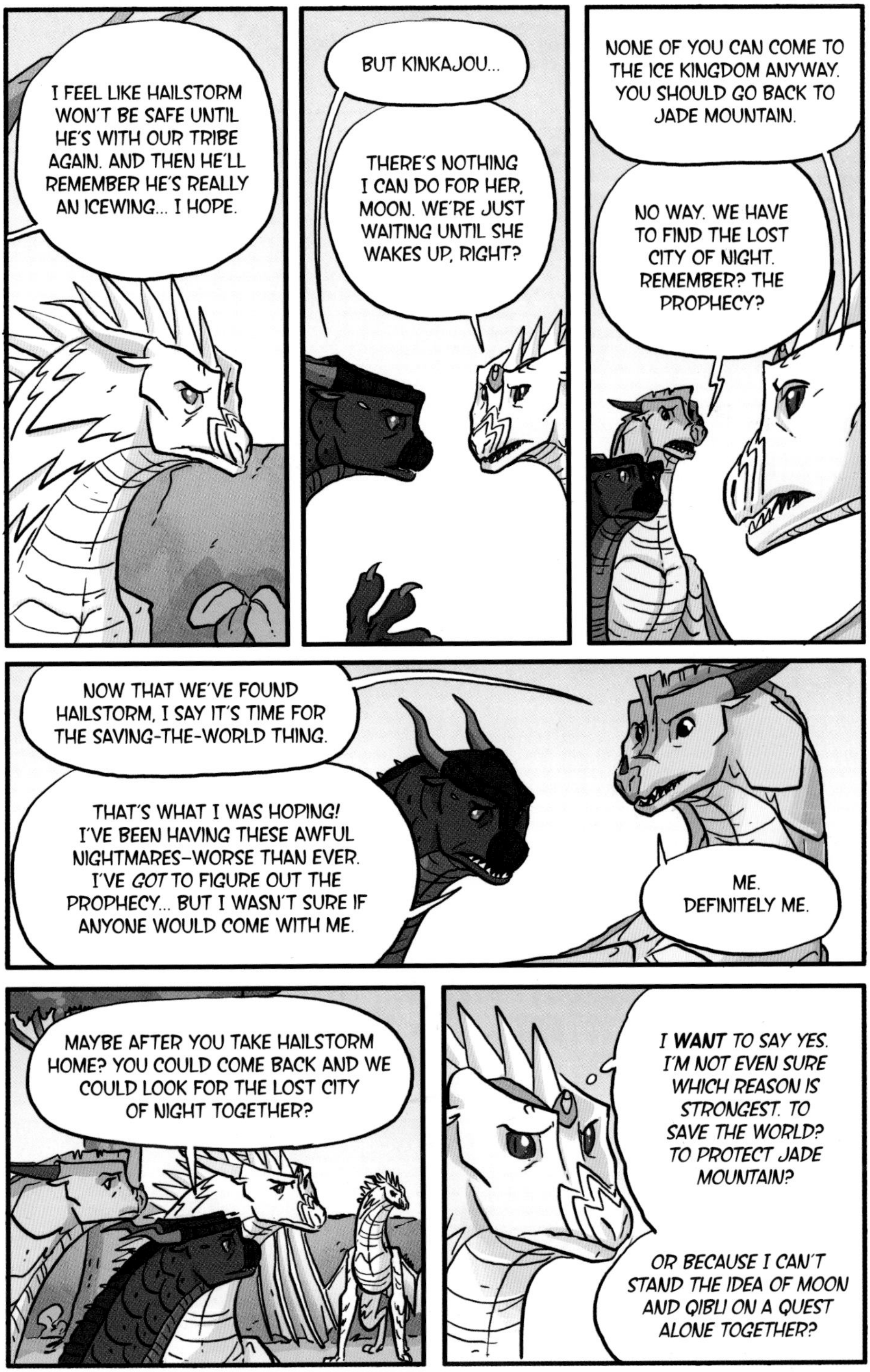
I FEEL LIKE HAILSTORM WON'T BE SAFE UNTIL HE'S WITH OUR TRIBE AGAIN. AND THEN HE'LL REMEMBER HE'S REALLY AN ICEWING... I HOPE.
BUT KINKAJOU...
THERE'S NOTHING I CAN DO FOR HER, MOON. WE'RE JUST WAITING UNTIL SHE WAKES UP, RIGHT?
NONE OF YOU CAN COME TO THE ICE KINGDOM ANYWAY. YOU SHOULD GO BACK TO JADE MOUNTAIN.
NO WAY. WE HAVE TO FIND THE LOST CITY OF NIGHT. REMEMBER? THE PROPHECY?
NOW THAT WE'VE FOUND HAILSTORM, I SAY IT'S TIME FOR THE SAVING-THE-WORLD THING.
THAT'S WHAT I WAS HOPING! I'VE BEEN HAVING THESE AWFUL NIGHTMARES–WORSE THAN EVER. I'VE *GOT* TO FIGURE OUT THE PROPHECY... BUT I WASN'T SURE IF ANYONE WOULD COME WITH ME.
ME. DEFINITELY ME.
MAYBE AFTER YOU TAKE HAILSTORM HOME? YOU COULD COME BACK AND WE COULD LOOK FOR THE LOST CITY OF NIGHT TOGETHER?
I ***WANT*** *TO SAY YES. I'M NOT EVEN SURE WHICH REASON IS STRONGEST. TO SAVE THE WORLD? TO PROTECT JADE MOUNTAIN?*
OR BECAUSE I CAN'T STAND THE IDEA OF MOON AND QIBLI ON A QUEST ALONE TOGETHER?

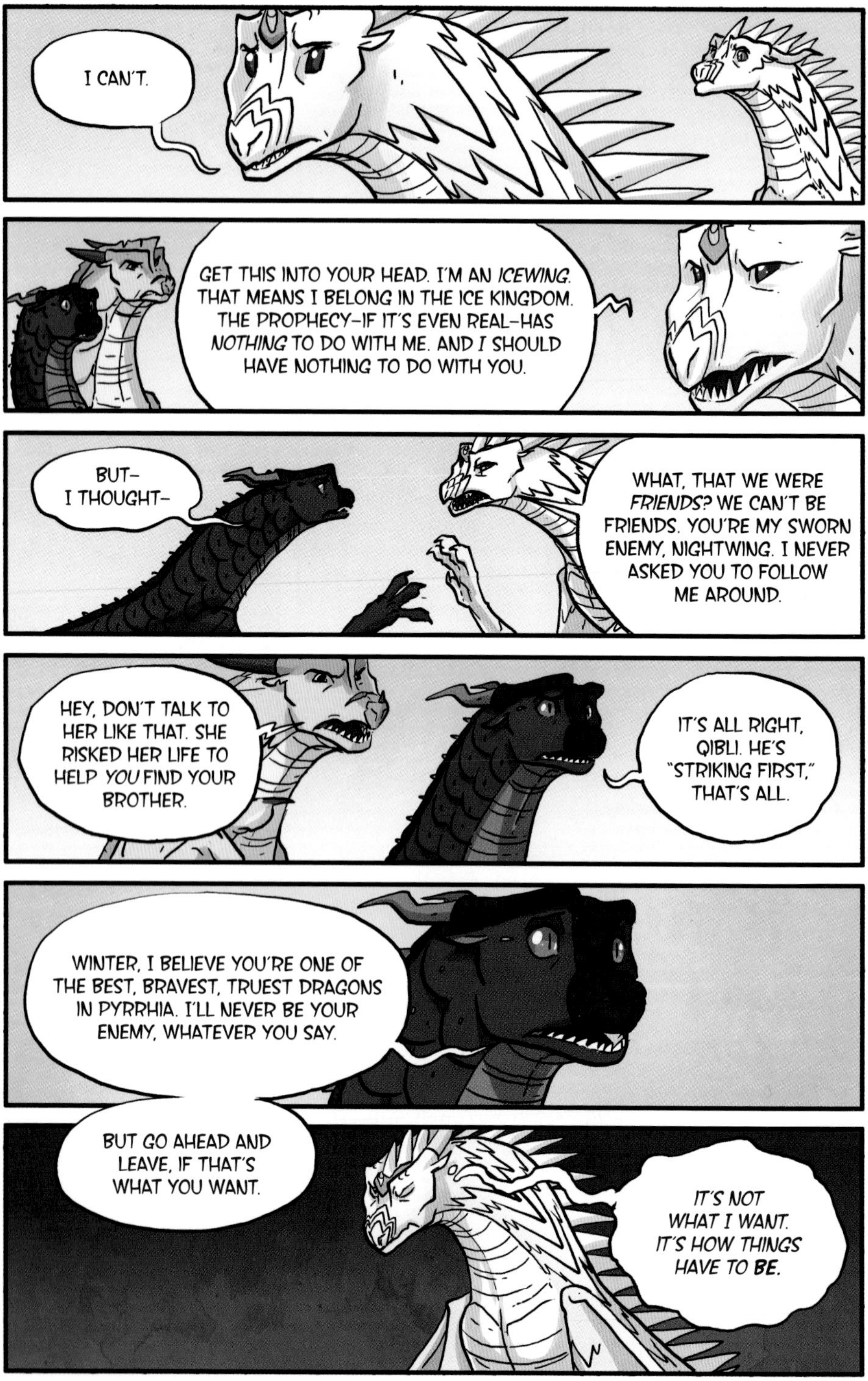
I CAN'T.
GET THIS INTO YOUR HEAD. I'M AN *ICEWING.* THAT MEANS I BELONG IN THE ICE KINGDOM. THE PROPHECY–IF IT'S EVEN REAL–HAS *NOTHING* TO DO WITH ME. AND *I* SHOULD HAVE NOTHING TO DO WITH YOU.
BUT– I THOUGHT–
WHAT, THAT WE WERE *FRIENDS?* WE CAN'T BE FRIENDS. YOU'RE MY SWORN ENEMY, NIGHTWING. I NEVER ASKED YOU TO FOLLOW ME AROUND.
HEY, DON'T TALK TO HER LIKE THAT. SHE RISKED HER LIFE TO HELP *YOU* FIND YOUR BROTHER.
IT'S ALL RIGHT, QIBLI. HE'S "STRIKING FIRST," THAT'S ALL.
WINTER, I BELIEVE YOU'RE ONE OF THE BEST, BRAVEST, TRUEST DRAGONS IN PYRRHIA. I'LL NEVER BE YOUR ENEMY, WHATEVER YOU SAY.
BUT GO AHEAD AND LEAVE, IF THAT'S WHAT YOU WANT.
*IT'S NOT WHAT I WANT. IT'S HOW THINGS HAVE TO **BE.***

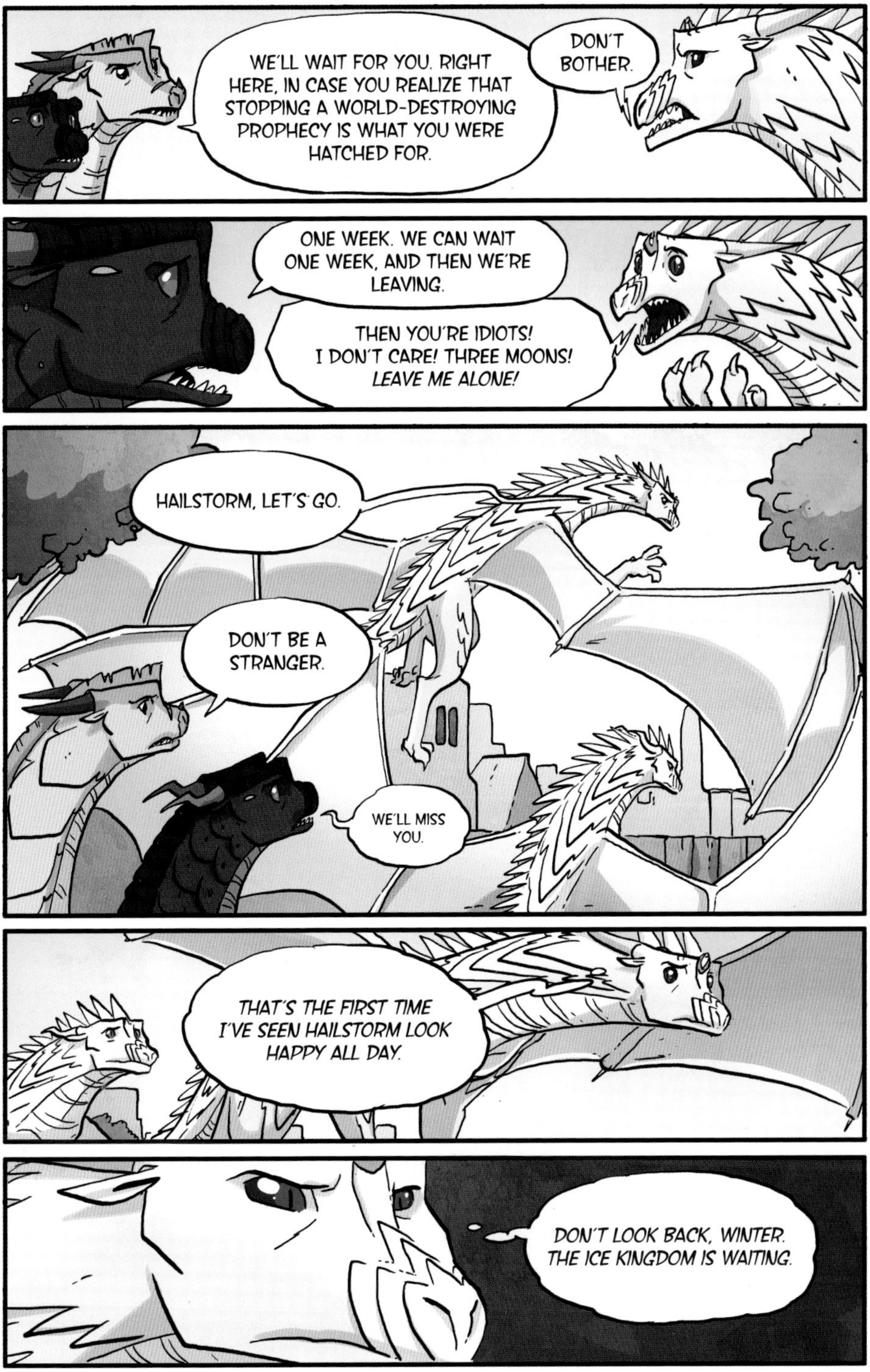
WE'LL WAIT FOR YOU. RIGHT HERE, IN CASE YOU REALIZE THAT STOPPING A WORLD-DESTROYING PROPHECY IS WHAT YOU WERE HATCHED FOR.
DON'T BOTHER.
ONE WEEK. WE CAN WAIT ONE WEEK, AND THEN WE'RE LEAVING.
THEN YOU'RE IDIOTS! I DON'T CARE! THREE MOONS! *LEAVE ME ALONE!*
HAILSTORM, LET'S GO.
DON'T BE A STRANGER.
WE'LL MISS YOU.
THAT'S THE FIRST TIME I'VE SEEN HAILSTORM LOOK HAPPY ALL DAY.
DON'T LOOK BACK, WINTER. THE ICE KINGDOM IS WAITING.

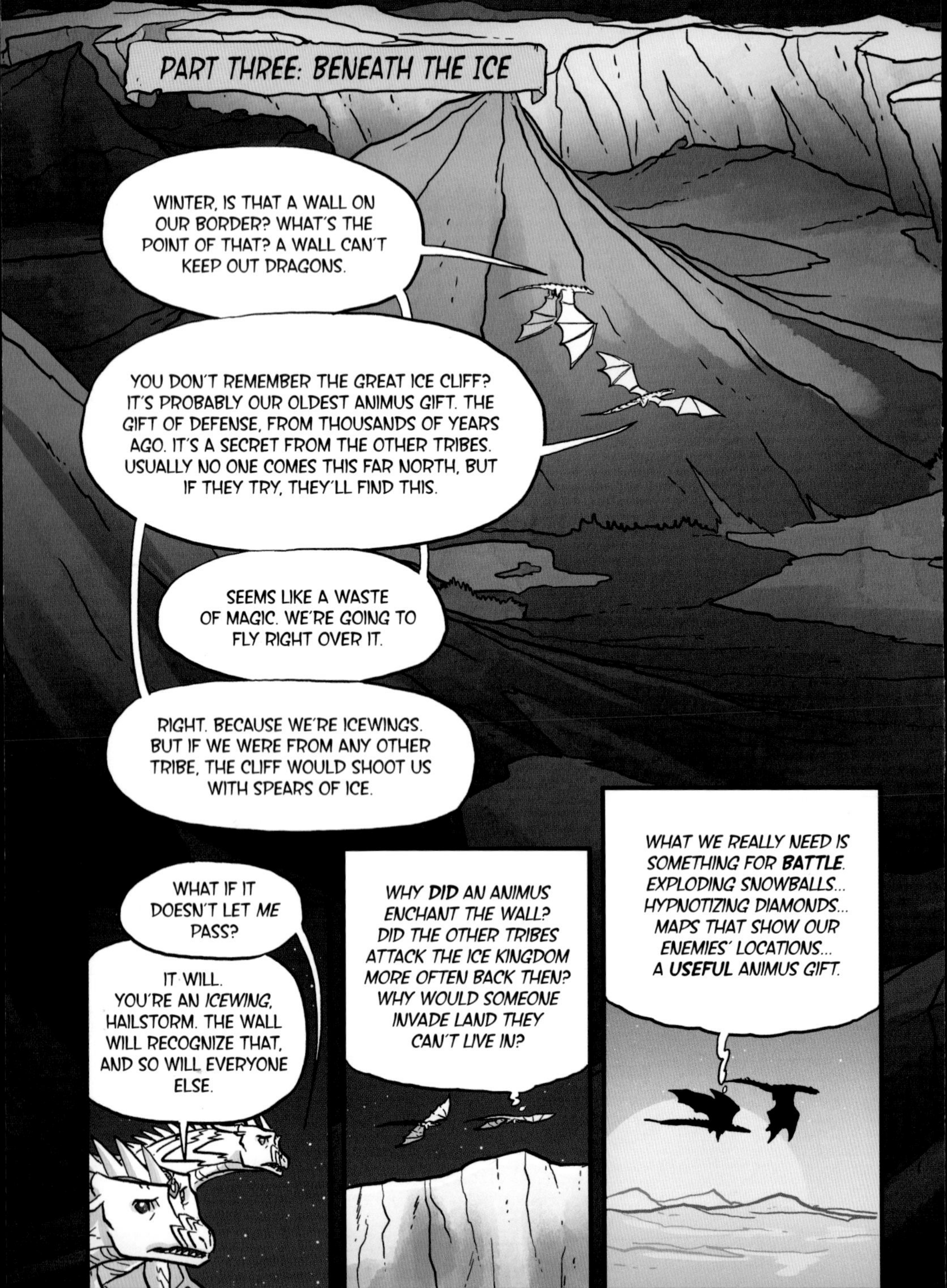
PART THREE: BENEATH THE ICE
WINTER, IS THAT A WALL ON OUR BORDER? WHAT'S THE POINT OF THAT? A WALL CAN'T KEEP OUT DRAGONS.
YOU DON'T REMEMBER THE GREAT ICE CLIFF? IT'S PROBABLY OUR OLDEST ANIMUS GIFT. THE GIFT OF DEFENSE, FROM THOUSANDS OF YEARS AGO. IT'S A SECRET FROM THE OTHER TRIBES. USUALLY NO ONE COMES THIS FAR NORTH, BUT IF THEY TRY, THEY'LL FIND THIS.
SEEMS LIKE A WASTE OF MAGIC. WE'RE GOING TO FLY RIGHT OVER IT.
RIGHT. BECAUSE WE'RE ICEWINGS. BUT IF WE WERE FROM ANY OTHER TRIBE, THE CLIFF WOULD SHOOT US WITH SPEARS OF ICE.
WHAT IF IT DOESN'T LET *ME* PASS?
IT WILL. YOU'RE AN *ICEWING*, HAILSTORM. THE WALL WILL RECOGNIZE THAT, AND SO WILL EVERYONE ELSE.
*WHY **DID** AN ANIMUS ENCHANT THE WALL? DID THE OTHER TRIBES ATTACK THE ICE KINGDOM MORE OFTEN BACK THEN? WHY WOULD SOMEONE INVADE LAND THEY CAN'T LIVE IN?*
*WHAT WE REALLY NEED IS SOMETHING FOR **BATTLE**. EXPLODING SNOWBALLS... HYPNOTIZING DIAMONDS... MAPS THAT SHOW OUR ENEMIES' LOCATIONS... A **USEFUL** ANIMUS GIFT.*

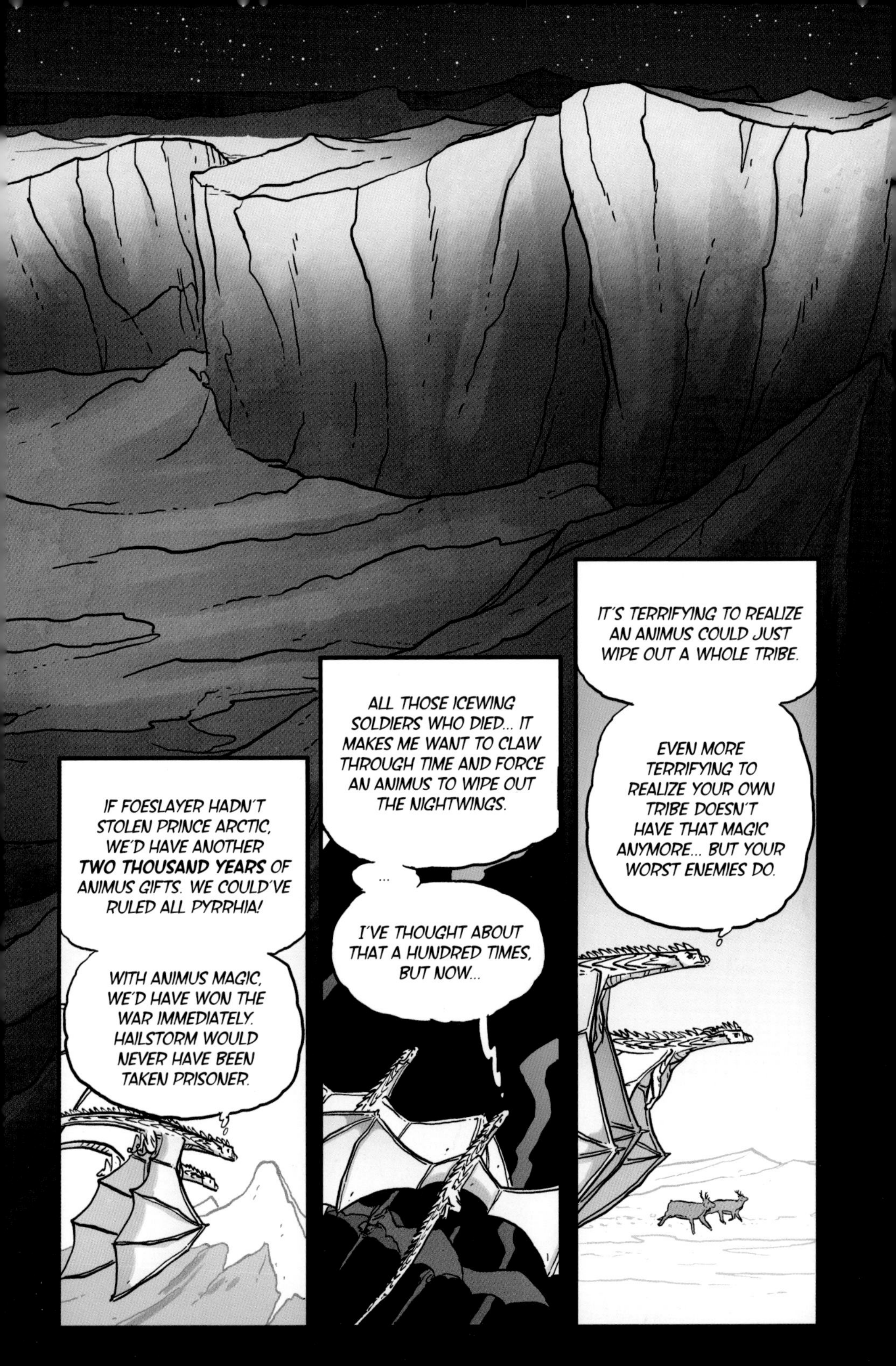
IF FOESLAYER HADN'T STOLEN PRINCE ARCTIC, WE'D HAVE ANOTHER **TWO THOUSAND YEARS** OF ANIMUS GIFTS. WE COULD'VE RULED ALL PYRRHIA!
WITH ANIMUS MAGIC, WE'D HAVE WON THE WAR IMMEDIATELY. HAILSTORM WOULD NEVER HAVE BEEN TAKEN PRISONER.
ALL THOSE ICEWING SOLDIERS WHO DIED... IT MAKES ME WANT TO CLAW THROUGH TIME AND FORCE AN ANIMUS TO WIPE OUT THE NIGHTWINGS.
...
I'VE THOUGHT ABOUT THAT A HUNDRED TIMES, BUT NOW...
IT'S TERRIFYING TO REALIZE AN ANIMUS COULD JUST WIPE OUT A WHOLE TRIBE.
EVEN MORE TERRIFYING TO REALIZE YOUR OWN TRIBE DOESN'T HAVE THAT MAGIC ANYMORE... BUT YOUR WORST ENEMIES DO.

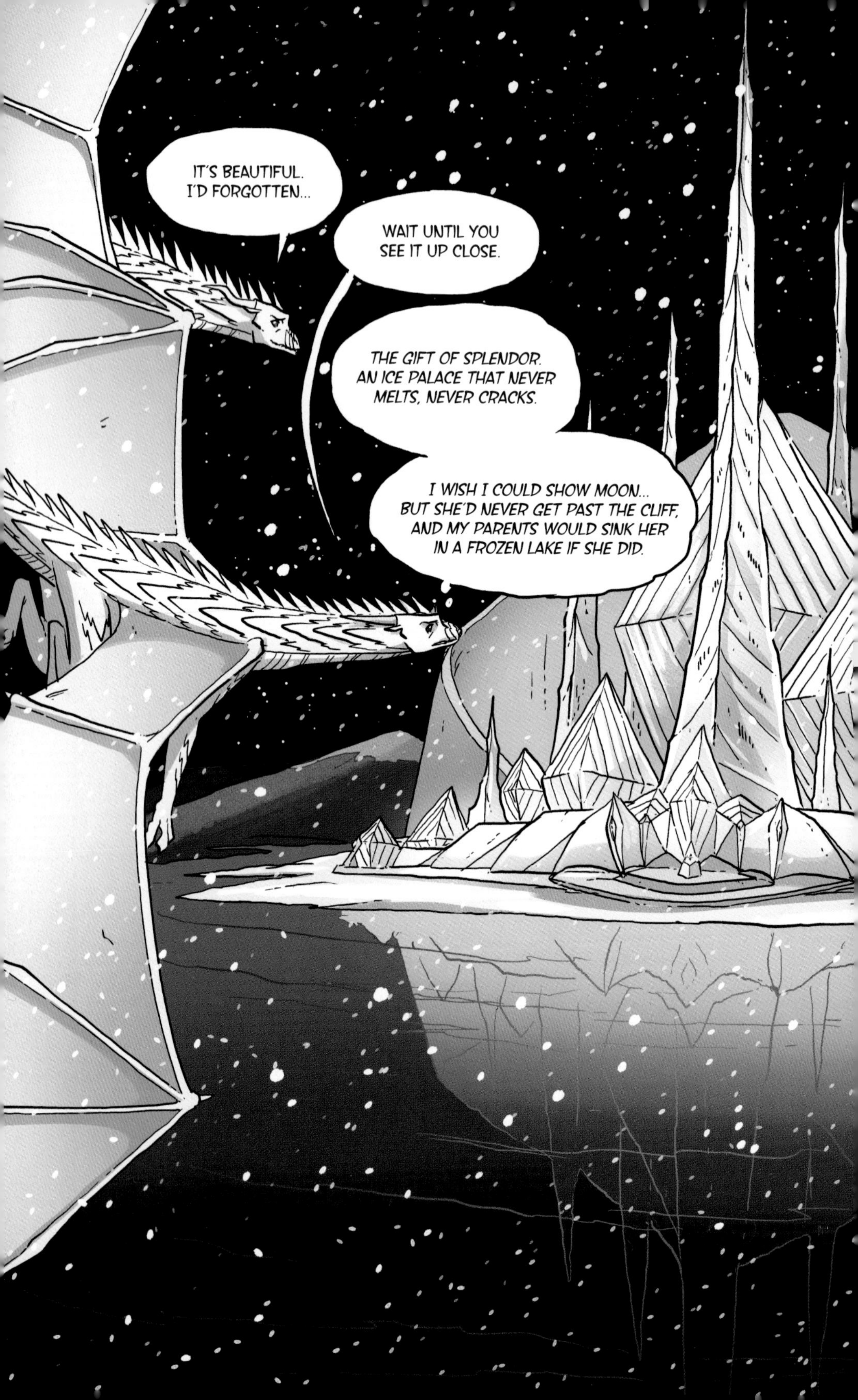
IT'S BEAUTIFUL. I'D FORGOTTEN...
WAIT UNTIL YOU SEE IT UP CLOSE.
THE GIFT OF SPLENDOR. AN ICE PALACE THAT NEVER MELTS, NEVER CRACKS.
I WISH I COULD SHOW MOON... BUT SHE'D NEVER GET PAST THE CLIFF, AND MY PARENTS WOULD SINK HER IN A FROZEN LAKE IF SHE DID.

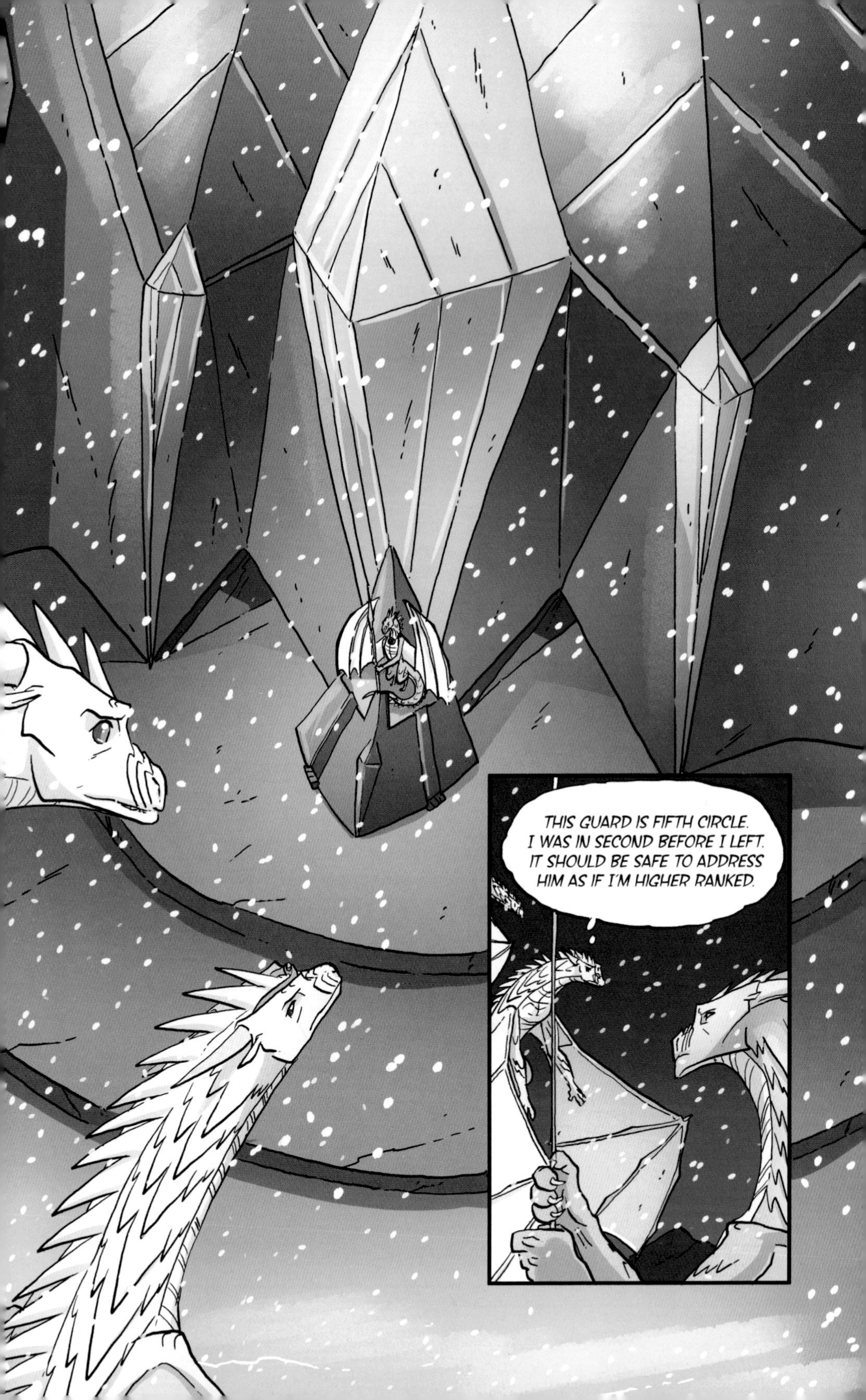
THIS GUARD IS FIFTH CIRCLE. I WAS IN SECOND BEFORE I LEFT. IT SHOULD BE SAFE TO ADDRESS HIM AS IF I'M HIGHER RANKED.

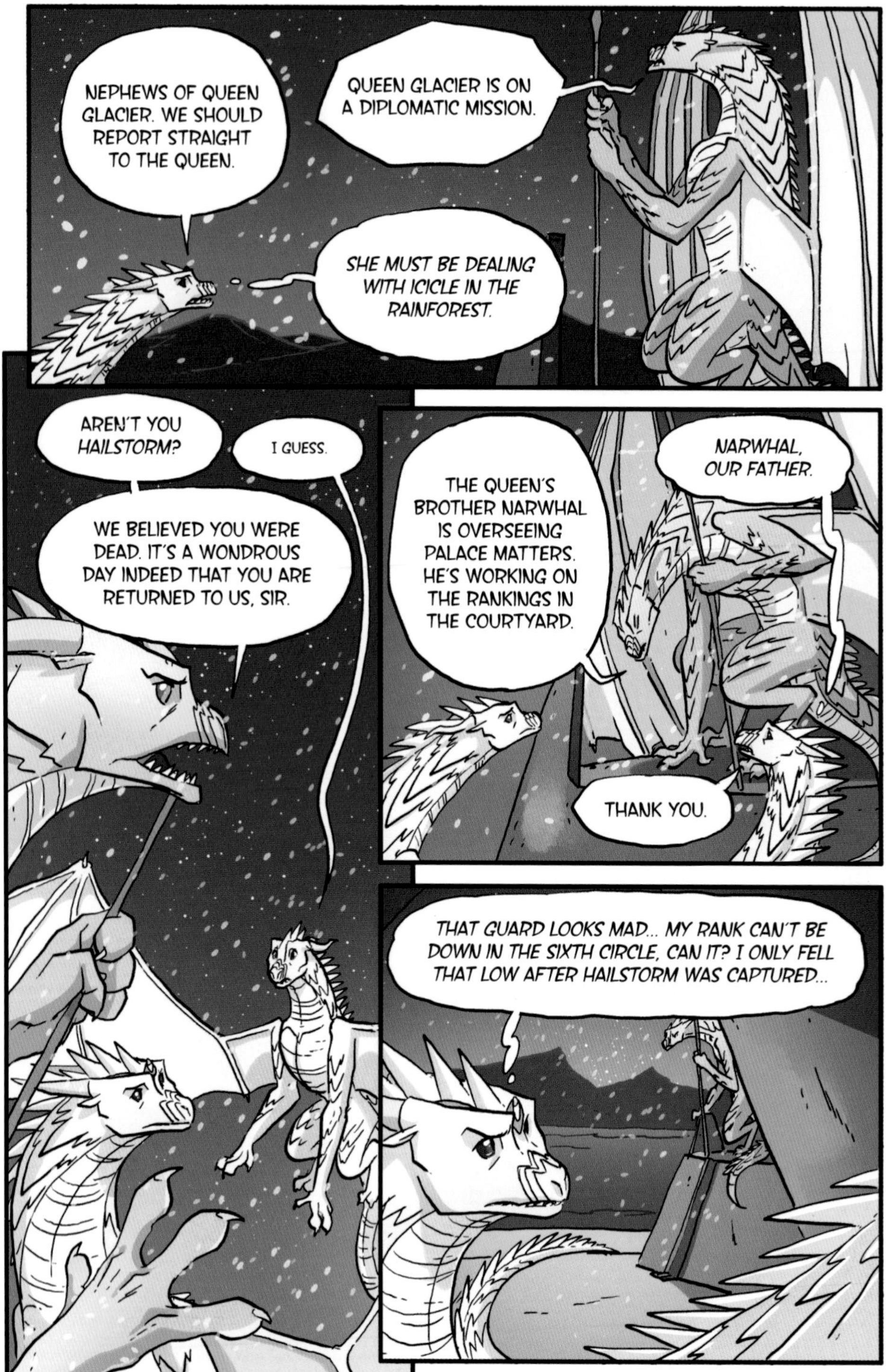
NEPHEWS OF QUEEN GLACIER. WE SHOULD REPORT STRAIGHT TO THE QUEEN.
QUEEN GLACIER IS ON A DIPLOMATIC MISSION.
SHE MUST BE DEALING WITH ICICLE IN THE RAINFOREST.
AREN'T YOU HAILSTORM?
I GUESS.
WE BELIEVED YOU WERE DEAD. IT'S A WONDROUS DAY INDEED THAT YOU ARE RETURNED TO US, SIR.
THE QUEEN'S BROTHER NARWHAL IS OVERSEEING PALACE MATTERS. HE'S WORKING ON THE RANKINGS IN THE COURTYARD.
NARWHAL, OUR FATHER.
THANK YOU.
THAT GUARD LOOKS MAD... MY RANK CAN'T BE DOWN IN THE SIXTH CIRCLE, CAN IT? I ONLY FELL THAT LOW AFTER HAILSTORM WAS CAPTURED...

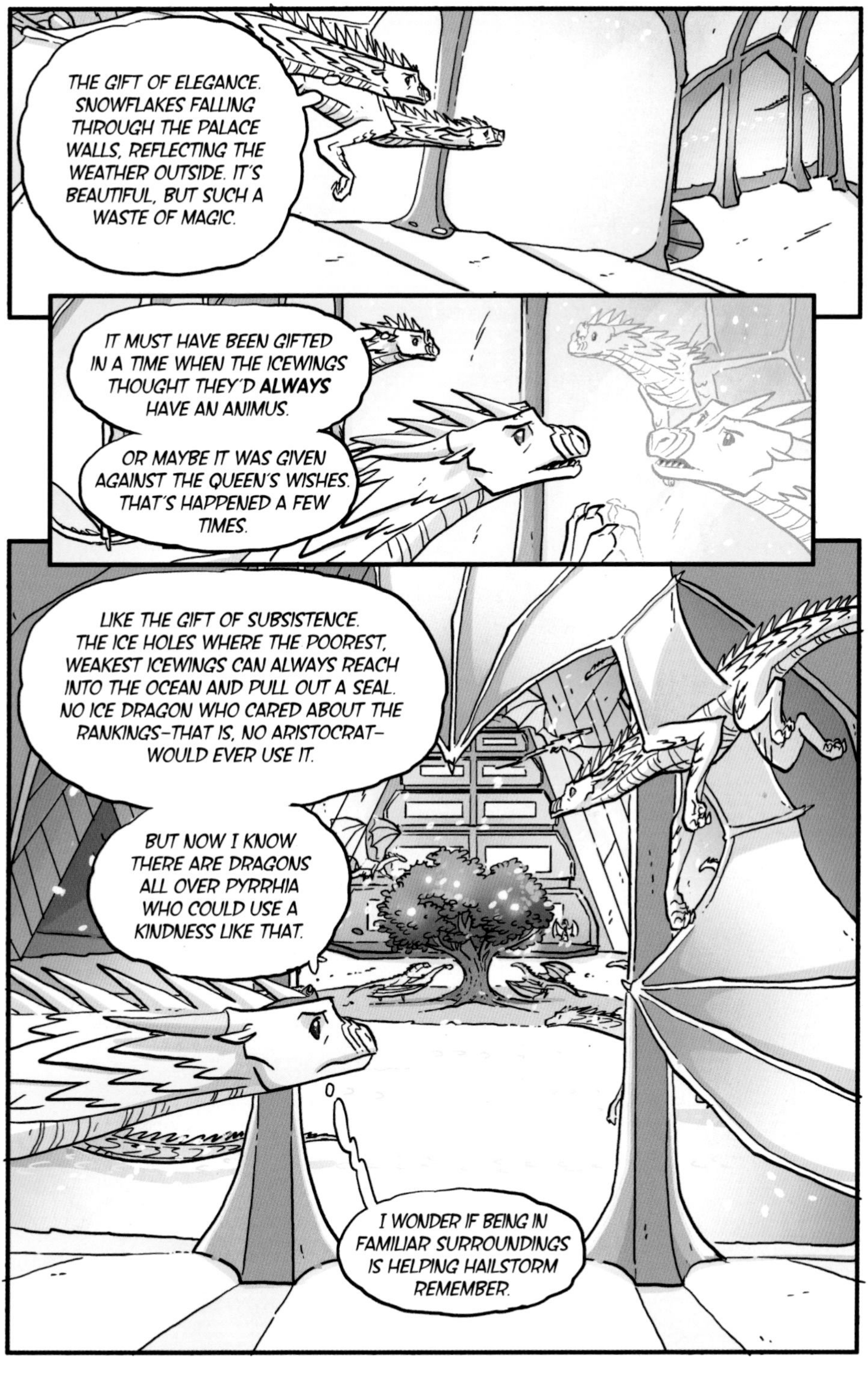
THE GIFT OF ELEGANCE. SNOWFLAKES FALLING THROUGH THE PALACE WALLS, REFLECTING THE WEATHER OUTSIDE. IT'S BEAUTIFUL, BUT SUCH A WASTE OF MAGIC.
IT MUST HAVE BEEN GIFTED IN A TIME WHEN THE ICEWINGS THOUGHT THEY'D **ALWAYS** HAVE AN ANIMUS.
OR MAYBE IT WAS GIVEN AGAINST THE QUEEN'S WISHES. THAT'S HAPPENED A FEW TIMES.
LIKE THE GIFT OF SUBSISTENCE. THE ICE HOLES WHERE THE POOREST, WEAKEST ICEWINGS CAN ALWAYS REACH INTO THE OCEAN AND PULL OUT A SEAL. NO ICE DRAGON WHO CARED ABOUT THE RANKINGS–THAT IS, NO ARISTOCRAT–WOULD EVER USE IT.
BUT NOW I KNOW THERE ARE DRAGONS ALL OVER PYRRHIA WHO COULD USE A KINDNESS LIKE THAT.
I WONDER IF BEING IN FAMILIAR SURROUNDINGS IS HELPING HAILSTORM REMEMBER.

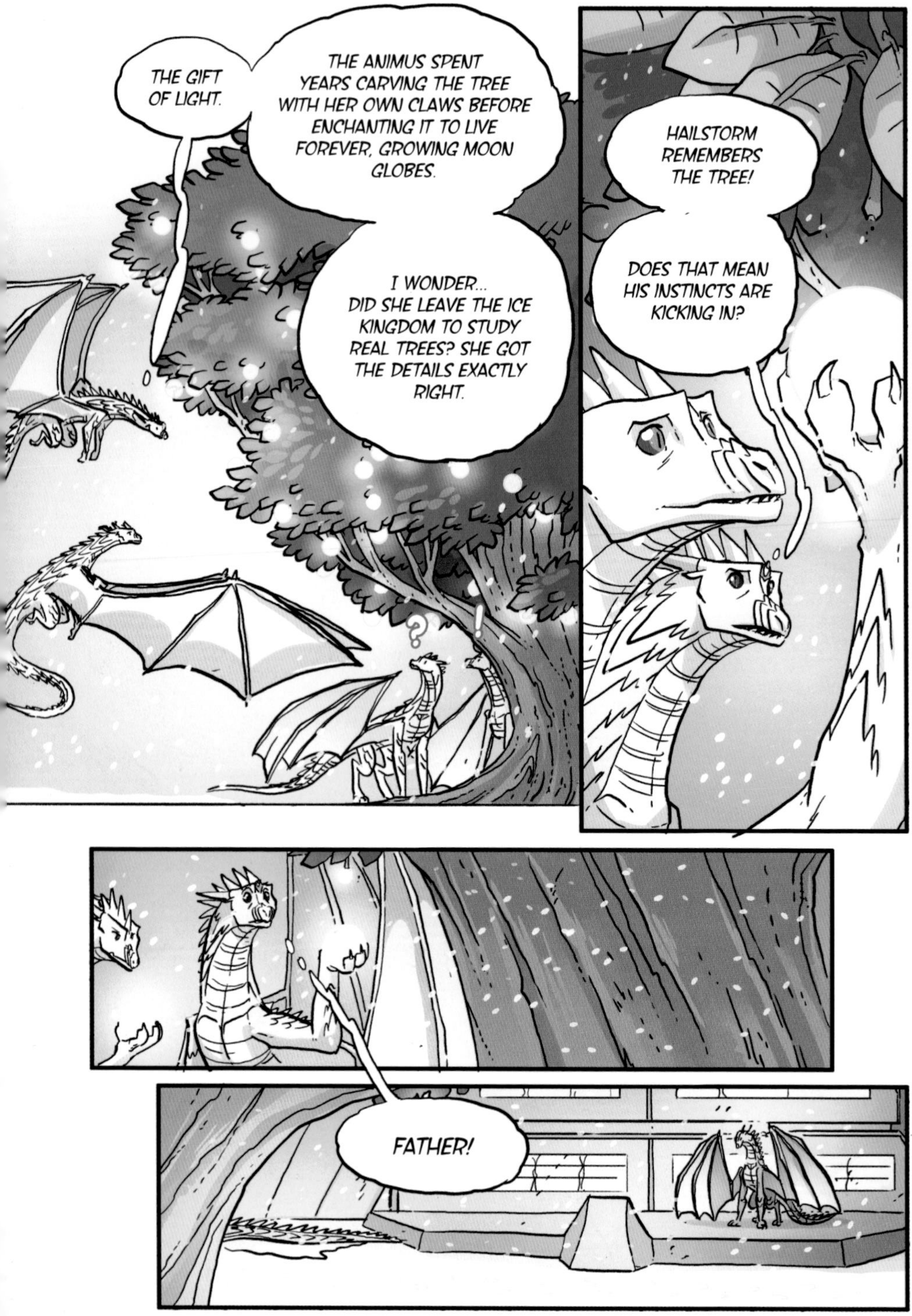
THE GIFT OF LIGHT.
THE ANIMUS SPENT YEARS CARVING THE TREE WITH HER OWN CLAWS BEFORE ENCHANTING IT TO LIVE FOREVER, GROWING MOON GLOBES.
I WONDER... DID SHE LEAVE THE ICE KINGDOM TO STUDY REAL TREES? SHE GOT THE DETAILS EXACTLY RIGHT.
HAILSTORM REMEMBERS THE TREE!
DOES THAT MEAN HIS INSTINCTS ARE KICKING IN?
FATHER!

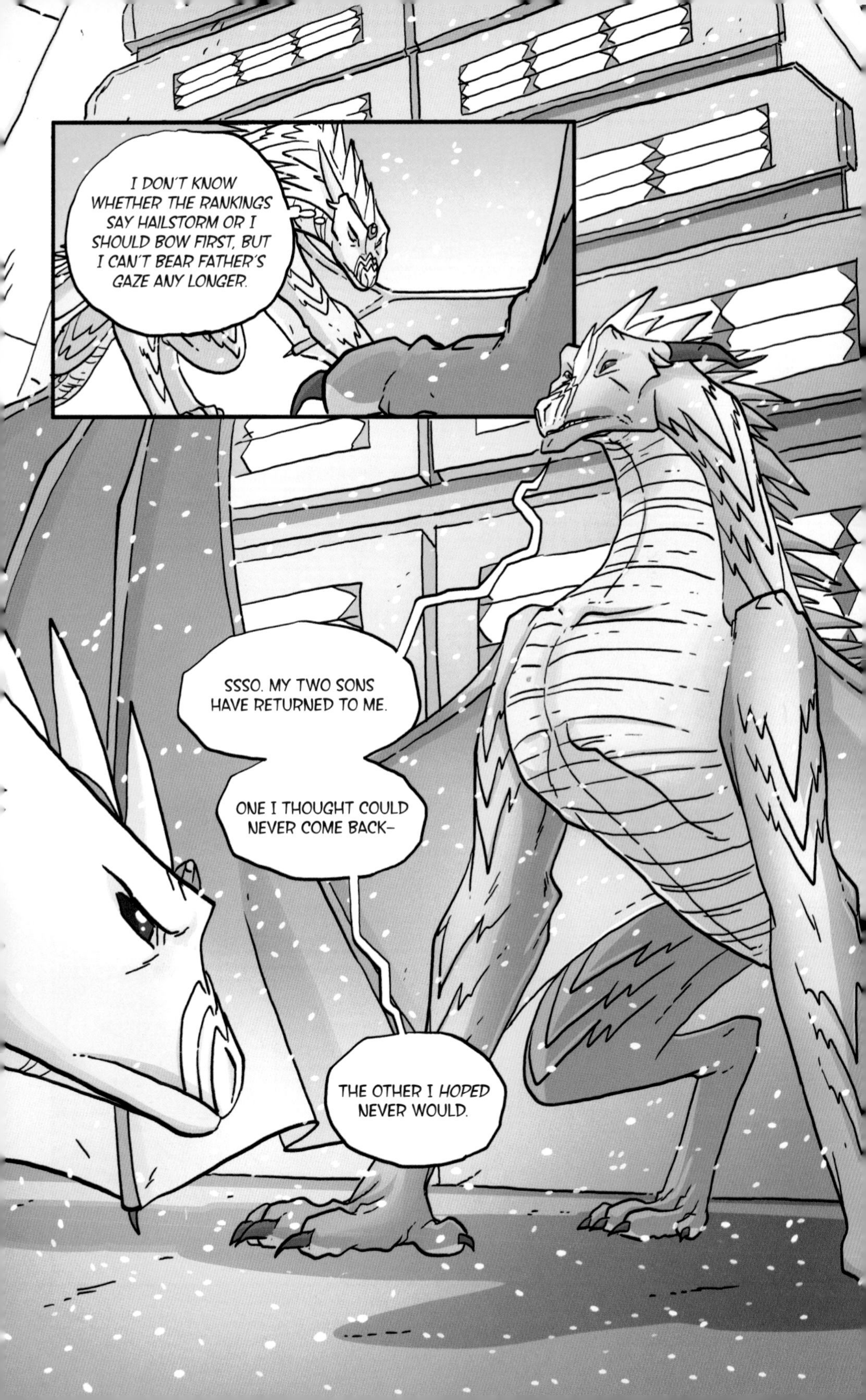
I DON'T KNOW WHETHER THE RANKINGS SAY HAILSTORM OR I SHOULD BOW FIRST, BUT I CAN'T BEAR FATHER'S GAZE ANY LONGER.
SSSO. MY TWO SONS HAVE RETURNED TO ME.
ONE I THOUGHT COULD NEVER COME BACK–
THE OTHER I *HOPED* NEVER WOULD.

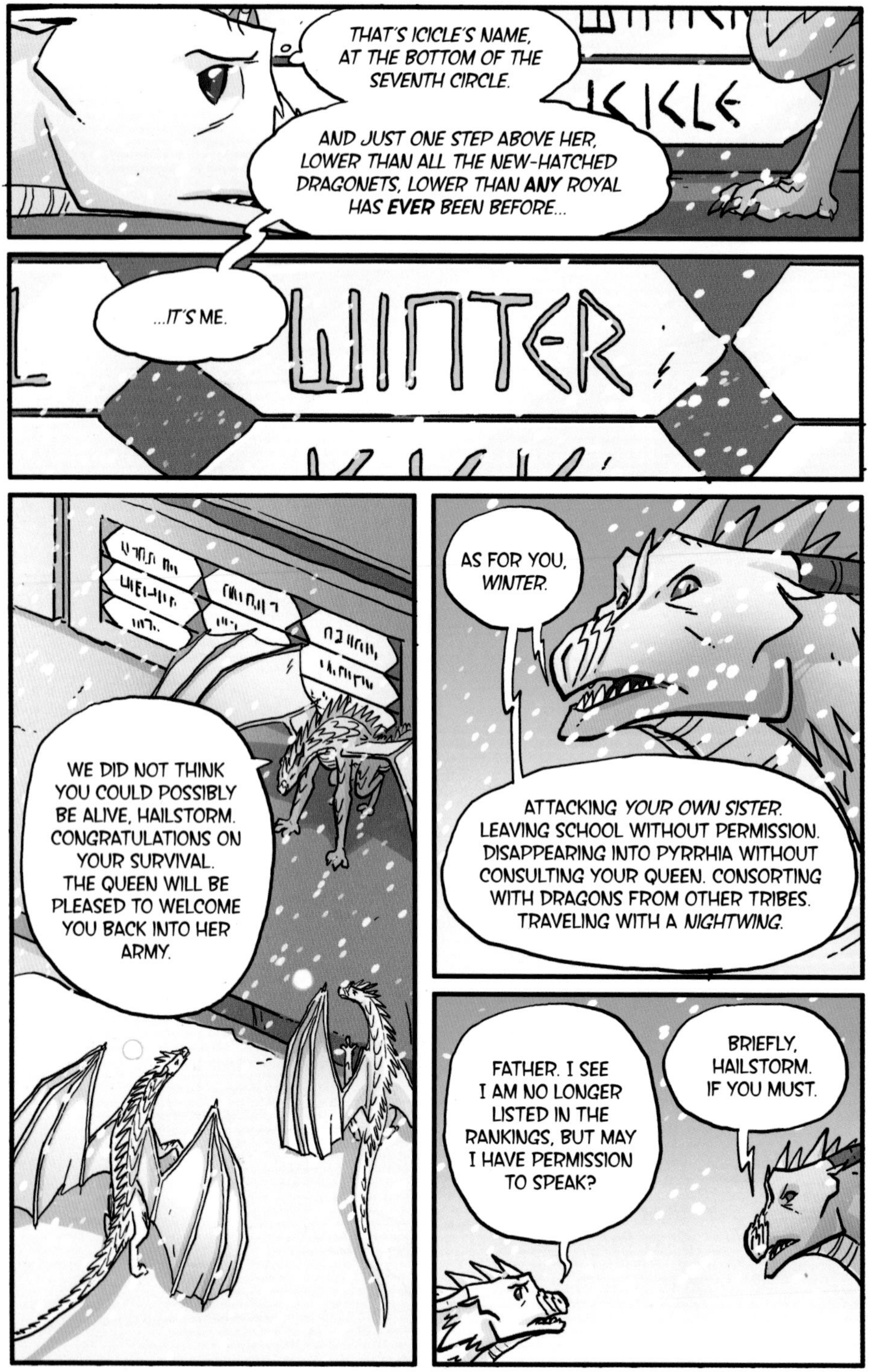
THAT'S ICICLE'S NAME, AT THE BOTTOM OF THE SEVENTH CIRCLE.
ICICLE
AND JUST ONE STEP ABOVE HER, LOWER THAN ALL THE NEW-HATCHED DRAGONETS, LOWER THAN **ANY** ROYAL HAS **EVER** BEEN BEFORE...
...IT'S ME.
WINTER
WE DID NOT THINK YOU COULD POSSIBLY BE ALIVE, HAILSTORM. CONGRATULATIONS ON YOUR SURVIVAL. THE QUEEN WILL BE PLEASED TO WELCOME YOU BACK INTO HER ARMY.
AS FOR YOU, *WINTER.*
ATTACKING *YOUR OWN SISTER.* LEAVING SCHOOL WITHOUT PERMISSION. DISAPPEARING INTO PYRRHIA WITHOUT CONSULTING YOUR QUEEN. CONSORTING WITH DRAGONS FROM OTHER TRIBES. TRAVELING WITH A *NIGHTWING.*
FATHER. I SEE I AM NO LONGER LISTED IN THE RANKINGS, BUT MAY I HAVE PERMISSION TO SPEAK?
BRIEFLY, HAILSTORM. IF YOU MUST.

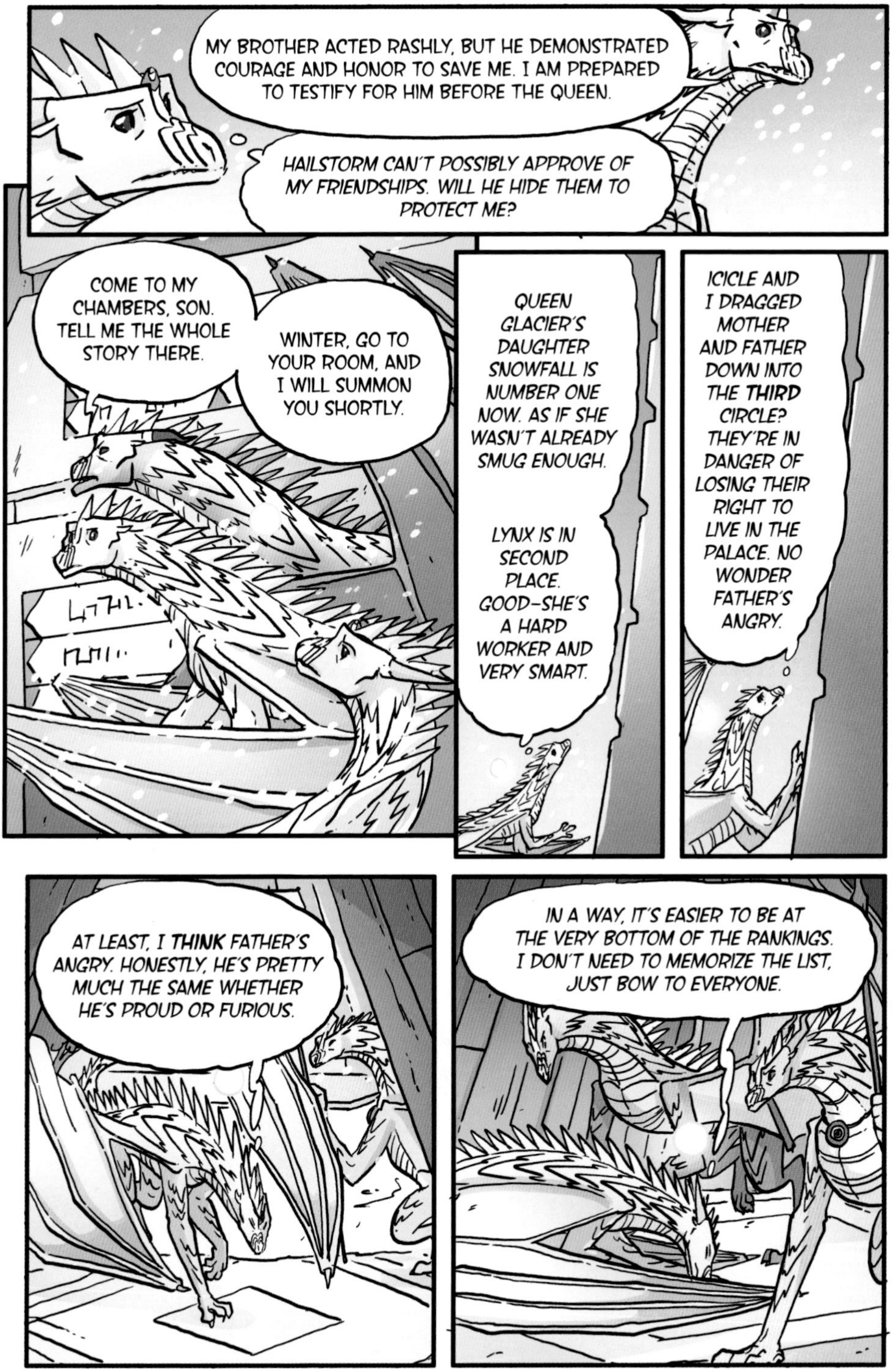
MY BROTHER ACTED RASHLY, BUT HE DEMONSTRATED COURAGE AND HONOR TO SAVE ME. I AM PREPARED TO TESTIFY FOR HIM BEFORE THE QUEEN.
HAILSTORM CAN'T POSSIBLY APPROVE OF MY FRIENDSHIPS. WILL HE HIDE THEM TO PROTECT ME?
COME TO MY CHAMBERS, SON. TELL ME THE WHOLE STORY THERE.
WINTER, GO TO YOUR ROOM, AND I WILL SUMMON YOU SHORTLY.
QUEEN GLACIER'S DAUGHTER SNOWFALL IS NUMBER ONE NOW. AS IF SHE WASN'T ALREADY SMUG ENOUGH.
LYNX IS IN SECOND PLACE. GOOD—SHE'S A HARD WORKER AND VERY SMART.
ICICLE AND I DRAGGED MOTHER AND FATHER DOWN INTO THE THIRD CIRCLE? THEY'RE IN DANGER OF LOSING THEIR RIGHT TO LIVE IN THE PALACE. NO WONDER FATHER'S ANGRY.
AT LEAST, I THINK FATHER'S ANGRY. HONESTLY, HE'S PRETTY MUCH THE SAME WHETHER HE'S PROUD OR FURIOUS.
IN A WAY, IT'S EASIER TO BE AT THE VERY BOTTOM OF THE RANKINGS. I DON'T NEED TO MEMORIZE THE LIST, JUST BOW TO EVERYONE.

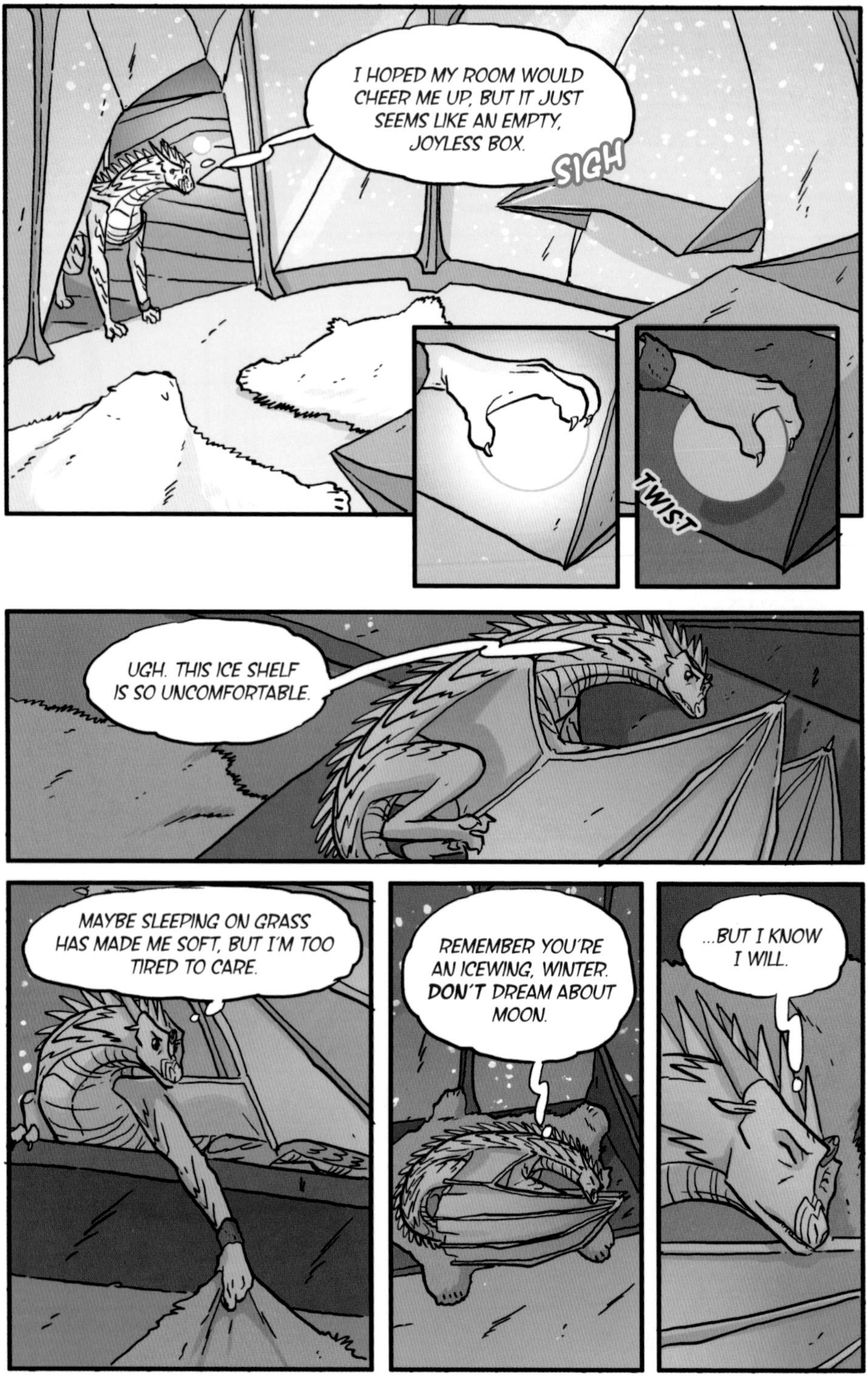
I HOPED MY ROOM WOULD CHEER ME UP, BUT IT JUST SEEMS LIKE AN EMPTY, JOYLESS BOX.
SIGH
TWIST
UGH. THIS ICE SHELF IS SO UNCOMFORTABLE.
MAYBE SLEEPING ON GRASS HAS MADE ME SOFT, BUT I'M TOO TIRED TO CARE.
REMEMBER YOU'RE AN ICEWING, WINTER. DON'T DREAM ABOUT MOON.
...BUT I KNOW I WILL.

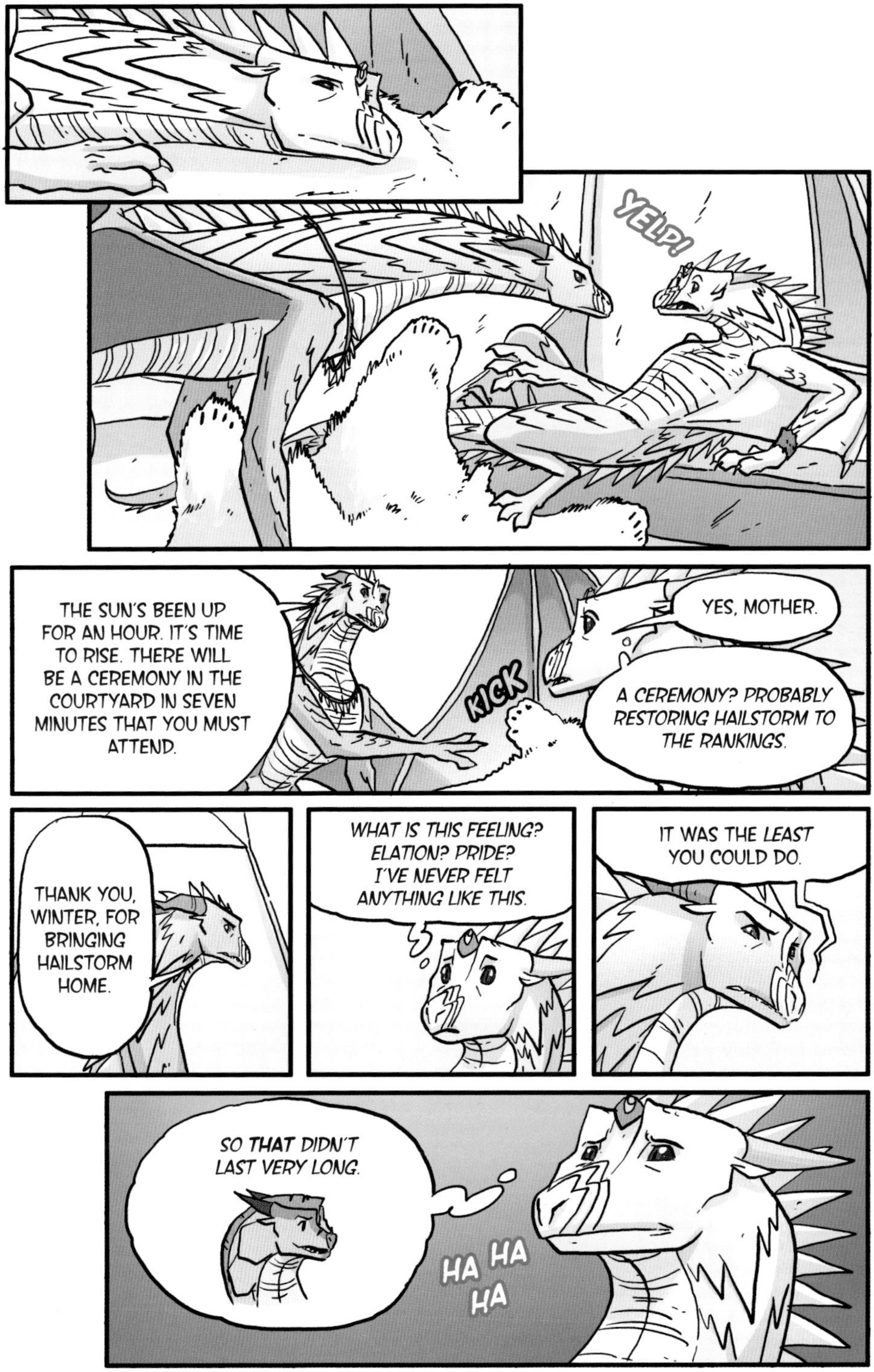
YELP!
THE SUN'S BEEN UP FOR AN HOUR. IT'S TIME TO RISE. THERE WILL BE A CEREMONY IN THE COURTYARD IN SEVEN MINUTES THAT YOU MUST ATTEND.
KICK
YES, MOTHER.
A CEREMONY? PROBABLY RESTORING HAILSTORM TO THE RANKINGS.
THANK YOU, WINTER, FOR BRINGING HAILSTORM HOME.
WHAT IS THIS FEELING? ELATION? PRIDE? I'VE NEVER FELT ANYTHING LIKE THIS.
IT WAS THE LEAST YOU COULD DO.
SO THAT DIDN'T LAST VERY LONG.
HA HA HA

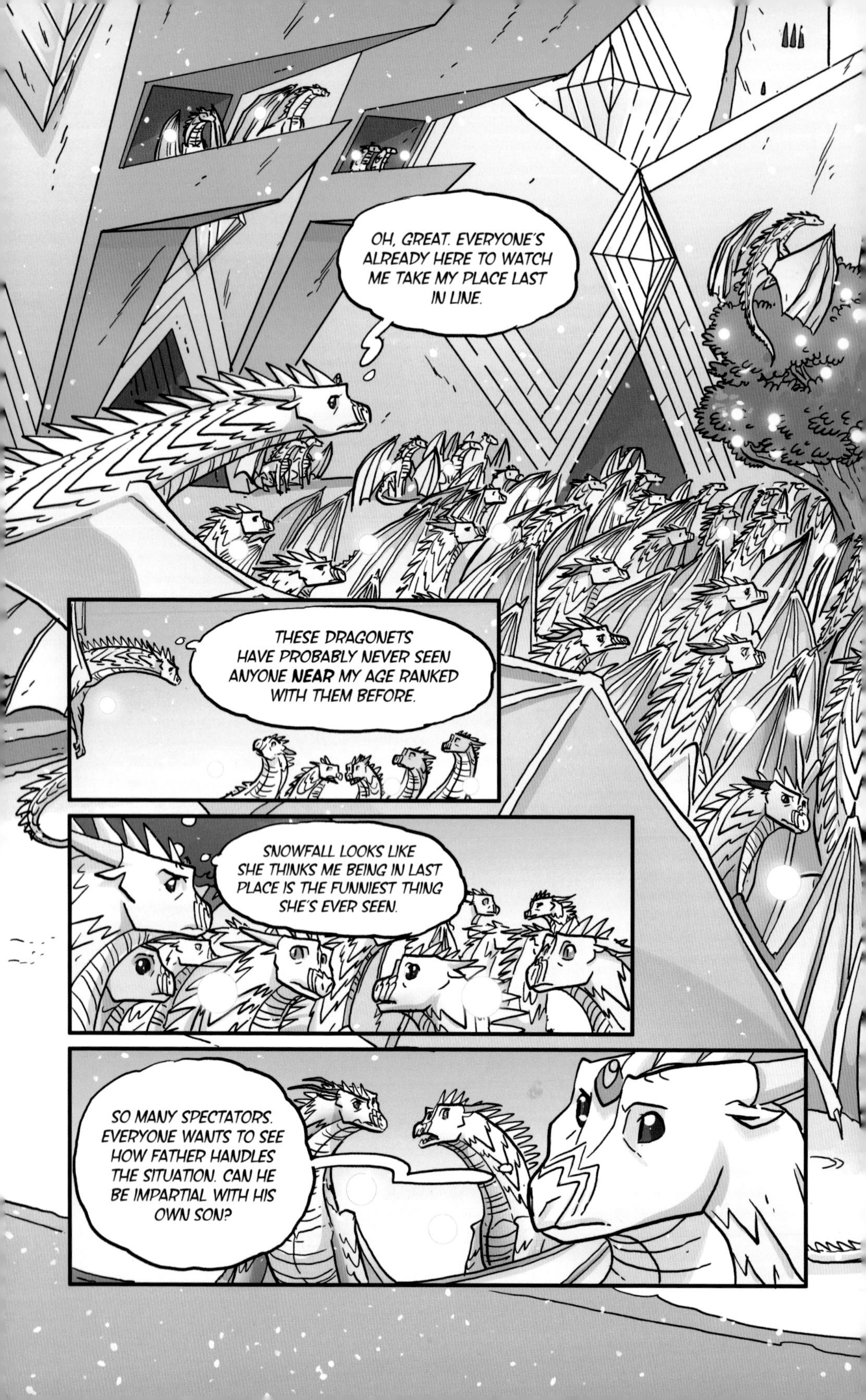
OH, GREAT. EVERYONE'S ALREADY HERE TO WATCH ME TAKE MY PLACE LAST IN LINE.
THESE DRAGONETS HAVE PROBABLY NEVER SEEN ANYONE **NEAR** MY AGE RANKED WITH THEM BEFORE.
SNOWFALL LOOKS LIKE SHE THINKS ME BEING IN LAST PLACE IS THE FUNNIEST THING SHE'S EVER SEEN.
SO MANY SPECTATORS. EVERYONE WANTS TO SEE HOW FATHER HANDLES THE SITUATION. CAN HE BE IMPARTIAL WITH HIS OWN SON?

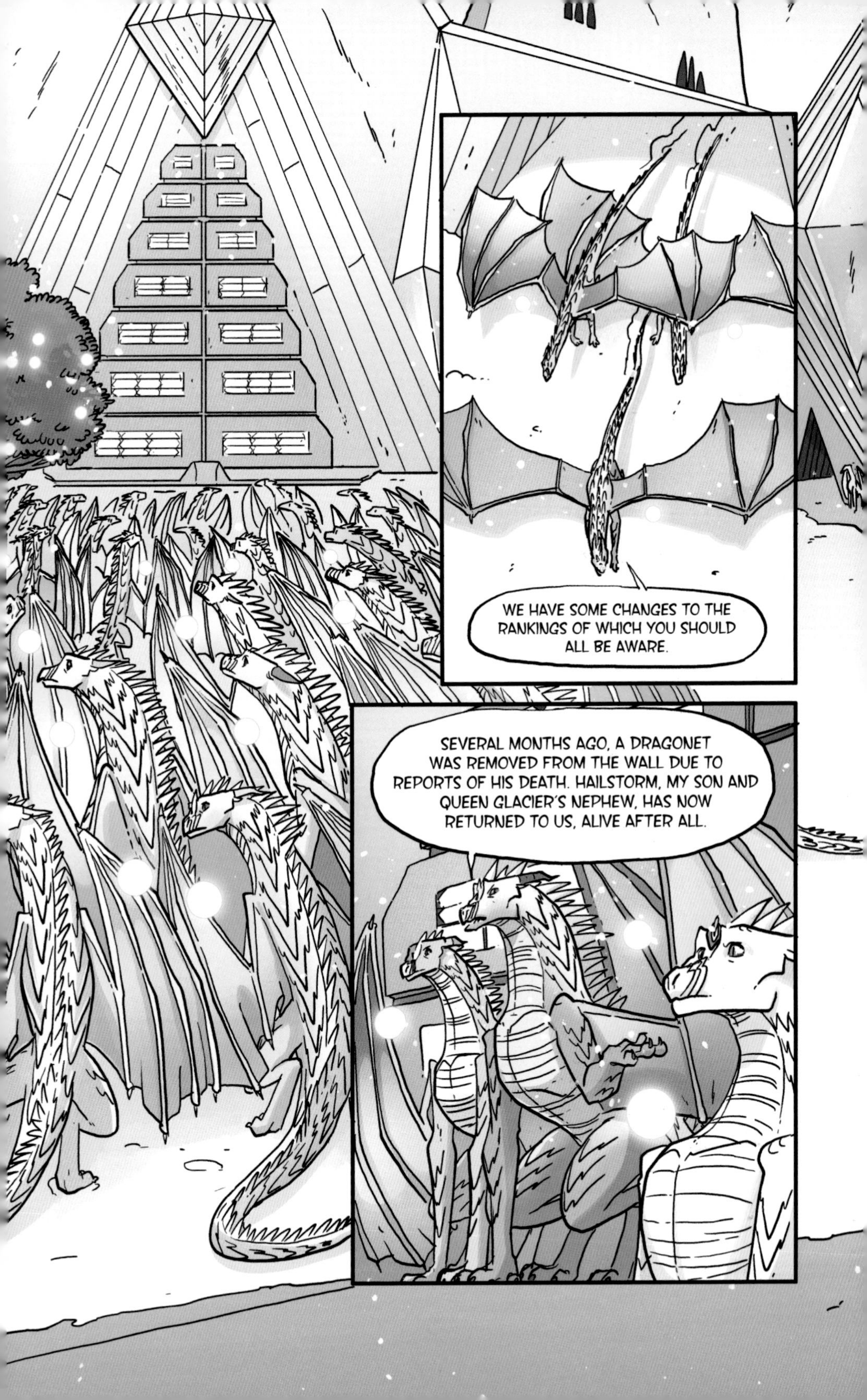
WE HAVE SOME CHANGES TO THE RANKINGS OF WHICH YOU SHOULD ALL BE AWARE.
SEVERAL MONTHS AGO, A DRAGONET WAS REMOVED FROM THE WALL DUE TO REPORTS OF HIS DEATH. HAILSTORM, MY SON AND QUEEN GLACIER'S NEPHEW, HAS NOW RETURNED TO US, ALIVE AFTER ALL.

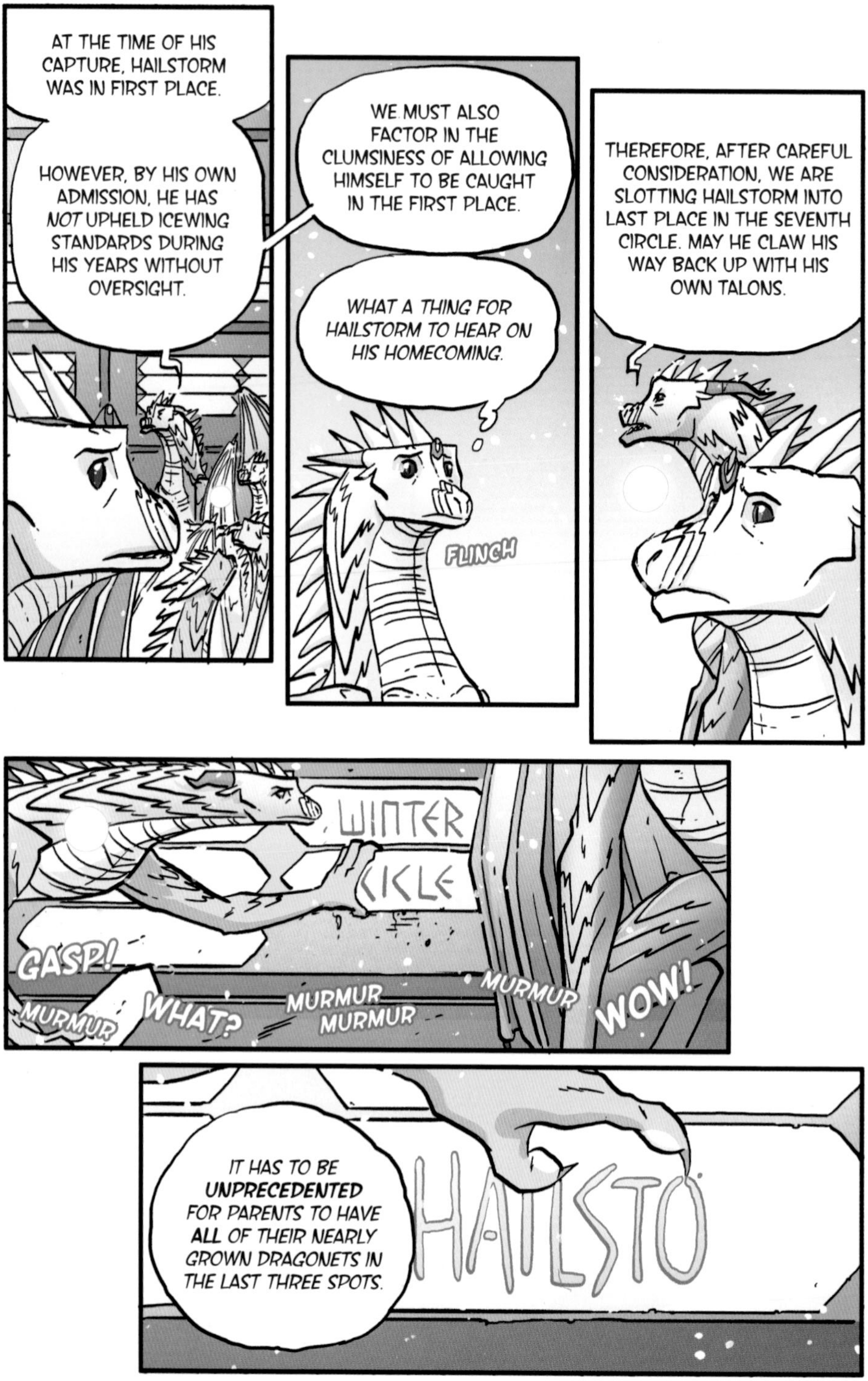
AT THE TIME OF HIS CAPTURE, HAILSTORM WAS IN FIRST PLACE.
HOWEVER, BY HIS OWN ADMISSION, HE HAS *NOT* UPHELD ICEWING STANDARDS DURING HIS YEARS WITHOUT OVERSIGHT.
WE MUST ALSO FACTOR IN THE CLUMSINESS OF ALLOWING HIMSELF TO BE CAUGHT IN THE FIRST PLACE.
WHAT A THING FOR HAILSTORM TO HEAR ON HIS HOMECOMING.
FLINCH
THEREFORE, AFTER CAREFUL CONSIDERATION, WE ARE SLOTTING HAILSTORM INTO LAST PLACE IN THE SEVENTH CIRCLE. MAY HE CLAW HIS WAY BACK UP WITH HIS OWN TALONS.
WINTER
CICLE
GASP!
MURMUR
WHAT?
MURMUR MURMUR
MURMUR
WOW!
IT HAS TO BE ***UNPRECEDENTED*** *FOR PARENTS TO HAVE* ***ALL*** *OF THEIR NEARLY GROWN DRAGONETS IN THE LAST THREE SPOTS.*
HAILSTO

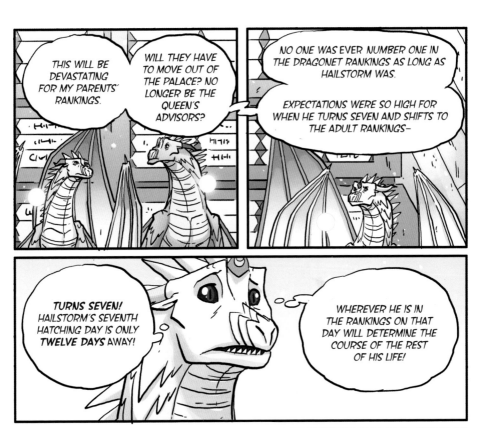

THIS WILL BE DEVASTATING FOR MY PARENTS' RANKINGS.

WILL THEY HAVE TO MOVE OUT OF THE PALACE? NO LONGER BE THE QUEEN'S ADVISORS?

NO ONE WAS EVER NUMBER ONE IN THE DRAGONET RANKINGS AS LONG AS HAILSTORM WAS.

EXPECTATIONS WERE SO HIGH FOR WHEN HE TURNS SEVEN AND SHIFTS TO THE ADULT RANKINGS—

TURNS SEVEN! HAILSTORM'S SEVENTH HATCHING DAY IS ONLY TWELVE DAYS AWAY!

WHEREVER HE IS IN THE RANKINGS ON THAT DAY WILL DETERMINE THE COURSE OF THE REST OF HIS LIFE!

CAN EVEN HAILSTORM RISE BACK TO THE TOP THAT FAST? WILL HE HAVE TO RISK THE DIAMOND TRIAL?

DID I RESCUE HIM FROM ONE TERRIBLE FATE JUST TO DOOM HIM TO ANOTHER?

ONE MORE ANNOUNCEMENT. ANOTHER DRAGONET WAS RECENTLY SHIFTED TO THE BOTTOM OF THE LIST FOR UNSUPERVISED, UNAUTHORIZED ACTIVITIES.

HOWEVER, ACCORDING TO THE NEWEST INFORMATION, HE CONDUCTED HIMSELF WITH COURAGE AND INTELLIGENCE BEFITTING AN ICEWING. IN THIS CASE, THE FINAL RESULT—RETURNING A MISSING DRAGON TO THE TRIBE—OUTWEIGHS OUR DISAPPROVAL.

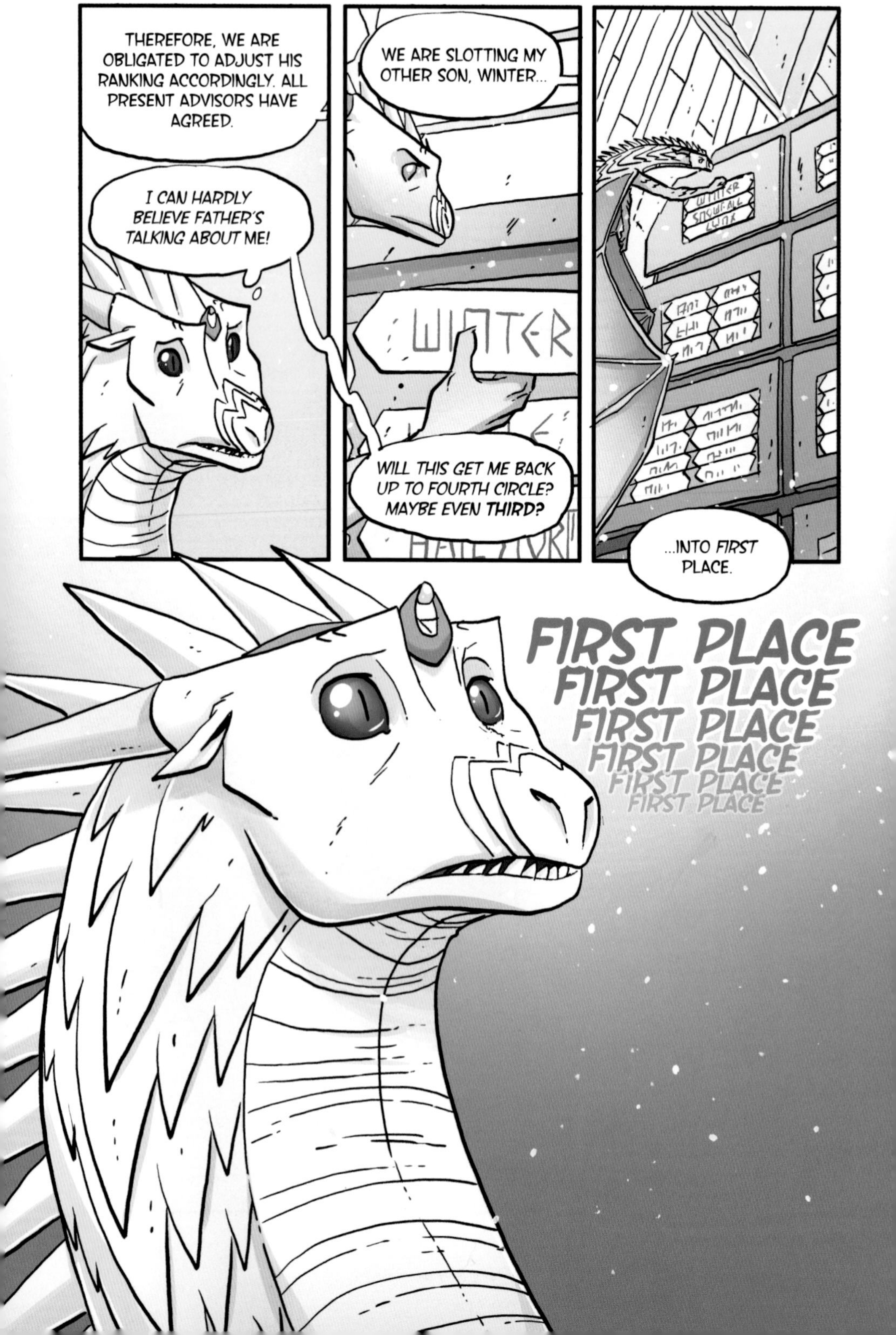
THEREFORE, WE ARE OBLIGATED TO ADJUST HIS RANKING ACCORDINGLY. ALL PRESENT ADVISORS HAVE AGREED.
I CAN HARDLY BELIEVE FATHER'S TALKING ABOUT ME!
WE ARE SLOTTING MY OTHER SON, WINTER...
WINTER
WILL THIS GET ME BACK UP TO FOURTH CIRCLE? MAYBE EVEN THIRD?
...INTO FIRST PLACE.
FIRST PLACE
FIRST PLACE
FIRST PLACE
FIRST PLACE
FIRST PLACE
FIRST PLACE

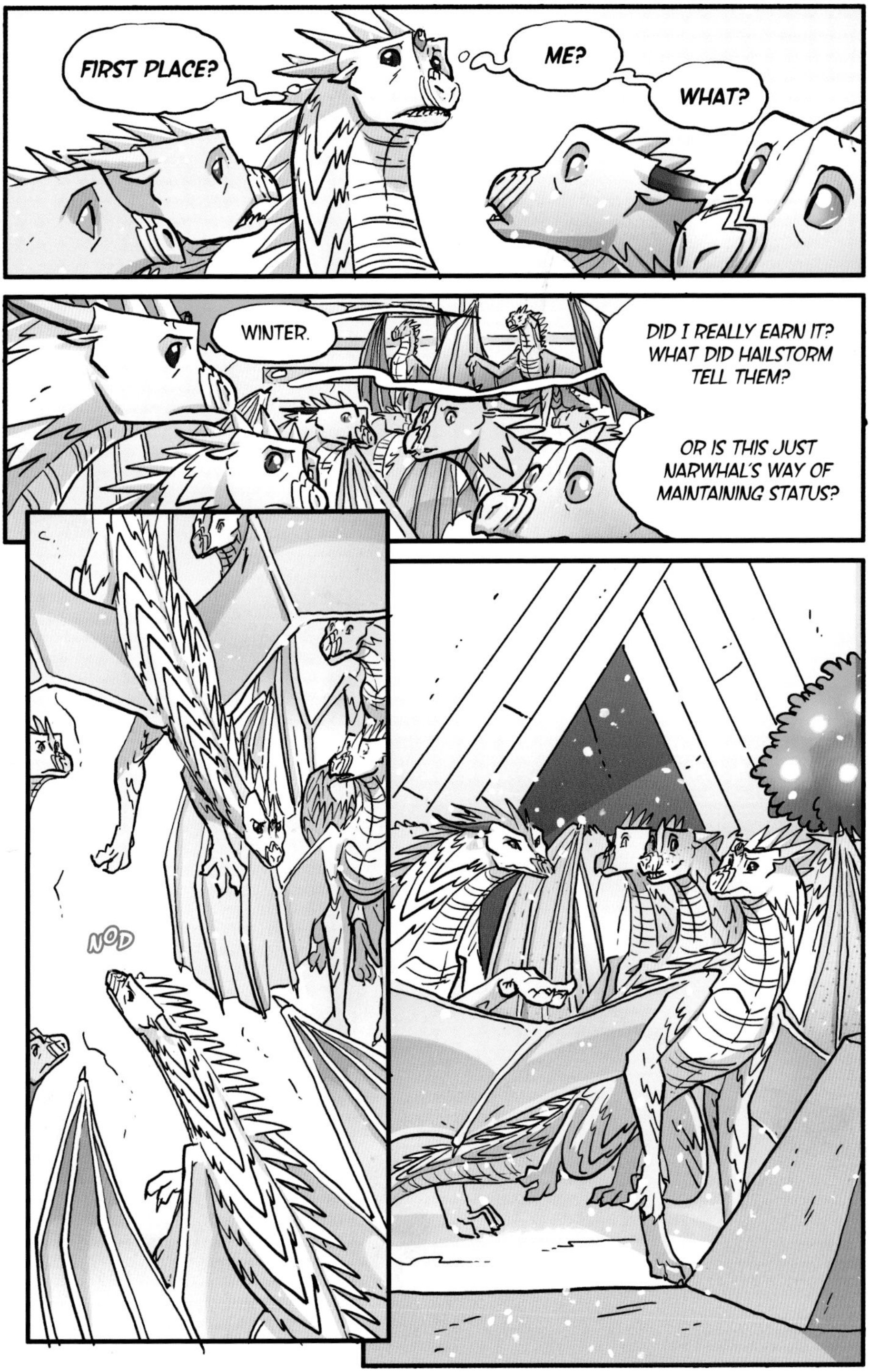
FIRST PLACE?
ME?
WHAT?
WINTER.
DID I REALLY EARN IT? WHAT DID HAILSTORM TELL THEM?
OR IS THIS JUST NARWHAL'S WAY OF MAINTAINING STATUS?
NOD

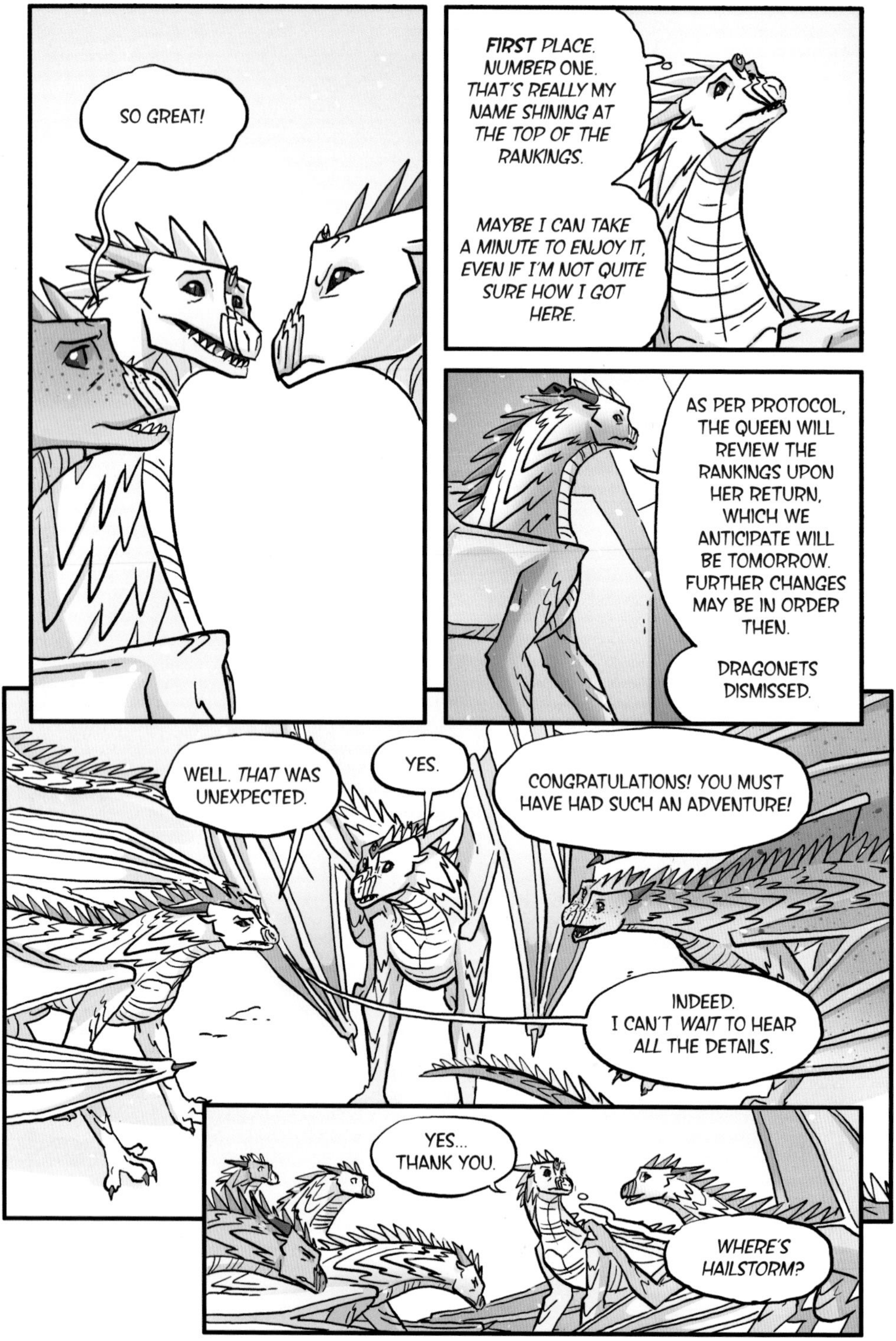
SO GREAT!
FIRST PLACE. NUMBER ONE. THAT'S REALLY MY NAME SHINING AT THE TOP OF THE RANKINGS.
MAYBE I CAN TAKE A MINUTE TO ENJOY IT, EVEN IF I'M NOT QUITE SURE HOW I GOT HERE.
AS PER PROTOCOL, THE QUEEN WILL REVIEW THE RANKINGS UPON HER RETURN, WHICH WE ANTICIPATE WILL BE TOMORROW. FURTHER CHANGES MAY BE IN ORDER THEN.
DRAGONETS DISMISSED.
WELL. THAT WAS UNEXPECTED.
YES.
CONGRATULATIONS! YOU MUST HAVE HAD SUCH AN ADVENTURE!
INDEED. I CAN'T WAIT TO HEAR ALL THE DETAILS.
YES... THANK YOU.
WHERE'S HAILSTORM?

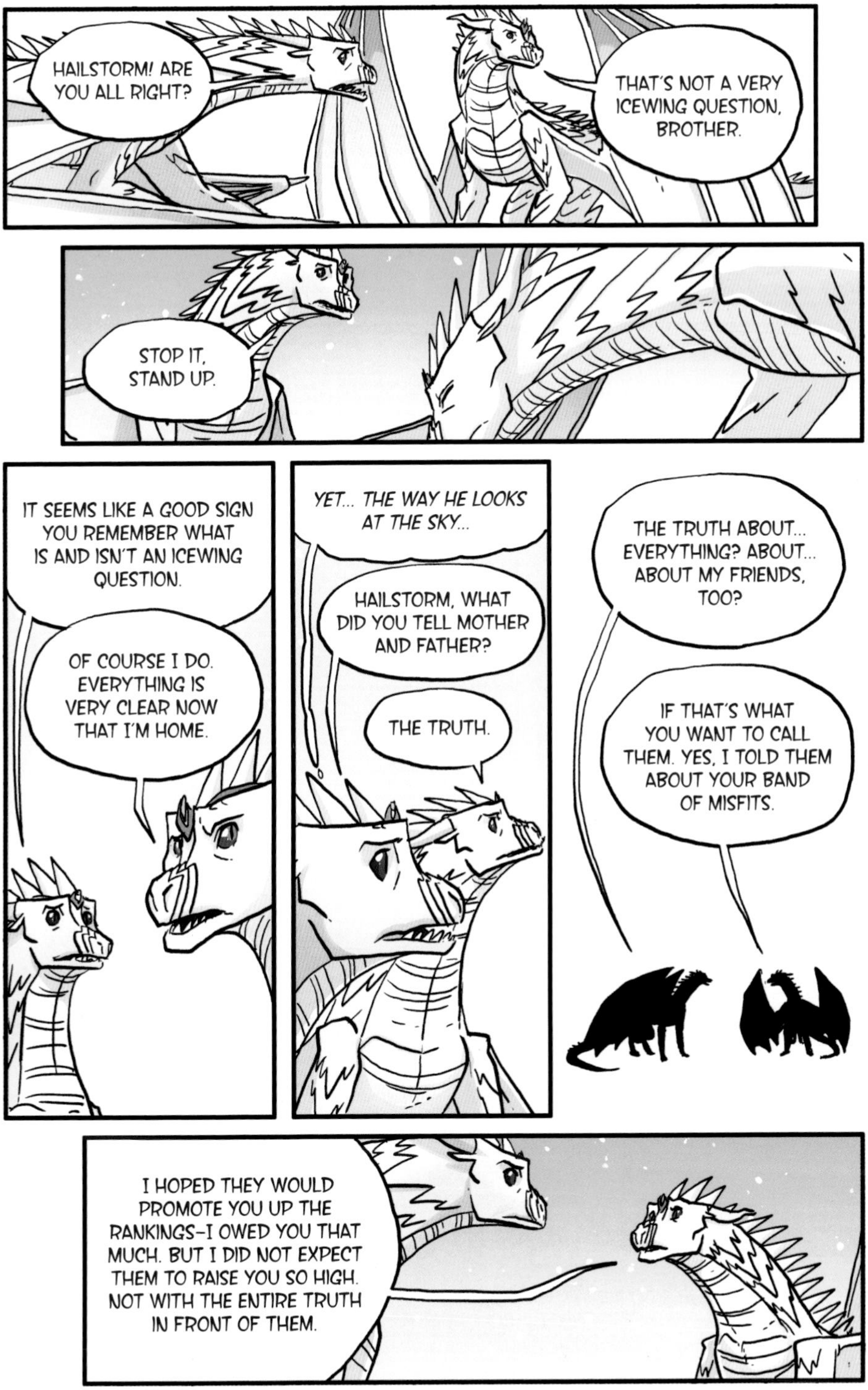
HAILSTORM! ARE YOU ALL RIGHT?
THAT'S NOT A VERY ICEWING QUESTION, BROTHER.
STOP IT, STAND UP.
IT SEEMS LIKE A GOOD SIGN YOU REMEMBER WHAT IS AND ISN'T AN ICEWING QUESTION.
OF COURSE I DO. EVERYTHING IS VERY CLEAR NOW THAT I'M HOME.
YET... THE WAY HE LOOKS AT THE SKY...
HAILSTORM, WHAT DID YOU TELL MOTHER AND FATHER?
THE TRUTH.
THE TRUTH ABOUT... EVERYTHING? ABOUT... ABOUT MY FRIENDS, TOO?
IF THAT'S WHAT YOU WANT TO CALL THEM. YES, I TOLD THEM ABOUT YOUR BAND OF MISFITS.
I HOPED THEY WOULD PROMOTE YOU UP THE RANKINGS—I OWED YOU THAT MUCH. BUT I DID NOT EXPECT THEM TO RAISE YOU SO HIGH. NOT WITH THE ENTIRE TRUTH IN FRONT OF THEM.

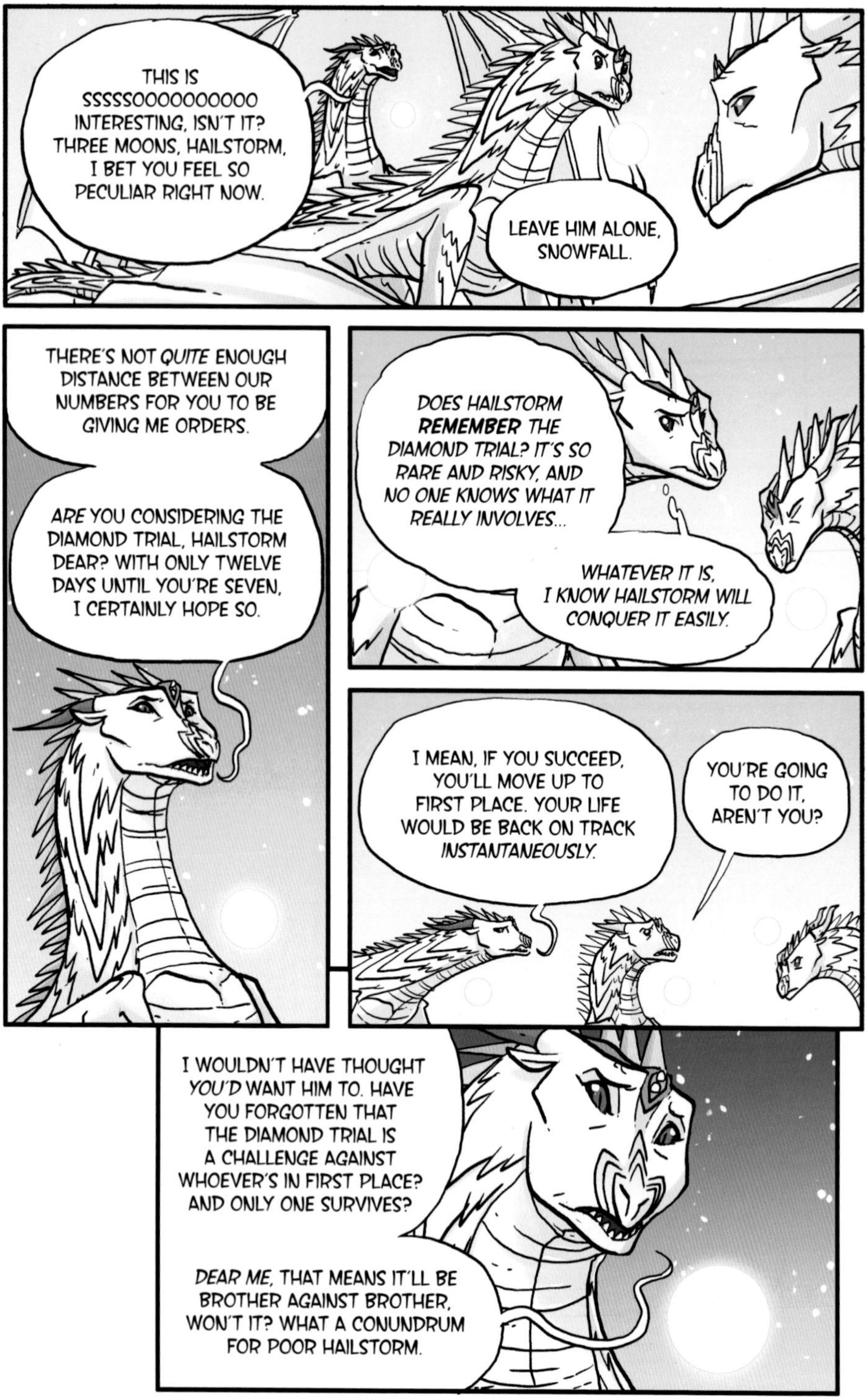
THIS IS SSSSSOOOOOOOOOOO INTERESTING, ISN'T IT? THREE MOONS, HAILSTORM, I BET YOU FEEL SO PECULIAR RIGHT NOW.
LEAVE HIM ALONE, SNOWFALL.
THERE'S NOT *QUITE* ENOUGH DISTANCE BETWEEN OUR NUMBERS FOR YOU TO BE GIVING ME ORDERS.
ARE YOU CONSIDERING THE DIAMOND TRIAL, HAILSTORM DEAR? WITH ONLY TWELVE DAYS UNTIL YOU'RE SEVEN, I CERTAINLY HOPE SO.
DOES HAILSTORM ***REMEMBER*** *THE DIAMOND TRIAL? IT'S SO RARE AND RISKY, AND NO ONE KNOWS WHAT IT REALLY INVOLVES...*
WHATEVER IT IS, I KNOW HAILSTORM WILL CONQUER IT EASILY.
I MEAN, IF YOU SUCCEED, YOU'LL MOVE UP TO FIRST PLACE. YOUR LIFE WOULD BE BACK ON TRACK *INSTANTANEOUSLY.*
YOU'RE GOING TO DO IT, AREN'T YOU?
I WOULDN'T HAVE THOUGHT *YOU'D* WANT HIM TO. HAVE YOU FORGOTTEN THAT THE DIAMOND TRIAL IS A CHALLENGE AGAINST WHOEVER'S IN FIRST PLACE? AND ONLY ONE SURVIVES?
DEAR ME, THAT MEANS IT'LL BE BROTHER AGAINST BROTHER, WON'T IT? WHAT A CONUNDRUM FOR POOR HAILSTORM.

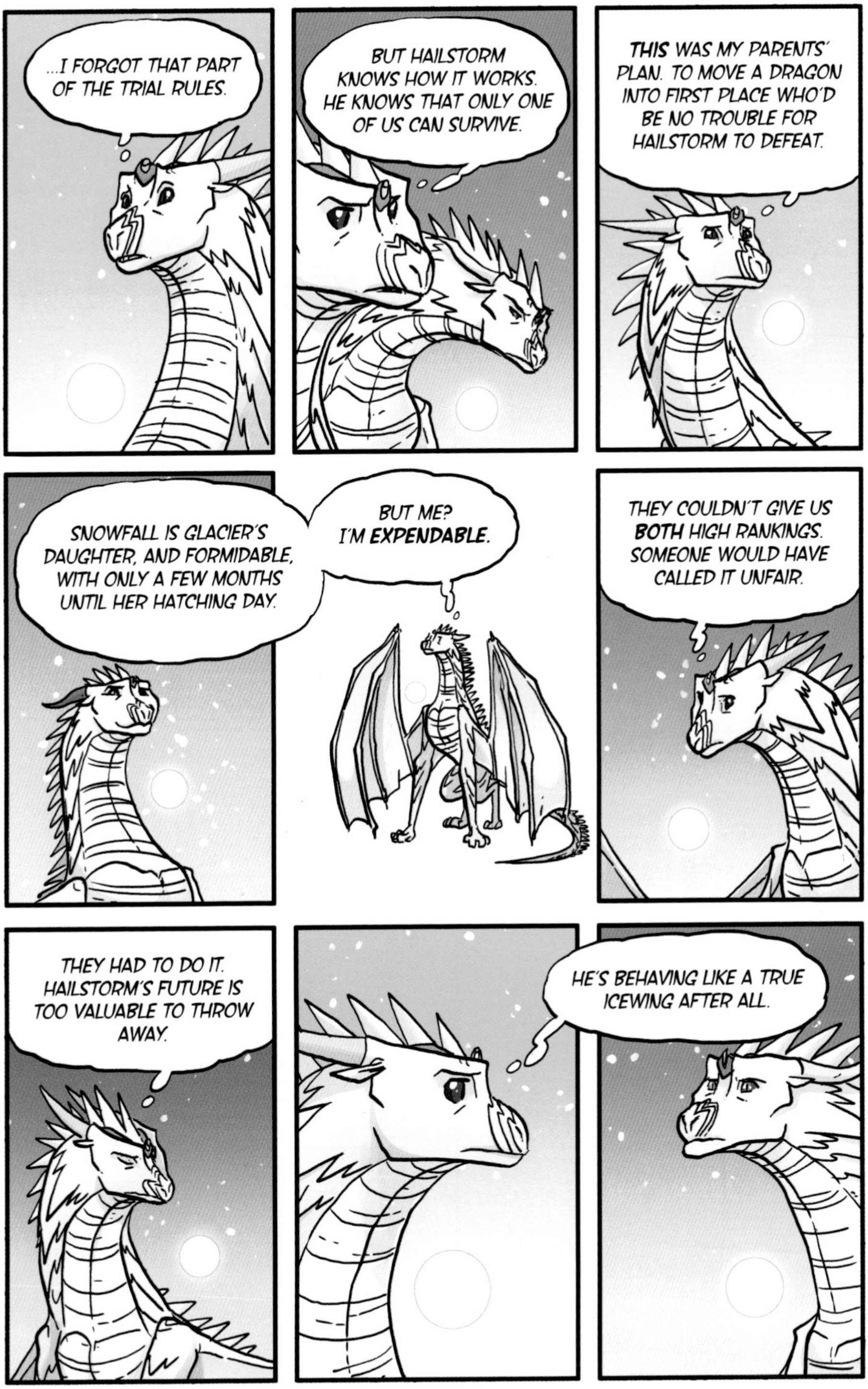
...I FORGOT THAT PART OF THE TRIAL RULES.
BUT HAILSTORM KNOWS HOW IT WORKS. HE KNOWS THAT ONLY ONE OF US CAN SURVIVE.
THIS WAS MY PARENTS' PLAN. TO MOVE A DRAGON INTO FIRST PLACE WHO'D BE NO TROUBLE FOR HAILSTORM TO DEFEAT.
SNOWFALL IS GLACIER'S DAUGHTER, AND FORMIDABLE, WITH ONLY A FEW MONTHS UNTIL HER HATCHING DAY.
BUT ME? I'M EXPENDABLE.
THEY COULDN'T GIVE US BOTH HIGH RANKINGS. SOMEONE WOULD HAVE CALLED IT UNFAIR.
THEY HAD TO DO IT. HAILSTORM'S FUTURE IS TOO VALUABLE TO THROW AWAY.
HE'S BEHAVING LIKE A TRUE ICEWING AFTER ALL.

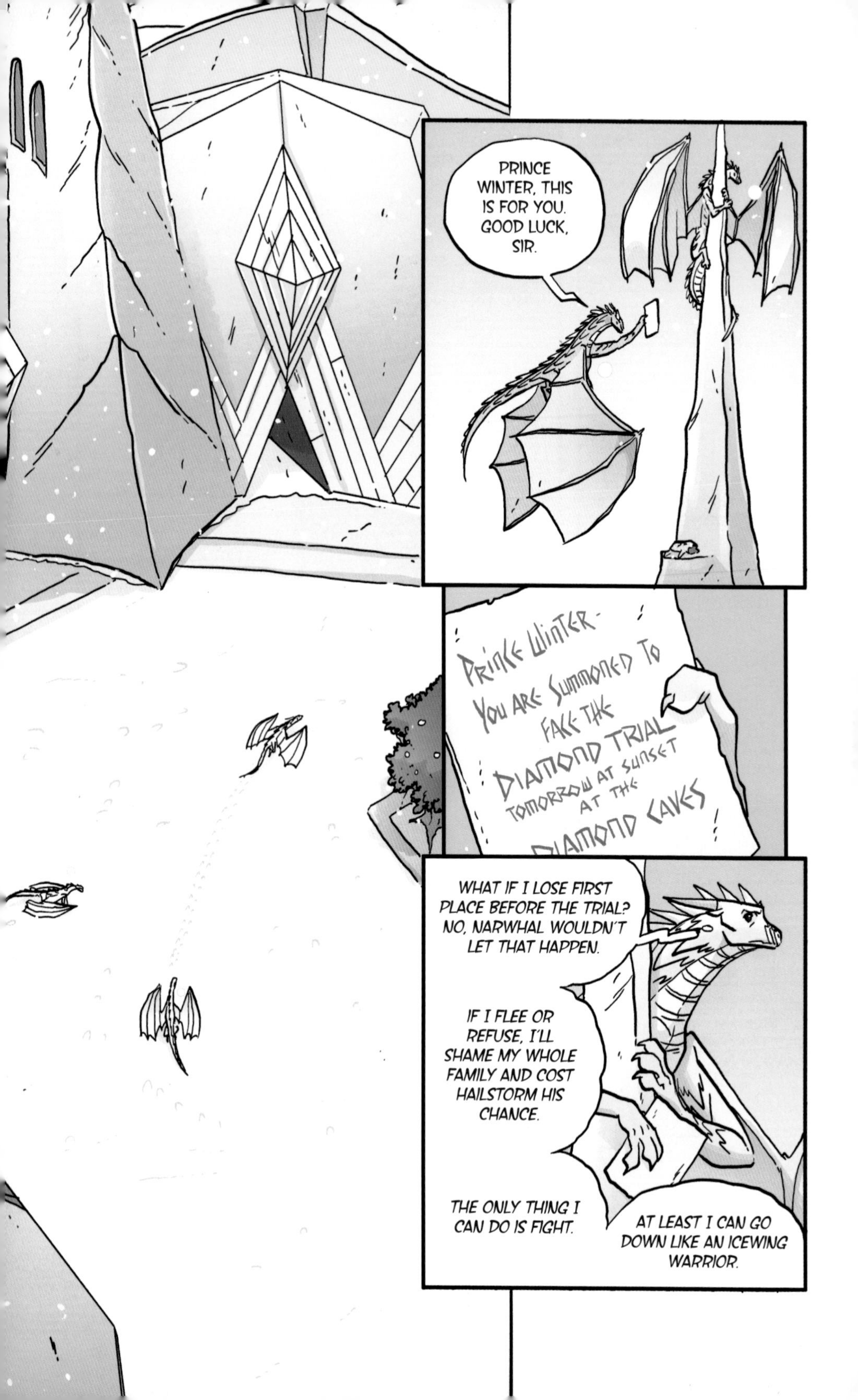
PRINCE WINTER, THIS IS FOR YOU. GOOD LUCK, SIR.
PRINCE WINTER-
YOU ARE SUMMONED TO FACE THE DIAMOND TRIAL TOMORROW AT SUNSET AT THE DIAMOND CAVES
WHAT IF I LOSE FIRST PLACE BEFORE THE TRIAL? NO, NARWHAL WOULDN'T LET THAT HAPPEN.
IF I FLEE OR REFUSE, I'LL SHAME MY WHOLE FAMILY AND COST HAILSTORM HIS CHANCE.
THE ONLY THING I CAN DO IS FIGHT.
AT LEAST I CAN GO DOWN LIKE AN ICEWING WARRIOR.

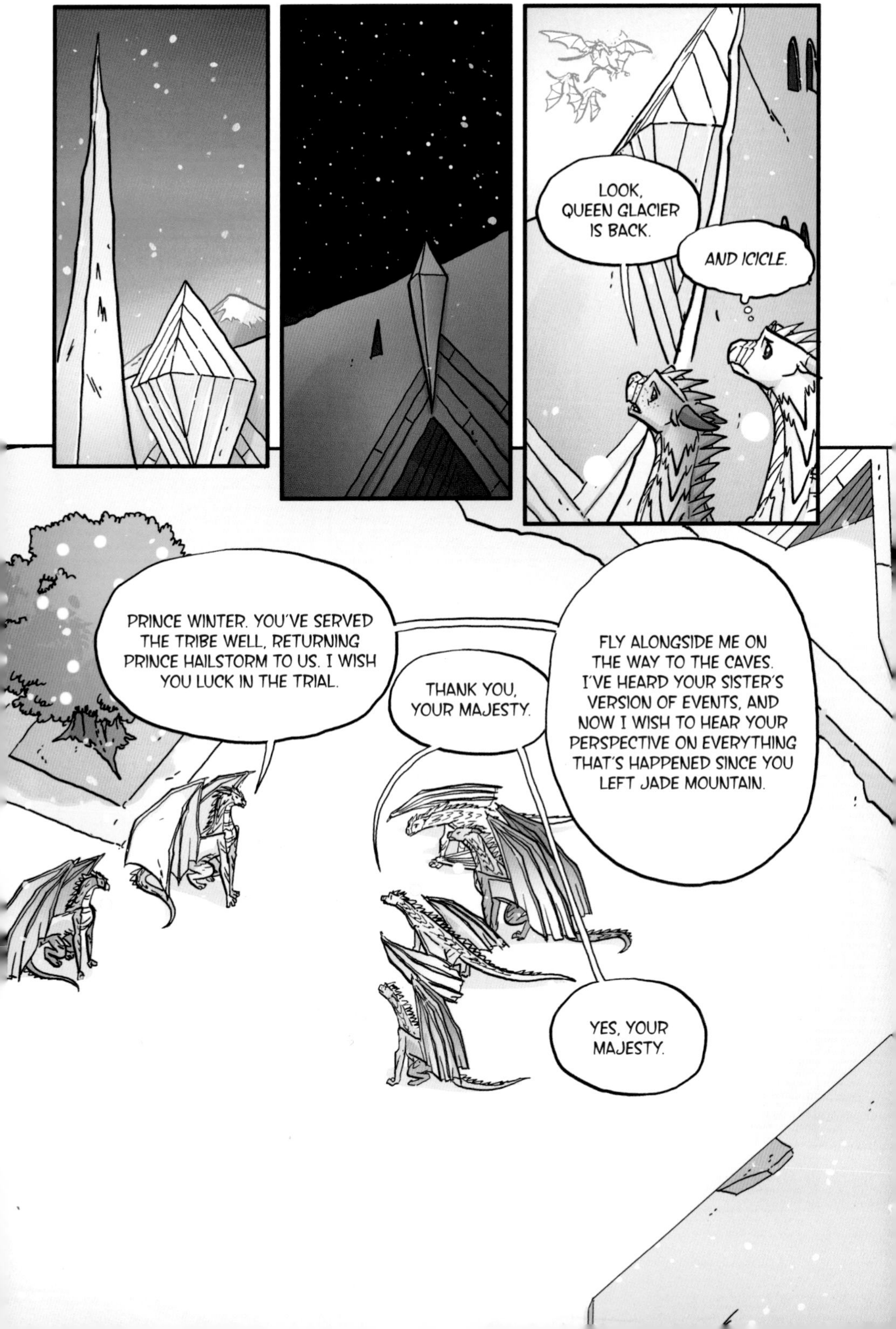
LOOK, QUEEN GLACIER IS BACK.
AND ICICLE.
PRINCE WINTER. YOU'VE SERVED THE TRIBE WELL, RETURNING PRINCE HAILSTORM TO US. I WISH YOU LUCK IN THE TRIAL.
THANK YOU, YOUR MAJESTY.
FLY ALONGSIDE ME ON THE WAY TO THE CAVES. I'VE HEARD YOUR SISTER'S VERSION OF EVENTS, AND NOW I WISH TO HEAR YOUR PERSPECTIVE ON EVERYTHING THAT'S HAPPENED SINCE YOU LEFT JADE MOUNTAIN.
YES, YOUR MAJESTY.

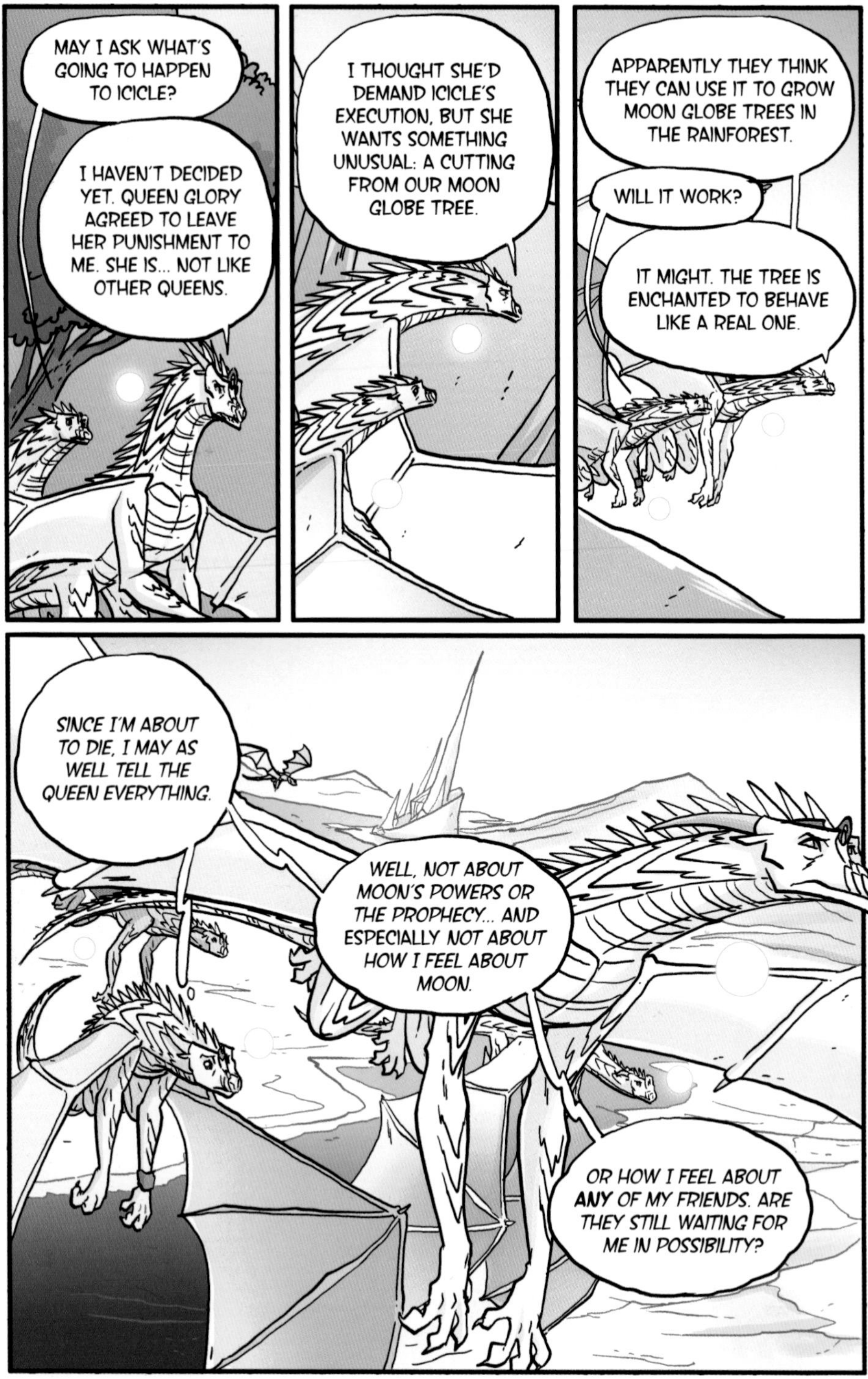

MAY I ASK WHAT'S GOING TO HAPPEN TO ICICLE?
I HAVEN'T DECIDED YET. QUEEN GLORY AGREED TO LEAVE HER PUNISHMENT TO ME. SHE IS... NOT LIKE OTHER QUEENS.
I THOUGHT SHE'D DEMAND ICICLE'S EXECUTION, BUT SHE WANTS SOMETHING UNUSUAL: A CUTTING FROM OUR MOON GLOBE TREE.
APPARENTLY THEY THINK THEY CAN USE IT TO GROW MOON GLOBE TREES IN THE RAINFOREST.
WILL IT WORK?
IT MIGHT. THE TREE IS ENCHANTED TO BEHAVE LIKE A REAL ONE.
SINCE I'M ABOUT TO DIE, I MAY AS WELL TELL THE QUEEN EVERYTHING.
WELL, NOT ABOUT MOON'S POWERS OR THE PROPHECY... AND ESPECIALLY NOT ABOUT HOW I FEEL ABOUT MOON.
OR HOW I FEEL ABOUT **ANY** OF MY FRIENDS. ARE THEY STILL WAITING FOR ME IN POSSIBILITY?

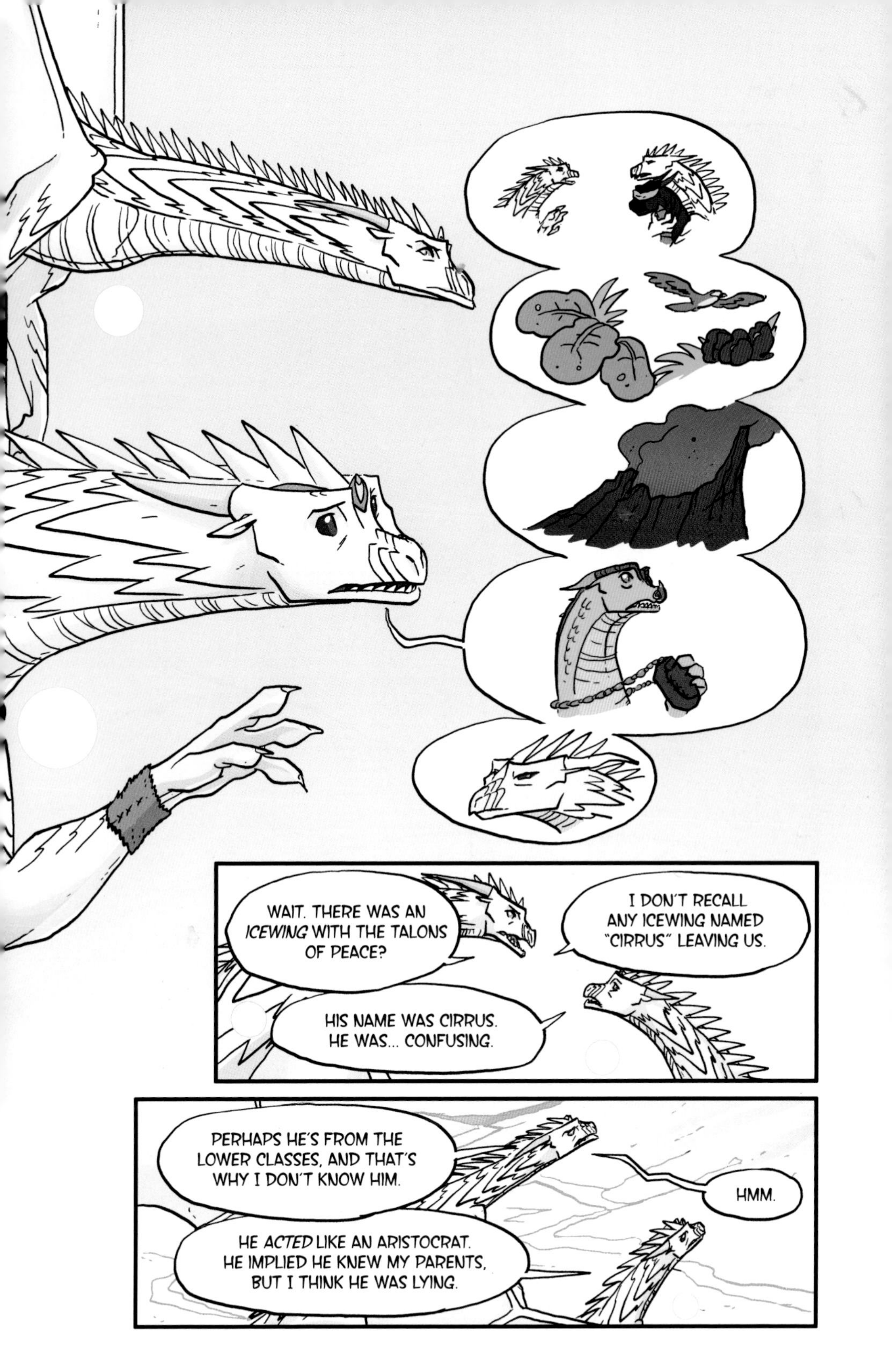
WAIT. THERE WAS AN ICEWING WITH THE TALONS OF PEACE?
I DON'T RECALL ANY ICEWING NAMED "CIRRUS" LEAVING US.
HIS NAME WAS CIRRUS. HE WAS... CONFUSING.
PERHAPS HE'S FROM THE LOWER CLASSES, AND THAT'S WHY I DON'T KNOW HIM.
HMM.
HE ACTED LIKE AN ARISTOCRAT. HE IMPLIED HE KNEW MY PARENTS, BUT I THINK HE WAS LYING.

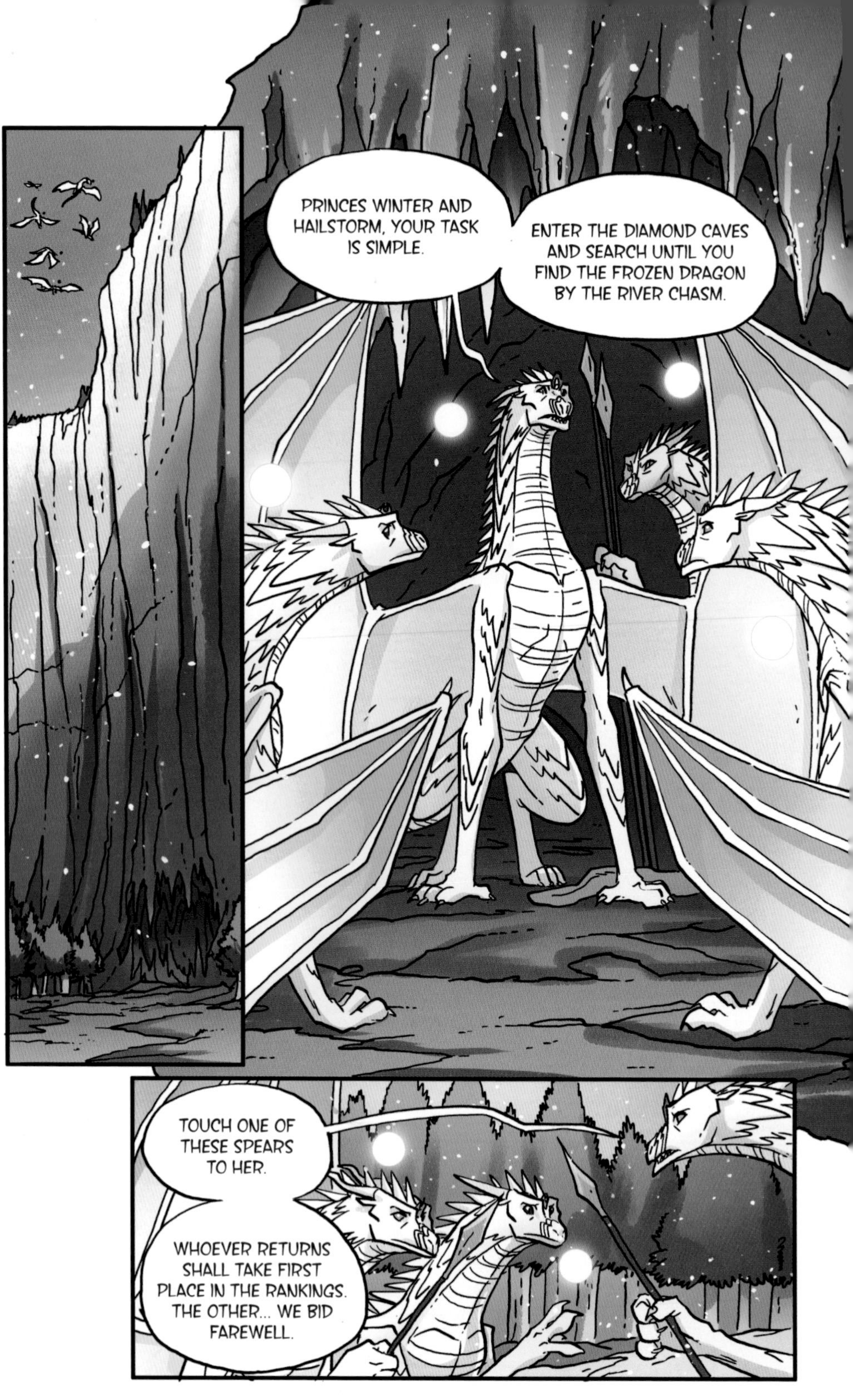
PRINCES WINTER AND HAILSTORM, YOUR TASK IS SIMPLE.
ENTER THE DIAMOND CAVES AND SEARCH UNTIL YOU FIND THE FROZEN DRAGON BY THE RIVER CHASM.
TOUCH ONE OF THESE SPEARS TO HER.
WHOEVER RETURNS SHALL TAKE FIRST PLACE IN THE RANKINGS. THE OTHER... WE BID FAREWELL.

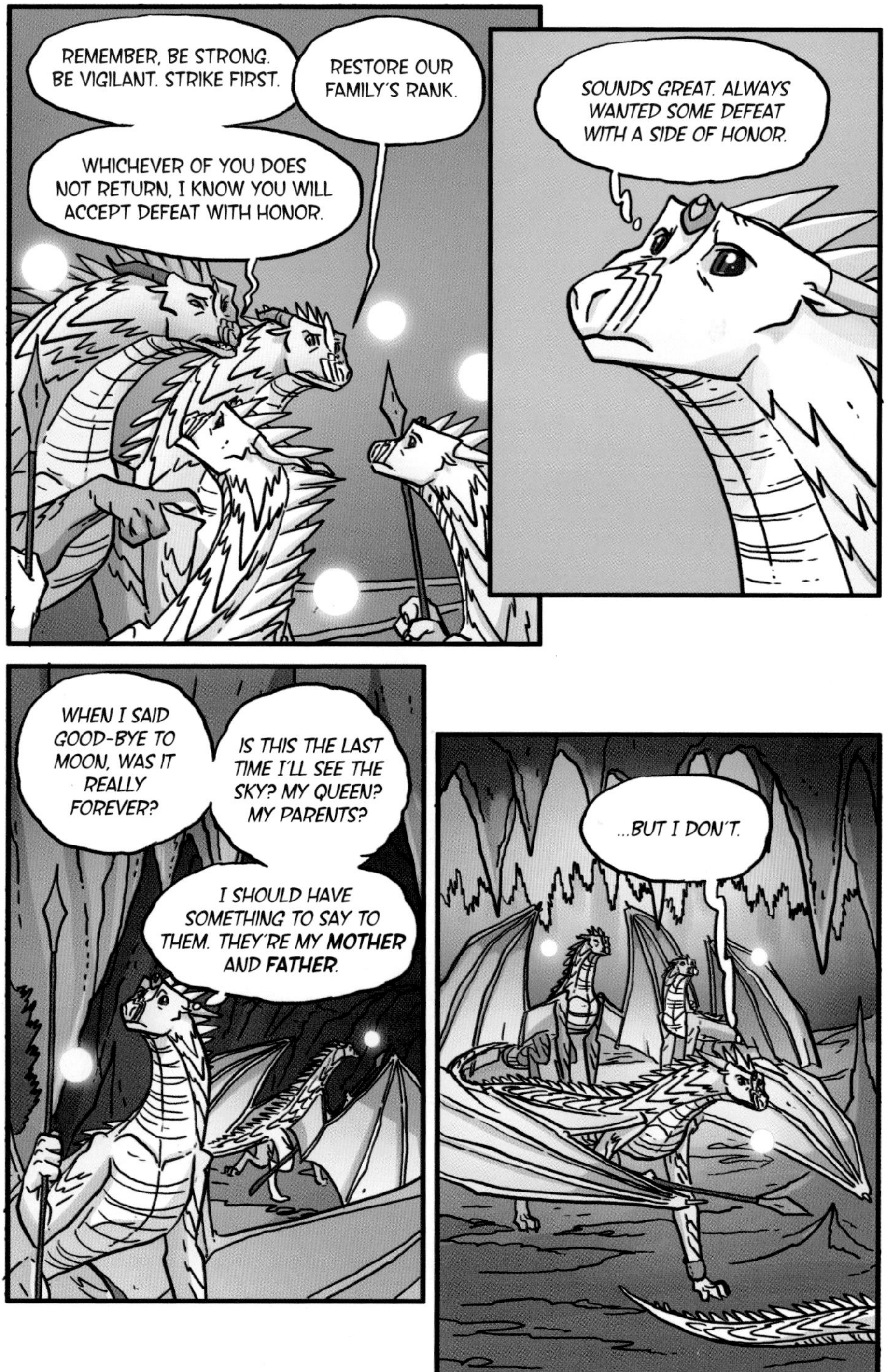
REMEMBER, BE STRONG. BE VIGILANT. STRIKE FIRST.
RESTORE OUR FAMILY'S RANK.
WHICHEVER OF YOU DOES NOT RETURN, I KNOW YOU WILL ACCEPT DEFEAT WITH HONOR.
SOUNDS GREAT. ALWAYS WANTED SOME DEFEAT WITH A SIDE OF HONOR.
WHEN I SAID GOOD-BYE TO MOON, WAS IT REALLY FOREVER?
IS THIS THE LAST TIME I'LL SEE THE SKY? MY QUEEN? MY PARENTS?
I SHOULD HAVE SOMETHING TO SAY TO THEM. THEY'RE MY MOTHER AND FATHER.
...BUT I DON'T.

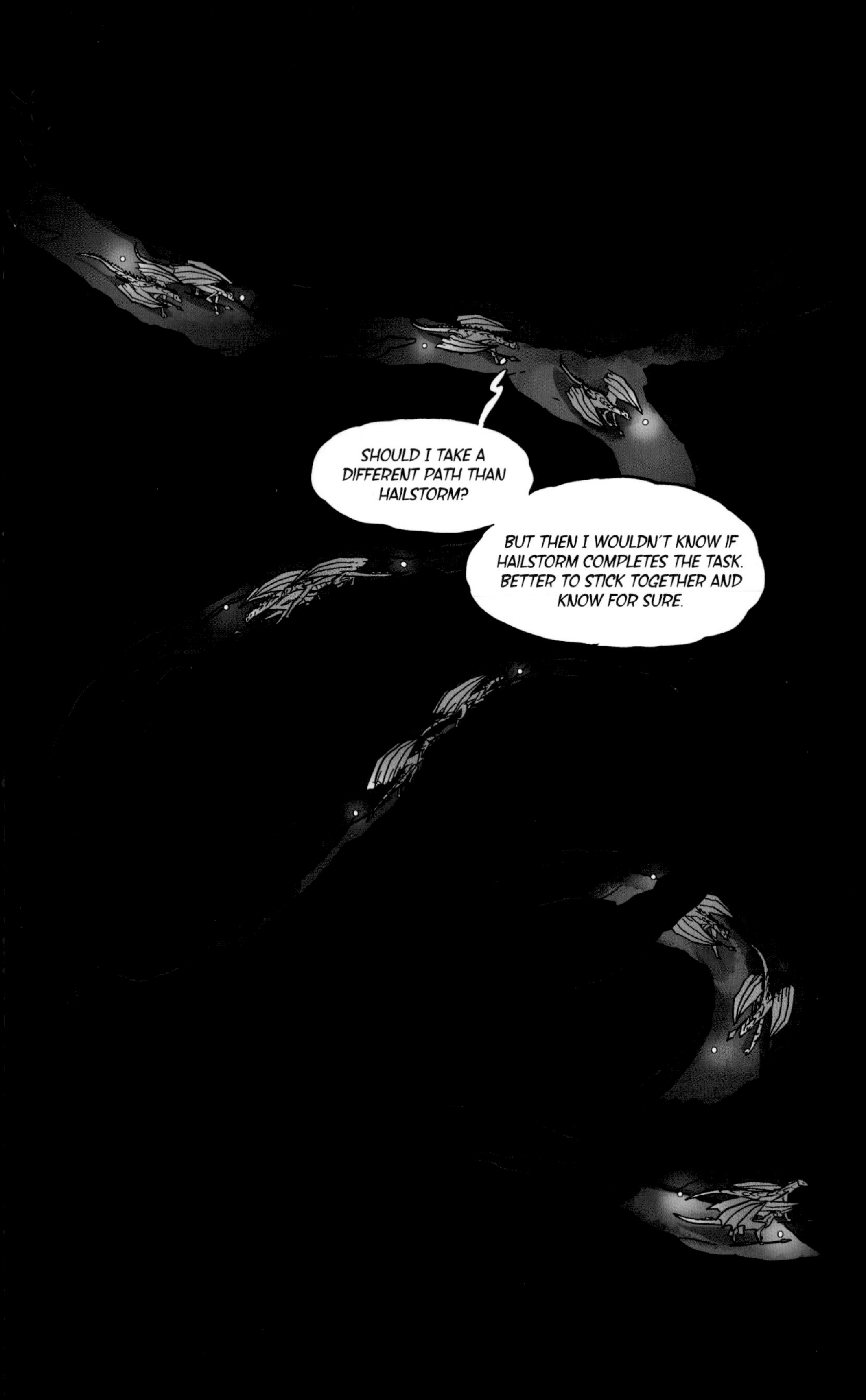
SHOULD I TAKE A DIFFERENT PATH THAN HAILSTORM?
BUT THEN I WOULDN'T KNOW IF HAILSTORM COMPLETES THE TASK. BETTER TO STICK TOGETHER AND KNOW FOR SURE.

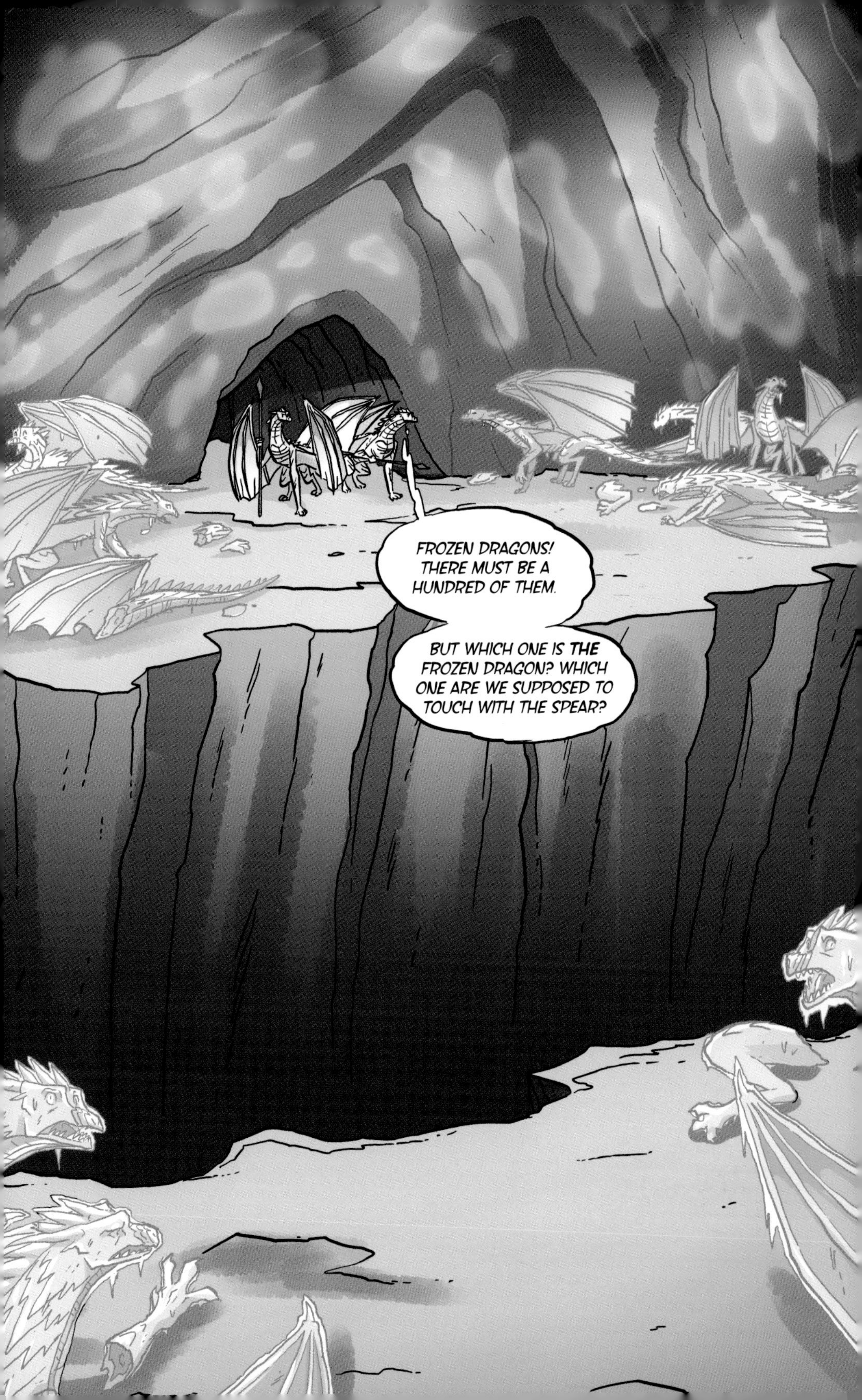
FROZEN DRAGONS! THERE MUST BE A HUNDRED OF THEM.
BUT WHICH ONE IS **THE** FROZEN DRAGON? WHICH ONE ARE WE SUPPOSED TO TOUCH WITH THE SPEAR?

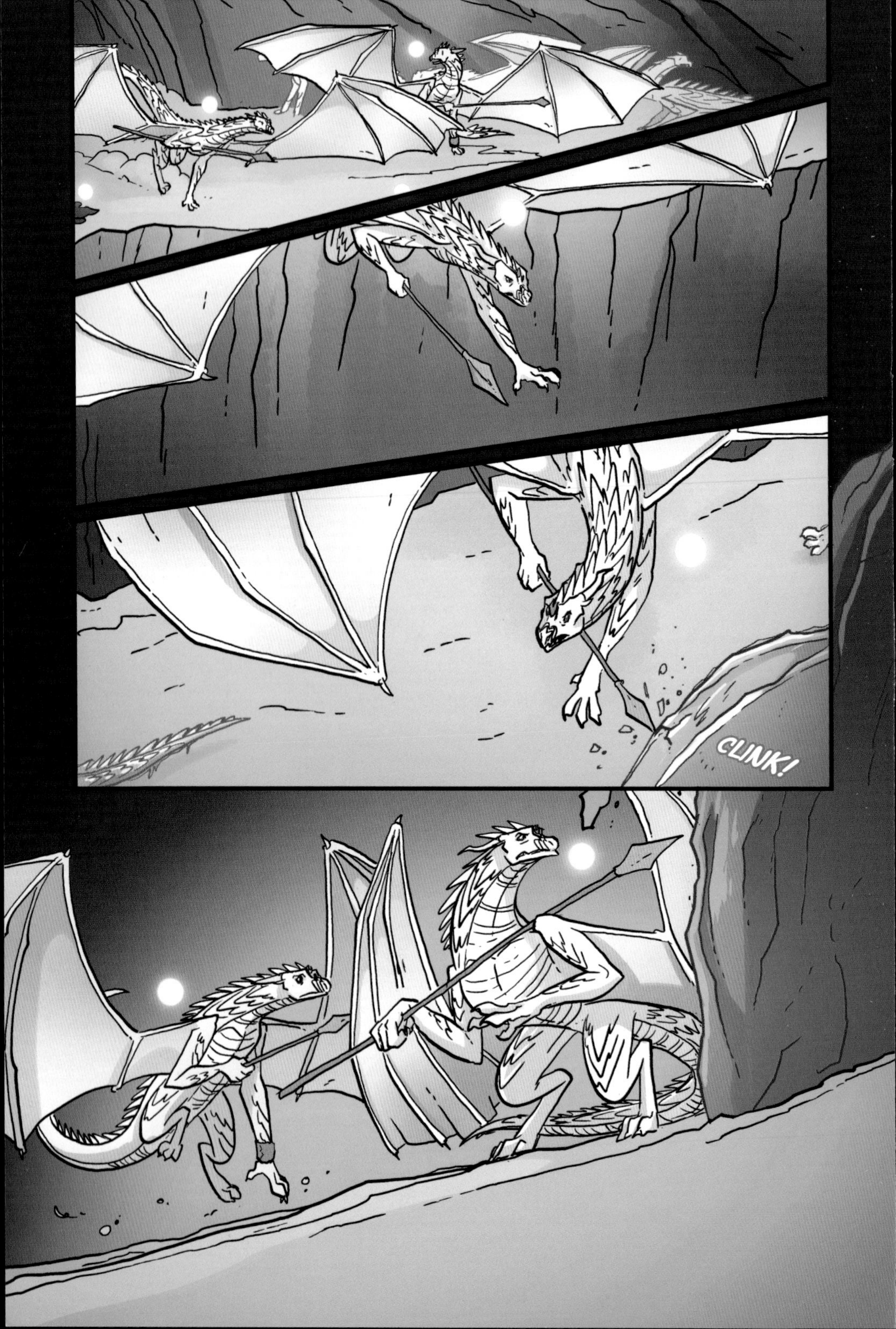
CLINK!

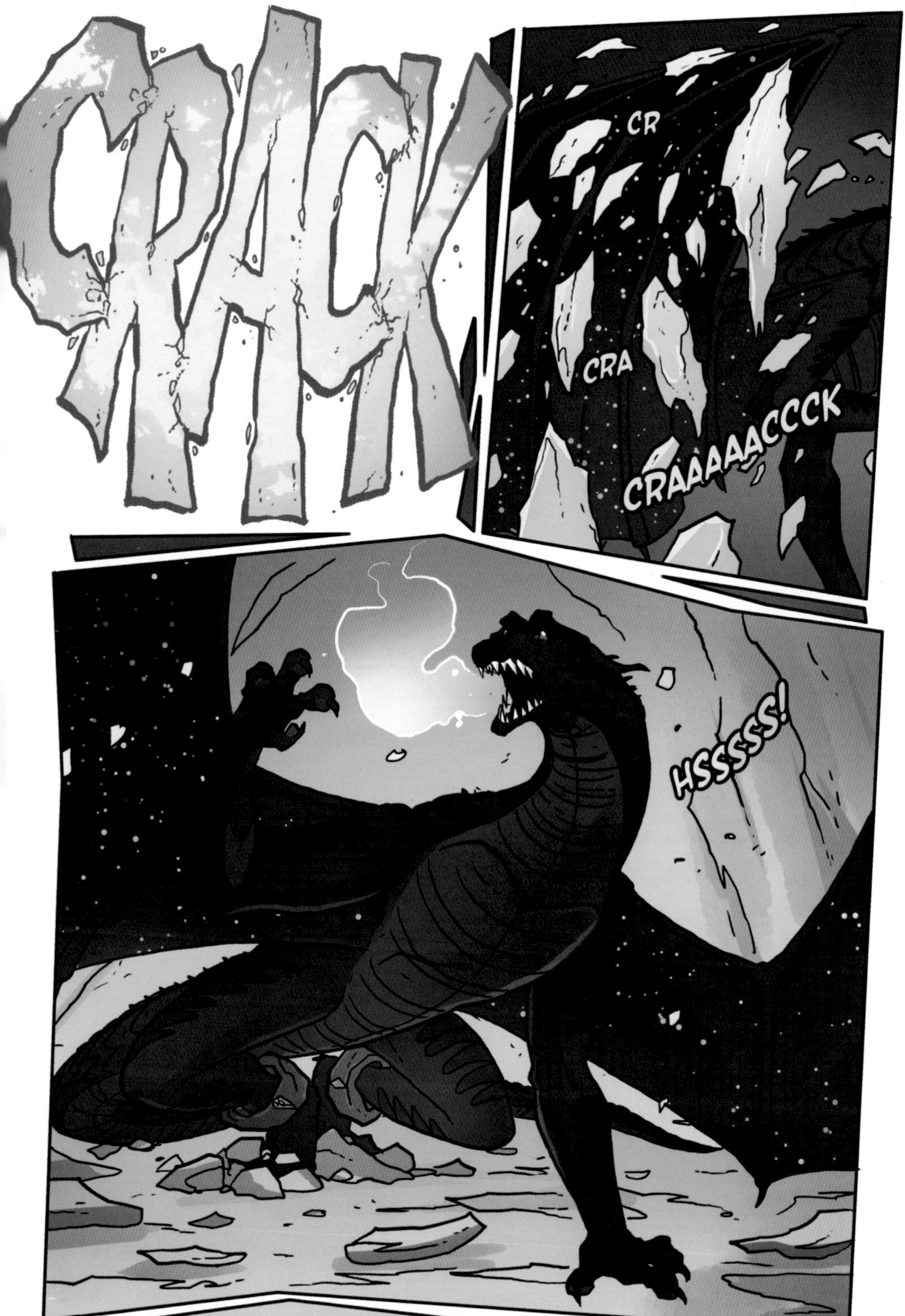
CRACK
CR
CRA
CRAAAAACCCK
HSSSSS!

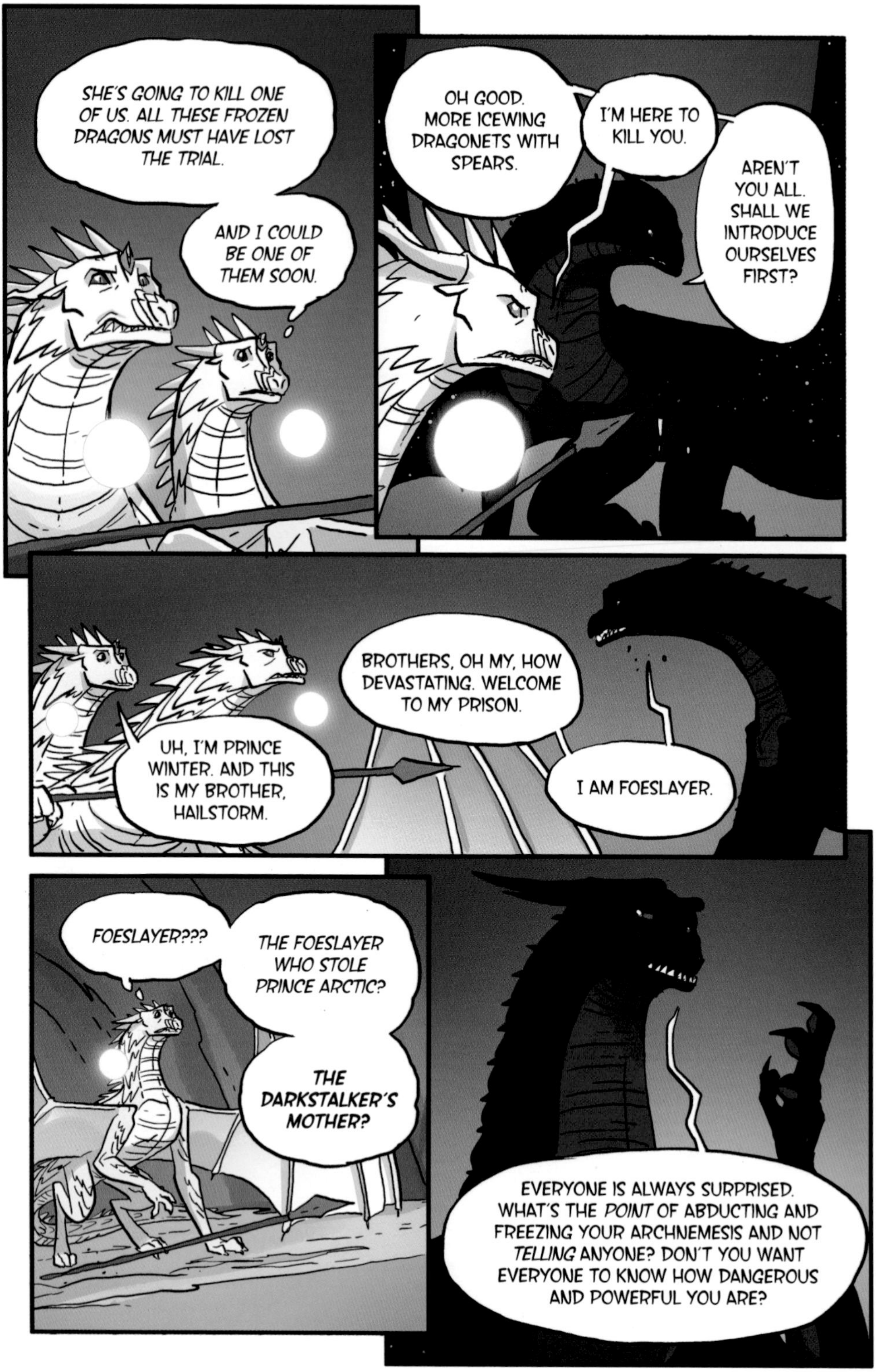
SHE'S GOING TO KILL ONE OF US. ALL THESE FROZEN DRAGONS MUST HAVE LOST THE TRIAL.
AND I COULD BE ONE OF THEM SOON.
OH GOOD. MORE ICEWING DRAGONETS WITH SPEARS.
I'M HERE TO KILL YOU.
AREN'T YOU ALL. SHALL WE INTRODUCE OURSELVES FIRST?
UH, I'M PRINCE WINTER. AND THIS IS MY BROTHER, HAILSTORM.
BROTHERS, OH MY, HOW DEVASTATING. WELCOME TO MY PRISON.
I AM FOESLAYER.
FOESLAYER???
THE FOESLAYER WHO STOLE PRINCE ARCTIC?
THE DARKSTALKER'S MOTHER?
EVERYONE IS ALWAYS SURPRISED. WHAT'S THE POINT OF ABDUCTING AND FREEZING YOUR ARCHNEMESIS AND NOT TELLING ANYONE? DON'T YOU WANT EVERYONE TO KNOW HOW DANGEROUS AND POWERFUL YOU ARE?

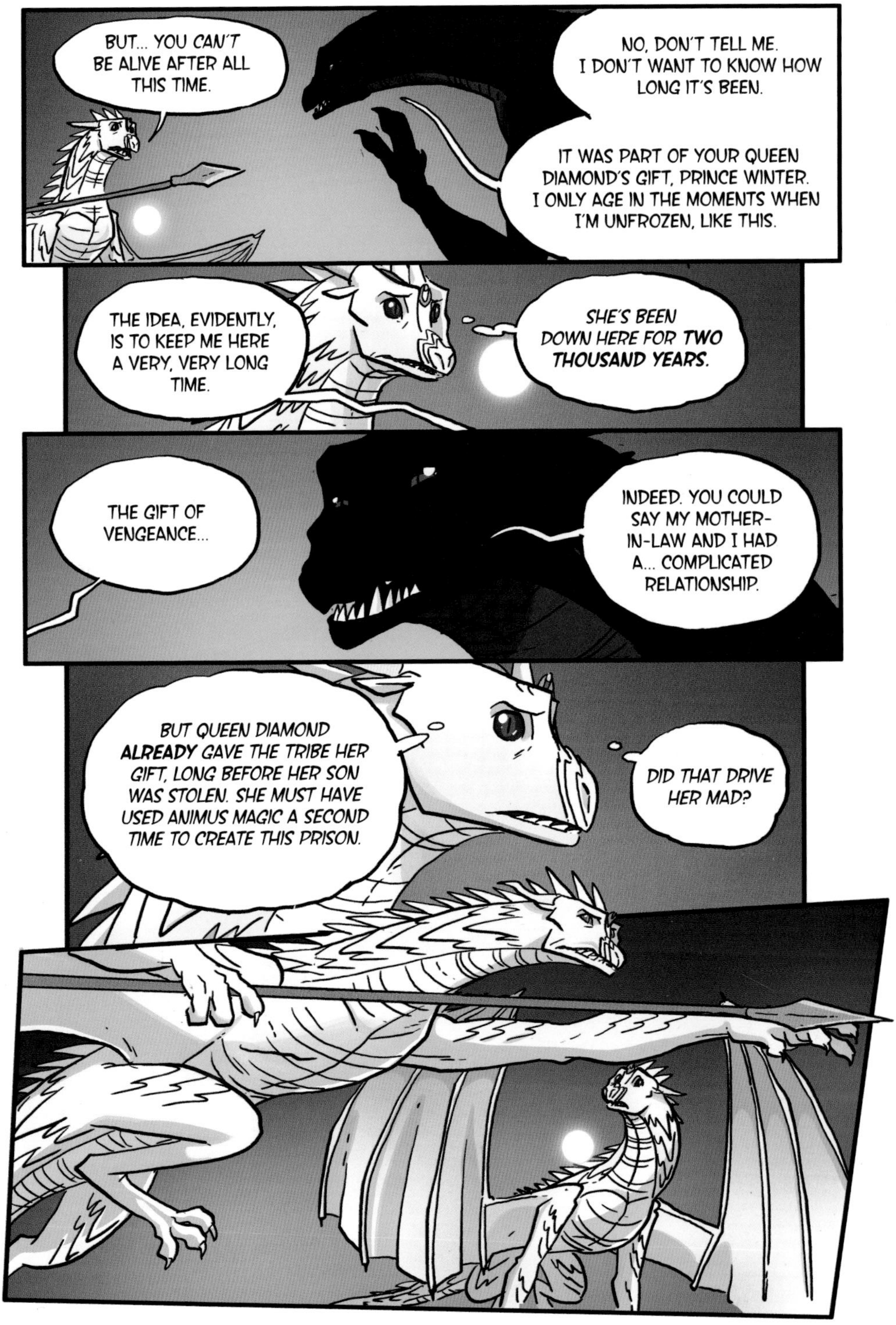
BUT... YOU CAN'T BE ALIVE AFTER ALL THIS TIME.
NO, DON'T TELL ME. I DON'T WANT TO KNOW HOW LONG IT'S BEEN.
IT WAS PART OF YOUR QUEEN DIAMOND'S GIFT, PRINCE WINTER. I ONLY AGE IN THE MOMENTS WHEN I'M UNFROZEN, LIKE THIS.
THE IDEA, EVIDENTLY, IS TO KEEP ME HERE A VERY, VERY LONG TIME.
*SHE'S BEEN DOWN HERE FOR **TWO THOUSAND YEARS.***
THE GIFT OF VENGEANCE...
INDEED. YOU COULD SAY MY MOTHER-IN-LAW AND I HAD A... COMPLICATED RELATIONSHIP.
*BUT QUEEN DIAMOND **ALREADY** GAVE THE TRIBE HER GIFT, LONG BEFORE HER SON WAS STOLEN. SHE MUST HAVE USED ANIMUS MAGIC A SECOND TIME TO CREATE THIS PRISON.*
DID THAT DRIVE HER MAD?

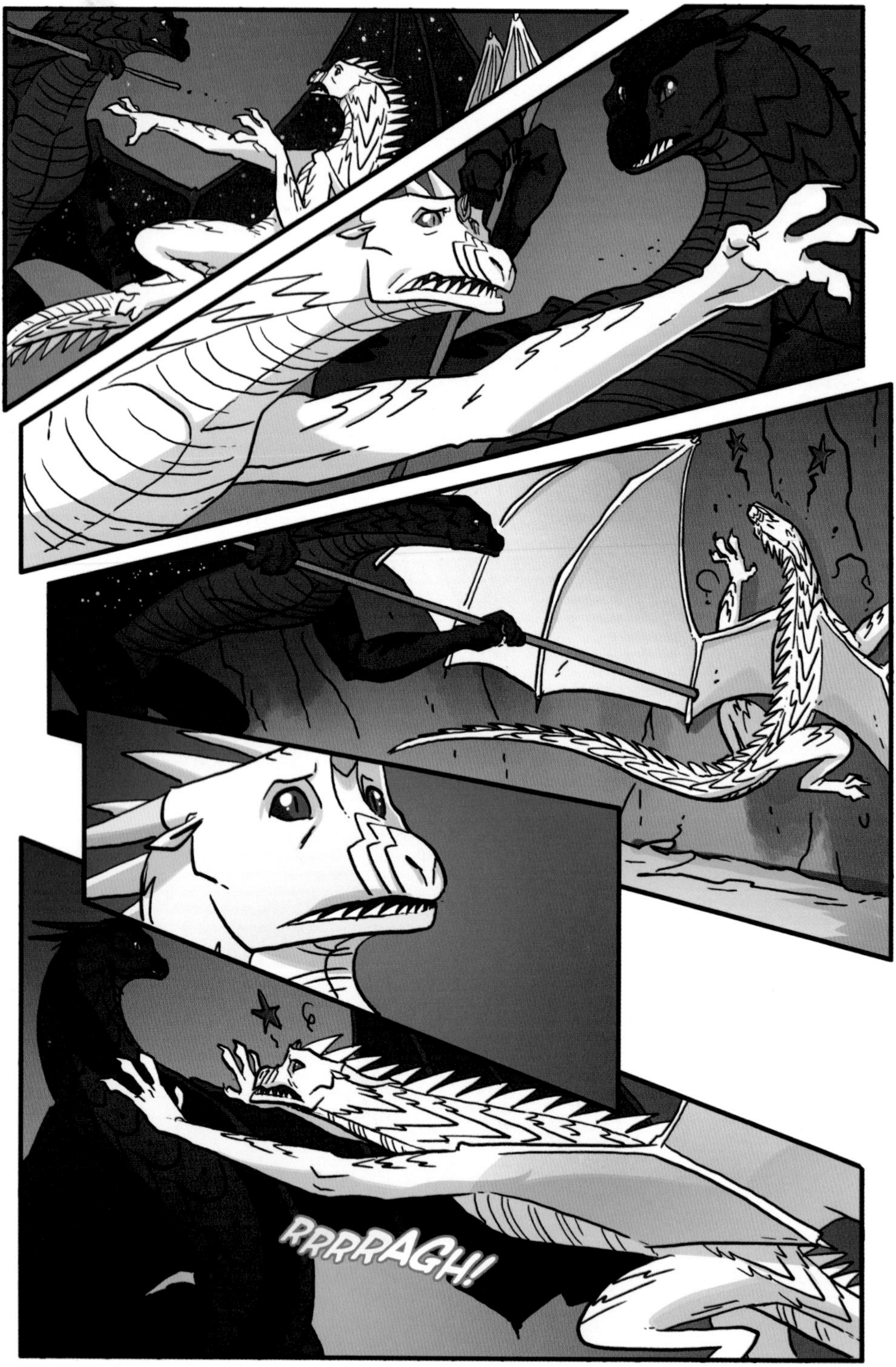
RRRRAGH!

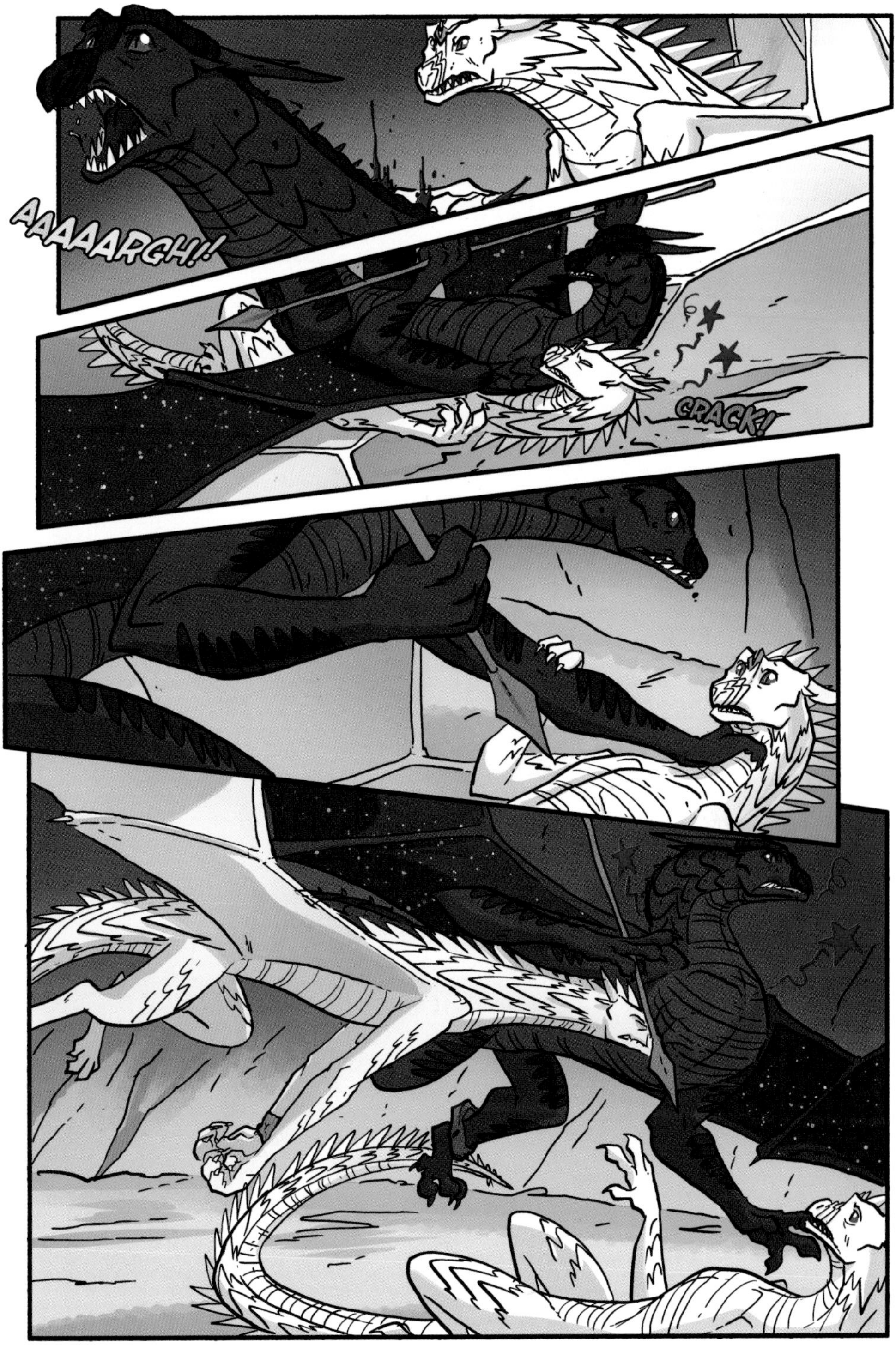
AAAAARGH!!
CRACK!

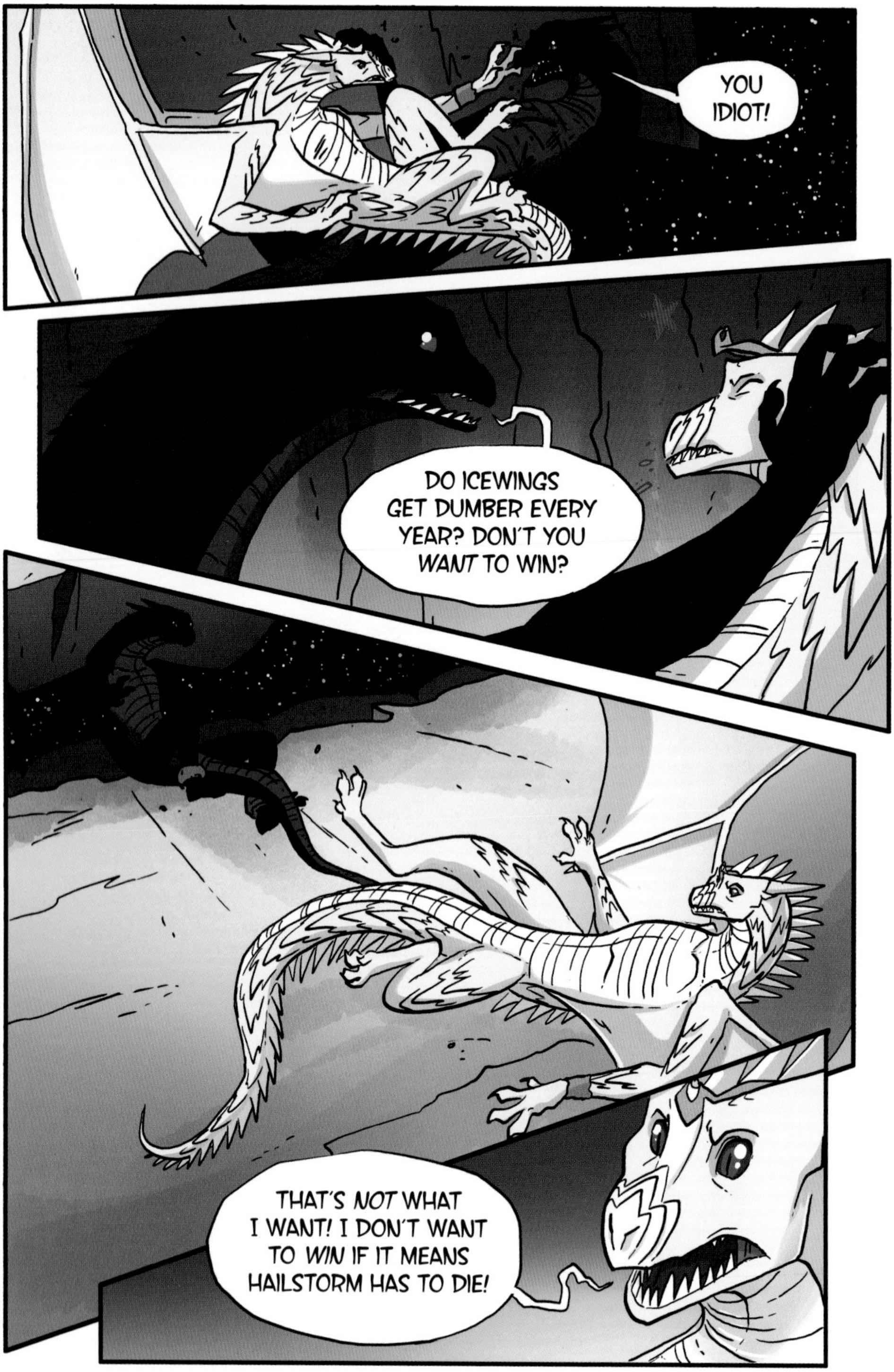
YOU IDIOT!
DO ICEWINGS GET DUMBER EVERY YEAR? DON'T YOU *WANT* TO WIN?
THAT'S *NOT* WHAT I WANT! I DON'T WANT TO *WIN* IF IT MEANS HAILSTORM HAS TO DIE!

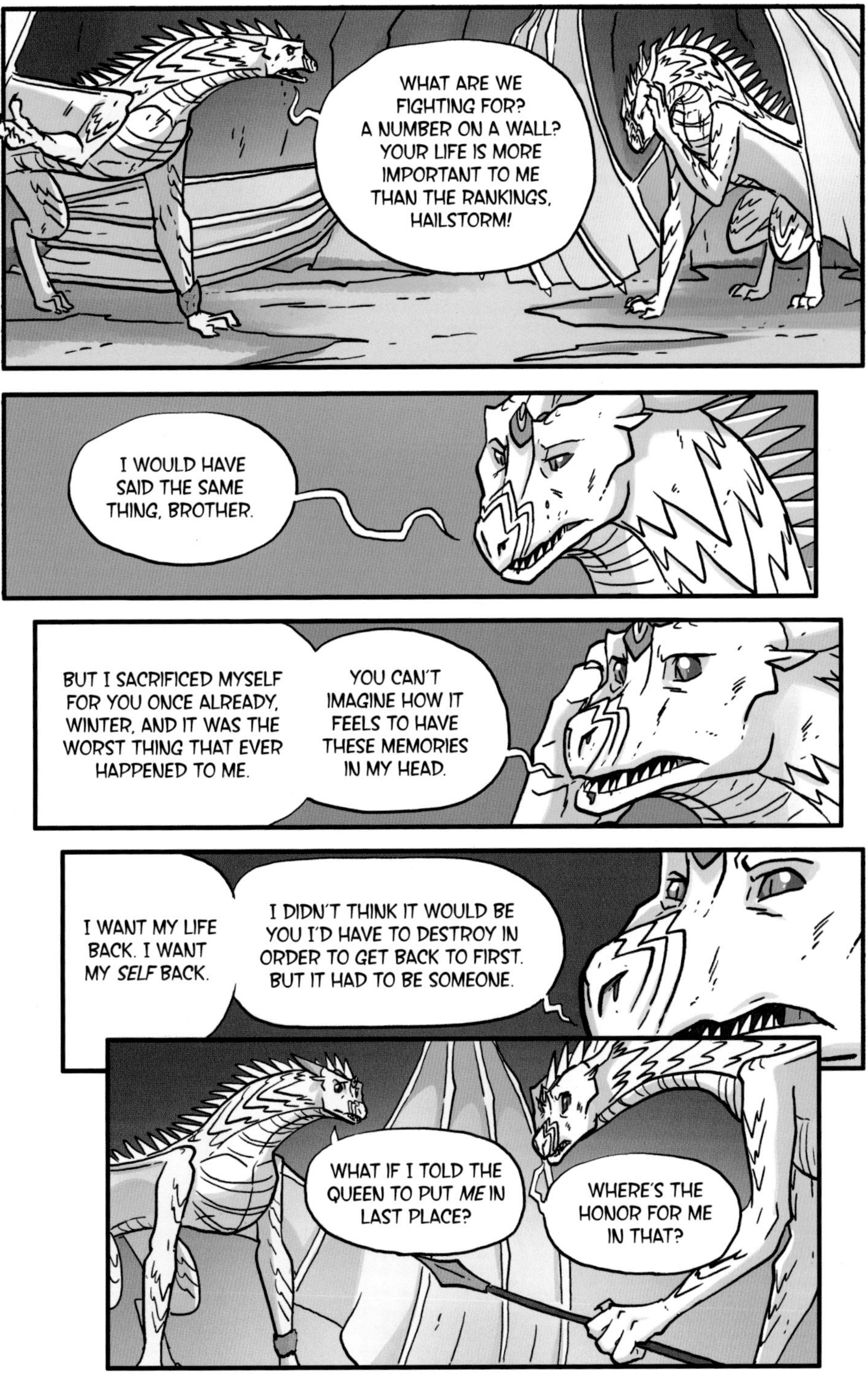
WHAT ARE WE FIGHTING FOR? A NUMBER ON A WALL? YOUR LIFE IS MORE IMPORTANT TO ME THAN THE RANKINGS, HAILSTORM!
I WOULD HAVE SAID THE SAME THING, BROTHER.
BUT I SACRIFICED MYSELF FOR YOU ONCE ALREADY, WINTER, AND IT WAS THE WORST THING THAT EVER HAPPENED TO ME.
YOU CAN'T IMAGINE HOW IT FEELS TO HAVE THESE MEMORIES IN MY HEAD.
I WANT MY LIFE BACK. I WANT MY *SELF* BACK.
I DIDN'T THINK IT WOULD BE YOU I'D HAVE TO DESTROY IN ORDER TO GET BACK TO FIRST. BUT IT HAD TO BE SOMEONE.
WHAT IF I TOLD THE QUEEN TO PUT *ME* IN LAST PLACE?
WHERE'S THE HONOR FOR ME IN THAT?

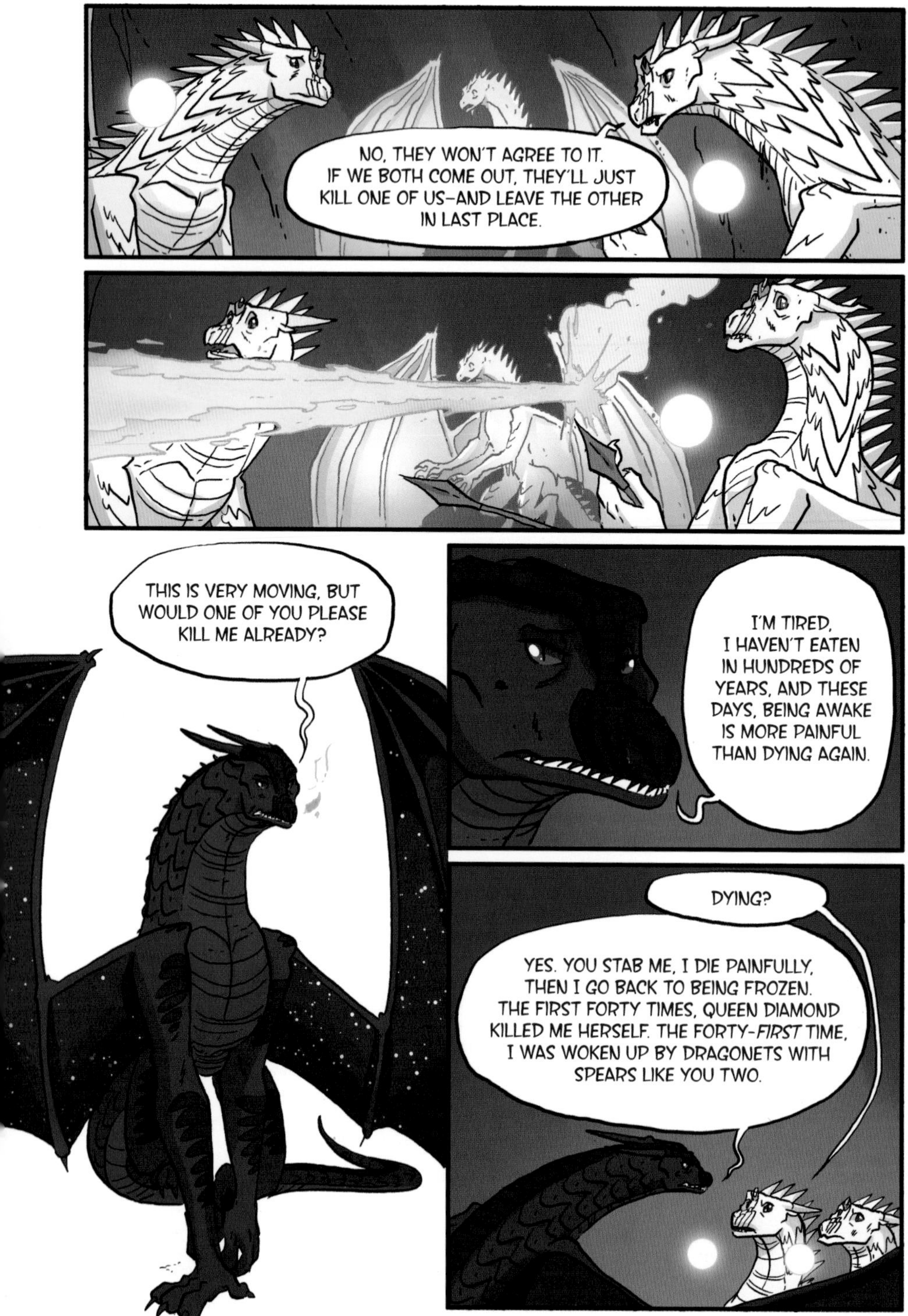
NO, THEY WON'T AGREE TO IT. IF WE BOTH COME OUT, THEY'LL JUST KILL ONE OF US—AND LEAVE THE OTHER IN LAST PLACE.
THIS IS VERY MOVING, BUT WOULD ONE OF YOU PLEASE KILL ME ALREADY?
I'M TIRED, I HAVEN'T EATEN IN HUNDREDS OF YEARS, AND THESE DAYS, BEING AWAKE IS MORE PAINFUL THAN DYING AGAIN.
DYING?
YES. YOU STAB ME, I DIE PAINFULLY, THEN I GO BACK TO BEING FROZEN. THE FIRST FORTY TIMES, QUEEN DIAMOND KILLED ME HERSELF. THE FORTY-*FIRST* TIME, I WAS WOKEN UP BY DRAGONETS WITH SPEARS LIKE YOU TWO.

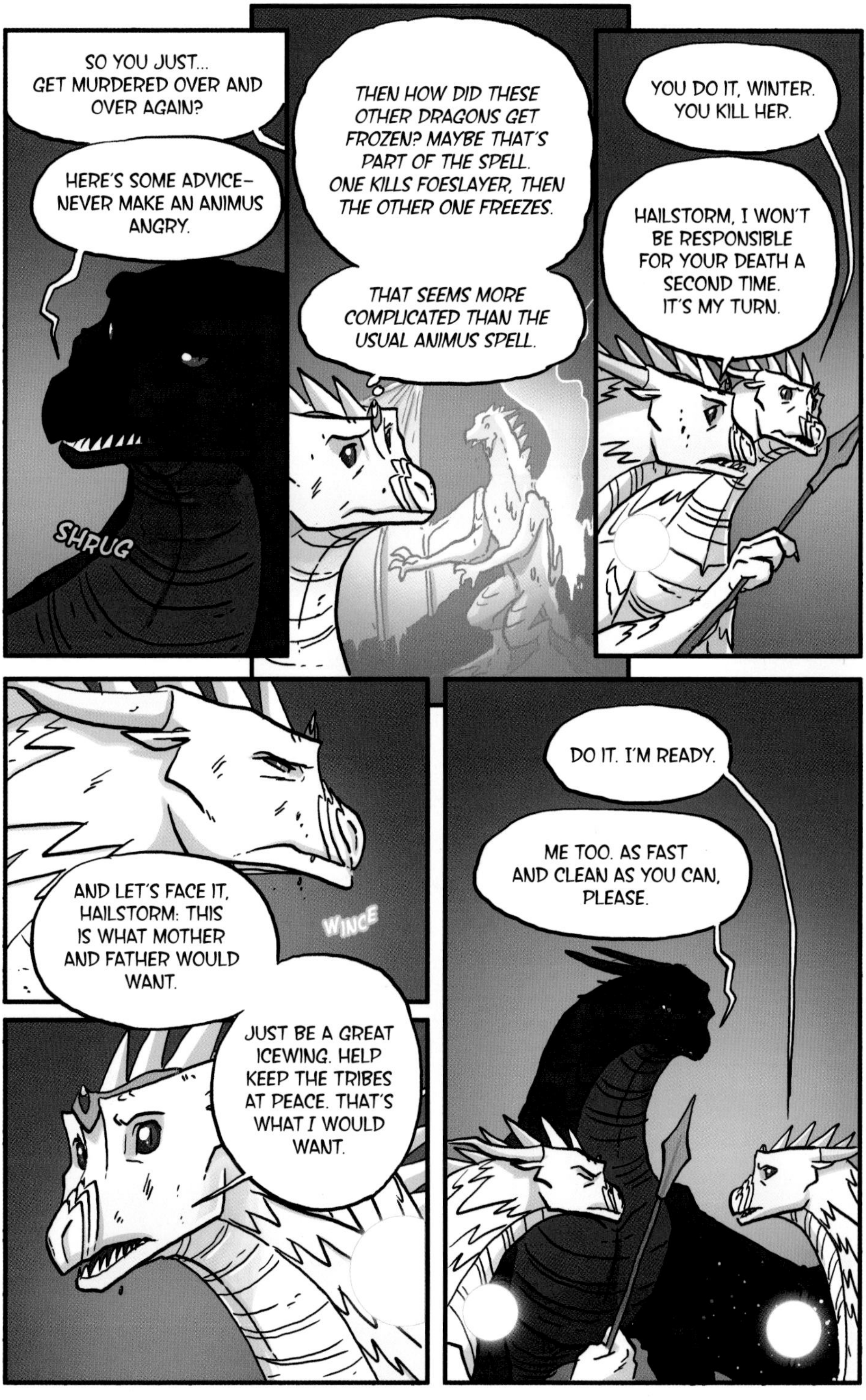
SO YOU JUST... GET MURDERED OVER AND OVER AGAIN?
HERE'S SOME ADVICE— NEVER MAKE AN ANIMUS ANGRY.
SHRUG
THEN HOW DID THESE OTHER DRAGONS GET FROZEN? MAYBE THAT'S PART OF THE SPELL. ONE KILLS FOESLAYER, THEN THE OTHER ONE FREEZES.
THAT SEEMS MORE COMPLICATED THAN THE USUAL ANIMUS SPELL.
YOU DO IT, WINTER. YOU KILL HER.
HAILSTORM, I WON'T BE RESPONSIBLE FOR YOUR DEATH A SECOND TIME. IT'S MY TURN.
AND LET'S FACE IT, HAILSTORM: THIS IS WHAT MOTHER AND FATHER WOULD WANT.
WINCE
JUST BE A GREAT ICEWING. HELP KEEP THE TRIBES AT PEACE. THAT'S WHAT *I* WOULD WANT.
DO IT. I'M READY.
ME TOO. AS FAST AND CLEAN AS YOU CAN, PLEASE.

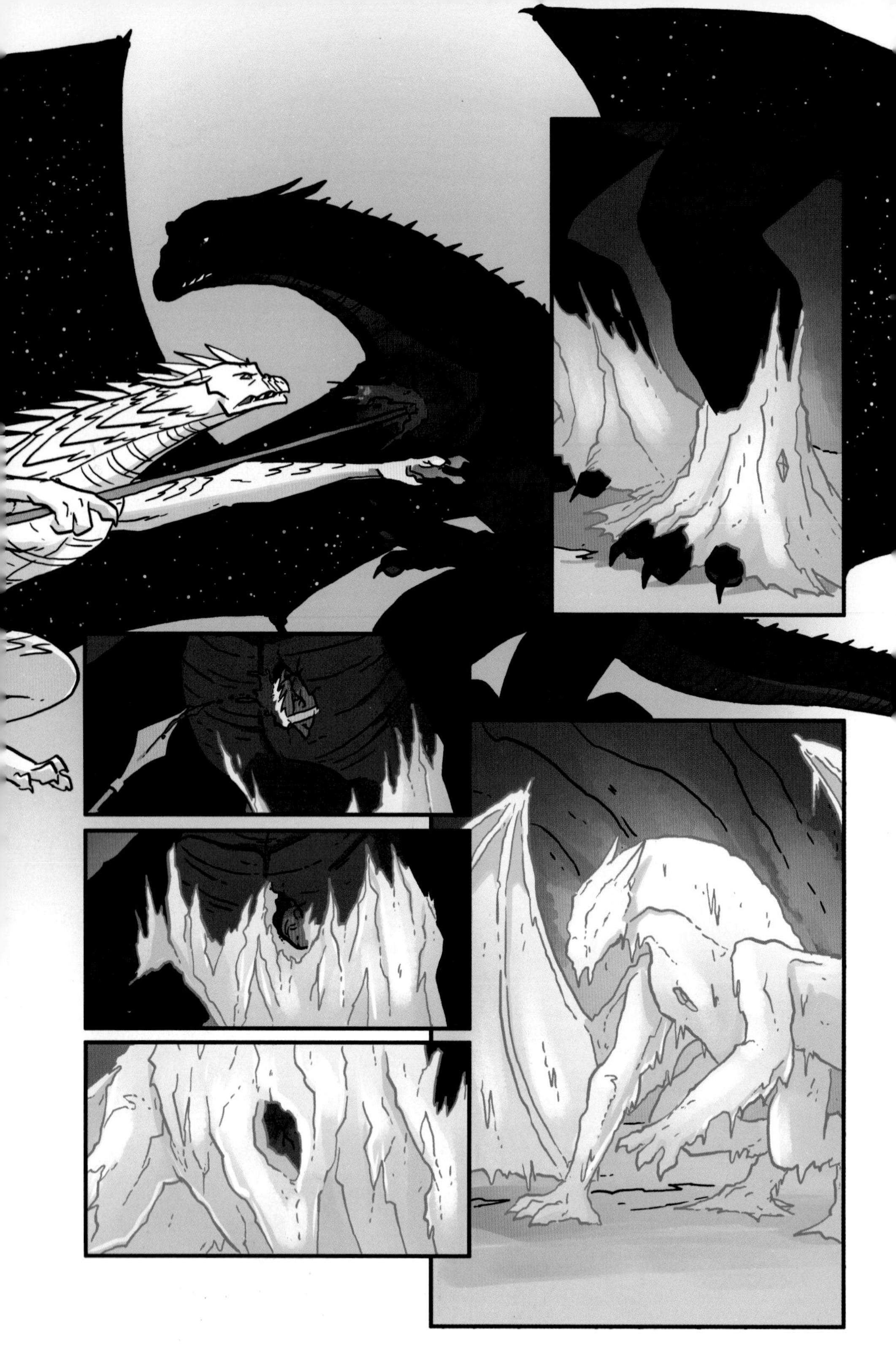

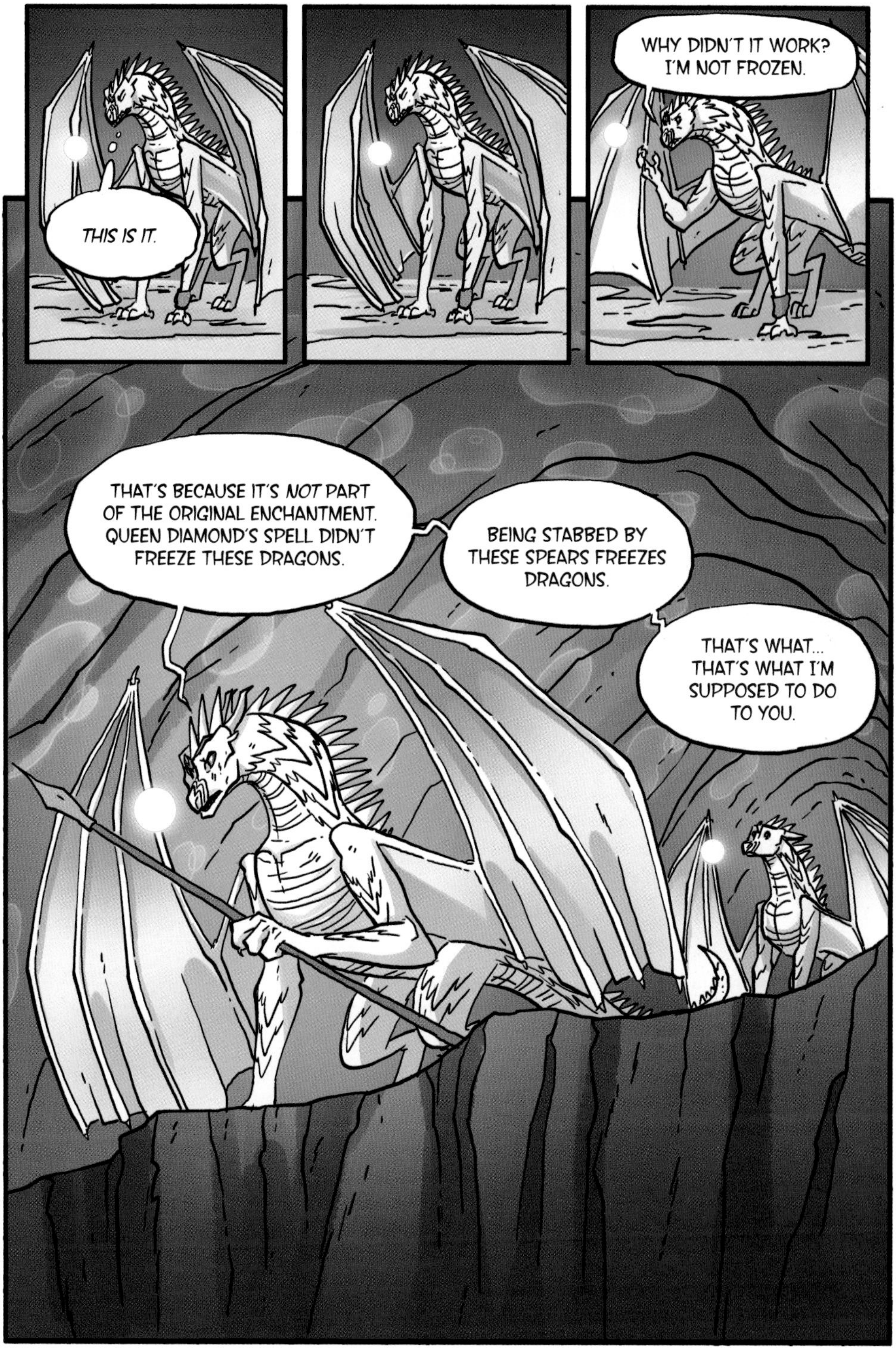

THIS IS IT.
WHY DIDN'T IT WORK? I'M NOT FROZEN.
THAT'S BECAUSE IT'S *NOT* PART OF THE ORIGINAL ENCHANTMENT. QUEEN DIAMOND'S SPELL DIDN'T FREEZE THESE DRAGONS.
BEING STABBED BY THESE SPEARS FREEZES DRAGONS.
THAT'S WHAT... THAT'S WHAT I'M SUPPOSED TO DO TO YOU.

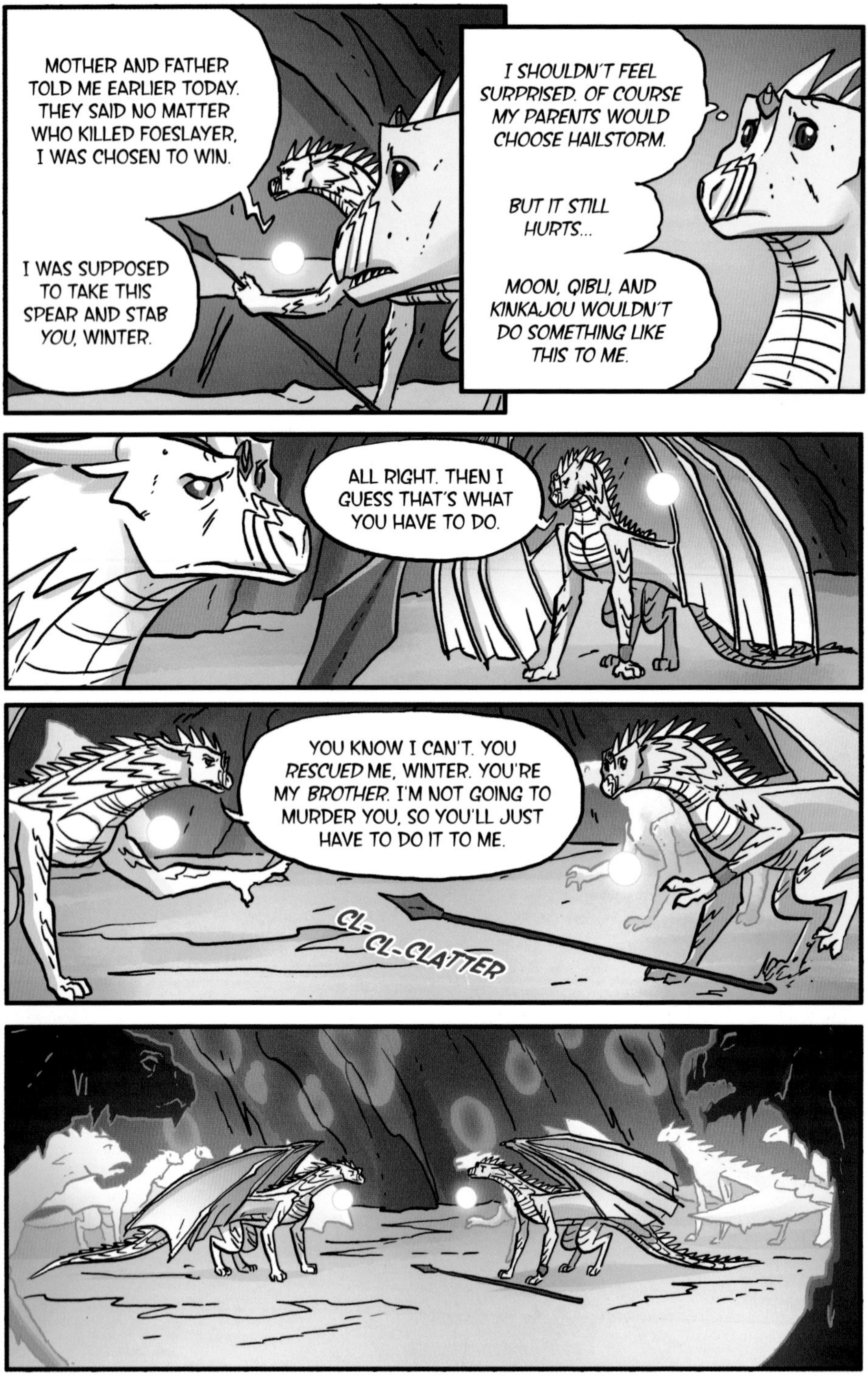
MOTHER AND FATHER TOLD ME EARLIER TODAY. THEY SAID NO MATTER WHO KILLED FOESLAYER, I WAS CHOSEN TO WIN.
I WAS SUPPOSED TO TAKE THIS SPEAR AND STAB *YOU*, WINTER.
I SHOULDN'T FEEL SURPRISED. OF COURSE MY PARENTS WOULD CHOOSE HAILSTORM.
BUT IT STILL HURTS...
MOON, QIBLI, AND KINKAJOU WOULDN'T DO SOMETHING LIKE THIS TO ME.
ALL RIGHT. THEN I GUESS THAT'S WHAT YOU HAVE TO DO.
YOU KNOW I CAN'T. YOU *RESCUED* ME, WINTER. YOU'RE MY *BROTHER*. I'M NOT GOING TO MURDER YOU, SO YOU'LL JUST HAVE TO DO IT TO ME.
CL-CL-CLATTER

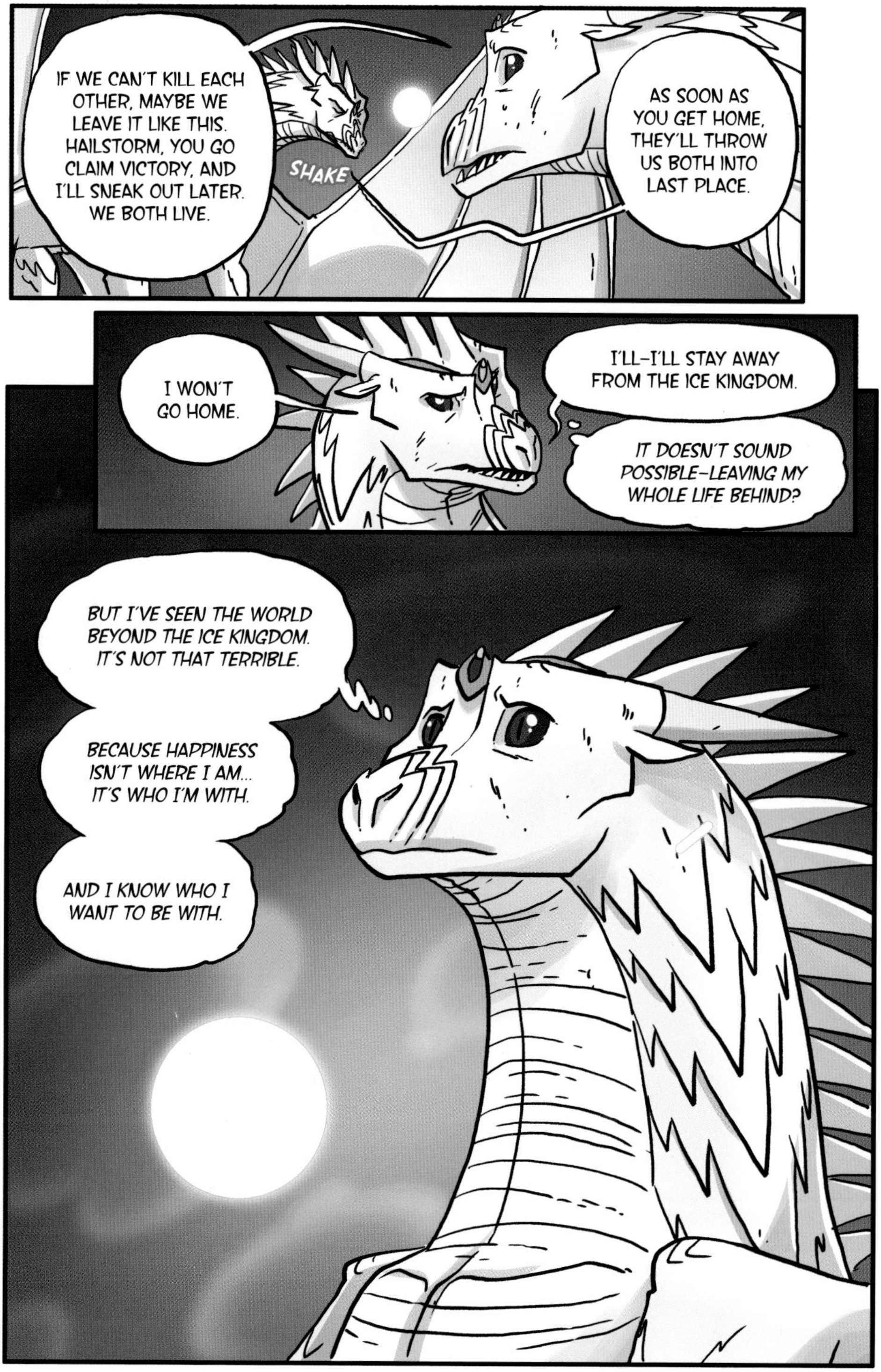
IF WE CAN'T KILL EACH OTHER, MAYBE WE LEAVE IT LIKE THIS. HAILSTORM, YOU GO CLAIM VICTORY, AND I'LL SNEAK OUT LATER. WE BOTH LIVE.
SHAKE
AS SOON AS YOU GET HOME, THEY'LL THROW US BOTH INTO LAST PLACE.
I WON'T GO HOME.
I'LL–I'LL STAY AWAY FROM THE ICE KINGDOM.
IT DOESN'T SOUND POSSIBLE–LEAVING MY WHOLE LIFE BEHIND?
BUT I'VE SEEN THE WORLD BEYOND THE ICE KINGDOM. IT'S NOT THAT TERRIBLE.
BECAUSE HAPPINESS ISN'T WHERE I AM... IT'S WHO I'M WITH.
AND I KNOW WHO I WANT TO BE WITH.

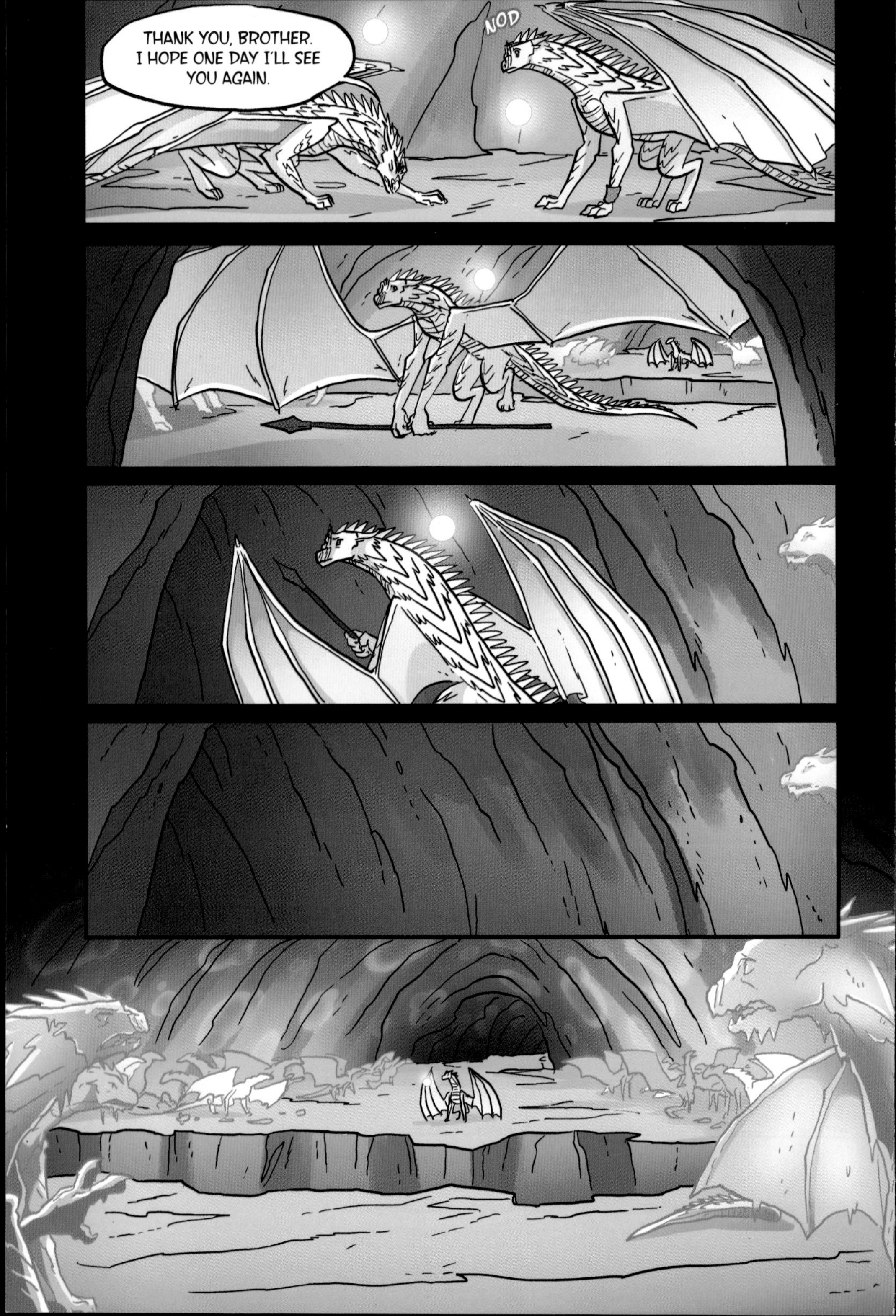
THANK YOU, BROTHER. I HOPE ONE DAY I'LL SEE YOU AGAIN.
NOD

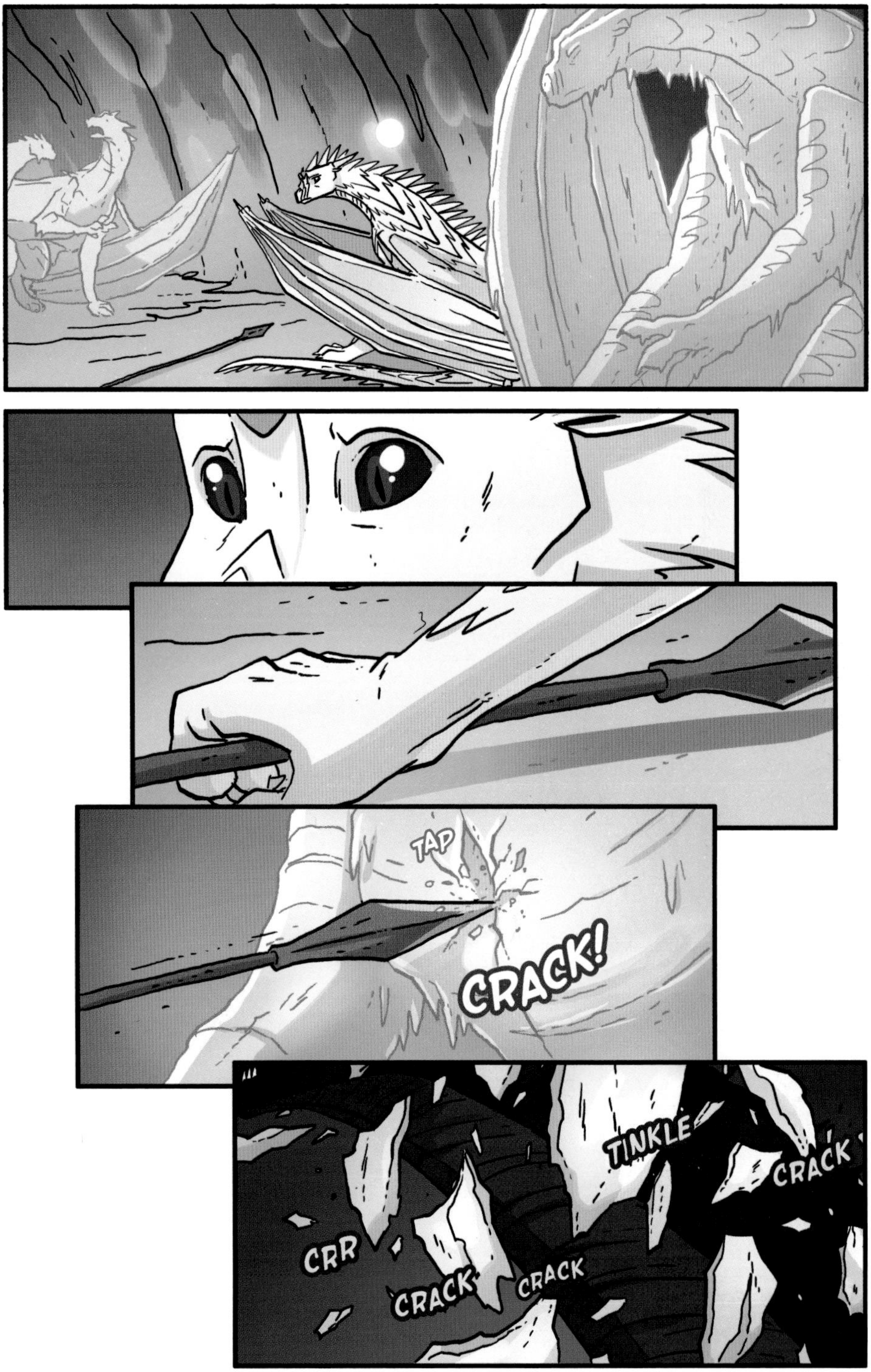
TAP
CRACK!
TINKLE
CRACK
CRR
CRACK
CRACK

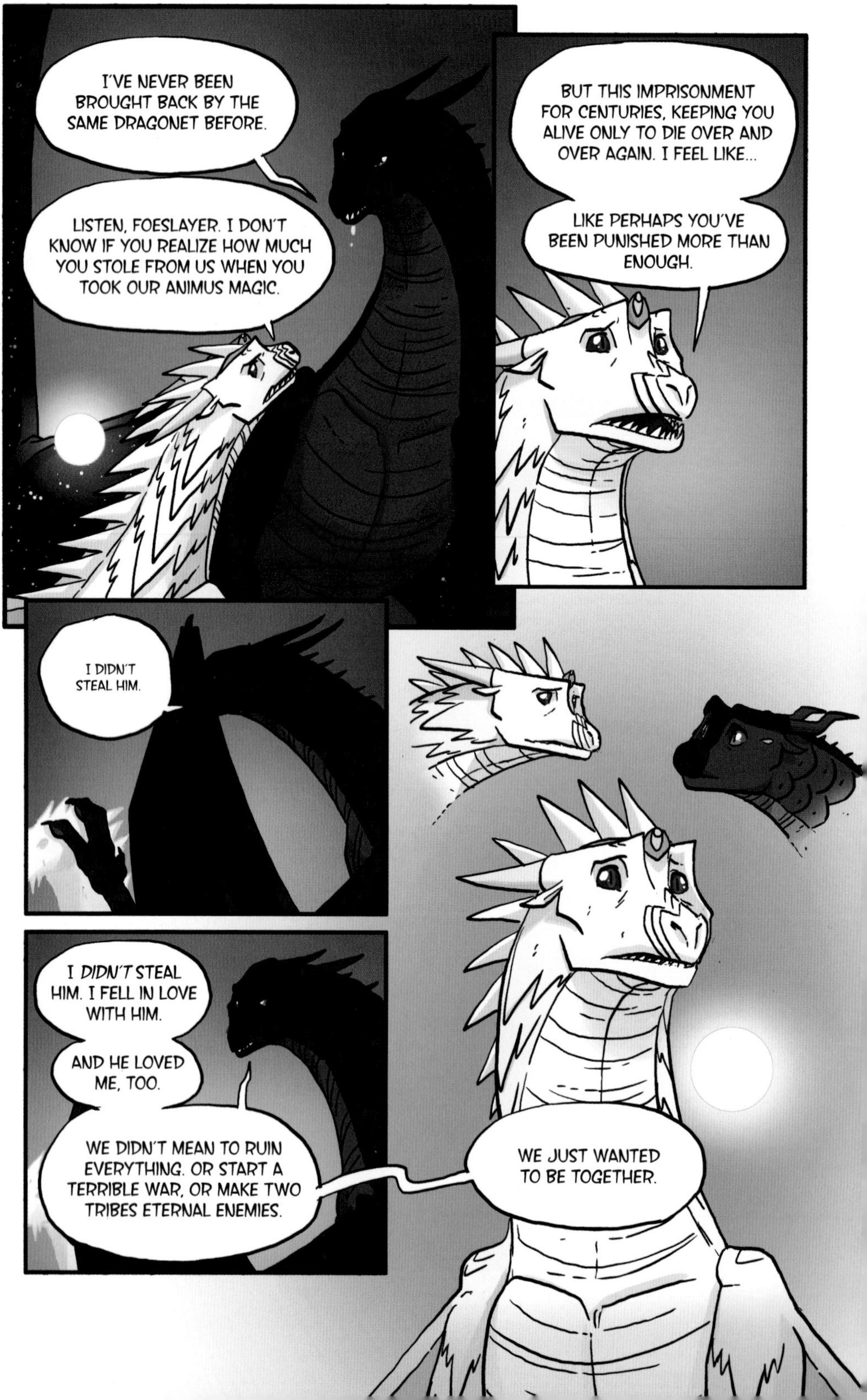
I'VE NEVER BEEN BROUGHT BACK BY THE SAME DRAGONET BEFORE.
LISTEN, FOESLAYER. I DON'T KNOW IF YOU REALIZE HOW MUCH YOU STOLE FROM US WHEN YOU TOOK OUR ANIMUS MAGIC.
BUT THIS IMPRISONMENT FOR CENTURIES, KEEPING YOU ALIVE ONLY TO DIE OVER AND OVER AGAIN. I FEEL LIKE...
LIKE PERHAPS YOU'VE BEEN PUNISHED MORE THAN ENOUGH.
I DIDN'T STEAL HIM.
I *DIDN'T* STEAL HIM. I FELL IN LOVE WITH HIM.
AND HE LOVED ME, TOO.
WE DIDN'T MEAN TO RUIN EVERYTHING. OR START A TERRIBLE WAR, OR MAKE TWO TRIBES ETERNAL ENEMIES.
WE JUST WANTED TO BE TOGETHER.

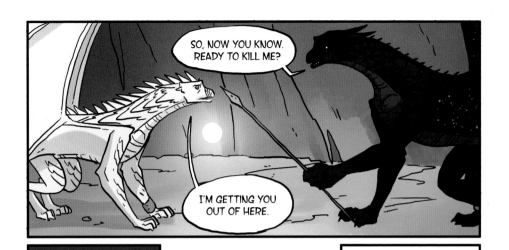

SO, NOW YOU KNOW. READY TO KILL ME?

I'M GETTING YOU OUT OF HERE.

THAT'S IMPOSSIBLE. THE ENCHANTMENT WON'T LET ME CROSS THE CHASM.

ICEWINGS ARE CAREFUL PLANNERS, ESPECIALLY WITH ANIMUS GIFTS. I'M SURE DIAMOND LEFT A WAY TO FREE YOU, JUST IN CASE.

IT MUST BE YOUR SHACKLES. THEY'RE ANIMUS-TOUCHED, RIGHT?

WELL, THEY'RE IMPERVIOUS TO FIRE, AND NOTHING HAPPENS WHEN I SMASH THEM AGAINST THE WALLS EXCEPT IT MAKES MY ANKLES HURT. SO, PROBABLY.

IF I KNOW ICEWINGS, ONLY A ROYAL FAMILY MEMBER CAN BREAK THESE. BUT YOU'RE IN LUCK, BECAUSE THAT'S WHAT I AM.

THESE DIAMONDS MUST BE THE LOCK.

AND I BET THE KEY IS SOMETHING ONLY AN ICEWING CAN DO. BECAUSE NO ICEWING WOULD EVER, EVER FREE A NIGHTWING.

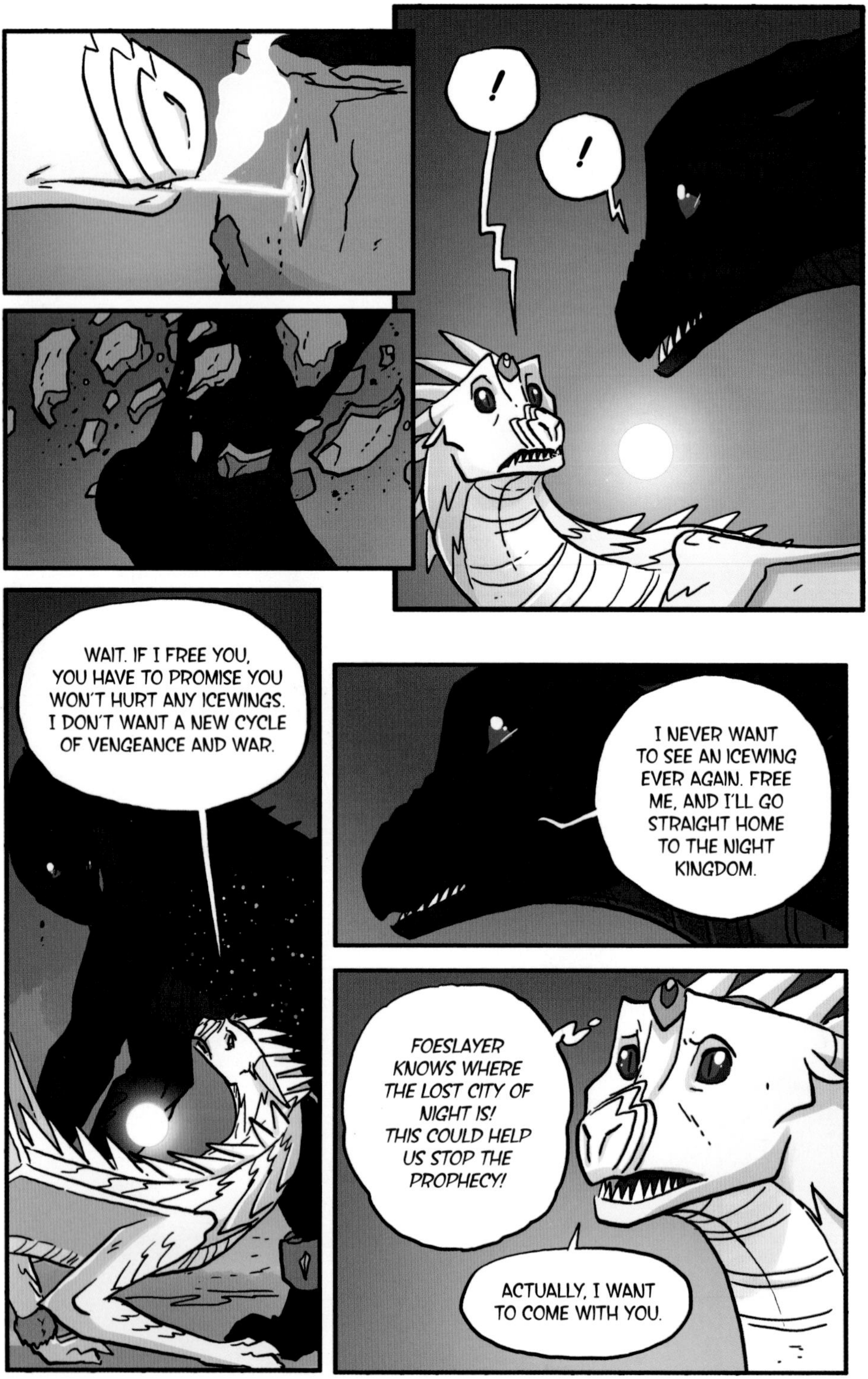
!
!
WAIT. IF I FREE YOU, YOU HAVE TO PROMISE YOU WON'T HURT ANY ICEWINGS. I DON'T WANT A NEW CYCLE OF VENGEANCE AND WAR.
I NEVER WANT TO SEE AN ICEWING EVER AGAIN. FREE ME, AND I'LL GO STRAIGHT HOME TO THE NIGHT KINGDOM.
FOESLAYER KNOWS WHERE THE LOST CITY OF NIGHT IS! THIS COULD HELP US STOP THE PROPHECY!
ACTUALLY, I WANT TO COME WITH YOU.

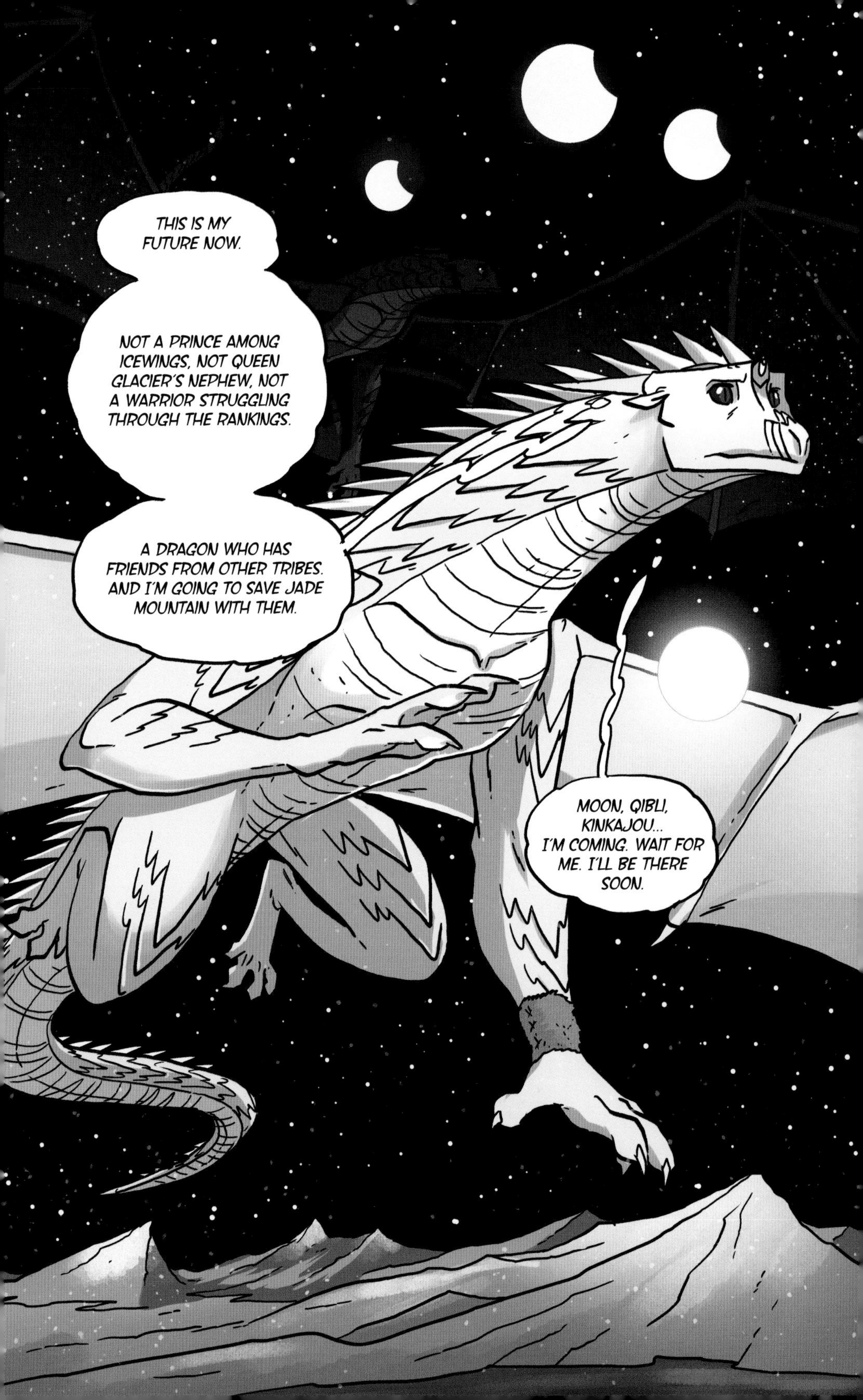
THIS IS MY FUTURE NOW.
NOT A PRINCE AMONG ICEWINGS, NOT QUEEN GLACIER'S NEPHEW, NOT A WARRIOR STRUGGLING THROUGH THE RANKINGS.
A DRAGON WHO HAS FRIENDS FROM OTHER TRIBES. AND I'M GOING TO SAVE JADE MOUNTAIN WITH THEM.
MOON, QIBLI, KINKAJOU... I'M COMING. WAIT FOR ME. I'LL BE THERE SOON.

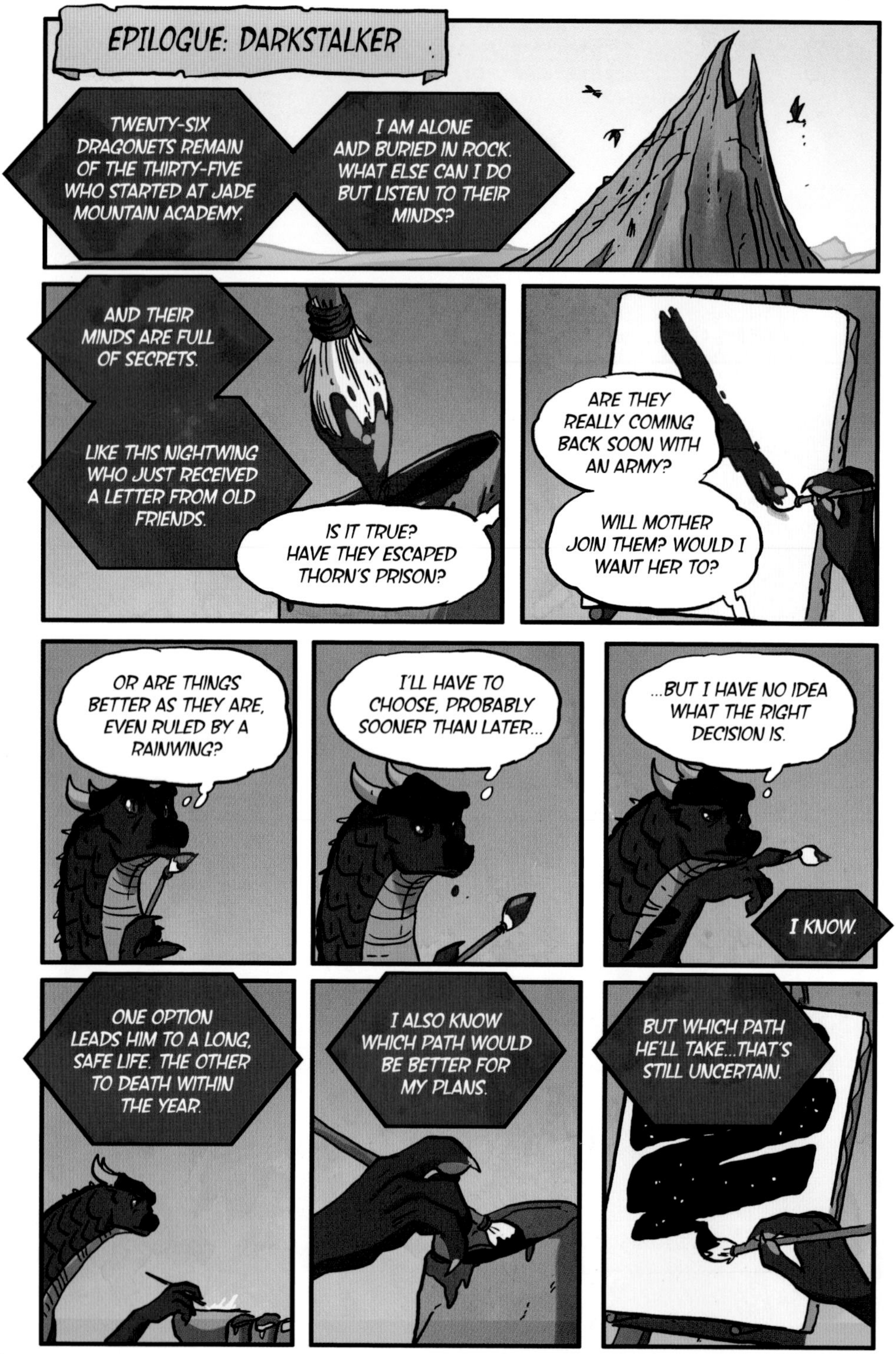
EPILOGUE: DARKSTALKER
TWENTY-SIX DRAGONETS REMAIN OF THE THIRTY-FIVE WHO STARTED AT JADE MOUNTAIN ACADEMY.
I AM ALONE AND BURIED IN ROCK. WHAT ELSE CAN I DO BUT LISTEN TO THEIR MINDS?
AND THEIR MINDS ARE FULL OF SECRETS.
LIKE THIS NIGHTWING WHO JUST RECEIVED A LETTER FROM OLD FRIENDS.
IS IT TRUE? HAVE THEY ESCAPED THORN'S PRISON?
ARE THEY REALLY COMING BACK SOON WITH AN ARMY?
WILL MOTHER JOIN THEM? WOULD I WANT HER TO?
OR ARE THINGS BETTER AS THEY ARE, EVEN RULED BY A RAINWING?
I'LL HAVE TO CHOOSE, PROBABLY SOONER THAN LATER...
...BUT I HAVE NO IDEA WHAT THE RIGHT DECISION IS.
I KNOW.
ONE OPTION LEADS HIM TO A LONG, SAFE LIFE. THE OTHER TO DEATH WITHIN THE YEAR.
I ALSO KNOW WHICH PATH WOULD BE BETTER FOR MY PLANS.
BUT WHICH PATH HE'LL TAKE...THAT'S STILL UNCERTAIN.

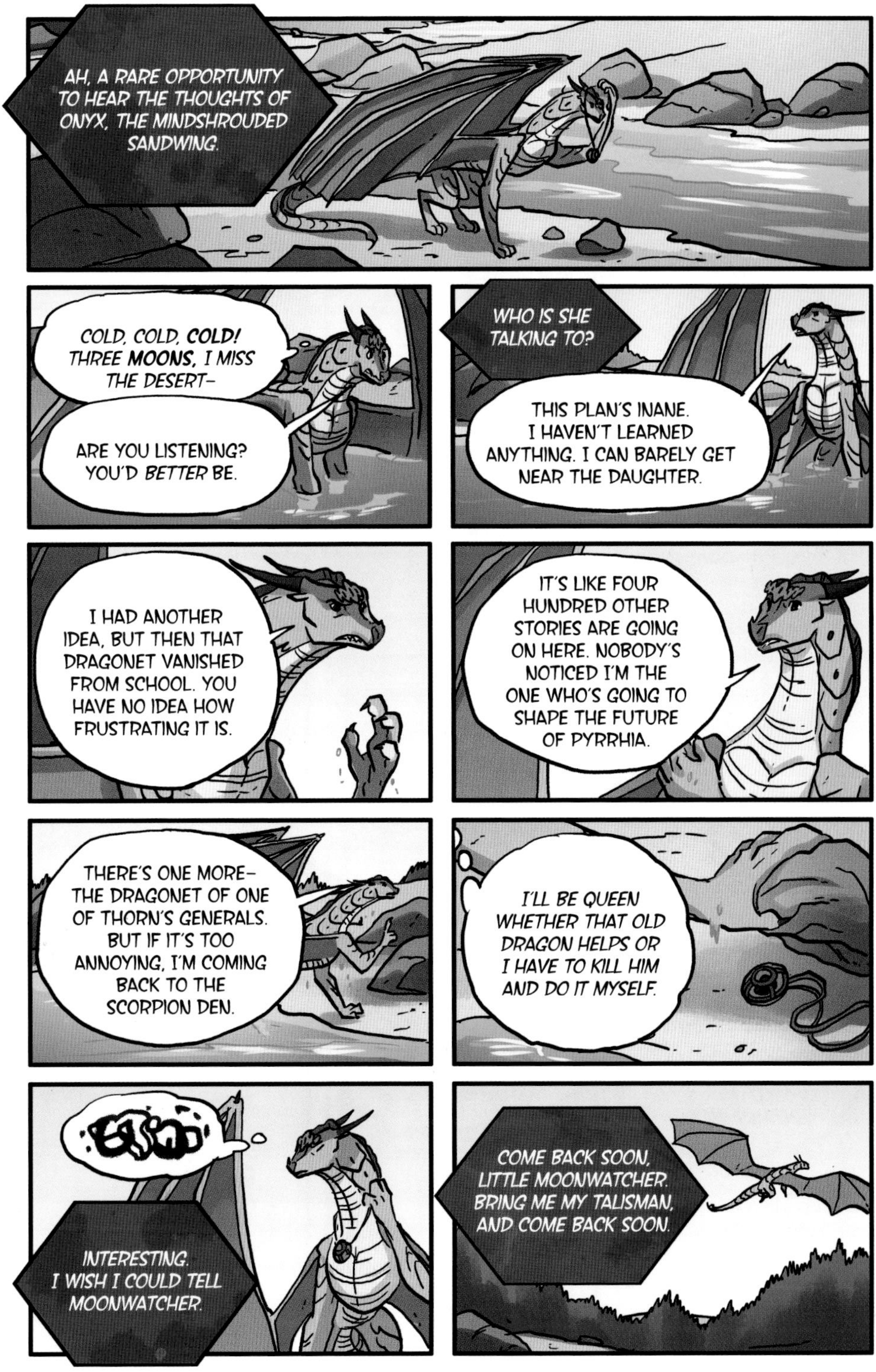
AH, A RARE OPPORTUNITY TO HEAR THE THOUGHTS OF ONYX, THE MINDSHROUDED SANDWING.
COLD, COLD, COLD! THREE MOONS, I MISS THE DESERT–
ARE YOU LISTENING? YOU'D BETTER BE.
WHO IS SHE TALKING TO?
THIS PLAN'S INANE. I HAVEN'T LEARNED ANYTHING. I CAN BARELY GET NEAR THE DAUGHTER.
I HAD ANOTHER IDEA, BUT THEN THAT DRAGONET VANISHED FROM SCHOOL. YOU HAVE NO IDEA HOW FRUSTRATING IT IS.
IT'S LIKE FOUR HUNDRED OTHER STORIES ARE GOING ON HERE. NOBODY'S NOTICED I'M THE ONE WHO'S GOING TO SHAPE THE FUTURE OF PYRRHIA.
THERE'S ONE MORE– THE DRAGONET OF ONE OF THORN'S GENERALS. BUT IF IT'S TOO ANNOYING, I'M COMING BACK TO THE SCORPION DEN.
I'LL BE QUEEN WHETHER THAT OLD DRAGON HELPS OR I HAVE TO KILL HIM AND DO IT MYSELF.
INTERESTING. I WISH I COULD TELL MOONWATCHER.
COME BACK SOON, LITTLE MOONWATCHER. BRING ME MY TALISMAN, AND COME BACK SOON.

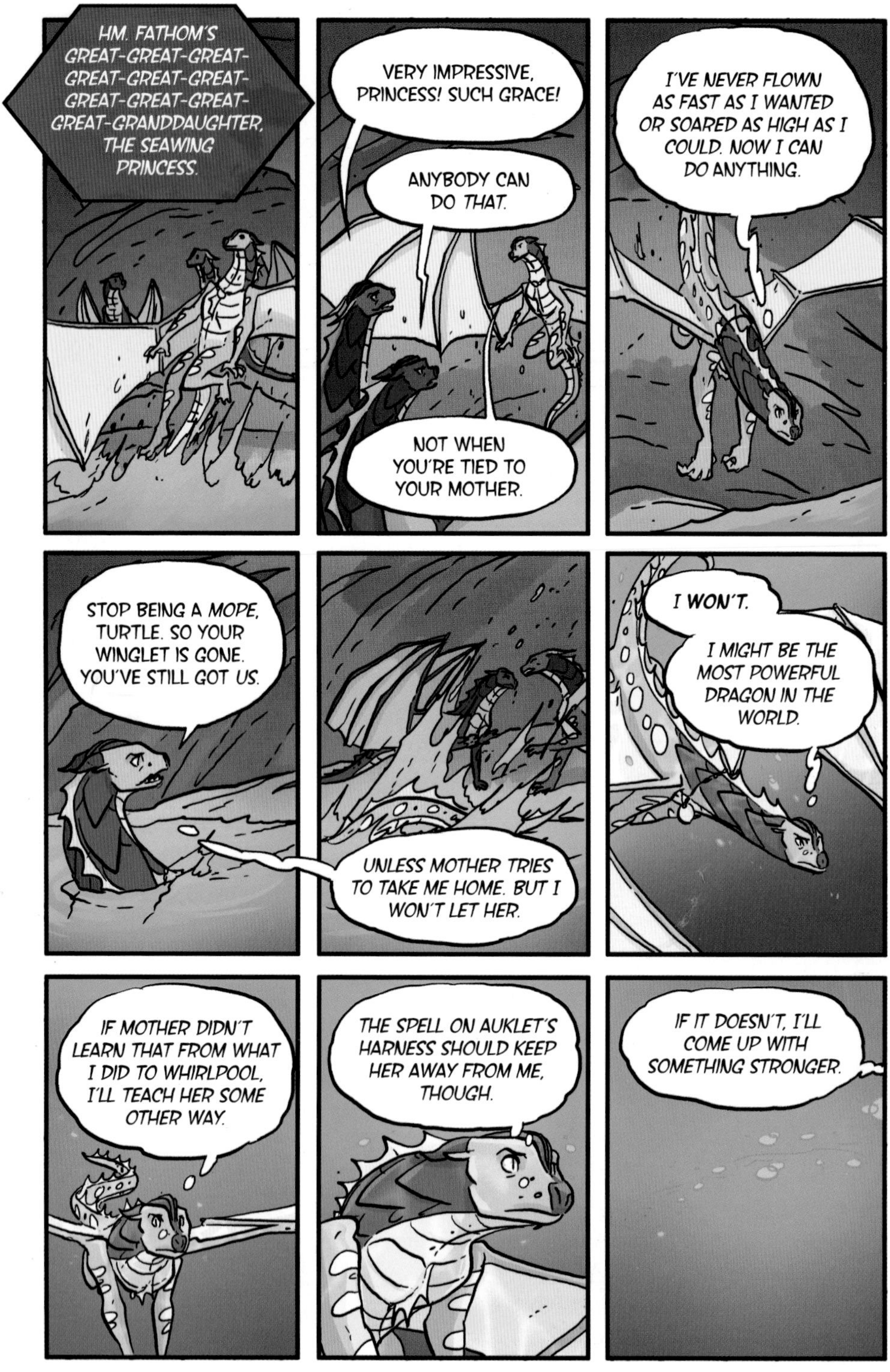
HM. FATHOM'S GREAT-GREAT-GREAT-GREAT-GREAT-GREAT-GREAT-GREAT-GREAT-GREAT-GRANDDAUGHTER, THE SEAWING PRINCESS.
VERY IMPRESSIVE, PRINCESS! SUCH GRACE!
ANYBODY CAN DO THAT.
NOT WHEN YOU'RE TIED TO YOUR MOTHER.
I'VE NEVER FLOWN AS FAST AS I WANTED OR SOARED AS HIGH AS I COULD. NOW I CAN DO ANYTHING.
STOP BEING A MOPE, TURTLE. SO YOUR WINGLET IS GONE. YOU'VE STILL GOT US.
UNLESS MOTHER TRIES TO TAKE ME HOME. BUT I WON'T LET HER.
I WON'T.
I MIGHT BE THE MOST POWERFUL DRAGON IN THE WORLD.
IF MOTHER DIDN'T LEARN THAT FROM WHAT I DID TO WHIRLPOOL, I'LL TEACH HER SOME OTHER WAY.
THE SPELL ON AUKLET'S HARNESS SHOULD KEEP HER AWAY FROM ME, THOUGH.
IF IT DOESN'T, I'LL COME UP WITH SOMETHING STRONGER.

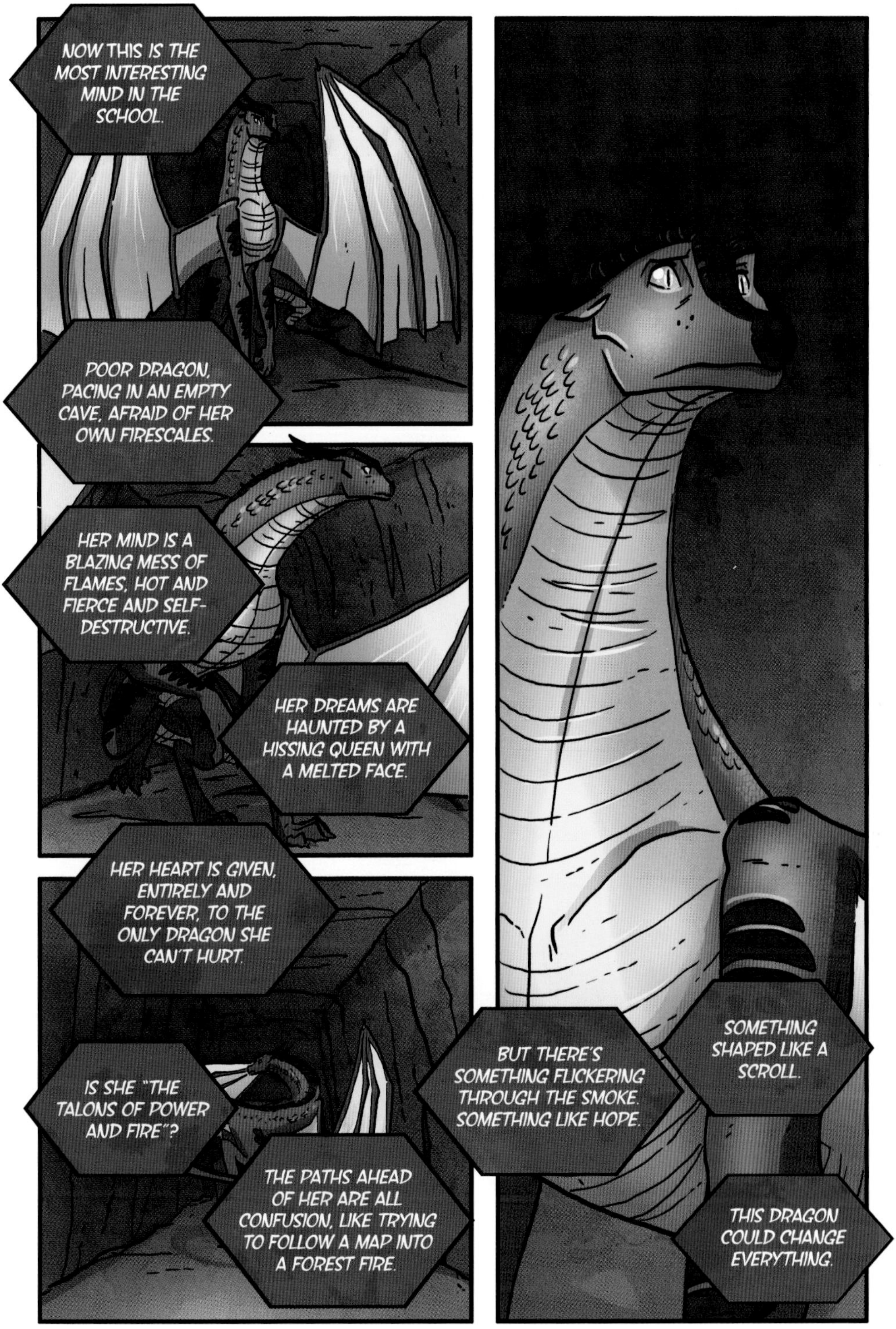
NOW THIS IS THE MOST INTERESTING MIND IN THE SCHOOL.
POOR DRAGON, PACING IN AN EMPTY CAVE, AFRAID OF HER OWN FIRESCALES.
HER MIND IS A BLAZING MESS OF FLAMES, HOT AND FIERCE AND SELF-DESTRUCTIVE.
HER DREAMS ARE HAUNTED BY A HISSING QUEEN WITH A MELTED FACE.
HER HEART IS GIVEN, ENTIRELY AND FOREVER, TO THE ONLY DRAGON SHE CAN'T HURT.
IS SHE "THE TALONS OF POWER AND FIRE"?
THE PATHS AHEAD OF HER ARE ALL CONFUSION, LIKE TRYING TO FOLLOW A MAP INTO A FOREST FIRE.
BUT THERE'S SOMETHING FLICKERING THROUGH THE SMOKE. SOMETHING LIKE HOPE.
SOMETHING SHAPED LIKE A SCROLL.
THIS DRAGON COULD CHANGE EVERYTHING.

TEN TRIBES.
TWO CONTINENTS.
THREE MOONS.

LIMITLESS STORIES — TOLD BY
THE DRAGONS THEMSELVES.

AVAILABLE NOW!